FAMILY SECRETS;

OR,

A PAGE FROM LIFE'S VOLUME.

A Romance.

―――――――

"There is a skeleton in every house."—OLD LEGEND.

―――――――

LONDON:

PRINTED AND PUBLISHED BY EDWARD LLOYD, 12, SALISBURY SQUARE,
FLEET STREET.

――

1846.

PREFACE.

IN concluding the Romance of " Family Secrets," the author has to congratulate himself on yet another instance of the fact, that pictures of real life are always acceptable to the public.

The notion put into the mouth of Nicholas Lowe, the real hero of the Novel, that there is a skeleton in every house, may, at the first glance, sound like a piece of harsh philosophy, but when we come to consider that the most favoured of mortals are certainly not without their cares and troubles, we shall find but little difficulty in coming to the opinion, that, go where we may, to the palace or the cottage, we shall find some corroding care, which may not inaptly be likened to a skeleton, in the house.

We cannot but attribute the great success of the Novel—a success which induced its author to extend its publication beyond the originally intended limits— to the fact, that its whole aim and object was to inculcate a great moral truth.

If, by inculcating that truth, the Romance of " Family Secrets" should tend in any way to make those who repine over their lot, and envy the apparent better fortune of others, more contented, it will have really achieved a practical benefit of vast importance.

That such has been our object we assert ; and we are most decidedly of opinion that the more human nature is inquired into, and the more the flimsy veil of Custom is drawn aside from the arcana of human thought, the more it will be found that happiness is distributed with great equality among all persons.

Thus, when we see some favoured child of Fortune, who appears to be in so enviable a position as to be beyond the possibility of knowing any care, we may safely say to ourselves,—

" We will not envy that man, for Heaven and himself only knows what skeleton he may have in his house."

LONDON,
November, 1846.

FAMILY SECRETS;

OR,

A PAGE FROM LIFE'S HISTORY.

𝔄 𝔕𝔬𝔪𝔞𝔫𝔠𝔢,

BY THE AUTHOR OF "THE RIVALS," "VARNEY THE VAMPYRE," &c.

𝔈𝔫𝔱𝔯𝔬𝔡𝔲𝔠𝔱𝔦𝔬𝔫.

HERE is an old proverb, which says, there is a skeleton in every house. Alas! that there should be so; but is it not true, reader? Not a skeleton such as may adorn or disfigure—call it which you will—a surgeon's laboratory—not a fleshless entanglement of yellow bones, but a skeleton of the mind—gaunt and terrible—a spectre of the imagination, such as in drawing-room or bed-chamber—attic or cellar—dining parlour or hall—will intrude its grisly form to spoil the purest pleasures, and say, " Be joy no more !'"

Is there an individual without his or her corroding care? Is there one happy mortal who can place his hand upon his heart, and say, with truth, all is peace here? Not one, we boldly say, not one. Evil that has been, evil that is, or evil that is to come, and has already sent its gaunt shadow before it to dim the heart's lustrous happiness, will prevent the possibility of any one, with truth, uttering such a sentiment.

Envy no one. Envy not the millionaire, as he rolls by, in his gilded chariot! Poor wretch—poor bankrupt! miserable perchance in all that constitutes real happiness; what can we know of the consuming care that may be tugging at his heart even then, and turning the very sunshine that dances on his gilded equipage to hate?

Envy not these children of fortune—these apparent heirs to happy destinies.   If they smile, envy them not; for in this world there are far more smiles hiding breaking, bursting hearts, than are really indicative of joy and mirthfulness, and that peace within which is the brightest jewel of the soul.

Who so happy—who so prosperous, as to have no drawback upon his felicity? Stop him, who there quietly steals along, and seems, by the costly value of his apparel, and the well-kept look of his whole exterior, to be one upon whom fortune has lavished some of her brightest smiles.   Ask him to be candid—Is he happy? Oh, mockery. He will tell you that, but for so and so, he is quite sure he should be happy— *He has his skeleton!*

See that young and beautiful girl! surely she is happy—very, very happy. What sweet dimples play around her mouth—what a world of beauty in her cheek—what heavenly lustre in her eyes. Fair maiden, are you happy? she starts—she, too, has a skeleton. We are told that the Romans at their feasts would have a skull introduced, to remind them that to that complexion must they come at last.   Oh, needless precaution—oh, senseless provocative to memory! The difficulty is to forget! not to remember quite sufficient cares and anxieties to dim the lustre of beauty, rob music of its melody, and dash the foaming wine-cup from the lips.

It is the doom of human nature. There never was, there never shall be, perfect happiness in this world. Fortune may smile—fame crown the brow with laurels—friends abound—plaudits ring upon the air; and yet the hero of them all, the popular idol, the man who shall be something more than man, shall yet have—his skeleton!

Where, perhaps, he has centered his whole heart's love he shall be betrayed. He has found falsehood, perchance, where he had alone looked for truth. The friend he trusted has betrayed him; the heart he loved has proved false; the child in whose welfare he has been content to sacrifice a life, has turned aside from honour, and his heart is breaking—the plaudits of mankind sound like mockeries—gold degenerates to valueless dross, and he looks but to the grave as a haven of rest.

CHAPTER I.

THE HIDDEN TREASURE.

RATEFUL labour—grateful labour—how the carts rumble along the stones. Well, well, I shall be done at last; for six nights, now, how hard I have worked, to be sure. I—I—could not have thought I had the strength to do it. Sixty years ago I should have thought nothing of it at all. Sixty years ago—did I say sixty? sixty—six——Ah!"

Old Jasper Barnacle sat down on a little three-legged stool, and wiped the damp perspiration from his face.

"Sixty—did I say sixty?"

He was an old man; eighty-five summers had passed over his head, and they had taken care, with the aid and assistance of the winters likewise, to leave some tolerably strong traces of their once presence behind them. He was a little, wrinkled, wasted old man. He looked a living piece of anatomical preparation, so hollow-cheeked, so wasted, so wan, so shaky, and apparently used up, was old Jasper Barnacle.

His dress was very old, too. For the sake of economy, he always purchased boys' clothing, and those second-hand. In truth, he was about the size of a very thin lad of twelve years of age, and he had on an old pair of patched corduroy trowsers, that had belonged to some urchin, and a jacket which had been most ingeniously mended. It looked amazingly strange and ludicrous to see that old man so apparelled.

In his old, shrivelled, mummy-looking hands, he held a spade, with which he had been at work, when the uncomfortable idea struck him that sixty years ago he could have got through the labour better.

The scene of his operations was a cellar—a large vaulted cellar; which, from its deviousness and length, seemed to have robbed half-a-dozen houses on each side of their cellars.

He had been working for some hours now, and it was the same work he had been at for nearly a whole week. His object appeared to be to make a new but much smaller vault at the end of the large one, for he had cut out a place just large enough for him to creep in at, and there he had been trying, with the most exemplary patience, to excavate it inside.

"Sixty years ago," he muttered, as he drew a long breath; "sixty years ago I was five-and-twenty. Ah! what would I not give now to be five-and-twenty. No, no, I would not give much—oh, no, I would not bring myself to want, even if I were five-and-twenty. I would give a thousand—I mean a hundred—that is to say, twenty, or ten pounds; and yet ten pounds is a good lot of money—ten shining, beautiful pounds. Oh, and I am a good life yet—a very good life yet. I don't know that I would give ten pounds. No, no; if it wasn't for the cough, now—I—eugh! eugh! eugh! I—eugh! eugh! Oh dear, oh dear. I always have it in the autumn; but what of that—but what of that? Let me see. Eighty-five!—eighty-five. How old was Old Parr? Ha! ha! I am yet a mere boy; and as for Henry Jenkins—He! he! he! what a funny idea! I might have been his little boy. Ha! ha! Eh? eh? Oh, Lord, oh! I thought—no, I didn't—that I heard some one laugh, too; or was it an echo, only an echo? it must have been an echo."

Trembling the old man rose, and recommenced his task. A rushlight lent him but little assistance, and that he looked at curiously, as it slowly wasted away, and talked about his substance going.

The hollow place he had dug was now large enough for him to creep fairly into, and nearly stand upright in. He was delighted at the progress he was making in his work.

And what was that work for? What was the object of this labour of the old man, who, sixty years before, could have done it so much better? It was to bury his gold. He had accumulated wealth, and the fear of losing it was the harassing thought that oppressed him by day and by night, never leaving him for a single moment, but adding, for every year, at least three to his life by incessant anxiety.

He inhabited the house to which the large cellar was attached alone—but let not the reader suppose that old Jasper Barnacle paid for it. Oh no. It was in Chancery. It had been in Chancery for forty years, and for forty years old Jasper Barnacle had lived in it unmolested by any one. It was now of no value to any of its claimants, for, as a property, it was completely swallowed up by the expenses of litigation.

And yet, once upon a time, it had been a handsome house, and gay laughter had made its now damp crumbling walls echo again. Music, lights, and merry hearts had once made it a region of sunshine and smiles, but all that had passed away, and, except the strange, hideous, most unmirthful chuckle which sometimes came from old Jasper Barnacle, no human sound was ever heard within its walls.

"—I—I shall be able to sleep in peace," the old man muttered, "when I have buried my money here. Last night I am sure I heard some sound as of some one trying to open the door. Of that I am quite certain. Oh, quite—quite—I am not easily deceived—not easily mistaken. I am sure I heard it. I—I am not so old as all that comes to. I—I can hear well enough. He! he! Old Harry Jenkins. He! he! he! They do say he married when he was ninety-four. Ha! ha! How imprudent. What an expense!"

The old man paused again, and sat down on the stool. He had brought it there on purpose to rest on, for he could not continue at work above half an hour at a time, so that he had been nearly a whole week in getting a job completed, which any ordinary labourer would have done in a couple of hours. But it was a labour of love, it was to hide his money.

Taking now the light in his hand he trotted slowly out of the cellar, and went into what had once been a pantry under the kitchen stairs, for the preservation of rare wines and costly liquors. From an obscure corner of the place he lifted up an old piece of board that looked as if it had been loosely cast there out of the way. Beneath was a very thin layer of earth, which, when he had removed, enabled him to see several little bags, such as money is tied up in—miniature sacks, with string round their mouths. There were four of these, and now he took two of them, which, along with the light, was as much as he could conveniently carry, and, with trembling steps, he again proceeded to the cellar and deposited them in the excavation he had made. Starting at his own shadow, and tremblingly alive to the least noise, he again went to the pantry and removed the other two little sacks. Twice or thrice as he went, he turned round and listened.

"All is still," he muttered. "I—I have done a famous piece of work now, I feel assured. If any people were to come here to hunt for money, what would they do? Why, why, when they found it not above ground, they would think I had buried it of course, and they would dig up the earthen floor of all the cellars. Ha! ha! ha! but they would not think of beginning upon the walls. Oh, no; oh, no. It's a good plan—a famous plan!"

With these two bags he crept into the excavation he had made, and then he arranged all against the wall, after which he chuckled again with delight at his own vast cleverness.

"If I live but another thirty years," he said, counting on his fingers as he spoke, "I shall double the amount I now have. How cautiously I will lend it out at good interest; when nobody sees me, I can creep down here. Ha! ha! Thirty years. I shall only be one hundred and fifteen years old then. What of that; what of that? I am rich now, tolerably rich now; but by then, what shall I be? Ah, and then there are those who would rob me, or borrow from me without interest, and never pay me, which is just the same thing. Sister Ann's children. D——n sister Ann's children! What the deuce business had sister Ann with children? She married for love. Love. Bah! I never loved anybody but Jasper Barnacle, myself—yes, myself. Ha! ha! ha!"

A heavy waggon came along the street, shaking the foundation of all the houses with a strange vibratory motion. Old Barnacle was alarmed, for it was just over his head. He would have got out of the small excavation, for a piece or two of the rubbish fell from the upper part upon him. Then there came a sudden rumbling sound, and a slight rush of earth. The partly earthern and partly brick wall, through which he had made the orifice, settled down, and he was imprisoned in the small vault he himself had made. Horror at first so froze up his faculties that he could not speak or move. He seemed death-stricken by the suddenness of the singular accident that had befallen him. Then he all at once appeared to think that there could not be much, if any danger in it, and he sank on his knees by the orifice which had become so choked up. He had not the spade with him, but he had his hands wherewith to work himself to liberty and life.

"But a few loose bricks," he muttered, "but a few loose bricks removed, and I shall be free again; surely, surely."

With trembling eagerness he commenced the work, and he got out one brick, but the rumbling noise came again, and the opening closed up by the weight of loose materials above. Then Jasper Barnacle began to tremble, and a cold perspiration broke out upon him from top to toe, as he said.—

"No, no, no! I, I shall not die such a death as this. I am choking. Help! help. I—I will give ten—twenty; fifty pounds for life and liberty."

The light began to burn dimly, a sure sign that the air was becoming vitiated; and yet he had not the courage to put it out; for darkness, absolute darkness, would, indeed, have been terrible in that place. He gathered up all his energies in one desperate effort, and although his hands bled, and his nails were broken by the exertions he made, he, for several minutes, worked hard to remove the mass of obstruction from the mouth of the narrow excavation.

All was in vain. It is true he did tear away bricks, and pieces of cement, and handsful of earth, but the pressure from above always brought it down again, so that when, from sheer exhaustion, he was compelled to pause, he knew that he had made no progress whatever. He leaned back, and rested against the wall behind him—his face assumed the hue of death, and he wrung his hands despairingly, as he cried,—

"All, all, all, for one breath of cold, pure air ; all, for one draught of water. Oh, God! that I were the poorest beggar in London streets, now. Help! help! God of Heaven, help me!"

Had he ever called upon that Heaven in his prosperity, to which he now prayed, when the finger of death was upon him? Never. Had he ever attempted to propitiate its mercies, and its goodness, and its blessings, by sympathetic acts towards its creatures? Had he ever done good to his fellow-creatures? Had he ever dried the mourner's tear? Never. Had he ever even spoken a kind word to man or beast? Never, never. How could he then, in his extremity, call upon Heaven for mercy?"

"A thousand pounds!" he shrieked ; "a thousand pounds for air!—air!—air!"

The shriek died away, and then the candle went out.

Oh! how he now panted for breath—how his heart laboured! He felt as if hot flannel was bound over his mouth. How he tried now to breathe, but could not. How he, in stifled sobs, implored the mercy of that Heaven whose highest, holiest ordinances he had outraged. He called upon the names of those he should have called upon in life, not in death.

"Ann!—Ann!" he shrieked,—"sister Ann, your little ones shall not want bread. Help me, sister Ann! help me! The children of your love shall not want. Oh, what a death is this!—what a death!—what a death!—what—a death!"

A convulsion, arising from his terrific efforts to breathe, came over him, and he dashed unconsciously one of his feet through the orifice into the outer cellar. There came a rush of cold air into the place in which he was, for although the rubbish held his foot now by the ancle, as if it had been in a vice, the whole of the air was not excluded.

"What a change — what a change!" he exclaimed. The life-blood again circulated in his veins. He lived again—he could draw his breath, but all was dark—dark ; all was still, and he was a prisoner. What was now to become of him ?

When the first delicious consciousness that he was not choking had passed away, this became a fearful question.

"What shall I do ?—what shall I do ?—oh! what will now become of me ?"

He tried to remove his foot, but it was in vain. He commenced shrieking for help, but the sounds he made were not likely to penetrate far [when they had but so small a portion of air to agitate as was in that confined space. Hour after hour passed away—hunger came upon him—thirst devoured him. He was getting weaker, but his cries for help were more and more incessant. They changed to groans, only now and then increasing to a shriek.

*   *   *   *   *

Two men were passing along the street, laughing and talking : one of them paused suddenly, as he said to his companion,—

"What's that ?"

"What's what ?—I didn't see anything."

"No, but didn't you hear something? Just now some strange sound seemed to come from the pavement here under my feet : it quite thrilled through me."

"Your fancy it must have been."

"Indeed, no ; I am sure."

"I tell you it's impossible. This house is uninhabited, and has been for years. They say it's in Chancery, and there, I suppose, it's likely to remain."

"It's a nice, large, handsome-looking house, too."

"Yes, it is : but come on—come on."

" Well, I thought I heard some strange noise, I assure you; indeed, I could have sworn I did, and just here, too."

" Oh, stuff, stuff! Well, as I was just about telling you, the Cumminge's are the happiest people in all the world. They have no cares, I know. Cummings has a good situation, and he has a good-looking and amiable wife, and healthful, fine children, upon my word, and I do believe, if there is a happy dog in the world, it is Cummings."

" Indeed!"

" You say indeed, as if you doubted it."

" Nay, I have no reason to doubt it, except that I, as you know, always doubt appearances. You took me to this happy house, and I can tell you that I did not fail to observe such a shade upon the brow of the wife as convinced me all was not as it might have been."

" You surprise me!"

" My dear friend, you may depend there are family secrets everywhere."

" There may be."

" And painful ones, too: most sad and painful ones, you may rest assured. I have been a student of nature. You know I have travelled much—you know I have mingled in all sorts of society—the grave and the gay—the high and the low—the apparently happy, who have been really miserable—the seeming miserable, who have been, or who ought to have been, happy. I have not in vain noted all this. From the great book of human nature I have copied some stray leaves. Often I have promised you some of the results of my experience."

" You have; and often have I reminded you of your promise."

" You shall not have any further occasion to do so. Society may be divided into two great portions—those who have committed murders, and those who have not."

" A strange division!"

" And yet so true. I belong to the former."

The friend of him who thus spoke started back in dismay, and stared into the speaker's face, by the light of a lamp beneath the rays of which they happened to be, with amazement.

CHAPTER II.

THE CHILDREN OF CHANCE AND THE DESERTED HOUSE.

s the friends spoke, there came a half-stifled shriek upon their ears, but where it came from seemed most mysterious, for no one was near at the time, and, from the peculiar nature of the sound, it did not seem to them to have come from any of the houses.

" We both heard that," said he who had listened with so much amazement to the declaration of his companion, with which we concluded our last chapter. What, in the name of Heaven, can it be?"

" It is like the too late shriek of some one suffocating."

" Too late shriek! What do you mean by a too late shriek?"

" That shriek which some dying wretch utters when he finds there is no hope of safety from his own exertions; a shriek which, had he given at first, might have brought assistance to him."

" But whence came it ?"

" Ah, that is a serious question ; but if from anywhere, I should say yon empty house echoes yet with the fearful cry."

" Say you so ? Then be it certain he shall not scream for aid wholly in vain. I will use one effort to save him."

The young man ran up the steps of the house, and plied the knocker vigorously. He heard the dull echoes of the sound he made ringing through the empty house, but no one answered the appeal for admission, nor did any cry of hope or of despair reach their ears again.

" All is in vain," he said. " I had hoped ——"

" Hoped what ?" said the other. " Come along—come along. You can do nothing, I tell you—will you come away ?"

" But some one, I am certain, was in mortal agony, or they could not have uttered that most fearful cry that we heard. I am loth to abandon all hope of assisting a fellow creature, if we could now but get in."

" See—see. You want to assist a fellow creature. Here is a wretched family of fellow creatures—one, two, three, four ; and so wretched and so wan, that you cannot doubt the reality of their misery."

A wretched group of four, miserable, half-clad, half-starved-looking children, had walked up to the spot. They sat down upon the steps of the empty house, and they looked a despair too deep and too long endured to be relieved by tears.

The eldest of these little unfortunates was a girl. Her age was about thirteen, and then there was a boy of about eleven, and two younger girls, the least of whom could not be above five—she was a small tottering thing, and looked famished. These unhappy beings sat close together, and they shivered as they looked ruefully in the faces of the two young-looking men who were the only persons near at hand. He who seemed to have something of the cynic in his disposition, folded his arms and leaned against a neighbouring lamp-post, as if with easier leisure to survey the group ; but the young man, who from sudden impulse rather than reflection had knocked so loudly at the door of the deserted house, appeared to regard them with very different feelings.

" Have you no home ?" he said.

The girl who was the leader of the wretched party looked in his face as if the word was almost a new one to her, and then she glanced at the little things that were with her as if she could have said,—

" Now what effect upon your hearts has this magic word, home ?"

The children only huddled themselves closer together, and one whispered something to her whom no doubt they all looked upon as one towards whom they felt a tie which binds the weak to the strong. It sounded like the word " bread."

" Have you no home ?" said the young man, again.

The girl shook her head, as she replied,—

" No, no—we sleep in the market, or under the archways in the Strand."

" Have you no friends ?"

" Not one, except poor mother. She is in a hospital."

" And uncle John," said one of the little ones—it was the least of all.

The eldest girl laughed bitterly. It was dreadful to hear one so young as she was laugh in that manner, and she was beautiful too. Had her lot cast her in a happier station she might been, and, no doubt, would have been, one of those fair, sinless creatures, who know not evil even by name, and are more puzzled than enough by the enumeration of enormities in the ten commandments. But want, misery, degradation, and the world's harshness, had given her a fearful and a peculiar knowledge of life, and she laughed bitterly—she whose lips should have only parted to give utterance to words of holiness and joy, or to laugh as laughs some happy child for the mere love of mirth.

" Uncle John," she said. " Uncle John—no, no, no."

" Then you have no uncle John ?"

" Yes. We have an uncle John—we saw him once. There are four of us. He met us and knew us. He took four farthings from his pocket, and he said he would not give them to save us all from being hanged ; and then our mother told him, God only knows if she knew truly, or if it ever will be so, but she told him the time would come when he would give all the money he was hoarding, and all that he ever hoped to hoard, for the sight of one of us."

As the girl concluded these words, so dreadful and strange a cry appeared to come from somewhere deep beneath the very steps on which the children sat, that they, with terror in their looks, rose hastily to move away.

"There, there—there is the cry again," said he, who had knocked at the door. "It makes me very uneasy to hear those cries. Here, children, here is some money for you. The night is cold and chill. Go somewhere, and get food and rest."

The girl looked at the shilling he gave her with surprise, and then, as if fearful that such an amount of generosity would be repented of, she hastily dragged the children away round the nearest corner.

"What can be done—what can be done?" he said, who had bestowed the alms. "Something, surely, it behoves us to do to ascertain from whence these cries have proceeded."

"I do not know what we can do," said the other. "Propose what you will, I have no particular objection."

"Then—then—I propose that we break into the house."

"And so get committed to prison for our pains."

"Nay, but ——"

"I say nay. You are by far too eager and too enthusiastic. All we can do, is to call the attention of the watchman to the circumstance. And here most opportunely comes one."

One of the ancient, white great-coated guardians of the night now made his appearance, awakening all the neighbourhood with the gratifying intelligence that it was past something o'clock and a cloudy night.

"Hilloa, my friend," continued he, who had been speaking. "Hilloa! we have heard a strange noise here, which seems to proceed from this house."

The old watchman moved his nightcap from one ear, as he said,—

"Eh? Eh? Did you speak?"

"We have heard a noise in that house."

"That house—that! oh that? Oh, very good, very good. Old John Penny lives there."

"John Penny! and who is John Penny?"

"Past twelve and a clou—dy night."

"Come away—come away. You see, now, there is nothing to be made out of this affair. Come away, Harrington, come away. Have you forgotten that I made an observation which I would have made to no living soul but yourself? Have you forgotten that I have denounced myself as a murderer?"

"I have not. The words you uttered, Nicholas Lowe, sunk deep into my heart. They were not likely words to forget."

"They were not indeed. But do they awaken no desire to hear more? You thought me happy; you thought me content because I have enough about me of this world's goods, and, to all appearance, no care, no anxieties, because I have neither wife nor child, nor any one in any way dependent upon me. Ah, Harrington, Harrington! I have taken upon myself to convince you that there is a skeleton in every house, and I will begin with my own."

Nicholas Lowe, who was he who had made so startling a revelation, drew Harrington away from the neighbourhood of the house near to which such strange sounds had saluted their ears. He continued speaking to him in low accents, and he did not notice that a man was watching their movements, although from the other side of the way.

"You know, Harrington," he said, "that the house I now occupy is my own. You know it is my freehold, and that I alone live in it, without servant and without companion."

"Yes, yes."

"And so shall I live until this mortal frame commences to resolve itself again into those elements of which it is compounded. When I am gone that house will be yours.—With it you will inherit something that may make my memory seem blacker than it ought to be. After a most severe mental struggle, I have resolved to confide in you."

" You know you may, Nicholas Lowe."

" I do know I may. I tell you I am a murderer !"

" Is he mad?" thought Harrington. " Is he mad?"

" How long have you known me?" abruptly demanded Nicholas Lowe.

" Five years."

" Yes, yes. It must be five years—

> ' Five times five, then half a score—
> Shall his years number—no more, no more.'

And I am thirty-five now."

" What, in the name of Heaven, are you talking about ?"

" A prophecy that was made at my birth, and which I have just repeated to you. Is not the night turning strangely close? Do you not feel a warm air blowing on your cheek? The clouds, too, hang low. There is that strange, mysterious stillness in the air which seems to herald some convulsion of nature."

" A little thunder, perchance. But here we are at your house."

Nicholas Lowe trembled so much that he could scarcely place the key in the key-hole, and the whole energy of his frame seemed to have left him. He appeared weak to an extent which astonished his companion, and more than once he was on the point of proffering to him the assistance of his arm, so utterly unable did Nicholas Lowe seem to be to support himself. The door, however, was at length opened, but the passage was very dark indeed. It was one of those intense, pitchy darknesses which appear like something absolutely tangible, and not a mere state contingent upon the absence of light.

" Come on," said Nicholas Lowe. " Come on, come on ; keep close to me and come up the staircase,—there is nothing to stumble over. Hark, hark !"

" What ?"

" Heard you nothing like the moans of a dying man ?"

" Certainly not. Nicholas Lowe, your imagination is excited to-night. You are not well I am certain."

" Are you not afraid ?"

" Afraid? Certainly not ! Of what should I be afraid ?"

" You are in this pitchy darkness with one who has shed human blood—with one whose hands have dabbled in the gore of his victim—with one who has taken a life in outrage of God's holy ordinance — with one are you who now for twelve years has not known peace."

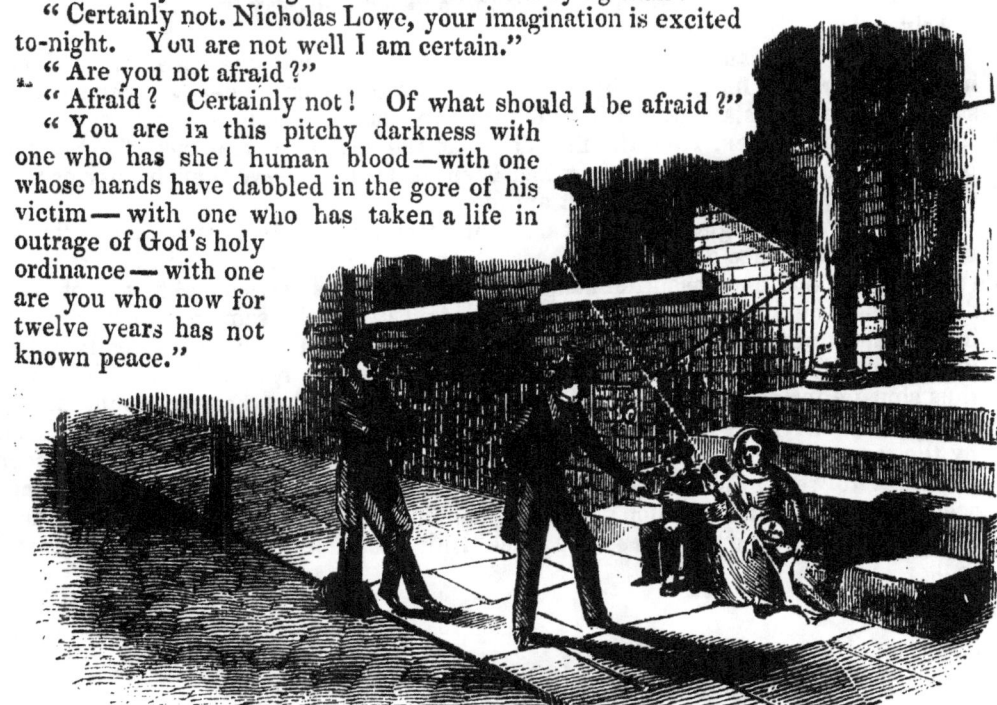

"I am not afraid of you, Nicholas Lowe."

"And yet I am he."

"I cannot believe but what your fervid imagination dresses up some circumstances with more guilt and terrors than they really deserve."

"Was that thunder?"

"It was."

"There will be a storm."

"Probably; but you must have seen many—heard many. Why should a storm to-night so much discompose you? Be more yourself, Nicholas Lowe, and shake off these gloomy fancies, I implore you. Why, man, I have seen you the gayest of the gay."

"While a serpent was eating my heart. 'T was a rare piece of acting. Come on, come on."

There was a dazzling flash of lightning, and as the lurid lustre flashed through the fan-light above the street-door, Harrington caught a momentary glimpse of Nicholas Lowe standing halfway up the staircase that was at the end of the passage, and looking so wild, so frightfully pale and wan, that the young man instinctively started back a pace or two in alarm.

"You fear me now; you fear me now," cried Nicholas Lowe. "Nature conspires against me. Oh, you fear me now!"

"No, no," said Harrington, rapidly recovering his self-possession. "No! I will follow you,—and now almost with the belief that you have really something to tell me."

"Almost, almost," muttered Lowe, as he slowly ascended the remainder of the stairs to the first floor. "God of Heaven! I have a proof here which may not be gainsayed!"

He paused on the landing, and Harrington heard him striking a light. He saw the showers of sparks as they fell among the tinder, and he saw him then ignite the match, the blue light of which gave him an unearthly and ghastly look. Then a candle was lit, and Nicholas Lowe turned and beckoned to his friend, saying, in deep, hollow sounds,—

"Having thus far come, come farther, and see all,—know all!"

He opened the door of the drawing-room, and led the way into that apartment, closely followed by his friend.

We might well pause to give the reader some insight into the appearance of that house, but we feel hurried on by events of a more exciting tendency. Suffice it to say that at some distant period it had been furnished in the most costly style, but that, to all appearance, from the first day that the elaborate and rich fittings had been put into it, not the least effort had been made to preserve their beauty or save them from the consequences of dust and decay.

There were costly glasses, so smeared with accumulated dust, that they reflected nothing on their once glittering surfaces. The gilding had already disappeared, and the elaborate and once beautiful hangings at the windows carried an amount of black dust almost equal in weight to themselves. And it was the same with every article in each apartment. It seemed as if it had been furnished with all the costly extravagance possible, and numerous little elegant bijouterie strewed about it, left to be thus shut up for many years. From the ceiling hung what had no doubt been a costly chandelier. It now was a dense black mass, and nearly rooted to the floor by the long pendant webs which the industrious spiders for many years had been permitted to weave undisturbed. Take it for all in all, that room presented a strange scene of beauty and desolation; it was a place into which one would tread with awe, for the very carpet, which was inch thick with dust, felt like treading on a funeral pall.

CHAPTER III.

THE TENANT OF THE ROOM.—THE CORPSE IN THE FLOORING.

NICHOLAS LOWE had entered the room first, and he held the light at arm's length above his head, although his hand shook so much, that it cast but a very unsteady radiance around it. Harrington looked around him with evident interest, as he exclaimed :—

" Why, Nicholas, you never showed me this room, it is quite a curiosity !"

" A horrible curiosity !" exclaimed Lowe, as he placed the candle, which his agitation had allowed him to hold no longer, upon the table, and then staggered to a couch which was in the room, on which he sank, with a deep groan.

The cloud of dust that arose from the couch almost hid him from view, and nearly choked Harrington, who, however, contrived to say :—

"'And what extraordinary whim has induced you to sacrifice all the property I see here by keeping the room in such a state ?"

" Hush, hush, hush ! speak low !" said Nicholas, with agitation. " See how the flame of the candle catches the spiders' webs, and makes them fly about like ghostly banners. Oh, God ! how this place is altered from that which once it was."

He wrung his hands as he spoke, and his voice had a dreadful wailing expression and tone.

" Pray be calm," said Harrington, " pray be calm. Your mind will be eased by your making a confidant of me regarding the mystery of this room."

" I feel that my career is coming to a close," he exclaimed ; " I cannot die and tell no one. I pitched upon you to tell five years ago, and now the time has come. Look about you."

" I have been looking about in wonder and amazement."

" Are there not sufficient marks of time's ravages here ?"

" There are, indeed. It amazes me where all the dust could have possibly come from. It lies like soot on everything, and is of an amazing thickness. I am surprised, and, I must say, astonished too. Is the carpet of black velvet ?"

" It was of dazzling brightness."

" Indeed ! and these massive curtains, and that black mass, which I cannot make out, which is hanging from the ceiling. Truly I am much surprised ; and what have we here on the table ?"

" Look again."

" Bottles and glasses ! some strange looking things which seem like shrivelled up pieces of bread. Why, it seems as if the room at some particular moment had been fully inhabited, and then as suddenly deserted."

" No human foot has trod in this apartment for more than twelve years."

" Twelve years !"

" Yes. For that time has the door been unopened. There was a small bolt on the outside, to which, twelve years ago, I affixed a seal ; it was not broken until to-night."

" I am astonished."

" The tenant of this chamber has been so long as that undisturbed."

Nicholas Lowe, as he spoke, grasped the wrist of Harrington with a pressure sufficient to be painful, and he shook fearfully, as Harrington, with unfeigned surprise, ejaculated :—

" The tenant of this room !"

" Yes, the tenant. It has always been occupied."

" He is decidedly mad," thought Harrington.

" Always, I say, occupied," added Nicholas Lowe. " Is there no strange odour here ?"

" There certainly is an odd smell, which, I suppose, arises from the want of fresh air in the place. I perceive the shutters are closed, and no wonder a room should have a strange smell after being, as you tell me this has, closed for many years."

" It is not that ; it is —— was that thunder again ?"

" It was. The storm which was prognosticated from the closeness of the air has not yet quite passed over, although it is by no means a severe one."

Nicholas Lowe now spoke in a strange, husky whisper, as he said,—

" Harrington, close the door, and trim the light. There—there. You will now know a secret which has never been breathed to mortal man—which is unsuspected completely, but which I cannot die and leave unrevealed to some human being—a secret of murder. There, again, how the thunder growls and rattles at me. I know, oh, God! that I am doomed ; I know it well. There are five words written in liquid fire upon my brain : " Thou shalt do no murder." I am doomed—I am doomed! and oh, I have already suffered—retribution begun early. I have carried about with me, beneath a careless, and sometimes a smiling face, feelings which were in themselves a hell."

As he continued speaking, his voice got louder and more discordant, and, by the time he had repeated the last word, it had changed almost to a scream.

" Hush—hush," said Harrington ; " hush ; for God's sake be calm, control yourself."

" Who was that ?" he said, suddenly ; " who was that ?"

" What ?"

" Some one screamed out the word ' hell !' "

" It was yourself ; why you are confusing your own intellect. Tell me, calmly and composedly, what you have to say ; depend upon it, that such advice as I can offer you in all the sincerity of the truest friendship, shall be yours.

" My case is now past all power of advice to better, or friendship to alleviate. I —I will endeavour to be more calm. Strange thoughts are flitting through my brain. This room conjures up a dim host of images. The dead now appear to move before me in terrible array. There—there—see how the spectres mock me. Look at that one ! There—by yon covered chair."

Harrington was not without some terrors as he looked in the direction indicated ; but he saw nothing, and he felt ashamed of himself that he should for one moment have given way to the impulses of superstition.

" My good fellow," he said, " there is nothing."

" Oh, God ! oh, God ! Look there—there, gliding behind yon curtain is one —one long since dead. There again, it stoops behind the couch. They are thronging round us. Oh, help me, Harrington. Save me from them."

" Hush ! hush ! We are alone."

" A face—a face only. I see a face—the face of the dead. Look, look, how it hovers about the room, so pale, so bloodless. I killed not you—God knows, I killed not you. Let him haunt me whose blood is upon my hands."

" Let me entreat of you," said Harrington, " if this room, as it seems to do, conjures up so many sad and afflicting images of the past, to leave it at once. Come down below to where you ordinarily sit ; you will be better there, and can as well there tell me whatever you have to tell."

" No, no ; here, although a hundred graves should give up their dead, must it be told. Here and here only, for here and here only is the proof. They have hidden themselves now to listen. The beings of another world are about us."

" Delusion. All a delusion."

" It is none—I know that they are here. Behind those hangings they are hiding themselves, and some beyond that massive curtain which half closes up the entrance to the next apartment."

" I will convince you that you are wrong," said Harrington, as he took up the light, " by at once examining the place you mention."

" No, no, no. Let them be—let them be. They have a right to hear me.

There are several that have a right to hear me. Set down the light upon yon sideboard, Harrington. Oh, 'tis guilt alone that can confer upon the beings of another world the fearful privilege of making themselves so hideously visible to the earthly senses. And I am guilty, Harrington, while I sit here, for I am nerveless and now have no power to help you move that table on one side."

Harrington wheeled along a massive table which was in the centre of the room. Its castors made deep ruts in the thick black dust that lay upon the carpet, and so rotten was the carpet itself that some of it went with the legs of the table, and a cloud of dust was evolved during the process. Nicholas Lowe's voice had now decreased to a strange whisper again, and he looked cold and wretched, as with clasped hands he sat watching Harrington, and telling him what to do.

"In the next room," he said, "beyond that curtain, Harrington, which divides the two apartments—in the next room, on the table, you will find a long flat chisel. Fetch it, fetch it ; but—but draw the curtain as you go, and I shall not then be quite in the dark."

"Yes, yes."

"God only knows what dreadful faces might show themselves were I alone and in darkness here. Go, go, at once."

Harrington took the light and advanced towards the curtain. He laid hold of it to draw it on one side, but the moment he did so, its supports gave way to the slight movement which he gave it, they having, no doubt, become completely rotted, and the whole of the curtain fell to the floor in a heap. A scream burst from the lips of Nicholas Lowe, and there was now such a dense atmosphere of dust in the room, that the light of the candle looked as if it were only dimly shining through some fog.

"What was that? What was that?" said Lowe.

"Don't be alarmed," said Harrington, as well as he could from the quantity of dust that got into his mouth, and choked his utterance. "It is but the curtain which has fallen. Do not let that at all disturb you."

"But—is there nothing?"

"In truth, I cannot see very well ; but I am sure it fell from its means of suppor being rotted away."

"You think so, Harrington, you think so. Oh, what a trial this is to me! And there is the thunder again, too. It comes like the voice of the Almighty to assure me of his vengeance against the murderer. Hark! there it is again—there it is again."

"You seem quite to forget," said Harrington, as he walked over the fallen curtain into the next room, "that Heaven's mercy is its highest attribute."

"But not to him who sheds man's blood. Have you found it, Harrington? Have you found the chisel? The light here is very small. Come back, come back, or I shall go mad ; Harrington, come back."

Harrington found lying upon a table in the room where he had now gone, and which was a smaller one considerably than that in which Nicholas Lowe sat, a chisel with a wide flat blade, such as had been described to him by Lowe, and the moment he had it, he, without waiting to look at anything in that room, hastened back with the candle.

"I have it," he said, "I have it."

"'Tis well," said Nicholas Lowe, "'tis well ; do not leave me alone here, good Harrington. I think I should go mad."

"I have no intention, I assure you, of leaving you for a moment. What more now would you have me do?"

"Hark at the thunder—hark—hark! Is not the storm increasing? How very strange. It was this night so many years since, and such a storm, too ; I knew it would be the same—I was sure it would. I am a doomed man. I feel the prophecy, which, perchance, was uttered in an idle moment, will now be fulfilled. You—you will remove the carpet, Harrington—that portion of it which was beneath the table."

"It has most of it come away with the table ; it seems wonderfully rotten."

"Damp exhalations," muttered Nicholas Lowe, "damp exhalations. Saw you ever, Harrington, a stain below upon the ceiling."

"In the room in which you usually sit, and which, from the construction of the house, must of course be under this, I have perceived a yellow stain upon the ceiling."

"Yes, yes—oh, God, yes. Did you guess?"

"Indeed, I did not. I never troubled myself about it. The whole place is in that state of dilapidation that I never gave a thought to any particular appearances I saw."

"And I never forget it, Harrington. Be quick, I—I cannot aid you. You will find several boards loose which you can easily raise with the chisel you have. It raised them once before. I—I will drag myself close to you to look upon a sight which may blast me for ever, which, while I yet linger in this world, may light up the hideous flame of insanity in my brain, and yet I must look—yet I must look! Oh, how many, many hours of the night have I lain awake, imagining what a fearful spectacle that object must prove."

"What—what object?"

"The corpse of the murdered man!"

"Good God!" exclaimed Harrington, as he dropped the chisel from his grasp on the blackened boards at his feet.

At that moment only he seemed to have awakened to a full consciousness that there was something far beyond the ravings of a distracted imagination in the words of Nicholas Lowe. A faint and strange feeling came over him, and he felt that, with the conviction that there was indeed a corpse below the floor, one half his strength of mind and body both had gone.

"Nicholas Lowe," he said, "you—you surely do not mean what you say."

"I have told you."

"But—a corpse here—here?"

"Ay, even where you stand," whispered Lowe. "For twelve years I have lived, eaten, drank, and slept here, with the knowledge of its awful presence, and felt that it was my doom to guard it; to keep a perpetual watch over its place of concealment. In mind and in body alike am I now wearied out, and prepared to die when I shall have told you all."

"I wish to Heaven you had kept the secret still locked within your own breast."

"No, no. There is a doom connected with murder—I laughed at it once, as an idle superstition, but it is not so—it must and will out some day, and if there be no likely means of others falling on the truth, sooner or later he who did the deed will make a confidant of some one, perhaps to his own destruction, but yet he must make it."

"I am full of sorrow to be made the depository of such a secret."

"You know it now."

"No, no. I have seen nothing; let me see nothing. I will restore the table to its former position, and having seen nothing but this long deserted room, I shall know nothing."

"You have heard me speak."

"I have; but am willing to set down those words to the account merely of a heated imagination, which prompted the lips to utter they knew not what."

"No, no, no," cried Nicholas Lowe, "it may not be. We have already gone too far. Remove the boards. On your soul's salvation I implore you to remove the boards, or I must do so. I have a horrible curiosity which must be gratified, even though at the moment it kill me. What evidences think you of a human form would remain after such a lapse of time?"

"I cannot tell."

"Then we must see; we must look, Harrington. Harrington, remove the boards, I charge you—I beg you."

There was a wildness about Nicholas Lowe's manner that made Harrington again begin to have his doubts whether it was not all a delusion after all. The only way to resolve the question was, certainly, now that he had the opportunity, to remove, as he was desired, some of the boarding, and really see what was beneath. He was a man himself of rather an imaginative temperament, and in the habit of acting from hasty impulses. Now one of them at once seized him, and turning to Nicholas Lowe, he said in a decided tone —

"Hold the light, and I will comply with your wish, since you are so urgent upon it."

The self-accused murderer crept forward. He said not a word; but he took the light from the hand of his friend, and then he sunk on his knees, and fixed his eyes on a piece of the blackened flooring which Harrington was clearing the dust off with the side of the chisel, in order to find the part where it joined to the next piece of timber.

As yet everything had been fully confirmatory of the statement of Nicholas Lowe. The stain upon the ceiling below, and the rottenness of the carpet above, results which might each arise from, as he had said, the damp exhalations from the dead body; and now, when he found where the floor-boards joined, and inserted the chisel, he found another confirmation in the looseness of the boards, which were evidently not fastened.

A slight scream of suppressed agony came from the lips of Lowe, as he saw the first of the boards move. Then, when it was partly turned over on one side, Harrington recoiled with horror, for the stench which arose was dreadfully nauseous, and his eyes fell upon a mass of something which he dreaded to look further at.

"Here, here," shouted Nicholas Lowe, springing to his feet as if he had been shot. "It is here! It will not decay, it will not pass away, and leave no recognisable trace behind. Look, look, look! The head which I battered down with my foot between the joists. There it is! there it is still! Ha—ha—ha! Ha—ha—ha!"

At this moment such a tremendous and uninterrupted knocking came at the street door that Nicholas Lowe dropped the light, and, with a scream, fell backward on the floor. A voice from the street then said,—

"Open, open in the king's name," and then another, in strange exultant accents, shouted, "Nicholas Lowe is accused of wilful murder!"

CHAPTER IV.

MRS. PADDLEBAT'S TEA PARTY, AND ITS CONSEQUENCES.

IT was in the October of the year 1805, just fifteen years before the period at which the events recorded in our last chapter took place, that Mrs. Paddlebat gave a tea party. But as the reader is extremely likely at this juncture to say, who is Mrs. Paddlebat? we consider ourselves bound at once to answer the inquiry.

Mrs. Paddlebat then, as may be naturally supposed, was the wife of Mr. Paddlebat, and Mr Paddlebat was a goldsmith, and one of the most eminent which the city of London could boast of.

He was very well to do now, and at the period when the tea party was given to which we wish to draw attention, he had long thought of giving up his business and retiring to some little snug country box, where he could have no doubt been to the full as unhappy as men of actual business habits usually are when they retire to snug country boxes.

But this was a design as yet only in embryo, and a very amusing thing to talk about, indeed much more so than to put into practice.

The family of Mr. Paddlebat consisted of himself and his wife, Mungo Park, Juliana, and Paulina.

Mungo Park was a very black-faced pug dog, with corpulent body and very small legs; Juliana was an Italian hound, as delicate and small-bodied as Mungo Park was given to obesity, and Paulina was a tabby cat of most unquestionable mousing powers, with other capabilities.

And a glorious time of it these animals had, for there were no children to get up a sort of inquisition on a small scale to torture them.

With so few drawbacks therefore it was, as everybody said, and of course what everybody says must be true, no wonder the Paddlebats got on amazingly well, and could retire and not be so very old either. The fact is, business then was not what it is now, when tradesmen go into business with three times the capital which their forefathers would have thought was quite enough to retire upon.

And there was often among old fashioned tradesmen a great degree of liberality too, for old Mr. Paddlebat fully intended, if he did retire to the aforesaid snug country box, to leave his business connection in the hands of the young men who had been for some years in his employment, and who were consequently well versed in the business.

These young men were respectively Jervis Rodwell and Nicholas Lowe. Two persons of more strikingly dissimilar characters perhaps never had the ill luck to be associated together in the same house and in the same pursuit.

Jervis Rodwell was the senior by several years of Lowe; he was good looking—of a flashy looking sort of exterior, but at heart utterly hollow and worthless. Selfishness was the grand characteristic of his character. He had but a limited education—never thought deeply or studied; but in worldly wisdom he was far above Nicholas Lowe, who had a shade of melancholy in his disposition, and was a great lover of all that was beautiful in nature and in art.

Lowe was as unselfish as the other was grasping, but there lay at the bottom of his heart passions of a far finer character than any which found a place in Jervis Rodwell's disposition, and which for good or for evil might be called into action according to the circumstances in which he was placed.

Rodwell hated Lowe, and Lowe had no feeling at all the one way or the other towards Rodwell; perhaps, had he been compelled to give some sort of a judgment upon him, he could have said, that he rather held him in contempt than otherwise, and did not consider him worth the thinking of or the talking of.

Both these young men had good incomes given to them by Mr. Paddlebat, so that both had ample opportunities, which certainly neither of them neglected, of presenting the outward appearance of gentlemen.

That such a very incongruous pair should ever be able to continue long together in partnership, was visible to everybody but Mr. Paddlebat. His wife loudly proclaimed her opinion on that head, and considered that Jervis Rodwell was worth fifty Nicholas Lowes, all rolled into one.

So much then in the way of introduction; and now, if our readers will please to imagine Mr. and Mrs. Paddlebat sitting after dinner and conversing, we shall have an insight into a matter which threatened a little to disturb the peace of the family.

Mr. Paddlebat had a yellow silk handkerchief over his bald head, a measure of precaution against catching cold which he always adopted after dinner. Mrs. Paddlebat was what ladies call laying down the law, i. e., arguing Mr. Paddlebat into something which he did not exactly like.

" You may go on talking, Mr. Paddlebat, till you can talk no longer, like the old gray parrot who ought to have been dead thirteen years ago. Still it won't do, Mr. Paddlebat, and you ought to know that as well as I know it, although somehow or other you never do know things so well as I know them. I don't believe it is in the nature of man to see anything with the eye of a woman."

Here the lady paused, and Mr. Paddlebat gave a sort of a grunt, to signify that he was paying the profoundest attention to what was going on.

" Very good," resumed Mrs. Paddlebat, who was long accustomed to hold similar discourse, and to receive similar answers,—" very good; and of course I have no disinclination to your retiring from business, especially seeing how very comfortably we are situated now, and after so many years have past and gone in the vale of what d'ye-call it; but it won't do, Mr. Paddlebat—it won't do. I told you so from the first, and I tell you so now, and I shall always go on telling you so as long as I am a suffering and a living woman."

" Eugh!" said Mr. Paddlebat, who was nearly asleep.

"What do you say, Mr. Paddlebat, that it will do; I can tell you that it won't do, and sha'n't do, and it's unmanly in you to say that it will."

These words were screamed out in such close proximity to Mr. Paddlebat's ear that he started fully awake, saying

"Eh! eh! what is it all about—what is the matter?"

"Now, really, Paddlebat, you are a trying man," said the lady. "You are an iron chain, Mr. Paddlebat, that's what you are. Nobody's nerves could stand you for a week; you know as well as I, that I alluded to Nicholas Lowe and Jervis Rodwell taking the business after you."

"Oh,' said Mr. Paddlebat.

"I tell you it will not do," continued the lady; "they are different young men. Nicholas Lowe! faugh! who is Nicholas Lowe? an oaf—a bear—a Corsican—a bruin! not at all a genteel young man; far from it. 'Twas but the day before yesterday, that I took Mr. Whiskin's beautiful portrait of me into the counting-

house, and I said to him, 'Nicholas, who is that intended for?' Well, what do you think he said?"

"Oh, I don't know," said Mr. Paddlebat.

"Why, he said he recognised my gros de Naples dress, but as to who I lent it to to have their portrait drawn, he could not for the life of him perceive, but, on the whole, he considered the picture was a label on humanity."

"I suppose you mean a libel," said Mr. Paddlebat; "but you always call a libel a label."

"Oh, dear, me!" said Mrs. Paddlebat, with an infinite number of little jerks of the head; "since we 've been in the volunteers, of course we can put everybody to rights."

"My dear, you know I went into the volunteers to protect our hearths, and our homes, and all that sort of thing, against that rascal Buonaparte. There's the French, as you know, got a hundred thousand flat-bottomed boats, waiting to bring seventy thousand men to pillage all the goldsmiths' shops and ravish all the women."

"Ravish a fiddlestick!" said Mrs. Paddlebat. "I should like to see 'em; but that 's not the question, just at present. I say it is no use to try it; Jervis Rodwell and Nicholas Lowe will never agree in the business; and, ah me!—lawks a daisy! when you come to think of Jervis Rodwell, what an elegant young man, so what-do-you-call-it, so thingummy and everything, and always a-smiling, like flowers in May, and such a voice! and so sentimental! Ah! there 's the young man, Mr. Paddlebat, as is worth his weight in gold."

"Always smiling, is he?" grunted Mr. Paddlebat. "D—d if I like a fellow with a perpetual grin upon his face."

" Mr. Paddlebat, it is your vulgarity that calls it a grin.   You may grin, if you like, but Jervis Rodwell is incapable of grinning."

" My dear, I never grin," said Mr. Paddlebat.   " If ever I have an inclination that way, I think of you, and that stops it."

" You monster!" exclaimed Mrs. Paddlebat.   " I only wish the French would come, that's all.   You may go on as long as you like, sir, with your jeers and your jerks; but I tell you, as I told you before, that they never will agree in business together."

" Now look you, Sarah," said Mr. Paddlebat.   " I have thought over this matter, in my own mind, and I have arranged it all; we've neither chick nor child, you know."

" And whose fault's that, I should like to know, Mr. Paddlebat? these sort of things is always somebody's fault and somebody else's misfortune."

" Mrs. Paddlebat, we have had quite enough argument on that head.   As I say, we've neither chick nor child.   You have no relations but old Skinner, the sugar-baker, who's quite well enough off without our assistance; nor have I any, for we have good reason to believe that my two sisters, Amelia and Alice, are both dead, poor things.   When Amelia married that scamp Leslie, and went with him God knows where—to the north pole, or the South Sea, or some such place—I gave her up for lost, poor thing, and that's a matter of fifteen years ago; and as for little Alice, who now would be so young even, you know very well she disappeared and we never heard of her again."

" And have you forgotten old Gilbert Paddlebat?"

" No, I haven't; but as he chooses to forget us, I think we may as well forget him.   The last time I met him was four years ago, come next Michaelmas, and then I invited him to take a glass of ale, which came to fourpence, and all the while we were drinking it, I saw him counting something up on his fingers, and when we had done, he gives a hideous kind of chuckle, and he says,—' You have spent a year's interest upon six and eightpence, at five per cent.   I disown you, ass; you'll come to want; never speak to me again.'   And I think, after that, we may as well be done with Gilbert Paddlebat."

" Oh, I know he's a brute," exclaimed Mrs. Paddlebat.   " I heard him say once, that he thought women a great deal more expense than they were worth; that was enough at once to show me what the man was."

" Well, then, my dear, it comes to this," said Mr. Paddlebat, laying his great fat hand with a bang upon the table; " I am going to leave the business myself, so Nicholas Lowe and Jervis Rodwell, both of them, I believe, honest men, may as well keep it as long as they like, and quarrel over it at last, as have the shop shut up at once."

" Whatever is all that row about?" exclaimed Mrs. Paddlebat; " did you ever hear such a lumbering and scrambling in all your life?"

These words were scarcely out of Mrs. Paddlebat's mouth, when the dining-room was opened, and a well-fed, rosy-cheeked servant girl made her appearance, saying,

" Oh, if you please, sir and ma'am, they are come."

" The French?" exclaimed the goldsmith.

" Good gracious! and the ravishing will begin directly," said Mrs. Paddlebat.

" No, ma'am; not the French, but a young chest and a great lady—no, I means a young lady and a great chest, and ever such a great dog, and Mungo Park's as dead as nothing.   Paulina's up the kitchen flue, and Juliana seems to take to it as if they had know'd each other in some other sphere."

This was not the most intelligent speech in the world, and no wonder that both Mr. and Mrs. Paddlebat looked at the girl, the former with a strong suspicion that she was a little deranged, and the latter that she had been at the spirit bottle.

" She's mad," said Mr. Paddlebat; " she's gone mad with too much to eat and too little to do."

" Mary, you hussy," said Mrs. Paddlebat, " you have been at the shrub again."

A sudden shriek from Mary, and a very precipitate manner of settling down upon the floor, told equally well for both these suppositions, and then there darted past her a huge Newfoundland dog, with a cold fowl in his mouth that he had found on the tray outside the dining-room door, and a coating of mud upon him which only left a small portion of his back visible.

The landing of the French would have been nothing to Mrs. Paddlebat, in comparison to this, and with a loud scream she flew to the further corner of the room, while the dog sat down by the hearth and commenced eating the fowl, with a relish which seemed to say he had been a stranger to such luxuries for some time.

"That's one of 'em," said the servant, and, even as she spoke, there came into the room such an apparition of beauty that the dog was forgotten, as well as all the ravages he had committed and the mischief he was doing, and Mr. and Mrs. Paddlebat seemed as if they would never take their eyes from off the doorway.

It was a young girl who produced this magical effect. She was plainly attired, but not in the coarse, homespun material in which the world would have clothed that native grace and form of loveliness. The half hat half bonnet of plaited straw which she wore had fallen back from her head, revealing such masses of beautiful hair, surrounding a countenance of so much sweetness, modesty, and beauty, that no one could gaze upon it a moment without being charmed, and feeling that, notwithstanding the numerous cases to the contrary, the human face might indeed be divine. It were in vain to say she had such eyes and such lips, while the buds of such and such flowers bloomed upon her cheek ; it were in vain to talk of the soft, rounded chin, and the dimples that played about her velvet lips ; suffice it, she was beautiful—beautiful in that beautiful innocence and grace which is only to be found in the young and the mentally gifted, long before the world's cares and the mind's anxieties have made war upon the frame.

She stood irresolutely about two paces within the room ; one hand held around her slender, sylph-like form, a very common shawl, while in the other she carried a letter. The great dog having contrived in a very few moments to convey the fowl down his capacious throat now walked up to her, and sat down at her feet, as much as to say, "Now here we are both of us ; what do you think of us ?"

"Dear me," exclaimed Mrs. Paddlebat, "am I on my head or my feet ?"

"My dear," said Mr. Paddlebat to the young girl, "you are very pretty, but we hav'n't the least idea as to who you are."

She spoke, and her voice was melody itself. The old goldsmith could hardly believe the sound of his own voice, when pronounced by the lips when it came from that sweet creature.

"This letter," she said, "is for Mr. Adam Paddlebat ; they told me he was here."

"That's me, my dear," said Mr. Paddlebat.

In an instant the young girl sprang towards him, and clasping her arms around his neck, and kissing him on the cheek repeatedly, exclaimed,

"My heart ought to have told me you were he. Oh, this is the happiest moment I have known for long."

Mr. Paddlebat was aghast, and Mrs. Paddlebat held up her hands aloft.

"This letter," said the girl ; "read it, dear uncle, and it will explain all."

"Uncle !" shouted Mr. Paddlebat.

"Uncle !" shouted the wife ; "I'm petrified. What's coming on us now ?"

The goldsmith placed the spectacles on his nose with a precipitation that nearly smashed them, and tearing open the letter he read aloud as follows, while, from the breathless silence that was in the room, every word came distinctly upon every ear there present, and from the nature of the contents, the reader will not only arrive at a knowledge of who the beautiful and mysterious young lady is, but may readily guess what must have been the sensations of Mr. and Mrs. Paddlebat upon her most unexpected presence.

"MY DEAR BROTHER,—I write to you, after years of absence, under circumstances of the most painful depression. I am on my death bed, and long, very long, before these words can reach your eyes I shall be no more and at peace in the grave, although that grave is far away from my native land and from all I love. I have repeatedly written to you since I left England with my husband, and for years I blamed you much for being so unkind as to return me no answer, a circumstance which I attributed to your strong disapproval of my marriage with Leslie.

" I have, however, but lately discovered that you were not to blame, but that the whole of my letters to you had been taken possession of by Leslie, and so prevented from reaching their destination.

" He is no more. Let his faults and his wickednesses rest with him in the grave, brother. For my sake forgive him, and, if you cannot do that, strive to forget him.

" And now, dear brother, I come to that part of my letter which is nearest to my heart. If no untoward accident occur on the long and weary voyage and journey, this letter should be placed in your hands by my only child, Fanny. She is good, and gentle, and amiable. Oh, brother, brother, for the sake of goodness, of mercy, and of God, be kind to her. She has no friend in the wide world but yourself. If you extend not to her the hand of love and friendship she is indeed desolate.

" And she will love you and yours ; for a more pure, and innocent, and kinder heart never beat in human bosom. She is your niece, your own poor sister's child, you know, brother. God bless you—God look down upon you, and prosper you if you are good to her. Oh, do not turn her from you. Brother, this is my last

prayer—this is my last hope. My last thought on earth is now divided between Heaven and you.

" Brother—brother Adam, you—you—God ——"
    *   *   *   *   *   *

Here the letter broke off abruptly, and at the foot of the page was the following memorandum :—

" These his toe scratifie has missus lessly his ded very and coodent finish this ear ןeter noe how hang me.   ANIAS GOTIGHTLY."

" Good God !" said Mr. Paddlebat, and the letter dropped from his hands, at the same moment that his eyes filled with tears, which ran down his cheeks profusely, in spite of all his exertions to restrain them. " Good God ! Poor, poor Amelia. My dear, my dear child, come to me. I—I am, as you see, a d—d old fool, but—but—when I desert you, I only hope I may be hung. Bless you, I won't be your uncle, I will be your father, you pretty darling. God bless you, bless you. Mind, I ain't crying; it's only a cold; I—I—ain't such a fool."

And, as he spoke, the old goldsmith clasped the little orphan to his breast, and gave her so many kisses, that she was half smothered.

" You are a dreadful fool, Mr. Paddlebat," said his wife, and then she set-to blubbering at a bountiful rate, and, catching the young girl away from her husband, she completely hid her for about a minute in a capacious embrace.

" Do you mean, Sarah, to be good to her?" said Mr. Paddlebat.

" Do I mean!" cried his wife. " Am I Buonaparte, or a Prussian? Do I mean! How dare you ask me, if I mean. My dear, don't you cry—don't now. You shall stay here as long as you will, and two days beyond, for ever."

Mr. Paddlebat moved his hands up and down like the fins of a large turtle, as he said, between laughing and crying,—

" I knew it, oh, I knew it; I always said, Sarah, your heart was in the right place; I always said so. Now we have got a child—a daughter—ready made ——"

" Will you hold your tongue, Mr. Paddlebat?"

" Without the trouble, and all the squalling, and the mess, and the napkins ——"

" Mr. Paddlebat!"

" My dear."

" Is this manly, sir? Is it proper, you wretch?"

" Oh, dear, oh, dear; I don't know what I'm saying. I—I don't know hardly what I'm doing. Don't you keep her all to yourself, Sarah. Come to me now, my dear. Why don't you let her come to me, Mrs. Paddlebat?"

" Because you are ridiculous, Mr. Paddlebat; that's the reason. I shall give a tea party this very evening, or I'll know the reason why; I will. Come along with me, my duck of diamonds. We shall be good friends, I know, bless your little heart. Well, well, who would have thought this. There's a family likeness, too, Come along, my dear; you shall always go out with me, and—oh, dear, oh, dear. everybody will be always thinking you are mine. Oh, you beautiful, nice creature."

The young girl might or might not have expected so kind a reception; but as it was, she was so overpowered by it that she could do nothing but weep; and, covering up her beautiful face with her long slender fingers, between which the tears forced themselves, she followed Mrs. Paddlebat from the apartment.

CHAPTER V.

THE DOG.—THE RIVALS.—A GREAT ALTERATION IN THE FEELINGS OF MR. PADDLE-
BAT.—THE NEW ARRANGEMENT.

HEN Mr. Paddlebat was alone, he did nothing but move about his hands for some minutes, in the manner we have before likened to the movements of the paws, or fins, of a huge turtle; and while he did so, he made that odd chuckling noise in his throat which many people use to give expression to their surprise.

" Well, well," he at length said; " well, well, who would have thought it! Here's ups and downs, and goings round. Here's a world. Leslie dead, and my poor sister, too! Well, well. Bless us, bless us; and here I've got a niece that all the young fellows in London will soon be quarrelling about, I can see. Dear me, dear me, dear me! what a dear, affectionate little creature she does seem, to be sure."

We will leave the good-tempered gold-

Smith to pursue his own cogitations, while we follow up stairs the young girl and her aunt. Scarcely had they got into a chamber above, than the great dog made such a sudden rush lest the door should be shut upon him, that he nearly knocked down Mrs. Paddlebat, and did upset several things that stood what that lady called " tottery" upon a table.

" Lie down, Leo !" said the young maiden, and in an instant the huge animal crouched at her feet.

" Oh, my nerves," said Mrs. Paddlebat. " My dear child, you don't mean to keep this great elephant of a dog about you, surely ?"

" The dog !" said Fanny Leslie, as she knelt by the side of her friend and favourite. " Ah, my dear, good Leo."

" Really, my love, you talk to the creature as if it were a Christian ; but I suppose you don't think of keeping him ? He's quite as big as a small donkey."

The young girl rose with a deep sigh, and moved towards the door, saying, as she did so, in a mournful voice,

" Come, dear Leo, come. We will go somewhere else."

" Somewhere else !" answered Mrs. Paddlebat. " Why, what on earth do you mean by that, my dear ?"

" You said Leo was to go, and so we must both go. If dear Leo goes, I must go too. We shall have both of us to beg."

" Lord have mercy upon us, I suppose, then, we must keep him. Come back here, and don't be so foolish. He is dreadfully big, certainly. I hope he is not growing, my dear, for really, if he gets the size of a bull I don't know what we shall do ?"

" No, no. Leo is at his full growth. He is a dear and old friend of mine. He has saved my life twice."

" Saved your life ?"

" Yes ; once when I was quite a child, he got me out of Patanamaowow, near to the rapids."

" Out of the what ?"

" It is a river in America ; and another time he saved me from a panther, and was nearly killed himself. You see one of his paws is a little lame, and half of one of his ears is gone. The panther did that."

" Merciful Providence ! What an animal ! and what's his name ?"

" Leo."

" Well, I suppose we shall get used to him, only he certainly has a dreadful way of running against one's legs and knocking one down ; and, you see, he occupies all the floor, and his tail stretches under the bed ever so far; really I cannot move."

" He will wait outside. Leo, begone, to watch."

The dog rose, and after a glance at the face of his young mistress, he left the room, and laid himself down on the landing outside the door.

" Bless me, he understands what you say to him, my dear, like any human being. Well, I am astonished."

" Ah, poor fellow," said Fanny, " he loves me, and will do anything that I tell him. He has taken a world of pains to understand all that I say to him. He will never intrude unless he is permitted."

" Well, that's a something, and as he has really saved your life, my dear, and given us the pleasure of seeing you, we will make a great pet of him, big as he is, and now you must consider yourself quite at home here, and you need be under no apprehension, about ever outstaying your welcome."

" Oh, how can I thank you ?"

" Not at all, my dear ; say nothing about it. That's the way to thank us. Eat and drink as much as ever you like, and make yourself comfortable. That's all we want of you ; we are old-fashioned folks, and require nothing else. You are a very sweet pretty creature, and I dare say you have been told that before."

Fanny laughed and shook her head.

" Well, if you haven't, you'll get told of it enough I'll be bound soon by the young chaps. You must know that Mr. Paddlebat is a common councilman of this ward."

Fanny Leslie knew about as much what a common councilman of a ward meant as if she had been told that he was chief man of Constantinople, but she made no remark about it, and listened with respectful attention to whatever her aunt chose to tell her of the dignities of the goldsmith.

"And besides all that," continued Mrs. Paddlebat, "he's a man wonderfully respected in the city, I can assure you, my dear, and one whose word would pass anywhere for a thousand pounds."

"Indeed, dear aunt."

"Yes, you may believe what I say, for it's a fact as I tell it to you ; we have no children."

"Oh !"

"At present—ahem !"

"Do you mean to have a few ?"

"Well, I don't know ; but never mind that, my dear. Now you must to-morrow have some new clothes made for you, but as I shall invite some friends to tea this afternoon, we must see what we can do for you out of my wardrobe. I's a pity my things won't fit you, in consequence of my being a little stouter than you are."

Well might Fanny Leslie open her beautiful eyes rather wider than before at the idea of her aunt being a little stouter. One of Mrs. Paddlebat's dresses would, without any exaggeration at all, have made at least three very handsome and full ones for the sylph-like form of Fanny.

However, with some management, Fanny was very easily fitted out, when all of a sudden Mrs. Paddlebat said—

"But, my dear, something was said about a large box that belonged to you surely."

"Oh, yes, aunt, it's full of bear skins."

"Bear skins, my dear !"

"Yes ; they were made a present to me by one of the Indian chiefs who wanted me to become his wife."

"Heaven be good to us ! The wife of an Indian chief."

"Yes. When, however, he found I would not, but that I insisted upon endeavouring to come to England to seek out those who were of kindred to my mother, he bade the great spirit to bless me, and he gave me the chest full of bear skins which I have brought with me. It was the only species of wealth he had to bestow upon me."

"What a singular thing, my dear ; I long to look at them. Let's have the chest brought up here ; who knows but he may have placed something else in it ?"

"He may have done so."

"Bless me, I'm all curiosity to open it ; we will have it up here directly, my love. The idea of an Indian chief wanting to marry you. Ah ! I thought somebody had told you before to-day how pretty you were."

While all this was going on in the family of the Paddlebats, there were two individuals who were ultimately to be most largely interested in the proceedings, who, strangely enough, knew nothing about them.

Those individuals were Jervis Rodwell and Nicholas Lowe.

Both these young men were in the shop, or, as it might more appropriately be called, warehouse, of the goldsmith ; and as Fanny Leslie, with Leo and the great box full of bear skins, came in at the private door, and as the direction in which they had come did not enforce the necessity of reaching that private door by passing the shop window, these two young men, although they knew that some bustle was going on, really knew nothing about it.

They were both seated, and both were making up accounts. The fact was, that they were compelled, the one as a check upon the other, not as regarded honesty, but for mere punctuality and business habits, to keep a separate account of books of the business, and old Mr. Paddlebat, once a month, looked over these books, to see that they corresponded in every particular with each other.

This was no bad plan. It was one he had found answer his expectations, and i^t was one therefore in which he steadily persevered.

The young men were both at work upon those very books, and there was an air of anxiety and care upon each of their countenances, which, had our readers seen them, would have tempted the question of—

"Have they skeletons?"

We, who are behind the scenes, are enabled to answer that they had.

After he had been for some time writing Rodwell looked up and said, in a tone of inquiry,

"There were four forks last Thursday?"

To this Lowe made no answer, and Rodwell, after a pause, repeated in a tone of anger, "There were four forks last Thursday—is that correct?"

"You can look in your day-book, Mr. Rodwell," said Nicholas Lowe. "I should have no objections on earth to answering you, were it not a direct violation of the orders of our mutual employer, Mr. Paddlebat."

"Indeed."

"Yes—that is the only reason why I cannot answer your inquiry, but feel myself as it were compelled to refer you to your day-book, which, if correct, will at once satisfy you with the information you seek."

"I'll tell you what it is, Lowe," said Rodwell, vehemently.

"What is it?"

"If I were such a d—d sneaking saint as you are, I would poison myself some of these days."

"If I was the fool you are I might," was the reply.

"Fool!"

"That was what I said. You want to pick a quarrel with me, Rodwell, and I know it. Let me, however, advise you to do it in some other point than because I will not keep your books and my own too. You will find that will not answer, and that Mr. Paddlebat will use his own judgment in matters of business, however much he may defer to his wife's in minor affairs."

"His wife's! What do you mean?"

"Oh! you know what I mean well enough; since you have been in the place your constant endeavour has been to make yourself amazingly agreeable to Mrs. Paddlebat; now, don't mistake me, Jervis Rodwell. I say you do this as a stroke of policy, and not at all from any mere sinister motive. You think it desirable and judicious, situated as you are, to be on good terms with Mrs. Paddlebat—perhaps you are right. You can do these things and I cannot."

"And, pray, what's that to you?" said Rodwell, audaciously.

"Nothing whatever—but you asked me for an explanation; and now you have got it. I gave it you more freely for fear of a misconstruction; having mentioned Mrs. Paddlebat's name, I felt bound to explain why and in what sense I had mentioned it."

"You are d——d careful," said Rodwell.

"I am, when I know I am speaking to those who are not at all likely to put the most friendly construction upon my words; and now that I have said my say, I would rather not talk any more upon the subject."

"Oh! no doubt you wouldn't. I never thoroughly believed, till I came here, what d—d sneaks there were in the world, fellows who are so precious careful and considerate, they couldn't do anything wrong on any account. Oh! dear, no; and, if they do, by a slip of the tongue, say anything, it can be so nicely and sweetly explained away to mean nothing. D—n me, don't you think the word sneak now is an emphatic one."

"Yes," said Nicholas Lowe, "I heard it most emphatically applied to you yesterday."

"To me!" exclaimed Rodwell, starting up and letting the ledger fall at his feet with a loud bang.

"Yes!" said Lowe, quite calmly, and adding up a line of figures at the same time— "fourteen and six are twenty, and eleven are thirty-one, and five are thirty-six, and ten are forty-six, and nine are fifty-five.   I believe I said I heard it applied to you, didn't I ?   Two pounds fifteen."

"You didn't—you never did—where and when was it ?"

Nicholas Lowe closed the ledger, and putting his two elbows upon it and resting his chin upon his hands as he looked steadily in Jervis Rodwell's face, he said,—

"Why, it was your friend, who rejoices in the odd name of Snookem, who called

yesterday.   I heard him call you a humbug and a sneak, both ; but, as you say, I think sneak the most emphatic, and the most happily descriptive of the two."

"Curse Snookem !" said Rodwell, as he sank back on his seat again, and turned very pale.

"Well, he's a friend of yours," said Lowe, "and you may curse him as much as you like, as far as I am concerned."

"A friend !" ejaculated Rodwell, with a jerk of his head, and a groan.   "I should like to see some wall plastered with his brains.   I should like to see him kicked to death, d—n him—he's the bane of my existence."

" Indeed !" said Lowe ; " you and I were talking the other day about there being an old proverb of a skeleton in the house, you denied your possession of one, and here you now talk of a man being the bane of your existence."

" Oh, you be hanged, and your skeletons, too ; it's like a piece of your gloomy philosophy."

" Most unhappily," said Lowe, " most philosophy is gloomy.   I regret it, but cannot alter the fact.   I say as I have often said, there is a skeleton in every house."

" A skeleton ?"

" Yes.   Not a matter-of-fact collection of the bony structure of the human form, but a skeleton of the mind—some hideous thought, or painful recollection—the ghastly and terrific particulars of some episode which clings to one with all the tenacity of existence itself—a something which, in our most pleasurable moments, will come with a sudden bang across the heart, and cloud the sunshine of our joy. I know it—I am certain of it ; if all men were honest and would make a full confession, you would find, indeed, there was a skeleton in every house."

" Oh, oh !" laughed Jervis Rodwell, discordantly ; " it's nothing to me ; there may be a skeleton in every house, for all that I care.   I ain't the housekeeper, therefore it makes no difference to me."

" A very witty and consoling speech, doubtless," sneered Nicholas Lowe ; " but yet it don't get rid of ——"

" Snookem," said one of the errand boys, popping his head into the counting-house at this moment.

" D——n !" said Rodwell.

" And as drunk as the devil," added the errand boy.   " He says he don't intend to go home till morning, till daylight doth appear.   There's a go for you !"

" Tell him," exclaimed Rodwell, springing to his feet, " that I am not here—that I have gone home—out of town—anywhere ; that I am ill—dead ; tell—tell—him that—that I 'll come to him in a minute."

" Blessed if I can recollect anything but the last of that ere message," said the boy.   " He 's been a-saying he 's been with somebody of the name of Mynheer Van Dunk, who never got drunk ; and blessed if I know what he is, for all that he said he was a friar of orders grey, and down in the walley he takes his way."

Rodwell walked sheepishly enough to the door of the counting-house, then he turned and looked at Lowe, who was laughing at him, and who said, before he crossed the threshold,

" Jervis Rodwell, there is a skeleton in every house."

Rodwell muttered a curse, and dashed out of the place.

" Indeed !" said Nicholas Lowe to himself, " and he doubts that which is so obvious.   He has no skeleton, has he ; and I—God of heaven ! if I could exchange mine for his,—and yet I know not ; ask a score of loaded porters, and each will think his burden the heaviest.   I have a skeleton, gaunt, gigantic, and terrific, but I would not exchange it for Jervis Rodwell's.   Yes ; I, too, have my skeleton, a hideous one that haunts me at bed and board, a skeleton I can never forget, one that rises before me in the long hours of the night, one that follows me through all the ordinary avocations in the day, that takes its post beside me ever, a spectre I can never banish, I cannot forget, and the philosophy that bids me assert there's a skeleton in every house, has been one to me that is fearfully practical.   What is the matter now ?"

The door of the counting-house was opened, and the servant put in her head, saying,

" Oh, are you alone here, Mr. Lowe ? have you seen her ?"

" Seen who ? what are you talking about ?"

" Oh, the sweetest and most angelictest young cretur as ever lived, a beauty and a half, Mr. Lowe.   Well, I do wonder as you have heard nothing of her ; master's niece, to be sure."

" What are you talking about ?   Do you mean Mr. Paddlebat ?"

" Yes, to be sure ; who else should I mean, Mr. Lowe? of course I mean Mr. Paddlebat."

" But he has no niece.   How can you be so absurd ?"

" Oh, that was all as he knew about it ; but you 'll soon find as he has a niece, though he didn't know anything about it ; people has lots of things they don't know anything about, till other people find it out for them.   Now there 's me ; I didn't know what I had got, till you found it out for me."

" What do you mean by that ?"

" Why, didn't you tell me as I had a skeleton one day, and I said as I hadn't, and then you sifted me."

" I sifted you ?"

" Ah, to be sure you did ; and after I had been sifted ever so long, I told you as how I had lent four pounds seventeen and sixpence to Captain Butler's young man, and then never sees him or the money again, and how I used to wake up in the night and think of it, and, as the novels say, bedew my tears with my pillow, and feel all the agony of the many sneezecences of the past."

" Do you mean reminiscences ?"

" Well, that's your way—t'other's mine.   The liberty of conscience, say I, and pronouncify your words as you like."

" Very good—very good !"

" Then, you know, you made out as that was my skeleton."

" I recollect now we had some such discourse."

" In course we had."

" But what has that to do with the discovery of a niece of Mr. Paddlebat ?"

" Well, I don't know, now, you've put it out of my head ; I know it had something at first.   Howsomever, that's neither here nor there, and no mistake ; and one of the sweetest creatures is she as never was."

" I should like to see her."

" And so, of course, you will.   Missus is going to have a grand tea party, and then you'll see her.   Oh, Mr. Lowe, master's niece, I am sure, has got no skeleton."

" Yes, she has—yes, she has.   It may not be very gigantic, or very hideous ; but she has one, or else she is not human."

" Human is as human does, Mr. Lowe, that is my motto.   Howsomever, I must be off now ; I heard the bedroom bell ring seven times, and missus will be getting a little impatient.   Oh ! she's a temper to deal with, I can tell you ; she's enough to be any poor servant's skeleton, I can tell you, without any other, right away off hand, and no sort of mistake.   I know what she is, and the worse luck in knowing it.   Talk of skeletons ! she's enough to make a skeleton of nobody in no time,— and there's the blessed bell ringing the eighth time, I declare !   How people will keep on ring—ringing is astonishing !"

" Perhaps the secret of that," said Nicholas, " is, that other people don't answer them."

" Oh, bless you, no, it's natural perwarication !—that's what it is.   Well, there she goes again !   Well ! of all the tiresome fidgets—I suppose I must go now, or there will be no peace.   Good bye, Mr. Lowe ; just tell me, to-morrow, what you think of the new niece."

And so saying, the servant at length condescended to go and answer her mistress's bell, which had only rung eleven times.

" Indeed !" said Nicholas Lowe, when he was alone.   " A new niece has come to-night, has she !   I never heard of old Paddlebat having any relations, but I suppose it's a fact.   And beautiful, too, it appears ; but that I have on very doubtful authority ; indeed, I may think very differently when I see her.   She may be some great country dowdy, for aught I know, and anything but beautiful.   However, it makes no difference to me one way or another ; for, after all, it was but a supposition that the old goldsmith might retire, and do something handsome, when he did so, for those who had been long in his service.   Old people, who have been long in trade, cling to it as an occupation, as well as being more and more enamoured of its profits. I know that he has talked of retiring, but that he ever will is quite another affair. I never believed it, and never shall."

At this moment Jervis Rodwell returned, and with a deep sigh, threw himself on a chair. He took out a handkerchief, and rubbed his head and face very hard ; he looked, and wished that Nicholas Lowe should ask him some question, but Lowe would do no such thing, but only busied himself the more earnestly with his books after Rodwell had made his appearance.

" D—n Snookem !" said Rodwell. But even that had no effect in stirring Lowe to make the least remark.'

" D—n everybody !" said Rodwell, but although he, Lowe, was included in the universal condemnation, he would take no notice of these strong remarks of his companion, but continued provokingly to count up, half aloud, long columns of figures.

Then Rodwell, whose impatience and fretfulness would not permit him to set to work, seized his hat, and with all the determination of a man who had suddenly made up his mind to what he should not, he rushed from the counting-house, leaving those books unfinished which should have been placed in the hands of Mr. Paddlebat on the following morning.

" Ah !" said Nicholas Lowe, " his skeleton grows more gigantic. Snookem, or whatever may be the name of that low associate of his, has some power over him, which he dare not gainsay. Well, well, that, too, matters not to me."

The door was flung open, and Mrs. Paddlebat herself walked into the counting-house. She was magnificently attired, for in looking over her wardrobe, in order to accommodate Fanny Leslie with some fresh apparel, she had been tempted to put on one of her showiest and most gala dresses. She looked one mass of crimson satin, and being, as we have before remarked, a lady of no ordinary dimensions, when she got into the counting-house, and her dress renewed its standing out propensity, it looked a perfect wonder how the door admitted her.

"Oh !" she said, " I thought Mr Rodwell was here."

" He was here recently, madam," said Lowe, " and has but just now left."

" Oh, indeed ! Well, then, should he come in, be so good as to tell him, Mr. Lowe, that we shall expect him to tea in the drawing-room, and you, too, Mr. Lowe, of course ; I am not one that makes fish of one person and flesh of another."

" I am much obliged," said Lowe, coldly.

" Oh ! You are vastly welcome. Our niece has come from America, and will be remaining with us. She's a young lady of great expectations, and of course will make a great match in the city—an alderman's son at the very least—and some of these days dance the minuet what-d'ye-call-it with the prime minister when she's lady mayoress. Mr. Lowe."

" Madam !"

" I hope as a nod's as good as a wink to a blind horse."

" Well, I should think it was, madam, quite as good."

" You understand me, Mr. Lowe. I am a woman of few words,—a plain woman."

Lowe made a slight inclination of his head only.

" But what I say I mean, and what I mean I say. Once for all, and all for once, no gallavanting or love-making to our niece,—that's all. She's brought a Newfoundland dog with her, but that's quite another affair, and an immense box full of bear skins, as some Indian chief gave her. You know all about it, Mr. Lowe. She's our niece. We take tea at six."

Mrs. Paddlebat gave a toss of her head, as much as to say " I have done that rather," and then by the same effort of dexterity by which she got into the counting-house she got out of it again, leaving Lowe not a little surprised at the particular caution he had received not to fall in love with our niece.

" She must be beautiful," he said, " or surely all these precautions would not be taken. I begin now to long to see her. Alas ! what right have I to think of love ; have I not already thought by far too much of it, by far too deeply for my peace ? Have I not already brought one of Heaven's masterpieces to degradation—to ruin—to despair? Is it for me, then, to talk of love ? Oh, no ! I do not want two skeletons haunting me. One is enough !"

CHAPTER VI.

LOVE AT FIRST SIGHT.—THE LETTER TO NICHOLAS LOWE.—THE NEW ANXIETY.—
MRS. PADDLEBAT'S ANGER.

AD Jervis Rodwell been at all aware of the honour which Mrs. Paddlebat intended him of inviting him to tea with "her new niece," he would most probably have come back much sooner than he did, and made every possible endeavour to calm his agitated spirits, so as to appear, with some satisfaction to himself, before the ladies.

It is very doubtful indeed if Jervis Rodwell would have had anything said to him about the nod and the wink and the blind horse, for such was Mrs. Paddlebat's exalted idea of him and his attainments, that she would have scarcely thought it a degradation to have the illustrious blood of the Paddlebats mingled with that of the Rodwells.

It is astonishing that such a really good woman as Mrs. Paddlebat was should be so dreadfully prejudiced; but, alas, it is a remarkable fact as regards poor human nature, that the best dispositioned species of it are by no means always the most acute.

So it happened, then, as regarded Mrs. Paddlebat: she had a thousand good qualities, and she never went wrong when she saw her way correctly; that is to say, she always intended to do right, while, at the same time, she took likings and dislikings to different people, from circumstances that justified neither the one feeling nor the other. And deplorably susceptible to flattery was she likewise, and that is a weakness which any child may play upon, so little skill does it require.

Vanity has a capacious swallow, and a strong stomach: it can digest almost anything in the world, and such was the reason why Jervis Rodwell got so far into the good graces of the lady. He told her abundance of pleasant lies about herself, and to these he added abundance of anecdotes about himself, the whole of which went to represent his own character in the most exalted, amiable, and generous light. She unhappily believed both: it would have been illiberal to receive one without the other, so she took in both as comfortably as possible.

Lowe never condescended to commit these little, petty, suggestive manœuvres, and hence he was out of favour. He never obtruded his opinion; but when asked it, he seldom shrunk from giving it honestly.

Rodwell came home, heated and angry-looking, a very short time before the hour at which the tea was to be had, and when he heard of the invitation, he made a rush up-stairs at once to his own bedroom, for the purpose of making such changes in his apparel as he thought would tend to give him a captivating appearance in the eyes of the new niece. Never, however, had Rodwell looked so pale; but that was an advantage, for however much his florid complexion might be admired by people of no higher cultivated taste than Mrs. Paddlebat, it certainly did not tend to make him look a bit more like a gentleman. But then Rodwell never could be a gentleman.

He put on a dress suit, and when he came down the stairs he had something folded up in his hand, which he was desirous of concealing. He trembled, too, very much as he met Lowe, and passing through the counting-house, he went out at a door leading from it to the kitchen. As he passed through, however, he dropped something, which Lowe had no opportunity of telling him of, in consequence of the quickness with which he was walking. What it was Lowe could not make out till he lifted it up, and then he saw that it was the wristband of a shirt, and that, for about one half of its extent, it was literally sopped in blood. Lowe turned paler than usual, and that was needless, as he exclaimed,—

"Good God! what awful suggestions does this give rise to? What am I to conclude from this? it is surely blood."

At this moment he heard the footsteps of Rodwell returning, and instinctively he placed the evidence of blood having been shed within his desk, and then bent over it as if he were reading. He heard Rodwell pause, and for a few moments he remained silent, then he said—

"Are you going to the tea-drinking, Lowe?"

His voice trembled very much as he spoke, and was strained and unnatural.

"Yes, I am going," said Lowe.

"Well, ain't you going to dress yourself?"

"I am dressed."

"Oh, ah! but I mean as I am, in full dress. Mrs. Paddlebat I know likes her guests to come full dressed, she would have them in court costumes if she could. You had better put on the best dress you have got, and what ornaments you have too."

"No," said Lowe, "I shall not do so."

Lowe divined the motive of Rodwell in wishing him to dress showily like himself. It was that if the taste of the new niece should happen to be of that character which liked personal decoration, he should be superior to Lowe in that respect, while if it went in the plain way, he, Lowe, would have no decided advantage over him in consequence of the absence of all ornament.

"Well, well," he said, "of course you will do as you like."

"Thank you. I shall go just as I am; I have a dress coat on, and that is sufficient, surely; I have a great dislike to any set costumes for particular occasions."

"The tea is ready," announced the servant. "La! how nice you do look, Mr. Rodwell, to be sure, you have a taste; but you don't seem well; you look as if you couldn't help it."

"Couldn't help what?"

"How should I know?"

"Oh, pho—pho."

"Well you do look very odd, for all the world like the man in the play."

"What man—what play?"

"The murderer."

"D——n! I—no. What a fool you are. Don't you hear, Lowe? The tea is ready, and we are to be introduced to the niece of the Paddlebats. I challenge you to a fair trial of strength as to who shall win her heart, if it should turn out to be backed by such a pretty face as to be worth the winning. We start fair, you see, we have neither of us had the advantage of the other. Ha—ha—ha! The house will have some life in it now in comparison to what it has had. A young girl in a house makes all the difference in life. Come on, come on, d—n me, I'd jump over the moon; I never was in such spirits in all my life."

Nicholas Lowe looked amazed. He thought that such a gush of animal spirits must be affected, and would soon fail; but whether they were affected or not, they certainly did not fail, and Jervis Rodwell never was in all his life, so Mrs. Paddlebat declared on the following morning, such good company.

How far the sight of Fanny Leslie transcended any idea of her beauty which either of the young men might have been favoured with, our readers may imagine. Rodwell looked for a moment confounded, and Nicholas Lowe involuntarily uttered the word—

"Beautiful!"

It met the ears of Fanny, and for a moment she rested her dark eyes upon his face, and a slight accession of colour came over her face.

"D—n it!" muttered Rodwell, "she don't seem to see my crimson and embroidered waistcoat at all; she has no taste; and yet—humph! I won't let that chap win her."

From that moment the two young men were rivals, and it was perhaps fortunate on that first evening for both of them that several other persons from the neighbourhood had been likewise invited to tea, in honour of the unexpected arrival of the lovely niece of Mrs. Paddlebat, to whom she was introduced, and who necessarily occupied much of her attention.

But Jervis Rodwell was determined to make an effort to shine, and he accordingly did so, going on with an innumerable quantity of nothings, and making himself, according to the taste of all present, excepting Nicholas Lowe, and probably Fanny Leslie, especially amusing, although not one really clever thing ever passed his lips. There is an amazing difference in nonsense. Nothing marks the strong division of intellect between the man of genius and the man of none more than the difference there is in what is called their nonsense; that is to say, that kind of rattling small talk which is always so pleasant in society, but which not one person in a million is gifted with the genius and the tact, for it usually requires both, of indulging in. The nonsense of some people it is a treat to hear, for it abounds with wit, with happy illustration, anecdote, admirable satire, and is full of intellect; but what a different thing is the incessant rattling small talk of some common-place personage, it is completely destitute of anything appertaining to the whole affair excepting the necessary amount of assurance. How pointless, how cold, how fearfully tiresome such nonsense becomes. It is not, as in the other case, the recreation of genius, but it is downright stupidity holding its own high carnival. And yet people laugh at it. How many a man of abounding intellect will sit neglected in a corner while some idiot becomes the lion of a party.

Nicholas Lowe and Rodwell watched each other closely, so that neither had an opportunity to say much to Fanny Leslie. What little Lowe did say to her, and what little he heard her say, only fixed her image more strongly in his mind.

Several hours passed as hours usually pass on such occasions, wearisome to some and amusingly to others, when the servant, as she came once into the room, placed in the hands of Lowe a letter sealed with black wax, and having on its edges the black funereal-looking border which prepares the recipient of the epistle for the news of death.

Nicholas Lowe turned as white as a sheet, but before any eye save Rodwell's, and he happened to be watching him, could notice his extreme agitation, he rose hastily, and at once left the room.

"Mr. Rodwell," whispered the servant.

"Well, what?"

"Come out a minute."

He did so, and then with much mystery and trembling, she added,—

"To save myself some trouble in the morning, I was cleaning out the counting-house, and what do you think I found?"

"What?"

"In the inside of the common desk, where you know Mr. Lowe sits, I actually, as true as I'm a living breathing soul, found this."

She handed him the wristband soaked in blood, which he himself had dropped, and for a moment, at sight of it, his presence of mind entirely forsook him, and he was compelled to stagger against the wall for support.

"Oh, I thought you'd be affected—I was."

"Give—give it to me," he gasped. "I will talk to you about it to-morrow, but, now mind, for your life's sake, say nothing about it."

"Oh, dear, no."

"To-morrow—I will find all about it, to-morrow. You must keep the secret, or else, whatever I learn, I will not communicate to you, mind that. To-morrow—we will talk over it to-morrow. Be till then as secret as the grave."

The tea party was over, and the house of the Paddlebats was again restored to its wonted tranquillity, but as regards the results of that day's proceedings, Heaven, in its omniscience, could only guess them. They were to be more deeply important than any of the after actors in the scenes of agony, bloodshed, and contrition, could possibly imagine. Had some of them so imagined them, and seen with the eyes of truth that which in the progress of time was to occur, there can be but little doubt that despair such as is akin to absolute madness would have taken up its abode in their brains.

But far better is it for mankind that Providence carefully draws a veil over the future, a veil so impenetrable that not even the most accurate knowledge of the past will enable any human being to hazard even the most likely guess of what will be again. All is dreary darkness and profound doubt. Conjecture even has not the slenderest resting-place, and mercifully, we repeat, is it so. It would seem sometimes as if the lives of several individuals had all reached some posterior point which enabled them to exercise a serious influence for good or for evil upon each other.

This was the case at the Paddlebats. There can be no doubt but that the most unexpected appearance of such a beautiful, young, intelligent, loveable creature as Fanny Leslie, at the house of the old goldsmith, was calculated to produce very serious results. If nothing more occurred than the rivalry for her affections, provided she chose to bestow them upon either, between Nicholas Lowe and Jervis Rodwell, it was calculated to cause a world of uneasiness to her, as well as to those kind and good relations who had with such ready philanthropy afforded her a home. Where now was the old goldsmith's plan of letting the two young men conduct the business for their mutual profit? If, before, their minds seemed to be composed of jarring materials, and if before there seemed to be, as undoubtedly there were, the elements of discord in their dispositions, how much more would these elements be added to by such a prolific source of constant strife as jealousy would be likely to produce. Truly, as Mrs. Paddlebat had remarked, it would never do.

We give that lady credit for her judgment, although not for the course of reasoning or feeling by which she arrived at it, merely by that admiration for Jervis Rodwell which we think so very much misplaced. And now Jervis had made up his mind that win Fanny Leslie he would, if any mortal means at his disposal would suffice to produce such a result. It cannot be doubted but that he was sensible of the beauty of the young girl, although at the same time nothing can be more probable than that which guided him equally was his determination to make her his wife if possible.

That she would now become the heiress of the property of the Paddlebats he felt certain. The manner of her reception, and the kindness he saw lavished upon her, even thus early, by the old man, convinced him of that much, and consequently whatever hopes he had of coming into a good share, if not the whole of the goldsmith's business, vanished into thin air, since such hopes were altogether based upon the known fact of the old couple having no relation for whom they wished to provide, and consequently no one but himself or Nicholas Lowe to look to or to care about.

There could be no doubt then in his mind as to the policy of paying his attentions in the best possible manner he could to Fanny Leslie. This he would probably have done, had nature been altogether as niggardly to her in the article of beauty as she had been bountiful, for Jervis Rodwell was a gentleman who prided himself upon having what he called an eye to the main chance, which we have generally found to translate itself, practically, into getting as much money as possible without being very particular how.

There was a great nervousness about his manner, as he, Jervis Rodwell, dressed himself on the morning following the tea party. He trembled so much that he was compelled to pause several times, and yet he kept muttering to himself some words of congratulation, which seemed sadly at variance with his general perturbed looks and manner.

"I, I, am free now," he said; "and, I, I, am free just at the proper moment, when I required all my energies to make myself as acceptable as I could to old Paddlebat's niece. This a great crisis in my fortunes, I am certain. How strange it is that I should be free of ——. I will not pronounce his name, even to myself. At the very moment when I most required to be so. That, that, wristband which the girl found, I must have dropped it in the counting-house when I passed through to destroy the other evidences of a deed of blood, which—— hush! hush! hush!"

He glanced cautiously around him, as if he fancied that the old saying of "walls have ears," was about to be verified, and he kept on for some moments saying, "Hush! hush! hush!" evidently unconscious that he was repeating the word, for his thoughts were most decidedly elsewhere.

He took a long time over his toilette, dressing himself with great care, for he considered Nicholas Lowe as rather a sloven than otherwise, and he thought he should have a decided advantage over him by a marked attention to costume.

"This young beauty," he said, "shall soon perceive who is the gentleman, and who is not. Lowe is saving money, but I put mine on my back; and the odds are, that let him do what he will with his cash, I am making the best investment. If I can but succeed in winning this girl, who surely cannot be very difficult to please when we come to consider her age, and, probably, the trouble and difficulties she has gone through, I shall be a made man. Nicholas Lowe will of course try his luck as well. I could see it by the manner in which he fixed his eyes upon her. I could see what was passing in his mind as well as if he had been candid enough to tell me in so many plain words; but, d—n him, I'll beat him out of the field."

The last observation arose from Jervis Rodwell having succeeded, as he thought, in giving his hair a most captivating twist.

Fatal mistake! Love depends not upon such matters; if a young girl take a fancy to a young fellow, he cannot, let him do what he will, entirely cure her of it, even if he wished; and if she do not take a fancy to one, not the wisdom of Solomon, the graces of Adonis, the wit of Apollo, nor all the qualities, human and divine, that could be imagined to be concentrated in one individual, could make her.

But Jervis Rodwell had a fancy that he was a decidedly good-looking fellow, and therefore, out of compliment to what nature had done for him, he chose always to do a little more.

Moreover, he had two modes of rising in the world, and of accomplishing any object upon which he set his mind. The one was by endeavouring to make his own deserts speak as loudly as possible for him, and the other was not to stop at any means whatever of effectually damaging his opponent.

Therefore he did not, although he had so very high an appreciation of them, rely solely upon his

[See page 35.

own attractions, but he made up his mind to do as much active injury now as he possibly could to Nicholas Lowe.

"I will take away from him," he said, "just what he values most, and what will kill him to lose; namely, his character. And now about this wristband, and the blood upon it; no doubt he placed it carefully enough, as he thought, in his desk, for the purpose of producing it to my destruction, but he has done himself more harm by such a course than he knows of. What footstep is that?"

Jervis Rodwell turned deadly pale, and grasped the dressing-table for support, as, in a moment, all his nerves seemed to lose their tension, and some dreadful agony of fear came over him.

There was a footstep, and then he heard a voice of some one humming a tune, and he knew it was the servant.

He drew a long breath, and sat down to recover himself, as he said—

"What a fool I am now, what a dreadful fool I am to be frightened at any little thing which before I should not have regarded at all. I—I had no idea I could possibly be so nervous, or—or perhaps I should have paused before I—I—hush, hush! How often a word has hovered on my lips which I could not even pronounce to myself for worlds. I am very safe. There was no one nigh when the fatal blow was struck. No—no, no one. I cannot be suspected of—. There again—there again! I was on the point of saying it again. What folly, what hideous folly! Never was man more secure than I am, and as for the wristband, if there be any danger from that, it shall light upon the head of Nicholas Lowe, and not upon mine—not upon mine."

He left his room, and as he descended the staircase he met the servant girl who had handed to him the wristband.

"I wanted to see you," he said.

"Lor, what for, Mr. Rodwell?"

"About that wristband, covered with blood, which you found in Mr. Lowe's desk. You have not mentioned the circumstance to any one."

"Oh, dear, no."

"Well, then, do not. I have been thinking over it, and as we really don't know at all how it became bloody, and as we neither of us can have any wish to injure Lowe, we had better say nothing about it at present. You understand."

"Oh, yes; but, sir, won't you tell nobody?"

"Not a soul. And you will remember, if ever I call upon you to detail the finding of that wristband in his desk, you will say that I persuaded you to say nothing about it before, out of good feeling and generosity to Mr. Lowe; you understand: and that I said I should be very sorry to do him any injury, as, after all, the circumstance might arise very innocently."

"I'm sure it's very good of you."

"Yes, yes. If ever you are called upon to say anything about it, you can add, that you thought it very good of me."

"Oh, of course I will."

"Then now let me beg of you to keep the circumstance entirely to yourself, and—and I will confide another secret to you."

"A secret!"

"Yes; to me a most important one."

"Oh! dear, Mr. Rodwell, I do so like secrets—what is it?"

"I love Fanny Leslie."

"And I don't wonder at it. A more charminger young lady don't live on this mortal spear, Mr. Rodwell. She's up now, and has been for some time, a looking over all the nice beautiful looking books as Mr. Lowe has sent her."

"Lowe sent her books?"

"Yes, he has."

"D—n him! he is determined to lose no time. Why, it wants half an hour now of breakfast time."

"To be sure it does; but last night he stepped up to his own room, and opened one of those boxes of his, as he has never before opened since he's been here, and he took out some of the most beautiful books as ever was, and he takes 'em into Miss Leslie's room, and places a little bit of paper on the top of 'em, and wrote on it, 'With Nicholas Lowe's respects,' and then he leaves 'em."

"Well, this is too bad. Upon my soul, this is coming it. D—n him! he thinks to get the better of me, does he, by beginning at once; but I'll—I'll think of something during the day. I say—where's the great dog?"

"I don't know; I think as he's making a door-mat of himself outside of Miss Leslie's door."

"Oh! I will propitiate the dog. That will be sure to please her. I dare say Lowe has not thought of that: I will run up, and make acquaintance with him."

Jervis Rodwell, as he came down from his room in the attic, had not noticed the dog upon the landing, and, as he had passed on quietly, the dog, who was coiled up exactly opposite the door of the chamber which had been appropriated to Fanny Leslie's use, had taken no notice of him. Now, however, the case was very different; for Jervis Rodwell stopped, and with such expressions as "Poor fellow," "Fine dog," &c., &c., he strove to make friends with Master Leo.

But Leo was, he considered, upon duty, and any coaxing, under such circumstances, he evidently considered as invidious; so all the reply he gave was in the shape of a low growl, which ought to have been sufficient warning to Rodwell to leave him alone; but he was fool-hardy, and would persevere, and, therefore, the moment he laid his hand upon the animal, Leo sprang up and laid hold of the intruder by the ankle, not sufficiently tight to bite him, but quite enough to hold him quite a prisoner.

Fanny Leslie heard the scuffle, and, in a moment, she opened her room door. Her hair was hanging in beautiful disorder down her neck and shoulders, and around her she had hastily thrown a shawl. Her small white feet were bare, for she had sprung from her bed; and, as he looked at her, Rodwell thought he had the evening before conceived but a faint idea of her beauty: and there he was, in the embarrassing position of being held by the leg by a great dog, while such a form of beauty was within two paces of him.

"What has happened?" said Fanny.

"Why—why—the dog; I was passing, and he laid hold of me.'"

"Leo, release him! You must have touched him or offended him in some way. He is very gentle, and touches no one unprovoked."

Fanny Leslie then, without waiting for any reply, closed her bedroom door again, leaving Rodwell entirely free from the gripe of the dog, for at the command of his young mistress he had released him, but dreadfully provoked at the whole occurrence. Do anything, however, he dared not, or even say anything angrily, for Leo kept his eye upon him as he slunk down stairs again, considering the whole affair as an utter failure, and muttering to himself,—

"A dose of arsenic shall soon rid me of such a hindrance as that d——d dog. Oh, how beautiful she looked!"

And Nicholas Lowe was to the full as much in love with Fanny Leslie as Jervis Rodwell could be, only that he loved her more for her own sake, than for any real or supposititious advantages which were at all likely to result from his achieving a conquest of her affections.

We have recorded that during the evening a letter had been placed in his hands, and he retired to his own room very shortly afterwards. The particulars concerning that letter will appear in another place; suffice it to say, for the present, that it relieved him from an entanglement which had become of the most serious consequence to his peace, and which, indeed, had been the "skeleton" he had alluded to as always haunting him. To be sure, memory still remained. He could not forget but that was not so bad as what had been going on, and comparatively his skeleton had dwindled down to a thin and far less tangible shade than it had been.

We hope and trust that our readers will go with us in the use of this word skeleton, and bear in mind in what sense we use it, namely, metaphorically, to delineate that one feeling of anguish, of sorrow, of remorse, or of anxiety, is the one bitter drop in the cup of every human being's happiness.

So firmly fixed was this opinion in Nicholas Lowe's mind, that everybody must have his skeleton, that he now trembled to think that surely something soon must happen to him in lieu of that deep anxiety that had passed away. If anything, however, could tend to banish from his mind obtrusive and disagreeable thoughts, surely it would be the constantly recurring image of the beautiful Fanny Leslie.

"I love her," he told himself, "and I must try to win her, and endeavour, by kindness and honourable conduct to one of God's beautiful creatures, to make up in some measure for, alas, a different line of proceeding towards another. But I must not think of that. I love Fanny Leslie, and the question of how to win her heart is the one now of most deep interest to me in this world."

He had decidedly got the start of Rodwell by sending her the books, which were most welcome to the fair young girl, and probably thus she had a far stronger feeling in favour of Nicholas Lowe than of Rodwell, although as yet she knew so little of either that she certainly was not qualified to form any opinion.

But not only upon Lowe and Rodwell had the charms of Fanny Leslie produced a great effect. There was a young man, or rather a lad we might call him,— for he was in that transition state between the boy and the man, during which the human animal, if not well controlled and directed, makes itself most supremely ludicrous,—who was smitten to a degree beyond all imagining.

This individual, Mr., or, as he was commonly called, Master Ebenezer Crump, was certainly as much in love with Fanny Leslie as anybody very well could be on a short notice. He was the only son of a doating mother, who carried on the business of a tallow chandler in the City, to which, of course, Master Ebenezer had a reversionary claim; and as the Paddlebats had known the deceased Mr. Crump intimately, the widow and "Neezey," as he was usually called for shortness, were always invited upon any special occasion.

Ebenezer was lanky and lamentably thin; that is to say, he looked lanky because he was so lamentably thin. The most prominent feature of his face, namely, his nose, was fearfully prominent, and stuck out of poor Neezey's face like the blade of a hatchet, giving him very much the appearance of the water-fowl called the spoonbill. Ebenezer Crump's shoulders measured across seven inches and a-half; his neck was long and his head was small, being shaped like a pear; he had long lolloping arms, and remarkably thin legs. Such was Master Crump, and as he is the representative of a large class of lanky boys in London, who think themselves men, and who are always to be seen in abundance in the streets, we must not describe him any farther, than just to say that such ill-put-together lads are always considered by all the female members of their family mighty genteel. Thus Ebenezer Crump was by his mother thought the pink of gentility, because he was so frightfully thin. A buxom servant wench from the country, who suited Mrs. Crump in every other respect, was discharged for want of taste, because she called poor, dear, handsome, genteel Ebenezer "an object." And an object he certainly was, notwithstanding his mother's advocacy of his charms; but he did not think so. On the contrary, he rather thought he was a fine fellow, and as, when he said anything silly, his mother cried it up for wit, and repeated it to her female friends as such, Ebenezer could not but accept so flattering a homage to his vanity, and believed it was just what she said, wonderfully clever.

This, then, was the third lover of Fanny Leslie. He had sat looking at her with his mouth open, and his weak watery-looking eyes distended with wonder, and during the tea-drinking he had likewise drank in deep draughts of love.

It was the next morning that, after a sleepless night, Ebenezer determined upon making his mother a confidant of his passion. He came down stairs looking whiter than usual, and with his dust-coloured looking hair in disorder. He had turned down his shirt collar after the most approved die-away Byronian fashion, and his whole appearance he calculated was quite sufficient to induce some sort of inquiry on the part of his mother which would warrant him in disclosing the secret of his heart.

Mrs. Crump was not,—the truth must be confessed,—one of the most refined of human beings. She had a good deal of low sagacity, which might be called cunning, but she was as ignorant as an elephant, and her manners were by no means according to the code laid down by my Lord Chesterfield.

When Ebenezer came down stairs to breakfast, he sat opposite to his parent, and looked abstractedly at the ceiling for several minutes, which had the desired effect of inducing his parent to say,—

"Why, Neezey, my love, what is the matter?"

"Oh," said Ebenezer, who was decidedly of a romantic turn, "what is the matter—that is the question."

"Ain't you well, my duck? Take an *apparent* pill, my dear, and a *sudlets* powder, my duck."

"A what?"

"An apparent pill; I thought it was a pain in your stomach, as you placed your hand there, my duck."

"Oh, how horridly unromantic, mother. Mother, my pain is at my heart."

"Oh, how you frighten me."

"Listen, listen. This morning, while the stars kept on holding a lonely watch, I burst——"

"Burst? Oh, gracious!"

"Into song. Do not interrupt me. The villanous editor of a most d——e work I could name, who refused my last week's effusions from the muses, will soon discover his loss, I can tell you; he will soon bitterly regret putting in his notices to correspondents that 'E. C. was an ass.'"

"Did he, my love?"

"He did. The iron nearly went into my soul, but not quite. 'Never mind,' said I, 'never mind.' I wrote the barbarian a note, asking if it was the measure of my poems he found fault with, and what do you think was the new insult in the publication of yesterday."

"Well, really, I can't say, my dear."

"It was this. 'If E. C. will furnish us with the measure of the exact length of his ears, we will print it among the odds and ends.'"

"Never you mind, my love. You place it in Mrs. Mouthmagnal's album instead. Then, you know, it will be admired."

Ebenezer laughed scornfully, like a neglected and snubbed genius, as he was, and then, drawing a scrap of paper from his bosom, where he had ensconced it, he read the following words :—

"Oh, love, why do you torment my bosom?
I love her, how I love her, so true;
She's beautiful, most beautiful to me,
    And with loveliness does my fond heart imbue.
I saw her but a moment, but I could look all day;
    Such charms so rare does never, oh, never, fade;
But, when envious years have flown over her, she still will be,
    In the valley where we met, my beautiful maid."

When Mr. Ebenezer had read these lines, he folded up the paper again and placed it majestically in his bosom, as he said,—

"I mean to send them to her."

"To who?" gasped his mother; "to Mrs. Mouthmagnals?"

"Curses not loud, but deep," exclaimed the insulted poet, "upon her. I mean to send them to my heart's empress, the beautiful maid of my soul—to Fanny Leslie; and if she don't respond responsively to my affections, there's the Serpentine, or Mount Vesuvius, or the fathomless ocean, or the Monument."

"The Monument?"

"Yes. I'll pay my sixpence, and then throw myself off into Monument-yard."

"Oh, good gracious, Neezey! you don't mean what you say. Do you want to break your fond mother's heart, and bring my grey hairs—no, I mean my new front, with sorrow to the grave?"

"Hush! I feel it here," said Ebenezer, giving his forehead a blow. "I love her like a child of the storm, with all the ardour of a fiery nature. Oh, if I were but a brigand!"

"Oh, goodness me, Neezey, you do frighten me out of my wits."

"I feel, mother, like a storm-riven cloud, precisely. She must be mine, or the peace of society at large shall be convulsed;—she must be mine. Oh, Fanny, Fanny, Fanny!"

"My dear, be calm, and take your muffin."

"My muffin! I despise muffins; the volcano that's in my heart rejects muffins. I am a desperate man; let society beware how it taunts me; I cannot forget that 'E. C. is an ass!'"

"Oh, my dear, never you mind. The man didn't know any better, you know."

"Mother, mother, mother!"

"Yes, my duck."

"When a new author appears, a man who knows he is like a spring in the desert, that goes on gushing away like anything, I am convinced that all the old ones have a meeting to try to crush him."

"You don't say so."

"I do; I am sure of it. Why was Byron tried to be put down? why am I tried to be put down? why is it that none of the penny periodicals will print the effusions of a genius which is like the fathomless ocean, when tossed by the wild storm of winds and the thunder of mighty and horrid cataracts?"

"Oh, what a mind!" ejaculated Mrs. Crump.

"Why is it that one editor calls me an ass, and another a donkey, if it was not arranged between 'em beforehand, eh? I ask of human nature that astounding question."

"Very true, my love."

"But I will win and wed the fair Fanny, and in some quiet spot, shut in by Alpine hills from the rude world, will sit and wander. Mother, you must go and speak to Mrs. Paddlebat about it, or you may take a lodging on Fish-street-hill, the more conveniently to pick up my mangled form when I throw myself off the Monument, which I most assuredly shall do."

"Oh, my love, don't think of it."

"I will, I will."

"But how can Fanny Leslie refuse you? how can anybody refuse you, my duck?"

"It would be difficult."

"Impossible, my dear. If so be as you wish it, I'll speak to Mrs. Paddlebat, and I dare say it will be all right. Don't now, whatever you do, say anything more about the Monument; you've given me quite a turn already, my love."

"'Tis well. I want half-a-crown."

"There it is, my duck."

"You will go to the Paddlebats, and you will say that Fanny Leslie sits enthroned in my heart. You may take the poetry. You may tell her that society will, in a very short time, become wide awake to the fact of my genius, and that the other fellows who write poetry will all be at a stand, for after I am begun they will all get nothing to do."

"I should think they wouldn't, my dear."

"I know it. Adieu, adieu. I go to Wilkins."

"My dear Neezey, how can you associate with Wilkins? You know he is only an errand boy; I really wonder at it?"

"He has a soul for feeling although he will not own it. I read him my effusions, and we discourse of great things together. I go to summon Wilkins from the base pursuits of ordinary life, to mount on the wings of fancy, and, as my poem says, which was rejected last week—

"'Let us dream, let us dream, ha! ha!
On the billowy foam, he! he!
Isn't the billowy foam the pirate's home, ha! ha!
So brave and so free, he! he!'

And the fool of an editor couldn't see the beauty of it, but calls such an author a donkey. Oh, human nature! Oh, everything!"

Master Ebenezer Crump dashed his hat on his head, and sallied out in search of Wilkins, who was a clothier's apprentice in the neighbourhood, and a distant relation of the Crumps.

CHAPTER VII.

THE MURDERED MAN.—THE TERROR OF RODWELL.—MR. PADDLEBAT'S GREAT SCHEME.

RODWELL and Nicholas Lowe were both in the counting-house, when Jem, the porter, popped in his head, and said—

"Oh, such a row."

"What about Jem?" said Lowe.

"A man murdered."

Bang went the lid of Rodwell's desk, as he said—

"What do we care,—what is it to us who is murdered and who is not? We didn't murder him; why do you bring such nonsense here? A man murdered, indeed! I don't believe any such a thing. Nonsense, nonsense."

"Well, Master Rodwell, all I can say is as they are bringing him along here in a shell. He was found just at the bottom of the steps by London Bridge, and his head is all smashed, they say."

"Oh, indeed!" said Rodwell, with such a sudden alteration of manner, that both Nicholas Lowe and the porter stared again. "Oh, indeed! well, well, it's dreadful to think of such deeds being committed in the open face of day. I suppose they have caught the murderer?"

"I don't know that; but if you come to the door, you may see him go by. I mean him as is murdered, not him as did it, you know."

Both Lowe and Rodwell went to the door, and it was amazing to hear how continually the latter went on speaking. Any one would have thought he had laid a wager to see how much he could say within a given space of time.

There was a crowd passing along the street, and two men in the midst, who were carrying a shell that had been procured from the workhouse, in which the remains of the murdered man were placed, and, as fortune would have it, the two men stopped just opposite to the goldsmith's door, and put down their burthen in order to wipe the perspiration from their faces, for the weight was considerable.

"Let me see him, let me see him?" said a wild looking woman, pressing forwards among the throng. "I know everybody, and can tell you who he is. They call me a witch, too—ha! ha! Well-a-day, perhaps I shall be witch enough to tell who did the deed."

"Come in, come in, Lowe," said Rodwell; "don't stay here to listen to that old woman's mad ravings. She goes about London, and pretends to be mad."

"Nay, but whether she is mad or not," said Lowe, "I have no objection, as a matter of common curiosity, to hear what she has to say."

"Then I won't; I don't care about raving, not I. I would not give a pin's head to know what she has to say about anything."

Yet he did not go. True, he retreated a step or two, but some sort of spell forced him to remain; so back he came again, and stood on the door-step gazing at the coffin, which was covered by a piece of coarse black cloth, kept at the workhouse for such emergencies along with the shell, which was of iron.

"Let me see him, let me see him!" shouted the wild-looking mad woman. "Let me see him; I know everybody."

"Be off with you," said one of the bearers of the corpse.

"No, no, I will not. Dare you deny me a sight of that corpse? No, no, you dare not. It is not every day, is it, friends all, that we have a murder in London streets?"

"Oh! let her see it if she will," said a man in the crowd, whose curiosity was thereby exited to see it himself. "Let her see it if she will."

"What business is it of yours, busybody?" said he who had formerly spoken, and who had completed the process of wiping his face, and threw his handkerchief into the corner of his hat with a bang; "what do you put your finger in the pie for? Eh?"

"Oh! what a great man you are," said he who was questioned. "How's your mother?   Is she aware of your absence from the maternal roof?   How came you to be trusted out alone with your father's hat—eh, old cut-and-come-again?"

There was a laugh at the coffin-bearer's expense, and the woman, taking a sudden advantage of the confusion caused by the altercation, gave the cloth which covered up the face of the dead a touch which at once withdrew it, and exhibited to all eyes the hideous, ghastly spectacle beneath.

Recognition of that body was out of the question.   Either the blow which had deprived the man of life had been originally dealt upon the face and had smashed the front of it in, or such extensive injury had been dealt afterwards for the purpose of destroying identity.

There was not a feature of the corpse visible.   The whole of the bones of the face were smashed in, and presented nothing but a blackened, hideous mass, with here and there a streak of blood, which had oozed from some brain that had not yet coagulated.

One of the eyes too happened to be visible.   It was hideously inverted, so that a large portion of the white of the eye was visible, and having been displaced from its orbit altogether by the violence that had been used, it occupied a strange situation in the middle of the face, and, with a glassy-looking lustre, seemed to be staring in at the goldsmith's door, as the head, the dreadfully mangled head, was turned in that direction.

Lowe was sickened at the sight; but Rodwell uttered a loud shriek of terror, and went backwards as if he dared not turn until he got into the counting-house, calling out all the way as he went, in the most agonized accents,—

"Take it away! take it away! take it away!"

The woman whose pertinacity had brought that dreadful object in sight clapped her hands, and screamed as if with intense satisfaction—

"I see him!" she said, "I see him!   Give me his eye, and I will find out who he was.   Let us all touch him, and see at whose touch the first blood flows.   Look at his teeth.   Saw you,—saw you ever such a sight as this?   Hark, how the man who did it shrieks.   Ha! ha! ha!   He did it—he did it."

The people stared at this sudden and extraordinary accusation, and the more ignorant of them showed a tolerable disposition to believe it, for the love of the marvellous is inherent in human nature, and as easily to be overcome by education.

Anything in the shape of a "prophetic greeting," or a revelation, is always acceptable to persons of unlettered intellects; and hence, among that throng which stopped the way at the goldsmith's door, there were many who would have taken the dictum of the mad beggar woman, probably, in preference to stronger evidence.

"Who did it?" cried one.

"He who screamed when he saw the face of the dead," she exclaimed; "and I saw that fresh blood flowed from some of the veins the moment he cast his eyes upon it."

"So did I—and so did I," exclaimed several.

"Confound you all," said the man, who was the irascible coffin-bearer, "if you don't get out of the way, I'll make you.   Come along, Bill."

He and his companions raised the shell again, and carrying it swaggering between them, after replacing the old piece of black cloth over the corpse, they pursued their way, and most of the mob, along with the mad woman, followed them.

Then Lowe went into the counting-house, whither Rodwell had retired in so much agitation, and he found him sitting on a chair, with his back to the wall, while his whole appearance showed what a state of extreme mental agitation he was in, and what sufferings he was enduring.

"Has it gone—has it gone?" he said.   "Have they taken it away?   By what d——e chance was it that they stopped here?"

"You mean the body?"

"Yes, yes.   Has it gone?"

"It has.   The bearers, I presume, only paused for a rest, and a crowd naturally enough collected to see such a spectacle.   I have seen a much larger concourse of people assemble upon much less provocation."

[See page 43.

"Yes, yes, and I. Of course there was no particular motive for stopping at this door?"

"Motive?"

"No, no. That is—the sight of death, to tell the truth, Lowe, is to me so dreadful, that I know not what I do, or what I say, when it is near me. Think nothing of this extreme agitation. It will soon pass away."

"There is a skeleton in every house," said Lowe, solemnly.

"What do you mean—what do you mean?"

"I have no hidden meaning. You have often enough heard me use that expression, to know what I mean by it. You know well enough what I mean."

"I don't care what you mean. What is it to me what you mean about your skeletons in every house? I have none—I have none."

"Indeed?"

"Ay, indeed. You speak incredulously, as if you did not believe me."

"I speak as I feel."

"Then you mean to say you do not?"

"Since you will have it, then," said Lowe, solemnly, "I most certainly do not. Why, your own terror at the sight of a corpse is enough to confirm my words."

Rodwell looked for a moment or two, as if he meant to be angry, and then, making a sudden effort to be quite the reverse, he said,—

"Excuse my abruptness, I am sorry to have said anything offensive."

"You have said nothing offensive to me," said Lowe. "You yourself broached a subject which I had no desire particularly to enter upon."

"I know I did—I know I did. But the fact is, that from the earliest childhood I have always been particularly averse to a corpse. The sight of one used to make me seriously ill, and although the reflection of maturer years has enabled me to get over that feeling, I am still, as you see, very nervous upon the subject."

"So I perceive."

"Well, we will change the subject. What, now, Lowe, do you think of Miss Fanny Leslie, the newly found niece of Mr. Paddlebat?"

There was a slight flush on Nicholas Lowe's face, as he said,—

"Concerning her there can be but one opinion."

"I agree with you there. She is loveliness itself, Lowe, and she would make a charming wife for whoever has the chance to get her, as well as a wealthy one. I think it is likely enough that Paddlebat will leave her well off—eh?"

"Mr. Rodwell," said Lowe, "I do not like discussions here of any kind whatever, in which the name of Mr. Paddlebat is introduced. I have, therefore, no opinion to give upon such a subject."

"Oh, indeed. Were the books interesting that you sent to Miss Leslie?"

"I hope so," said Lowe, and he was tempted at the moment to add, "Did the dog bite you very hard at the door of Miss Leslie's chamber?"

"Who told you that?"

"I heard it from my own room above. I was on the point of descending when I heard Miss Leslie reprove you for interfering with Leo."

Rodwell cast a furious look at Lowe, and muttered something between his teeth which the other did not hear, and then Lowe, as he opened his desk, uttered an exclamation of surprise.

"What now?" cried Rodwell.

"Not much, only some one has been to my desk."

"Do you mean me?"

"I do not, because I cannot know that it was you, Rodwell. Something has been taken from my desk."

"What," said Mr. Paddlebat, who at that moment entered the counting-house, "what has been taken from your desk, Mr. Lowe? I hope that the tones I heard you conversing in, both of you, just now, were not those of disagreement? You are only two of you here, and surely you might agree. Young men, you will never get on in the world with a petulant disposition. Beware of it, I say, beware of it."

The old goldsmith appeared to have lost sight of his original question to Lowe, in the bit of practical wisdom he had followed it up with, for, without waiting for an answer, he left the counting-house, and went up stairs, from whence he only came to get a book, which he knew just where to lay his hands upon, and, therefore, came himself for instead of sending.

This broke up the conversation, for Lowe set to work upon his ledger, and Rodwell, after several bitter looks at him from beneath his knitted brows, affected to do the like.

Mr. Paddlebat walked up stairs, where his beautiful niece and his wife were at breakfast; and never to the old, domesticated goldsmith's eyes had the room, and the table, and all the place, with all its comforts, looked so nice and agreeable as it did now, with the extra presence of Fanny Leslie.

He watched her every movement with as much attention and interest as if she had been some favourite child of his own, from whom he had been for many years separated, and had but now known what joy it was to meet again.

And she, too, with a grace that was far, far above the reach of art, watched and tended upon him, handing him what he wanted, and in some instances anticipating his wants before he could express them—all of which was done greatly to the admiration of Mrs. Paddlebat, who was too corpulent to move with great rapidity herself, but was quite pleased to see how well Fanny Leslie seemed to understand Mr. Paddlebat, and to wait upon him with so much affection.

And there was something, too, in the contrast between the two parties which made the scene look well. Old Paddlebat was far, very far from being a romantic-looking personage ; while she, Fanny, was like the embodied spirit of a poet's dream, so beautiful and so sylph-like was she.

Thus the morning meal passed away, until Mrs. Paddlebat suddenly said,—

" My dear child, if you recollect, yesterday, Mrs. Deputy Fauburg came in just as we were going to open your great box of bear-skins."

" Yes, dear aunt, I recollect."

" And we did not open it at all. I do so long to see them ! Mr. Paddlebat, suppose you ask Peter the porter to bring it in here ?"

" Just as Fanny likes," said the goldsmith.

" Oh ! then we will have it here at once. Bear-skins can't make any mess. They are not like the bears themselves, at any rate, who must be dreadful creatures to be continually meeting with, when you ventured out of an evening, which I suppose is the case in America, my dear."

" Not always, aunt," said Fanny. " I certainly saw some when I lived a month in an Indi n village."

" An Indian village !"

" Yes. The settlement in [which we lived was burnt completely down, so a friendly tribe of Indians offered us a shelter and food for some time, and I, along with others, accepted the kind offer."

" Really !"

" Yes ; and it was one of the chiefs, or sachems, as they call them, of the tribe, who gave me the chest of skins."

By this time Peter, who had received his orders from Mrs. Pattlebat, made his appearance with the chest, and placed it on the floor, with some muttered exclamation of surprise concerning its great weight.

" Well," said the goldsmith, " it doos look heavy."

" Heavy, sir !" said Peter ; " it's ekal to St. Paul's. I never did carry up such a weight. Bear-skins lie uncommon close, surely."

" Well—well ; that will do, Peter."

" Much obliged, sir. I would a deuced deal rather carry that box about for a week, sir, nor a fortnight. Bless your bright eyes, miss, you may laugh, but it's a fact, I can tell you."

And so Peter went away, as great an admirer, in his way, of Fanny Leslie's beauty as any one else, only Peter made no ambitious projects on the occasion, but contented himself with telling everybody, that to his judgment—and he took care to let you know that such judgment was quite conclusive—Miss Fanny Leslie was the prettiest girl in London, and no mistake in any way whatsomdever.

" Well, now, as we have the box here," said Mr. Paddlebat, " we may as well open it at once, my dear Fanny."

" Yes," said Fanny.

" Oh !" said Mrs. Paddlebat, " I see now everything is as Fanny likes." But she did not say this in any way but good-naturedly, so the goldsmith and Fanny both only laughed at it, and made no remark upon it.

The whole three now assisted in undoing the box, which, with the aid of a knife to cut the leather thongs with which it was fastened instead of cords, was very speedily accomplished.

There were certainly in that box some of the most magnificent skins that could be found in the country from whence they were brought ; and as Mrs. Paddlebat drew out one after the other, her expressions of admiration were unbounded.

" Well, I never did ! Look, Mr. Paddlebat, here's beautiful skins. I do declare that Mr. Scoppy, the great furrier of Leadenhall, has nothing at all equal to them in all his stock.   How very beautiful!"

" They are, indeed," said Mr. Paddlebat.   " What a famous winter coat one of them would make me, to be sure !"

" Yes ; and no end of boas, and capes, and muffs, for Fanny and me."

" Well, you are certainly set up for some time in the fur line," said Mr. Paddle-bat.   But what have you got there ?"

" Well, I—really—don't know," said Mrs. Paddlebat, turning something round and round in her hand, which looked like some very badly manufactured wig. " It looks very odd ; but, really, I can't exactly say what it is.   Fanny, my dear !"

" Yes, aunt."

" What's this ?   I see there are several of them."

Fanny Leslie clasped her hands when she saw what Mrs. Paddlebat had got, and at the same time she exclaimed,—

" How could he fancy that I should be pleased by such a present as this ?"

" As what, my dear ?"

" Oh! aunt—aunt! to us these things are revolting.   Place them away."

" Lor ! why, it's a wig."

" No, aunt—no.   The Indian chief has placed them among the skins to show me how truly he was inclined to give me articles considered of great value among his people.   I am sorry to say that these are human scalps."

" Scalps !" shrieked Mrs. Paddlebat, as she dropped the one she held, as if it had been a hot poker.

" Yes, aunt."

" Why, good God!" said Mr. Paddlebat, " you don't mean, Fanny, to say that these are actually what we read of as being lugged off the heads of people ?"

" Yes, uncle ; those are some scalps which have been dried in the wigwams of the Manatoes, and no doubt they were taken from the heads of some of their enemies.   A present of these, among Indians, is considered to show an amount of friendly feeling which knows no bounds."

" Oh, dear me !" cried Mrs. Paddlebat, " I feel as if the hair on my own head was a creeping off all by itself.   How very dreadful !   What shall we do with them, Mr. Paddlebat ?"

" Why, I propose that they be sent to the British Museum, to be placed among the other rubbish, in the shape of old bones, petrified black beetles, and flints. They are fit for nothing else.   I don't know anywhere else where they would get house-room, except in that lumber-room of the nation."

" Ah !" ejaculated Mrs. Paddlebat, as she went to the sideboard, and took a small glass of something, as she said, to bring her round again.   " What a turn those *scallops* have given me, to be sure.   Only to think that I should hold up somebody's human *scallop* by the hair, and not know what it was.   Oh, I shall dream of savages as long as I live."

" I am very sorry, aunt," said Fanny ; " but I had not the least idea that he who presented to me those skins had added to them a present, which, to us, conjures up the most frightful images.   I quite, however, acquit him of any idea beyond that of paying me the most delicate attention."

" Mighty delicate, my dear.   However, I couldn't wear any of those skins now, if I was to be paid for doing so.   I should always be thinking of how they came all the way from America along with the skins of peoples' heads.   What a dreadful idea, to be sure ; it's really enough to make anybody ill for a whole week."

" My dear Fanny," said Mr. Paddlebat, as he saw that the young girl looked very much vexed, " you could not help it, you know.   You did not scalp anybody."

" No, uncle—no."

Fanny laughed as she spoke, and Mr. Paddlebat added,—

" I shall have one of those skins made into a coat for me, notwithstanding it came from America along with some scalps, and when I put it on, and feel it warm and comfortable, I shall always say to myself, ' This is a present from my dear Fanny.' "

"Mrs. Crump," announced the servant, "and a dead body, and a shell."

Certainly that servant of the Paddlebats had the oddest way of making announcements in the drawing-room that could be conceived. She generally had two or three things to say at once, and she as generally jumbled them up together so oddly, in the same tone of voice, that it was quite a matter of impossibility to separate the one from the other. It would have required a conjuror of no mean powers to find out what now she meant by announcing Mrs. Crump, and a dead body, and a shell, to her astonished master and mistress.

But the Paddlebats were a little aware of this propensity on the part of their servant, and Mr. Paddlebat said,—

"What do you mean? First of all, there's Mrs. Crump."

"Yes, sir. And then there's been by the door a dead body."

"Oh, oh."

"In a shell."

"That will do—that will do. Now we understand, and you can show Mrs. Crump up stairs."

"Mrs. Crump," said Mrs. Paddlebat, in a tone of vexation. "What can she want now this morning after having been here till God knows the hour last night? What can she want?"

The inquiry, however, into the cause of Mrs. Crump's visit was cut short by the sudden appearance of that lady, whose errand our readers will be able to guess, although Mrs. Paddlebat was not, from the recollection of the conversation which had taken place between the unappreciated Ebenezer Crump and his most amiable mother.

In truth, the lady had come, in pursuance of her promise to Ebenezer, to break the ice for him to Mrs. Paddlebat, and make that lady aware of the great affection which her darling had for Miss Fanny Leslie, the new found and beautiful niece of the Paddlebats. But, while that lady is so urging her son's claim to the hand of her whose beauty was likely to be so great an element of discord in that house, we will introduce the reader to another personage in our story, with whom as yet no acquaintance has been made, except by reputation—we mean Gilbert Paddlebat, the miserly elder brother of Mr. Paddlebat, the good-tempered and kind-hearted goldsmith of the city.

CHAPTER VIII.

GILBERT PADDLEBAT TAKES AN ADVANTAGE OF HIS PARTNER'S BLINDNESS, AND RETIRES FROM BUSINESS.

GILBERT PADDLEBAT, at the period of these interesting occurrences in the family of the Paddlebats, was a money scrivener in very good circumstances. He was in partnership with another old man, for Gilbert was old, of the name of Sheepy, and two more acute business men, or two men more likely to see an advantage and at once take it, than Sheepy and Paddlebat, the great city of London could not boast of. But, if Sheepy was able to see an advantage in business, it was with the greatest difficulty he succeeded in ever seeing anything else.

The fact was, that old Sheepy's eyesight had never been very good, and latterly he had become almost blind. Notwithstanding this, however, neither his partner nor any one else was enabled, metaphorically speaking, to get on the blind side of him, and he often took now occasion to remark,—

"Mr. Paddlebat, I can feel the money, and I can hear it chink and make its pleasant music, though I cannot see it."

And so he went on adding to his share as much as he possibly could, and finding, in the mere love of money, and the intense pleasure of accumulating it, a compensation even for the great physical deprivation that was coming over him. And who shall say, after this, that Providence does not in some way or another send us an antidote to our evils?

These two old men, then, were childless, wifeless. They owned no human ties of any kind or description. They separated themselves from the great family of mankind completely so far as interest and sympathy in them, and their cares, and their feelings, went.   All the sort of communication they ever had with anybody, or ever wished to have, consisted in lending money on good security and at good interest. Old Sheepy had been originally in the business, but feeling the want of a partner, he had taken in Gilbert Paddlebat, who had brought in an adequate amount of capital to the concern.   But they were both getting very old men, and once or twice old Sheepy had said to Gilbert Paddlebat,—

"I can't help thinking, friend Paddlebat, that your voice is failing, and that you are not so strong and hearty as you were."

"Can't you?" Gilbert would say with a growl.   "I ain't blind."

"Ha! they say blind people always live to a great old age."

"Do they?"

"So I have heard."

"Then you have heard wrong, Sheepy."

"Ah, well, well.   Have you made your will, Mr. Paddlebat?   That's what I want to know.   Have you thought of making your will?"

"My will!   What the devil puts that in your head?"

"Well, well, don't be angry—don't be angry.   You know you are old, very old; you know you are."

"You are remarkably young?"

"No, no; not young; but I am dreadfully strong and hearty; I sometimes could cry over my own appetite, it is so expensive."

"So it is.   But what are you driving at, Sheepy? I know you have some crotchet now in your mind?"

"No, no, no.   I—I only thought about your will.   I thought if you had not made your will, what a pity it would be."

"Why a pity?"

"Why a pity,—why a pity, Gilbert Paddlebat?   Would you like, after you were dead and gone, and mouldering away in the grave, and being eaten by worms and turning to dust, and ——"

"D——n!" cried Gilbert Paddlebat, "what's the use of saying all that?   If you had just said, when you are dead, it would have been enough, without adding to it an account of one's decomposition."

"Well, well, well.   You have turned short-tempered of late, Paddlebat, which of itself is a bad sign,—a very bad sign,—but enough of that."

"Quite enough," growled Gilbert.

"As I was a saying, how would you like the money you have taken such pains to hoard to be wasted away, and given in all directions to the poor, perhaps.   You know how you and I hate the poor, don't we, Paddlebat?"

"I can answer for myself.   I would have it placed in the coffin with me, or if I could by some means annihilate my money at the same moment that I breathe my last, it would be very satisfactory indeed."

"So it would."

"But I ain't going to die yet.   I am strong yet, I can tell you, and have a constitution of iron,—yes, of welded iron.   Ha, ha!   I don't give up yet awhile."

"With all my heart, with all my heart, Paddlebat; but you know if you die without a will, that extravagant brother of yours, who spends such a quantity of money, would be your heir-at-law, and would get it all, and laugh at you while he spent it."

"D——n him!"

"And he would make such a merit of giving it away to all sorts of idle vagabonds who had become poor through their own bad conduct, as everybody does."

"Of course."

"Only think of all that, Paddlebat.   The money that you have sat up night and day to earn,—the money that you have so much exerted yourself to make, shilling by shilling, to be scattered right and left in pounds."

"I—I will adopt some plan to prevent it."

"Do so.   Do so.   And—and, Paddlebat, what plan so good as making me your heir? You know that I would not spend it. You know that I would give none of it away to the idle and dissipated who have become poor. Why not make a will, Gilbert Paddlebat, and leave it all to me, and so cheat those who are exulting to themselves that they will come in for all your money and spend it?"

" I tell you what I will do, Sheepy."

" What, what?"

" We will both make our wills, and he who dies first shall have the other's money."

" Agreed, agreed."

" Well, then, agreed!"

It was strange to see with what eagerness these two old men fell into this proposal, each of them feeling so confident that he would outlive the other, and so become possessed of his wealth.

They drew the two wills at once themselves, for they were well qualified so to do, and besides the matter was so very simple; and then they got witnesses and signed them, so that in the course of an hour the whole affair was concluded.

" The old fool!" thought Sheepy; " why, he will soon die, for I am sure he gets weaker every day,—I can tell it by his voice."

" Ha! ha!" laughed Paddlebat to himself, " I shall not be kept long out of Sheepy's money. He is failing fast. I have seen that for some time, though of course it is not very likely that he will believe it—old people never do."

And so they were both well pleased with the arrangement that had been made, and although both might be said to be tottering on the brink of the grave, they waited as eagerly for each other's death as young expectant heirs for their estates.

There was a very old dilapidated well staircase which led to some of the upper rooms of the house which these two old men inhabited, and the lower part of which was devoted to their business arrangements.

The house was their own freehold, and therefore it was little enough, in the way of repairs, they could ever bring themselves to do to it; and the only circumstance that kept the old dilapidated staircase from falling long ago was, that under it was a cupboard, and in that cupboard was an iron safe, upon which the beams of the staircase actually rested, and from which, no doubt, they derived all their main support. The old men, however, did not think of this. Whenever they ascended the staircase they felt that the stairs were firm, and did not creak much, although the balustrades were in a very tottering condition indeed.

But it so happened that this iron safe, which had been there a long time, wanted some repairs, and in order to do them effectually, and to fresh paint it, which was a measure actually necessary for its preservation, it had to be taken away to the house of a maker of such articles. This was accordingly done one morning while the partners superintended the process, and saw it, at least one of them, fairly off the premises.

"You are quite sure now, Paddlebat, you left nothing in the safe?" said Sheepy.

" Quite—quite. You have asked that a hundred times."

" No, no; not a hundred. How do you feel to-day, Paddlebat?"

" How do I feel?"

" Yes—in health?"

" What do you ask that for? Eh? eh?"

Paddlebat was a little poorly, and his partner, who was much too blind to see that he was so, asking him how he was, quite frightened him, for it seemed to have something ominous about it.

" I am very well," he added. "Of course, I am,—very well."

" Well, well; I asked you only because I felt so wonderfully well myself; I never was better in all my life,—never, never."

" Indeed?"

" No. I—I seem to-day quite young again. Not that I can call myself old. Oh, dear, no; but—but I have a juvenile feel."

" Juvenile fiddlestick!"

" Eh? eh?"

"Nonsense!"

"Well, well, Paddlebat, you may say nonsense as much as you like; I do feel wonderfully well, 1 can tell you that. Where are the two wills we made, eh?"

"Oh, they are all right."

"No doubt, Paddlebat, no doubt. When you are gone, you know, I shall take as much care of the business as I do now, you may depend upon that."

"Oh, indeed! When you are gone I shall retire."

"Ha—ha—ha! When I am gone! He—he—he! Well, well, Paddlebat, we won't dispute about that now, old friend. Although my eyesight is very bad indeed, I am wonderfully strong. 1 shall renew all our leases if I can."

"Oh, do. But you ought to be aware that to feel wonderfully well is always a very bad sign."

"Is it? Ha—ha!"

"D—n him," muttered Paddlebat, "what spirits he is in, and I have passed a very bad night, and am far from well. He seems to know it. Curse him, I wish I saw him a corpse at my feet. How he goes on laughing. It's aggravating to see him—desperately aggravating, upon my soul. Really he's quite an old fiend to-day. Now, I could find it in my heart to knock him down and brain him. What are you laughing at?"

"Nothing—nothing. I am going up stairs. I am not laughing. It's your wonderful and active imagination, Paddlebat, makes you think so. Are you any better?"

"Better! 1 am not bad."

"I thought you said you did not feel quite the thing. Well, well, don't be offended. How very short tempered you have become lately, to be sure. You talk of bad signs—now that's a bad sign, if you please. I am going up stairs. If you want me you can call me, or come for me, you know."

"Very well—d—n you."

Old Sheepy went up stairs, laughing to himself, and when he reached the top, he said,—

"How wonderfully the old staircase shakes to-day."

Then he walked into the room where he usually sat, and which he knew so well, that, had he been totally blind, instead of only partially so, he could have found as well every article it contained. He left Paddlebat in a terrible fume below. The fact is, old Sheepy had made him positively nervous, and when he was alone he sat down and fancied he had never felt so ill in all his life as he did just then. Alarm increased upon him, and had not some one come in on very important business, no doubt he would have frightened himself into very serious indisposition.

As it was, however, it saved him, that a person came in to pay him some money on account of a mortgage deed, and the very words, money and pay, seemed to have quite a magical effect upon the old man. His fit of the blues passed away, and he was in a few moments immersed in a profound calculation regarding the precise amount of interest that he had to realise. This was, at length settled, for he who came to pay was not of that class of men who look twice at a farthing, so he let old Paddlebat impose upon him a little without caring about it much. It was necessary, however, that the signatures of both Gilbert Paddlebat and old Sheepy should be placed at the back of the parchment deed on which the payment was duly recorded.

"Is your partner within, Mr. Paddlebat?" said he who came to pay the welcome cash.

"Oh, yes," said Paddlebat. "He is up stairs. I will call him down in a moment to you. We like to have everything done regular, I assure you, and he shall sign the acknowledgement for what you have paid, as well as I."

It was quite an everyday occurrence this for old Paddlebat to call down Sheepy when he was actually wanted, but somehow or other the old man did not hear him, and in a great passion Paddlebat went up stairs as quietly as he could.

Now, Paddlebat was a much heavier man than Sheepy, although, Heaven knows, he was no great weight, and the moment he set his foot on the stairs, he felt the great alteration that had taken place in them. A sudden fear came over him

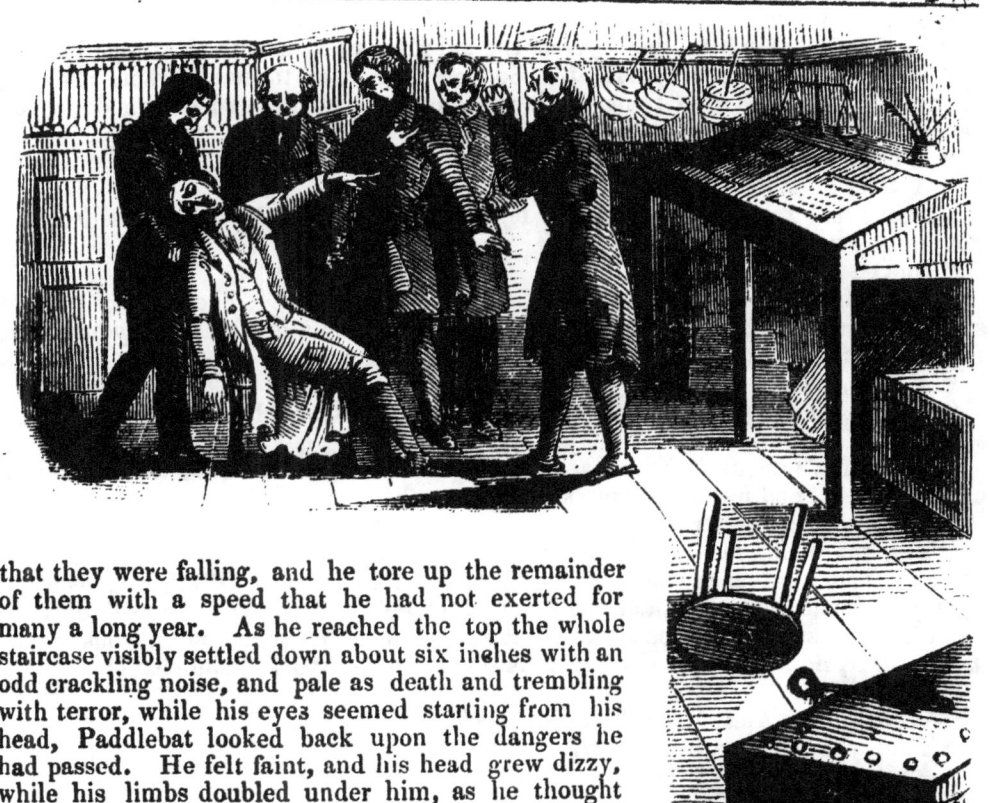

that they were falling, and he tore up the remainder of them with a speed that he had not exerted for many a long year. As he reached the top the whole staircase visibly settled down about six inches with an odd crackling noise, and pale as death and trembling with terror, while his eyes seemed starting from his head, Paddlebat looked back upon the dangers he had passed. He felt faint, and his head grew dizzy, while his limbs doubled under him, as he thought how almost certain would have been his destruction if the staircase had fallen with him, for the height was considerable.

It was some minutes before he could recover his presence of mind sufficiently to move or speak, and then he still trembled as he said, in a faint whisper,—

"What an escape—oh, what an escape! The—the weight of a cat would now bring the whole staircase down. A cart rumbling along the street would do it. What an escape I have had to be sure!"

He wiped the cold drops of perspiration that intense fear had forced out upon his brow, and then he suddenly assumed an attitude of deep thought. A strange flush of colour came across his face, and then vanished, leaving it more deadly pale than it had been before.

"Hush—hush," he said. "Be calm—be calm."

And then he walked into old Sheepy's room. He found his partner, as he had expected, fast asleep. Old Sheepy lately had been in the habit of dropping off in that way, but never till this time had Paddlebat looked with complacency upon him while in that state. But now he could have smiled to see him, had not his mind been full of something too dark and terrible to make him to do so.

"Hilloa," he said, "hilloa!"

A snore was the only reply he got from Sheepy.

"How sound he sleeps," muttered Paddlebat. "I have his will. It's all left to me. How very sure he has always made of outliving me. It's wonderfully odd now that—that something should turn up that alters the prospect a little."

Old Paddlebat went out of the room to the head of the stairs again, and listened. All was still below. The man in the counting-house was waiting with the most extraordinary patience, and then back again went Paddlebat, determined at once upon awakening the sleeper.

He placed his hand upon his arm, as he said,—

" Hilloa—hilloa!   Sheepy, you are wanted."

" Eh ? murder—what's that ?" cried the old man, starting with a terrified look.

" It's only I, Gilbert Paddlebat.   So you have been to sleep again, Sheepy ; your old habit.   I have to transact all the business, and then when it's done you have half the profits.   Ain't that it ?"

" What a dream !"

" A what ?"

" I have had a dream.   I thought I fell from a great height and was killed, and you had all my money."

" Indeed !"

" Yes.   How—how odd, and yet how very improbable.   The way to prevent such a dream as that from coming true is never to go to a height.   Are you better, Paddlebat, than you were ?"

" A little.   How are you ?"

" The dream has put me out a little, but I am tolerably well, thank you ; I shall see you out yet."

" Well, that's all as it happens.   There's Mr. Hewit, down stairs, has come to pay his money, and he wants your signature at the back of the deed ; you understand ; so you had better go down to him and sign it."

" Yes, yes ;—oh, yes, of course.   And yet you say you do all the business, Paddlebat.   That's rather too bad, upon my soul ; it is, indeed.   Well, well, you are getting old and querulous, and very bad tempered.   That I have noticed of late, and it's a bad sign, a very bad sign ; but I don't want to make you nervous about it ; oh, dear, no ; oh, no.   Ha ! ha ! ha !   Are you nervous, Paddlebat ?"

" Not very."

" Well, well.   Ah ! Mr. Hewit, you say ?"

" Yes ; you will find him below."

" Ain't you coming ?"

" I will follow you."

" Very good, very good.   By the bye, as you came up just now, Paddlebat, did you notice how the stairs creaked ?"

" Creaked ?"

" Yes.   We shall have to go to the expense of doing something to them, you may depend ; nothing but expense, nothing but expense."

" Oh, just so."

" Well, well.   You weighed Hewit's money ?"

" Oh, yes.   It's all right, you may depend upon that ; why don't you go down ? he will be getting impatient."

" Well, I'm going now."

" Be careful," said Paddlebat, as he stood far back on the landing, " be careful how you go, Sheepy.   Remember, you have made your will.   Hold on to the balustrades.   Do the stairs creak ?   What a pity it would be if you were to hurt yourself.   You are a very reckless old man."

Sheepy had got to the middle of the staircase, and then he felt some sudden movement of them, and, instead of going on as quickly as he could, he turned round and shouted,—

" Help ! help !"

In another moment, down went the whole staircase, with a tremendous crash, carrying the old man with it, and burying him amid the ruins, from whence arose such a cloud of black dust, that Paddlebat was compelled to go into the room above and close the door, for fear of being suffocated, and there he sat down and shook, as if his last hour was come, while he kept moving his hands up and down and muttering,—

" He's killed, he's killed, he's killed ! and I shall have all the money.   He's killed, and I shall have all the money.   I—I didn't do it ; I didn't do it ; I didn't do it."

CHAPTER IX.

MR. WILKINS AND EBENEZER CRUMP HAVE A DIFFERENCE OF OPINION ABOUT
THINGS IN GENERAL.

LET us leave old Gilbert Paddlebat for a time to see if he is any the happier for his acquisition of Sheepy's money, especially considering the mode in which it was acquired. We will leave him to his own thoughts and reflections, and to settle the somewhat knotty point of whether he who will not save a fellow creature from destruction when he could so at no risk to himself, is not equally morally guilty with the man who deliberately achieves the deed which deprives his fellow of existence. We know not how far Gilbert Paddlebat's philosophy may carry him in a consideration of this subject, but our own opinion is very unequivocal upon it, and we dare say the opinions of our readers coincide with ours to the effect that Gilbert Paddlebat was to all intents and purposes morally guilty of the murder of his partner.

But, as we say, we will leave him for awhile to introduce to our readers no less a personage than Mr. Wilkins, the friend of Ebenezer Crump, and the confidential adviser of that neglected genius and very great man. Now, at first sight, considering the rather low spoke in Fortune's wheel to which Wilkins clung, it would appear derogatory to the character of so stupendous a genius as Ebenezer Crump to hold companionship with him, but when we come to reflect upon the subject, we shall find that in such a circumstance there is nothing inconsistent with the ordinary course of human nature and the ordinary workings of the human heart.

It will be recollected that Ebenezer Crump, although a genius, was a neglected one, and therefore he could not be expected to be on those terms with society at large, which a petted *feted* idol of the public may be. The consequence of this state of things was, that Ebenezer Crump was compelled, of course by the jealousy of contemporaneous authors, to go and get applause where he could. Hence then did he, to use his own lofty language, descend from the Parnassian mount to converse with a Wilkins.

Poor Wilkins was a good kind soul, totally destitute of education, except so far as he could read print, and made always a desperate attempt at writing. But he had about him a natural shrewdness of observation and a practical knowledge of human nature, such as Ebenezer Crump could not pretend to. Moreover, Wilkins had an imagination and a flow of ideas which enabled him not unfrequently to give the most felicitous turn to his thoughts, and to illustrate them in the happiest manner. He was in these respects vastly superior to Ebenezer Crump, who really was but a small-minded person, only he made fully up in vanity for whatever other deficiencies he had—that is to say, he made up to himself all deficiencies by that commodity; but it has this evil attendant upon it, that however well personal vanity may get an individual over a personal difficulty, it by no means has a corresponding effect upon society at large, which is very apt to call the aforesaid individual a humbug in addition to a fool, and it is with great grief we say it, that Ebenezer Crump was certainly something of a humbug.

When he left his maternal abode after uttering the dreadful threat concerning the Monument which so much alarmed Mrs. Crump, but which need not have alarmed her at all, Mr. Ebenezer made his way to Mr. Wilkins, and summoned that individual to hold conference with him. In the clothier's where Mr. Wilkins devoted his genius to assisting, there was generally some out-of-door business to perform, which at any time would give Wilkins an opportunity of getting out, so that it very rarely happened that when Ebenezer Crump passed the door several times with his usual tragic struts that Wilkins had not some parcel or another to take somewhere, who he could embrace that opportunity of taking, and so enjoying *en route* the society of the great neglected genius.

The fates were on this occasion sufficiently propitious for the accomplishment of such an object, and accordingly Wilkins made his appearance with so small and genteel looking a parcel, that Mr. Crump was not shocked and ashamed to walk with him, as was sometimes the case, when he would come out with a great pack that was sufficient for a donkey's load.

"How are you?" said Wilkins. "As blessed melancholy as usual is you?"

"Melancholy? Ha! ha!" said Crump, by which no doubt he intended to put some great slight upon the world at large.

"Oh, well," said Tom Wilkins, "I can't make much out o' that."

"Hush!" said Crump. "Hush! Tom. List! Oh, list!"

"List. Do you want any list? There's lots at our shop. Oh, oceans of it, I can tell you. We rolls it up in jolly great balls."

"Tom, you are an ignoramus and an idiot."

"I'm very much obliged to you. They do say as one donkey always knows another when he sees him."

"What do you mean by that insinuation?"

"That *sinivation*? Nothing at all. But what is the matter? You don't look the thing at all."

"Ha! ha! Do I look sardonic?"

"I don't know, but you look as if you'd lost a shilling and found a fourpenny piece, and didn't know whether to grin or to cry."

"Oh, ye gods!" exclaimed Crump, "that the noblest feelings of an exalted and terrifying intellect should be so comparisoned!"

"Greek," said Tom. "Greek that is, I supposes."

"Once for all," added Crump, "let me warn you. Do not—oh, do not tamper with feelings that are like slumbering giants."

"The deuce!"

"It is so, Tom; did—did you ever love?"

"I believe you."

"And—and was she all that youthful poets fancy when they dream?"

"I really don't know; I likes it with the kidney."

"The what?"

"The kidney. A *line* o' pork to be sure."

"Oh, wretch! wretch! wretch! Oh, Fanny Leslie! Fanny Leslie!"

"Hilloa!" cried Tom. "Fanny Leslie? Hilloa!"

"What on earth are you calling out in that way for?" said Crump. "Don't you see that the people are staring at you with amazement?"

"I thought you seed her somewhere, and was a calling to her, so I thought as I'd help you a little, that's all about it."

"Very good."

"Oh, heavens!"

"You do not know, Tom, what I suffer. I saw her last night; she beamed upon my soul last night for the first time. Oh, I cannot describe her, Tom, in prose. It is not possible. No, no!"

"Indeed!"

"But in verse."

"Oh, it's a coming," said Tom.

"Step aside under this archway, and give me your candid opinion of the following lines. They were dashed off in a moment of enthusiasm—in one of those dear precious moments when the airy fancy on its etherial car is wandering in the realms of space. When the—the——You understand?"

"Oh, of course; do you think anybody could miss understanding anything as was so wonderfully clear and distinct as all that? I ain't such a fool as not to see a nose upon a person's face. Come, let's have the poetry. Is it funny?"

"What?"

"Funny. I rather like myself a good chorus."

"Oh! oh! oh!"

"Lor, what's the matter? Ain't you well? Have half a pint of half and half with the chill off, and a bit of ginger in it."

"No, no. Tom, I am very much afraid you are a Goth. That's my candid opinion of you; but, however, I will not deprive you of the intellectual treat of hearing the lines to Fanny Leslie."

"That's kind; drive on, for these here are waistcoat pieces in this parcel as has got to be showed to somebody to choose among, and they ought to have gone a hour or two ago."

"Listen, then, listen."

Mr. Crump produced from his pocket the following lines to Fanny Leslie, which he read with great fervour to Tom, who listened with the profoundest gravity :—

TO FANNY LESLIE.

> "Oh, Fanny Leslie, beautiful and wonderful creation ;
> Fairest, dearest, best of all this nation ;
> My heart for you is in a vast commotion,
> Like the stormy ocean when it's going to make a motion.
> Oh, Fanny, look upon my burning flame,
> And tell me with a sigh that you feel just the same.
> Ah me !—ah me ! I am a tender lover,
> And from my idol ne'er will prove a rover."

"What do you think of that, Tom ?"

"It's difficult to know what to think," said Tom.

"But you must have some idea of the beauty and sublimity of such poetry ?"

"Not yet. They've a'most took my breath away, that's the fact. What does she say to em, eh ?"

"I have not yet shown them to her."

"Well, then, I wouldn't."

"Why not ?"

"You may depend as she'd be diffident of writing of herself to such a genius as you is. She'd be afeard as you'd set the Thames a fire some day, and she'd get burnt along o' everybody else. I wouldn't show 'em her, if so be as you really wants to have her, you know. If it's only a lark, why, you may as well ; but them verses is enough to stun everybody as hav'n't very strong nerves."

"Well, I will say this much for you, Tom : with all your want of education and genius, you certainly have a very correct notion of poetry."

"Oh, yes. I always had since I was never such a little chap ; but it's your blessed confusions as have made me the out-and-out one in judging of poetry as I really is."

"You mean effusions, Tom, not confusions."

"It's all the same, you know, call it which you will. Ain't you a-going to print them lines ? What a out-and-out sensation they'd make."

"I would ; but after the manner in which I've been insulted, I think myself quite justified in refusing to allow the world to participate in the efforts of my muse. You appreciate me, and there may be many others ; but unfounded jealousy and agonising feelings of being completely cut out, call me an ass."

"You don't say so ?"

"For the sake of human nature I regret to say that it is a melancholy fact. When a hundred years after this my life is written, and my memoirs collected, it will be a dreadful anecdote to tell that the editor of an obscure periodical did actually call me an ass."

"Did he indeed ? I say he's no fool."

"No fool ! What do you mean ?"

"Why, you know if he'd let your poetry be put in his blessed obscure periodical, it would have smashed in another week altogether, in consequence of the beauty of these lines being so very superior to nothing else as was never put into it, and all as was is, and as is, you see, you understand, it wouldn't have been no go, and down it would have gone."

Crump looked dreadfully puzzled at this speech, which no doubt had been purposely uttered so obscurely by Tom to get out of the scrape of having condemned the poetry.

"I really cannot comprehend you," he said.

"Well, it's only tit-for-tat, for I can't comprehend you, you know—leastways, very seldom."

"That fact, Tom, arises from your not being acquainted with the muses ; but what would you do now, candidly speaking, if you loved ?"

"Oh, I couldn't help it, I suppose, and should have to put up with it."

"I don't mean that. How would you proceed?"

"Just as usual."

"Well, what would you say to the fond object of your heart's idolatry? What would you do to win her best and dearest affections? You are more in the world than I am. I mingle not with the crowd of humanity, but sit, as it were, apart from kith and kin, in meditation, with genius soaring at my side."

"Well, then, I'd ask her what she liked best, and if it turned out to be the Eagle ——"

"The what?"

"The Eagle, in the City-road. I'd take her there and treat her like a trump, I would, and hang the expense. Then I'd tell her as I'd make her Missus Wilkins, if so be as she wouldn't mind living in a front attic, and finding herself."

"Oh, horror, horror."

"Don't you like it? You asked me what I'd do, and I've told you."

"Ah, I see. It is in vain to talk to you. You are a groveller."

"Well, if so be as a groveller is a fellow as gets his own living, and don't make such a fool of himself as to induce editors of obscure publications to call him a ass, I'm deuced glad I am one, that's all."

"Do you mean to insult me?"

"Insult you!"

"Yes. Your language seems to be of that tendency. I repeat, do you mean to insult me?"

"I couldn't, I couldn't."

"Why not, permit me to ask—why not?"

"Cos you are like the pig that had his tail curled into two knots. He was so precious proud of it that when anybody insulted him, he just turned round his head, and looked at it, and says, says he, ' I'm composed and reconciled to anything; I've got two knots in my tail.' Now that's the way with you; ' I'm a genius,' says you, ' and where's the odds,' says you, ' what anybody says?' and that's the way you gets over it."

"Once for all, now," said Ebenezer, with great dignity, " I consider you a fool, and decline any further conversation with you. You will be so good as not to consider me as patronising you any longer. I find I am mistaken in you, that you have not that soul for poetry which I, at one time, was willing to give you credit for. Do not now boast that you are acquainted with him who will yet be the great and the celebrated Crump."

"I won't," said Tom. " Make yourself quite easy."

Ebenezer did not condescend to say any more; but he walked away with, as he thought, very great dignity indeed. But if Tom Wilkins had been as anxious about keeping up the acquaintance as he was indifferent to it, he knew well, from experience, that he need not at all put himself out of the way on account of this little difference of opinion; and as Ebenezer Crump must read his poetry to somebody, and as nobody else would endure it on any account, except his mother, he was pretty sure to come again to the clothier's in a few days, and summon his patient listener, who certainly did not often take upon himself to speak so candidly as he had done on this occasion.

"Ah me!" thought Ebenezer Crump, as he walked alone down the Strand; " what a state of things is this! that an individual who is qualified to electrify the world, and whose autograph a couple of hundred years after this will be eagerly sought for as a wondrous literary curiosity, is now, at this present moment, walking along just like anybody else."

This was a very shocking state of things certainly, and what with his reflections upon it, and the deep-seated conviction which he scarcely liked to own to himself, that Fanny Leslie rather laughed at him than otherwise, when he ventured to make any elaborate poetical remark to her, Ebenezer Crump was about as miserable as any forlorn lover could be.

"My fate cries out aloud," he said; " I feel as if I was born to be not like my fellow-mortals. I have a soul far, far above getting my living like ordinary people; and, as for tallow-chandlery, I detest the very name of it. It's dreadful to think that my mother will not sell the business and retire to the Regent's Park; but, despite all that, I feel that I must be great. I know that the time will come when I shall be the great something, or the great somebody."

" That time has come already," said a man, who had been walking behind Ebenezer Crump for some distance, and had heard the muttered breathings of his troubled spirit.

" Eh?" said Ebenezer, turning abruptly, and expecting some admirer, in the shape of some one who, perhaps, had heard some of his poetry.

" Yes, you are quite right," replied the man; " that time has come, for you are evidently now the great goose."

Here was another blow of fate! Thoughts of the Monument actually, for a moment, did pass through the excited brain of Crump, and he rushed home in a state of agony, which, as the newspapers say, can be better conceived than described.

He darted up stairs to the attic, which he called his study, and then with a deep groan he threw himself into a chair to await the coming home of his mother, who he was told was out, and who he felt assured had gone according to promise to break the ice for him at the Paddlebats'.

CHAPTER. X.

MR. PADDLEBAT SETTLES WHAT IS TO BE DONE WITH HIS BUSINESS, AND SENDS FOR HIS BROTHER.—THE RIVALS IN EARNEST.

MRS. CRUMP was on this very expedition on which so much of the future happiness of the great Ebenezer depended, when she called so unexpectedly upon the Paddlebats, as to induce Mrs. Paddlebat to wonder what she could possibly want, seeing that she had been there on the preceding evening.

Now Mrs. Crump was certainly a clever woman, and she knew a great many things from practical observation, among which was, that a great number of people can be at once overcome by downright assurance, and that many an object is carried by a great assumption of independence, which otherwise would drag its slow length along for an indefinite period.

On her road to the Paddlebats', she settled in her own mind that there might be a great many more things of a much worse tendency, as regarded the future prospects of Ebenezer, than his marriage with the goldsmith's niece.

" They are both too young," she soliloquised; " but then that is a fault that is daily mending; and if it is at once settled and understood that she is engaged to Neezey, it will keep off others, who might, perhaps, attempt to entangle her affections. The Paddlebats are easy enough people in their way, and I dare say I can manage them tolerably; and as poor dear Neezey likes the girl, why he may as well have her; and I dare say old Paddlebat means to do something handsome for her, as he has no children of his own to look to."

Armed, then, with this prudential reasoning, and a full determination to carry it out to the utmost, Mrs. Crump, as we have seen, arrived at the Paddlebats'.

" Oh, my dear Mrs. Paddlebat," she exclaimed, " how do you do? You see I come without any sort of ceremony in the world, to give you a morning call. How do you do, Mr. P., and how are you, my dear Miss Leslie? How well you are all looking, to be sure! what a pleasure it is."

" Thank you," said Paddlebat, drily.

" My dear love," added Mrs. Crump, in a whisper to Mrs. Paddlebat, " I should not have troubled you again so soon; but I have a piece of good news to tell you."

" Good news?"

" Oh, dear, yes. I don't know but what I ought to tell it to you alone; but, at all events, I don't want Fanny to hear it. Young people, you know, are, after all, young people."

There was no disputing such a proposition as this, so Mrs. Paddlebat did not attempt it, but, turning to Fanny, she said,—

"My dear, will you go into the next room, and amuse yourself with the piano for a little while?"

"Yes, dear aunt," said Fanny, who was not at all offended that her absence was required, and who seemed to have a sort of intuitive horror of the amazing volubility of Mrs. Crump.

When she was gone Mrs. Crump turned to Mr. Paddlebat, and in her most insinuating tones she said,—

"Mr. P., I have been telling Mrs. P. that I have something for your private ears, which has induced me to come here this morning; and as good news, you know, ought not to be kept, why, I have come at once, you see, though it is rather early, and I said to myself, 'Who knows,' says I, 'but I may be taking the Paddlebats at a nonplus?'"

"Not at all," said Mr. Paddlebat, to whom Mrs. Crump was by no means a favourite. "Not at all; good news don't need such a string of apologies."

"Now did you ever hear the like of him?" said Mrs. Crump, appealing to Mrs. Paddlebat. "He's always got something short and witty to say; now, hasn't he really?"

"Well, what is it you have come to tell us?" said Mrs. Paddlebat.

"Ah, what's it about?" said Mr. Paddlebat.

"Why, it's about your new-found niece, then, if you must know."

Well might Mr. and Mrs. Paddlebat stare at each other, and at Mrs. Crump, at the very idea, that she should have any news about the beautiful girl who was thrown on their kindness and protection, and of whom they themselves, as yet, knew so little.

Mrs. Crump felt now, that if anything was to be done successfully, it must not be done timidly or hesitatingly, so, with a profusion of smiles, and such a redundancy of language that we almost despair of being able to faithfully record it, she added,—

"Yes, and well you may look surprised. I can tell you I was surprised, though perhaps you'll say, in your funny way, Mr. P., that you and I have now come to an age when we ought to be surprised at nothing. However, that's neither here nor there, says you, and no more it isn't. I know well that you will both feel with me as I feel, and of course can't help feeling, as it's natural I should, when I absolutely tell you, my dear Mr. P. and Mrs. P., that my Neezey admires Miss Leslie."

"Indeed!" said old Paddlebat.

"It's a fact, sir; so now you know it. Ain't it pleasant? ain't it delightful? ain't it just what we should all have wished now if we had been asked? Really, when I heard it, I was just like you, quite—quite, in a manner of speaking, astonished, because Neezey, you know, is such a genius, so clever, and so—so—you understand. Ain't it pleasant, Mr. P.?"

"Very."

"Yes, yes; a-hem! It shows how young people will be young people, don't it, Mrs. P.?"

"Very," said Mrs. Paddlebat.

"Oh, to be sure, that's just what I knew you would say. He actually admires her; he told me so in his beautiful way. You know his beautiful way—bashful, but so full—of—of what do you call it?"

"Exactly," said Mr. Paddlebat. "He's not such a fool as I thought him."

"A fool, Mr. P.!"

"Yes, ma'am. I am, however, willing to give him credit for his taste in admiring my dear niece, Fanny, who everybody admires; so, as far as that goes, he would have been rather singular if he hadn't. But what's the good news you came to tell us, Mrs. Crump?"

This was rather disconcerting, but Mrs. Crump was equal to the emergency; she laughed loudly, as she exclaimed,—

"Oh, what company you are, to be sure, Mr. P.! That's what poor Crump used

to say, before he was happy. 'If,' said he, ' you want good company, go to Mr. Paddlebat ;' and how true it was."

"But you really have not, you know, told us the good news, Mrs. Crump," said Mrs. Paddlebat, who very judiciously took the cue from her husband of battling the loquacious Mrs. Crump, who replied rather hastily,—

"Why, that's the good news."

"Oh, that—oh !" said Paddlebat.

"Oh, indeed !" said Mrs. Paddlebat. "Oh, oh."

Now this was enough to try the temper of Job himself, and Mrs. Crump said,—

"Of course that's it, and I don't anticipate any obstacle to the wishes of the young people from any quarter."

"Nor will there be any," said Paddlebat.

"Very good, my dear Mr. P. I knew you were only joking. We will consider the affair as completely settled."

"Just as you like, Mrs. Crump ; we have nothing to do with it. We cannot help your son admiring our niece ; and if we could, I don't know that it would be worth our while to do so ; so you may consider it settled, if you please, that he does admire her, and that we have no sort of objection to his doing so."

"And, of course, you prevent anybody else from paying any attention to her; because poor Neezey is dreadfully jealous."

"Prevent anybody else!"

"Yes, Mr. P., you agreed it was settled."

"Yes, that your son admired her; but it don't follow, you see, Mrs. Crump, that she at the same time admires him."

"Mr. Paddlebat!"

"Mrs. Crump!"

"I came here, sir, to tell you that my Neezey would, in a couple of years, make your niece Mrs. Crump."

"Oh!"

"And you treat me with derision. Are you, or are you not, agreeable to the little affair, Mr. P.? If you have other views, it would be more manly to say so, than to trample on a lone widow who has nobody to protect her."

Mr. Paddlebat was not often really angry, but he was rather now.

"Madam," he said, "whatever my views regarding my niece may be, I don't just yet mean to put them into the hands of the parish crier; and as for your son, poor young man, I don't want to have to say anything about him, because it is an ungracious subject; but if you fancy I am standing in the way of the young people, I will soon put that matter to rest. Fanny—Fanny, my dear."

"Yes, uncle," said Fanny, as she came from the adjoining room. "Yes, uncle."

"Did you, my dear, see a thin young man here last night, with very light hair and his collar turned down?"

"Oh, yes, uncle."

"Well, Fanny, he admires you, and wants to know if you admire him?"

"Admire him, uncle!"

"Yes, do you, dear, or do you not?"

Fanny laughed, as she said,—

"I thought he had escaped from some lunatic asylum, by what he said to me. Admire him! Oh, dear, no, I pity him."

This was too much for Mrs. Crump's nature. That lady rose indignantly, and while the tip of her nose hung out a red flag of defiance, she said,—

"You are low people. You are all low people, and I pity you—I sincerely pity you, you abominable low-lived set. I wonder I ever condescended to come into such a house. Oh, you low set. Vulgarians you all are; and as to you, Miss Pert, you may think yourself pretty, but you'll soon find out that that's a delusion. I look upon you as a little contemptible half-bred hussey."

Fearful that some reply might be made by Mrs. Paddlebat, Mrs. Crump rushed from the room as she uttered the last words of her philippic against the Paddlebats, nor did she stop until she gained the street, when she strove to console herself for her disappointment by saying,—

"I had the last word. It was quite clear the wretches did not know what to say; and as for the niece, with her airs and her graces, I am strongly of opinion that she is no better than she should be, and that after all it's quite an escape for poor dear Neezey not to have anything to do with her."

And thus, like the fox and the grapes, did Mrs. Crump go home affecting to disparage what really now had an immense importance in her eyes, but which she felt convinced was past all hoping for, namely, an alliance of a matrimonial nature between the houses of the Crumps and the Paddlebats.

Indeed, so overcome by her feelings was Mrs. Crump when she got home, that she had to take something an amazing deal stronger than water to compose her fluttered spirits.

When she was gone, Mr. Paddlebat said to his wife,—

"My dear, there's nothing without its use in this world. This visit of Mrs. Crump's, ridiculous as it was, has set me to thinking."

"Thinking about what, Mr. Paddlebat?"

"I will tell you another time, when—a-hem!"

Mr. Paddlebat glanced towards Fanny very cunningly, to indicate that the other time when he would tell her would be when Fanny Leslie was not present ; so there the matter stopped for the present, but an opportunity occurred in the course of the day for its renewal, and then Mr. Paddlebat said,—

" My dear, you must see, as well as I, that Fanny will have abundance of admirers ; and now the difficulty that we experienced about the disposal of the business here, which I wish to leave, is easily set aside."

" How do you mean, Mr. Paddlebat ?"

" Why, I just mean this, that whoever wins Fanny Leslie shall likewise win the business, and until she is settled in life, I will retain the shop in my own hands."

Mrs. Paddlebat was silent for some moments, and then she said,—

" Do you exclude the two young men, Mr. Paddlebat, from this matter, or do you mean that if Jervis Rodwell or Nicholas Lowe should win Fanny's heart, you would let either of them have the business ?"

" I have no will in the matter," said the old goldsmith, " but the happiness of Fanny Leslie.   I do not mean foolishly to say, that I shall not keep a good watch upon whoever has access to her society, and I have only to hope that she will make choice of some one who is worthy of her.   I have no intention whatever of excluding either Rodwell or Jervis from the choice of a good wife and a good business."

" Very well," said Mrs. Paddlebat ; " I consider you have made a very proper and very prudent resolution."

" I hope so."

" I am sure of it ; and I don't mind wagering anything that Jervis Rodwell will be the man for Fanny."

" I know he is your favourite, but I hope, my dear, that you will not allow yourself on that account to do any injustice to Lowe."

" Oh, of course not."

" Then I am satisfied.   Let Fanny have her own unbiassed choice.   Our duty will only be to take care she has no opportunity of choosing badly."

" That we can see to."

Mrs. Paddlebat was evidently well satisfied with this arrangement of her husband's—probably that, and his determination to afford a home to Fanny, were the only two things in which she had thoroughly agreed with him.   The one was because she really had an admirable opinion of Rodwell, and the other was from downright native goodness of heart.

" There is another thing I feel inclined to do," said Mr. Paddlebat, " which I should not have dreamt of under any other circumstances."

" And what may that be ?" said his wife, in a tone of interest, for the old goldsmith spoke with earnestness and solemnity.

" It is," he replied, " to send for my brother, Gilbert."

" For Gilbert !   Send for Gilbert !"

" Yes.   Poor Amelia, the mother of Fanny, is his sister, as well as she is mine, or, rather I should say, was.   I do not, therefore, want to give Gilbert an opportunity of saying that I kept him from a knowledge of the existence of his niece."

" Well, there is something in that, Mr. Paddlebat.   Everybody says that Gilbert is very rich, and I am sure if he is, he cannot do better than to leave all his money to Fanny, which, of course, he cannot do if he doesn't know there is such a person in the world."

" I will write to him to come here on particular business," said Mr. Paddlebat, " and when he comes I will introduce Fanny to him, and, if he has any heart left at at all, he surely must have some feeling of affection towards her."

Accordingly Mr. Paddlebat sent a note by one of his shop lads to the offices of his brother, whose peculiar position, as regarded his partner, Sheepy, he had no knowledge of, for the circumstances regarding the death of that individual, which we have detailed, had not yet become generally known, and, as there was no correspondence of any description between the brothers Paddlebat, it was only by a common report that the old goldsmith could know anything of what Gilbert was about, or of any changes in his position or prospects.

While Paddlebat's boy is taking his time in carrying the note, as boys always do, and stopping at every object in the street which promised five minutes' amusement, we may as well precede him to the office of Gilbert Paddlebat.

It will be recollected that we left that exemplary character congratulating himself upon old Sheepy having broken his neck down the crazy staircase, and so leaving him, Gilbert Paddlebat, sole legatee to all his money.

It was an odious, as well as a sad thing, for a man of Gilbert Paddlebat's age, who ought to be weaning his thoughts from this world, and thinking of that eternity to which he was hastening, rubbing together his old shrivelled hands, and chuckling like some supernatural fiend at the prospect of fingering the gold which it was utterly impossible he could ever enjoy.

Indeed, view the matter which way we may, it was utterly impossible that Gilbert Paddlebat should enjoy either his own or his partner's money. In the first place, he was far too old, and in the second, if the capacity for taking any enjoyment that gold could purchase had still belonged to him, he never would have had courage to disburse the necessary funds to produce them.

He did not love money for the money's worth. He did not wish for gold because of its vast power in the purchase of those things which will, where the heart and conscience are free from corruption, make life one dream of beauty and romance. Far, far from it. He might—which no doubt many do who begin to hoard—have at first thought what a glorious thing it would be to have abundance of money to spend ; but soon the love of the mere money itself became his ruling passion, and he was content to know that he possessed a power which he never had the courage to use, and the idea of which would be sure to impart to death, whenever it might come to him, its bitterest pang, because he was compelled then to leave it behind him. But such is always the miser's misery—for ever grasping at something in the shape of an enjoyment, which is for ever eluding him, until at length death comes to snatch him from the hoards he has toiled to produce, and leave them, as is too commonly the case, to be scrambled for by rapacious heirs, and squandered eventually, perhaps, by the very person against whom above all others, the miser had been most bitter.

Gilbert trembled, and felt very ill, as he sat in Sheepy's room, after he had heard that individual fall down the staircase with such a crash. He dared not go out on to the landing to look at what had taken place. He thought he ought to do so, and that it would be better if he were ; but he could not summon sufficient courage. He tried to rise from the chair, but he sank back again, his limbs refusing to support him.

"I—I should like half a pint of porter—small beer, I mean," he gasped, "to give me strength now, for I am wonderfully weak and agitated. I—I hope he is dead ; I hope he is quite dead. How still everything is !"

The stillness did not last very long, though. It was only that stillness which for a few moments succeeds some startling occurrence, before those who have witnessed it have time to make an alarm, or to give utterance to the feelings which come over them at the moment. Then suddenly there arose a loud cry for help, and Gilbert Paddlebat thought it was the voice of the man who had come to make the payment who was calling out so lustily.

"What an alarm there will now be !" he gasped. "The place will be full of people. Good God ! somebody may take something—who knows? and I up here, and no staircase to enable me to go down by."

This harrowing thought, that somebody might possibly steal something, although, Heaven knew, there was little enough to steal in the offices of Sheepy and Paddlebat, did quite as much towards the restoration of the old man from the state of weakness and agitation into which he had fallen, as the half pint of beer he, in so reckless a manner for him, thought he would not have minded paying for a short time before.

He rose, and now, although he still trembled and felt anything but comfortable, he cautiously opened the door of the room. The clouds of dust that had arisen from the falling staircase had now partially settled and subsided, so that without much inconvenience to his breathing he could walk out on to the landing ; and the moment he did so he heard the voices of a number of people below, and he guessed that assistance had been called in from the street.

He could not hear distinctly what was said, because so many spoke at once, which, whatever effect it has in saving time, does so, unfortunately, at the expense of intelligibility.

" I—I cannot go down," said Gilbert : " I must call for help, and they will have to bring a ladder. What a wreck the place looks !"

The place did indeed look a wreck. The whole staircase had gone down together, and in its progress it had torn away much of the plaster from the wall, leaving a most fearful-looking chasm below.

Gilbert dared hardly look down in the nervous state he was in, although he held fast by some of the top rails that were left, and which had no connection with the balustrades of the staircase. The noise continued below, and then, mustering all the breath he could, he cried aloud,—

" Help ! help ! help !"

In a moment several persons appeared in the passage, and one man, in loud, strong accents, cried out,—

" Hilloa ! Who's that ?"

" It's I—Gilbert Paddlebat. Help ! help !"

" Wait a bit—wait a bit. Don't attempt to come down," said several.

This was quite a needless caution, for Gilbert Paddlebat certainly had not the remotest intention in the world of coming down, so with great truth he said he would not.

In the course of five minutes a ladder was brought and placed up to the landing, and then, while it was held carefully in its place by several persons below, the old man came cautiously down, holding fast by the sides, and feeling every step before he trusted it.

" Come on—all's right," said the same man who had first spoken. " Here you are !" and when old Gilbert came within reach, he found himself seized in some herculean grasp, and fairly lifted off the ladder, and right into his office, before he was placed upon his feet again.

" What has happened ?" he then said, wringing his hands, and affecting an ignorance of the catastrophe that had occurred. " Good God ! what has happened ?"

" The staircase has fallen down."

" The—the staircase only ! I thought the whole house had gone, and gave myself up for dead. Where is Mr. Sheepy ?—Oh, where is Mr. Sheepy ?"

" Here," said a deep, solemn voice ; and the little throng of people separating that were around Gilbert, he was enabled to see his dying, but not dead partner, sitting in a chair, and looking more like some exhumed corpse than anything human.

" I am here," said Sheepy ; " I am a dying man. Gilbert Paddlebat !—Gilbert Paddlebat !"

" What, my dear sir ?"

" God forgive you, Gilbert Paddlebat !—God forgive you !"

" Amen !" said Gilbert, as if he were at church ; and very clever it was of Gilbert, too, under the circumstances, to pretend to take a religious view of old Sheepy's words.

Then Sheepy raised his hand and pointed at him, as he made an attempt to utter some inarticulate words, which died away in his throat. His breast heaved, and his face assumed a horrible expression. Then he fell from the chair before any one could support him, and when they picked him up he was dead.

CHAPTER XI.

FANNY LESLIE GIVES HER UNCLE AN ACCOUNT OF THE INDIAN VILLAGE AND ITS
INHABITANTS.—THE AUDACIOUS ATTEMPT OF JERVIS RODWELL.

OH, what a relief it was to Gilbert Paddlebat that old Sheepy was really dead. From the first moment that he had heard him speak, the dreadful idea had come over Gilbert, that his old partner might after all survive the accident he had met with sufficiently to make another will, and yet dispossess him, Gilbert, of the money he had certainly gone through thick and thin to make his own. But when he heard them say he was quite dead, the words came sweetly to Gilbert's ears, and he whispered to himself,

"Safe, safe, safe!"

A surgeon had been sent for, and he now arrived and pronounced the old man to be quite dead, so that there could be no doubt about it, and then old Gilbert spoke, saying,

"Take him somewhere—to a public house—anywhere but here. There is no accommodation here for him,—nothing but offices. He cannot lay here obstructing business. Take him somewhere."

"Who is he?" said one.

"His name is Sheepy," replied Gilbert. "He was my partner in business."

"Has he no friends?"

"No, no, no!"

"That's odd."

"Odd or not, it is the fact. Come, now, he may as well be removed at once. I will pay very handsomely any of you who will take him away."

"There's nowhere to take him to, master," said a rough-looking man. "He must remain here, except he was took to the workhouse. You wouldn't like that?"

"Yes, I should. Anything—anything!"

"Mr. Paddlebat," said a man who was attired in faded black. "Mr. Paddlebat, don't you know me, my dear sir?"

"No; who are you?"

"My name, my dear sir, is Leech. Mr. Leech, your neighbour, the undertaker, you know."

"Indeed."

"Yes, my dear sir; and all I have to say is, that if you intend that the deceased shall have a respectable funeral, I will send a shell and have the body at once taken to my house, out of your way. We think nothing of dead bodies, you know. Business is business, and it's nothing to us."

"Take him, then, take him," said old Gilbert. "What do you want?"

These last words were addressed to the goldsmith's lad, who had arrived in the midst of the uproar, and who was wonderfully delighted to find something of an unusual character going on, and much blamed himself for not getting there sooner, as, if he had done so, he might have actually had the fun of seeing the stairs fall down, which of course would have been famous.

"What do you want?" repeated Gilbert angrily.

"What does I want? eh!"

"You scoundrel, get out!"

"I've got a letter for old Gilbert Paddlebat, I have. It comes from my master, Mr. Paddlebat, the goldsmith."

"Give it to me."

"Oh, is you the cretur?"

"Give it to me, I say, you rascal."

Old Gilbert snatched at the letter and opened it, wondering much as he did so what should have induced his brother to write to him, considering the terms they were on. The note was a brief one, and merely requested that he, Gilbert, would call as soon as he could at the goldsmith's.

"What can be the matter?" thought Gilbert. "I wonder if he feels unwell and thinks of making his will. It's odd; I'll go most certainly. I don't feel well myself. I want some stimulant, and I may as well go there and have it at his expense as not. He is quite extravagant enough to offer me something to drink. I'll go, I'll go. Boy!"

"Here you is."

"You can tell your master that I will come."

"You will, sir?"

" What makes you doubt it ?"

" Oh, nothing. I only heard missus say as she didn't suppose the old hunks would come."

" Indeed. You can tell her, then, that the old hunks will see her in the grave, and that, out of grateful remembrance of the word, the old hunks will attend her funeral."

" Oh, there's too much of that ; I can't recollect such a long message as all that comes to. It won't do. I 'll say as you 're coming, and that's all as I can say ; so good-bye."

Away went the boy, and then old Gilbert Paddlebat began to consider if his brother really wanted him to make his will, and the more he considered the more he thought that such a thing was probable, and the more he exulted over the idea that he might come in for more money still.

" He would hardly send for me to make his will," thought Gilbert, " unless he intended to leave me something, and what else he could send for me for, I really cannot very well imagine. I will go as soon as I see Sheepy fairly off the premises."

The undertaker was as good as his word. He sent two men with a ready made coffin, which was used for such emergencies, and into that old Sheepy was laid and carried off. Then Gilbert began to think of going to his brother's, to whom the message he had sent had been duly delivered by the errand-boy, and who, in expectation of his coming, told Fanny Leslie who he was, and what were some of his peculiarities of habits and character.

" You need say very little to him, my dear," said the goldsmith ; " and mind, I do not send for him with the wish, the hope, or the expectation that he will do you any service, but I know I should be blamed by almost everybody if I did not introduce you to him."

" I shall be glad to see him," said Fanny ; " surely, dear uncle, as he is your brother he cannot be so very unlike you."

" My dear, there are great differences in brothers. I don't know really what has made Gilbert what he is, but we do, I think, differ in feelings, habits, and opinions quite as much as any two people possibly can."

" And is he old ?"

" He is older than I am, considerably, and he looks miserable, because he denies to himself those indulgencies which a man of his years ought to have."

" It 's very strange. I am glad, though, that you have sent for him, dear uncle, because, if ever we should meet, I should know him again. Kinder to me than you, he could not be, and if he treat me with harshness, I shall feel the more acutely the vast amount of gentleness and goodness you have already lavished upon me."

" My dear, that is not much ; but I hope that time will show that I wish to lavish kindness upon you, which I have not yet had the opportunity of doing. I look upon you in every respect as a dear child of my own, and if you will regard me as you would some indulgent father, who had no thought concerning you that was not for your happiness, you will please me."

Fanny flung her arms around the old man's neck, and kissed him, as, half sobbing, she said,—

" Oh ! dear, dear uncle, I can never hope to be so good to you as to recompense you for your goodness to me."

" Yes, you can, dear, and you are now. I bless the hour when first you came into the house. I have been much happier ever since. Heaven has denied me a child of my own, but it seems to me to have sent you to supply the place of one."

" And I will be one in duty and in affection."

" Of that I am well aware ; but now, Fanny, before your other uncle Gilbert comes, I wish you to tell me some particulars of how you came to be placed in such strange situations in America."

" Willingly, dear uncle."

" Very good ; and not to give you the trouble of repeating these particulars twice, my dear, go and fetch your aunt now, if you can find her, and tell her to come here and listen to you."

Fanny darted off on her errand, and on her road she met Nicholas Lowe, who moved aside with a low bow, to allow her to pass, as it was upon the staircase that they met.

"Oh! Mr. Lowe," she said, "I am so much obliged to you for the books you sent to me."

"I am, indeed," said Lowe, "most amply repaid for presenting them by the pleasure they have given to you."

"They are very pleasing. I am not well acquainted with English literature. They have, therefore, to me all the charms of novelty as well as excellence. In America we have very little imaginative literature that does not take some portion of the vast continent as its scene of action; and it is scarcely possible to read a page without at once perceiving the origin of the author."

"I have noticed as much in American works," said Lowe. "There is generally something about dollars before you get far."

"There is, indeed," said Fanny, with a smile; but her aunt at this moment made her appearance, and she bade Lowe a courteous adieu, which he returned rather confusedly, because he saw that Mrs. Paddlebat's eyes were upon him not with the most approving glance. However, she said nothing to Fanny upon the subject of holding any conversation with Nicholas Lowe, but accompanied her to the drawing-room, where was the goldsmith, who said,—

"Now, my dear, I want you to hear Fanny tell us, before brother Gilbert comes, something about her history, and particularly about how she came to be among the savages, and then if Gilbert should ask any questions, we can answer him."

"Certainly," said Mrs. Paddlebat; and then Fanny, in her sweet, low, melodious tones, commenced, as follows, to tell those whom she now loved and esteemed so well how she came to spend some time among the Indians :—

I lived nearly a year in an Indian village, and therefore became well acquainted with their manners and their customs. It happened that we were situated in a very lonely but beautiful spot, near the far-famed Hudson river, and more beautiful scenery than is there to be found can scarcely be imagined.

The country thereabouts was but thinly populated, and therefore exposed to the attacks of the Indians. They were in the habit of associating much together and by this means aiding each other when an attack was made. This did not often happen, save during war; but every one has heard of Indian cruelty, and few would care to live after they had been taken by an Indian. The worst that could happen to an adverse warrior was to be wounded, and left to fall into the hands of the natives. Death was a thousand times more preferable, and suicide, or any means of escape, was most readily flown to.

One autumnal evening, when the trees in the forest were exhibiting the most splendid and beauteous colours the mind can imagine, I walked along the banks of the Hudson, and gazed upon the waters. The air was calm and serene, and the evening beautiful. There was scarce a breath of air to ruffle a leaf in the forest, though here and there a few would fall from the trees—but they fell dead.

The beautiful hues of an American forest are delightful to look upon, and cause many pleasing images to fill the mind. What is there to equal the efforts of nature? In spring, progress, or decay, all alike are beautiful, and surpassing all that man can imitate.

I walked along, until the broad shadows of the forest trees reminded me that I was late, and might meet with some prowling party of enemies, though such were not expected; yet every one knew, that when the Indians did make an attack, it was always by surprise, and therefore not to be expected at one time more than another. As I walked home, I thought dark shadows more than once appeared in places that I thought strange, but shadows I thought but very little of, and yet I could not pass them without feeling some unpleasant sensation.

When I reached home I remarked that I had seen some dark moving objects in the woods, and could not tell what to think of it.

"Do you think it was the Indians ?"

"No ; I can hardly think that : for they would never have let me by, but would have captured me at once."

They would, most likely ; as the season's growing late it may be a bear or two, they have not yet gone to their winter quarters, and therefore it is no matter of surprise.

This was a very natural explanation, and I could not attempt to disturb it. I cannot say that I thought it was the best, and yet I knew of no other. We knew that the Indians were at war with each other, and were likely to make any attempt to injure and destroy those who might aid, or might have been the friends of, their enemies.

That night I could not undress myself; I merely laid down on my bed : I could not sleep, and lay awake counting the minutes. The house was buried in repose. It was well and strongly built, and made to resist any sudden attack; but, unfortunately, ny such places were unable to do w.

The night came, and we sat round a cheerful fire and conversed freely about many matters, and amused ourselves with games and books, and when we were tired we began to converse about the different occurrences that had taken place, and, among others, the attack upon, and the massacre of, a white family by the Indians that had but lately occurred.

"And how was that?"

"They made a night attack," said a gentleman who was present.

"And what became of them?"

"They were either killed or carried away, either as slaves, or else they took them to torture."

"The Indians are a cruel and blood-thirsty set of beings."

"They are; but then we must blame them only so far as we may consider it unnatural in people so brought up and educated to it. They know no other system of action, and have been taught that to do as they do is the highest pitch of virtue and heroism."

"I would rather they practised their virtue and heroism on any one else, little as I could wish evil to any one, rather than on me."

"I hope we may none of us have occasion to experience any of these wild people's cruelties."

"Or know any one who may," said I.

"Or know any one who may," he repeated; "but this I am sure of, if it were my fate to be engaged with any of them, I would sooner die than for a moment submit to them. Or if I were, unhappily for me, taken prisoner, I would, if there was an opportunity, take my own life and fall by my own hands."

"It is forbidden."

"I would sooner than be their prisoner," replied the gentleman, firmly; "it may be wrong, but I would do so."

We said no more on this subject, and about an hour after this we all parted for the night, but, as I said, I could not sleep that night—oh, no—I lay awake thinking of the words of the gentlemen and the dark shadows I had seen in the forest as I returned home. The longer I laid the more I thought of them, and the more vivid did the recollection return to my mind, and what then seemed merely shadows and indistinct, were now plain and palpable, and made me very uneasy.

I may say I lay in a perfect dread that each moment would produce some fatal and dreaded event. Why I should think so I cannot tell, or why such a sense of impending evil should hang over me I cannot say. But I did feel it, and that too most wretchedly. Oh, how I longed for the morning! but morning seemed afar off, and time passed slowly.

> "Upon the middle of the night,
>   Waking, I heard the night-fowl crow,
> The cock sung out an hour ere light,
>   From the dark fen the oxen's low
> Came to me, without hope or change."

There I lay wishing for sun-rise. Suddenly I was aroused and everybody body else within the house, by a wild and terrific yell. There could be no doubt as to the cause, but I sprung from my bed as if I had been thrown out by a powerful arm. I approached the window and carefully peeped out, and saw numbers of dusky forms as they hurried to and fro with wild demoniac gestures.

Every one in the house were fully alive to what was the cause of the dreadful announcement. It was the war-whoop. The Indians had set upon us, and rushed with wild frantic gesticulations to the house, believing we were at once in their power, and they endeavoured to force the doors. These, however, withstood their efforts, and afforded those inside time to dress and arm themselves as well as possible for the fray.

Oh, 'twas dreadful in the still hours of the night to hear that discordant cry; 'twas dreadful to hear, when awakened from a peaceful slumber or pleasant dreams, that ominous death-shout which these merciless savages uttered! Many lay paralysed, barely believing in the evidence of their own senses, and then thinking it could be but a startling and dreadful dream. But not long did this last ; the discordant yells were repeated, and in the noise of their attempts to force the doors, soon brought the few inmates to the windows to see what was the matter, or rather to ascertain who their enemies were.

Then came the report of the rifle, **sharp** and clear, on the night air, and a flash here and there indicated the situation of the assailants.

Things went on thus for nearly two hours, and many shots were exchanged, when there was a cessation of hostilities on the part of the savages. This gave us hope that they would either draw off and retreat, as they do sometimes when foiled in their first attempt, or that they would be held at bay till daylight, and then there would be a chance of succour from our neighbours. However, we were not long kept in suspense, and then our doubts were relieved in a manner that chilled our blood. The savages were collecting a quantity of dry brushwood and materials for lighting a fire. We at once understood the dreadful alternative that was presented to us—either that of yielding, or being burnt to death. I could not repress an involuntary shriek when I saw these preparations ; but, the moment they advanced, several rifles from the house discharged a volley of bullets, and they took effect, for several of the dusky figures carrying combustable materials were seen to fall. This occurred more than once, but they were in sufficient numbers to disregard all our efforts, and they assailed so many parts at once, that we could not prevent the house from being fired in more places than one at the same time.

What could we do ? Remain there, and be burned to death ? we could scarce do that ; human nature rebelled against suffering, what I may term, a passive death, inflicted by a foe, and unresented ; nature compelled us to seek the open air, and to make a desperate attempt to reach some of the neighbours, and cut our way through. The gentlemen believed that the Indians would not stand a charge, but fly and, therefore, in the rapidity of flight there might be a chance for some of us. At all events, it would be some satisfaction, they said, to die fighting, and bravely defending themselves with arms in their hands, and inflicting the same death they were about to suffer under. This was no sooner determined upon than executed, and the females were placed in the middle for protection. The house was in flames, and we could hear the crackling of the wood, as well as see the light it emitted around, and enabled us to see what we were doing, and exposing our foes to us. Our people fired one volley, and reloading hastily, they, finding the heat and smoke so intense as to threaten destruction, boldly made a dash at the largest body, who recoiled before us, and we made our way to the open ground towards the river with all the speed we could.

We hadn't got far when we heard a discharge of rifles, and so true were the aim that only the males were struck by them. They make slaves of the women whom they take in battle, or make wives of them, which is precisely the same thing, being indeed a worse species of slavery than all others, for you are regarded as a moveable, and valued and treated accordingly. Then came an attack before which our few defenders could not stand. I could not see what was done, for they seized me, and hurried me away, but I could hear the yells of the Indians who fell, the shots, and the blows.

Oh, how each sound went to my heart ! A tall savage had seized me, and hurried me along with considerable force. I could not resist—alas ! it would have been unavailing, and merely a prelude to ill-usage of one kind and another.

Who was or who was not injured in the dreadful affray I could not tell. All passed before my eyes like a frightful and hideous dream, and one, too, of the reality of which I could scarce persuade myself : indeed, all seemed the effects of a vision. But there were the savages and the burning house : the flames were high, and cast a lurid gloom upon the dark forms that moved about in the red light that was cast below, looking like so many demons. I was soon hurried from the scene, and the party who had captured me being apprehensive that I could not travel quick enough, lifted me up between two of them, and carried me along at a running pace until we reached the woods.

Here they stopped awhile, and procured some branches and made a kind of litter, which they carried between them, and I was laid upon it. We went through the woods until the morning dawned, and by that time we had passed over many miles of ground through the pathless forest. That night we stopped nowhere, and it was not until the morning dawned, and the sun rose, that they thought of a halt. Then, on the banks of a beautiful stream, they prepared a temporary encampment, and began to see about getting some food and rest. They lit fires, and shot some wild animals: they shot a buck that crossed their path by accident, and then they soon contrived to cook some of the most choice parts, and after having eaten to repletion, they lay down and soon fell to sleep, like so many beasts. Not one remained awake: they knew they had bound me securely, and they believed themselves free from all surprise.

It is well known, that these people, though their whole art of war consists in surprise, yet they never take any precaution against them. Their whole art seems exhausted in making an attack, but not in guarding against one, or providing for any contingency that might arise during an excursion.

I could not sleep, as may well be imagined. I lay secured to my couch, with two of the most wakeful of the tribe on either side of me—for they are proverbially light sleepers—in case I made any attempt to escape. This, I am persuaded, would have been useless, had I attempted it, for they would easily awake, at even a movement.

They slept thus for nearly two hours, and the day was far advanced towards noon, when I thought I saw shadows in the wood. I started at first, for I thought of the experience of the previous night and trembled; but I remembered that this would affect me but little; that I was a prisoner, and therefore took but little interest in what happened. It was no doubt, I thought, another party of the same tribe, who had been detached for a similar purpose as that in which the one I had become a prisoner to, had been engaged in. I expected to see them come loaded with prisoners and pillage. This was not the fact. The first that came in sight was a tall chief, as I could tell from his ornaments. He stopped and listened to the slightest sound, and at the same time, he motioned to his followers, who came creeping and crouching forward until within a few yards of the spot where we lay. I was in some fear, for I perceived that their motions were hostile, and had a natural dread of anything happening. He approached within about twenty yards, when one of those who lay by me started and looked around, and then uttered a cry of terror, and jumping up, seized his rifle. His cry immediately brought the whole tribe to their feet, and at the same time a shower of bullets were poured in with deadly effect, and one half of the tribe were stretched lifeless and bleeding upon the earth.

With the same wild shout, the war whoop, the assailants rushed on with their hatchets, and a deadly conflict ensued, which could last but a very few moments. The numbers were so few against the assailants that they were soon overpowered, and the few who did escape made the best of their way to the woods, and there eluded all pursuit.

I shuddered as I looked upon the number of the slain; the dead bodies lay where they had fallen, and those who but a short time before were conquerors, and had been successful, were now, by a change in fortune, lying dead, and despoiled of their victory.

When there was no longer any opposition they set to work and commenced the disgusting operation of tearing the scalps from the heads; and this done, the chief of the party turned to me, and with his own hand unbound me, at the same time he looked earnestly at me, and made signs that I should not be frightened, that no harm was intended me. They then took the litter I was on and proceeded onwards at a rapid rate, until the sun was sinking in the west.

The forest was here to be seen in its full splendour, the leaves were of all hues, and the sun's sinking rays fell upon them, reflecting back a thousand different tints. The heavens, too, seemed all to watch these beauties, and were lighted up with rays of a thousand dies; the clouds presented the most gorgeous scenery that the mind can imagine, and not a spot but what had its peculiar beauties. The sun sunk and all nature seemed to sink in repose, and then night came on apace. My guides hurried on, and came at a late hour to another small party of their own tribe, and then encamped for the night.

There were here provisions all ready prepared for us, and I must confess I was compelled to eat. I had eaten nothing since the night of the attack. I was very faint, and was compelled to accept of the food which the chief proffered me, and extreme hunger caused me to eat with eagerness. That night we slept in the forest, and I must say very great care was taken of me to prevent the night winds from reaching me.

The next morning we again resumed another day's march, and at length came to a large body of water, the very edges of which were clothed with tall trees, whose boughs overhung the water's edge. Here an incident occurred that alarmed me much, and that was, the party, while searching along the banks of the lake for some canes, disturbed a large rattle-snake. The venomous brute raised itself up above the tall sedges, and gazed around at the cause of the disturbance. In an instant the Indians fled, and secreted themselves behind some trees, while I was carried to a yet greater distance, and my guides stood by me ready to fly yet further, if there should be any necessity for so doing. The creature was soon in motion, and I was afterwards informed that no doubt it had been disturbed after a long sleep, for it gorges itself to repletion, and then lays idle till it has digested its meal, which may take weeks in doing; it had been disturbed before it was yet hungry, and therefore did not dart upon them the instant they came in sight. When they had got to a distance and saw the snake rousing himself to attack them, and began moving after them with great rapidity, and turning about, they fired several times at it, but the motions of the snake were so rapid, and never remaining an instant in the same posture, it offered a bad mark for the Indians to shoot at, and often more than a dozen shots had been fired, and it had not been more than twice wounded. One of the Indians, however, at length, with an arrow pierced it right through the body.

I shall never forget the fire of its eyes, and the rapidity of its movements, which but for its danger I should have thought extremely beautiful. However, the Indians did not now fear it, and wounding it fatally in the head, the animal was destroyed. It was of almost incredible length; and, as we stepped over it, we got a full view of it—it must have been an inhabitant of the forest for a considerable number of years. The Indians say they do not grow so large as formerly, and the reason is, they are destroyed whenever they are met with, and thus they decrease in number.

When we crossed the great lake, as it was called, we came to an Indian village, and there our journey was at an end. I must confess I had been passive; but what else could I do? there was no aid or help at hand, and besides, I really thought that my present captors would use me gently, and that I should suffer no ill treatment from them. Why I should think so I know not, save that these were enemies to the former tribe, and that was a very insufficient reason. I remained here nearly a year, and had slaves to attend upon me, and everything that could be done to please me was done, and I had nothing to complain of, save my liberty. I knew not where I was, or how far I was from the place I had been taken, and could, therefore, take no steps to release myself.

The chief who had re-captured me paid me every attention, and, after a time, hoped to make me his wife, and promised that he would even discharge all his other wives if I would consent, and, moreover, he would have no more. But I was proof against such blandishment, and refused all his offers, and remained obdurate, much to his disappointment and vexation. However, he after that time promised me I should be sent home, and, as he had no longer any war with rival chiefs, he would conduct me home. Glad was I to hear this, and I betrayed my joy so unquestionably, that he noticed it, and feared he had not done enough, but I told him he had, and could never forget his care. This pleased him, and he gave me a valuable box of skins and other things.

* * * * * * *

There was so much sweetness about the manner in which Fanny Leslie told her simple history, that neither her aunt or uncle thought proper to interrupt her during its continuance, and when she had concluded, they wished that she had had more to tell them, so deeply interested had their love for her made them feel in the narrative of events which had concerned her so nearly.

"Oh, what danger," said Mrs. Paddlebat, "you must have been in, my darling; I should have died of the fright, myself."

"Oh," said Mr. Paddlebat, "I should have wished for my volunteer gun if I had seen these Indians."

"I was younger, then, than I am now," said Fanny, "and, therefore, really did not feel or estimate the danger I was in. I certainly at times felt much fear, and much anxiety, but nothing in comparison to what I fancy I should now feel under similar circumstances"

"No doubt, no doubt."

"Oh, if you please, sir," said the incomprehensible servant, popping her head into the room, "here's Mr. Gilbert Paddlebat, sir, and a skrimagee."

"A what?"

"A skrimagee atween Mr. Lowe and Mr. Rodwell and the plug in the street."

"I cannot understand you, and never could," said the goldsmith. "The first part of what you have said is all that is intelligible to me, and, as that is no doubt of the most importance, we will give up the remainder in despair. Tell my brother to walk up here."

"Very good. A chimney and an ocean."

"Gracious goodness, what do you mean?" exclaimed Mrs. Paddlebat, and then, by dint of cross questioning, it was ascertained that Gilbert Paddlebat had happened to come in at the same time that Rodwell and Lowe was having some disagreement, and that co-existent with those circumstances, there had been an alarm of fire in the neighbourhood, which had occasioned a plug to be opened, but it was found only to be a foul chimney, in which was an ocean of soot.

When all this was satisfactorily ascertained, old Gilbert was shewn up, and he entered his brother's drawing-room with a snarling look of supreme contempt for any article in it, which he thought it behoved him to put on, for fear the goldsmith should think he greatly admired any of the furniture or the decorations of the apartment. He planted himself in the middle of the floor, and then placing his hands behind his back, as if for security against any one venturing to shake hands with him, he said, in rough accents,—

"Well? well?"

"I have sent for you, brother Gilbert," said the goldsmith, "because I considered it was my duty to do so."

"Humph!"

"And from no other consideration. I did not expect any pleasure from your society, but yet you shall not say you came here without being offered some hospitality. What will you take, brother?"

"Something of the best and most expensive article you have," said Gilbert. "Wise men drink at fools' expense."

Without taking any notice of the offensive remark which was made to him, the goldsmith ordered wine to be placed before Gilbert, who at once partook of it without any scruples.

Gilbert Paddlebat never did have any scruples at partaking of anything expensive at some one else's cost.

"Ha!" he said, as he poured the generous liquor down his throat. "Go on; what did you send for me for?"

"Gilbert, you remember our sister Amelia?"

"Amelia, Amelia! Ha! she who, married a vagabond, who far from being able to keep her, could not keep himself; a thief—a cut-purse."

"Hush, Gilbert! Hush, hush!"

Fannie Leslie burst into tears.

"Leslie, our sister Amelia's husband, is dead," said the goldsmith; "let his faults die with him. He is now out of the world, and to be judged by his Creator. What he was need not now be alluded to."

"Stuff—nonsense!" cried Gilbert. "Was that what you sent to me for?"

"Not exactly, Gilbert."

"What then? I'm a man of business, and cannot be wasting my time at this part of the day. What do you want with me? Say it at once, and then let me go."

"I will, Gilbert. I have no wish to detain you. You seem to me to be in a worse and a more ungracious humour than usual to-day, which I am very sorry indeed for, because it never before happened that I so much wished you to appear, at all events, a little otherwise."

Gilbert made a gesture of impatience, and then the goldsmith added,—

"Our sister Amelia is no more. She has died in another land, and among a people whom no one would either live or die among, if they could help it."

"Who may they be?"

"The Americans."

"Ah! thieves all of them. Go on."

"You heard me, Gilbert? I said Amelia was dead."

"Well; I ain't deaf."

"And is that all the feeling you have to show upon such news? Oh, Gilbert, Gilbert, have you really, as some people say, no heart?"

"What's that to you, or to anybody else? Have you said your say? Because if you have I'll say mine, and be off."

"Not quite. Amelia has left a child."

"What?"

"A child—destitute and helpless."

Old Gilbert Paddlebat's face became livid with rage, as he said hoarsely,—

"And you want me to keep it—and you want me to keep it? That's what you have sent for me for. D——n I ought to have suspected something of the sort was coming. I won't—I won't. Not a farthing does it get from me; no, not a pinch of salt to save its life. D—n all poor people's children! they ought to die."

"Shame, shame upon you," said the goldsmith. "Gilbert, I would not trust a dog or a cat to you, far less a sister's child. I never dreamt of asking you to keep Amelia's child. She is here, the good and beautiful girl, my adopted daughter; I have only sent for you that you might not say I never told you of her, and that she might know what a mass of folly and of selfishness she has for another uncle."

"Indeed! And that's all, is it? I'm wonderfully obliged to you all. You have got her, and you may keep her. Now, I suppose, as I was only sent for here to be abused I can go."

"Go as soon as you like."

"And a remarkably good riddance, too," said Mrs. Paddlebat. "You'll come to some bad end—I know you will. Oh, you old wretch! I hate the sight of you, and I always did, and I always shall. It gives me a cold feel to see you come into the house, you odious old man with one foot in the grave."

"Go on, go on," said Gilbert, "go on—I like it. It's a good thing to be abused by a fool; it gives me a notion that all's right, and that I have acted with great wisdom. He—he—he! Go on, madam, go on, you must be a tolerable expense."

"You old monster!"

"Peace—peace," interposed Mr. Paddlebat, "my dear, you have no occasion to say anything to Gilbert. I sent for him on a family affair, and we can settle our business together—so don't say another word. Brother Gilbert, for the last time, have you no kind word to say to your niece?"

"For the first, and the last, and for every time," said Gilbert, with bitterness, "I tell you, I don't mean to give a penny-piece to anybody, or to acknowledge any relationships at all."

"Very well; then I have no more to say to you—our interview is over. There's the door, Gilbert, and the sooner you pass out of this room the better I shall be pleased."

"No doubt. I have had three glasses of wine."

" Never mind that."

" Yes, but I do though. This wine is worth, I dare say, five shillings a bottle, and a bottle won't run above nine such glasses as these. That comes to about sixpence halfpenny and a fraction each glass, so you are the worse of my visit to the extent of nearly twentypence, and that is a whole year's interest on one pound six- teen shillings at five per cent., and where are you to get five per cent. now ? Who's the fool—eh ? Ha—ha ! Who's the fool now—eh ? Ha—ha—ha !"

Chuckling to himself, old Gilbert Paddlebat walked from the room, fancying in his own mind that he had acted very cleverly, and achieved a great triumph over his brother.

Poor Fanny was weeping, but the old goldsmith drew her towards him tenderly, as he said to her,—

" My dear, don't fret yourself. The love of money and dreadful selfishness, an exhibition of which you have seen, is little better than a species of lunacy, and you will consider it as such, and rather pity Gilbert Paddlebat than blame him."

" I will, dear uncle, I will."

" Think no more of him now, my darling, but just let circumstances take their course. I fully expected he would behave in the way he has ostensibly, although I did not think that there could have been such a total absence of all feeling. But never mind, my darling, you shall be our dear child, you know, and you need not care for any one in all the world."

Fanny Leslie controlled her tears, and looked up affectionately in the face of her uncle, as she thought to herself,—

" And can these two men be brothers ? One the soul of kindness, honour, and noble generosity, while the other is totally destitute of such feelings. Ah, how happy have I been that my lot has cast me where it has ! Had I gone first to Gil- bert Paddlebat, what would have become of me ?"

CHAPTER XII.

THE GRATEFUL FEELINGS OF FANNY.—THE OLD GOLDSMITH'S INCREASED AFFECTION FOR HER.—JERVIS RODWELL AND THE DOG.

The conduct of Gilbert Paddlebat was so far from having the least effect upon the old goldsmith in inducing him to imitate such unkindness, that if possible he certainly loved Fanny Leslie the better now that he found she was so entirely dependent upon him.

It seems to be a principle of human nature to feel some degree of affection for those living things which are wholly dependent upon us, and we are inclined to think that if in many cases the overweening fondness of people for all sorts of animals was sifted to its foundation, it would be found in the utter helplessness of the animal, and the feeling of perfect control and power which can be exercised over it.

It is with our equals we are disposed to quarrel, and to stand upon points of etiquette and nicety, but not with those who are so very far below us that any clashing of thoughts, feelings, or sensations, is out of the question.

Of course this was not the case as regarded the old goldsmith and the beautiful Fanny. Her helplessness and her entire dependence upon him, no doubt added firmness to his attachment to her, but still he loved her for herself, and without the extraneous aid of the feelings which the harshness of Gilbert had produced, she would have been, from the intrinsic qualities of her own heart, from her beauty, and from the many kind and good feelings that continually showed themselves in all her actions and in every word she uttered, most dear to him.

Old Paddlebat, too, was childless; but not on that account had he lapsed into insensibility as regarded those dear domestic ties which bind heart to heart. Often, with a sigh, had the old man regretted that age was stealing upon him, and that there was no one loved form, with the freshness of youth, to hover round him and call him by the endearing name of father.

As year after year passed on, this regret had almost grown into a bitterness, and, indeed, to follow out the proposition with which we commenced these pages, it almost became the old man's skeleton.

It was the shadow on the sunshine of his heart. All was prosperous with him. His business throve ; his health was good; and Mrs. Paddlebat was a very good sort of woman indeed, and, barring little occasional ebullitions of temper, made him as comfortable a home as he could well expect,—but he had no child. There was not one object around which all his affections could centre.

Unlike—most unlike—his brother Gilbert, whose constant aim had ever been to repel humanity, and to live for himself alone, the goldsmith had ever felt keenly all the social amenities of existence. With all their foibles, and with all their faults, he loved his fellow-creatures.

And truly there had seemed not the remotest chance that the void in his heart would ever be filled up. A void it was which each day he felt more and more acutely, until the blessed chance came that at once gave him something to love, which his judgment, equally with his feelings, approved.

No. 10.

Fanny Leslie, his own dear sister's child, the little one of that sister whom he had ever felt affection for, one in whose face too he could trace the remembrances of times gone past; she came to him, and from the first moment that she twined her arms around his neck, and he felt the soft pressure of her cheek, the old man was happy.

The brightest dream of his ambition was now fulfilled. He had something to love—something which filled his whole thoughts,—and had Fanny been ten times his own child he could not have lavished upon her more tenderness than he now did. And yet, although it had the appearance of one, we will not call this love of old Paddlebat for his sister's child an infatuation. Ah, no! it was a far, far better feeling, and it was a lasting one, too, and so may well be taken out of such a category. He loved her as the tenderest father might love a child. To his feelings and perceptions she could say nothing wrong—she could do nothing wrong. The very fact that anything wrong was said or done by Fanny was in his mind sufficient to sanctify it.

This was, we will readily admit, a weakness; but then there are some weaknesses which we are almost inclined to prefer to some virtues; at all events, the weaknesses and the prejudices of some people are far more loveable than the virtues of others. Moreover, too, when there exists this extravagance of affection, much of the good or of the evil which shall spring from it will wholly depend upon the object on which it is lavished. If unworthily bestowed, of course the evil predominates, and many little heart-breaking consequences may ensue. But who could love such a one as Fanny Leslie too much? Happy was the old goldsmith that he had met with such a one as she, on whom to expend so much affection. And Fanny repaid well the love which was lavished upon her. With the keen perception of an intellect far above mediocrity she saw the single-mindedness of her uncle, and in every word he said to her she saw how much he loved her. Gratitude filled her heart towards him with the liveliest emotion, and there was nothing, let it involve what risk it might, that she would have shrunk from, to give him some return for his generous adoption of her.

In a rough school had the gentle Fanny been of late nurtured; but like some delicate and beautiful summer flower, which has outlived the severity of a winter of storms and frosts, and then again in the sweet spring-time blooms with some new beauty, did she shake from his mind the past with all its terrors and all its anxieties, becoming again what she should have always been, the darling of all hearts and the cause of as much joy in others as she was herself capable of feeling and appreciating.

The old goldsmith, when he now thought of his brother Gilbert, did so with strange feelings of curiosity and pity, and could not for the life of him understand the feelings that could actuate such a man. The love of money, except that it was a medium of exchange for many desirable things, was a sensation he had never for one moment experienced; and why, or with what imaginable or tangible motive an old man, such as Gilbert was, should deny himself all the sweetest luxuries of life for the sake of hoarding wealth he never could enjoy, puzzled the old goldsmith amazingly.

By degrees, however, the acerbity of his feelings towards Gilbert softened down into a sort of pity, and he thought of him as a sort of curiosity, and as one whose mind must have become warped, perhaps, by some circumstance which he knew not of. There was some pleasure, too, in the reflection, now that Fanny was left entirely to him, that Gilbert had had the fair opportunity given him of doing something, and had not done it. Not only, too, had he not done it, but he had taken good care to couch his refusal harshly, so that by no means, or under any circumstances now, could he come forward with any claim upon the affection of his young and beautiful niece.

" Well, well," old Paddlebat said to himself, " I am very glad I sent to him. If I had not done so, he would always have hinted at what he would and might have done if I had not, as he would probably have called it, smuggled up our sister's child all to myself. I am very glad Gilbert has seen her. He refuses to do anything for her ; so now he has no sort of right ever again to interfere with her or to claim the least portion of her regard."

And no doubt Fanny's philosophy was sadly at fault to reconcile her mind to the wonderful disparity between the two brothers; but hers was a disposition which led her far more readily to dwell upon the happy present than to perplex herself with the affliction of the past, so that old Gilbert the miser had a very fair chance of being soon forgotten by his beautiful niece, as he was nearly by all the world beside. The dog, too, made himself quite at home at the goldsmith's, and soon came to be considered as one of the family, even by Mrs. Paddlebat herself. He took to the old goldsmith wonderfully, and would take his station at his feet, as if he had known him for years. The old man would have it that the dog saw what good friends Fanny and he were, and acted accordingly. And as for Mrs. Paddlebat, her heart was won by the great creature striking up an acquaintance with her favourite cat.

It was an odd thing to see these two creatures, so dissimilar as they were in size and in habits, become such great friends as they did. If the dog met puss in the passage, he would take her up in his mouth, and carry her up stairs as tenderly as possible, bringing her into the drawing-room, and placing her by the fire quite comfortably. Then in the morning, or after the dog had been out for some time, it was quite ridiculous to see what a fuss in the way of friendly recognition the cat would make. With her tail perpendicular, and crying at a prodigious rate, she would walk round and round him, spreading out her claws and taking them in again, while every moment she would give her head a hard rub against him, as if awaiting a caress.

"Well, I declare," exclaimed Mrs. Paddlebat, " these creatures are, for all the world, like two Christians."

" Christians !" said the old goldsmith. "Well, I never saw one Christian walking round another like that before, and making such an odd noise."

" Mr. Paddlebat, you always take me up, you know, in that sort of way. How can you do so ? Of course, I didn't mean that the cat was a Christian."

"Oh ! ah !"

" But I do say it is wonderful to see them both, and now, Fanny, that the dog does behave himself as he ought to do, and has made friends with the cat, I have no objections to him."

" I am very glad, aunt, to hear you say so. I am much attached to him, and I should like all whom I love to love him likewise."

" Besides," added Mr. Paddlebat, " you know he sleeps on the mat outside your bedroom door, Fanny, and I think him a very great safeguard to all the house."

" You may depend he is," said Fanny. " I should pity any one very much who should come in the night and get into the clutches of him."

" Well, that is something," said Mrs. Paddlebat. " I shall sleep all the sounder. I always have had a dread of being murdered in my bed some night. You know, Fanny, that the quantity of gold and silver plate on the premises offer temptation to thieves."

" You need have no apprehensions, aunt, indeed, now," said Fanny. " The strength of my four-footed friend here is very great, I assure you. Unless you really saw some exhibition of it you could not believe it. No man could stand against him, I am convinced from what I have several times seen of his strength and courage."

The dog gave a low anxious sort of growl at this moment, and Fanny looked astonished.

" What is he thinking about now?" asked Mrs. Paddlebat. with some feeling of alarm.

" I don't know," said Fanny. " He hears something that he does not like probably, or some one may be coming up the stairs of whom he has some suspicions. That sound, however, is merely a note of dislike ; unless I were to tell him he would do no sort of violence."

The dog continued to growl, and left his station by Mrs. Paddlebat to come close to Fanny, into whose countenance he looked with a steady gaze, as if waiting for instructions what to do.

The cause of the disquietude of the dog was soon explained by the appearance of Jervis Rodwell, who entered the room to bring some message to the goldsmith.

"That dog is always growling at me," he said.

"Well, it's a very odd thing," said Mrs. Paddlebat. "He must mistake you for some one else."

"No," said Fanny, quietly. "When you know him better, aunt, you will feel convinced that he never makes mistakes. Down, sir, down."

The dog immediately crouched at her feet, but now he kept his eyes fixed upon Rodwell, who hesitated to advance into the room for fear he should be suddenly seized by an animal of such weight and strength, that to contend against him would be out of the question.

"He will not touch you," said Fanny. "He will not touch you, you may be assured."

This assurance enabled Rodwell to recover his usual pert audacity, and he said,—

"I am quite surprised, Miss Leslie, that he should growl at me, because I am so particularly fond of dogs."

"You must have offended him."

"Unconsciously, then, I am sure, Miss Leslie. Poor fellow—poor fellow."

The poor fellow evidently regarded the advances of Rodwell with anything but an eye of satisfaction, for he exhibited as a reply such a formidable row of white teeth, that Rodwell rapidly retreated the two steps he had advanced.

"You had better say nothing to him," remarked Fanny. "If he will not be friends with you, you can never induce him."

"I suppose, then, if I meet him alone he will fly at me."

"No, no. If you meet him let him pass, but I warn you not to attempt to interfere with him."

Rodwell had some difficulty to prevent himself from duly d——g the dog, but he did keep the words to himself, and he said,—

"I have merely come, Mr. Paddlebat, to tell you that Alderman Plumby has sent to say he would be glad to see you, if you can spare an hour, any time before four o'clock to-day."

"Very well: I will attend to him. You can send and say so, Rodwell."

"Yes, sir."

Rodwell left the room, and when he was gone, the dog gave a short sound of satisfaction, and Mrs. Paddlebat said,—

"Well, I do wonder what objection the dog can have to Mr. Rodwell; it's quite a mystery to me."

Fanny stooped to caress the dog, and made no reply to this remark her aunt's.

CHAPTER XIII.

GILBERT PADDLEBAT AT HOME.—HIS NIGHT THOUGHTS.—THE MISER'S MISERIES.—
INFATUATION.

Was old Gilbert Paddlebat quite satisfied and contented with what he had said and done at his brother's? Did no vision of the beautiful girl he had there seen haunt him? Could he be so utterly inhuman—so entirely destitute of all earthly feelings as to have no pang of regret?

We shall see, we shall see. Assuming the cloak of invisibility we will follow him to his dreary, comfortless home. We will listen to his lonely communings with himself, when he thinks that no eye—not even that of Heaven is upon him —when he thinks there is no ear to drink in the faint mutterings of his perturbed and conscience-stricken spirit.

In the broad daylight, and when all is bustle—all activity around them, many men are very different to what they are at other times and periods. The salient points of their characters do not come out under such circumstances. They are playing a part, but it is a part that has become so habitual to them that they play it naturally and well, so naturally, indeed, that thousands are deceived, and think they are the real man, when such is not the actual case.

But surely with Gilbert Paddlebat there need be no disguise. He need not be a miser unless he pleased. He need humble to no one for gold—not he. He is wealthy—very wealthy, and can look and say what he pleases. It is such men as he, with such ample means as he possessed, that can, if they choose, make slaves of the prodigal and the spendthrift, and not be slaves themselves of that glittering metal which they may command if it so please them.

But what amount of mental degradation or slavery can exceed that of a miser to his hoards? Where shall we find a more abject wretch than he, who no doubt has first commenced by fancying the delight of exercising the power that money will give him, and ends by becoming the money's victim?

The day has closed—night has come over the giant city. The business, to a great extent, of London is over, and the pleasure—alas, in too many cases but a nickname for vice—has commenced with thousands.

The busy streets are crowded. Friend meets friend, and many kindly greetings are exchanged. Lights flash from the windows of the houses, and the general bustle and animation which is to be found in London an hour after sunset, has now fairly commenced and will last till nearly midnight: after that hour the hilarity is not of the right sort, it begins to savour too much of late hours, neglected occupations on the morrow, and dissipation.

There are very few on an evening in London but who are glad of some occupation—some friendly interchange of thought and feeling—some one or more kindred friends with whom an hour or two may be passed; but among the few who are deaf to these calls of sociality and humanity—and we rejoice that they are but few—was unquestionably old Gilbert Paddlebat the miser.

Yes, he was alone. He courted no friendly salutations—not he, he had no appointment with anybody; he called nowhere to take his place in some friendly domestic circle; no, he stood apart from all humanity, like a thing accursed, and wrapped up in his own selfishness. His place had never been cleaned for many years, and consequently the walls of his room were covered with dust and cobwebs, and the floor was as black as ink.

"There is warmth in all that," he would say. "If there is a hole or a crevice anywhere and you leave it alone, it gets filled up of itself by degrees."

His supper consisted of some dry bread and cold water, and as he went to bed early, he got through his time generally speaking sufficiently to his own satisfaction. But there were times, when, in the dead hours of the night, strange feelings of dread would creep over him. He would fancy that the house contained thieves and murderers, and in all the frenzy of horror at the supposition, he would rise and go prowling from room to room with a light, shielding it from sudden draughts with his hand, which made it cast a strange, spectral light upon his face.

And thus, at times, he would wander about till the dawn of day, when, feeling somewhat exhausted, he would snatch an hour's slumber before it was time to rise and proceed to business.

These attacks of depression had not, however, been very frequent, so that he founded no specific line of conduct upon them; but after the death of his partner, a change came over him, and he became painfully alive to the least unusual sound that disturbed the stillness of the place in which he dwelt.

It is night now. He is seated in the old arm-chair—a crust of bread is in his hand, and on the table by his side is an earthen jug with water. These form his frugal repast. There had been indications of rain early in the evening, which old Gilbert Paddlebat always liked to see, because it spoiled people's pleasure out of doors, and he thought to himself, "What right has anybody to be pleasant?"

The appearances of the early portion of the evening had not been deceitful, for about an hour or so after sunset, the rain came down in torrents, and a squally sort of wind arose. Against the windows of the room in which Gilbert sat, the rain dashed now and then with violence, and he smiled grimly as he said,

"Humph! a stormy night. It will spoil the pleasures of a goodish many, and a good job too. Besides, it will spoil their clothes, the fools; and nothing wears out boots and shoes equal to wet weather. What a destruction of people's means. Well, well, it serves the improvident right. I'm glad of it,—I'm very glad of it. I don't care who comes to ruin, because nobody comes to ruin except by their own wild and wilful extravagance. There's my brother now—ah, ah—there's my brother ——"

He paused a moment or two, and shifted his position in his chair, and then he added,

"He drinks his wine—very well, very well. That costs the interest on a large sum. Suppose now his wine costs him a hundred pounds a-year, that's the interest of two thousand pounds at five per cent. What a dreadful proposition! To sink two thousand pounds for the doubtful gratification of tippling wine. Ah, ah! and there's that girl, too—why do I think of her? What is she to me—what am I to her? uncle—uncle. Psha! all the world knows I think nothing of relationship; that, indeed, I hate the very name of such a thing, so I won't make myself nervous on such a subject, not I. I never was better in my life—never, never, and old Sheepy's dead too, which is quite a release—a release for him as well as for me."

Thus did old Gilbert Paddlebat try to talk himself into an easy and a pleasant frame of mind; but he found it impossible to do so. His nervousness and his fears each moment increased considerably; until at last he really began to get seriously unwell.

"What's the matter with me," he said; "what is it—what can it be now that affects me so much to-night? I did not kill old Sheepy, not I. If staircases will break down, how can I help them? Of course I cannot, and as for giving away money because one's sister has been so absurd as to make an improvident marriage, I could not dream of such a wilful waste. Why do I keep thinking of Sheepy—what is he to me? Nothing, nothing. He might fall or he might not, and if he did, how was I to take upon myself to say as a consequence that death would result —no, no, no—I will get a light. Let me have a light. I think I must be so extravagant as to get a light on such a night as this."

He tottered to the mantelshelf, where he always kept the means of procuring a light, and with nervous hands he commenced striking with a flint and steel for that purpose. To go to the expense of any more artificial mode of procuring a light, would have seemed to Gilbert Paddlebat like going to ruin headlong; a steel cost only one penny in the first instance, a flint could always be got for nothing at all, and any old rag, picked up in the street, would make tinder, so that, on the score of economy, no wonder that the miser stuck to the flint and steel.

After many abortive efforts, in consequence of his extreme state of nervousness, he did succeed in getting a light, and in igniting the rushlight, which was at hand. Then, with a timorous look, he cast his eyes around him, as if he expected them to rest upon some dreadful apparition.

"There is nothing—nothing," he said, with a long sigh of relief; "after all, there is nothing; it was the storm of wind and rain that is without that has deceived me; I am alone—quite alone, of course. How foolish of me to give way to such terror, and to waste a candle."

He turned about to blow out the light, but he did not do so. The feeble puff he gave it did not produce that effect, and then he paused and said,—

"I think for to-night, as I do not feel quite myself, I will let the candle burn a little while, in spite of the expense. I—I did not kill him. If a staircase is rotten, I cannot help it; I am not to blame; it cracked under me, and it might only have cracked under him; I was not to make an outcry because the staircase shook; and, besides, would he have interfered to save me, knowing, as he did, that at my death he would come into all I possessed? Certainly not—oh, most certainly not; and so—so I'm not to blame—no, not in the least."

Thus did old Gilbert Paddlebat strive to still the pangs of a disturbed conscience; but he strove in vain. He was arguing a bad cause, and well he knew it. Well he knew himself to be virtually the murderer of his late partner; and, say what he would, do what he would, he could not silence that still, small voice, which will be heard.

"I think I will go to bed,' he said, as with trembling steps he sought the miserable couch which was in the next room ; "yes, I will go to bed—to bed, and then I shall forget. I do not often dream—not very often ; and I do not think I shall to-night ; what have I to dream about ?"

The poor light from the candle he carried cast but a dim and a sickly lustre around it. It could not be said at all to illumine the room, for, at a distance of about a yard from it, the same gloom prevailed as if there was no light in the place.

"Now for—for calm repose," muttered Gilbert. "I will think of my money—ay, my money, which always brings pleasant images before me. I am rich ; much richer, too, by the death of him whom I did not kill, and, therefore, concerning whom I need have no terrors whatever—not me—not me. Was—was that a sound ? What—what was it ?"

He shook like an aspen for some moments, and then, as usual, muttering that it was nothing—that he was sure, quite sure it was nothing, he took off the old cloak, and hung it behind the door.

"I shall soon go to sleep—very soon ; I always do very soon go to sleep ; why should I not ? What have I done that should prevent me from soon going to sleep ? —nothing—just nothing. Surely a man is completely and entirely justified in keeping his money if he likes, and not throwing it away upon his needy relations ; and—and as for Sheepy. Eh?—eh? What—what was that? Oh, it was nothing—nothing again. How foolish of me to allow myself to be so easily disturbed. But—but when I get to sleep, all will be well."

It did not take the old man long to prepare for bed ; he had no prayers to utter. He never prayed. The words would have stuck in his throat. Upon what plea could such a man as he have asked anything of Heaven ?

The bit of rushlight was short, and now the idea came over him that it would be a comfortable thing to go to sleep while it was burning, and let it go out of itself, which it naturally would at the end of its existence.

"A good idea," he muttered, "although an extravagant one ; but for once, I do think I will be rash enough to do so. There is not above an inch of the candle left, and that cannot come to much. To-morrow, I will calculate the amount closely, and manage to save it somehow during the week, so that I shall not be a loser by the transaction."

This was consolatory. He made up his mind actually to allow the candle to burn out of itself. He hung over the same nail on which he had suspended his cloak the dirty white cravat he wore, and then he lay down on his miserable bed—that man, who, if he had chosen, might have slept on down, with a silken coverlet.

He placed the small piece of rushlight in such a position that it did not attract his eyes, but it shed around the room its pale, sickly-looking light, making the size and the shape of everything obscure, so that old Gilbert began to suspect he would have been more comfortable in the dark altogether than with so dim a light.

"I can see nothing plainly," he said ; "and yet, somehow, I do not like to shut my eyes. I think I had better put out the light after all."

He turned and glanced at it, and he saw that it was so nearly burnt away that it must of itself go out in a very few moments.

"There is no occasion," he muttered ; "there is no occasion : it is going ; it is going of its own accord. There, I hear it beginning to fret and crackle, as a candle does often before expiring. I suppose some salt is among the tallow, and gets to the extreme end. I wonder if anything could be made by extracting the salt from candle ends—eh ?"

The piece of candle certainly spluttered considerably as it approached its dissolution, and the old man now turned away his eyes from it, for the flame was very irregular, and made odd, fantastic-looking shadows dance upon the walls of the room.

"What do I care," he said, "for anything or for anybody ? I am rich, though not so rich as I ought to be, or as I think, if I am very careful, I shall be: Yet I am beyond the chance of want, I think, unless the nation becomes bankrupt, and all the banks break, or thieves come and rob me. What noise was that?"

He cast his eyes towards the door on which he had hung his cloak and cravat. The light from the candle end was dim and flickering. Horror froze the life-blood in old Gilbert's veins, for there, against the door, to his perception, stood old Sheepy. The cloak and the cravat had accidentally become so arranged together, as, with the assistance of the excited imagination of the miser, to form a very tolerable outline of a human form. He named it to himself Sheepy, and with a shriek of dismay his senses left him at the same moment that the last portion of the wick of the candle dropped into a little pool of fat, and was at once extinguished. All was darkness. The rain still beat against the window, and the wind roared in the chimney, but old Gilbert heard nothing now.

———

CHAPTER XIV.

FANNY LESLIE ASKS HERSELF AN IMPORTANT QUESTION.—LEO DECIDES IT FOR HER.— THE NEW FRIENDS.

THE goldsmith had such a horror of Mrs. Crump, that he was glad, as soon as possible, to invent some excuse for getting out of that lady's way whenever she called; sometimes, without manifest rudeness, which he was too kind-tempered to bring himself to exercise at all towards any one, except, indeed, upon very serious provocation, he could not avoid her, and at other times he was more fortunate.

Fanny, however, had not so much acquaintance with Mrs. Crump as to make it necessary for her to remain long with her; and indeed Fanny had been now for some time longing for the seclusion of her own room, in order that she might ask herself a very serious question.

That question was one which we shall put in her own words; and when she was alone, she said, after some time spent in silent thought,—

"Why is it that at the sound of the name of Nicholas Lowe I change colour— for I can feel that I do—and tremble, as if—as if the name were painful to me? Ah! no—not painful; it is a pleasure to hear him speak, to see him, or to think— what am I going to say? 'What is Nicholas Lowe to me? I love my uncle, and Lowe has no claim of even the most distant relationship upon me, therefore— therefore I do not see why I should ——"

Fanny started at the words she was about to utter, and a crimson flush suffused her face, as she said, in a lower tone,—

"What is the meaning of this? Was I really about to confess to myself that this comparative stranger was dearer to me than those to whom I am bound by every tie of gratitude, and esteem, and relationship? No, no, no—that would be very wrong and very foolish. Surely we may esteem a person who possesses great and engaging qualities, and yet incur no blame. One may esteem without loving, surely; and therefore I will esteem Nicholas Lowe."

Alas! poor Fanny, how much you are deceiving yourself! Under the garb of this esteem you speak of, how often, alas! there lurks a far higher passion! You love Nicholas Lowe; your own heart has told you so. You love him, and thank Heaven that as yet he is so worthy of all the love you can bestow upon him.

Fanny was silent now for about ten minutes, and then she was suddenly aroused from her trance of thought by the sound of some voice on the staircase. She rose and approached the door, and then she discovered that it was not quite closed, and she heard Leo whining to some one in a peculiar tone, which she knew he always adopted when fondled by some one whom he chose to be great friends with.

Did some freemasonry of love tell her who it was that Leo had made such acquaintance with, or had the slight and few tones she had heard convinced her of the fact? Be it which way it may, she certainly became aware that it was—that it must be—Nicholas Lowe who was talking to the dog.

Her first impulse was to make known to him in some way that he was over-heard, for to such a nature as Fanny's, the idea of playing the part of a listener was most repugnant; but she felt so agitated, that she did not like to show herself, and abruptly to close the door would be to induce in him a belief that he must have offended her in some way, and that she shrank more than anything else from doing.

While she thus hesitated between what she thought she ought to do, the opportunity had altogether passed away, and she had become a listener, at all events, to some of what had fallen from Lowe's lips. He was caressing the dog, and speaking to it in a low tone of voice.

"Poor Leo," he said; "fine fellow. How glad I am that you seem so inclined to be friendly with me, for I will love you, and do love you for your dear mistress's sake."

Fanny could hear the dog prancing round him with pleasure, and she sank into a chair that was near to the door, now so overcome by her feelings, that it was quite out of her power if she had wished ever so much to do so.

"He loves me—he loves me," was all she could say, and that was in a whisper to her own heart.

"Fine fellow, Leo," added Lowe. "Fine fellow. Ah, I envy you the regard of her who loves you, Leo—your dear and beautiful mistress. Happy, happy Leo!"

Fanny could have wept to hear him speak thus. She sat and trembled, and although the words he had uttered were as music to her ears, such was her agitation of spirits, that she felt it was a great relief when she heard him go down the remainder of the staircase.

"He loves me—he loves me," she again said, and then tears gushed from her eyes, and she wept freely; but they were tears of joy, surely they were tears of joy.

Do not let our readers for one moment suppose that Nicholas Lowe knew of the proximity of Fanny, when he spoke to the dog. The fact was, that his sleeping chamber being at the top of the house, he was compelled, whenever he had occasion to go to it to make any changes in his apparel, to pass the door of Fanny's chamber.

He had been on this occasion up stairs to his own room, and as he was coming down, he saw Leo ascending from the lower part of the house. They met at the door of Fanny's room, for Leo never went any further, and here was it that the little interesting conversation, if we may call it such, had occurred.

The very fact, too, that the door of Fanny's chamber was not quite closed, would have been sufficient to convince Nicholas Lowe that she was not there, had he observed that circumstance, which, however, he did not, for he knew she had been in the drawing-room so recently, that he believed, as a matter of course, she was there still.

Poor Fanny was in by far too agitated a state of mind to think of removing from her room; she only sincerely hoped that her aunt might not come to her until she had quite recovered herself, and was better able to conceal, than at this time she could hope to be, the emotions of her heart. And yet pleasure predominated. She was agitated, and she wept and trembled; but there was still the blessed consciousness of being beloved by that one person whose love was alone acceptable.

"Yes—yes, he loves me. Nicholas Lowe loves me. He now loves poor, fond, faithful Leo for my sake, merely because he belongs to me; and how strange, too, that the dog, who is not apt to make great acquaintance with strangers, should be so kind to him."

She called Leo into the room, and, as she caressed him, she could not help feeling that she should ever look upon him as the interpreter of Nicholas's love.

"But for you, my noble Leo, I should not have known that secret which now warms my heart, and occupies my mind to the exclusion of all minor topics. But for you, my Leo, he would not have spoken; he would have passed on, and my ears would not have been greeted by those words which have sounded to them like pleasant music."

A new world of beauty and delight seemed now to be opening before Fanny Leslie. Never before had her mind been so filled with pleasant dreams of the future. Never before had she felt how great a charm might be lent to existence. Those words of magic power, which she felt she could now with truth pronounce, of "Nicholas Lowe loves me," were the talismanic charms that lent such wondrous beauty now to everything. The sunshine she now felt assured would look to her far more resplendently beautiful than it had ever been, because it would be a reflection of the still more glorious sunshine that shone upon her heart.

"And will he," she asked herself—"will he tell me that he loves me? Will he make a confidant of Leo, and not of me myself? Ah, no! soon—soon he will seek some opportunity to breathe to me in fervent words his honest, holy passion; and what then can I say to him?"

She paced her room with agitated steps. This was a question which she felt she could not too soon answer; for she could not tell how soon now she might be called upon probably to carry it out.

Our readers, who can, of course, look on all the circumstances with the calm eye of spectators, may easily answer Fanny's self-put question. She might hesitate— maiden modesty might, as doubtless it would, chain her tongue from the utterance of an affirmative when Lowe should ask her for her love; but as she did love him, the result, come it slow, or come it fast, must be the same. She must and would at last confess to him that she was his—by word, by gesture, or by look, she must do so at last, and then how happy might they be. And, in the meantime, Nicholas Lowe was to suffer all the pangs of hope deferred. He was to love as truly as man ever loved, or ever could love, and yet he was, for a time, to shrink from proclaiming his passion to the fond object of his heart's idolatry, for fear of that repulse which we know, although he did not, was very far from awaiting such a declaration. There was, however, an excessive refinement and a delicacy about the mind of Nicholas Lowe, which was likely to make him backward, beyond ordinary precedent, in the declaration of such sentiments as those which he felt towards his employer's beautiful niece. He would have liked her to know more of him before he spoke to her of his heart's feelings, so that she might be the better able to judge from an opinion of his sincerity.

Alas! Nicholas Lowe, you do not know as much of the female heart as more extended experience will teach you. You have yet to learn that love is not a matter of calculation but of impulse, and all the knowledge in the world of any particular individual cannot create that passion, which is, almost invariably, the growth of a moment. Oh, if you could have but known, poor Nicholas Lowe, that already was Fanny aware of your attachment, and disposed so favourably to receive it as she really was, what hours of deep anxiety and care would you have been spared. But that was not to be. On the contrary, Fanny was now likely to be more guarded than ever, for fear the secret of her heart should prematurely escape ; so that there was by far less chance than before of Nicholas being able to flatter himself that he might be received, if not with favour, at all events with some feeling which should enable him to hope.

Then did Fanny make an effort to leave her room and go down stairs to the draw-ing-room, and then did she shrink back to look again at herself in the glass, to be sure that there were no traces of emotion visible in her countenance sufficient to induce a question from her aunt or her uncle. Each time she fancied that she looked flushed and in a state of excitement, so that she dreaded to venture down.

" I will remain here until they seek me," she said. " Each moment is in my favour, and, perhaps, by the time my aunt misses me and comes to seek me, I may be better able than I am now to look calm and serene."

It then occurred to her that if she could withdraw her mind from what had taken place, by filling it with new images, she would have the best chance of recovering her composure, and she at once hastened, as a resource of that character, to the books which Nicholas Lowe had sent to her.

" If my aunt does come while I am reading," she said, " I may be able to ascribe any traces of recent tears she may see in my eyes to the tale I am perusing."

Was Fanny already—already learning duplicity?

She opened one of the books and soon found material which possibly might, if it did not wholly banish from her mind its present thoughts, so mingle with them as to render them passive. She read as follows, and soon her whole attention became enchained to the page over which she leant :—

In Cumberland, there are many farms that are of small dimensions. Their average is less than those in the more southerly counties. The owners of these farms are not rich, but they are independent and sturdy, the only remains of a still wealthy peasantry we once possessed. They are yeomen—of, in many cases, ancient families, for they know not the time, nor ever heard of the time when their fore-fathers possessed not the land they lived on, and hoped to live on.

This honest class, who prided themselves upon their own standing, were indeed a respectable class, and men mourn that their numbers are decreasing and the small farms are being broken up, and turned into larger ones, to suit the avarice of land-lords or the speculative mania of capitalists.

Day after day the prodigality of some, and the chapter of accidents bring these hold-ings within the reach of the man of money ; and then instead of a respectable class of small farmers, there is nothing between the large capitalists, or a numerous and poorly paid peasantry.

Ridge Farm was one of this sort, but somewhat larger than the usual size of these holdings ; but then it had some extent of sheep-walks attached to it, which made it appear a large farm ; but these had been added to it. Farmer Copeland was a hale, hearty man, of scarce eight-and-forty ; and, in the ideas of himself and neighbours, was a rich man. Not in money, because he had but a little, com-paratively speaking ; but then his farm was his own, and his stock was good, and numerous, and the crops he had gathered in at the harvest, were of some value, and he cared not to send it to market until his leisure served him. He had no neces-sity to sell, but he sold when he pleased ; and his sheep, too, and cattle, they were the pride of his heart, and his whole care.

Farmer Copeland felt delighted to walk through his farm-yards in winter weather; and to examine his well filled barns and granaries filled him with pleasure, and his hardy servants were well fed, and treated with respect befitting their station. The stable and the barn gave out sounds that pleased—the merry sound of the hard flail on the floor, resounded from daylight till dark, and the cheerful neigh, and the lowing of the herds. Come what would, be the weather as inhospitable and cheerless as it would, still there was always enough at Farmer Copeland's to make the heart glad and merry.

Ridge Farm was situated on a high piece of level land, from which ran several large hills—hills that might be said to merge into mountains, and protected his lands on the north and east, while the farm-yard and house were protected by a tolerable plantation, or wood, of larch and fir.

The winds whistled round the old farm-house, and the old chimney roared with the violence of the storm that seemed to be coming up. The day had been windy and cold, the cattle had not been turned out, and little could be done in such severe weather; the ground had been for some days moist and soppy, from previous rains, and this stayed all operations.

The farmer sat at the head of the board; by him sat his wife and children—two athletic young men, the eldest about five-and-twenty, the second about three years younger; and then his daughter, a girl of eighteen, the rose of all Cumberland, a perfect picture, the pride of her father's heart, and the delight of her mother. There was none so universally beloved as Rose, for she was as good as she was beautiful. Kindness, love, and mirth, seemed to be perpetual to her; she had no other thought, and to her clung a younger sister, scarce fourteen, a black-eyed, dark-haired beauty, whose laughter-loving, roguish-looking eyes, caused her to become a familiar and a favourite of all.

See page 81.

We have said the wind howled round the old farm, that the chimney roared, and that every now and then it would sink to a low moaning and wailing sound, or rise, with a fury that could scarcely be credited, to a whistle and scream, as if the sturdy walls of the farm house were too strong to be easily pierced, and the storm and tumult was owing to the disappointment and rage of some demon who guided the blast, but could not enter the farm house.

Farmer Copeland sat with his family near the fire; and with him sat such of the farm servants as were boarded in the house; and, save occasional aids and extra hands at harvest time, the farm servants all lived in the farm house, and all at the same table as the farmer himself and his family. The large fire roared, and the flames threw a glare and light over the kitchen beside the hearth, that rendered every part light and comfortable; the logs crackled with a pleasing sound. The farmer had been gazing at the fire some time in silence, when awakening from his reverie, he said,—

"How the wind howls to-night. If the wind goes down before morning we shall have a fall of some sort, I shouldn't wonder."

"Yes," said one of the men, "I think it will be snow, for it's very cold, and the ground, too, has been getting harder and harder."

"Yes, I think myself the winter has now set in in its worst colours ; but it will do no harm—not a bit, not a bit."

"It will do much good," said an old man ; "after a hard winter come a good summer and a good harvest."

"We cannot complain of that gone by ; it has been an abundant one."

"So it has, and so much the better ; still a hard winter is a good sign."

"But," said Rose, " what will be the sufferings of many who are not so well off as ourselves ; to the cottager and the poor ?—they will feel it."

"They will ; but they will also feel the reverse, and profit by it in proportion, of a good harvest, and so none can complain."

"And then the poor animals," said Mary ; "think of the birds, what a number will die of starvation and stress of weather."

"Not so many as you would suppose, Mary."

"Indeed."

"No ; nature furnishes them with the means of resisting the effects of the cold, unless it be of a very extraordinary intensity and duration."

"I don't know what tensity and duration may mean," said one of the men, " but I know that, after a time, there's no food to be had in the fields, and the birds get famished, and then they become cold, and are frozen to death."

"That's true, may be," said the farmer, "when it does happen, but that ain't so very often. But come, lads, haven't you any tale for the fire-side to-night ? Here, Bill, get in some more logs, and you, Rose, just fill a can of right good October."

Those orders were right willingly executed ; the ale was placed in a huge flagon, and the man brought in the logs which were placed on the fire, adding a new blaze, and a great crackling ensued, and the red sparks flew upward.

"It's a coming, master," said the man, as he sat down after placing the logs.

"What is coming, Bill?" said the farmer.

"The snow."

"Is it ?"

"Ay, it just does come ; you can't see three or four yards off. The night's very dark, but the white flakes give a kind of curious light to the place."

"Has much fallen ?"

"Enough to cover everything ; and you can't hear yourself tread."

"Ay, ay ; then if we have a heavy fall, we may have a change in the weather—it may get warmer, you know."

"So it may."

"And now a tale," said the farmer, as he tasted the ale and put down the cup.

"Did you ever hear tell of the mysterious miller and Matlebury mill ?" inquired one of the servants—he was an old man who seldom spoke.

"No, never, that I remember, Robin," said the farmer ; " have you, lads ?"

"No—no—no," was the response.

"Then fill your mug, Robin, and tell us what you know about him."

The old man filled his mug, and drawing his seat close against the whitened walls, he looked around him, and then at the fire, before he began to speak ; then sinking against the support thus afforded him, he began,—

"I don't know anything of it myself, but my uncle—who is dead and gone, peace be with him—has told the story often enough. If you don't mind my rough way of expressing it, I will give it you at once, and it may serve to while away an hour :—

Matlebury mill was situated on a small but rapid stream ; the strength of the stream added much to the power of the mill, which was usually kept working night and day, and yet it was a wonder to many how the miller contrived to do so, because they believed he had not sufficient corn to grind.

There was another singular thing, too, and that was, there were many fatal accidents in that part of the stream. Just below the mill was a ford where the river could be crossed, but it was said to be dangerous; and many people really were killed there; somehow or other they lost their footing and were carried away. Now the poor people could cross this stream, and scarce such a thing was heard of as an accident among them.

There was no accounting for it; nobody could understand it; everybody said it was mysterious, and they supposed they must have deviated from the right track, and gone into some holes that were above and below the ford.

These accidents were the cause of some disturbances, and it was talked about all over the country, and something was said concerning a new bridge, but nobody saw one.

The miller allowed any one to pass through his mill, and ferry them over for a small sum if they chose, and for this those who could afford it went to the mill. This for a time stopped the accidents; at least they were not so frequent; but still it did happen now and then that some of those whose appearance betokened means were found floating down the stream for some distance. People used to mark these circumstances, and say,—

"Well, well, they deserve no pity; for the trifling sum of a few pence they could cross in safety, and yet they chose to run the danger that in the end proved so fatal to them; they must be mad—quite mad."

There was one curious thing about this that those who were thus drowned, though they appeared to be men carrying money, yet never was anything found upon them.

"It was very strange," everybody said; but so it was, and so everybody agreed that that was all that could be said.

It was autumn; the days were drawing in and the nights were increasing, but the weather was lovely and warm. The evenings were almost as beautiful as the day, save the white mists that covered the earth, which rendered it difficult to find your way about, except upon well-beaten tracts.

A village alehouse, one night at this period, was filled with guests, as soon as the evening set in, and the farm-yards cleared.

"Well," said one to the landlord, "how gets on the river? Any more drowned to-day?"

"Yes," answered the landlord.

"The deuce there is. It is a very strange thing to me that people should get drowned in that manner; I can't understand it, neighbour."

"Nor I."

"Has he any money about him?"

"Yes, a few halfpence."

"No more?"

"No."

"What sort of a man is he?"

"You can see him up stairs," said the landlord; "he is there."

"Is he?"

"Yes; go up and then you'll see."

"No, thank you," said one.

"Why not? He's dead, and can't bite you. I have, unfortunately, seen too many to think much about it. Go up. It is a very strange thing to me how he came by the blow on the head."

"A blow on the head, did you say?"

"Yes; go and see."

"It might have happened in the water, you know, against some obstruction or another."

"It might."

Up stairs the guests went, and there was the dead man, sure enough, stretched out on a board. Over the left temple was a large wound, or rather bruise ; it felt soft, as if the skull had been beaten in.

"That must have been a heavy blow," said one, as he looked at it.

No remark was made, but all looked at it. They saw the dress was an expensive one, of the first quality ; and it did seem strange that such a man should have no money.

The guests returned to the parlour, and sat for some time in silence, when the landlord entered the room and sat down too.

"Well," said he, "what do you think of the dead man, neighbours ?"

"Think," said one ; "I hardly know what to think. How many are drowned at that ford every year, do you know ?"

"About twelve or fifteen."

There was a dead pause at this, and the guests looked at each other in astonishment, or rather with some strange, uncomfortable feeling.

"Well, what do you think of the bruise ?"

"I think it looks very like a blow," said one. "I don't think it could be done in the water. The river is not so swift or so deep, nor are there many places where he could be thrown against with force sufficient to do it."

"That's what I say," said the landlord.

"Then how could it happen ?"

"I am sure I can't tell ; but it does seem to me that something very mysterious is going forward. He has no money, you say ?"

"None ; but nobody that's drowned there ever has ; they are cleared out, and every vestige of paper and memorandum gone that could be of any use in the way of discovering who they are."

"Yes ; that's true."

"But this man was here the day before yesterday," said the landlord.

The guests looked hard at the landlord as he was speaking, as though they would not lose even his looks.

"Had he any money that you saw ?" inquired one of the guests.

"He had."

"Much ?"

"He changed a sovereign, and inquired for the ford. I told him the danger, and he said he should go to the mill and get over from that, as he was a stranger to the place. Besides that sovereign, he had, I should say, a bag full."

Here was a pause among the guests, and they looked at each other, while they repeated the words "money" and "mill" to each other.

"And now he has but a few pence," said the landlord. "I don't know what to think of it ; but it seems to me to be very extraordinary ; and I am sure of this, that some of those who have been drowned before have had money."

"Indeed !"

"Yes."

"And why ?"

"Because they have called here—several of them I am sure did—and they must have had some money ; they couldn't all be beggars, and well dressed. I'll never believe it ; and I'll tell you what, neighbours, I am sure there's something wrong about it."

Everybody agreed it was wrong, and, moreover, that it was very mysterious. And so it was.

The guests talked over the affair the whole evening, and not a word was said by way of suspicion, only all agreed that some foul play was being carried on which they could not understand.

It was singular that every one had some undefined suspicion of one man, but that man was not named during the whole evening—his name was not uttered. The man they were suspicious of was no other than the miller himself. Yes, everybody suspected the miller himself.

He was a tall, stout man, dark and ill-looking, with a forbidding countenance, and at times he entertained strange guests. He had always plenty of money, and cared but little for his business. He always looked upon the people who lived in his neighbourhood with suspicion, and discouraged all attempts at intimacy, and did not like any one visiting his mill, and staying in the neighbourhood.

The guests stayed late that night, and two of them stayed behind the rest; and these two eyed each other for some time, and the landlord sat still and silent. At length one of them said,—

" Landlord, I'll tell you my opinion freely about this matter. We are among friends, and what is said need go no further."

" Certainly net," said the landlord.

" You can depend upon me," said the other.

" Well, then," resumed the first, " I can't drive it out of my head but this miller has more to do with this affair than he ought."

The landlord nodded, and the other, who had not spoken, added,—

" And I feel convinced of it. See how he lives, and the many curious things connected with him. I think he ought to be watched."

" Decidedly."

" Then," said the landlord, " this ought to be kept to ourselves."

" It ought."

" And if you be so minded, I will make one of a party to watch, and endeavour to detect where the evil lies."

" Agreed," said he who spoke first.

" And I am agreeable; and now for the plan, landlord."

" There are two ways."

" Name them."

" In either case you two must be concealed thereabouts long before any one is seen coming either to the mill or the ford."

" Which ought it to be ?"

" The ford," said the landlord; " for if it be the mill, any one may be admitted, and he would be killed before you could come to his assistance; and if you attacked the mill prematurely, you lay bare the suspicions, and the plan, and all is lost."

" I see we had better conceal ourselves in the vicinity of the ford; there are plenty of hiding-places, from which you can see all that passes, and rush out in time to save anybody who may be in danger."

" And you ?"

" I will come after any body that is coming this way; not so quickly that I shall be up so soon as to disconcert the affair, but in time enough to aid you both."

" Then it is agreed between us ?"

" It is as far as I am concerned."

" And I."

" Then to-morrow you will take your station; if you want a good stick or two come to me and I will supply you."

The two guests departed in company, and the landlord felt some comfort in having done so much; for it was to his interest to have the affair found out, as in absence of all proof any innocent man might get some share of suspicion and blame.

The next day came, but no one went to the ford; but on the second day some one called at the house, and inquired the way to the mill.

" Let me advise you to go to the ford, sir."

" I was advised to go to the mill, as the ford was dangerous."

" Not at all," said the landlord, " if you walk over at the ford and neither go up stream nor down you are safe."

" The mill is safer."

" Well, sir, as you please, but I would not go through the mill; in my opinion it's not so safe; the miller is a strange man, and has more than once insulted people, and you have no redress."

" Very well, I will take your advice."

The man started off and made for the ford; the landlord followed close—at least, almost within sight, but he took care to conceal himself as he neared the man, and took another path, the one by the river side, and crept up along beneath the trees, and got within a short distance unperceived.

The stranger approached the ford, and debated in his own mind what he should do, whether he should go to the mill or cross over. Just as he was about to do the latter, he saw the miller coming towards him. He paused until the miller came up—he had a small ash stick in his hand, with which he walked.

See page 84.

"Is this the ford?" said the stranger.

"Yes," replied the miller, "take care of the holes."

"Holes?"

"Yes, there's one."

"Where?" inquired the stranger, looking about in the water. The miller making no reply, the stranger was about to look up, but he received a stunning blow on the head with the loaded stick, which prostrated the unfortunate man

No. 12.

without a sound or a groan. The two spies immediately rushed forward from their hiding-place, exclaiming—

"Villain, we have detected you at last."

"All lost," said the villain, as he made an attack upon the two, but seeing the landlord of the inn advance, he turned and fled to the mill, which he gained and barricaded and secured.

"Look to the wounded gentleman," said the landlord; "we had better take care of him; we can get the miller afterwards."

He was accordingly lifted up, and being quite insensible they at once carried him back to the village in haste, both for assistance and because they believed the miller would issue out with his men and attack them. It was quite dark when they reached the village, and the whole affair being generally known, the place was in arms, and a strong body armed themselves, determined to go and take the miller. However, they had not got half way there before they beheld a great blaze in the direction of the mill. They all suspected he had burnt the mill; and this was true, for he and his men were never heard of since. It was supposed that knowing he was detected in such a crime, he had determined upon self-destruction in the way related, while some averred that he died in wretchedness and misery befitting his life. However, the ruins of the mill stand to this day; it was never rebuilt.

CHAPTER XV.

THE OFFER.—FANNY'S MISTAKE.—MRS. PADDLEBAT'S WARM RECOMMENDATION.

FANNY locked up from the volume which she had been perusing, and as she did so she heard some one try the lock of the door. It was opened, and Mrs. Paddlebat entered the room with an expression of countenance which seemed to indicate that she had something to say of more than common importance.

What it could be Fanny was quite at a loss to conjecture, and yet, when she looked a little more narrowly at Mrs. Paddlebat, she fancied she detected some lurking smile about her mouth which appeared to indicate that whatever she came about was not altogether a grave subject of deliberation.

"Why, my dear," she said to Fanny, "where have you been for so long? I have been wondering what had become of you for the last hour."

"I have been here, aunt," said Fanny, "and nowhere else. The time slipped past easily, for I have been reading."

"Well, lay down your book, Fanny, for I have really something now to say to you that requires undivided attention."

"Indeed, aunt!"

"Yes, my dear, I have. Just think now and tell me if, among all the people you have seen since you came here, there is any one of whom you have reason to believe you have made a conquest."

Fanny looked astonished, as well she might, and she repeated the word conquest as if it bore some hidden meaning, which thought might elucidate.

"Why, how astonished you look!" exclaimed Mrs. Paddlebat. "Is there anything so extraordinary in a young girl of more than common attraction making a conquest?"

"Aunt, you are jesting with me."

"Not I, indeed. You have won the heart of a gentleman, and I am commissioned to break the news to you."

Fanny's colour went and came as she asked herself,—

"Can it be possible that Nicholas Lowe has confided the secret of his heart to Mrs. Paddlebat, fearing a repulse from me?"

"Why, my dear, you seem agitated."

"No—no—no; only you did alarm me a little, aunt. The strange subject of your conversation was calculated to make me feel some degree of agitation. Who is it?"

" Cannot you guess ?"

" No, I cannot indeed. There are several, you know, aunt. But who has sent you on so strange an errand ?"

" Nay, now, Fanny, surely you cannot but have some notion upon the subject. You must have seen that you were much admired by some one."

" It must be Nicholas Lowe," said Fanny. " It surely must be Nicholas Lowe."

" What do you say, my dear? You speak in such a whisper, that I cannot hear you."

" I was considering, aunt, who it could be. Has he made you for long a confidante ?"

" No, Fanny ; only a short time since. He says he loves you, and I dare say he does."

Poor Fanny was in such a state of bewilderment, that at the moment she was not able to judge of how extremely unlikely it was that Nicholas Lowe should make Mrs. Paddlebat a confidante of his passion. She had her mind so filled with his image, that she could not think of any one else loving her, and now it was with evident interest, and marked agitation, that she said,—

" Do not keep me in suspense, aunt. If he—he really has told you that he loves me ——"

" Well I never !" exclaimed Mrs. Paddlebat. " Well I never ! Why you don't mean to say it's what's-its-name, *reciprocity*, do you, Fanny ?"

" I—I have said nothing, aunt. Name him—oh, name him !"

" Before I do, let me tell you that he offers marriage when you shall be a year older. He ain't altogether badly off either, and it is for you to judge."

" What is wealth compared to true affection ?" sighed Fanny.

" Well, I don't know exactly; but I must confess I am surprised at your taste. He certainly is about as odd a looking young man as ever I saw."

" Odd-looking ! Why, can you think him otherwise than very handsome ?"

" Handsome ?"

" Yes, aunt, on that head there can be but one opinion, surely."

" Well, you must see him with very strange eyes ! Ebe... zer Crump handsome !"

" Who ?" exclaimed Fanny.

" Why, Ebenezer Crump, to be sure. Who did you suppose it was ?"

" Ebenezer—Crump ? He ? That—that boy ?"

" Yes, I thought you guessed it was him, Fanny, and I was very much surprised indeed to hear you speak as you did about him."

" I—had forgotten his existence."

Mrs. Paddlebat paused for a moment; she was thinking of who it was that Fanny supposed it to have been ; for she saw the instantanous change that took place upon her countenance when Ebenezer was mentioned, and now poor Mrs. Paddlebat fell into as great an error as Fanny had done, and she thought to herself,—

" Who can she have supposed it to be whom she calls handsome, but Rodwell ? She must mean him—she must mean Jervis Rodwell. Oh, it's quite clear she means him, of course."

" Fanny."

" Yes, aunt."

" You know that it must be all a joke about Crump. It's true his foolish mother has been here to make an offer for him, but I never for a moment expected you to think of such a person, you know."

" You are right, aunt."

" Of course I am ; but you were thinking of some one else. There that colour that comes and goes so quickly on your cheek convinces me that such is the case. You were thinking of some one to whom you have no objection at all. You need not tell me that such is not the case, because I see that it is so Fanny."

Fanny gently answered that she had no intention of saying that such was not the case, and Mrs. Paddlebat continued,—for she was very well pleased at the idea of her great favourite, Rodwell, having made an impression, as she supposed, of so favourable a nature upon Fanny's heart; it was a great triumph over Mr. Paddlebat, who, although he was not disposed to find any particular fault with Rodwell, certainly of the two, as his wife well knew, esteemed Lowe the most ;—

" I don't wonder, my dear Fanny, at your calling him whom you mean handsome. He is a most elegant young man, as everybody admits."

" There can be no mistake now," thought Fanny.

" But," added her aunt, " if he loves you he has said nothing to me about it. Has he to you ?"

" No, no. Oh, no."

" Well, he will in good time, no doubt, my dear. You know you are very young now, and there's plenty of time yet before you, and as he is in the house you have an opportunity of studying his disposition."

Fanny felt now no doubt whatever. She threw herself with childish artlessness into the arms of her aunt, as she said,—

" Dear aunt, I do not know how you came to be aware of this cherished secret of my bosom ; but do not blame me, I will not listen to him if you disapprove."

" Disapprove ! My dear child, I am very far, indeed, from disapproving, I can assure you."

" And, my uncle ?"

" Oh, never mind him. I don't think he has any objection, but there's time enough for all that. Now compose yourself, and when you meet him again, let him not imagine that you are altogether indifferent to him ; which you can manage so as not to give him more encouragement than a young lady may with perfect propriety give to a gentleman, and yet to let him see that you prefer his company to that of any one else. You understand ?"

" I think I do, aunt. I cannot do wrong if I follow your advice, surely."

" Of course, not. I believe I know by this time what's right and what's wrong, and have been accustomed to society that enables me to tell you what you ought to do, and what you ought not. You be guided by me, my dear, and you will be all right ; of course, men don't feel like women—how can they ?— and, therefore, Fanny, you need not mind what Paddlebat says to you. You always come to me when there's any difficulty at all, and in a few words I'll put you right."

" How can I sufficiently thank you, dear aunt," said Fanny, as the tears sprang to her eyes, " for so much kindness ?"

" My dear, don't mention it. I am only very glad, indeed, that you have made so worthy a choice."

" He is worthy."

" To be sure he is ; and clever, too, as well as handsome."

" Yes ; oh, yes !"

" The life and soul of a party, and quite the ladies' man."

" Yes, yes."

Poor Fanny, under the supposition that Nicholas Lowe was meant, was ready to agree to anything of a laudatory nature that her aunt chose to say, and when Mrs. Paddlebat rose to go, she said,—

" Dear aunt, let this secret rest between ourselves for the present. You have made me happy, indeed, by the kind manner in which you have spoken to me ; but as he has not yet made mention of his love to me, except with his speaking eyes, do not give the remotest hint of my feelings to him or to any one."

" Rely upon me. Do you think I would, now ? No, no. Let the lover always speak first, and when he does speak, Fanny, it will be better for you, without being too cruel, you know, to treat him a little coolly. When Mr. Paddlebat first came courting me I refused him altogether, and nearly drove him mad."

" You did not then love him ?"

" Oh, that has nothing to do with it at all. He came again, and then I was not quite so cruel ; but still I would scarcely speak to him ; and he said he would sell his business and emigrate to some dreadful place, so, out of pity, I at last consented, just now and then, to see him. Oh, my dear, it won't do to be too easily won, I can assure you. The men like you all the better for treating them badly, I can tell you, so mind you frown and put on a look of great disdain at first."

"Ah, I fear I could not."

"But you must."

"But that would be very insincere, you know, aunt, and what a violence to my feelings. I think, if he were to come to me, and say, ' Fanny, I love you,' I could not speak harshly to him."

"Then you are a very foolish girl, I can tell you, Miss Fanny. What would you say to him?"

"I do not think, aunt, I should speak ; but I think that I should look into his eyes and smile, so that he would see the joy that was beating at my heart."

"Stuff, stuff!"

"Well, dear aunt, of course I will endeavour to do as you bid me ; but you will remember that I am not well accustomed to the usages of European society. You know how strangely my life has been spent. Sometimes among the Indians, and sometimes among the settlers in the wildernesses of America, who were scarcely so civilised as the natives."

"Never mind—never mind. I have moved in all sorts of society, and know what's what. My family, before I knew Paddlebat, always lived in a square, which, of course, introduced us to a good circle ; and, therefore, you have but to depend upon me."

"I certainly will do so, aunt."

"That's right, and now come down stairs as soon as you can, for your uncle has been asking for you, and, somehow or another, when he don't see you for an hour or two, he don't seem at all comfortable now, poor man."

"I will come, directly," said Fanny. "My uncle is so good to me that it is impossible I can too much return his affection."

Mrs. Paddlebat left the room, and Fanny sat down to think upon the wonderful and sudden alteration that had taken place in her views and prospects within so short a space of time.

"How very strange," she thought, "that so shortly after I should have overheard Nicholas Lowe talking of his love for me, I should have had so interesting a conversation with my aunt, and have instantly confessed to her my affection for him. Surely my good star is now in the ascendant, and fortune smiles upon me. If my aunt had not approved of my choice, I cannot but feel that I should have had much to fear from her opposition ; and, probably, my only resource would have been in the affection of my uncle, which would have prompted him to side with me ; but then, again, that might have produced most lamentable family dissensions on my account, from which, Heaven knows, how much I should have shrunk."

This was a view of the case, which to the sensitive mind of such a girl as Fanny, was most afflicting, and over and over again did she congratulate herself upon the fortunate and most delightful circumstance, that Mrs. Paddlebat should, in such an unhesitating manner, not only approve of her choice, but encourage her in it.

"How unjust was I towards my aunt," thought Fanny, as she was about to leave the room, to proceed to the drawing-room ; "how very unjust was I towards her ! I actually fancied that she regarded Lowe with an indifference amounting to dislike, and that in what she said to him when she was compelled to speak to him at all, there was a marked coldness ; but now she admits that he is handsome, intelligent, and in every way most worthy."

Alas, Fanny, what a serious mistake you are making ! Your first observation was most correct. Mrs. Paddlebat did not like Lowe at all, and she did invariably treat him with a coldness, which bordered so closely upon rudeness, that it might in many instances have been mistaken for it. Could you, Fanny, for one moment have imagined that it was James Rodwell whom your aunt was so enthusiastic about, what a different feeling in your breast would her praises of that individual have produced."

But now all was sunshine about the heart of Fanny—she saw no obstruction to her happiness. That she herself loved Nicholas Lowe, she felt well assured of; and had he not in her hearing convinced her how dear she was to him? Most certainly. The few words he had addressed to Leo, bore too much the stamp of truth to be doubted for a moment. They were uttered from the heart—that mint from where no spurious coinage arises. Moreover, they were not intended for her ear, and hence was it that to her perceptions there was a charm about him even of a dearer character, than if they had been with more eloquence actually addressed to her.

"I shall be very, very happy," said Fanny to herself with a smile, as she descended the staircase. "I shall surely be very happy indeed. Oh! what a recompense has Heaven's goodness prepared for me after all that I have gone through. If now my poor mother were but living, I should have no wish ungratified; if I had but been blessed by seeing the smile of joy upon her lips; I had been—too—too happy."

She paused a moment, and blamed herself for adverting to so painful a theme, for she felt the tears ascending to her eyes, and now she feared that her uncle might detect their presence, and be anxious to learn the cause. She therefore composed her feelings as well as she could, before she would enter the drawing-room, and when she did so, she was pleased to find that it was darkened by the blinds being for the most part drawn down, so that she considered it was not likely Mr. Paddlebat would notice that she had been at all agitated. Mrs. Paddlebat was not there, so that she had no opportunity of adding to Fanny's confusion by any of those nods and winks which such a personage was very likely to indulge in; for a secret to some people is so burthensome that they must be always making telegraphic signals about it even if they do not actually divulge it.

CHAPTER XVI.

THE MEETING OF THE FRIENDS.—THE DESPAIR OF A POETICAL TEMPERAMENT.—
THE DREADFUL THREAT.

SOMEBODY has truly remarked, that great events from trifling causes spring. The observation is so true, that it almost becomes trite, and we shall see a most notable example of it in what is now occurring at the Paddlebats'.

Who would have supposed, who could have supposed, that such a person as Ebenezer Crump should, by a freak of fortune, or by a strange concatenation of circumstances, exercise any control over the fate of such a being as Fanny Leslie! What imagination could have supposed that this boy, without the respectability of a boy, because he aped to be the man, should be the actual cause of Mrs. Paddlebat's serious mistake, and of that flush of delightful feeling that had come over the heart of Fanny!

But so it was. If Ebenezer Crump had not conceived that wonderful passion which his poetical temperament indulged in for Fanny, the respectable Mrs. Crump would not have called upon Mrs. Paddlebat upon the subject. Mrs. Paddlebat would not then have sought the chamber of Fanny as she did, and the misapprehensions and mistakes which then occurred, could not have taken place.

Mrs. Crump had quite penetration enough to discover that the addresses of Ebenezer in that quarter would never be acceptable. As she returned home, visions of the Monument and Ebenezer descending from the top of it into Fish-street-hill, crossed her bewildered imagination. He had threatened as much, and if he did not make his exit in that manner from a non-appreciating world, there's no saying what a job he might give the Humane Society to drag him from the Serpentine.

Now these were not pleasant personal reflections for Mrs. Crump; and, besides, that lady had some pity upon the world, and asked herself what would become of society at large, and the *bell letters*, if Ebenezer was to find earth's mists with his pure pinions disagree, and rejoin the stars unlaurelled.

"I must break it gently to him," soliloquised Mrs. Crump; "it will never do t° tell the dear boy all at once. What a sad want of taste there is at the Paddlebats. He mightn't see it, bless him, in its proper light, and treat them with the contempt they deserve, and which I am sure I feel most devotedly for every member of the family. She'll go further and fare worse. I know old Paddlebat's niece. Who knows who she will put up with at last? Pride will have a fall. I shall just tell Ebenezer she ain't worth his attention, and perhaps that may induce the dear boy to think of her as she deserves. I've no patience with such people giving themselves airs and graces above their neighbours, and fancying themselves too good for anybody, indeed; who's she, I should like to know? A stuck up minx that's been brought up amongst savages, and would think no more of scolloping anybody than taking her breakfast. Who knows what she might do to Ebenezer when she got him all to herself?"

With these thoughts and feelings, Mrs. Crump proceeded homewards, reconciling herself, like a prudent person, to that which was inevitable. It was a great relief to her to find that, when she did get home, that Ebenezer had not returned. The reader will recollect that after the obscure threats of self-immolation he had uttered to his mother, Ebenezer had betaken himself to one Wilkins, an apprentice to a clothier in the neighbourhood, who, in addition to his claims on the Crumps, on the plea of distant relationship, highly appreciated Ebenezer's poetry, or at least he seemed to do so, although there was a rough simplicity and a tact about Wilkins that might have led one to a contrary assumption.

There is something, however, so delightful to amateur authors and actors, and such like, in the breath of popular applause, that we have long ceased to wonder at it being prized, whoever may accord it. Ebenezer Crump reasoned upon it in a, to him, very satisfactory manner. "The individual," he would say, "who admires my poetry, shows by that act alone what immense judgment he must possess in comparison with the fools of editors of all the stupid periodicals, whose private jealousies, or whose ignorance prevents their inserting my effusions." Consequently, when Ebenezer met with any disappointment, or wished to unburden his soul, as he called it, he was in the habit forthwith to repair to Wilkins, who heard all he had to say, and let him talk on without offering him any interruption, beyond what was of a satisfactory nature.

Wilkins had an hour to his dinner, and it was during that period of time that, generally speaking, any conferences between him and cousin Ebenezer, as he usually called that illustrious individual, took place. Ebenezer had timed it very well, for, as he reached the clothier's door, Wilkins was emerging therefrom.

"Ah, cousin!" said Wilkins, "how is you?"

"Do not ask me," said Ebenezer, solemnly. "The iron has commenced entering my soul. The world's out of joint."

"Gracious!" said Wilkins; "you don't say so! Is it owing to the comet, do you think?"

"The comet! How could the comet make the iron enter my soul?"

"Oh, I didn't mean that. I understand that. I meant about the world's being out of joint."

"And what may you understand," said Ebenezer, "concerning the iron entering my soul?"

"Why, a blessed nail in your head, to be sure. What else is it? In course, I didn't get your edication; but I knows what's what."

"Oh, ye muses!" exclaimed Ebenezer. "Listen to me, Wilkins, I am going to unfold my tale to you."

"Lor'!" said Wilkins.

"Wilkins, did you ever love?"

"Oh, I believe you! lots o' things; but if you really want to give me a treat ever, make it Epsom sausages fried in fresh butter. Lor! the very thoughts of such a thing makes one quite desperate."

"Oh, ye gods!" said Ebenezer; "I allude to the tender passion."

"So they is tender—tenderer things nor them couldn't be."

"But divine woman, Wilkins. That's the cause. There is a piece of perfection, called by the profane world, Fanny. Ah, me! love's ensign is waving to and fro in my breast. I love her as never hero worshipped goddess. Oh, my mother."

"Ah," said Wilkins, "does she know you're out?"

"I tell you what it is, Williams," said Ebenezer. "It strikes me you have no soul."

"Ah. haven't I? I don't see why I shouldn't have a soul as well as anybody else. I've been wanting to see you, Ebenezer, because I've been making some poetry myself."

"You make poetry? What profanation!"

"D—n it, I don't see that. Come, now, Ebenezer, you've read me a lot of yours at different times, now I'll read you some of mine."

"Ah, ah!" said Ebenezer. "Ah, ah!"

"Thank you, it's intended to be funny."

"Then you worship the comic muse?"

"No, I doesn't. I don't *wash up* any *mews*. I've quite enough to do to sprinkle the shop."

"Go on, go on. I never knew you so fearfully supine."

"There's nothing the matter with my spine, Mr. Ebenezer, as I knows on"

"Oh, heavenly powers, can human nature support this? Now, Wilkins, really you have become terrific. Listen to me, and when you hear that fearful narrative which should harrow up your soul, if you have one to harrow, then, oh, then, you can say what you please, for my thoughts will be far away. Ah, me! oh."

"Well, that's polite of you, however."

"What's polite?"

"Why, to promise me that your thoughts shall be never so far off when I'm talking to you; but, howsomdever, say what you've got to say, for my hour is a rolling away like bricks, and I shall perhaps be forced to go back to the shop in the middle o' some of your fine speeches, if you don't look sharp."

"Listen!" said Ebenezer, and he tried to look as like Macready as he could. "Last night I looked upon a form—I gazed upon a face—I loved! but she—oh, despair, she did not seem to notice me, and yet she is beautiful."

"But you ain't, you know," said Wilkins, "and perhaps that accounts for it."

Ebenezer looked daggers.

"Genius," he said, "is always beautiful. always lovely. I'll trouble you not to make such remarks as that, Wilkins. "I have mentioned my heart's passion to my mother—she knows what my despair may be if the cherished object of my affections melts not into ambrosial sighs at mention of the passion which now fills my heart."

"Melts into what?"

"Sighs—sighs"

"Is she sizeable?"

"Oh, great God, Wilkins, do you want to drive me mad?"

"I should not have fur to drive you," said Wilkins; "but, come, come, who is she?"

"The niece of one Paddlebat, a goldsmith; but there is no gold in his shop so precious as that heavenly creature."

"Oh, I know Paddlebat—he deals with us."

"But you have not seen the radiant creature! the beautiful Fanny! Ah! me, my soul bursts into song."

"All round my hat," said Wilkins.

"Base metaphor. When I returned home last evening, and Sol was in his ocean bed, when the mass of humanity had closed the leaden eye of slumber, and the dreamy effulgence of wrapt repose was upon the giant city, I alone sat up."

"Lor!"

"Thus I wrote. Inspiration dawned upon me."

"Now, I do wonder at you, Ebenezer, with your edication, to make such a mistake."

"What mistake?"

"About that ere word," returned Wilkins. "You said inspiration. You meant *perspiration*."

Ebenezer cast upon Wilkins a withering look, and then he took from his pocket a folded paper, as he said,—

"Come into this doorway, and you shall hear what mortal ear has not yet drunk in. You shall become aware of those strains which in time to come will captivate and enchant a world; and when you in after years, perhaps when time has silvered your locks, and lent furrows to your brow, hear of the great, the celebrated, the immortal Ebenezer Crump, you will be able to say, in gasping accents, ' I knew him—I knew him—I actually knew him.' "

"Drive on, then," said Wilkins, who did not seem to be much affected by this burst of eloquence; but then, as Ebenezer said afterwards to himself, "what can be expected from people who have no souls?"

But it is not a trifle that will stay an author in reading his productions. The delight of doing so to such amateurs as Ebenezer is too strong to be lightly overcome. The book writer, who is forced to take things in a business way, soon has the romance of the thing knocked out of him; but Ebenezer was an amateur in the full sense of the term; and as nobody, somehow, would publish his works, he was compelled to find a private audience where he could. With abundance of gesture, he now read to Wilkins the following lines—we were almost going to call them verses :—

> "Oh, fairest Fanny, look on me,
> While my bounding bark is on the sea.
> The moon may shine in lustrous beams—
> The stars look down, as if in dreams,
> But I must worship thee.

> " Niece are you of a man of gold :
> My love's despair can ne'er be told.
> If you smile not, my mind is bent
> On a fall from the top of the mon-u-ment,
> To Fish-street-hill so old."

" There," said Ebenezer, as he folded up the paper and dashed it into his breast-pocket. " There—there !"

" Where ?"

" I mean, what do you think of that ?"

" Beautiful—beautiful! I always did say, you know, Ebenezer, that if you could do nothing else, and never did do nothing else, you was an out-and-out hand at poetry."

" You consider those lines beautiful ?"

" I does."

" You are right. Of course I would not say as much to everybody, but with you I can be confidential, and when you say they are beautiful, I have no hesitation whatever in assuring you that you are perfectly correct."

" Thank you; I can't read you any of my poetry to-day, because there ain't time, for my hour has just about gone, and I must go back to the shop."

" Well, well," said Ebenezer, with a patronising air, "another time will do just as well. But, before you go, there is one thing you can do for me."

" What is it ?"

" Here is a note which I want given into the hands of Fanny herself."

" Yes."

" You say you know Paddlebat's shop. I want you, by some means, to get this note conveyed to Fanny."

" There's nothing improper in it—is there ?"

" Improper ! Angels and ministers of grace defend us ! It is but to ask her to meet me in the Adelphi, at the quiet terrace near the Thames, that I may there breathe to her my heartfelt vows, and, in strains of poetic melody, assure her that she is all my own, and reigns supreme mistress of my heart."

" Oh, I have no objection to that. Mind, though, I mayn't be able, for I can only go after the shop's shut up ; and then I don't know her."

" Ah ! you cannot but know her. The rose-tint blooms upon her damask cheek —her step is like the fawn."

" Well, I'll do my best, Ebenezer, you may depend upon that ; and if I don't succeed, you know, you must take the will for the deed."

" I shall—I shall. When you have delivered the note, come to me at once, and let me know ; and now adieu, for I see your hour has almost come. Adieu—adieu !"

" Adoo—adoo !" said Wilkins. " The hour has come, and old Martin, the clothier, will be furious if I don't be in the shop in a minute. Whatever you do, Ebenezer, don't you go apprentice to a clothier."

" I—me—apprentice? Good Heaven ! Fancy the wild chamois tied to a child's cart, and compelled for ever to trudge through the miry streets of London with a squalling infantine brood behind him ! Fancy the wild horse of the desert in a night cab ! Fancy what you will that is wild, horrible, afflicting, and preposterous, but do not fancy me an apprentice."

" Very good. I don't think anybody would have you, with all your fancies, if they only know'd 'em as well as I do ; but, as I say always, you can write poetry ; whether it's worth while or not, I don't know, in course, and whether sich things will ever get you a living or not, I don't know; but for all the good as it is, whether it's much or whether it's little, you can do it, cousin Ebenezer."

"Ha! ha!" said Ebenezer, gloomily, and like a great genius, as he walked away. "Ha! ha! I can. Let me perish as a poet, rather than live as anything else. I feel that I can never stoop to get a living. Perish the thought. Ha! ha! Let lots of iron enter my soul first, and a nation's tears embalm my sepulchre."

CHAPTER XVII.

LOWE'S SKELETON.—AN EPISODE OF EARLIER LIFE.—THE DESERTION.

It is now time to return to the consideration of the letter which Nicholas Lowe received during the time that the party had been given by Mrs. Paddlebat, in honour of the arrival of the niece of Mr. Paddlebat.

When Lowe escaped from the drawing-room, he hastened to his own room. There, in extreme agitation, he looked at the letter, which he threw down before him on a table, and walked to and fro for several minutes to regain composure enough to take the letter and break the seal.

He took the letter, and, tearing it open, read the following :—

"Abney-house, Shooter's-hill.

"Sir,—I beg to inform you that Laurelle is dead. She died last night. I wish to receive your instructions relative to the disposal of her remains, as well as to inform you of some expressions she used towards you before she died. She was perfectly sensible and sane a little while before her death. She died in peace and Christian forgiveness of all; but you shall hear more of that when I see you.

"I am, sir, your obedient servant,

"JAMES SPALDING, Proprietor."

The letter fell from Lowe's hands as he finished it, and a deep sigh escaped his breast, and tears stood in his eyes. He leaned his head upon his hands, and there gave vent to his grief in audible sobs, which he endeavoured to suppress. But Nature was powerful, and would have her sway; and the deep grief that now sat heavy on his soul, found a vent in deep groans and long-drawn sighs.

"I will go," he murmured, "on the morrow. Yes, I will go and see the last sad office performed for poor Laurelle—she whom I have ruined and destroyed— she who loved me so unsuspectingly and so fervently. Yes, yes, I will see her carried to her last home, where I would gladly join her, but my hour is not yet at hand. I was her skeleton, and she has been a fearful one to me, haunting my mind by day and night. But have I not deserved it?—have I not deserved it? Yes, yes, too surely have I."

Leaving Lowe to the deep grief that seemed to prey upon his heart, we will take a retrospect of an earlier period of Lowe's existence, and seek for an explanation of his grief, and the contents of the strange letter from the proprietor of a madhouse, for such Abney-house was.

*   *   *   *   *   *   *

Some years ere this, when Lowe was in the north—at least north from London— he met with an incident that introduced him to a family, of which, indeed, the members were few, but they were happy and peaceful.

They laid down at night with no fear hanging on their minds, and no sorrow to cloud their brows; and had they been compelled to declare what wish they most desired, it would have been some wish uttered for the health and happiness of the other; and the only fear that could be felt was that some event might happen to destroy this felicity; and an event did so happen that plunged them from happiness to extreme misery.

There was a ball given in the town, and Laurelle was invited. She was beautiful and innocent, gay and charming. She had many friends, and was an ornament in any party.

With a relation she attended the ball—it was a cousin, who, at the same time, took his own sisters to the same place, for her parents did not go : the one being unwell, the other was necessarily unable to attend.

But Laurelle was well taken care of by her cousin, who otherwise was a wild young man, but he was presumed to be sufficiently capable of taking care of his sisters, and of course his cousin, as well the presence of one being the protection of the other.

Lowe was at this ball, and was stricken by the beauty of Laurelle. He saw and noted her well-formed features.

" She is beautiful—really and truly beautiful," said Lowe; "there is no other present that is at all like her. She dances to perfection, not showily, but with a graceful, swan-like movement, nothing in the least constrained or ill-suited to the occasion."

Long did he gaze upon her before he made up his mind to introduce himself to her, but an opportunity soon occurred after he had done so.

The dancing had been kept up some time, when her hand was begged by an individual who had more impudence than manners, and, fearful of giving offence, she consented.

Laurelle had reason soon to repent of this, for the stranger was insolent, and his warmth of manner bespoke him no gentleman.

When the dance was done, instead of leading her back to the seat occupied by her friends, he led her to an unfrequented part of the ball-room, and thence to an ante-chamber, where he became rude and insulting.

Concluding what was the object of the gallant, Nicholas Lowe followed them softly, and when he saw the stranger attempting to force her hand to his lips, he felled him with a blow, without uttering a word to him, and then offering his arm to Laurelle, he said,—

" Allow me to take you from this place to the dance, or your friends."

" I am much obliged," said Laurelle; " I knew him not ; is he hurt?"

" Nothing to speak of ; but you will soon see him out, I dare say. The dance is about to begin : will you favour me with your hand, and then we will place ourselves ?"

Laurelle could not refuse, but consented, and they were soon in the maze of the dance, which was danced with much grace and animation by them both. Lowe then had good spirits, and he was so placed that he felt all the pleasure he showed, and when the dance was over he was introduced as being her protector.

After some opposition, she was permitted to remain till a late hour in the evening ; and during the time she remained there she was wholly under the protection of Lowe.

The individual who had so insulted her they saw afterwards, but prudence was the better part of valour, and he kept his own secret ; and a large bruise, which was fast becoming too plain to render a protracted stay in the ball-room prudent, forced him to leave without presuming to take any notice of his discomfiture.

Of course there was much conversation that passed between them during that evening, and Nicholas Lowe discovered from her that her father was an invalid, always confined to his room, and her mother never left him ; and that while her father lived they were independent, for he had a pension, or an annuity, she could not tell which.

This was an introduction that gave Lowe much pleasure ; for he would listen to the soft sweet accents of Laurelle with evident delight. Her conversation was often animated, and always pleasing ; for one so young, too, it was wonderful how reasonable she was, possessing a good fund of information, which came naturally to her as she spoke.

Lowe certainly felt a strong attachment to this unfortunate young girl ; indeed, he loved her there can be no doubt ; and when the warm gush of affection first filled his heart he certainly cherished it with ardour. He knew—he felt he loved. He was often a guest at the cottage where they lived ; he was often there as early as when the golden tints in the eastern sky awoke the lark to his matutinal song. He watched the progress of the shadows, the change of colour in the leaf of the vine that was carefully trailed over the white wall of the cottage; he would watch how each flower grew into sight out of the darkness and mist that often enshrouded the beauties of the cottage garden that was the especial care of Laurelle.

Laurelle, too, would, when the sun had well illumined the horizon, but before even the labourer was at his work, arise and come into the garden, and would often say,—

"Ah, Mr. Lowe, you are an early visitor. I see you want to steal the sweetest odour from my garden."

"Incidentally I do; but all is so fresh, so beautiful, and the mind, too, has so little of the cares of the world upon it to take from it any of its elasticity, that this is by far the most propitious hour."

"It is so; and yet how many lose it."

"But you and I, Laurelle, we will not—we do not—even when all the world are asleep, we live, and love, and speak those affections our hearts feel; say, is it not so, sweet Laurelle?"

"It is so, Nicholas, since you say so."

"Happiness is certainly found most frequently in such a spot as this; at least, to me it is doubly welcome—it is enhanced."

"Indeed; I am pleased my garden so well pleases you. But see, here is some fresh rose blossoms; they came out but yesterday."

"Indeed! they are the emblem of you, dear Laurelle; you are the rose of this place, and by far the sweetest and most beautiful."

"You speak flatteringly."

"Indeed I do not. You know my heart too well to think I could flatter; the love I bear is not such that I could; I would as soon flatter myself—I should be as capable."

"Well, Nicholas, I must give you credit for sincerity; I should be greatly mistaken, but I think you are to be believed."

"I know from my own heart that I say what I mean, and therefore think I may. But, Laurelle, how is your father?"

"Much as usual."

"No better, nor worse?"

"No, but unusually cross; but then he is a great sufferer."

"Do you think he will allow you to go to a ball that I have a ticket for?"

"I really don't know; he is sometimes so very strange in his notions that I know not what to think."

"Cannot we ask your mother alone? she will not refuse you."

"If she were to give permission without his leave, she would get into sad disgrace. No, no; I had better not do that—I will risk all, and ask him to let me go."

"And if he will not?"

"I must decline going there without his permission; it would cause so much unhappiness that I am sure you will not ask me."

"I will not, under these circumstances; but I will come by-and-bye to see how you have sped with your father."

"Do so. But will you not stay to breakfast with us?"

"No. But do you think I should do any good if I were to put the question to him myself, Laurelle? if so, I would do so."

"I think you had better not; he may give a short answer—he has lost much of his equanimity of temper lately."

"Then, farewell, dear Laurelle, for the present; I will be back with you in the evening, in time to take you if you can obtain permission to quit your home for a few hours."

"Farewell," added Laurelle, as she held out her hand; this he pressed warmly, and then suddenly stealing a kiss from her lips, he evaded her playful attempt at chastisement, and left the garden.

Toward sunset Nicholas Lowe again made his way towards the cottage of Laurelle; and when he came there he saw both Laurelle and her mother walking in the garden together. Nicholas entered, and saw they were engaged in conversation, but he heeded it not, but walked up to them both.

Laurelle seemed both flushed and somewhat displeased; but when she saw him she held out her hand to him, saying,—

" You have come at a happy moment, Mr. Lowe; my mother has been scolding me on your account."

" Indeed! I regret to hear that very much; but let the blame, if any there be, rest on my shoulders."

" You give me a taste for balls, and gaieties of one character or another."

" Indeed; then I tell you I would rather do the reverse. But yet I hope such an enjoyment is not to be denied us now and then; it is but seldom, indeed, that I feel a pleasure in such places—but have you permission?"

" Her father will not permit her to go, Mr. Lowe; he says it's scarcely right to do so with a gentleman to whom she is almost a stranger."

" I had hoped I was no stranger, or that my love for Laurelle would have been understood and seen; for my feelings and intentions are of the most honourable character. I believe the time will not be long hence before I can make some provision, and then I trust I shall not be as unsuccessful in my applications as I am now."

" That is certainly speaking to the point, Mr. Lowe; but her father is so great a sufferer that he cannot control himself—however, I would say no more to him about it now."

" So you must excuse me for this time, Mr. Lowe," said Laurelle; " and I shall be perfectly reconciled to your having another partner for the evening—I hope you may spend a pleasant evening."

" Where, Laurelle?"

" At the ball."

" No, no; I shall not go since you are not going with me."

" Do not stay away on that account."

" I shall; and if you do not mind a walk, we will stroll about for an hour or two."

The pleasure that this proposition met was very evident in Laurelle's face. She really felt it was an act of self-denial on Lowe's part to abstain from a place that was so well suited to his years, and she herself had felt strongly the unkindness of her father in refusing her permission to go with him.

But the old invalid was much too short-tempered to consider anything; he merely acted from some impulse, and that generally consisted of some sharp pang, that was enough to destroy any temper.

It was not long before the lovers walked from the house to enjoy a ramble across the meadows, and watch the setting sun.

Never before had they been so happy—never before did they think they ever loved each other so well, or that their future happiness so entirely depended upon themselves, and upon no others—that they were all in all to each other.

It was late that evening before they returned to the cottage, and then Laurelle hung upon his neck and sobbed, as he pressed her to his heart, and then parted.

Lowe returned to his home, and Laurelle paced the garden for some time to regain her composure and tranquillity, before she entered the presence of her parents.

*   *   *   *   *   *   *

The meetings used to be frequent, and Lowe was as heretofore the constant and assiduous lover as ever he had been. But somehow or other the position of the two seemed changed—there was a difference that no stranger would have failed to remark.

Laurelle grew pensive and melancholy—she sighed often when alone, and was much more thoughtful than usual. Indeed, she was a shade paler, and her step was less elastic.

What was the cause of this, it was difficult to divine. There was no apparent cause for it. Lowe was as often at the cottage now, if not oftener, than he used to be.

She used to watch for his coming with a pensive countenance, and sometimes a tearful eye. She took less care of her flowers too, a sure sign with her that she was unhappy—that her mind had some deep sorrow, or something that she mourned over in secret.

When Nicholas came, she greeted him with pleasure, and while he was with her, there was an end of her sorrow, and her weight of care all seemed lightened, and she was no longer sad and sorrowful.

There was a tone of love and confidence about her when Nicholas was with her, that shewed the power he swayed over her, and how dependent now were all her prospects of future happiness and bliss ; and how great would her misery be, should aught happen that would separate her from her lover. Then, indeed, the worst that could happen to her would follow, so wholly and entirely was she dependent upon his honour and truth, for life and happiness.

Lowe loved her, but they now sought the quietest and most retired spots that could be found—there they contemplated the beauties of nature, and the happiness of all living and breathing objects.

Laurelle looked up into the face of Lowe as he spoke, as if to catch from the very expression of his face, if he were pleased with her, or with what she said. Numberless little traits did she exhibit, which told, as plainly as words could speak, that he had her very heart—she was his most entirely. No woman could love more devotedly than Laurelle. She looked upon Nicholas Lowe as the perfection of human nature, of honour, and of truth.

Alas, what an exemplification of the mind was all this! he had won her young heart, but the denouement will come.

Time passed on, and days and weeks were come and gone since this occurrence, and Laurelle each day grew more melancholy, and watched for him her heart had chosen more earnestly than before—saw him come with more satisfaction, and depart with a bitter pang. Yes, she often wept when he left her—she would have detained him had she dared, or could she have done so, but she could not.

Time wore on, and one evening when she saw him coming, she could not refrain from tears, and as he entered the small arbour, he saw she had been weeping.

" Laurelle," he said, " are you weeping ? you cannot have cause to do so."

" Ah, Nicholas, Nicholas, you know not what you say when you say so. You, alas, know too well that I have."

" This must not be, dear Laurelle. We must mend this—me must have all sunshine and happiness where we are."

" I would we could, Nicholas, and you certainly have the power of making it so."

" Indeed, Laurelle."

" Yes, I have loved you too well."

" That cannot be."

" It is, and will be, unless you will prevent my utter ruin, nay, destruction. You often swore so solemnly, and such have been the nature of the dreadful oaths you have taken, that I cannot believe it probable or possible that you would break your promise."

" You are right, Laurelle. I would not, and I could not perjure myself ; but wherefore weep, dearest—you know my love ?"

" Alas, yes ; but unless you will do what remains to be done, all will be discovered, my disgrace will be complete. There is now no time to lose, if you would save me from ruin, disgrace, aye, destruction. Do it, Nicholas, do it—but it must be done at once."

" I will, Laurelle ; but you are aware of the reasons that have hitherto delayed the moment I with yourself so urgently desire."

" But they must give, dear Nicholas, they must give way, or my ruin is complete—my destruction will be effected. My mother and father would be brought to a premature grave ; and then, oh, God, what shall I not have to answer for ? my career will have been short, guilty, and miserably unhappy."

Laurelle wept bitterly, and Nicholas Lowe felt uneasy ; he could not look upon so much beauty, and so much grief, unmoved.

" Dearest Laurelle," he said, " listen to me. What you desire shall be com‑plied with, and that very speedily, too—very speedily."

" Ah! could I believe it !"

" You may. What you have said has made me determined to brave all, and you shall have what you desire, the marriage ceremony performed ; but we are united in heart already, but you shall be satisfied."

" Thank you! oh, thank you, Nicholas. I shall be grateful! You know not how grateful I shall feel for this kindness. I will be a slave to you, and be happy."

" Laurelle," said Nicholas, reproachfully, " you mustn't talk thus, or else I shall think you doubted my heart, my intentions."

" No, no—I do not doubt ; and yet, Nicholas, if you knew the anxiety, the dreadful anxiety I have suffered on account of this, you would scarce say an angry word about it, for I have been almost mad."

" Be so no more, dearest. I regret you should have suffered—I hope now you will be quiet, and rest in peace, for what I have promised I will perform, and that in a very few days."

" Ah! it was so dreadful to contemplate being a mother and not a wife. I could not bear it—my heart would burst. You can have no conception of the dreadful feelings I have had, it has been before my eyes sleeping and waking. I could not hide the fearful thoughts that crossed my brain. Death—death—death was all that stared me in the face, the only thing I could think of."

" But come, dearest, think no more of it. To-morrow I will do all I can towards putting things in train for our immediate marriage, and then you will feel no more of these sad thoughts, but all will be sunshine and happiness."

" All will be sunshine and happiness, indeed, Nicholas. Thank God such a moment is so near at hand. Oh, Nicholas, my very heart will burst with joy, I can scarcely bear it."

" Moderate your feelings, Laurelle, and our happiness will be the more lasting."

" Yes; but you know not the life I have been leading of late,—the dreadful depression of spirits—the horrible idea of the misery and desolation I must suffer. The grief and sorrow of my parents, all combine to render me most miserable."

" My dear Laurelle, we will say no more of this. I have said this much, and I will abide by it, be assured of that ; and now, dearest, shall we make a home of our own, and leave this place—you will then go with me ?"

" Yes, yes, anywhere—to the world's end with you, Nicholas, when I am your wife—then I will be your slave."

" My wife, love, and not my slave."

" As you wish, Nicholas," said Laurelle, who was much agitated at the pro‑spect of an immediate union with the object of her affection, who might now have left her.

She was somewhat extravagant in her gratitude and joy—she hoped so strongly to escape the stigma that now seemed impending over her.

They remained for nearly two hours ere they parted, and when Nicholas walked to the garden-gate, she hung her head upon his shoulder, and shed tears of joy.

"Then you will not forget your promise to poor Laurelle?" said she.

" Oh, no, no, no—believe me, no, dear Laurelle. I will be here again in a day or two—as soon as I have taken the first step."

" What is that ?"

" I will obtain a licence."

" What happiness!"

" And then we will leave this neighbourhood at least for a year, you know."

"Oh, Nicholas, how considerate and kind you are! This is kindness!"

" But we will do it; and now farewell, dearest. We will meet never more to be parted. Farewell, for a very short time."

" Adieu! Oh, how long will it be before we meet again! It will seem like an age! Time will creep on so—so very slow, I shall be able to count every pulse between this and then ; but if you must go, adieu."

" Adieu."

See p. 97.

Thus they parted.

Laurelle looked after the departing figure of Lowe: she seemed spell-bound. She strained her eyes as the fast disappearing figure of her lover became more and more indistinct in the distance, and then it suddenly disappeared behind the hedge.

Then she was alone—not a sound could be heard, save the throbbing of her own temples.

"He will be back in a day or two, at the farthest;—yes, yes; and then I shall—shall bless the hour we—we met."

She heard her own name pronounced at the cottage-door by her mother; she started, and turned towards the house, and obeyed the call of her mother, and went in.

Nicholas Lowe passed onwards for nearly half a mile, and then he said to himself,—

"So, so, it has come to this. I am sorry, very sorry; but marriage now would not mend the evil—must cause some more. Her name may indeed be saved; but what is that? It is useless. It will produce great mischief. I must to London and escape it.

"Aye, the coach—the coach that passes here at five will take me. I will prepare all things for the start, and then away for London. She will forget me, and some one else will fill my place, and she will, moreover, be better off with her parents. She has a home."

CHAPTER XVIII.

THE REPENTANCE.—THE MARRIAGE AND THE MADHOUSE.

LOWE kept his word with himself—he hurried homeward, packed up such necessaries as he should require, and came to London. He sometimes thought of Laurelle, but he consoled himself as many young men did upon such matters.

If he had committed an indiscretion, he was sorry enough for it, but he could not be chargeable with any great amount of criminality in loving a beautiful girl any more than she in loving him. Indeed they had both been indiscreet, and the worse consequences certainly fell upon her; but to marry her would be to sink two into misery, and tie two people together, who would pass a life of torment and unhappiness; it was by far the best that things should remain as they are. " She will soon forget me," he thought, " and I will endeavour to do so by her. It is the best."

Thus Lowe reasoned, and thus he acted. Day after day he walked about, and thought no more of the matter, save as a passing reminiscence.

Many, many months had elapsed—Lowe had scarce counted them, and yet no tidings were heard of Laurelle, as indeed it was most unlikely he should ; he gave up the idea, and he even ceased to think occasionally of her. She was to him a something that was past, and in process of being entirely forgotten.

* * * * * *

One day—it was some time after the above occurrence—Nicholas Lowe was walking through the streets, when he saw a woman, whose dress bespoke her wretchedness and poverty, soliciting charity in the public thoroughfare.

She came to him, but he tried to avoid her, and in doing so—for she stood in the middle of the pavement, he was compelled to turn on one side, with his face towards her.

She held out her hand, and in a low, sad accent, besought alms, but she never raised her eyes to the face of the person whom she thus besought, and Lowe said,—

" My good dame, I have nothing, indeed."

The sound of his voice acted as a charm, and she looked in his face, and exclaimed,—

" Merciful God ! do I indeed behold the author of all my misery !"

" What do you mean, good woman ? I never saw you before."

" Have wretchedness and misery so altered me, then, that you know me not ? Have poverty, and want, and hunger, so changed my features and voice that you cannot even remember the accents of the mother of Laurelle?"

" Of Laurelle !" he exclaimed, staggering backwards.

The shock was great.

" Yes ; of the deluded Laurelle. You have brought her to despair and ruin, and me to poverty, and ruin, and want. I feel even now I am dying ! I——"

" Stay," said Lowe ; " stay. Say no more now. You have some place you call a home ?"

" Yes, indeed I do call a shelter by that name ; but what of it ?"

" I will go with you, then, and hear all you have to say. I thought not of this. I thought not of this."

" But you are the author of it all ; every pang of sorrow and misery I feel, you are responsible for, and the sharp pangs of hunger that at this moment beset me, are caused by you."

" Here," he said, " take this, and relieve your immediate wants, and then tell me all about her I fear to name."

The unfortunate female took the silver offered her, and purchasing some of the necessaries of life, she tottered towards the lodging—if such a miserable hole as that in which she slept deserved that appellation.

He followed her to one of those wretched old houses in which there are a vast number of rooms, and each room is let out to at least one separate tenant.

This was one of that class, and the street-door stood always open. Mrs.

Mansell entered it, and Nicholas Lowe followed her. The stairs were many, and creeky, and a bannister every here and there was gone, in some places four or five. The stairs were clogged with dirt, and the room she occupied was at the very top.

This was the back room, too; the door was opened, and Nicholas Lowe entered a small room, more like a loft than even an attic.

The floor was bare, indeed the room was bare; there was scarce an article in it of any kind. There were two badly constructed seats, scarce safe, and a table, that would only stand when propped up against the wall. Two-thirds of the glass in the small window had been superseded by the use of paper, which permitted but a very subdued light indeed to enter the room. There was no fire, and there were no signs of one having been there recently. Such a scene of poverty and misery had never before been seen by Nicholas Lowe. He shuddered as he looked around him.

"This—this," he said, "is all my doings! God of Heaven, what have I not to answer for! What have I not to answer for!"

The old woman now sat down upon one of the questionable seats, and began to eat with great avidity. She was dreadfully thin and emaciated, and looked the picture of gaunt starvation, and Lowe shuddered as he watched her eat mouthful after mouthful with such eagerness that showed she had been a stranger to food for some time, and he trembled at the consequence of the rapid way in which she ate.

"But—but," he stammered, "where is Laurelle? I do not see her."

"She is not here. I—I do not know where she is, except she is somewhere in London, living as I do."

"Good Heavens!"

"Aye," said Mrs. Mansell, "if that had not been appealed to in vain, I and Laurelle had not been starving upon Christian charity."

"But how came all this about?"

"I will tell you, now some of the pangs of hunger are appeased. I will not upbraid you, because if you have the ordinary feelings of a living and breathing fellow creature, you cannot look upon your own doings—misery of your own creation, without feelings of remorse and sorrow, and I beg and implore you to restore me my unfortunate child."

"Alas! I know not where she is! I knew not she was in London."

"Well, you remember the last time you parted from her?"

"I do—I do."

"She expected you on the second day after that. She waited that evening in the garden to a very late hour, but you came not. She was unhappy and dejected; not, however, wholly despairing.

"'He will come—he will come, I am sure of it, he said so. I will not doubt him. I loved him, and he cannot be false.'

"She came in that night; she shed no tears, but I could see that something was amiss. I questioned her; but all she would say was,—

"'He has not come—he has not come; but he will come, mother.'

"I saw her heart was filled with grief, and here eye was wild and unsettled. She went to bed that night, but in the morning she was very unwell. She, nevertheless, arose and sat at her window watching; but you came not.

"This was repeated several days, and she became wan and pallid, and then she expressed her fears to me, and informed me of your promise.

"I then guessed her situation, and upon my accusing her she burst into tears and confessed all. Well, I saw it was no use adding to the poor child's misery by reproaches, and the first burst of my anger was soon turned to sorrow.

"She left home that day to inquire at your lodgings, and there she found you had left.

"She was so stunned at this intelligence that she returned home, and for several days did nothing but mope about the house. She was not perfectly sensible to her deplorable condition.

" Suddenly, one evening, about the usual hour at which you used to come, she sprang up in her chair, exclaiming, with a shriek,—

" ' He will not come—he will not come.   I am alone now, and shall never see him more.   I am ruined and deserted, God help me!'

" She fainted, and I had great difficulty in bringing her to, and then, in getting her up stairs, and she fell violently ill for many days.

" About the time of her recovery she seemed more composed ; but she had made a resolution of which I knew nothing.

" Her father now divined the cause of her ill-health.   You know he was almost bed-ridden, and his pains were an aggravation that completely destroyed both reason and temper.   He was greatly enraged, and reviled her bitterly. Nothing in the whole extent of language was too bad for her, and whenever she made her appearance he cursed her.   You may guess what were my feelings when my child was used so, both by lover and father."

Lowe groaned, and his features showed the intensity of the feelings agitating his breast.

" Laurelle had heard you had gone to London, and it seemed she was determined to make an attempt to reach London and find you out, and see if you could not be induced by prayer and entreaty to restore her to society.

" Her father seemed daily to grow more and more enraged against her.   His revilings were truly terrible, and I could not hear him, but was compelled to leave the room whenever he began, which was very often, so that he was much alone ; and a fit of pain coming on, he grew frantic.

" I took leave of Laurella.   I went into her room after the usual hour, and found her prepared, and this was the cause of her confessing to me her determination to come to London.

" I gave her what advice and money I could, after having in vain dissuaded her from such a project, so fraught with danger to herself, and which promised her so little advantage.

" ' Mother,' she said, ' I cannot be worse off.   Here I cannot stop; I would prefer death first.   My father's unkindness has so much increased since my misfortunes that I cannot stay here ; it is impossible.   Do not endeavour to stay me, mother; rather give me your blessing mother, and when I am away I may think upon one act of kindness, and know that misfortune, at least, has not deprived me of your love.'

" What could I do ?   I did as she begged of me, blessed her, and went to bed.   I arose early the next morning and got some breakfast for her, and then saw her to the coach, else she would have endeavoured to have walked the whole way.

" ' God bless you, Laurelle !' said I.   She returned the prayer, and kissed me. Tears moistened her cheek, which was cold.   She endeavoured to hide this from me, and then mounting to the roof of the coach, she waved her hand as it drove rapidly away.

" There was a strange feeling came over me, as if I had parted with all I loved best.   I watched the coach out of sight, and stood transfixed to the spot long after it had disappeared, and when I recovered from my grief, I turned and walked homewards.

" Here another scene awaited me ; Mr. Mansell had missed me, and was calling for me, and was in a dreadful rage ; and fell into a fit of awful swearing, and when I told him of what I had done, that he made his own daughter desert her home by his ill usage, he seemed struck with remorse, and he repented of what he said to her.

" After that a paralysis came on, and he was unable to move, and lost the use of speech.   He could no longer demand what he wanted ; he was perfectly senseless.

" He could not remain long in this state.   About a fortnight it was a piteous sight to me.   I believe myself that passion and remorse had been the cause of it. The doctor said it was very likely to have arisen from such causes.   God knows, but it would never have happened but for you; and had it happened, it would have been less a misfortune to me had I my poor daughter—my unfortunate Laurelle by my side.

"As it was, I was alone. No one was there to share my grief—no one to whom I could look for consolation—no one whom I could love. Ah! it was a desolate moment for me; full of grief and sorrow.

"Mr. Mansell died. My sorrow could not be greater; indeed, I had no cause to be so; he was released from a state which caused him to be miserable. Heaven knows if he suffered any pain; but he groaned, and some half-formed words were uttered when the parson came to pray to him.

"He said he was praying—it may be so. I hope it was; to me they sounded like the half formed oaths and curses he used to make use of when he was vexed. It might have been the case, and so it is, most probable. The same night he was released, and a week after he was buried.

"When all was realized—debts paid, and everything sold, and money paid both ways, I had just twenty-five pounds.

"This was but little to begin the world with; but had Laurelle been with me, innocent and happy, we should have lived in some way or other; I firmly believe in that.

"'How could you have done?'

"We must have done something or other for our living, of that there can be no doubt. We had every motive to exertion—every inducement—every hope would have been within us, we could have aided and condoled with each other; but now we were separated.

"Mother and daughter were cast loose upon an unfeeling and ungenerous world, that would look with indifference upon our exertions, and when one slight misfortune would reduce either of us to the very brink of despair, and cast us into the depths of misery and wretchedness.

"This has been my fate—it has—it must at this moment be hers. I came to town, determined to hunt out my daughter, but she has eluded my search; or, rather, I have not been successful in doing that which I would be too glad should be done.

"She would now be glad, indeed, to see her mother; to hear her talk to and soothe her; but yet she could not aid me in this search. She cannot even know of it, and to go back whence I came she would not.

"I spent all my money, was reduced to despair, and compelled to beg my bread; and such has been the history of the unfortunate wretch who is now before, and who has suffered all this through you. I would you had never been born; I should not have suffered what I have, and my daughter would still have been a daughter to me.

"I should not have suffered distress, biting hunger, and piercing cold. Want, age, and sickness now come upon me, and a few days more and my troubles are over, to suffer no more."

Nicholas Lowe sat motionless all this while, his face buried in his hands; deep sighs escaped his breast, and the tears fell silently down his cheek. He could not control the emotions he felt; grief had too strong a mastery over him, and he wept, ay, wept like a child, at this recital of grief, of woe, and of wretchedness.

When the old woman, for she looked extremely old and infirm, had finished, he looked up, and saw she was in the last stage of disease. A rapid consumption had seized upon her frame, and she was wasting away.

Lowe in all this saw the work of his own hands; he saw that he had been guilty—extremely guilty and criminal—and he felt, now, all the horrors and repentance that could be felt by any human being.

Thus torn, he felt that all he could do was reparation full and complete; nothing short of marriage could atone for what he had done, and even that might be too late.

"Oh, take me," he said, "take me to Laurelle; I will do all I ever promised—

I will do all that man can do; but that I feel will never compensate her for what she has suffered, or for what you have suffered."

The old woman looked at him with an inquiring glance; she seemed as if she either did not comprehend him, or disbelieved the promises made under such circumstances.

"Oh, God!" exclaimed Lowe, "and have I caused so much misery; and yet you cannot have felt what I feel at this moment; tell me where Laurelle is to be found, and she shall indeed become my wife, if she will not refuse one who has done her so much injury."

"Do you not know, Nicholas Lowe, I told you I have been begging my bread in London, and have not been able to do so? I know not, man, if she be living. I would I could find her; I would I could find her."

She rocked herself backwards and forwards in the old chair, that caused it to sway so that it was a mercy it was not broken.

"Yes, yes, I would give my best limb to know where the dear girl is. God knows what misery she has endured, spirit broken and heart-broken. Who knows what necessity and temptation may ——"

"For the love of Heaven cease, and pursue the picture no further. I feel that whatever has happened, has happened through me. I, alone, am responsible for it, and will abide it."

"Ay, but when?"

"When I can find her."

"Will you swear to seek her, heart and hand, by day and night, and that you will not cease to look for her while you have life, and pursue every means that is in your power?"

"I will, I will."

"Swear it."

"I do swear it, solemnly and without reservation. I will go to all the haunts of poverty and misery, of crime and want, and every conceivable place, to find out her whom I have so deeply injured. Say—say you forgive me. Say you will look over my past conduct, and believe in my future. I will make reparation."

"Do; but do not do it merely as an act of forced justice, but do it from your heart, and never let her think you love her less for what she has gone through."

"Oh, no, no; that would be but adding to my own misery."

"If you keep this promise, and keep it well," said Mrs. Mansell, solemnly, "I forgive you all that I have suffered—and that is no little; my life is fast passing away, but should you fail in doing so, may the bitterest curse of a bereaved and dying parent rest upon you for ever. May you never know sleep nor peace; may you never know happiness or prosperity, but be always haunted by the picture of the misery you have caused one whose only fault was in having loved you too well, and may the workings of an evil conscience lay heavy on your heart as long as you are a living man."

The old woman spoke in solemn and impressive tones; it seemed as if the love she bore her daughter, together with the circumstances connected with them both, had inspired her with a momentary power and eloquence far beyond what usually is met with in females; her voice was measured and affecting, it trembled as it uttered the last few words, and then a pause of deep silence, which lasted about a minute, elapsed before another word was spoken.

Lowe was completely bowed down in spirit before the old woman; it seemed as though some weight lay upon his spirit, or as if some gigantic spirit spoke, before whom he shrank in dismay and with a guilty conscience.

At length he said, in a subdued tone, and clasping his hands together,—

"May all this, and more, come to pass upon me, if I keep not my promise."

"Then," said the old woman, relapsing into her former manner, "I forgive you all I have suffered; and though I fear I may not see it come to pass, yet I will leave behind me my dying blessing upon the union when it shall take place, and a hope that happiness may yet be the portion of that bruised spirit."

Some time elapsed, yet before Lowe quitted the house, some more conversation passed between them, and then he left the unfortunate woman by herself, having left her some money to relieve her wants.

To set about finding Laurelle was his next task, and this he pursued with great diligence, but, as may be imagined, London is too large a place to enable any one to discover another human being; far from it; it would be an impossible matter, except by mere chance or accident.

He called a night or two after upon the mother, with the intention of communicating with her, and affording her any information he might obtain, or receiving any she might get, and in aiding her with the means of existence, which she had not.

He, however, could not get into the room, and upon going to inquire of the landlady what was the cause of it,—

" Oh, the old 'ooman's gone," said a red haired specimen of female loveliness, with a dirty white face and a ditto cap.

" Gone!" said Lowe.

" Yes, clean gone; nobody knowed of it, but the doctor said she choked herself, and that's how it was."

" Gone away, and choked herself?" said Lowe ; " I do not comprehend you."

" Lord, hang the man," said the red-haired lady ; " I means she swallowed too much food, and then she was boughed up. She had killed herself through eating ravenously, so doctor said ; that's all as I knows about it ; she must a bin gallus hungry, I expect, and made a bolt of what she had been eating."

" Good God! and so soon ; couldn't they get any aid to her?"

" Nobody know'd anythin' about her; we suppose she couldn't halloo, and so nobody took any notice of her whatever, 'cause, you see, nobody know'd anythin' about it."

" But where is she?"

" In the work'us."

" I can see her there?"

" Ay, to be sure you can ; that is, if you are there in time, but you'll not be there in time to-day."

" They won't bury her before to-morrow."

" Well, she died the night afore last ; yesterday the 'quest was sat upon her."

" What ?"

" The jury and coroner sat upon her yesterday, and I dare say she's buried."

" Indeed ; so soon?"

" Oh, bless you, what do they care for paupers? She was a pauper; nobody knowed her, and she lived by begging. As sure as you've a nose on your face, she's been put underground ; they knowed she was dead, so what's the use, they'd say, of keeping her out of the ground."

" Where did they bury her?"

" Don't know; never saw a pauper buried ; they say they are buried, however ; but I never knowed anybody say they see 'em buried except the parson and some of them folks ; but that's all my eye, I don't believe it—however, that's neither here nor there ; my child, od drat it, is a squalling, so I can't tell you any more now."

With a melancholy and sorrowful heart Nicholas Lowe turned from the house.

It seemed as though there never was to be anything to prosper with him; the very means which he had provided for her use, had been turned into the means of her destruction.

" What misery," he uttered, wringing his hands, " what misery have I not caused, turn which way I will! Oh, Laurelle, better had it been by far for you that I should have been dead before I had ever met you. You, your mother and father, might yet be happily enjoying yourselves, and I should not have the dreadful knowledge on my mind that I have been the cause, the only and sole cause, of so much misery."

*   *   *   *   *   *

The next day Lowe did call at the workhouse, but he was informed that the body had been interred, and he could not see it.

Upon his demanding to know the spot where it was buried, an old man went with him after much grumbling, to a corner of the pauper burial ground, and there he pointed to a spot that had a small mound upon it, saying,—

" There she be."

" Who?" demanded Lowe.

" The woman."

" What woman?"

" The woman you came about. Don't you know her name?"

" What is the name of the woman you say is buried there?" inquired Lowe.

" Margaret Lindsey."

" That's not the one I want. Mrs. Mansell is the name of the female. I wish to ascertain the place of her interment."

" Oh, Mansell—that's her to be sure. That's what I said, only we have no missus's here ; they are just what they were christened, and no more ; and I don't see why they should be ; if she be Mansell, why let her be Mansell. What's the odds ?—eh, What's-your-name ?"

Lowe made no reply. It was useless to contend with ignorance and brutality, and he could do nothing without making the matter public, and that he shrank from. It would answer no good purpose, but confine him in his efforts to discover the unfortunate daughter of an unfortunate parent—his Laurelle."

He quitted the workhouse, and directed his steps towards the neighbouring dens, that were inhabited by the poorest and most lowly ; but it was dangerous to wander among them.

" Where shall I go?" he muttered. " How to direct my steps I know not' The curse of the dying mother still rings in my ears, and yet I know of no way by which I can discover her abode. I must and will continue the search, though it may only end with my death."

*   *   *   *   *   *   *

Day after day—day after day, did Nicholas Lowe walk the streets, frequenting every quarter of the town, in hopes of meeting with her whom he hoped to save and yet no tidings could he gain of her.

He made inquiries at all the shops that she was at all likely to be found to deal at ; but it was all useless—nobody knew of such a person, or any one like her, or if they did, it was sure to turn out some mistake.

Indeed, on several occasions there were some disagreeable explanations to b made ; but yet this did not deter Nicholas Lowe from continuing his inquiries, and he was resolved to do so, come what would, until he himself should no longer be able to walk about.

It was a long and a wearisome task, and one the success of which was so very problematical—one, indeed, that had for every chance of uccess, some ten thousand chances of odds against him.

How long this might have continued, Heaven knows, but it wo uld only have ended with his life, because the scene he had witnessed with Mrs· Mansell was enough to turn his very heart, had it been of adamant. He had resolved never to desist from making constant search for the unfortunate girl.

Some time passed—a long while—and yet no tidings could he gain of her whom he so assiduously sought ; and yet nothing was heard of her, and nothing could be seen of her, or anything that could, in the remotest way, lead to a discovery of the spot where Laurelle had concealed herself and her sorrows, as she was known to no one.

One day he was standing by the counter of a chemist's shop, when a girl came in. She was a low, ragged, mean and dirty creature ; but she was used to it, as any one might see, as the chemist remarked.

" I wants the physic."

" What physic ?"

" What you were to get ready for me against I came again."

"Oh, I remember now ; you come from thirty-four in the lane?"

"That's just it, mister, so hand over the pison, will you ?"

"You are a nice article," said the assistant ; "you'd pison, as you call it, a whole community with your dirt."

"Never mind my dirt ; you ain't got the job of washing me, so it makes no difference to you, Mr. Gallipot."

"You young devil's imp, you deserve to be sent back without.'"

"Well, what's the odds ? Jem's got to eat it, you know ; I'd sooner die quietly, and be buried decently and respectable, than torment my inside with your drug, though it does look pretty."

See page 117.

"You would hardly believe, sir, would you," said the chemist, "that there was so much impudence in life."

"I should not," replied Lowe, "have done so long ago ; but I have been amongst such a variety of characters of late, that I can almost believe in anything, though I own she is a specimen in her way."

"Oh, yes, a very perfect specimen. She can swear, I believe, can't you, Betsey ?"

"Yes, and be d—d to you. What are you poking fun at me for ? Hand over the mess, or I won't wait. You lazy fellow, if I was your master I'd scrape your back-bone with an oyster-shell, and heal it up with saltpetre ; I'll warrant you wouldn't sleep over your business."

"There, give that to the young woman—is she any better?"

" Ax," said the young girl.

" Didn't I do so ?"

" Yes ; but what's the odds ?"

" There, get out of the shop ; you are going the right road to the mill.   Don't come here any more ; I won't serve you."

The girl only grinned, winked her eye very hard, and made some hieroglyphics with her fingers from the end of her nose ; but, before the enraged shopman could get round to turn her out, she was gone.

" Well, that girl and I shall, some of these days, come to a sharp row—I won't be insulted by a girl like that.   Certainly, it's not treatment we ought to receive, especially as Mr. Hall gives the medicine for nothing to the young girl."

" Indeed."

" Yes, she has been a long while ill."

" Any relation of this girl's ?"

" No, merely a lodger ; a young woman who has been lodging in extreme misery and destitution in one of the rooms in her mother's house."

" Indeed ! what is her name ?"

" Laura, I think.   Laura something ; but I don't know, now."

" I think you say she is destitute."

" We have every reason to believe so.   They would have sent her to the work-house, there to die, had it not been for Mr. Hall, and some humane persons ; but she remains in a very precarious state, because she has not the means of pro-curing proper nourishment.   She has been, and even is now, very beautiful.   I suspect it is a seduction case myself, though there's no child ; but still I have my reasons for thinking so."

" If you will give me her right name and address, and if she be a deserving object, I will endeavour to afford her some temporary relief, at all events," said Lowe.

" Certainly," said the assistant, " you shall have it."

At the same time he turned over the leaves of a large ledger, and coming to a particular leaf, he said,—

" Oh, I see, it is not Laura ; but Laurella Mansell.   Yes, that's her name."

Nicholas Lowe nearly gasped for breath, and held convulsively on the brass rail that ran along the ledge of the counter, while the assistant, taking a small piece of paper, wrote the address at full length, then handing it over, he said,—

" As far as we know, sir, she is a deserving object ; she has evidently been used to a different kind of life.   Some scoundrel, no doubt, has been the cause of the poor girl's destitute state ; he deserves a worse fate than her's."

Nicholas Lowe took the paper, and folded it up, and placed it in his pocket with as much coolness and collectedness as he could assume, and said,—

" I dare say it is as you say, sir.   I am obliged to you ; I will see her at once. Good day to you."

" Good day, sir," said the shopman, and he bowed as Lowe walked out.

" Thank God !" he exclaimed, " I have found her out at length.   It was a mere chance—a mere chance—and it is in time.   I have now kept my oath with her mother.   How shall I tell her all ?   How can I tell her the misfortunes of her family, and say this was done by me ?   How, indeed, shall I enter the place and look her in the face ?   Will she, indeed, forgive me ?   Will she accept of the reparation I come to offer ?   May she not even spurn one from her who has so much injured her, who has bereaved her of all she holds dear ?   Oh, it will be a terrible interview ; but it must be attempted.   Come what may, I will see her."

CHAPTER XIX.

THE MEETING.—THE REPARATION.—THE BRAIN DESTROYED BY UNEXPECTED
HAPPINESS.

DESPITE the tremor that caused Lowe so much uneasiness, lest he should fail in his attempt to see Laurelle, when he came to the door he paused for some minutes. He could not venture into the presence of one whom he had wronged so terribly as he had Laurelle.

"I have sworn," he said, "to marry her, and I will. She may think that I will shrink from the performance of the promise, because she has suffered so much, suffered so dreadfully as I have caused her. But how can I present my-self to her? To go in unannounced would be, perhaps, to cause her death, or some catastrophe that ought to be avoided. If I send my name to her, she may refuse me an interview. What can I do, then? I must see her, that is certain. I will send up word that some one wishes to see her from the doctor's; ay, that will do."

Just at that moment the girl who had been at the chemist's came to the door; when she perceived him,—

"Do you want to see her?" she inquired.

"Yes, show me her room."

"Don't you wish you may get it?"

"Come," said Lowe, "don't play any of the nonsense off upon me you played off at the chemist's; you will be the loser, not I."

"I?"

"Yes, you show me Miss Mansell's room, and I will give you this."

"Give us hold of it, then."

"When you shall have done what I want you, but not before."

"Miss Mansell; well, I'm sure, if beggars are to be miss-ed in that way, I suppose they'll call me my lady; but, come along, if you don't keep your word I'll play the devil's tattoo on the door. All the while you are in there you sha'n't have any peace."

"You shall have it; now, just go in, and say that a gentleman from the chemist's wants to see her, will you?"

The girl nodded her head, and began to stride up the stairs with an agility that would have surprised many.

The house was the counterpart, or, at least, of the self-same class as the one in which Nicholas Lowe had entered to see Laurelle's mother, and he could not but shudder, as this strongly reminded him of the fate of the mother, by the appearance of the abode of the daughter.

After some exertion he contrived to reach the top of about five sets of stair-cases, each one more dilapidated than the former, until the last appeared to be so closely upon the verge of the dangerous, that the girl turned round in doubt as to whether he would follow her up the dangerous ascent.

"Don't be afraid, sir, it's only a little gone; but quite safe yet. I goes up and down, and don't care for it."

"I am here," said Nicholas, as he ascended and stood upon the landing.

"I'll just step in first."

"Do."

"What am I to say?"

"Say!—oh, say a gentleman wants to speak to her, and then come out."

"Shall I wait for an answer?"

"Never mind—never mind; and yet, if she offer to speak, listen to her."

"Oh, yes," said the girl, "I have no objection to listen."

She then, without further ceremony, opened the door, and entered the room, saying,—

"A gentleman wishes to see you."

"Me!" said the invalid, in a soft sweet voice; but so sweet and soft came its tones, that it was painful to hear it.

However, in these sweet tones, Nicholas Lowe at once recognized the voice of Laurelle.

"Yes."

"Who is he?"

"Don't know."

"What does he want?"

"To see you."

Nicholas Lowe pulled the girl out; he could not hear such tones and such words addressed to the unfortunate Laurelle.

"What are you up to, mister?" said the girl, as she came backwards into the landing; "didn't you tell me to listen?"

"Yes, but that will do," said Lowe, in a strange and unnatural voice, that made the girl stare again. "Here is what I promised you; now begone, and that quickly."

"Well," said the girl, as she walked slowly down stairs, and putting the six-pence in the corner of the handkerchief, where she tied it, "I never saw such a rum chap in all my born days. I wonder who he is—he made my blood curdle when he took hold of me in that manner. I think he'd frighten mother, leave alone me, and I am sure father can't do so."

Nicholas Lowe watched the girl down stairs, and then he turned towards the apartment, such as it was, and, after a desperate struggle of emotions within his own breast, he entered.

He closed the door after him, and for some moments he was stupified. He could not move. He stood in the same room, and he breathed the same air with the much injured Laurelle.

The room was almost devoid of furniture; but up in one corner stood a kind of bed, the name of which we cannot give; but it had no posts at the ends, and those that were up at the top had long since been sawn off, for what reason we cannot say.

It was a small bedstead, and by the thickness of the bedding, or thinness, we should say, there was scarce enough to prevent the ropes from being felt.

A few bed clothes, but very few, and these not sufficient to hide the form of her who reposed beneath them, was all the covering that was given the poor girl.

He advanced towards the bed. God! what a change was there. Laurelle lay extended much on one side. Her face was pallid, even to death; her hair thrown all back, which caused the features to show more prominently and more sharply than they would have done but for this.

Her lips were parted, her eyes half closed, and she seemed to be incapable or unwilling to move.

Lowe approached the bed, and, with a tremulous accent, he uttered the name of Laurelle.

For a moment it produced no effect. She seemed to listen, as if something had stricken upon her senses that she could not for a moment recollect. At length she said, raising her voice,—

"Who calls upon Laurelle?"

"I call upon you, Laurelle. I, Nicholas Lowe, your own loved but treacherous lover, who now comes to ask forgiveness for the past and hope for the future."

While he spoke, she raised herself upon her elbow and looked at him stead-fastly for a moment or two, and then, with an hysteric laugh, she said,—

"Ha! ha! ha! come at last, come at last. Ha! ha! ha! I knew he would come at last."

"Laurelle, Laurelle," he said, "my own Laurelle, do not speak in that dreadful tone; it kills me more than reproof, however well deserved. I am here—here to ask you, upon my bended knees, the forgiveness I so much need."

But Laurelle heard him not; she wept and beat her forehead with the palms of her hands, and then, after a minute or so, she became perfectly senseless. She had fainted, and gone off in a fit.

"Good God!" exclaimed Lowe, "I have been the cause of her death, as of her mother's."

However the moment was one of emergency; there was standing on the shelf a cup with some liquid in it that Nicholas presumed to be water, and so it was; he threw it over her face and did all he could to restore animation, and succeeded in a short time in recovering her from her trance, and then she gazed about her wildly.

"Said he not that he was here?" she exclaimed; "said he not he was come back to me;—come to see me before I die?"

"I am here, dearest Laurelle; here to make what atonement I can for the evil I have caused you; here to redeem the broken promises I made; here to restore happiness to your heart, if you will not drive me away from you. Receive me, Laurelle, and forgive me, and my life shall be devoted to amend the past."

"Do I dream, or am I indeed in the world of spirits, and the happiness I had hoped for is now about to be realized? Do I indeed hear aright, or do I dream? Break not the fond delusion."

"Laurelle, Laurelle, it is no delusion; awake! look up! here am I, your lover —a repentant one, who loves you and implores your forgiveness for the past."

"And do I indeed again see you, Nicholas Lowe?" she said, after a pause, and gazing earnestly on his face. "Do I again see you? You whom I thought had long since entirely forgotten me. Oh! Nicholas Lowe, you know not what has happened since we parted. The time has been long, and I have suffered much misery; but let it pass, let it pass; this moment of happiness would drown years of misery in oblivion. Oh! thank God that he has permitted me to live till this moment."

"And can you indeed forget and forgive your treacherous lover for his perjury and falsehood? Can you—can you, Laurelle?"

"Ay, all for this, all for this, I would almost go through all I have suffered to hear you at such a moment, and to know you yet love me, and that you will not despise me; that you still love me."

"Oh, Laurelle, what volumes of reproaches does this not convey to my mind; how great must be the chasm that separates my unworthiness from your truly greatness of soul."

"Oh, no, no, no, Nicholas, you could not be cruel; you never intended, you could not mean it. It was a mere waywardness of the time, a phantom that crossed your mind, but was no substance; it was but a shadow, and now that it is dispelled, see, see, here you are again, my own, my long-lost lover."

"I am here, and I am your own, dear, sweet Laurelle; and I were worse than brute did I give you one hour of uneasiness after this. Do you know, Laurelle, I feared to come to you; I thought I should receive what I know so well that I deserve, severe but well-merited reproaches."

"Reproach you, Nicholas! when did I ever think ill of you? Not when pain and disgrace hovered around me, and I had no one but strangers—mercenary, hard-hearted strangers—around me; then, even then, I thought of you, and prayed you might be spared, and that one day we might meet again."

"We have met again, dearest Laurelle, and I hope it is a happy meeting, that we may never part again, that we shall be firmly united and never more separate."

"And do you, Nicholas, say this to me?"

"I do, Laurelle; and if you will not spurn me, you shall be what you ought to have been long since—my wife, before God and man!"

"Oh, Nicholas!"

"Yes, Laurelle; do not agitate yourself, do not flurry yourself, but so soon as you are able to get about and to attend church, so soon shall you become my wife."

" Oh! it has come to pass at last, I knew it would ; all my dreams by night, my thoughts by day, tend towards the same point,—I always said you would do so."

" And now, Laurelle, I have no motive to seek you out and tell you a falsehood ; I will make you my wife, and we will spend a happy life yet ; this day will I put up the banns between us, and in three weeks' time we shall be married. Be careful of yourself, and get well."

" Oh, I will be very careful ; yes, for your sake, I will be very careful of myself. I feel, I am sure that God will grant me health and strength to go through this happiness. I feel, I know you will do all this, Nicholas ; indeed, why should you say so if you would not ?"

Nicholas wept as the head of the unfortunate Laurelle lay on his bosom. She was pallid, and her flesh had wasted away ; her eye was bright—it was very lustrous— and dilated as she gazed upon him, while a flush of crimson settled on her wan cheek, that had but borne a death hue for weeks past.

Nicholas talked more calmly to her and she to him, yet she hung upon him and listened to his accents with a feeling of the most perfect self-abandonment that can be felt.

It was impossible to remove Laurelle for some days from this wretched apartment, but a change was immediately effected in the comforts of the room ; more bedding and clothing were immediately produced, and every convenience that could be required, while a large fire was lighted—one that made the room look so different that any of its former occupants would not have known it again, but believe that they had made a mistake and entered the wrong house.

Food, too, such as she most needed, was sent in, and any spare hour that Nicholas could obtain he spent with her, and passed the time in conversation that sufficed to rouse the drooping spirits of the young and beautiful Laurelle.

Day after day she gathered strength, and Nicholas could see the absent beauties one by one slowly but imperceptibly return to her face.

She got better, and the first thing Nicholas did was to procure other lodgings, where she would be more comfortable and more properly attended to. Laurelle was passive, she submitted to anything that Nicholas proposed, she deferred to him in everything, and the chief thing that seemed to delight her was to listen to Nicholas as he recounted the many hours of happiness they would hereafter enjoy.

She could sit and listen to this for hours with a delighted ear, she loved to hear the sound of his voice when conversing upon this theme, and would smile so sweetly and so thankfully that Nicholas often paused to gaze upon her.

Nicholas, however, thought proper to say nothing about the fate of her mother or her father to her, but evaded all the questions she could put to him, which were not many, as she could have no idea of the calamities that had befallen them, much less could she think that Lowe was acquainted with them. She was much too weak to bear many more mental trials ; the shock to the system might prove fatal to life or reason.

The time passed on, and the day came when they could be married by banns. What a morning that was to poor Laurelle ! she scarcely knew whether she was living in a land of spirits or not, where all was happiness and pleasure, and where sorrow could not come.

It was a fine Sunday morn, the bells rang out merrily from some five hundred steeples of the metropolitan churches ; every one seemed gay and happy, every one was dressed gaily ; it seemed a day of bustling gaiety and happiness, nobody but looked more willingly happy than on any other day ; they were hurrying to and fro more rapidly than at other times.

Nicholas and Laurelle were to be accompanied by their landlady, who promised to attend at the ceremony as a witness, and to support the bride ; and in the after-noon Nicholas proposed, that if Laurelle's strength would permit her, he would take her an excursion to some pleasant suburban retreat, there to spend the day and increase the happiness and health of Laurelle. She had now been confined for many months, and scarce knew what the fresh a████s, save that which blew in at the window.

She indeed rode by the side of her lover to the church ; she expressed the happiness she felt, and often would she turn to look at him, and assure herself that it was not all a dream—a delusion.

"Oh, Nicholas!" she exclaimed, as the coach in which they were drew up at the church door; "now I know that this is not some pleasant dream, but real happiness ; this is a moment we used to dream of at the cottage, but which, until very lately, I thought was very far off indeed. Will not my poor mother be overjoyed to hear all? She knows not what I have suffered, Nicholas. I would not make her unhappy by letting her know it all; on the contrary, I have refrained from writing, thinking that even doubt and uncertainty are much better than the knowledge of positive evil."

"It is well, my dear Laurelle, you have done so ; but come, the moment, though long delayed, has at length arrived when we shall be united together. Come along, dearest."

He gave his hand to her, and she leaned on his arm, with a sweet smile of happiness upon her lips, and thus they ··ked into the body of the church, accompanied by Mrs. Mundell, their landlady, and witness for the occasion.

There were but few moments spent before the officiating minister was in readiness to perform the service, which he did.

During the whole of the service there was a strange expression about the eyes of Laurelle—a something that Nicholas had never noticed in their early acquaintance ; but this he laid to the amount of long illness, which had altered her looks greatly, and she had not recovered her wonted appearance, or even strength and health.

The ceremony passed off well enough—there was no interruption, and they left the church; but Nicholas had to lift Laurelle, fainting, into the coach, and during their ride back, it was but a succession of fainting fits, in which, indeed, she did not entirely lose her senses, but very nearly so ; she did not faint so as to become insensible, but slight hysterics followed.

"Poor thing—poor thing !" said the compassionate landlady ; "poor thing, she seems very weak—that's what it is, sir ; she should have waited another week—she would have been stronger, then, much stronger; but she'll be better soon."

"She has suffered much from illness of late," said Nicholas ; "and she has scarcely yet recovered from it ; but she will daily get stronger."

"I hope so—I hope so. Her mind will be more composed soon. But here we are at home now, and we will see what we can do for her. Some cordial will restore her spirits."

They now returned to the house whence they had set out, and Nicholas lifted Laurelle out of the carriage, and carried her into the parlour, where he placed her on a couch.

"It is done now—it is done now ; I knew he would do it—I knew he would do it. They said he was false ; but see—see, there's the ring. Is that a proof of truth or falsehood? Oh, no—no ; he is true—he is true !"

"Laurelle ! Laurelle !" exclaimed Lowe, in fearful accents ; "Laurelle, be calm —compose yourself; you are with me—your own Nicholas ; be calm and composed —you are safe, and with friends."

"Yes, he is true," said Laurelle, without heeding him. "Say what they will ; he is true ; I always knew it ; one look at this golden circlet—what does that not say for his truth and honour. Oh, he could never be cruel or unkind to me."

Lowe stood by, the picture of despair. The landlady lifted her hands in amazement, and said,—

"Poor thing—poor thing ! she is going mad—she is going mad !"

"Good Heavens!" exclaimed Lowe, "can nothing be done for her ?"

Before the landlady could reply, Laurelle set up a loud shriek, and beat her hands together, and then with a discordant and hysterical laugh, she went off into a very strong fit.

It was long before she could be recovered. Medical means were compelled to be resorted to, and she was ⬛⬛⬛ up stairs to her bed, with orders that she should be kept quiet.

Nicholas Lowe, appalled at the occurrence, inquired anxiously of the medical man who was called in, what was his opinion of the affair.

"I am a stranger, sir, to all the preceding occurrences, and therefore can give but a very limited judgment. These affairs generally are got over with safety ; but, I know not if I be right, she seems to have been suffering severely from illness."

"She has—she has, most severely."

"Then this will be trying to her strength ; but I hope she will recover. Has she suffered much in mind ?"

"She has, as much as in body ; indeed, the disease of the mind, sorrow and disappointment, preceded the latter."

"Poor thing ! I know not what to say ; I will call again towards evening, and then I may be a better judge of her condition."

The medical man left Lowe in a state of mind bordering upon distraction.

"Am I to be always the bane of her existence ?" he exclaimed. "Is she to know no rest, no happiness, because she has loved me ? God of Heaven ! what have I done that I should not be punished, instead of an innocent and suffering girl ?"

When Laurelle recovered from her insensibility, she was raving mad ! She knew nobody—spoke incoherently and rapidly, and the phrenzied fire of madness lit up her eyes.

The old physician shook his head, and sighed deeply, as he said to Lowe and the landlady, who were whispering in the room,—

"You need not control your voices—she hears you not ; she never will understand you rightly again. Reason has fled, and will never return until some other mental shock restores it—most probably death alone will do it. She is mad !"

Lowe sank on the floor with a loud groan, and became insensible.

    *   *   *   *   *   *   *

By the advice of the physician, poor Laurelle Mansell was sent to Abney-house, Shooters'-hill, where, he said, she would be taken care of, and the air and situation were salubrious.

His advice was complied with ; and thus Lowe's wedding-day was terminated by so fearful a catastrophe, and truly placed a skeleton in his house of the most fearful character.

———

CHAPTER XX.

THE DEATH.—THE FORGIVENESS.—THE LONELY FUNERAL.—THE QUESTION AND ITS
ANSWER.

THE unfortunate Laurelle was, as we have stated, sent to Abney-house asylum— a private madhouse ; and for a long while did Nicholas Lowe pay out of his salary a sum for her maintenance in comfort at this place

She was harmless, but quite mad, and unfit to be trusted to herself for any time, however short, in society ; but here were gardens and places where she could ramble about.

This she did, and used to wait at one spot—a gate, and look earnestly and long in one particular direction, murmuring to herself,—

"He does not come ; wherefore comes he not ? He will come ; I know he will come ; he will not desert me ; he has sworn he will come, and I am sure he will be here—if not now, at least to-morrow. Yes, yes, he will come."

And thus she would continue to murmur, day after day, and to continue to watch at the same spot, as if she waited some one's coming. It was melancholy and sad to see her eyes always straining to catch a sight of something that she never could see.

She knew him not when he came to see her, which he did ; but she was wholly unconscious of his presence. She appeared to forget all past events, save one, and

See page 124.

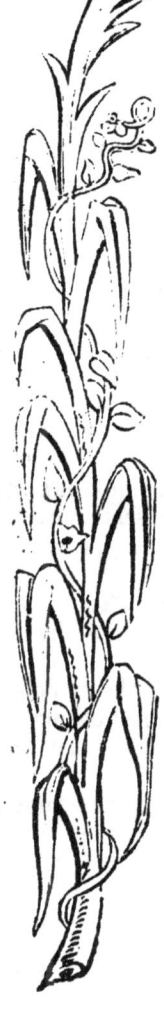

that was that she used to wait for him at the garden gate, and there watch for him, and the last time she did so was that on which he cáme not.

A remembrance of this, and this only, seemed now to float upon her errant senses.

Nicholas Lowe sat often and looked upon the wreck of beauty and youth before him; and he would sigh as he beheld her walk towards the spot she so constantly frequented.

"And this," he said, "is my doing—my work. I have caused a waste, a destruction of youth, innocence, and beauty. One of God's fairest creatures has been blighted in the bud; and I—I, worse than criminal, have done this deed. Oh, Laureile, Laurelle, sad, sad as your fate is, mine is yet worse—mine is yet worse."

Who could sit unmoved, and witness such a spectacle as that before him? She was beautiful, but there was such an air of me-lancholy about her, that it was heart-rending to see and watch her.

The keepers had at night, at the hours at which they closed the doors, to lead her back to the house. She was perfectly passive and obedient, but she was almost helpless—at least, she would not exert herself, and were she not conducted to the place where she ate and drank, she would suffer the pangs of acute hunger before she could be induced to seek for food to alleviate her misery.

There was no other trouble with her. Perfectly passive, obedient, and tractable in every way that could be desired, but without the aid of care and kindness, she would perish.

"Thus," said Nicholas to himself, as he gazed upon her, "thus have I ruined thee, Laurelle; you are wasting away—your life is not chequered by any of the gleams of happiness and warm sym-pathies which our nature gives us. No, no, all is cold oblivion with you—a simple life of forgetfulness, a mere blank. Oh! what would I not give to be dead—to forget all that I h··· done. Ah, how willingly would I not lay down in my grave to restore you to your former state. Wretched, wretched man, what a skeleton have you not raised up to haunt your house, one that will make you curse your nature, the hand that made you. Oh, God!"

Wringing his hands, he q█████ed a sight to him so appalling, so full of misery and sorrow.

* * * * * * *

The day after that on the evening of which Nicholas Lowe had received the letter from the proprietor of the asylum in which Laurelle had been kept, he obtained leave of absence under plea of ill-health of some relative or private business, and set out for Shooter's-hill, where Abney House was situated.

He was sad, very sad, indeed. He took his way to London-bridge, and there engaged the aid of a waterman to carry him down as far as Greenwich; the remainder of the journey he would perform on foot, and by himself.

The morning was serene and calm, but there was but little sun—it was chilly, too, but Nicholas Lowe felt not the chill—he was cold at heart, colder by far than the atmosphere. He felt it not, therefore, but sat in moody silence.

He saw not the shipping, he saw not the host of men and things that are to be seen on the river; he, might, indeed, have gazed at them with his eyes, but it conveyed not the slightest idea to his mind; he was deeply busied in thought—such thought that absorbs all other faculties.

The very boatman was amazed; once or twice he spoke, but he received no answer, and he, too, was silent. Once after he did indeed say,—

"The Pool's full to-day, sir. Yonder vessel coming up has come from the Indies."

There was no answer returned, and the boatman muttered to himself,—

"He's a d—d nice fellow for a long voyage. I'm blessed if they'd ever get a yarn out of him if they were to sail alongside the Flying Dutchman. He'd do to play dummy."

He rowed on, but spoke no more, but ill pleased with his customer.

After some time he was safely landed at Greenwich-stairs, and when he got out, Lowe placed a piece of silver in the waterman's hands, and then turned abruptly.

"Vell, my hearty, what have you got there?" said another waterman, who came out of the public-house; "is he a fat 'un?"

"Better 'an I expected; he's a rum un, he is, any how, and no mistake."

"What's amiss?"

"Nothing amiss, mate, only he wouldn't speak the whole way down."

"Not a word?"

"No, not a word, mate; though I did speak, but as he said nothing to me, why, I couldn't say much to him."

"In course not. Has he paid you?"

"Yes, very well. I can't complain much—just double fare, and a drop o' beer."

"Well, he's a good un. I was brought here for only my bare fare, think of that, Jack—wasn't that a shame? and to aggravate me, he said I didn't row fast enough."

"Well, that was blessed aggravating. I would a run foul o' something, and up-set the boat, myself and all, in such a case."

In the meanwhile Nicholas Lowe hurried on towards Shooter's-hill. There was some distance to walk, especially as the house was situated on the farther side of the hill from the place where he was.

The morning was highly conducive to enjoyment in this way, but Nicholas could not feel any pleasure in aught that he saw; the beauties of nature were nothing to him, he cared for nothing—he was sad at heart, and he knew nought of what was around him.

True it was, that, after walking about an hour, he was much warmer, and much better than when he was on the river. This had its effects, he felt his grief more active, but less of that dead, sullen, stagnant feeling that before beset him.

Now he could weep, he could sigh, and yet he continued onward without any intermission of pace, and soon he came within sight of the house where the remains of his wife lay.

"There, there!" he exclaimed, "all that is mortal of her, lies—lies for me to see, to notice well the havoc and desolation I have made. She could with her dying breath have cursed me, and I should have deserved it—ay, I should have deserved it; but, no, no, angel-like, she has forgiven one who merits her misfortunes and end."

Somewhat relieved from the excitement the first view of the house had excited, he pushed his way onward, resolving within himself to exhibit as little as possible of the intense feelings of self-accusation and deep grief when he arrived at the house to see her body.

"These people are used to this kind of thing," he said, "and they look but coldly on grief, and they reason correct enough, perhaps, that it ought to be a matter to rejoice at, when any of these unfortunate creatures are released from their troubles, for a life of madness or insanity must be very dreadful."

He rang at the outer gate, and soon after he was admitted by the attendant, who knew him at sight; he was next shown into a comfortable enough parlour, and in a few moments after, Mr. Spalding entered the room.

"Ah, Mr. Lowe," he said, "this is a sad occasion you come upon this time. Sad in one sense, and yet it may be considered as an event that is more to be rejoiced at than deplored, for where there is no hope of amendment, it is a sad thing to know they are always in a state which is life, without any knowledge of self or of existence."

"It is true," said Lowe, "very true; and yet when there are circumstances which endear another to us, we can feel little else than sorrow at their departure, though their life is useless to themselves."

"Yes, that is true. I, of course, reason more, and feel less than if I were placed as you."

"Precisely. Can you inform me what took place at her death?"

"Yes; I was with her during the last hour she lived," said Spalding.

"Was she sensible? I believe your letter said so, though, at last?" said Lowe.

"Yes, she was restored to a state of perfect consciousness before she died, perfectly sane. It was a sure sign her death was at hand, and knowing that I would not leave her, in case she should have anything she desired to say in her last moments."

"Yes, yes; it was very right and considerate," said Nicholas Lowe, with a long breath.

"She mentioned several particulars to me," continued the proprietor of the house, "and the last thing she remembered was her wedding-day, the day she fell ill on."

"Yes, yes," said Lowe.

"And then she inquired what had become of herself, and you, too, since that period. Of course I answered that she was incapable of doing the smallest thing for herself, or even to keep out of the way of accident, and that she had been taken care of here. She said she could recollect nothing, and had no doubt she was well used. After that, she inquired where you were, and if you could come and see her.

"'I am dying,' she said; 'I see and know all now. Oh, send for him, send for him! I wish to see him, to assure him that I do not blame him, I do not curse him. I love him—ay, to the very last. Pray assure him of it, and yet, if I could but see him, I should die happy.'"

Lowe could not contain his emotion. His self-accusing conscience told him how little he deserved such love, such devotion.

"I told her I would send for you, but you could not possibly arrive until to-day.

"'That will be too late,' she said, 'too late; but tell him I die contented and happy. But charge him to seek my mother and father, and tell them I thought of them. Give my love to them and let them believe I am in peace.'

"A little while before she died, she again said she was perfectly satisfied with you, and begged I would not let you think for a moment that she felt aught that could in the least be construed into regret or anger.

"'Tell him,' she said, 'that if there has ever happened anything with which he could blame himself, tell him now to forget it, it is all over; and if I have anything to forgive, I do forgive it most freely, and most heartily. May Heaven bless him, is the last and dying wish of his Laurelle.'

"Then, after a while, she added,—

"'Tell him to think of me after I am gone; tell him not to forget me. I would I could see him; but since I cannot, I must be content. I die in peace and good-will to all.'

"These were her last words, sir; and they, to my mind, seemed to represent her in a truly amiable light. She was very sincere; her tone and manner showed she was sincere; her whole heart seemed thrown into her assurance."

"What was the immediate cause of her first illness?" inquired Nicholas.

"Some symptoms of general derangement—nothing in particular. I'm inclined to think it is a decline, she has fallen away so much less in her face than elsewhere. No doubt the seeds have been long since sown."

"No doubt, no doubt," said Lowe; "she has suffered much at one time and another—very much, indeed; she deserved a better fate."

"If she were ever like what she was yesterday, in her moments of health and sanity, then I must say she was a rarity that deserved to be prized."

"She did deserve to be prized. She was ever what you saw of her then," said Nicholas, despondingly. "She was always good, beautiful, and amiable. But, alas! she is now no more."

"No," replied Mr. Spalding; "but that is our common lot; it does not belong to her only; we all of us must come to that complexion at last, sir. It's a common fact."

"Can I see the body?"

"Certainly."

Nicholas now summoned up his courage to look upon the face of the dead—that dead whom, while living, he had so much injured, but who had, at the last moment of life, so freely forgiven him of all his unkindness.

"Will you follow me," said the proprietor, "and I will lead you to where she lies."

"Lead on," said Lowe; and he followed Mr. Spalding from the parlour to a large light room at the back of the house.

"Here," he said, taking a key and unlocking the room door; "here we have placed her; it is an unoccupied room, and has been used for a similar purpose before."

As he spoke, he pushed the door open, and then walked up to the window, which he opened, and drew up the blind to let in light enough.

The room was bare of furniture. There was a bedstead in the room, but the furniture had been stripped off, and a sheet was the only covering of the bed.

Nicholas Lowe trembled, despite all his efforts to the contrary. He could not stand without the aid of the bed, against which he stood in uncertainty of what to do.

He raised his hand to turn down the sheet, but his hand shook so violently that he could not do it.

"Allow me," said Mr. Spalding, as he stepped forward, with some politeness, and turned down the sheet, and then left the apartment.

Lowe stood still; now he was transfixed, nay, fascinated to the spot, by the sight of those beautiful features reposing in death.

Notwithstanding the grim hand of the destroyer had visited her, yet there was much sad beauty in that calm face, with its closed eyes—nay, there was a smile even on her lips, and a slight dimple on her cheek, at least Lowe thought so; there was an air of the most perfect sweetness and kindness in the face—so expressive of kindness and love that it was scarce possible to believe in death.

"Great God!" exclaimed Lowe; "and is this death?"

He paused, with clasped hands, as he gazed long and steadfastly on the body.

"So young," he murmured; "so young, so beautiful, and withal so good, to die so early, and such a death, is truly horrible. What has life been to thee, thou unfortunate one?—a scene of toil and trouble, of disappointment, want, and woe—all else was denied thee ; and he who should have cherished thee, and kept thee, and stood between the world and thee, wronged thee, and brought misery and madness upon thee. Oh, Heavens! and yet Laurelle, thou forgavest him all his sins and all his transgressions, and died with his name and a blessing on thy lips. Good Heavens! what a monster of selfishness and criminality must I not be to live, and know all this. Oh, Laurelle, had you but lived, I had been happy; but thou art gone to a happier sphere than this, where no treacherous lover will seek thy ruin."

He paused. Tears dimmed his sight; deep sobs burst from his bosom, and he bowed his head on the breast of the corpse, in utter prostration of all spirit. He remained thus giving vent to the wildest grief until its violence somewhat subsided, and then he kissed the cold lips of the corpse ; then, replacing the sheet over the face, after one long, last look, he turned and left the room.

He was allowed some time by Mr. Spalding to recover himself—for that person had been a spectator to some of his grief, and considerately kept out of the way, and when he did enter, he said,—

" Well, Mr. Lowe, this is a very sad affair. But is there anything else you would have had done ?"

" Nothing, Mr. Spalding. Though this is an unhappy affair, yet there is nothing, as things go, that I would have had otherwise."

" I did all that I could think of at the time, sir ; but strangers are not always so happy in their attempts as relations ; however, since you are satisfied, I am."

" Did she say anything about where she would like to be buried ?"

" She never mentioned the subject once."

" Or anything connected with her relations—whether she left any messages ?"

" Nothing more than what I have informed you of already, sir ; but have you any particular desire for her burial ?"

" None—none."

" Then you will have the burial, I presume, in the neighbourhood ?"

" Yes ; in some place near at hand, where there is a quiet, unpretending grave-yard."

" There is one, then, sir, that I have often admired, not far hence. The funeral —how would you like it attended to ?"

" Plain—quite plain, but respectable ; and a gravestone, for which I will furnish you with the inscription ; and last, not least, I will leave you funds in hand to de-fray all these things, and then tell me when the funeral will take place."

" On Sunday morning next, sir, I think we shall have all in readiness, and then every mark of respect that can be paid her will be shown."

* * * * * * * *

It was with sad and bitter thoughts, that he came back to London a sadder man than even he had that morning left it.

* * * * * * *

The graveyard was an old-fashioned one ; the church was one of those old, grey, turreted buildings, square and plain, of which many are to be seen in different parts of the country, at a distance from town.

It was well known to the villagers and inhabitants there about that one of the unfortunate people in Abney-house had died, and would be buried there that morn-ing. A burial to them was something of a rarity ; it was not with them as it is with the metropolitan districts, where they are frequent and numerous, and each hour the passing bell tolls for some human being who has lapsed into eternity, and become what he was before he existed.

There were a few of the inhabitants gathered together in different groups, to wit-ness the burial—such a sight was looked upon by them as a curiosity ; and they were eager to see what sort of people would follow the mad woman to the grave— whether she had any friends or not, and if they could discover what they were by their appearance.

The morning came, the sun shone on the old churchyard, and there was the sexton, too, in his vocation—a great man was he on burying days ; it was e one on which he esteemed himself equal to any thereabout.

And then the admiring rustics, too, as they gazed over the deep pit, shuddered and thought it was an awful time when it would be necessary for them and their friends to inhabit such deep pits in the earth.

Here and there, too, were bits of bones, the remnants of some being who has long since been forgotten, and whose very bones were becoming, and had in parts become, entirely amalgamated with its parent earth.

Alas! what sad thoughts such sights conjure up in the busy minds of contemplative men. How short a time seems to enable the living to forget the dead; and then those who have but few relations—men and women who have few to care for them, or whose peculiar circumstances or dispositions did not endear them to the living—how soon they are forgotten; and yet they belong to the great family of man—they had their hopes and fears; they, too, would have had the same fear of death, they breathed the same breath of life with the living.

And yet all are subject to the same law, and the man who would be rich and beloved, can no more escape the doom of man, or, having paid the debt of nature, he can no more preserve his bones from the cankerous decay, or his flesh from the worm, than could the poorest and most contemned among men.

But such is the nature of humanity; the world goes round in the old way, never heeding the great truths, or, heeding them, caring but little for them, and not fearing, or deeming the events too distant to merit attention.

The hour came, and the tolling of the bell sounded dismally on the ear, and at variance with the clear light air of the morning, and the rays of the sun which shone, while the lark soared high in the heavens, heedless of the solemn occasion below, and carrolling the joyous notes of thankfulness out on high.

" When will they be here ?" inquired one of the bystanders.

" Oh, soon enough," said the sexton.

" Ay ; but is that the hour ?"

" Yes, as far as I know."

" Who is she ?" inquired one of the females. " Is she young ?—is she beautiful ?"

" I have heard she was both, missus, but I can't say, as I never saw her She'll have no need of youth or beauty now, you know ; you won't be able to tell her from her coffin a hundred years hence, you know."

" I should say not, old fellow," said a young man standing by him. " How long is it before anybody does the pleasant office of digging a hole to pop your carcase into ? It strikes me you won't be long before you are dried, and of a deep mahogany colour, eh ?"

" Are you there, young Jackson ?"

" To be sure I am ; and you are down there, ain't you, you old bone-grubber ?"

" Ay, I shall have many a job yet, and you'll be a customer of mine ; old as I am, I'm a green'un to you yet."

" Green as a turnip top, my rum 'un."

" You've been to Lunnun to larn summut, young scapegrace."

" You've no grace, even in your cups."

" You may talk the largest, lad, but you are too fast to live long."

" A short life and a merry one."

" That's the thing to make old bones before you are young meat."

While this dialogue was going on, the bystanders were applauding this trial of wit between the aged, hard-featured sexton, who was seldom known to travel beyond the precincts of the place, and a youngster who drove a team to the great city.

" Here they are, here they are !" exclaimed a voice in the crowd.

" Who—who ?"

" The funeral and mourners."

" All's ready, then," said the sexton ; and as he flung up his spade, he added,— " Take that."

In another minute he was standing up among the spectators, eyeing his own work with the eye of an artist.

" That's wot I call a tidy grave for a young 'un, at all events."

" Why ?"

" Because it is deep."

" Were there any orders to that effect ?"

" They always has their graves deep, these people at Abney-house."

" The mad people ?"

" Yes ; they are afraid of their being inclined to get up again."

" There's very little fear of that."

" None at all ; the clay will lie much too heavy to think of it."

*   *   *   *   *   *   *   *

That morning Nicholas Lowe had taken his last look of the pallid corpse of one whom he was now about to follow to her last long home, where she would never know sorrow more.

The coffin was screwed down in his presence. He forced himself to view all— to see everything ; he thought it a duty that should not be slurred over because it pained him. Pain him it might, but still he would perform the sacred duty.

The funeral procession left the house. Mr. Spalding attended with Nicholas as chief mourners ; there were but few besides, and they from curiosity, but none from sympathy, feeling, or friendship.

Slowly it wound its way down the remaining declivity of the hill, for the church-yard was built in a hollow.

Sad, silently, and solemnly they paced along, and all the while the bell tolled mournfully on their ears.

As they neared the churchyard, the people who had assembled to witness the procession arranged themselves on either side of the grave, but, at the same time, with a view to obtain a good sight of the ceremony.

The procession slowly reaches the gate, and is met by the officiating clergyman, who leads it back to the church, and then, after a while, they all come to the grave.

Here, then, the ceremony must finish ; and with what depth of feeling did Nicholas Lowe see the coffin lowered into its grave. Then, indeed, he felt truly that she was gone from him most certainly and most truly.

It was a pang to his breast to hear the sound of each clod of earth as it fell upon the coffin.

The ceremony was very affecting, and well calculated to inspire awe and melancholy in the mind of a mere spectator, and much more was its effect likely to be stronger on those who were so closely connected with her who had been so silently cast into the tomb.

He stopped to see the last duties performed ; he stopped to see the grave filled up to the last shovelful of earth ; and, when all was over, he walked silently and serenely from the churchyard.

Not unmoved was Nicholas Lowe a spectator of the scene in which he had taken a part.

*   *   *   *   *   *   *   *

Nicholas Lowe returned to London that night. His bosom was torn by conflicting emotions ; and he asked himself if, now that she was dead and gone, was he not rid of the skeleton that haunted his mind.

" No," he replied ; " the memory of the past will be an efficient skeleton to my mind, either asleep or awake.'"

CHAPTER XXI.

LOWE'S MENTAL FREEDOM.—THE VISION OF THE PAST, AND THE REALITY OF THE PRESENT.—THE DECLARATION.

LOWE was correct unquestionably when he considered that episode in his existence, from which he had just emerged, would cling to him with life ; but still it would not be so bitter as it had been, because accompanying it would be two or three reflections, which would tend, in a great measure, to assuage the agony of memory.

One of these, and perhaps the most cogent of the two, was that the circumstance in itself was over; nothing more could result from it than had resulted—that there was nothing to dread concerning that unhappy being who had now been consigned to the friendly repose of the tomb, except the occasional memory of her manifold wrongs.

His other source of consolation consisted in the reflection that, at all events, at last he had done all that was in his power to soothe an anguish that he could not entirely cure, and hence a partial process of reasoning upon the subject tended to make him feel easier upon it than he could ever have supposed it possible he could be; and gradually the image of the betrayed and heartbroken girl began to fade from his memory.

It is a natural order of things that the more vivid present should exercise an obliterating influence over the past. We may not forget, but we may remember so slightly that remembrance may cease to be a pang, or, at all events, so severe a pang as once it was.

And thus it turned out with Lowe. The beauty and vivacity and the intelligence of Fanny Leslie charmed him sufficiently, almost entirely, to chase away the skeleton of the mind which had oppressed him, and to make him look upon the future as a possible career of delight, which he saw nothing of any very great moment to obstruct.

The only shadow upon his path now was Jervis Rodwell, and he could scarcely be called such, inasmuch as Lowe greatly despised him, while, at the same time, he believed that Rodwell had a secret of his own of a character too fearful for him to hazard its examination.

The only point, likewise, he evidently strove to rival him in regarded Fanny Leslie, and without being able to accuse himself of any amount of personal vanity in the matter, Lowe could not help feeling that Rodwell's chance against him in such an adventure was but as a feather in the balance.

He had seen quite enough of Fanny to know which way the preference went. That language of the eyes, which he was better skilled to translate than she to conceal, had been amply sufficient to convince him that she was far from indifferent to his good opinion.

With a niceness of discrimination, which Rodwell could never aspire to, he, Lowe, felt certain that, on the very first interview, an impression had been made in his favour, and against that of his companion, which could never be effaced.

A day or so now passed away before it might be said that the mere gloom of the actual scene in which we have shown Lowe so recently an actor, had passed sufficiently away, to make him feel that he could enter with spirit into the little cabals and intrigues of the goldsmith's house, and then he began seriously to turn his attention to some still more decisive step as regarded his social and domestic position. He felt, and he felt truly, that the struggle between himself and Rodwell now was something more than a mere struggle for the hand of Fanny Leslie. It was no doubt a struggle likewise for actual existence, so far as regarded the establishment of old Paddlebat, the goldsmith; and, hence, the view he took of it became more enlarged and serious, and the more anxious he became thoroughly to come to an understanding with Fanny, so that Rodwell should feel the contest to be a useless one.

We certainly acquit Lowe of being actuated solely by motives of self-interest in the affair; we only mean to say that it was a coincidence of circumstances which made the jealousy between the two young men view them as a matter of such vital importance to their pecuniary interests.

They had been long enough with Mr. Paddlebat to be well aware of his intention of ultimately rewarding them with a permanent business; and had they not happened to have been of the discordant materials they were, and had not such an apple of discord as the beautiful Fanny Leslie been thrown between them, there can be very little doubt but that eventually a business under the name of Rodwell and Lowe would have been as prosperous as it had been under that of Mr. Paddlebat, with a fictitious "Co." at the end of it, to give importance to the heading of a bill of parcels.

Now, however, it was quite an understood thing between them both—one of those understandings by implication being as plain as any words could possibly make them, that whoever won Fanny Leslie would win the business; after which, the sooner the disappointed suitor crossed the doorstep never to return, the more prudent, necessary, and quiet a step it would be of his.

See page 132.

Just imagine two young men, each of strong and violent passions in his way, placed in such an antagonistic a position—Rodwell without principle entirely; and, notwithstanding some partiality we have for Lowe, we must confess that even he, oftener than we are pleased to contemplate, gave way to expediency.

How far their mutual successes and their mutual defeats might induce them to carry the deep hatred which either of those contingencies were likely to engender, we shall perceive as we proceed; and, come from what side the first act of violence

No. 17.

may, we are not at all prepared to say that it would not have come from the other, had the circumstances been reversed.

It was after some anxious thoughts, and revolving in his mind every little circumstance in the way of hope and encouragement that he had received, Lowe made up his mind to embrace the very first opportunity of so completely establishing himself in the good graces of Fanny Leslie, that Rodwell should have no chance of success, even from any accident; and fortune favoured him earlier than he expected, by enabling him to carry out this project, and at once place himself in the enviable condition he so much coveted, and which was to him of such vast importance.

During that day, as if to further the purpose of Lowe, Mr. Paddlebat announced his intention of getting up a party to visit Vauxhall.

"Fanny Leslie," said Mr. Paddlebat, "was a great stranger to such scenes; she had never seen any similar assembly of people and sights. She would be entertained, and she ought to become acquainted with such sights and places, now she was but newly arrived, and unacquainted with London life; and his great object was to initiate her into some of its mysteries."

Accordingly, the party was made up. Several individuals were invited, and promised to come. Both Lowe and Rodwell were included.

This, Lowe thought, would be productive of some such opportunity as he so earnestly desired should occur.

Mrs. and Mrs. Paddlebat had more than one consultation upon the matter, and ˗ latter made many long lectures to Fanny Leslie upon the proprieties of conduct ˗ observed there.

"˗ou will there see such things, my dear," said Mrs. Paddlebat, "that will ˗u—perfectly astound you; there will be such lights, all sorts of colours— ˗g and dancing, the like you could never have heard in the land of the sa ˗ ˗are say—indeed, it would be quite impossible."

"1 ˗ ˗ ˗en many strange sights," said Fanny; "but, I must confess, I have never seen Vauxhall."

"Well, then, you shall, my dear; you shall—you'll be quite dazzled. I used to be; but I have seen more of life now than I had then; and as for the fireworks, why, they are not to be described, but the fire is all sorts of beautiful shapes and colours."

"It will be very magnificent, I dare say," said Fanny.

"I am sure of it—I am certain of it. If it don't produce a change on you, I don't know what will, except dropping your feet suddenly in cold water, which, I know, takes away my breath, and makes me shiver all over, and that is enough to produce a change in any one."

"But a more uncomfortable one than will be produced by seeing the sights and partaking in the gaieties of Vauxhall Gardens?"

"Certainly, my dear—certainly," said Mrs. Paddlebat, gravely; "that is what I was about to observe."

The intermediate hours passed away, and the moment arrived when they were all preparing for their departure from the residence of Mr. Paddlebat.

The party occupied three coaches, which were waiting at the door for them, and then, when they were fully occupied, about dusk, they were driven along at the true old hackney-coach speed. They rumbled over the stones until they came to the more even roads that surrounded the gardens for some distance.

They alighted at a small wicket, and were admitted upon presenting their orders or tickets, which Mr. Paddlebat had purchased before he came.

They now entered the gardens to take a short walk together, for the purpose of pointing out to Fanny the different places, and the use made of them.

The garden was beautifully illuminated by thousands of variegated lamps, arranged to represent fantastic figures, and in contrast to their colours, which caused a beautiful and novel sight, and shed a subdued light upon the walks of the garden.

There were many long and circuitous walks leading to different parts of the garden, and in some parts the foliage was so thick that the light could scarcely be said to penetrate them.

Here were lonely, unfrequented walks, and there were others brilliantly illuminated, and filled with the gayest of the inhabitants of London.

The saloons and refreshment-rooms were splendidly furnished and arranged for the comfort and convenience of the visitors ; and, notwithstanding their great extent and spaciousness, and the number of attendants, yet it was frequently a matter of difficulty to obtain what you desired.

Dancing was carried on to some extent, and the place became heated and warm. Then the visitors could walk out into the cool walks that led to the more unfrequented parts of the gardens, and refresh themselves, and enjoy the change of the heated rooms and lively scenes to the cool, refreshing breezes that floated through the trees.

Here the whole party of the Paddlebats were walking about apparently more desirous of moving from place to place, from object to object, than in settling down in any part of the gardens.

The various amusements which the royal property contained and presented to its visitors were, even at that time, when the glory of Vauxhall may be said to have in some measure departed, amply sufficient to entrance the spirits of the young and the enthusiastic. With all the magic of its millions of lamps, and the artificial means which were resorted to to give a boundless perspective to the scene, those gardens seemed in themselves to realize some of the most vivid descriptions of eastern magnificence.

And although to only one of that party was the scene entirely new, yet to all it had its charms, and not the less so that there was one whose delight knew no bounds, and who discovered a subject for fresh rapturous exultation in every new vista or pageant that presented itself.

"Oh, this is indeed beautiful," said Fanny Leslie, as she hung upon the arm of Lowe, and looked down the long Italian walk, which was before her, in all its prodigality of lights, fountains, and statues. "What an immense extent must that be, Mr. Lowe!"

"I would not," said Lowe, "destroy the charm of a picturesque delusion ; but the walk is comparatively short to what it seems. These arches of lamps are so arranged as to give a false perspective to the scene."

"Is it indeed so?"

"Yes, Miss Leslie ; and if you will accompany me down the walk, you will soon perceive that what appears a long arcade of beauty is but a cheat upon the senses."

"Nay," said Fanny ; "we will not part company. Where are our friends?"

She turned hastily, and found that they were alone, a few paces down that picturesque promenade.

"Ah, they have all scampered off," said Lowe, "to some tight-rope dancing. Heard you not a bell ring while we were conversing?"

"I did, but noticed not any one's departure. This spot was crowded a few minutes since, and now how silent and deserted it appears. Let us join our friends."

"This way, then," said Lowe ; and he led her down the avenue for some distance, after which, turning abruptly to the left, they came upon a wooded spot, where the pathway was extremely narrow, and but here and there, placed over the bushes, a glimmering light to mark the devious track.

"Let us be quick," said Fanny. "What place is this?"

"This is called the dark walk," said Lowe ; "sacred to lovers' meetings and the whispering of lovers' vows of affection, which, whether true or not, borrow a romance from the beauty of the spot."

"Indeed!"

"Yes ; but we are alone here, Miss Leslie. It is not often, until the amusements are over, that soft footsteps tread this Arcadian grove."

He had paused, and Fanny Leslie lingered likewise, although in a low, faint voice, she said,—

"Why do we stop here? We ought certainly to hasten and join our party."

" Nay," said Lowe, " haste is needless ; they are no doubt enjoying an exhibition more consonant to their tastes than to ours. Miss Leslie, will you hear me for one moment, and pardon that which I am about to say ?"

" Pardon, do you say, Mr. Lowe ?"

" Yes, Miss Leslie, yes."

" Can you have anything to say which requires a pardon from me ?"

" Indeed, I fear I have."

" Then leave it unsaid."

" No, that I cannot—I dare not. I will not play the traitor to myself, after having so long sighed for an opportunity like this to disclose to you a cherished secret, which Heaven only knows if you have guessed the existence of."

Fanny Leslie was silent ; well she knew the secret to which he referred—a secret no longer such to him, since she had heard the few words he had spoken to Leo on the landing of the stairs of her uncle's house. She trembled, and felt as if at one moment she would have given the world to leave that spot, while at another she listened with the intensest anxiety to hear what was about to fall from his lips.

Still in gentle accents she urged him to go, yet making herself no onward movement, and while he clasped one of her hands in his, he whispered in her ear,—

" Miss Leslie, do not despise the expression of an honest passion, because it may come from one in a more humble station than your desert should promise you. The opportunity I have long coveted has now arrived, and I am enabled to tell you I love you. Yes, Miss Leslie, from the first moment I looked upon you, I loved you. Need I say that every further observation a generous fortune has enabled me to make of you has but confirmed the passion of my heart. You are silent. Let me not, oh, let me not think that for ever I have offended, by this too hasty a declaration, one who holds in her keeping my whole future happiness."

" I must not hear this," said Fanny ; " it is madness, Mr. Lowe. You forget to whom you speak."

" No, no—I am fully aware of the extent of my presumption ; but my feelings are too strong to be guided by the dictates of prudence. I am fully aware of my own presumption in this affair ; but, Miss Leslie, may I at least hope for pardon for my crime ?"

" It is no crime, Mr. Lowe ; but—but, to say the least of it, unexampled, and very improper in you to hold this kind of language to me. Recollect, we are but very recent acquaintances, and—and—I hope my conduct has not been the cause of this hasty, imprudent, and I think I ought to call it by a harsher name ——"

" No, no," interrupted Lowe ; " do not do that. I have at least acted honestly. I am sincere even in my presumption, for, I confess, Miss Leslie, how much greater the presumption had it been otherwise. No, be my fate what it may, my love is as deep as it is sincere."

Miss Leslie felt she could not keep up the appearance of disdain or coldness, though she was much inclined to evade any expression of her real opinion whatever at the present moment.

" Mr. Lowe, let me beg of you to forget what you have said, and allow me to return to our party. This matter may be forgotten, and your indiscretion will have produced no unpleasant results."

" Can you, Miss Leslie, think so lightly of my feelings," said Lowe, " as to imagine that having once told such an one as you are, that I love you ——"

" Sir ——"

" Yes, that I love you fondly, dearly, and devotedly. Do you imagine that I could ever forget ? Oh, no, believe it not in human nature, that a sincere and honest heart can forget its love. I am not your equal in position. Fortune, alas ! has decreed it otherwise ; but with such an object to gain, with such hopes and prospects as may flow from your love, what may I not hope for or achieve, or, at the least, make myself more worthy of happiness ? Say, Miss Leslie, that I may hope, and the hand of fortune will then open upon me, and this will be her first gift."

" Mr. Lowe," said Fanny, " I have listened to you not with anger, but sorrow, to hear this declaration. Say no more now—another time, and it may be more in place."

"I cannot be better timed. What oaths and protestations could I not sincerely utter; but I believe you are above that, and yet I should say much, but your coldness freezes me. Give me but one kind word, one token of forgiveness, and you will render me the happiest of men."

"Oh, Mr. Lowe, say no more now. You—you must say no more. I do forgive you. What would my aunt say to me if she were present?"

"I know not, but she could not say I have acted wrong—only presumptuously. But, heavens! what happiness is mine. I may hope that your love may one day be mine, at no distant day, too."

He took her hand within his own—she did not withdraw it.

"Will you add to my happiness by one kind word? I, too, sensible of this condescension to wish to hazard your good opinion by a too sudden and urgent pressing you to speak, but in such matters where the dearest hopes of my heart are concerned, I have the strongest feelings."

"I fear I have already said too much," said Fanny Leslie, "enough to prove myself ungrateful to my kind protectors, my aunt and uncle; but let it suffice, Mr. Lowe, when I say we will talk no more of this subject now. I scarce know my own mind."

"If not now, permit me to speak upon the same happy theme at some more favoured opportunity. I have not Mrs. Paddlebat's good will. I believe I have not paid that petty court to the good lady which Jervis Rodwell has—there is too much trifling and hypocrisy in it; but, I believe Mr. Paddlebat has some discriminating powers, such as men of business usually have, and I have his good opinion, and I have every reason to expect being treated with more consideration than one merely depending upon his employer; but of that I will say nothing more, and should not have said this much, but that you are a stranger here, comparatively speaking. Indeed, Mr. Paddlebat treats us more as he would his friends than his clerks."

"I have seen as much."

"Can I express my gratitude to you sufficiently for having added so much to my happiness—my future joys and hopes are all centred in you, and believe me I will do the utmost I can to make myself worthy of your preference."

As he spoke, he gently pressed her hand, which pressure was slightly returned, and then, emboldened by success. he pressed her lips to his own. She spoke not, a slight tremor ran through her frame, and she resigned herself, and made no more remonstrances of the impropriety of saying that he loved her, which he did over and over again, and extracted a half declaration from her, that she was not indifferent to his good opinion—that she, in short, preferred him before his rival Rodwell.

Just at this interesting juncture, the bushes, or ornamental shrubs parted, and a man hastily flung himself in their path. It was Jervis Rodwell.

"So, Mr. Lowe," he said, as fury flashed from his eyes. "So, sir."

"Well, Mr. Rodwell," said Lowe, in cold, and even disdainful accents. "What do you do here?"

"Oh! I presume the gardens are as free to me as they are to you, for the matter of that, though from what I have heard, I should say ——"

"That you have played the eaves-dropper," interposed Lowe.

"No, sir; but accident has made me acquainted with what is passing. 'Tis most improper towards such an employer as Mr. Paddlebat."

"Allow me to tell you, Jervis Rodwell, that this assumption of hypocrisy is useless with me. You may deceive Mrs. Paddlebat with it, because it looks smooth and pleasant, but not me; and I tell you once, and for all, that I will not be meddled with in my own affairs."

"And I tell you, Lowe, that you have acted wrong in inducing Miss Leslie to stray from her friends."

"I will have none of this impertinence; stand aside; or, if not, I will seek some other path to rejoin those who will be amazed to hear of your violence and indiscretion."

" You go not without me; nor go you at all unless by yourself."

Nicholas Lowe stepped forward, and in an instant seized Jervis Rodwell by the collar of the coat, saying,—

" If you do not instantly rid me of your presence, I will take measures that shall speedily effect what you are so much disinclined to do of your own good will."

" Take your hands off me, sir; or, by Heaven, you shall repent your insolence."

" When you leave the spot, and apologise for your intrusion."

" Then, take that," and, as he spoke, Rodwell aimed a blow at the head of Nicholas Lowe, who, however, avoided it by shifting his position; but he gave one in return, which shook Rodwell.

Miss Leslie, as soon as she saw that violence was about to take place between the young men, instinctively stepped behind Lowe, and when she saw Rodwell, as she believed, strike him, she uttered a loud scream, and rushed from the spot to seek for aid.

Lowe was now thoroughly aroused, and a desperate struggle ensued between the two young men; but Lowe had the superiority, both as regards coolness and strength, and he succeeded, after some difficulty, in hurling Rodwell to some distance, and, as he did so, said,—

" Let that suffice, Jervis Rodwell; do not provoke me further. I am in no mood of mind to put up with this insolent interference. You have sought this, and as you know so much, know that you cannot alter any one particular; be satisfied, I say again. I shall take this path, do you take that."

" No, by Heavens! chance has given you a momentary advantage; but it lasts no longer. You pass not on this path ere you have again tried your strength, and this time it will fail you."

" That must be tried before it can be established," said Lowe, stepping forward at the same moment.

When Fanny Leslie ran screaming away she knew not whither she was going. She desired, however, to meet with Mr. Paddlebat, and, by his interference, put an end to the contention of the two young men.

Fortune favoured her, for, before she was aware of their presence, and blinded by suddenly turning a corner, and coming full upon a blaze of light, she ran against old Mr. Paddlebat.

" God bless me, my dear Fanny," said Mrs. Paddlebat, looking at her in surprise. " Why, we missed you, and were looking for you; but knowing you were in good company, we thought you could come to no harm."

" Oh, no, no ——"

" Well, but what's the matter?"

" Oh, Mr. Paddlebat, uncle, hasten up there, and stop them."

" Go up there!" said Mr. Paddlebat. " Go up there! why, it's nearly dark."

" Oh, you don't know what may happen—part them—part them."

" Part who, Fanny? You speak in riddles, child."

" Mr. Lowe and Mr. Rodwell," said Fanny, who hesitated about pronouncing their names at all, since the declaration that had been made her by Lowe.

" Oh," said Mr. Paddlebat, " what is the matter with my child?"

I daresay," said Mrs. Paddlebat, " that Lowe has said something uncivil to Mr. Rodwell, for I am sure he would never offend so much as a fly, and, as human nature is human nature, it won't be trod on as a worm, which will turn again."

" I'll see to this," said Mr. Paddlebat, and he walked forward at an increased pace; but the curiosity of the party induced them to walk almost as fast as Mr. Paddlebat himself, and they would have gone faster, but for fear he might have over exerted himself on the occasion.

As it was, however, they permitted him to keep about six or seven yards a-head, and when he came up with the belligerents, they remained a short distance in the rear.

However, there was nothing shocking, nor was there anything to faint or scream about. They were standing apart, with angry and flushed countenances; but nothing had passed that could give any character to the scene.

"What is the meaning of this?" inquired Mr. Paddlebat. "Is this decent or decorous in you two to frighten a young lady, because you preserve your disagreements, and allow them to break out at such a moment?"

Both Rodwell and Lowe were silent, the latter waiting till the former spoke, endeavouring, if possible, to ascertain the nature of the explanation he would give before he would venture to give one.

"I say, what is the meaning of this?"

"Mr. Rodwell," said Mrs. Paddlebat, "I am sure you will not hesitate to tell us the whole truth."

"It is a thing that has sprung from a trifle, I believe," said Rodwell to Mrs. Paddlebat, for he strove to gain her goodwill, and thus establish himself in the favour.

"Then why allow it to spoil the harmony of a party like the present?"

"I regret, exceedingly regret it; but we have had a quarrel; but that is passed now."

"Are you sure?"

"Yes, sir."

"And what was the quarrel about?" inquired Mr. Paddlebat.

"Oh, only some of the illusions that have taken place this evening. I say they are illusions, and we quarrelled."

"Yes," said Lowe, "they are, I am perfectly sure, with Mr. Rodwell, illusions in one sense of the word; but not in the sense he takes them; however, 'tis now passed, and I have no more to say."

"Then do not let us remain here; we shall have a crowd of persons about us directly. We shall return home very soon."

"We had better remain and show Fanny the fireworks. Some of the best," said Mrs. Paddlebat, "will soon now be seen; they don't send them off very early, usually."

"Very well," said Mr. Paddlebat, "we'll wait and see them; in the meantime, we will walk about and admire the place. This, you see, that we are in now, is called the dark walk. It is used for different purposes to that which we found it just now, being intended for love making instead of quarrelling."

Lowe, Rodwell, and Miss Leslie, were all three silent. They saw, or believed they saw, that Mr. Paddlebat was quite abroad as to the cause of the quarrel between them.

"Mr. Lowe, my dear," said Mrs. Paddlebat to Fanny, "is anything but a nice man; now, Jervis Rodwell is so much the gentleman, and such a nice genteel young man, too."

"Indeed! aunt."

"Did you not instantly perceive it, my dear? it is very plain."

"I dare say, aunt; but you see I am a stranger almost to him, and cannot say much, but listen to your opinion."

"You are a good girl," said Mrs. Paddlebat, much pleased at what she thought was more than a delicate hint of her own superiority in matters of judgment and discernment. "You are a very good girl, and I am sure will be happy, that is, if you attend to the advice I shall give you; but where are we?"

"In the gardens, aunt."

"Yes, yes, my child, I know that—I haven't forgot that; but, I mean, where were we in our discourse?"

"Oh, you were speaking about Mr. Lowe," said Fanny.

"No, not Mr. Lowe, but Mr. Rodwell—Jervis Rodwell, that is ——"

"Ah, one or the other I knew it was."

"I see you don't hardly know the one from the other; but that is no need for your doing so; but you'll see them often enough for that; but there's a great difference between the two young men."

"That I can easily perceive," said Fanny; "they are of very different habits and tempers, I dare say."

"They are indeed. Mr. Rodwell's a nice young man, always civil and obliging. Indeed it is seldom that he has not got some civil thing to say; and then he is so entertaining, and so very sensible—very sensible indeed. Now do what you will with Lowe you can never get anything but a straightforward answer, and that sometimes not what you want and expect to hear."

"That is strange!" said Fanny, who could not help looking upon her aunt's commendation and dispraise as placed upon the wrong object, and given for qualities that ought to be withheld."

"My aunt is kind, and means well," thought Fanny, "but she has not the tact of discovering merit, or escaping the gross snares of flattery. Lowe is no doubt a gentleman, who feels too deeply to be enabled to shine among the flippant talkers of nonsensical compliments."

"You saw they quarrelled," concluded Mrs. Paddlebat.

"Yes, aunt, they quarrelled."

"And you could easily see which was right."

"Indeed, aunt, I was too much terrified to take particular notice; and as you may have observed, I ran away, lest any harm should happen."

"Ay, quite right, my dear, quite right. You did just as I should have done at your age. I should have run away from such contention; but no doubt poor Rodwell was much provoked by the conduct of Lowe. But come and look at the fireworks. There—there isn't that grand?"

"It is beautiful!" said Miss Leslie, glad of any subject of conversation rather than the one upon which she was talking, for she and her aunt much disagreed in this matter; and yet it was scarce worth while to enlighten her upon a subject upon which she believed herself invulnerable, and about which she and Mr. Paddlebat often conversed on the opposite sides of the question.

The fireworks were very beautiful indeed. The variety of form and colour was an agreeable sight, and often grand and startling.

The rockets flew high in the air until they were almost lost sight of, and then they paused a moment, burst, and threw a number of coloured sparks, and then were seen no more.

Suddenly blue lights appeared, followed by others of various colours, that gave and unearthly appearances to the people and buildings while their influences lived.

These strange alternations continued for some time, until indeed they were all nearly exhausted.

"I think, my dear," said Mrs. Paddlebat, "that we had better now leave the gardens; what more fireworks they have to light we shall see as we go home."

To this proposition there was no objection, and they forthwith prepared to depart, and took one more turn round the garden, and then they emerged therefrom.

Now came a scene of confusion and noise, arising from the shouting of linkmen, the plying of coaches, and all the assembled mob of disorderlies who had gathered on the outside.

Their departure, was however, effected without anything disagreeable, and the only peculiar circumstances that occurred at all was the manœuvre that was performed by Lowe, who contrived to get into the same coach with Miss Fanny Leslie, to the exclusion of Jervis Rodwell, who was filled with rage and vexation.

They quietly arrived at Mr. Paddlebat's house, where the whole party alighted, and were entertained to an agreeable supper.

When the guests were all gone, and they were all alone again, Mr. Paddlebat resumed the subject of the quarrel, and said he did not like to see ill-blood between them, and he would insist that they should shake hands, in token of good will and amity.

As they had said their quarrel was about a trifle, and they bore no animosity they could not refuse, and Nicholas Lowe at once stepped forward, and offered his hand, which Jervis Rodwell was compelled to take with the best grace he could, vowing in his heart to be revenged at another time ; and in this he was not less sincere than Lowe himself.

See page 133.

CHAPTER XXII.

NICHOLAS LOWE'S ANTICIPATIONS OF HAPPINESS.—GREAT CHANGE IN THE GOLDSMITH.

NICHOLAS LOWE felt now so happy and contented with the idea of his own felicity, in having, as he considered, so completely won the heart of Fanny Leslie, that he was almost tempted to doubt the accuracy of his own gloomy philosophy with regard to the skeletons.

"Surely, ' he said to himself, as he attired himself with unusual care on the morning following the party at Vauxhall, " surely, if there be any circumstances in this world which could place a man in the enviable position of saying, I have no skeleton now to haunt me, it would be those in which he had succeeded in obtaining the love of one who shall concentrate in herself all that he had ever imagined of loveliness and fascination."

Such was Nicholas Lowe's opinion; and perhaps he was right, so far as regarded the decrease of that feeling which creates the most dismal skeletons of the imagination.

But memory soon came back to him, and he shuddered as a voice seemed to whisper to him,—

"Nicholas Lowe, can you forget the past? Can you obliterate from your mind the madhouse and its maniac occupant? Do you not remember that funeral at which there was but one mourner, and that mourner yourself?"

"Yes, yes," he said, "I do remember. My skeleton has come back again. I feel its ghastly presence; I have a skeleton still. The philosophy, terrifying as it is, is still correct. There is a skeleton in every house."

With a brow on which sat pensiveness now, instead of joy, he came down to the breakfast-room. The inevitable consequence of a great flow of animal spirits had resulted in his mind—namely, in a corresponding reaction and depression.

He looked extremely wretched; so much so that Rodwell remarked it with a pleasure he did not attempt to conceal, and began to think that after all he must have deceived himself with regard to the proceedings of the evening before, for Lowe looked far more like a rejected lover brooding over his disappointment, than one who had, at all events, received all the tacit encouragement he could expect from a very young and an exceedingly sensitive and beautiful girl.

The reader, however, we have no doubt, has seen already enough of Nicholas Lowe to be able to come to a tolerably fair opinion with regard to his character.

He was one of those persons who are easily depressed and easily elated; a state of mind which did not arise from any want of power, but, on the contrary, from the activity of an imagination which at once grasped the whole scope and bearing of any particular circumstance, and so, with all its concentrated effect, brought it at once to act upon the mind and the animal spirits.

He rose happy and elated; there had come across him the gloomy recollection of the past, and he was depressed. Reflection after a time reduced that state of depression within its more ordinary and natural limits, and he became what he usually appeared, rather serious than gay, but to all outward seeming perfectly serene and at ease.

The eye of affection, however, cannot be deceived. Fanny Leslie saw that there was something the matter with Nicholas Lowe, although he had an idea that he had successfully eluded any such observation.

She had no opportunity of asking him if anything was amiss; perhaps, if an opportunity had offered itself, she would have shrunk from embracing it; so that she was only left to her own conjectures. Alas! how wide were they, in her limited knowledge of the world and its ways, of the truth.

She rather fancied that doubts of her affection had brought the cloud of depression upon his brow.

Besides, she could not but see with what looks of hatred Rodwell regarded him, and she felt that the pretended reconciliation which the goldsmith had effected was but, after all, a mockery.

In her own pure and beautiful mind she blamed Nicholas Lowe for holding out the hand of apparent forgiveness to Rodwell, unless with all his heart he chose to be friends with him; but still she could not know that he was not sincere, while, from the expression of Rodwell's countenance as he looked at Lowe, she felt certain he was not.

But the whole of these uneasy reflections passed away when she saw that Lowe had recovered his spirits, and the glance of affectionate meaning that he gave to her when he was compelled to leave her presence in order to proceed to the business of the day, banished every other feeling from her bosom but one of delight, that she was beloved by one whom her judgment could sanction her admiration of as well as her eyes.

A new world seemed now suddenly to have sprung into existence around the beautiful orphan, and she began to fancy that surely now the remainder of her existence would present to her a glorious compensation for the evils of the past.

"The troubles and disasters that I have gone through," she considered, "will enable me fully and thoroughly to appreciate my present happiness. Am I not, in a manner of speaking, now in possession of dear parents, for my aunt and uncle could not behave with greater kindness to me if I had been a dear and much-loved child of their own?

"Ought I not to be most supremely happy, for, in addition to that state of domestic blessing, have I not been, with all the eagerness which bespeaks the fondest affection, sought and wooed by the only human being whom I can love with a different feeling than that which moves my heart's affection in the case of my dear friends who have so kindly provided me with a happy home?"

These were the reflections of Fanny, and we are tempted to ask where was her skeleton?

Alas, she was not left long in ignorance upon that point. It seemed as if the fates had conspired to give full effect to Nicholas Lowe's philosophy, for some few hours after the morning meal, Mrs. Paddlebat called Fanny into her own room, and assuming a wonderfully serious aspect, she said, with a wise shake of the head,—

"My dear Fanny, I want to warn you."

"Warn me, aunt?"

"Yes, my dear. Yes—a-hem—a-hem!"

"Have you a bad cough?"

Mrs. Paddlebat looked vexed, for she could scarcely make up her mind whether this question of Fanny's proceeded from genuine simplicity or not. When, however, she looked inquiringly in the open ingenuous countenance of the beautiful creature before her, she gave her credit for the latter feeling, and she said,—

"My dear, you know very little of the ways of the world, for although you have been to a number of places, yet London is a different place from all those, and you have much to learn in London."

"I do, indeed, believe I have, aunt. I have not yet, you know, as I have been promised to be, been at the top of St. Paul's."

"Oh! fiddlestick."

Fanny looked surprised.

"When I said London, my dear, I meant the people."

"Ah, I do not want to know more people than I am at present acquainted with, dear aunt."

"That's not it either."

Fanny was more puzzled than ever, and her countenance plainly intimated the question of "What, then, do you mean?"

"My dear, you don't know some of the people that you think you do know; that's what I mean to say to you."

"Indeed!"

"Yes, indeed; and you must be extremely careful, Fanny—oh, amazingly careful you must be."

"How, aunt?"

"Why, in everything."

This was rather a sweeping admonition, and Fanny replied,—

"I hope I am careful in everything that it is worth troubling oneself to be careful about, aunt; but if there is anything in which I have been careless, or in which I have not been careful enough, believe me I shall listen to any admonition from you with all the respect that gratitude and affection can dictate."

"That's very right and proper, my dear, and just what I knew you would say; and, therefore, I have no hesitation, at any time, in giving you the result of all my great experience in the world."

Fanny made a proper acknowledgment, and then Mrs. Paddlebat continued,—

" My dear, you don't know the men."

" The men ?"

" No, you don't know them ; now I do.   All their ins and outs, and their wheels within wheels.   There's somebody in this house as is casting sheep's eyes at you."

" Casting what ?"

" Sheep's eyes."

" I assure you, aunt, no one has had the rudeness to cast anything whatever at me since I have been here."

" You don't understand me.   What I mean is, that there's somebody here as wants to be connudling with you."

" Well, I am as wise as ever, aunt."

" One of the fellows—one of Mr. P.'s shopmen—I am sure of it, wants to make you his, but he sha'n't."

" I can assure you, aunt, that he shall not."

" That's right ; you must have a spirit.   He, indeed !—ah, pitiful fellow—a man without a taste.   Psha ! I think I see him marrying into the family of the Paddlebats."

" Give me leave to assure you, aunt, that there is no fear of such a result.   I think him quite as tasteless and pitiful a fellow as you possibly can, and I assure you he has not the smallest place in my esteem, nor never had."

" Indeed !"

" It is so, aunt."

" Why, I thought—I was afraid—I really had apprehensions that you did like the wretch a little."

" You are much mistaken, aunt."

" Well, I am glad."

" I can assure you, that from the first moment that I saw him, I seemed, in my own mind, to place a proper estimate upon Mr. Rodwell.   It is wrong to despise any one, for we are all God's creatures, and as he has chosen to fashion us ; so I will not use that word, but my feelings towards him amount to dislike."

" Rodwell !"

" Yes, aunt."

" Jervis Rodwell ! You—you don't mean all for to say, for to think, for to imagine that I meant him ?"

Now, if our readers were to ask us candidly, and we were put upon our confessions, and compelled to be conscientious, we don't know whether we should be able to give Fanny entire credit for simplicity in this affair or not.   We are rather, on the whole, induced to think that she was willing,—while she practically punished her aunt for entertaining, upon insufficient grounds, a bad opinion of Nicholas,—to give utterance, once and for all, of such an opinion as regarded Rodwell, that no hope could for the future be entertained that she could ever be brought to look upon him in a favourable light.

Fanny could not be ignorant that Rodwell was a great favourite with her aunt, and it would be denying an amount of penetration which she most certainly possessed, to say that she did not perceive exactly from what circumstances Mrs. Paddlebat's good opinion had arisen.   Rodwell had her own taste in dress, and he now paid to her the most fulsome compliments—compliments which, however she might have aspired to raise thirty years before, the world had left off paying to her long before her taste for them had declined, consequently from Rodwell they became welcome, as well for their own sake as for their curiosity.

Alas ! for poor human nature.

CHAPTER XXIII.

THE CANDOUR OF FANNY, AND THE FAMILY DISTURBANCE.

MRS. PADDLEBAT's vexation at finding her prime favourite, Rodwell, so spoken of, and so mistaken as the individual against whom she wished Fanny to be particularly on her guard, that for some moments she could not speak, but kept allowing her face to get redder and redder, until it resembled the Saracen's Head, on Snow-hill, in brilliancy and complexion.

"Do you mean to tell me, Miss Fanny Leslie," she said, "that you look upon such a perfect gentleman as Mr. Rodwell, with contempt?"

"Rather so, aunt."

"Do you mean to tell me you look upon him as a person of no taste?"

"None whatever."

"Well, of all human obstinacy that ever I heard of, that is the worst. I can tell you that it was not Mr. Rodwell I meant."

"Who then, dear aunt?"

"Oh, don't dear aunt me; you know well enough who then. It's that sneak, Lowe."

"Aunt, aunt!"

"I say sneak."

"How can you apply such an epithet to one who, in both manners and appearance, is a gentleman."

"A gentleman! He a gentleman! Look at Mr. Rodwell, then you may see a gentleman, especially when he's dressed for a party, with his beautiful *brass* coat and the *blue* buttons," cried Mrs. Paddlebat, transposing, in her excitement, those fascinating articles of Rodwell's costume.

Fanny could scarcely forbear a smile, as she said,—

"Well, you know, aunt, these are all matters of opinion, and as such, should not have the power of destroying our good and perfect understanding. Believe me, that when I respect an individual as I do you, I can respect your opinions; but in order that your kind advice to me may not be thrown away, I promise you that as regards both Mr. Rodwell and Mr. Lowe, I shall never forget who and what I am."

Now this happened to be not the sort of thing which Mrs. Paddlebat had been aiming at. She had no objection whatever to alarming Fanny's pride as regarded Nicholas Lowe, if she could, but she wanted all that to redound to the advantage of Rodwell, whom she had made up her mind, so far as it was possible for a third party to achieve such a result, to be the husband of Fanny.

After a slight pause, she said,—

"My dear, I do not wish to make any reflection, but the fact is, I happen to know that Mr. Paddlebat is particularly fidgetty on your account, and he wishes to see you comfortably settled."

"Yes, aunt."

"Oh, it's all very well to say yes, aunt."

"But what would you have me say?"

"Listen to me. There's Mr. Rodwell, as likely a young man as you'll find in a thousand. There's no doubt but he'll have the business. Indeed, he's most competent to take it. He loves you, and some of these days if you have him, you may be lady mayoress,—who knows?"

"But if I don't happen to love him?"

"Not love him? oh! why—why, you may, you know."

"Certainly. But, until I do, I presume I may be excused from entertaining his addresses?"

"Ah, well! my opinion is, that love matches never do turn out well."

"But you would not, on that ground, recommend people to marry, who did not entertain some mutual respect, if not affection?"

"And do you mean to say you do not respect Mr. Rodwell?"

"Aunt," said Fanny, with much real emotion, "I hope that one of the things that made you and my uncle love me, was a conviction of my truth. Therefore, I am certain that you will not be offended with me for candidly saying, that I do not respect Mr. Rodwell."

"Oh, very good—very good. Of course a young girl like you is amazing competent to form an opinion. When I was a young girl, I wouldn t have dared to form an opinion, I can tell you, no more than I would have dared to have—a—a-hem !"

Baby, Mrs. Paddlebat was going to say, but she kept it to herself, and when she saw that Fanny turned aside to hide some tears that were starting to her eyes, she felt some little compunctious visitings of conscience at the part she was playing.

Probably she could have said something of a soothing character, and the little fracas might have ended much more pleasantly than it began, had not a very sincere, but impudent friend of Fanny interfered.

This was no other than Leo, the dog, who had crept into the room, and appeared to have been listening to the dialogue very attentively. Now Mrs. Paddlebat's last words to Fanny were certainly uttered angrily. There could be no mistake about that, and they had produced tears in Fanny's eyes, all of which Leo heard and saw, so just as Mrs. Paddlebat was relenting Leo walked up to her, and without so much as a " by your leave," he laid hold of that lady's ankle.

The attack was so sudden, and so utterly unexpected, that Mrs. Paddlebat believed that her last hour had surely come, and gave a scream to correspond with so very uncomfortable a situation.

Fanny, who was looking another way, could not divine the cause of the alarm, and in the hurry of the moment she gave a scream likewise, when who should bounce into the room but Nicholas Lowe, who chanced to be going up stairs at the moment, and heard the cries of alarm.

" Good God !" he cried ; " Fanny, are you hurt ?"

" Murder !" shouted Mrs. Paddlebat.

Leo gave a low growl, which at once let Fanny know the cause of the disturbance.

" Down, Leo, down !" she cried.

The dog let go his hold of Mrs. Paddlebat's ankle, and crouched at the feet of Fanny, who wrung her hands in despair, as she considered that after this, there could be no hope of inducing Mrs. Paddlebat to continue Leo's presence in the house.

But the good lady had gone into hysterics, and was probably unaware that Leo had been the cause of the effect, so that Lowe said,—

" Fanny, send Leo away out of the room, and Mrs. Paddlebat may not, when she comes to herself, accuse him at all."

This was a happy thought, and at once carried into effect ; Leo was ordered off, and he went at once in obedience to the command of Fanny, who then said to Lowe,—

" Lowe, leave this room at once, I beg of you, Mr. Lowe. If you are found here, Heaven only knows what may be said."

" Dear, dear Fanny."

" Hush, hush ; go at once."

He folded her unresistingly in his arms for a moment. He kissed her soft cheek, and then in a delirium of joy he dashed from the apartment, meeting on the landing immediately outside Rodwell, who was as pale as death, and looking all the hatred that he felt.

" So !" he said, " so !"

" Well, sir."

" This is well with a vengeance."

" Mr. Rodwell, don't stand in my way."

" D—n you, I will stand in your way, and as often as I like too. You are a pretty fellow indeed, who is to get out of the way of ——"

" Are you mad ?"

" No, but I think you are. What do you suppose Mr. Paddlebat would say, to Nicholas Lowe being in his bedroom ?"

" Nothing to Jervis Rodwell."

" But it shall be something to Jervis Rodwell, and something to Mr. Paddlebat, when I can tell him who comes sneaking up stairs to seduce his niece, that he thinks so much of."

" Repeat that word again, and ——"

" Seduce. That was the word."

" Base traducer !"

Lowe sprang upon him, and after a struggle of a few moments' duration, they both rolled down the staircase together, but at the bottom of it Rodwell took from his pocket a knife, and made a stab at Lowe with it, after, with a furious look and gesture, he had opened it with his teeth.

The attempt failed, and it was not necessary for Lowe to resent, for Leo, who had darted down the staircase after them, now pounced upon Rodwell, and got a good grip of him by the throat, despite several attempted stabs with the knife, which were abortive. The capability of Rodwell to continue any sort of struggle was now out of the question, and he must have been strangled by the dog, who was really angry, had not Lowe called loudly to Fanny to come down and save his, Rodwell's, life.

This she did, as good luck would have it, just in time, for Rodwell had turned black in the face, and had become perfectly insensible.

The whole house, as may well be supposed, was in a state of the greatest confusion, and the only wonder was that, in the midst of it all, old Mr. Paddlebat never made his appearance, although everybody knew, or thought they knew, he was in the breakfast-room reading the *Morning Herald*, according to his custom.

Why he did not appear, we shall presently see.

CHAPTER XXIV.

THE DANGER OF MR. PADDLEBAT.—THE ATTEMPT TO MURDER LOWE WITH THE AIR-GUN.

STILL there was no appearance of Mr. Paddlebat, notwithstanding all this. We do not mean to say that the non-appearance of that gentleman struck any one with surprise, for, to tell the truth, everybody was so wonderfully busy with what was more particularly concerning himself or herself, that Mr. Paddlebat was not thought of for a moment.

We, however, who are in the capacity of spectators of the scene, more than actors in it, have time to speculate upon what mysterious circumstances, or what amount of philosophy enabled Mr. Paddlebat to keep away from the scene of riot and unequalled disturbance that was taking place in his house, and the noise accompanying which was quite sufficient to have awakened the seven sleepers, let their repose be ever so sound.

Mrs. Paddlebat, of course, had no notion of anything quiet in the way of hysterics ; but always when she did patronise that popular female disorder, took good care that it should assume the kicking and screaming aspect, and, accordingly, the row and the noise she managed to make upon a small amount of provocation were alarming and threatening to the peace of the whole house.

Then Rodwell, when he did get sufficiently released from the gripe of Leo to enable him to do anything in the vocal line, set up a loud shout of murder, and everybody who, in any capacity whatever, was employed upon the goldsmith's premises, was, in a very few moments, on the scene of action, as well as two or three people who happened to be passing the door at the moment, and heard the cry of murder, which they conceived, and very properly too, to be quite a sufficient justification for running into anybody's house.

It would seem as if Mrs. Paddlebat above, and Jervis Rodwell below, were trying which of them could keep up the disturbance the longest, for at every scream that good lady gave, he uttered a shout of murder.

Therefore, it may be well imagined how, between them, they managed to keep the game alive.

This state of things, however amusing though it might be, could not last very long, and, accordingly, both the lady and the gentleman, in a short time, got tired and gave up the vocal duet.

Then Lowe thought it time to say something, and addressing himself to the strangers who had rushed into the place, he remarked,—

"There is no danger. The whole of this outcry has arisen because yon dog, which you now see is perfectly quiet, laid hold of that man."

"Is that all ?"

"It is, I assure you."

"Well, now, the idea of a fellow calling out murder because a dog laid hold of him. I never heard anything better than that in all my life."

"Absurd as it appears, I assure you it is the real and only cause of all the tumult you heard."

The people looked, as well they might, very angry at Rodwell ; for to have one's feelings excited with the idea of a murder, and then find out after all that it's only an affair of a dog, is really aggravating."

As for the discomfited ruffian himself, he now sat on the lowest stair of the flight, down which he and Lowe, in their struggle, had been precipitated, looking so confused that he was unable to say one word in his own exculpation or defence, to the people.

Nicholas Lowe whispered to Fanny,—

"Get up stairs to your aunt, dear Fanny, and leave me to manage with this fellow ; he is not dangerous now."

Fanny gave Lowe an appealing glance, which said as plainly as any language could have spoken it,—

"For my sake, be careful of your safety ;" and then she followed his advice, and at once ascended to her aunt's chamber.

Nicholas Lowe, reasonably enough, certainly, entertained a notion that the affair which had just taken place might be represented in such a light to Mr. Paddlebat as to do him a vast amount of injury.

There could be no mistake whatever about his being where he could have no business at all, namely, in the bedroom above stairs, and that Rodwell had had the good fortune to be peeping at the very moment that he, Nicholas Lowe, had the temerity to clasp in his arms the beautiful Fanny Leslic, which had been made sufficiently manifest by what Rodwell had said.

Under these circumstances, although Nicholas Lowe did not, perhaps, adopt the most dignified course he could, he adopted a very politic one, which consisted in endeavouring to make an implicit bargain with Rodwell.

Approaching that individual, he said,—

"Mr. Rodwell, you used a knife in your encounter with me just now. It lies now on the floor. You must be aware that for that circumstance only, independent of any causes of quarrel, I could have an ample revenge upon you by giving you over to the law."

Rodwell looked at him as if puzzled to know to what this exordium was likely to lead, but what Lowe added soon enabled him to see his drift.

"If," continued Lowe, "you endeavour to make any mischief in this family, by carrying any tales of what you have seen, or what you suppose you have discovered, to Mr. or to Mrs. Paddlebat, be assured that I will lodge a complaint against you, on account of this knife business, before the lord mayor."

"Indeed !" sneered Rodwell.

"Yes ; you understand me ?"

"Oh, of course I do ; there's not much difficulty in that. You are afraid I should tell Mr. Paddlebat that you kissed his niece."

"I disdain to parley with you. I have said all I wish to say."

"Well, Nicholas Lowe, be it so. That's a bargain."

"I know nothing of bargains."

"Psha ! Why need you be so squeamish, man? You are afraid that old Paddlebat should kick you out of the house, as most likely he would, if I were to tell him what I saw ; and as for me it would be inconvenient to be plagued before a magistrate about this knife business, which I tell you I'm glad went no farther than it did ; so it is a bargain.'

See p. 152.

"Call it what you please."

"I say nothing, and you say nothing; so that's understood."

"Well, well."

"Good. All is right then. I shall go and put myself a little to rights up stairs. You had better do the same. By Jove, here come the women."

The fluttering of garments on the stairs announced the approach of some one, and Fanny appeared.

"Do you know where my uncle is, Mr. Lowe?" she said.

"I believe in the breakfast-room," said Lowe, for the first time, amid all the confusion, wondering very much why the goldsmith had not made his gracious appearance upon the scene of action.

"Thank you," said Fanny, and she passed on to the breakfast-room; which, indeed, was, as regards the construction of the house, the dining-room, but at breakfast time, and all the morning, until dinner time, was called the breakfast-room.

Both Lowe and Rodwell followed her with their eyes, and then the latter said, in an under tone,—

"By Jove, I never saw her equal."

Lowe started, for at the moment so fascinated were his eyes by the sight of the beautiful girl, whom he believed was destined to be his, that he had completely forgotten the presence of Rodwell. He, however, made no remark, but ascended the stairs very slowly, for he was fearful that Rodwell might stay until Fanny emerged from the room again, and say something to her.

"Oh, you needn't trouble yourself," said Rodwell, who divined his motive.

"I am not troubling myself," replied Lowe.

At that instant there came a scream from the dining-room, which had so startling and sudden an effect upon Lowe's nerves, already rather unstrung as they were, that he nearly fell down the portion of the stairs which he had just the previous moment ascended.

As for Rodwell, he gave such a start that one would have thought he had been shot, so frightened was he.   And then, with one accord, they both rushed into the dining-room.

"Oh, my poor uncle, my poor uncle!" cried Fanny.

"What is the matter?" said Lowe; "good God! what is the matter?"

"He is dying."

"Dying!"

"Yes, yes; look at him,"

Mr. Paddlebat was seated in the large arm chair, which he had been accustomed for so many years to occupy.   The newspaper he had been reading lay upon the ground at his feet, and he was perfectly motionless, with the exception of a slight movement of the lips, and a strange kind of breathing.

Lowe was really alarmed, and turning to Rodwell, he exclaimed,—

"For God's sake run for a surgeon."

"Run yourself," said Rodwell.

"I will, I will," said Fanny.

"No, no," cried Lowe, "I must."

He dashed from the room, and as he did so, he had the satisfaction of hearing Fanny ring the bell with a violence which was sure in a few moments to bring every one in the house to the room.

In the immediate neighbourhood of the goldsmith there were plenty of medical men;—in fact, where are there not in London now?—and Lowe very soon procured the company of a surgeon back to the house.

"Apoplexy," said the surgeon, the moment he looked at old Mr. Paddlebat, who remained precisely as Lowe had left him.

"And fatal!" cried Fanny.   "Oh, uncle, uncle!"

"Not necessarily fatal," said the surgeon.   "Do not be alarmed.   These attacks often occur, and produce no serious mischief."

"Then he will not die?"

"I cannot say that.   We will do all we can."

The surgeon had Mr. Paddlebat conveyed to bed, which process let Mrs. Paddlebat know what had happened, so that she showed symptons of a fresh attack of the hysterics.

"My dear madam," said the medical man, "if you are going to make a noise, I must beg you will shut yourself up somewhere, where you will not disturb my patient."

"Shut myself up!"

"Yes, if you please."

Mrs. Paddlebat's anger sufficed to keep off the attack of hysterics, as a different mental impression not unfrequently will, and so, after calling the surgeon a brute, she made herself as active as any one else, in attending upon Mr. Paddlebat, who, after being bled by the surgeon, showed evident symptoms of returning consciousness.

"Will he recover?" anxiously asked Fanny.

"I think I may venture to say," replied the surgeon, "that this attack will pass off."

"Thank Heaven."

"Has it been induced by any mental emotion?"

"I think not.   I am not aware of anything which could have produced such an effect."

"Well, it certainly is not necessary that there should have been any immediate exciting cause in the matter."

"Perhaps, aunt, your going into hysterics might have done it."

"Me!" cried Mrs. Paddlebat.

"Did this good lady favour the house with any screaming?"

"Yes."

"Well, of course I cannot assert so much, but where a strong predisposition exists to any brain affection, sudden shocks to the nervous system are extremely likely to produce such results as we have here exhibited."

"Oh, of course, say it's me!" exclaimed Mrs. Paddlebat. "Say it's me all of you. That's right—oh, dear, yes."

Mr. Paddlebat was now sufficiently recovered to speak, and he said, faintly—

"What was it? Who screams?"

"There," said the surgeon; "some scream which he heard suddenly, has been the immediate cause of this affair, but from that circumstance we may gather more hope, that the attack will not be a serious one."

"What is it—what is it?" again murmured Mr. Paddlebat.

"Nothing," said the surgeon; "keep yourself quiet. It was only some cock and a bull affair."

"No, indeed it wasn't," said Mrs. Paddlebat, "a cock or a bull. It was a Newfoundland dog; so you see doctors are not always right."

"Madam, I admit the fallibility of the profession," said the surgeon. "Mr. Paddlebat, do not rise till I see you again, when I shall be able to come to a better judgment on your case."

He left the sick man, and Fanny followed him to ask him his candid [opinion about her uncle.

"Why, it is just possible," he said, "that some serious illness may ensue, and you know your uncle——I believe you said he was your uncle?"

"Yes, yes."

"Well, you know he is not a young man, and therefore we cannot expect to do a great deal for him."

"True—most true."

"But hope for the best, as the best I think is most likely to occur, than what we may call the worst."

This opinion was rather ambiguous than satisfactory, but Fanny was compelled to be satisfied with it, and to extract what hope and consolation from it she might, although her fears pointed to the worst result.

It will be remembered that Nicholas Lowe, in consequence of the coming down stairs of Fanny, and then her sudden alarm in the breakfast-room, had not had time to repair to his own room to free himself from the consequences, in the shape of torn apparel, of the contest he had with Rodwell.

Now, however, that all was done for Mr. Paddlebat that could be done, he went at once to perform his ablutions and put on another coat.

While intent upon these common-place operations, a circumstance occurred which filled him with suspicion, that Rodwell yet meditated towards him some serious mischief.

CHAPTER XXV.

THE NIGHT ATTACK.—THE MYSTERIOUS BULLET.

HE had taken off his coat and had washed his hands and face, when, upon pouring out some water from a toilette bottle into a glass, he fancied he saw some singular looking white floating particles of something in the glass, which evidently came out of the bottle along with the water.

This discovery he just made in time to save himself from drinking the water, which he had fully intended to do, and suddenly as it was possible for such a thought to enter any mind, came the idea across his, that this was an attempt to poison him.

He laid down the glass and shuddered, while a cold perspiration broke out upon his brow, at the dreadful thought of how near he had been to a terrible and an agonising death.

It was some moments before he could command himself sufficiently to speak, or think clearly upon the subject, and then his first movement was to close his room door carefully and lock it.

Then he sat down, and as he wiped from his brow the perspiration that had started on it, he said,—

"This is an attempt to poison me, and such being the case, by whom, in all this house, would it be done but by Rodwell?"

Certainly admitting the first proposition, that it was an attempt to poison him, the second formed a very fair and rational consequence to it.

After a time he strained off the water very carefully, and succeeded in retaining a portion of the white powder which certainly must have been placed in it by some one.

For fear of accident he threw away the water, and even then, lest some portion of what he supposed to be deadly poison, should be lingering in any corner of the bottle, he thought it safest to break it, which he accordingly did. The glass was easily thoroughly cleaned out, so that there could be no occasion to destroy it.

He then placed the powder he had obtained where it would dry, and locking his door outside lest any one should go in and disturb it, he proceeded down stairs to the shop with as unconscious a look as he could assume.

Rodwell was there.

He saw that the moment he entered, Rodwell cast upon him a quick, strange, hasty glance.

"The villain," thought Lowe; "he fancies now that he has destroyed me."

Nothing was said upon either side for some minutes, and then Rodwell, in a voice of affected friendship, suddenly remarked,—

"Mr. Lowe, I have been thinking over matters this morning more deeply than I usually do."

"Have you?"

"Yes; and I think that, situated as we both are, we are both very much to blame."

"Indeed!"

"Ay; we ought to be the best of friends, instead of cutting each other's throats in this way that we are continually doing."

"I never have had any objection."

"Objection to what?"

"To be the best of friends."

"Well, well; perhaps it's my fault. I'm short tempered and I know it. I now see my error, and after that, you don't, I suppose, want me to say any more upon such a subject matter."

"Certainly not."

"Why should not we pull together, Mr. Lowe, instead of different ways? Now, there's Mr. Paddlebat, he cannot last long you know."

"No, not very long. Life is proverbially uncertain."

"It is indeed. We are, in a manner of speaking, here to-day and gone to-morrow."

"Most true."

"Well, then, let us be friends."

"Agreed."

"I will own to you, that from the first moment that I looked upon her, I loved Miss Fanny Leslie, but I am not so blind, Lowe, as not to see that she prefers you, and that I can have, consequently, no chance; I give up the pursuit then at once and frankly, with all its attendant jealousies."

"That is frank and candid."

"I am glad to hear you say so. And now, if you will say to Fanny and to Mrs. Paddlebat, and to Mr. Paddlebat, that you and I are good friends, and that you are convinced of my good feelings towards you, I shall feel much more comfortable."

"I will take an early opportunity."

"Now, do so now. There's nothing like striking while the iron's hot, you know, Mr. Lowe."

"Yes, I know that—but ——"

"But what?"

"Why, somehow or other, I—I ——"

"What?" cried Rodwell, eagerly. "Speak, speak."

" Why, I don't feel very well somehow."

Rodwell sprang up from his seat and uttered an exclamation, after which he sat down again, and said hurriedly, and in a general tone and manner which was quite sufficient to confirm all Lowe's suspicions,—

" Not very well, did you say? Oh, nonsense. You will be better presently. It's only one of those passing indispositions which often attack all sorts of people. You will soon be better."

" Well, I don't know, I am rather worse than better."

" Are you really. What—what do you feel ?"

" A kind of burning sensation at my stomach."

" Oh, oh."

" Yes, that's what I feel, I never before experienced such a sensation. It's both painful and alarming. And yet, after all, I think it's only imagination."

" You think it's only imagination !"

" Yes."

" What makes you think that, Nicholas Lowe ?"

" Because it's decidedly better. The fact is, I found something up stairs I did not like, and it affected my digestion a little, to think how, if I had been fool enough to take it, it might have affected it a great deal more."

Lowe, as he uttered these words, looked fixedly at Rodwell, and he saw him turn pale and red by turns, for he was conscious-stricken, and now felt that he had been foiled in his dastardly attempt upon Lowe's life, and that he had exposed himself to all the dangers arising from a suspicion of such a deed, without, in the smallest degree, achieving any result beneficial to his interest.

" You understand me," said Lowe, meaningly.

" Indeed—I—I—do not."

" Very well. Perhaps, if you continue carefully the train of thought which you say you command this morning, it may enable you to come to a correct conclusion."

" What—what—do you mean ?"

" That I know you."

" You speak in riddles."

" And yet to you most oracularly. Now, Jervis Rodwell, beware. I am not, and you know it, in a condition just at present to prove anything, however my suspicions may be abundant. But if anything happens to me, you may rest assured that I shall have made such precious communications to persons whom you do not know, as shall point the finger of suspicion at you, and perhaps place you in an extremely awkward position."

" Suspicion ?"

" Yes, suspicion."

" How dare you, or anybody, accuse me of ——"

" What ?"

" I said nothing."

" No, you paused in time. The word was upon your lips. I say beware, Jervis Rodwell, and look to it."

" You are mad."

" Be it so. I well know that, say what you may now, the words which I have uttered during this interview shall sink so deeply into your brain, that you will never forget them. They are words of terror to you."

Lowe walked out of the place, and after a few moments' silence, Rodwell shook his fist in the air, and with a dreadful imprecation, muttered—

" His life or mine—his life or mine. He suspects me now. Curses on him. It shall be his life or mine. Let me think. Ah! there is a chance. Yes—the air gun—the air gun. I have one that may do me good service yet. Yes—yes; the air gun."

CHAPTER XXVI.

MR. PADDLEBAT GETS WORSE.—LOWE'S DANGER IN HIS EVENING WALK.

BEFORE many hours had elapsed, the medical man came again to see Mr. Paddlebat. Indeed, to tell the truth, that gentleman was more anxious concerning his patient than he chose to tell anybody but himself.

At any rate, and under any circumstances, the attack which Mr. Paddlebat had had would have been amply sufficient to justify the gravest apprehensions, but at his age it would have been something wonderful had he recovered completely from so very serious an affair.

The verdict of the medical man, when he came again, was not so favourable as it had been in the morning, if indeed what he had thus hazarded, of a mere conjectural character, could be called a verdict at all.

"I will not say that he may not recover sufficiently," were his words, "to be up, and to transact the ordinary affairs of life; but that he will ever be restored to the condition he was in before this attack, I cannot hold out to you the slightest hope."

"But is there any surety," said Mrs. Paddlebat, "of his getting over it at all?"

"No surety, certainly."

Fanny and Mrs. Paddlebat now prepared themselves for the worst, so far as it is possible for people so circumstanced to do so.

Now that Mrs. Paddlebat had become fully alive to the real danger of her husband, she seemed to have got rid of a great deal of the frivolity of her character, the better and brighter traits of which now came out in strong relief against her ordinary behaviour, which always had a seeming tendency to some amount of selfishness.

Fanny was much pleased, if anything under the present distressful circumstances could be said to be of a pleasurable character, to see this great change which had taken place in her aunt. She had loved her uncle dearly from that first moment when he had given her so kindly a reception upon her coming to him with that dismal letter, which introduced her to his notice.

But, as regarded her aunt, she had taken time to reflect upon her character before she yielded to her her affections.

The result of that reflection, however, had deen decidedly favourable to Mrs. Paddlebat, and Fanny perceived that all she did not like in her aunt's conduct were but the foibles upon the surface of her character, while a fund of kindly feelings lay beneath that were sure to exert their sway, when any circumstances of real importance called them into action.

This judgment of Fanny's, as it turned out, was amazingly correct. Mrs. Paddlebat was a very good sort of woman, but not being well educated, she gave way to a number of little foolish foibles, which tarnished the lustre of her higher and better qualities.

Now, however, that there was a strong call upon her feelings, no one could possibly have behaved with more tenderness and affection than she did towards that husband whom she really loved with the tenderest and most devoted affection which a wife could feel.

If anything, therefore, could have alleviated Fanny's acute distress at the illness of her uncle, it certainly would be such conduct as this on the part of her aunt, whom she now loved without the slightest alloy.

"My dear," whispered Mrs. Paddlebat to her, "let what will happen, you and I will not part; and if it be the will of Heaven that Mr. P. should be taken from us, we, who both love him, will find some consolation in being together, and in talking of him, and how good and kind he was to everybody."

"Yes, aunt, yes," said Fanny; "that will indeed be a great consolation to us both."

"It will, my dear."

" But yet we will hope for the best."

"Yes. Heaven forbid that I should anticipate any evil before it really comes upon us. We ought to be as well prepared as we can for the worst; and yet I know if it should come, it will, as these things always are, be as great a shock as if we were not prepared for them at all."

Nicholas Lowe found during the morning, as well as the latter part of the day, several opportunities of conversing with Fanny ; and even at that time, when her heart was so full of affliction, she could not help occasionally feeling that glow of satisfaction which is sure to irradiate the young and sensitive heart, when it finds itself loving and beloved.

These interviews were however necessarily brief, since, as regarded Lowe, they could only be obtained when a sufficient lapse of time had taken place to enable him consistently to walk up stairs softly, and inquire how Mr. Paddlebat was since last he made a similar inquiry.

But brief and few as these meetings were, they were to him most delightful, inasmuch, as at each of them he became more and more assured of the affection which he had succeeded in originating for himself in the mind of that beautiful and interesting young girl.

As for Rodwell, after the strange conversation he and Lowe had had together in the counting-house, he had disappeared from the house. Nicholas Lowe was not altogether now without a hope, that the fears of Rodwell had been so great as to induce him to abscond altogether from the place.

The very idea of such a consummation was certainly delightful, but a little further reflection soon convinced him how very unlikely it was that Rodwell had taken such a course.

There was no evidence of such a nature as would suffice to being any consequences upon his head, to connect him with the poisoning of the water in the bottle in Lowe's bed-room ; so that as far as regarded that affair, he had but to keep his own counsel, and he was quite safe.

With respect too to his use of the knife during his contest with Lowe, the latter himself had made an arrangement that that affair was to be allowed to rest where it was.

When Nicholas Lowe came then to consider all this, he gave up at once the flattering idea that Rodwell had left the place.

That he was about some manœuvre, however, which had for its object to do him, Lowe, probably some further and more serious amount of mischief, was but too probable, and he made up his mind to be most specially upon his guard.

He likewise thought it prudent not only to ascertain by a chemical analysis what the white powder was which he had been so near swallowing, but if he found it to be as he supposed it, some poison, to communicate with some solicitor upon the subject, so that if any successful, or partially successful attempt were again made against his life, the finger of suspicion, as he himself had said, should be immediately pointed at Rodwell.

The absence, however, of Rodwell from his duty in the business, compelled him, Lowe, to remain at home the whole of the day, so that it was not until the evening that he could get out.

That, however, was a tolerably early hour, for the goldsmith's shop was always, from immemorial custom, closed at dusk, as the class of customers he had were not such as were likely to come to him later, and he cared nothing for the chance sale of some petty article which might have been the result of lighting up the shop, and keeping it open till a late hour of the night.

Hence Lowe was liberated quite sufficiently early to be able to go where he pleased within reasonable hours, and transact all the business he intended with reference to the dastardly attempt which had undoubtedly been made against his life by Jervis Rodwell.

He ascertained, before he left the house, that Mr. Paddlebat was in a sound sleep, and seemed considerably easier, and, after telling Fanny that he would not be gone above two hours, he at once started.

His first object was to take the white powder he had obtained from the water bottle to some chemist, with a request that he would subject it to an analysis which should enable him to pronounce positively what it really was. After that he intended to go to a solicitor of whom he knew something, and state to him the whole of the affair.

The chemist said, that to all outward appearance the powder was arsenic, but he would not take upon himself to say positively that it was so, until he had submitted it to tests, which could not be applied at the moment.

Under these circumstances, therefore, Lowe had no resource but to leave the powder with the chemist; but he did not think that should be any hindrance to his proceeding to the attorney, which he accordingly did.

This attorney lived in St. John's-square, a very quiet and retired spot indeed to what it once was in its high and palmy days. To get there, Lowe passed down Wilderness-row, in which there chanced to be just then very few people indeed.

When he reached about the middle of the thoroughfare, which, no doubt the reader knows, is flanked on one side by a dead wall, and never very well lighted, a sudden feeling of danger came all at once over him, and he trembled in spite of himself.

Nicholas Lowe could not be said to be a man who was likely to give way to those kind of superstitions which are called presentiments, but the mind will attempt in vain, let it be as powerful or as educated an one as it may be, to battle against them when they really occur.

He unquestionably trembled, despite his better judgment, and despite all he could say to himself about the folly of his fears.

Still he would not go back, although more than once he wavered and thought of doing so.

He walked on until he came to a very gloomy part of the place indeed. It was gloomier then than it is now, and he paused a moment, from some impulse which even to himself he could not define.

At that instant of his pause he heard something whistle past his ear, as if some bird upon the wing had suddenly passed him almost close enough to touch him.

Then there was a blow upon the wall opposite—a sharp, well-defined, cracking sort of blow—and Nicholas Lowe, with an immediate feeling of what had happened, cried,—

" That is a bullet!"

There could be no mistake about it. It was a bullet. Nothing else could, by any means, have passed him so as to produce such an effect.

The moment he came to this most positive conclusion, he at once darted towards the direction from whence it came, or seemed to come, and, before he was well aware of it, he found himself in the shop of a tailor.

The aspect of Nicholas Lowe was sufficiently alarming. A man does not exactly preserve all his equanimity when he believes he has just had a bullet so near his head that an inch or two on one side or the other would have been immediate and certain death to him.

The tailor who owned the shop was at work upon a board fitted up in his window, and when Lowe, with such a look of frantic excitement, rushed in he might well, as no doubt he was, be to a certain extent rather terrified.

" What—what," he stammered, " can I do for you, sir?"

" Who is here," cried Lowe, " beside yourself?"

" Beside myself?" said the tailor; " I think you are beside yourself."

" Do not trifle with me. Have you any stranger here?"

" Not as I knows on."

" I am confident that from here came a bullet which was aimed at my life."

" A bullet?"

" Yes; a bullet."

" What from a gun, do you mean; a real bullet?"

" Yes, yes; and I shall instantly apply to the police to search this house."

" Search away; I only rent the shop and parlour, so I haven't much to do with the house. You won't find anybody with guns or bullets here, I can tell you."

Nicholas Lowe looked irresolute, and then he said,—

" I assure you that I have been shot at by some one as I passed down the row."

" Well, but it wasn't me."

" I do not say it was. All I know is, that from this direction the bullet must have come. What neighbours have you?"

" The houses are all let, and to different people, some of them by the landlords, and some by those who have rented them and live free themselves by letting them room by room."

"This affair is most mysterious."

" I didn't hear any noise, sir."

" No, nor I. An air-gun would produce all the effect without any sound of an explosion."

" An air-gun?"

" Yes. You will oblige me for the present by not mentioning this circumstance to any one. Allow me to take my own course in it."

" Oh, certainly ; I ain't given to gossipping, not I."

" Thank you, thank you."

" If so be, sir, you should want anything in my line, perhaps you wouldn't mind taking one of my cards."

" Oh, I shall never forget this place, you may depend."

Nicholas Lowe left, and hastily walked towards the attorney's, to whom he now had additional and grave matter of suspicion to detail, which he still considered bore a close relation to Jervis Rodwell.

The moment he was gone, the tailor jumped off his shop-board and hurried on a dilapidated coat, exclaiming as he did so,—

" I must go to the St. John's Head, and tell them all about this. There has not been such a good story there for I don't know when. Not say anything about it, indeed. I think I see me. A fellow comes into one's shop with a bounce, and makes never such a disturbance, and then expects as one is not to say a word about it. A likely joke. Here I go to the St. John's Head. I wouldn't miss going to-night for half a sovereign ; that I wouldn't."

Nicholas Lowe felt very much disturbed in his mind by what had occurred: The certainty that Rodwell sought his life now was of a nature which could not for a moment be doubted. First the poison—for that it was poison there could be no reasonable doubt—which had been placed in the water bottle in his chamber, was a proof positive that some one would be glad to see him numbered with the dead, and was making what exertions were possible to accomplish that object.

And if anything were wanting to confirm all his suspicions, this dastardly attack upon him in Wilderness-row would be amply sufficient.

It is no imputation upon his courage to say that, after he had left the tailor's, he trembled at every step he took until he was fairly housed with his friend the attorney, and then he became so faint, in consequence of the violence of the mental emotions he had gone through, that, before he could speak, he was compelled to accept of some stimulant which was offered to him.

The lawyer was astonished, as well indeed he might be, to see Lowe in such a condition, and when he heard the causes in full detail, to which he listened with marked attention, he said,—

" And do you intend to do nothing, as a consequence of all these proceedings, Mr. Lowe?"

" I will do whatever you advise."

" Then the direct course would be to apply to a magistrate the first thing in the morning."

" Do you not think that such a course would only have the effect of putting my enemy upon his guard?"

" It might, but then you know the next time he commits himself in any way, you may not be so lucky as to escape all the consequences of the act."

" True ; but I would incur some danger, rather than that such a scoundrel as Rodwell should escape justice."

" As you please. I admit with you, that there is nothing direct in the shape of evidence against him."

" Nothing whatever. I cannot really accuse him of placing the white powder, which, no doubt, will turn out to be arsenic, in my water bottle at the goldsmith's, although I have no moral doubt whatever upon the subject, in my own mind."

" Nor I. But a man's manner, and his looks, however convincing they may be to private individuals of his guilt, have very properly no effect against him in law."

" I am averse to asking as yet for magisterial interference then, as I do not see what could be gained by it."

" Nothing but a publicity of the fact that your life had been attempted, and that you suspect somebody whom you need not name, which would have probably the effect of frightening him from a repetition of any such offence, because he, if no one else was, would be well aware that the person you suspected, but would not name, was no other than himself."

" Well, well, I will think of it. And, at all events, I will wait until I hear the result of the analysis of the poison."

" Certainly."

" You, then, if anything should happen to me, are sufficiently aware of all the minute circumstances of my condition, to know in what direction to point inquiry."

" Yes. True enough, I am."

" And you might depend that a patient investigation would enable you to point to Rodwell eventually, as the author of the criminality."

" I think so, too. And now, as your nerves have been unstrung by what has passed, you had better take a bed here, and go home to-morrow morning in broad daylight."

" Under any other circumstances than those in which I am now placed, I would do so, but you will remember in how precarious a situation is Mr. Paddlebat."

" Ah! I had forgotten."

" And as Rodwell has been absent the whole day, he may not yet have returned, therefore my presence at home may be absolutely necessary, as in case of any sudden emergency, there is no male person in the house capable of doing anything."

" Well—you are right, but I will walk with you."

" For that I am grateful."

" Come on, then ; you seem in the fidgets to be gone, so I will accompany you at once."

They both started towards the goldsmith's house, and as they went, the strange circumstance of the shot which had been fired at Lowe, in Wilderness-row, fully found them in conversation until Mr. Paddlebat's door was reached.

It was then just ten o'clock, and the attorney, before he parted with Lowe, said—

" By-the-by, did you happen to notice what was the precise time at which you were passing down Wilderness-row when the shot was fired at you, which so narrowly missed you ?"

" I did not notice the precise time, but it was not much past seven when I left here, and I was not, I am sure, ten minutes at the chemist's, where I left the supposed poison, therefore it must, I think, have been a few minutes before eight."

" I think so, too, for you were with me at a quarter past that hour. Good night."

" Good night, and thank you."

Lowe let himself in with a latch-key, and closed the door carefully behind him, and with as little noise as possible.

———

CHAPTER XXVII.

RODWELL'S MANŒUVRING.—THE VISIT OF CONDOLENCE OF GILBERT THE MISER
TO HIS BROTHER.

NICHOLAS LOWE, when he had secured the street-door, went to the head of the kitchen stairs, and in a low voice called to the servant,—

" Hilloa ! hilloa !"

" Who's that ?" said the girl.

" Hush. Don't you know my voice, Susan? It's Mr. Lowe. I did not know if you were there."

" What do you want ?"

" I want particularly to know, Susan, if Mr. Rodwell has come home. Has he?"

" Yes."

" Very well. I'll come down stairs directly, Susan ; I want to speak to you particularly."

Nicholas Lowe hurried into the kitchen, and when he got there, he said to the girl, in such a mysterious manner that he quite alarmed her, and made her think that something of an extremely uncommon nature must have occurred,

" Susan, I want you to tell me particularly, and truly, to the very best of your ability and judgment, when Mr. Rodwell came home?"

" Oh ! when he came home ?"

" Yes, yes."

" To-night, you mean ?"

" Of course. Cannot you understand me? I wish to know as nearly as possible when he came home ?"

" Well, then," said Susan, looking up at the face of the kitchen clock, as if by consulting it now, she would get an accurate appreciation of time past. " Well, then, Mr. Lowe, since you is so particular, I should say as Mr. Lowe came home about half-past seven."

" What ?"

" Half-past seven, I should say, Mr. Lowe."

" Oh ! nonsense. You must, Susan, be under some serious error. Why, I did not myself go out till some short time past seven."

" Well, I knows."

" Then do you mean to tell me that Jervis Rodwell came home almost directly afterwards ?"

" It does seem funny, but you know, Mr. Lowe, a kitchen clock is a kitchen clock."

" Certainly, certainly."

" And all I can say is, as I heard Mr. Rodwell come in, and down stairs he came to take off his boots, because he wouldn't make a creaking, he said, on the stairs, as he went up to his room, which was considerate. So then he says to me, ' Susan,' says he, ' I don't want,' says he, ' to catch cold,' says he, ' by going over the passage oil-cloth,' says he, ' in my stocking soles,' says he, ' so if you will oblige me,' says he, ' by just,' says he, ' trotting up stairs and getting me my slippers,' says he ——"

" Good God ! all this only comes to your getting his slippers for him."

" Well, what else did you want it to come to ?"

" Nothing, nothing. I was foolish to interrupt you."

" So you was."

" Well, well."

" Very good. So as he asked civil enough, up I goes and gets him his slippers, and down I come again promiscuous like."

" What then ?"

" Why, then he looks up at the clock, and he says,—' Humph !' says he, ' it's half-past seven, about.' ' Gracious !' says I. ' Yes,' says he. ' Why,' says I, ' I thought it was later.' ' No,' says he, and then he shewed me his watch, and there it was the same, sure enough."

" Indeed ?"

" Yes ; and it bothered me, for, if you'll believe me on my bible oath, I'm always willing to swear, I was an hour and a half washing up six cups and saucers."

" How ?"

" Why, I went into the scullery to do so, while Mr. Rodwell was putting on his slippers, and when I came back, you might have knocked me down with a small feather or a pin."

" Why ?—why ?"

" Because it was nine o'clock."

" Susan—Susan, can you be so foolish as not to be quite certain about how these phenomena were accomplished ?"

" How what ?"

" I mean how it was that an hour and a half appeared to pass so quickly ?"

" Well, how ?"

" Why, Jervis Rodwell had his own reasons for altering the clock ; and while you were fetching his slippers, he put it back, and while you were amusing yourself in the scullery, he put it right again."

"Do you really think so, Mr. Lowe?"

"I do, indeed; and I particularly desire and request of you, Susan, that you will pay marked attention to this circumstance, so that, at another time, you will be able to recollect it, and relate it as you have related it to me."

"Well, but what has he done it for?"

"That, at present, is but conjecture, founded upon circumstantial evidence, which, some day, Susan, when I have more time, I will fully state to you."

"You really will?"

"Yes, most assuredly; and now, where is Mr. Rodwell?"

"I rather think as he went up stairs to inquire after Mr. Paddlebat."

"Who is better, I hope?"

"He ain't any quieter, because, you know, he hasn't hardly said anything since he was took ill; but Miss Fanny seems to think as he was more composed."

"That is satisfactory, at all events. I sincerely hope he will soon get better. I will now go myself, and inquire concerning him."

Nicholas Lowe left the kitchen. The manner in which Jervis Rodwell had attempted, in case he should be accused of the attempt upon his, Lowe's, life, to prove an *alibi*, was sufficiently transparent; and if anything was wanting in Lowe's mind to fix the guilt, completely and thoroughly, of that attempt upon Rodwell, it would have been supplied by this circumstance most clearly.

Now he might be said not only to know that he had an implacable enemy, but that enemy was sufficiently bold and desperate, brutal and unscrupulous, to adopt any means whatever that should put him out of existence.

This would be to any man a serious consideration, but, situated as Nicholas Lowe was in the family of the Paddlebats, it became doubly serious and most fearfully harassing.

It was not as if he could conveniently fly from such a danger. All his prospects in life consisted in his remaining, and since the affection which had sprung up in his heart for the beautiful orphan girl, Fanny Leslie, he felt that, quite independently of any pecuniary matters or considerations, it would be impossible for him to leave the Paddlebats.

Then, again, how was he to stay with any regard to his personal safety? That was a fearful question, for, notwithstanding his own firm conviction that Rodwell was the man who had twice now attempted his life, he had no evidence which could, in a court of justice, make such a fact apparent.

No wonder, then, that deep anxiety sat upon the brow of Nicholas Lowe, as he took his way up the staircase, in order to make personal inquiries concerning Mr. Paddlebat.

He had not got above halfway up, when he heard a footstep descending, and, upon casting his eyes upwards to see who it was, he observed Rodwell coming down, with a chamber-light in his hand.

Nicholas Lowe felt confident that he had not been observed, by the quiet and easy way in which Rodwell was descending; and now he stepped on one side into a niche on the staircase, which looked as if it had been originally intended for some statue.

Unless Rodwell should happen to cast his eyes actually into the niche, which, at candle-light, was not likely, he would inevitably pass Lowe without seeing him; and this he would have done, had not a sudden idea crossed Lowe's mind of trying an experiment upon the villain's nerves.

He let Rodwell pass him by the amount of about two stairs, and then he stretched out his hand and grasped him by the back of the neck, as he, at the same moment, exclaimed, in a sepulchral tone,—

"Murderer!"

Rodwell, for about a space of time sufficient for any man to have counted twenty, seemed absolutely paralysed, and stood as still as if he had been by the far-famed Medusean head transformed to stone. What pangs of terror his guilty heart endured during that terrific interval, we can only imagine ; no doubt they were almost of a character sufficient to overset the reason.

But this unnatural state could not last. The candlestick dropped from his hands, and, in a tone of voice that frightened even Lowe, the conscience-stricken ruffian shrieked out,—

"No, no—not yet ! Mercy ! mercy !"

Then he took but one tremendous flying leap, like a man plunging into the ocean, and cleared the whole of the remainder of the staircase, falling in the passage with a noise that was sufficient, one would have imagined, to break every bone in his skin.

Lowe was sufficiently satisfied with the experiment he had tried ; nay, it had turned out, in one respect, beyond his most sanguine expectations, for he had been able to go through with it admirably, without, to Rodwell, at all compromising himself ; for, as the former had not turned round to catch a glimpse of who or what it was that had spoken the word which could not fail to find such an answering echo in his heart, he had no idea, and never could have anything beyond a suspicion, that it was a trick of Nicholas Lowe's.

"The punishment is well deserved," said Lowe. "Villain, it is your own conscience which lent all the sting to an incident that might have startled an innocent man, but could have done no more."

Lowe was right. "Conscience doth make cowards of us all."

He knew that as well as Rodwell. If the latter's "skeleton" was more gaunt and terrific than that which haunted Lowe, still he, Lowe, had one that was quite sufficient to make the shadow upon any sunshine he might, in a moment of forgetfulness, picture to himself.

Lowe felt this after he had spoken the few words we have recorded as coming from his lips, when Rodwell went down the staircase so terrifically fast, and then the sudden pang that came across his own heart made him feel that he might be even so frightened as Rodwell had been, although not from the same cause or to the same extent.

There was one circumstance connected with this little *fracas* which, until it was over, Nicholas Lowe did not consider. That was the disturbance it was likely to produce in the house.

The incoherent exclamation which Rodwell had uttered, and then his sudden fall, were events not likely to be unnoticed, and as this thought flashed across his mind, he trembled to think how he might be blamed by Fanny Leslie for being so unthoughtful of Mr. Paddlebat's condition.

This seemed a just enough fear, for a loud scream from the kitchen now spoke very intelligibly of Susan's fears on the occasion, and what a fright she experienced from the sudden and quite sufficiently alarming noise in the passage.

While Lowe, then, was in a state of hesitation to know which he should do—ascend or descend the staircase—he heard the voice of Fanny Leslie calling to him from above.

This, of course, was decisive ; and Lowe answered the call, and proceeded up the remainder of the flight of stairs.

"Oh, Mr. Lowe," said Fanny, "what dreadful noise was that ?"

"A fall which Rodwell has had, dear, which I will blame myself for, and account to you about as best I may."

"But you should have remembered my poor uncle."

"I should indeed. Can you forgive me ?"

"Can I ? Ah ! can you ask ?"

"It was very wrong, Fanny, very wrong, indeed. How is Mr. Paddlebat ? Was he disturbed ?"

"Yes. He is, I think, better ; but I fear his medical attendant does not share that thought with me. He was sleeping, and the noise aroused him. How came it about ?"

"I cannot tell you now ; it is too long a story. But ——"

A loud rat-tat at the street-door announced not only an arrival, but either a very incautious and unfeeling one, or one who had no idea of the state of affairs, as regards illness, at the house of the goldsmith.

This instantly put an end to the colloquy which had been proceeding between Lowe and Fanny ; and which, with the peculiar facility of lovers to keep together, if it be but to say nothings when they ought not, might have lasted until some other source of interruption arose.

"Leave me," said Fanny ; "I hear my aunt's step."

The door not being opened so quickly, it is to be presumed, as he who demanded admittance thought it might be, the knock was repeated louder than before ; and then, notwithstanding her fright, Susan, with a sort of mechanical energy, ran up from the kitchen, and opened it.

The moment she did so, a person rushed into the passage, and that with such an amount of precipitation as to tumble over Rodwell, who was either too much frightened or too much hurt yet to have risen, and whose prostrate form had been avoided by Susan with no small difficulty.

CHAPTER XXVIII.

LEGACY HUNTING.—THE MEETING OF THE BROTHERS.—THE COMMON ENEMY.

THE individual who came into the goldsmith's house with such a madness of precipitation was a little weazened-looking old man, whom one would have thought would have been in a hurry about nothing, but to shake off with his life the load of years which oppressed him, and seek the quiet and repose of the grave.

He kicked, and swore, and plunged, however, when he thus fell over Rodwell, with all the energy of a younger man. Some sort of absolute insanity seemed to have come over him, and all he said was,—

"Where is he? where is he? Why was I not told before? Where is he? You want to rob him, of course, all of you. Where is he? I ought to have known."

By this time Lowe reached the passage, as well as Mrs. Paddlebat and the alarmed Fanny. It was Mrs. Paddlebat, however, who was the first to name the noisy and troublesome visitor, and she exclaimed,—

"Gracious ! it's old Gilbert Paddlebat, the miser."

"Is it old Gilbert Paddlebat, the miser?" cried Gilbert, for it was indeed he. "Is it, indeed? How do you know I'm a miser? Who says I'm a miser? I got my money by lawful trade; that is to say, the little money, the very little money, I have, for I am a poor man, quite a poor man."

"Mr. Gilbert," added Mrs. Paddlebat, "you are not wanted here. You are an unfeeling wretch,—and I can tell you that your brother is very ill."

"I know it; I know it; and that's why I came here."

"Then more shame for you to knock at the door of a sick house in such a way as you did."

"Pho, pho, madame! pho, pho! A knock at a door never killed anybody yet. All a delusion. I ought to prosecute you for letting people lie down in your passage, madam, just on purpose for other people to fall over."

"In the passage !"

"Yes ; who's this?"

All eyes were turned upon Jervis Rodwell now, who, with a bewildered look, was slowly gathering himself up from the floor.

"Mr. Rodwell !" exclaimed Mrs. Paddlebat.

"Ah ! Rodwell !" said Lowe.

"D—n him, whoever he is," said old Gilbert Paddlebat ; "I'll have the law of him ; it's the same as an assault."

"What—what's the matter?" said Rodwell. "What are you all looking at me for? What have I done? If anybody has got anything to say against me, let them say it at once. Who was it? what was it? Did anybody see anything strange upon the staircase?"

As he uttered these words, Jervis Rodwell shook like a leaf in autumn, and cast his eyes around from face to face in such a strange, imploring manner, that Lowe began to think that the shock he had given him would probably be more permanent in its effects than he had anticipated.

"Why, what is the matter, Mr. Rodwell?" said Mrs. Paddlebat.

"Nothing—nothing; I only—oh, it's nothing—nothing at all. How foolish."

"A madman!" cried old Gilbert. "What do you have him here for? Is this the care you take of my dear brother?"

"Your dear brother!" shouted Mrs. Paddlebat.

"Your dear brother!" exclaimed Fanny.

"What hypocrisy!" said Lowe.

"Willany, I calls it," chimed in Susan, who stood, open-mouthed, listening to all that passed. "I calls it willany; that's my idear, and my werdict. Oh, you skinny-looking old wretch."

"Go on, go on, all of you," said Gilbert; "I like it, because it only confirms me in my opinion that my brother is surrounded, now that he is ill, by a set of blood-suckers, who want to get his property from him in defiance of his will and kindred, who of course ought to have it."

"And pray," said Mrs. Paddlebat, marching up to old Gilbert, who looked like a little boy before her, and was completely hidden from everybody's sight; "and pray, you horrid-looking old piece of anatomy, what do you call me?"

"A fat woman."

"A what?"

"A fat old woman."

Mrs. Paddlebat, as she afterwards declared, was so thunderstruck at this atrocious insult, that, at the moment it was uttered, the smallest possible new-born baby might have knocked her down perfectly flat.

But even such an amount of indignation as this had its limits, and when Mrs. Paddlebat recovered sufficiently to do so, she made a demonstration of attack upon old Gilbert, which might have crushed him; but with wonderful agility, considering his age, he started back, and himself opening the street door, he called aloud,—

"Mr. Pink! Mr. Pink!"

A long, thin-looking species of humanity, with a most villanous expression of countenance, made his appearance in answer to the name of Pink. He was attired in a rusty suit of black, which, from repeated brushings, had long since bidden an adieu to any particle of nap, while the collar, cuffs, and pocket-flaps presented a shining appearance, as if composed of oil cloth.

A dirty white neckcloth encompassed the throat of Mr. Pink, and as he came into the house in an odd sidling sort of a manner, as if doubtful to the extreme of fear as regarded his reception, he impressed every one who saw him with the belief that he was one of those crawling reptiles who sneak through society doing the dirty work of anybody—for a consideration.

"Come in, Mr. Pink, come in," said Gilbert, almost in tones of affection; "I am remarkably glad I brought you with me, Mr. Pink—come in, come in."

"Thank you, sir," said Pink; "you are too good."

"I don't know," added Gilbert, "but what I should have been murdered here if I had come alone. Indeed I am inclined to believe I should."

"Murdered, sir?"

"Yes, Mr. Pink."

"You may depend upon it, sir, if you had been murdered, I would have marked them all most terribly for it afterwards."

"No doubt, Pink, no doubt. Ladies and gentlemen, this is Mr. Pink, my solicitor—what do you say to that? My brother is—very ill; well, I come to see him, and bring with me my man of business, in order that proper steps may be taken to do anything that my poor sick brother wishes."

"Yes, yes," said Pink.

"By mere accident, only," continued Gilbert, "I found out how ill my brother was; of course there was no one here who could send to me—not one, not one."

" You would have been sent to, and at once, sir," said Fanny Leslie, " but you cannot forget that the last time you were here you repudiated all the ties of relationship, and in the most marked manner you ——"

" Who spoke to you?" interrupted Gilbert, passionately ; " who told you to speak?   I believe, Mr. Pink, I am right there?"

" Very—very right, sir."

" I came here to speak to my brother about business."

" That then you cannot do," said Mrs. Paddlebat, " if you were twenty times his brother, and not the wretch you are, for he is not capable of conducting any business."

" You hear that, Mr. Pink," said Gilbert, with a twinkle of his little grey eyes. " You will remember that ?"

" Certainly, sir.   Dear me, yes—I am quite delighted to have come."

See p. 142.

" Then we shall be delighted when you go again," said Mrs. Paddlebat ; " for your absence will be extremely good company ; and yours, Mr. Gilbert.   It's bad enough, once in a blue moon, to see something of you when everything is going on well and pleasant, but to be bothered by such a person when one has other anxieties is too trying, so go away."

" Really, madam," said Gilbert, " you talk finely ; I can tell you that I have come here to see my brother, and see him I will."

" I should really advise," said Lowe to Fanny, in a whisper, " that he be permitted to see the state that Mr. Paddlebat is in, after which he can have no resource but to leave the house at once."

"Perhaps it would be better; I will speak to my aunt."

Fanny took Mrs. Paddlebat a little on one side, and whispered to her, —

"Dear aunt, do not contend with the unfeeling man. Do not give him the triumph which, after all, is what he wants, of being able to say, that he called to see his sick brother, and was refused admittance to him by those who could not say their claims of affinity were so near."

"Do you think so, Fanny?"

"Indeed I do, aunt. I think that, to let Gilbert Paddlebat go up stairs and see my uncle, will rather disappoint him than otherwise."

"Then he shall."

"But not the person who is with him, aunt."

"He? I think I see him. Now, Mr. Gilbert Paddlebat, there's the staircase, and you can come after me if you like, and see your brother."

"Can I really. Well, madam, I am rejoiced that you have got those about you who are more prudent than yourself. It's said my brother is a rich man, and from what I see here he ought to be; although how he became such, with people about him who think nothing of standing in a passage with no less than three candles, and one of them guttering down, is to me a mystery."

"You had better skin a flint," said Mrs. Paddlebat.

"Indeed! What a felicitous illustration. I'll follow you, madam, bless you. Come on, Mr. Pink."

"Ye-ye-yes," said Pink, hesitatingly.

"No, no," said Fanny.

"But I say yes!" cried Gilbert.

"No," said Nicholas Lowe; "Mr. Paddlebat is ill, and unable to say who shall, or who shall not, be in his house. During that state of things, Mrs. Paddlebat may order anybody out she pleases, and if she says the word, I will, on her authority, turn Mr. Pink into the street."

"Mind now, mind," cried Pink; "you must not use more violence than necessary. Don't be in a passion, young man."

"Come on, I say," cried Gilbert. "I authorise you to come up stairs."

"But, my dear sir," said Pink, "legally speaking, this is rather a trespass which, although on your part, as the brother of the party, allowed, may, you perceive, on mine be objected to."

"A trespass!"

"Yes, my dear sir, and so you see if anybody were to give me ever such a small kick, after I had refused to go, they would rather be justified, you see, my dear sir, than otherwise, always legally speaking."

"You will not allow him here, aunt?" said Fanny.

"Certainly not, my dear."

"And will you authorise me to eject him?" said Lowe.

"Of course I do."

"Come, come, now," said Pink, giving a spring to the street-door and laying hold of the latch. "No violence. Order me off these premises, and off I go."

"Why, you cowardly cur," exclaimed Gilbert; "what was the use of bringing you, if you intended to turn tail in that way?"

"Now, now, really, my much respected friend and client. My dear sir, anything legal that you ask me to do, you will find me as bold as a lion about. But you know, as a professional man, my dear sir, you know I compromise myself dreadfully by doing anything that is not exactly and strictly according to law."

"It's always the way with one's tools," muttered Paddlebat; "they foil one when most wanted." Then he said aloud,—"Madam, since it must be so, I will see my brother then alone."

"And—and," said Pink, "may I wait here?"

"No," said Lowe.

"Very good."

Pink opened the street-door, and bolted out in a moment, for he thought he saw the most unequivocal symptoms in the world of Lowe kicking him out, and Mr.

Pink rather knew the difficulty of proving that just a little more violence than was absolutely necessary had been used in turning out a trespasser.

No doubt it was a great disappointment to Gilbert not to have Pink with him up stairs. The fact was, that by mere accident he had heard something of his brother's sudden indisposition, and likewise of its character, which he knew was such as almost to preclude the possibility of his attending to business, or executing any testamentary documents. Now, Gilbert had a great hope that the goldsmith had made no will, in which event he, Gilbert, would put in his claim as heir-at-law to his estate, and Mrs. Paddlebat would just be entitled to her third of the personalities.

If his brother had already made a will, of course he, Gilbert, knew well that he had nothing to expect, but although once the goldsmith had asserted he had done so, the miser doubted the fact.

His present visit then had the object of seeing what sort of condition he was in, and whether he was likely to make any disposition of his property. If he found him in such a state of collapse as he supposed likely, he meant that Pink should be a witness to the fact, so that if any document of a testamentary character were to be produced, dated after then, he should be, he considered, in a good and fair condition to dispute it in a court of law.

If, on the contrary, he should find his brother so much better, that there could be no doubt of his ability to dispose of his property how he pleased, there could only be a little wrangle between them, and there an end of it.

It was very far from being with good grace that Mrs. Paddlebat ushered Gilbert up the staircase. Fanny, after a glance of intelligence at Nicholas Lowe, followed them, and then when she was gone, Lowe walked into the counting-house, for he had no desire to have any conversation with Rodwell.

The latter appeared to be in such a lamentable state of nervousness, that, doubtless, at the moment he would have felt thankful if Nicholas Lowe would have associated with him. Loneliness was terrific to him, and after finding now that Susan was the only person upon whom he could inflict his society, he snatched his hat from the stand in the hall, and rushed from the house.

No doubt he went to seek what consolation he could in a neighbouring tavern, as was his custom.

"There, Mr. Gilbert," said Mrs. Paddlebat, when she and the miser reached the door of the goldsmith's chamber, "there, sir, walk in, and you will find what a world of good your visit here has done you."

"Oh, you are very kind," said Gilbert. "You wear a silk dress in the house do you, madam? Well, well, of all the pieces of insanity in the way of expenditure that a man can be guilty of, I do think that of allowing an old woman to convert herself into a mountain of silks and satins, and other expensive fabrics, is the worst."

If Mrs. Paddlebat could have exterminated Gilbert by a look, no doubt that he would then and there have terminated his mortal career.

She bottled up her rage, however, until they should go down stairs again. Fanny, too, gave her an appealing look, which plainly said, "Let him make what remarks he pleases, aunt, his object is to provoke you."

And no doubt that was really the case, for the dismissal of Pink had dreadfully annoyed Gilbert, and he was malicious enough for anything, as we well know.

Gilbert had the kindness to wait a moment, in case Mrs. Paddlebat chose to make any rejoinder to this speech, but when he found she would not, he pushed open the door of the sick chamber, and at once walked in.

He was by no means careful how he stepped, not he. In addition to the feeling of carelessness as to whether his brother lived or died, which he really had, there was to be added now a thorough belief that his dying now without ever becoming sufficiently sensible to make a will would be the only chance he had of his dying intestate.

After such an attack of indisposition, it was not to be imagined that any man would, when he got well enough, neglect to put his affairs in order, unless he were a remarkably weak-minded man indeed.

Therefore, as regarded the fact of whether Gilbert was to get anything or not by his brother's death, it was certainly now or never.

He made ample noise enough to have awakened the goldsmith had he been sleeping, but it was evident that the state in which he lay partook more of the character of disease than sleep.

"Hilloa!" said Gilbert, "I have come to see you."

The goldsmith did not speak.

"Ah!" snarled Gilbert, "I didn't expect to be thanked, so I'm not disappointed at all. What do you have the room so dark for?"

"The light," said Fanny, "offends the eyes of my uncle."

"Does it? Lend it to me."

"Not if you are going to the bed-side with it. We always place it here, at a distance, and here it shall remain."

"Really you are too obstinate to live long, I should say. What stuff! you ask me to come up stairs, and I shall see my brother, and then you place the light so, that when I look I can see nothing but a heap of bed-clothes."

"Draw the curtains, Fanny, for the old wretch!" said Mrs. Paddlebat, "and tell your uncle who is here. He always seems to hear you better than any one else."

"I will, aunt."

"Ay," said Gilbert, "draw the curtains for the old wretch. You cannot think, madam, how much obliged to you I am."

"Hush! aunt, hush! Let him say what he likes," said Fanny. "Nothing tires of its own company so soon as malevolence."

"Indeed!" sneered Gilbert.

Fanny now drew aside the curtains of the bed, and stooping to her uncle's ear, said, in her low, distinct, musical tones,—

"Uncle, uncle, there is your brother Gilbert come to see you."

"What does he say?" asked Gilbert.

"Nothing."

"Tell him again."

"Will you not speak to him, dear uncle? Only a few words, if you are able, and then he will go, and leave you to repose again."

"Eh?" said Gilbert; "what does he say?"

"He has not spoken. I'm afraid he's worse!"

"You are, are you?" cried Gilbert; and before either Fanny or Mrs. Paddlebat could stop him, he snatched the candle from where they had placed it, and went to the side of the bed, saying,—"Come, I must and will see how you are."

The light from the candle fell full upon the goldsmith's face. Old Gilbert started back, and dropped the candlestick from his nerveless grasp.

"Help! help!" he said. "He's dead! he's dead!"

CHAPTER XXIX.

THE CORPSE.—THE CONFUSION AT THE GOLDSMITH'S, AND THE EJECTION OF GILBERT.

YES, the kind, warm-hearted, generous old goldsmith, was no more. He had breathed his last without a sigh; placidly, and no doubt contentedly, he had given up his spirit to his God; and on that bed lay in that long sleep of death which, as regards the mortal tabernacle of the spirit, is eternal, all that remained of the man, who, during his sojourn on earth, had ever striven to do a good man's duty, and who had gathered around many a fond affection, and many a kind heart to love him, and lament his loss.

He was dead. Oh! who shall hope to describe befittingly, the pang of desolation that came across the heart of Fanny Leslie, as she heard the fearful fact announced from the lips of Gilbert Paddlebat!

We cannot say that she was unaware of the danger of her uncle; but what is the fear of death compared to the actual presence of the fell destroyer? What mode, form, or shape of preparation can enable us to look upon the direful event, when it comes with any less degree of terror and affliction than it must always bring with it when one loved, trusted, and revered, is taken from us?

All she could say for a moment or two was,—

"No—no—no—no."

Mrs. Paddlebat sunk into a chair, and then she fainted, and fell on to the floor, while Gilbert stood by the bed-side, from which he seemed afraid to move, as all was darkness around him, and he did nothing but shout,

"Lights!—lights!—lights, here! Lights!"

This noise soon reached the ears of those who were in the lower part of the house. They only consisted of Lowe and Susan, both of whom rushed up the staircase with a frantic speed, that nearly extinguished the lights they carried.

Lowe, the moment he heard the confusion, had a sort of presentiment of what had occurred; and he said to himself, "The goldsmith is dead;" while Susan's idea decidedly took the turn of "Fire!"

It was not to be supposed, however, that Susan could get so soon up stairs as Nicholas Lowe. In fact, her apprehensions had rather the effect of impeding her progress, than accelerating it; for, after she got nearly to the top of the kitchen stairs, she stopped to scream, and, overbalancing herself in the effort, she fell down again to the floor beneath.

With amazing rapidity, Lowe reached the apartment; and, as he went, by some sort of instinct or impulse, which could not be accounted for, inasmuch as he had no knowledge of the fact that the candle in the bed-room of Mr. Paddlebat was extinguished, he snatched from a niche on the staircase a lamp, which it was customary to have burning there after nightfall, and, with it in his hand, he arrived at the scene of confusion.

His first exclamation that Mr. Paddlebat was dead, he found in a few moments to be a true one. The appearance and general aspect of the parties who were in the room was more than sufficient to convince him of the melancholy fact.

The shrinking, terrified, paralysed look of old Gilbert was awfully expressive; he stood cowering with his hands clasped, and looking towards the bed, as if he now expected its ghastly occupant to rise, and reproach him for a long life of hatred and bad conduct.

Mrs. Paddlebat was in a state of insensibility. That lady had a convenient habit of fainting upon occasion of any circumstances of emergency; and it was, perhaps, as well that such was the fact, for she was not likely to be of any very great use in moments of flurry or peril.

The shock to Fanny Leslie had been great; and although, as we have before insinuated, she took but a despairing view of her uncle's condition, his actual death came upon her with fearful suddenness.

The relief she experienced when she saw Lowe enter with a light was immense; she flew to him, and clasped his hand; tears then came to the relief of her overcharged heart, as, in sobbing accents, she cried,—

"He is gone—he is gone! my poor uncle is no more!"

"Hush! for Heaven's sake!" cried Lowe; "be calm."

"As calm as grief will let me," she replied; and she hung heavily upon his arm, while the tear drops fell like rain from her sweet eyes.

For a moment Lowe forgot the presence of Gilbert Paddlebat; he forgot even that he was in the chamber of death; every event and every anticipation was forgotten in the one blissful feeling, that he held in his arms the beautiful being in whose heart he believed he had awakened a sentiment of attachment which would be undying.

"Dear one," he whispered, "be tranquil; death, at the best, I grant ye, is an evil; but when it comes in the ordinary course of nature, and snatches not from us the young, we ought to look upon it as a more ordinary phenomenon than we generally do."

"I am desolate," she said; "I am desolate."

"Nay; now is that not a cruel speech to make to me? Can you be desolate while I live? Can you be desolate while I love you, as you know I do, with an affection above all comparison? Oh, do not—do not wrong me by saying you are desolate!"

"No; I will not, Nicholas—I will not—I did wrong you."

"Your heart is your accuser; but mine shall forgive you. With a deep but a chastened regret, we will think upon this blow of fate, which has deprived you of a relation you revered and loved, and me of the best friend beneficent fortune ever placed in my path."

"True—most true," sobbed Fanny.

"But we will love each other; and all the regrets, all the sorrows of the past, shall merge into that one happy feeling. With that blissful confidence, dear Fanny, we will hold at arm's length the greatest evils which unkind fortune can inflict upon us; the future shall be to us a reality of delight, while we will still cling to all that is happy in the recollection of the past, and all its sorrows shall fade from our memory, like some dimly-remembered dream, which, if we would, we could not retain."

"Yes, Lowe, yes; that shall be it; you speak the language of my own heart; but you can place it in those full and appropriate words which my excited feelings will not allow me to do."

"Ah, dearest, one word from you ——"

"Mighty fine—mighty fine!" said old Gilbert Paddlebat, stepping up, and poking his hideous face between them; "this is all very fine, young people, very fine, indeed; perhaps you forgot there was anybody here."

Lowe started, and Fanny uttered a faint cry, for she had, indeed, forgotten, at the moment, the presence of Gilbert Paddlebat.

"Ha! ha!" continued the old man; "and there's another thing you forgot; it's all very fine to talk about clinging together, and hearts and flames, and the memories of the past, and the happiness of the future; bah! Have you thought of the expense?"

"We want no advice from you," said Lowe.

"Oh, dear, no; I dare say you don't; and I'm a fool to waste it upon you for nothing. However, stop a bit—do you know who I am?"

"Yes," said Lowe; "you're Gilbert Paddlebat, the brother of him who lies there in the embrace of death."

"He! he!" said the old man; "and I'm something else, I'm something else; nobody can impose upon me. I knew him well. I ought to know him; a man always putting off till to-morrow what ought to be done to-day—ha! ha! Mrs. Paddlebat—Mrs. Paddlebat, where are you? Come, no nonsense and fainting now. I don't believe in anybody fainting. I never fainted myself, nor never mean. Come, come, woman, stir yourself; let's have none of this nonsense."

"Are you mad, old man," said Lowe, "that you make this disturbance, even in the very chamber of the dead?"

"No, I'm not mad, but I think you are, to doubt my right to make what disturbance I like here."

"What do you mean?"

Old Gilbert paid no attention to the question, but, turning to Mrs. Paddlebat, he gave her a great shake, exclaiming,—

"Come, come, old 'un, I want to speak to you; you and I must come to an understanding. I'll let you all know soon that I'm the heir-at-law, for, as sure as my name's Paddlebat, and that the sun will shine to-morrow, he left no will."

A disagreeable chill came across the heart of Lowe, as he heard these words. We do not, and we never did, claim for him a great amount of generous feeling; and probably, at that moment, something of the feeling which induced old Paddlebat to ask if he'd considered the expense came across Lowe's mind.

If the goldsmith had omitted to make some provision for his orphan niece, it was to her rather a serious affair, for she would become then completely dependent upon the bounty of Mrs. Paddlebat, who could, as the widow of the deceased, claim a third of the personalities.

If he, Lowe, then wedded Fanny, it would assuredly be to poverty, for he knew that he was no favourite with Mrs. Paddlebat ; and that, with all her real good feeling, she was a woman full of prejudices, and one much governed by personal likings and dislikings.

This was rather an uncomfortable view of his position, and, turning to Gilbert Paddlebat, he said,—

" Sir, this is not a place in which to discuss such a matter ; but, from the great affection which Mr. Paddlebat had for his niece, I cannot doubt that he has made, out of his ample means, an adequate provision for her."

" Cannot you, indeed ?" said Gilbert. " You'll be troubled, young man, to prove that fact. As I'm here, I'll place my seal upon everything. I claim to be heir-at-law. Produce a will, and dispossess me if you can; but, until you do produce such a document, mark me, I'm master here."

" Nay, you have got to prove that yourself. You must be well aware," said Nicholas, " you will look but awkwardly in such a business as this, if, after you have spoken in this way, a will of the deceased Mr. Paddlebat is produced."

" Produce it."

" I have it not. It is not likely that I should."

" I knew you had it not. When you, or any one else, can produce such a document, I will give you leave to say I look in an awkward situation. Until then, however, I am master here, I tell you, by right of being the heir-at-law. Hilloa, Mrs. Paddlebat, do you hear that, or do you still think it's better to do a little of fainting business ?"

" You old brute !" said Mrs. Paddlebat, suddenly, " how dare you talk to me in such a way ? You abominable old wretch !"

" There, there," said Gilbert. " I knew it, I knew it. How do you do, madam, with your third of the personal estate of the deceased Mr. Paddlebat ? How do you feel ? You know there is no will—no will, I say. Do you hear, woman—no will. Eh ?"

" I don't know any such thing," said Mrs. Paddlebat ; " and, besides ——"

" Aunt, aunt !" exclaimed Fanny, " is this a place in which to entertain such a discussion ? I pray you not to condescend to speak again to this person, who shews so unfeeling a heart, and so much disregard for others."

" You are right, my dear, you are right," said Mrs. Paddlebat. " Heaven help me, now I am a widow. Alas, alas! he was always a good husband to me. I little thought to be left alone now, in the decline of life ; but what must be, must be."

Mrs. Paddlebat would doubtless have run on for some time longer, much in the same strain, but her feelings overcame her, and she wept bitterly, shewing some symptoms of lapsing into hysterics, which rather alarmed old Gilbert than otherwise, and he said,—

" Mind, all of you, it's felony now to touch anything, or to move anything out of the house. I will go now, and come again to-morrow evening, at about this hour, you understand, and not before, with my professional gentleman, Mr. Pink, whom I have a perfect right now to bring into the house if I please, and when I please."

Without waiting for any answer to this speech, Gilbert walked to the door of the chamber, and trotted down the staircase.

" Come away, aunt, come away," said Fanny, " from this room—all is over now. Affection can do no more for him who has gone."

" No, no—nothing."

" Then do not stay here to make yourself more unhappy. Come, aunt, come. Mr. Lowe will do whatever is necessary to be done, and spare you all the trouble of arranging anything in the house."

" Mr. Lowe, did you say ?"

" Yes, aunt; he is here."

" Oh! very good; but I don't think there will be any need to trouble Mr. Lowe."

Lowe quite understood with what feeling these words were uttered towards him, but he made no reply to them.   In the consciousness of the affection of Fanny, he cared not what she might say, but turning to the object of his love, he said,—

" Pray command me in anything whatever."

" Yes, yes," said Fanny ; " I will speak to my aunt."

Mrs. Paddlebat tottered from the chamber of death, leaning on the arm of Fanny, so that Lowe was, in a manner of speaking, thrown completely in the shade, and compelled to feel that his absence would be considered by the widow as a good thing, whatever great difference of opinion Fanny might have concerning it.

After hesitating for a moment at the head of the stairs, he felt conscious that it would be extremely impolitic of him to force himself upon the company of Mrs. Paddlebat at such a moment, so he summoned to his aid a little philosophy, and a little hypocrisy, as he said, in as winning a tone as he could assume,—

" I hope and trust, madam, that a night's repose will do you much good.   I bid you good night with all the best wishes in the world for your welfare."

" Oh, thank you, thank you," said Mrs. Paddlebat, indifferently.   " Thank you."

" Good night, Mr. Lowe," said Fanny.

She spoke in that gentle tone of voice which goes direct to the heart of the hearer, and is most peculiarly significant of the best and the tenderest of feelings.

Nicholas Lowe felt himself most amply repaid for the almost rudeness of Mrs. Paddlebat, by these few words of gentleness, and he went down the stairs with his regret for the death of the old goldsmith considerably tempered by the thought that he was beloved by his beautiful and, in all respects, most amiable niece.

He congratulated himself much that Rodwell was not within during the occurrences that had passed, for, had he been so, he, Lowe, doubted not but that Mrs. Paddlebat would have bestowed upon him some especial mark of her confidence, in preference to him, Lowe, which might have produced some rather unpleasant collision between them.

Had Rodwell for one moment suspected what was going on, how eagerly would he have hastened to show himself at home.

Let us take a peep at what he is about.

CHAPTER XXX.

RODWELL AND HIS CONFIDANTE.—THE RESULTS OF INTOXICATION.—ADVICE FOL-
LOWED, AND THE SHOCK.

THE failure of Rodwell in the various designs he had attempted to carry into execution against the life of Nicholas Lowe, enraged as well as terrified him beyond all former precedent.

It was a wonder that he had sufficient presence of mind even to take that precaution he did, as regarded the kitchen clock, which certainly placed Susan, the servant at the Paddlebats', in a position, if she chose, to prove something like a very respectable *alibi* in his favour, if Nicholas Lowe should think proper to accuse him of firing an air-gun at him in Wilderness-row.

The public-house in the neighbourhood where Rodwell was in the habit of spending his dignified leisure, was one of those houses which are to be found in all neighbourhoods, and which are regularly frequented by the same people night after night, and, from long experience in what these people take, the landlord is able to calculate almost to within a few pounds what they were worth to him in a year.

Rodwell had lately gone to this house, but he was considered by some of the best off and most substantial tradesmen who regularly attended there, as something in the shape of an interloper.

He was known, after all, to be only a shopman, or something between that and a confidential clerk to Mr. Paddlebat, the goldsmith, and hence his rank was not considered such as to qualify him to mingle on terms of equality with Mr. Paddlebat's equals.

However, he managed with some of the frequenters of the house to get over these scruples, and to find sufficient society whenever he went there.

He always drank rather hard and recklessly.   Long habit had enabled him to do

so with an amount of impunity which persons not so seasoned could not pretend to, but, upon this occasion, half maddened as he was, by the whole of the day's occurrences, and in a very tolerable fright as regarded the ultimate result of them, he, to drown reflection, drank at a rate that surprised those who were in the habit of seeing him.

Among the frequenters of this house, however, there was one whom no one knew any more of than that he called himself a Mr. Johnstone, but who had been for a long time a frequenter of the place, and as he had always paid for what he had, and never obtruded himself in a marked manner upon the company, was regarded as, no doubt, in the absence of any knowledge to the contrary, a very good sort of respectable man.

This man looked hard at Rodwell, when he saw that, on this evening in particular, he seemed inclined to indulge himself with potations of more than ordinary depth.

Presently he came and sat down by him, and then, after making some ordinary remark concerning some current topic of the day, he said, in an under tone,—

"Mr. Rodwell, something has vexed you ; now, I don't like to see a good fellow, as I know you to be, put out of sorts. I am an idler. Can I be of any service ?"

"Service ?"

"Yes. Can I do you any good by advice, assistance, or personal trouble ?"

"No," said Rodwell ; "no. You are mistaken ; I am not out of sorts at all, or in any difficulty. Still, I am obliged to you, of course—it's friendly of you."

"Thank you—thank you, sir. I'm a blunt fellow, and, I believe, say too often, and too readily, just what I think, or I should be a richer man than I can lay claim to being at this present time. However, we will have a bottle together."

"With all my heart."

The bottle was had, and then Johnstone began a long rigmarole about his own affairs, which was of so complicated and troublesome a nature to understand, that, although at first Rodwell paid some attention, he found, after a little while, that he was thoroughly confused.

"You understand me ?" said Johnstone.

"I'll be hanged if I do."

"Well, I'm sorry for that. The fact is, I am myself in a little difficulty, which requires the assistance of a friend."

"Are you ?"

"Yes ; but don't mistake me ; I don't say this for the sake of drawing you into any trouble on my account ; I would not have it. Why don't you drink ? No, I would not have it ; but the fact is, Mr. Rodwell, I have got into a scrape or two. I am not very scrupulous about how I accomplish what I set my mind upon, provided I do accomplish it. You understand me ? You are not quite comfortable, somehow or another. Can a ready hand, a ready wit, and a steady heart help you in any way ?"

Rodwell paused for a moment or two. He had taken almost enough drink to throw him off his guard, but not quite—no, not quite. Some of his cunning still clung to him—he was not yet to be caught.

"No, no," he said. "Much obliged ; thank you—no !"

Johnstone looked a little mortified, but he replied, promptly,—

"Well, I'm as glad to hear it as if any one had laid me down a fifty-pound note—that I am—very glad to hear it. But you don't drink."

This was a most uncalled-for reproach, for Rodwell was drinking at the very least two glasses to Johnstone's one, and he was rapidly approaching such a state of intoxication that if he did not get thrown completely off his guard, and become confidential to his artful companion, it would be in consequence of inability to speak.

This was a state, though, into which Johnstone was determined that he should not fall, if he could help it ; so when he thought Rodwell had had nearly enough, he attacked the liquor himself, and it seemed to have no more effect upon his seasoned frame than so much water would.

"What do you say to a little stroll in the fresh air ?" said Johnstone.

"Very good," replied Rodwell, who could just manage to stand only. "Very good. Come on—come on, my boy."

"I must see him home," remarked Johnstone, in an apologetic tone to the company, as he turned to them for a moment. "He has taken, you perceive, gentlemen, the other drop."

So completely had Johnstone, up to this moment, absorbed the attention of Rodwell, and so much had he managed to sit between him and the company, that no one had perceived, until they rose, what a state Rodwell was in.

He was watched with looks of disapprobation by every eye in the room as he left it, for the old topers who came there, although they, every night in their lives, took enough to muddle and confuse their faculties, contrived always to be able to walk home steadily enough, and being, under ordinary circumstances, none of the brightest specimens of humanity, any little extra stupidity consequent upon gin-and-water, or other villanous and mind-obscuring compounds, was not observed.

For any one, then, to get quite drunk was an offence which served them to dilate upon for a whole evening.

When Johnstone and Rodwell got out into the open air, the effect upon the latter was that he got a great deal worse than he had been in the house, and he lost all sort of caution. In a short time, enough was drawn from him by Johnstone to use on another opportunity, although what he discovered really amounted to no more than that he was at war with Nicholas Lowe, whom he considered to be his mortal enemy, and knew to be his rival.

After this he got into a such a state of bewilderment and stupidity, that his companion was glad to leave him on the doorstep of the goldsmith's house, where he, Rodwell, in a few moments, fell fast asleep.

It was at the private door of the goldsmith's abode that Johnstone left Rodwell, and as the entrance of that was very deep, and defended by a gate, Rodwell might, without much probability of interruption, have slept there until the morning.

As it was, however, a disagreeable dream awakened him, after about a couple of hours, and he glanced about him with looks of astonishment.

A racking headache put him in mind that he had by far exceeded the bounds of common prudence in what he had drunk, and, after a few minutes of painful thought, the events which had been antecedent to his presence at the doorstep, came dimly across his mind.

A cold shiver came across him, and, with a groan, he said to himself,—

"Oh, fool! fool! What have I told to that fellow, who, for all I know, may, even now, be in possession of enough to hang me? Hush—hush! Good God, did I say hang?—what—what a word to pass my lips! What did I tell him? Let me think—let me think—or, rather, what did I not tell him?"

He rested his head upon his hands, and a painful idea crossed his mind that he had certainly used the name of Lowe, but how far he had gone in his perilous confidence with this real stranger he could not tell. He only, as was natural enough, suspected the very worst, and believed that he might possibly be, even now, standing on a mine, which, for all he knew to the contrary, might, in a few hours, explode beneath him.

Then, as thought after thought chased each other through his aching brain, a new idea sprang up before him, and he asked himself,—

"What would he get but trouble, and difficulty, and worry—not to say suspicion, by betraying me, even if I have been so imprudent as to tell him all? I suspect, though, yet, the end will be demands for money as the price of secresy. Curses on my heedlessness. Already have I once waded through—through—blood—yes, blood—it may as well be spoken at once—to rid myself of such an incubus, and now I have aimlessly, and without an object, involved myself again in some such a dilemma. Oh, fool! fool! fool!"

He rocked himself to and fro upon the door step for some time, partly with a sensation of bodily indisposition, which was growing upon him momentarily, and partly from mental anguish, to think that he should have been so fearfully imprudent as to trust a stranger with secrets that concerned his very existence, and that quite aimlessly, too.

Once or twice despair nearly got entire possession of him, but at last he began to fancy that he saw a way out of his difficulties—a way which, in his soberest judgment, he probably would have at once condemned, but which now presented itself to him in rather alarming colours.

"How am I situated?" he said. "There is not the shadow of a chance that Fanny Leslie will be mine; she has certainly made choice of Lowe, and consequently there's an end of all my chances. Mrs. Paddlebat may say what she likes, she won't persuade a young girl into a marriage contrary to her inclination. Let me see; ah, the goldsmith cannot live long—I am quite clear about that; and then what a fine chance I shall have. Especially when I come to consider this fellow Johnstone, who will no doubt be now continually begging at me for money as the price of his silence concerning what I suspect I have told him; what is to hinder me, with the knowledge I have of where to lay my hands upon the most valuable property in the warehouse, from at once possessing myself of all that I could expect under the most favourable circumstances, and getting clear off with it ?"

He pondered over this idea for some time, and the more he thought of it, the more feasible did it seem to him. He knew where to lay his hands upon portable, and actually intrinsically valuable property, to the amount of some thousands of pounds.

"Yes," he said,—"yes. There cannot be a better scheme than that. It would be capital then, if, from a distance, I could manage to accuse Johnstone of the robbery. Who knows?—I may hit upon some scheme of doing so, as well as perhaps of involving Lowe in some way."

His head ached fearfully, and he pressed his hands tightly upon his brow, and groaned again, as even the slight exertion of rising to his feet made his brain throb again as if it would burst.

"Brandy," he muttered. "Brandy, which I have up stairs in my own room, will cure me of this horrible headache; at least sufficiently to enable me to set about what I undertake, and what I will execute."

After considerable fumbling in his pockets, he found a latch-key, which admitted him to the house, and then, as he slowly groped his way up stairs, he thought that the plan of robbery he now meditated would be incomplete, unless he could get hold of Mr. Paddlebat's cash-box, which he knew was always kept in the goldsmith's chamber.

"There's always," he thought, "a few hundreds there, and ready money will be to me everything, because it will enable me to seek a foreign market for what valuables in the shape of jewels and gold I take, as well as supply me with the most efficient means of quick travelling, and so a thousand times better chance of escaping detection."

By the time he had reached his own room, he had quite made up his mind not only that he would have the cash-box, but that he would secure it first, so that he should not have to go up stairs again, loaded with the costly booty he intended to appropriate to himself from the warehouse or shop below.

He had in his room the means of procuring a light, and then his first movement was to a cupboard, which he unlocked, and from a shelf in which he took a bottle of brandy.

A brimming glass of that potent liquor certainly imparted sufficient of a reaction to his system, to have soon a marked effect upon the throbbing pain in his head, which subsided into a kind of confused consciousness of all not being quite right with the animal economy, which was, however, infinitely preferable to the dreadful pain he had been enduring, which had nearly reached a climax which was enough to drive him distracted, had it continued.

"Now, now," he said, with something of a feeling of exultation about him, "now I will at least show them all a trick they little suspect ; and, when I am gone, and they find what I have taken with me, they must admit that I have out-generalled them, at all events."

There were, however, yet some things to be well considered before his scheme could be fully carried out, and the only difficulty which at all seemed likely to be one of a very serious nature, consisted in the possibility, to his mind, of finding some one awake, and watching in Mr. Paddlebat's chamber.

He knew that since the illness of the goldsmith, either Mrs. Paddlebat or Fanny had kept watch by him in the night, and probably they relieved each other. The cash-box, he knew, was placed under the dressing-table, and it could, if no one were stirring in the room, be laid hold of in a moment, so that he need not be above two minutes in the room at all.

In the two minutes what an alarm there might be given! Either Mrs. Paddlebat or Fanny might alarm the whole house in less than that, and then Lowe would be certain to make his appearance, and the whole plan would be knocked on the head at once.

This was not a pleasant idea, and after some time spent in anxious thought upon it, he said, with a savage aspect,—

"I will not be foiled by a woman, now that my fortunes are so completely at stake in this affair. I am resolved to carry it out. Woe be to any one who interrupts me."

With these words he took from a box a pistol, the priming of which he carefully examined, and thus with it in his right hand, and the bundle in his left, he with slow and cautious steps descended to the second floor.

All was profoundly still in the house. For all the movement there was of aught living except himself, every one as well as Mr. Paddlebat, might have been in the arms of death.

Little did Rodwell suspect that he was going to the chamber of one who was sleeping the long sleep which knows no waking. How coward-like he would have shrunk back, could any one at that moment, when he was crawling so thief-like down that staircase, have whispered to him,—

"Jervis Rodwell, the goldsmith, is a corpse."

But there was no one to give him such a piece of news, so on he went to the commission of the crime he meditated, prepared for a kind of resistance which he was not doomed to meet with in the the deserted chamber of death.

"Whoever is there," he muttered, "will be sure to get up a scream, and to threaten ; I wonder, now, if it would have been my best plan at all events to get together below what I mean to take with me, so that when I secure my prize of the cash-box I shall be delayed but a moment or two before I leave the house."

He paused upon this mental suggestion, and it certainly was a sufficiently feasible one for him to consider it closely.

After a few minutes' thought, he said,—

"Yes, yes, of course, the best plan, obviously the best plan that will be. I will prepare all down stairs first, because after I have left the chamber of Mr. Paddlebat what security then have I that an instant alarm may not be given? While I remain there I may enforce the silence of terror, but when I have left what is there to prevent the whole house, ay the whole neighbourhood, from being set upon me?"

Even as he uttered these extremely reasonable reflections, he glided past the bed-room door of the goldsmith, nor paused until he was in the shop.

When there, from his knowledge of the place and where the most valuable portions of the stock were to be found, he in about a quarter of an hour made up a small parcel which was worth about 3,000l., and, besides, he stowed about him a number of costly watches and gold chains to the amount of 1,000l. more.

Highly gratified then with what he was about, and already feeling himself master of enough to secure him an independence, he turned his attention once more to the staircase, and with cautious footsteps ascended to the goldsmith's chamber.

The door was closed, and it was a circumstance that gave him some uneasiness, because he dreaded that upon the first effort he should make to open it either Fanny or Mrs. Paddlebat would take the alarm ; for that one or the other of them was there he had no manner of doubt in the world.

He placed his ear close to the door to listen if he could detect any sound which should enable him to judge if she who watched were sleeping or waking.

All was so profoundly still that he came to the conclusion that whoever was that night keeping watch in the sick chamber had become tired out and lapsed into repose.

"It must be so," he said. "It surely must be so, and therefore all that is required of me will be extreme caution and noiselessness."

He placed his light upon the landing, and the pistol in his pocket, but yet so handily that he could lay hold of it at a moment's notice, and then, with the greatest care any one in the world could have taken, he turned the door handle.

To his surprise the door did not open, and then he saw that the key was sticking in the lock, and that it had all the appearance of being locked on the outside.

This discovery, while it dispelled his apprehensions of any one disturbing him in the chamber, caused him great wonder and much conjecture. Yet, somehow or another, the real truth never for a moment occurred to him.

He waited nearly five minutes, and then, being quite confident that nobody was in the room but the goldsmith, who probably was not in a state to interrupt him, he with more boldness turned the key in the lock and opened the door.

All was darkness; but that did not surprise him. He had heard that light was prejudicial to the goldsmith in his situation, and therefore he did not expect to find one. Why, however, they had locked him in, was a mystery.

"No matter—no matter," he thought. "All is still; he sleeps, and the cash box will be mine."

Before, however, he possessed himself of the object of his peculation and his visit to that chamber, he thought he should like to satisfy himself thoroughly that the goldsmith was sleeping, or in that state of insensibility which he was frequently, since the first attack of his indisposition, in the habit of relapsing into.

With this view, and shading the light he carried in his hand, he slowly approached the bed.

For all he knew the goldsmith might be watching him. Had he been so, we have not sufficient faith in the humanity of such a man as Rodwell to doubt for an instant but that he would have put an end to the illness of Mr. Paddlebat along with his life.

The curtains were all closed with the most scrupulous care, and Rodwell drew one aside most slowly, in order that he should make no rattling with the brass rings on which it ran.

Then he bent himself forward to look at the goldsmith. The bed looked wonderfully smooth, and there was not the least sound of any one breathing, which rather surprised him, but when he did see the goldsmith's face he was transfixed with guilty terror.

In one moment the whole truth flashed upon him. The goldsmith had died—was laid out, and hence, of course, no one was required to watch in his chamber, and the door was locked.

It so happened, too, that in the case of the dead goldsmith, one of those strange and frightful changes had taken place in his aspect which prevented him, to all intents and purposes, from being what women so much delight in describing—namely, a handsome corpse.

The face was of a strange livid colour, which was anything but agreeable to look upon, while here and there were streaks of a muddy-looking yellow. One eye seemed to be looking direct upon Rodwell, as if with a mute denunciation of him for the deed he had meditated.

The fright of the villain who came to rob, but who certainly would not have hesitated to add murder to it, was, as we have said, so excessive, that all he could do for some moments was, with a dreadful kind of fascination, to glare with distended eyeballs upon the face of the dead.

He forgot the cash-box, he forgot the valuable parcel he had made ready below, as well as the costly articles with which his pockets were lined; he forgot the danger, even, that he exposed himself to, and, with a shout of alarm that awakened every one in the house, he rushed from the chamber, nor paused until he had reached his own and closed and locked the door.

CHAPTER XXXI.

THE NIGHT ALARM.—RODWELL'S ACCOUNT OF HIMSELF.—THE ARRIVAL AGAIN OF GILBERT.

UNTIL he was fairly in his own room, and a feeling of comparative safety come over him in consequence, Rodwell did not at all awaken to a consciousness of his extreme imprudence in making the alarm that he had done,

When such a thought did occur to him, he was so angry with himself that he could almost have found it in his heart to turn the pistol with which he was provided against his own life.

But men like Rodwell, however much upon the spur of a temporary excite-ment they may think of suicide, are generally by far too cowardly to carry into effect any such thing.

This idea, therefore, was not likely, nor did it for long hold a place in the mind of the villain Rodwell, who soon found that he had no resource but to wait patiently, or, at all events, with an appearance of patience if there was not its reality, for the effect which the disturbance he had himself created was likely to produce.

He had not to wait long, for Fanny Leslie was awake, and had heard the alarm which had been given, so that she sprang to the door of her apartment and called loudly,—

"Leo! Leo! Leo!"

The dog was immediately on the outside of her room door as usual, and he at once, when he heard her voice, sprang up and responded to her call by a loud bark.

If nothing else had done so, this, then, was amply sufficient to have alarmed the whole house; for his voice was none of the gentlest when he really chose to make it heard. Susan, who occupied one of the attics, uttered a succession of screams, and her prevalent idea concerning fire, as usual, took possession of her, filling her with terror, although she was without question in the very best position in the house for escaping the consequences of such an event, inasmuch as the attic which she occupied had a window that opened on to the parapet, close to which she could have crawled until she got to the adjoining house, or even the one next that had she preferred.

Mrs. Paddlebat had gone to sleep, but the succession of noises awakened her at once, and, as may well be supposed, she was not the sort of person to be slow in adding to them. Lowe, too, had, after remaining awake, thinking over the events of the evening, and wondering if, after all, he was ever destined to call Fanny his wife, fallen into a light slumber, and he was the only person who, having heard that there was some disturbance going on, sprang from his bed silently, without adding in any way to the uproar.

In a few moments he was sufficiently dressed to leave his room, and our readers will not blame him, that, in the first place, he made his way at once to the chamber of Fanny.

He found her with Leo upon the landing, immediately outside her bed-room door, and his delight at seeing that, whatever had happened, she was at all events safe, was very great.

"What has happened?" dear Fanny, he said; "oh, tell me what has happened?"

"That I cannot," said Fanny; "I hoped to get the information from you."

"I heard a noise."

"And I."

"Then something must be amiss. Perhaps thieves in the house. I will search it at once. I wonder if Rodwell has come home!"

"Do not, Lowe,—oh! do not expose yourself to danger. Call aloud from the windows for the watch, but do not alone attempt to face, perhaps, dangerous ruffians, who, disappointed of booty, may stop at nothing in the shape of violence."

"Nay, housebreakers are proverbial cowards. Besides, you shall spare me Leo, and he is a better companion than a man would be."

"And I will go with you likewise."

"No, no."

"Murder! murder!" shouted Mrs. Paddlebat, rushing from her room, and nearly falling over Nicholas Lowe. "Murder! murder!"

"Hush, aunt, hush!" said Fanny. "For Heaven's sake, be quiet. Here is Mr. Lowe, willing to search the house."

"Where is Mr. Rodwell?" exclaimed Mrs. Paddlebat. "There was a noise. Where is Mr. Rodwell? He is as bold as a lion."

"Madam," said Lowe, for he felt really provoked at this infatuation of Mrs. Paddlebat's madness, "an imputation upon the courage of a gentleman by a lady, however insulting or groundless it may be, of course cannot be resented. With regard, however, to your favourite Rodwell, I not only believe that he is as great a cur as regards courage, as ever lived, but I think it highly probable that he is to blame for all this nocturnal disturbance which has given you such a fright."

" He to blame ?"

" Yes, madam, he."

" And pray, how ?"

" Why, probably by leaving the street-door open, as he did once before, when he came home in a state of intoxication."

Mrs. Paddlebat looked furious at Lowe, for this had been a little affair in which she had shielded Rodwell from the just anger of the goldsmith, and she had not been aware that Lowe knew of it.

"Oh, of course," she said, "if a bad word can be said of Mr. Rodwell, it comes from you."

Lowe had made that speech which we have recorded, at a moment of irritation, and even when the moment he had uttered it, he felt its extreme impolicy, and much regretted that for one moment he should have given way to such an impulse and made, as no doubt would be the case, Mrs. Paddlebat a much worse enemy to him than she ever had been.

Fanny, too, looked the regret she felt that Lowe should have committed himself so far with her aunt, but still, while she did so, she felt that he was right, and that he was insulted, and had, unquestionably, amply sufficient cause to say what he had said.

"Very well," added Mrs. Paddlebat, "very well, Mr. Nicholas Lowe, we shall see what we shall see soon. You are not quite master here yet, Mr. Lowe, and I very much doubt if you ever will be. Wait a bit—wait a bit."

That Mrs. Paddlebat fully intended in the morning to discharge him from his employment he felt assured, and the thought that he should so soon be separated from her who now constituted the great charm of his existence was gall and wormwood to him. If, without seriously and fatally, in the eyes of Fanny, compromising himself, he could have said anything that would have had the effect of restoring himself even to his former standing with Mrs. Paddlebat, he would have done so, but it was impossible, so he merely said,—

" I regret any misunderstanding, and will now search the house, to see if any one be secreted in it. Come, Leo."

" Oh ! gracious !" exclaimed Mrs. Paddlebat, suddenly.

" What, aunt, what ?" said Fanny.

" It's body-snatchers !"

" It's who—what ?"

" Body-snatchers ! The bed-room door of your poor uncle is wide open, and there's where the noises has come from. I see it all now. Help ! help ! They have taken his body to put it along with the petrified black beetles in the British Museum !"

Certainly the door of the chamber of death was open, but both Nicholas Lowe and Fanny were inclined to place a much more rational interpretation upon that circumstance than Mrs. Paddlebat did.

What so natural, if any daring and expert housebreakers had made their way into the residence, than for them to expect booty of value in the best bed-room of the house ?

Lowe snatched Mrs. Paddlebat's light from her trembling hands, and, unarmed as he was, he at once made his way to the goldsmith's chamber.

At a command from Fanny, the dog followed him, but the search there afforded no grounds for any suspicion that anything wrong had happened. No articles were taken away, and there were several of considerable value laying upon the toilette-table. The only change in the aspect of the room consisted in the curtains of the bed being drawn back, when Lowe distinctly recollected himself closing them all with great carefulness.

As he came out of the room he saw, however, to his great surprise, a pistol

lying on the floor, and then he felt convinced that some one had been there with the hopes of plunder, and had probably been disturbed.

It was, he thought, certainly just possible that this disturbance might have arisen from finding the room tenanted by the dead instead of the living, and yet, when he came to reflect upon that view of the case, he much doubted if men, of such dispositions as public robbers were likely to have, would shrink from carrying out an adventure of a promising nature as regarded booty, for any such simple cause as finding that there was a dead body in the house.

He then proceeded down the staircase, still followed by Leo, but he found that in the lower part of the house all was quiet, although the door, by being just left on the latch, exhibited unequivocal testimony that either Rodwell had not come home at all, or had been sufficiently intoxicated, or sufficiently careless when he did so, to leave the door in a very insecure state.

From the cursory glance which he took round the shop, Lowe could not perceive that anything had been disturbed, and among a number of parcels and packages which lay about, the one which Rodwell had prepared to go off with, presented nothing calculated to attract particular notice.

Lowe fastened the street-door securely, for he was resolved that if Rodwell was not in, he should now remain out until the morning, and then he went up stairs to give an account of his search to Mrs. Paddlebat and to Fanny.

They were both waiting with anxiety, and more particularly the latter, who had all her fears awakened for the safety of Lowe, notwithstanding the presence of Leo with him, which she justly enough considered as a very great protection indeed.

Her countenance, when he appeared, sufficiently testified how glad she was again to see him in safety, and Mrs. Paddlebat observed as much, although at that time she said nothing on the subject.

" There is no one down stairs," said Lowe. " If anybody was on the premises, he has made his escape ; and whether anything has been stolen from below, or not, of course I have no means immediately of knowing."

" But there must have been somebody," said Mrs. Paddlebat, " or else how could the bed-room door be wide open ?"

" There is ample evidence," remarked Lowe, " of some one having been in Mr. Paddlebat's room, but who it was, or for what purpose, I cannot say. Nothing is, as far as I can see, missing from there, and the whole affair to me, I must confess, wears the most mysterious aspect."

Things had now, as regarded the alarm, come to a juncture, when to do anything more seemed just then not very easy, and Mrs. Paddlebat muttered something about having a Bow-street officer in the morning, and then retired to her own room; but she took good care, before she went, to see Fanny in hers, and the doors closed, so that Lowe had no opportunity of saying one word of an affectionate character to her, beyond the few which he had uttered before Mrs. Paddlebat had got a sufficient quantity of her voluminous apparel to justify her, in her own eyes, in making her appearance.

Reluctantly Lowe retired again to his own room. There was an uncomfortable impression upon his mind that all was not right, and he could not help fancying, although he once or twice accused himself of prejudice for so doing, that Rodwell was at the bottom of all the disturbance that had taken place.

" I should like much to know," he thought to himself, " if Rodwell is in or not. His room-door is closed, and I don't like to go and try to open it, considering the strange terms on which we are, and considering that I am morally certain he has attempted my life."

Still he could not make up his mind to go to bed, but carefully extinguishing his light, he placed the door of his room about an inch open, and sitting down by it, he made up his mind that, at all events, he would watch for some time, in case Rodwell should be in, and make some demonstration of such being the fact, from his bed-room.

Our readers may well imagine for themselves what a miserable state of nervousness and apprehension Rodwell must have been in during the last half hour.

There can be no question but that his best policy would have been to shew himself along with the other individuals of the house, affecting to be alarmed from the same cause which had alarmed them, while he could have assumed the same ignorance concerning it.

But this he really had not nerve to do. He knew it was his best course. He told himself that it was, and yet, although more than once he went to the door of his room, intending to sally out and demand what was the matter, his courage as often failed him, and fearing that, in his state of trembling confusion, he should betray himself, he thought he had better remain just where he was, and trust the issue to chance.

There were, however, circumstances which rendered it extremely desirable that he should not attempt to go to rest.

In the first place, if he did not intend to carry out now his scheme of robbery, it was highly desirable for him that he should get rid of the evidence of ever having had such an intention, for he feared that upon him, and upon him alone would suspicion alight.

There was the parcel below in the shop, which in the morning would most assuredly be discovered, and cause a great commotion. Then there was his pistol—a weapon which, for all he knew, might be proved to be his, lying on the floor in Mr. Paddlebat's chamber—at least he hoped it was lying there still—he could not know that it had been taken possession of by Lowe, who at that very time had it in his hand. And last, although not the least in importance, he had about him the watches and other costly articles with which he had crammed his pockets, as part of the valuable booty with which, no doubt, had all gone smoothly, he would, ere this, have been a considerable distance off.

Bitterly, most bitterly, he now blamed his own folly for allowing himself to be terrified at the very circumstance which afforded him the greatest possible facility in carying out his original plan of robbery. By the death of Mr. Paddlebat, and the consequent desertion of his chamber by the family, he got rid of the only chance of detection in the infamous plan which he had suggested to himself, and which he had so nearly succeeded in executing.

But now he knew not what obstacles might be placed in his way. An alarm had been given, and the suspicions of the whole household aroused to the fact that something was wrong, so that what before might have been attended with some little risk only, no doubt now would become a downright dangerous enterprise.

But yet, when he came to reflect upon his position, a strong desire still to carry out his plan arose in his mind. He thought of the danger he had, by his own ill-timed intemperance, and consequent imprudence, drawn himself into with that man Johnstone, and he thought then of how unlikely first of all it was, that the gold-smith had made any will; and, secondly, if he had, how still more unlikely it was that it should be a document that would in any way benefit him.

Thus he remained in what people call two minds for a considerable time, not knowing what would be the most desirable for his interests to do. At length, however, hearing all was profoundly still in the house, and believing that everybody had gone to bed again, and most probably to sleep, he fully made up his resolution to prosecute his original plan as regarded the robbery, with the one exception of the cash-box.

He felt that he could not, that he dared not attempt again to cross the threshold of the chamber in which lay the corpse of the goldsmith.

"After all," he reasoned, " there may not be much in it; and, besides, I cannot tell but that Mrs. Paddlebat herself may have had the prudence to remove it to her own chamber, in which case I should still be foiled."

This reasoning was all very well, now that he had made up his mind not to go to the goldsmith's chamber. Before, when such formed a portion of his plan, it would not by any means have sufficed him.

He was now, however, thoroughly frightened, and as no man likes exactly to own such a feeling, even in confidence to himself, he tried to persuade himself that it was from other reasons that he declined again visiting that chamber.

" I'll be off," he muttered, " and before morning I shall yet have time to get a considerable distance from here. I must turn into cash, with what expedition I can, and even at any sacrifice, some of the property I take with me, and then to the continent at once."

Before he would venture from his room, he listened very intently for about five minutes, and then the apparent intense stillness of the place reassured him that all was right, and he cautiously opened his door, and crept out on the landing.

Lowe had been watching for so long, that his patience was very nearly exhausted, and in a few moments more he would most likely have gone to bed with a conviction on his mind that Rodwell had not come home, but the moment he heard the lock of Rodwell's room cautiously turning, he was on the alert.

" He is at home," he thought; " he is at home, after all, and now is coming from his room to complete some enterprise in which he has been disturbed. The villain!"

Now Rodwell was fairly out upon the staircase, and treading as softly as foot could fall; and when he had commenced descending, Lowe armed with the pistol he had picked up close to the door of the goldsmith's room, stepped lightly from his own apartment, and determined upon following him.

Rodwell carried his light, so that all behind him was cast into deep shadow, and in that shadow Nicholas Lowe crept after the man who he knew had attempted his life, and who, he suspected, was now bent upon some enterprise that would enable him, Lowe, to be amply avenged upon him, and pursue him to his destruction.

Lowe felt that his best policy would be, not to interrupt Rodwell, but to let him do whatever he projected. If that was robbery, he resolved that he would even let him leave the premises before he interfered with him, and then have him apprehended with his booty actually in his possession.

This was certainly good policy on the part of Lowe, and no doubt he would, had he been permitted, have carried it out to the full, and so completely got the better of Rodwell, who, had he been apprehended with the valuable articles in his actual possession which he contemplated taking away, could really have made no defence.

The case would have been too clear against him to admit of the least cavilling, and Nicholas Lowe would have had the satisfaction of getting rid of his arch enemy.

But such, as we shall perceive, was not to be, and why it was not, affords but another of those most abundant instances of how trifling an occurrence will alter the whole aspect of the affairs of a number of people, and produce results of the most stupendous character.

Nicholas Lowe had not got many stairs down in his pursuit of Rodwell, when his foot caught in a loose stair-rod, and he made, in order, on the impulse of the moment, to save himself from falling, more than enough noise to induce Rodwell, with some such a cry of terror as he had before given utterance to in the goldsmith's chamber, to turn round and face his pursuer.

Lowe's first movement was to present the pistol full at Rodwell's head, and there, for the space of about half a minute, they both stood as immoveable as statues, gazing at each other with such feelings of bitterness and hatred, as few men are ever placed in circumstances to entertain.

CHAPTER XXII.

THE ALTERCATION.—THE PISTOL-SHOT.—MR. PINK'S FRIGHT.

WHAT feelings for that brief space of time found a home in the breasts of those enemies, may be to some extent imagined by our readers.

The temptation which Lowe now felt to pull the trigger of the pistol, and so rid himself and society of Rodwell for ever, was very great, and he really found no small amount of difficulty in refraining from such a course.

As for Rodwell, completely foiled as he was, and in circumstances of present as well as prospective danger, he was so confounded, that he was incapable of such collected thought as might enable him to make the best of a bad affair.

It was Nicholas Lowe who spoke first, and, in a voice struggling with passion, he said,—

"Detected villain! What can you now say to clear yourself from the consequences of guilt? Robbery, and perchance murder, have been your objects to-night; but you are foiled now, and you feel that you are known."

"What do you mean?" gasped Rodwell, for the fact was, he knew not what to say. "What do you mean, Nicholas Lowe? I was doing no harm to you."

"Villain! what was your object in creeping down stairs so stealthily?"

"I—I thought I heard a noise—I was afraid thieves were in the house, and so came down stairs for the purpose of attempting to discover them."

"You were not afraid thieves were in the house," said Lowe.

"How do you know?"

"Because I know you knew one thief was in the house, and if you are not afraid of yourself you were not afraid of him."

"I don't understand you."

"You do, and well too. But for the accident which made the fact, that I was following you known to you, I should, I have no doubt, have had the pleasure of detecting you in the very act."

During this short dialogue, Rodwell was recovering himself from his first fright, and beginning to think that if anything could now save him altogether from the consequences of his completely defeated scheme of robbing, it would be insolence, and a great show of confidence.

Accordingly, as the saying is, he plucked up a spirit, and, confronting Lowe more boldly, he said,—

"I have as much right, and perhaps more, to accuse you of bad designs against the house than you have to accuse me. You are armed and I am not."

"But whose pistol is this?"

"Your own, or some confederate's."

"This affrontery," said Lowe, "shall not save you; I will call in the police, and a magistrate shall, in the morning, decide this affair."

"A magistrate?"

"Yes. No doubt the proposition is unpalatable to you—I did not expect it would be otherwise."

"Well," said Rodwell, "let a magistrate decide between us, if you will have it so; but remember, Michael Lowe, there have been events in your life which you might not like exactly to hear repeated."

Lowe shrank back a little, and Rodwell perceived that he had an advantage.

"She," he continued, "who died bereft of reason, and whose funeral you ——"

"Madman!" cried Lowe, "have you no regard for your life?"

Rodwell would not have ventured to utter these words, had he been aware of the fury which they produced in Lowe, who, for the first time, became aware that somehow or another a secret which he had thought was confined to his own breast, had been committed, by some one, to the man, above all others, whom he would have been most anxious to keep such an episode from.

"I have you there," said Rodwell. "I know all. How I came to know it I shall not tell you, but I do know all, let that suffice for you. I had no bad intention in coming down stairs, so don't you go out of your way to accuse me of one, that's all."

"And—and you ——"

"Keep your own secrets, I don't want to open my mouth to fill other people's; what is it to me, I say? only don't accuse me"

Nicholas Lowe groaned. Well he might, at finding himself thus forced into a kind of armistice with the very man, above all others, whom he had no desire to keep peace with, before he became aware that by some inexplicable means he had acquired a knowledge of events which, if, in all their fulness of detail, were repeated to the Paddlebats, would go far to destroy him for ever in the opinion of so pure-minded and noble-hearted a creature as Fanny.

At this anxious moment, and before Lowe, in the state of confusion into which he had been thrown, could think of a reply to make, there came such a loud dab of a knock at the street door, that without at all meaning to do so, he, Nicholas Lowe, in the flurry of the moment, pulled the trigger of the pistol, and off it went with a tremendous report, sending a bullet just over Rodwell, and clean through the panel of the street door.

"By Heaven!" cried Lowe, "it was an accident."

"D——n!" said Rodwell, "you wanted to shoot me."

"Say so again," cried Lowe, "and I have a couple of witnesses to swear they saw you fire an air-gun at me in Wilderness-row."

"The devil!"

Nicholas Lowe was much terrified at the idea, that possibly the bullet had taken effect upon the person who had knocked at the street door for admission, and he sprang now down the remainder of the staircase, and past Rodwell to the door, which he opened with great precipitation, and in fell a man to the passage, who, for all the movement he made, might be dead.

"Good God!" he said, "this is indeed an unlucky chance."

"Is he dead?" said Rodwell.

"Yes, yes!"

"Stop a bit—let me see—why it's daylight outside."

Both Rodwell and Lowe, as if they had been the best friends in the world, now knelt by the body of the man who had tumbled into the passage, and looked carefully at him, but they could not discover any wound, nor did they know him.

The street door remained open, and now, apparently from a post which was immediately opposite to the door, there came a voice, saying,—

"Ha! ha! so you can commit murder, can you, among you?"

"Who's that?" said Lowe, starting up.

"Gilbert Paddlebat," said Rodwell. "There he is, hanging against the post."

"Then I know this man, for he came here before; his name is Pink; I thought I had seen him, but at the moment could not call to mind where."

"Ah!" said old Gilbert, as he advanced, "you are right, it is Pink. You'll be hung, there's no doubt about that, whatever. He was my professional man, and a very clever one too, I can tell you. And now he's gone—alas! poor Pink. Well, well, it's one comfort I sha'n't pay anything to your executors, Pink."

"Is he dead—is he dead?" exclaimed Lowe.

"I don't think he is," said Rodwell, "he breathed just now. Perhaps if the sharp blade of a penknife were to be poked down his thumb nail he might revive."

"Murder!" said Pink, suddenly starting up. "You want to murder me, though you have not yet succeeded. I'll have you all up, unless I get compensation."

"Thank Heaven!" said Lowe.

"Ha!" cried old Gilbert, "I congratulate you, Pink."

"Thank you," said Pink; "and I shall be able to send in my own bill."

"Confound you."

"What do you all want here?" asked Rodwell.

"I came," replied Gilbert Paddlebat, "to place my seal, as heir-at-law, upon the whole of the property. I said I'd come later, but I thought it prudent to come at once, so here I am. As for who fired the pistol at Mr. Pink, that, I presume, will become a question for judicial inquiry; but it's no business of mine."

"I'll take care of that," said Pink. "Somebody must pay me something, or else somebody must suffer in some way. Now we'll begin, Mr. Paddlebat, if you please. Will you hold a candle, and I'll go through the house with you, sealing up everything of any value; and, I think, to begin, we had better lock up the shop and place a seal over the keyhole of the door; what do you think, sir?"

"Yes, yes," cried old Gilbert, "anything for security—anything for security. Come along, Mr. Pink, come along; I rather think we have stolen a march on the enemy. Eh! eh!—who knows what would have been, perhaps, removed from here in the course of the day. There's nothing like being a little beforehand in matters of business.—Eh! eh!—ha!"

———

CHAPTER XXXIII

THE FINDING OF THE WILL. —THE DEMAND OF JOHNSTONE AGAINST RODWELL.

A WEEK has elapsed. The proceedings of Gilbert Paddlebat, as regarded the placing his seal upon the property in the house of his deceased brother, had been resisted at first by Mrs. Paddlebat, but afterwards acceded to, on the advice of a solicitor, to whom she sent, who told her that if she could not produce a will which would shut out old Gilbert, he was justified, at law, in the act.

There was no such will, to her knowledge, and, therefore, with as good a grace as she could command—and that was not a very good one—she did submit.

The old wretch was what Mrs. Paddlebat always called Gilbert ; and when the morning arrived for the funeral, she said to Fanny,—

" I was always at your uncle, Fanny, about making a will, but, with that usual obstinacy of men, all the answer I ever got was, ' Time enough, time enough ; I am not going to die yet.' "

" Ah, aunt," replied Fanny, " while all the feelings and the evidences of life are about us, it is difficult to think of death."

" Well, it may be to some people ; but still I mean to say that he ought to have made a will, knowing as your uncle knew better, or ought to have known better, than anybody, what a wretch of a brother he had, and what you and I would have to contend with when he was gone."

" But still, now, aunt, that he is gone," remarked Fanny, tearfully, " we will only remember his excellencies, and none of his failings."

" Well, I know it's of no use making any fuss or grumbling now. I don't pretend to know, for one moment, what my thirds may come to, only I say this much, Fanny, that so long as you remain single, or don't make some match that would be a disgrace to the Paddlebats, I will be your friend."

" I am as sure, aunt," said Fanny, " that you will be my friend, as I am that I shall make no match that can be, by any possibility, a disgrace to anybody."

" Very well, very well—a-hem !"

It was quite plain to Fanny that her aunt, by this oblique hint, alluded to Nicholas Lowe, for she had been continually, since the death of Mr. Paddlebat, apparently in a high fever of apprehension upon the subject of the supposed preference of Fanny for Lowe—a preference which the beautiful girl was too ingenuous wholly to conceal, and, indeed, which she had, on more than one occasion, all but admitted to her aunt.

But now the day of the funeral arrived, and the usual most uncomfortable commotion attendant upon such a circumstance pervaded the goldsmith's house.

Fanny was in a state of great depression and uneasiness on that morning, and so, indeed, was Mrs. Paddlebat, whose feelings partook more of that character which is commonly denominated the fidgets than any other.

The breakfast, which was spread as usual in that room which Mr. Paddlebat had sat in for so many years, remained untouched ; and never since his death had the vacuum he had left in the small family circle been so painfully apparent as it was on that day when his mortal remains were about to be consigned to their last resting-place.

Although dead, there, perhaps, had been an undefinable feeling that he was still present so long as his body was beneath the roof ; but now, when all sort of vestige of him was about to be removed, Fanny and the widow began truly to feel all that amount of desolation which the death of any principal member of a family makes so painfully apparent in the minds of those who are left to mourn.

" He should have had," said Mrs. Paddlebat, " a very nice funeral, but you know, Fanny, that once since his illness, when he was conscious enough to know who we were, and what he was about, he said,—

" ' Let my funeral be private and plain, and only four mourners.'

" He did, aunt."

" Yes ; and then, you know, I tried to be cheerful, and said to him, ' Fiddlededee, Mr. P., you won't want a funeral at all, plain or expensive, yet for many a long year ;' and then, you know, Fanny, he shook his head and said, in the most remarkable manner,—

" ' You are wrong ; this is my death-bed.' "

" I remember the conversation too well," sobbed Fanny.

A knock at the street-door announced some arrival, connected, probably, with the approaching dismal ceremony. It was the most unwelcome of all persons, the undertaker.

This individual and his assistants were admitted, and then the ceremony of screwing down the corpse was to be performed.

Of course this was a moment for the display of feeling. Indeed, whatever feeling existed in the hearts of those left, was shown at such a moment. It is a moment of all others that is felt the most severely, for then the last view of the dead is taken.

The ceremony is indeed a mournful one; the turning of the screws, and the business-like application of the men as they are called upon to screw the lid of the coffin on; the sound of the screw as it turns in the wood, all tends to tell one more strongly than is possible by any other means, that the unfortunate deceased is about to be hidden for ever from the sight of the living.

Mrs. Paddlebat and Fanny Leslie came to take their last farewell of the body. They were sad, and tears trickled down the features of both the widow and niece.

"Ah! poor dear soul, I shall never—never—never——"

Mrs. Paddlebat could get no further; the rest of the sentence died away in sobs, as she bent her head over the coffin in grief and sorrow.

Fanny Leslie was no less affected; she shed tears of sorrow at the death of her uncle, who was both a good man and a kind one. He had given her every reason to revere his memory, and love him, and she did so fervently.

"Poor dear soul, he is happier than we!" said Mrs. Paddlebat. "Yes, he is far happier than we!"

"I hope so, aunt."

"Hope so! Oh! he never wronged anybody; he never did a wrong action; did all he was commanded to do, and what more is there to make a good Christian? He had his faults, Fanny—men always have; but then they were trifling in comparison to what men usually have; quite trifling."

"Yes, aunt, I know they were trifling."

"God bless and save him!" she sobbed aloud.

"Amen!" sobbed Fanny. "He was a kind protector to me, and a generous one too. Heaven have mercy on him!"

The undertaker's men stood by while this burst of feeling took place. They could not be altogether unmoved, though they had become used to such scenes. It was to them an every day existence, a thing that continually occurred to them.

Nicholas Lowe entered the room to take a last view of his old employer, which he did, at the same time,—

"Mrs. Paddlebat," he said, "this is a melancholy and sad occasion; but grief must have an end. Allow me to take you away. The last ceremony must be performed."

"One more last look at my poor Paddlebat," she said, as she again leaned over the edge of the coffin.

Nicholas Lowe presented his hand to Fanny, and taking hers, drew it through his own. Fanny's eyes were swimming with tears, but Lowe could see the look of love that shone through them, and taking Mrs. Paddlebat, he was about to lead her away.

"You see, Miss Leslie, that this ceremony must be gone through. It is sad and mournful, but necessary."

"Ah, Mr. Lowe, I can never forget this day."

"There is no need," said Lowe; "but it must come to an end, and if you remain here much longer, then you may find grief even too strong for reason."

"Aunt," said Fanny, "we must go."

"Yes, yes," said Mrs. Paddlebat, turning from the coffin, "I am going. Farewell, Paddlebat! you were ever good and kind, and a worthy man. Farewell! farewell!"

Nicholas Lowe endeavoured to lead her away, but she said to him, in a passionate tone of grief,—

"Do not leave the room, Mr. Lowe; do not leave the room. See this ceremony performed before you do."

"I will," said Lowe.

"Thank you, thank you. Come, Fanny, we will retire," said Mrs. Paddlebat, with more composure than they had anticipated she would have possessed.

Fanny Leslie and her aunt quitted the room in which the body lay, and then proceeded to their own room.

"Now," said Lowe, to the undertaker's men, "you can proceed, and get this ceremony over with what expedition you may."

At this moment Rodwell and Gilbert Paddlebat entered the apartment to see the corpse.

"Is he screwed down?" said old Gilbert, as he walked up to the coffin of his brother, who, when alive, was truly his big brother. "Ay, you haven't screwed him down?"

"No," said one of the undertakers, "we have not, but are about to do so now, as there is no time to spare."

"Has the widow seen it?" he asked, turning to Lowe.

"Yes, she has."

"Then screw away. People don't change much in a short time. If he had lived upon less he might have been alive, like me ; but you see, when people live upon the fat of the land, it makes them gross, and liable to disease."

Lowe looked at Mr. Paddlebat as he lay in his coffin, and said, as he did so,—

"Mr. Paddlebat was never one who took anything in excess."

"Ay, but he ate as much as he could. He drank beer and wine ; and all these things help to disease the body, as well as to lighten the pocket."

"Life itself," said Nicholas Lowe, "must be kept up at an expense, and the amount differs in individuals as much as the shape and fashion of their garments."

"That's true," said Gilbert ; "but then, I never like throwing away any money in adorning my person. Look what in the course of a life it would come to, interest and compound interest."

Nicholas Lowe looked at the thin, spare form of the miser, and thought it was not necessary to adorn such a person as that, it was scarce worth the while ; but he said,—

"Then, taking all things into consideration, the state of death is the most preferable, since it puts you to no future expense. You can lie in your coffin, and let your wealth accumulate, while you are not at even the expense of a pitiful living."

"That's very true ; but you can't take advantage of the markets. You must lose all opportunities."

"But if you have no extra gains, you have no loss, nor unexpected expenses, you know."

"But it isn't so comfortable."

"Comfort is expensive."

"So it is ; but, unfortunately, it is a great defect in nature, that we must be at some expense ; and so the art is, not to live entirely without expense to somebody or other, but to live on as little as possible, and by that means to live long and healthily. No, no, I am convinced that had my brother lived as I have done he would have been alive now."

"In that case, you wouldn't have been heir-at-law," said Rodwell, as he stood by.

"No, no, I shouldn't ; but it's a fact, nevertheless."

"For my part," said Rodwell, "I like to live."

"And so do I."

"But I prefer ease and enjoyment, when I can get it, to a life of penury and poverty in the midst of plenty."

"Ah! young man, you don't know what penury and poverty is—you don't know what plenty is."

"You miscalculate what that is," said Rodwell.

"Plenty," continued the old miser, "ain't a full stomach to-day, and an empty one to-morrow."

"I grant it ; and yet it is the plenty of the day."

"Such plenty would bring me to beggary."

"But, now," said Lowe, "the body is screwed down, the last of poor Mr. Paddlebat has been seen."

"Not the last; we have to follow him."

"Do you go ?"

"Surely. I am chief mourner."

Nicholas Lowe, though he had heard of it, yet he could not help looking at the little odd figure beside him, and he could not avoid imagining in his own own mind what a figure he would make at a burial party, where he appeared rather incongruous, on account of his clothes ; for he could not believe it at all possible that Gilbert Paddlebat would go to the necessary outlay for a suit of mourning, even for one that had done duty for a century before.

At that moment Mr. Pink was announced.

"Ah! Mr. Pink ; just let him come in ; he's the very man I want ; a useful man is Pink, very useful indeed, has got a good knowledge of his profession, and knows how to use it too, and don't mind, that's why I like Pink."

Nicholas Lowe left the room, and proceeded to the room in which Mrs. Paddlebat and Fanny Leslie were seated, awaiting the moment when they should see the funeral ceremony pass out before them.

"It is done, Mr. Lowe," said Mrs. Paddlebat; "poor Paddlebat is now—is now——" She couldn't utter the words "screwed down," but paused with a deep sob.

"Yes, madam, all is prepared. I would not have left the room had it been otherwise."

"Thank you."

"When—when—will all be ready?" she inquired.

"For the funeral?"

"Yes."

"In less than an hour, I should imagine," said Lowe, "which will be about the time appointed. When we reach there the hour will have arrived that was agreed upon."

"Very well. Mr. Lowe, you will attend?"

"Yes, certainly."

"Have you seen Mr. Gilbert? He will attend, I believe."

"Yes, he has expressed his determination to do so."

"So I believe he has before," said Mrs. Paddlebat. "Who would have thought of such a man as Gilbert Paddlebat attending a funeral? I declare he is a disgrace. Of course he has no mourning? He would not have such a thing under any circumstance. He would think he was going to ruin himself. Oh, dear! if poor Paddlebat were alive, I am sure he would laugh, poor soul. Now, if Gilbert had died instead, how much happier we should all of us have been!"

There can be no doubt but Mrs. Paddlebat meant what she said; at the same time she did not wish that death might suddenly seize old Gilbert, but of the two she would much rather the latter had died. Indeed it was but just, she thought, that the miserly, disagreeable men should be taken first.

Nicholas Lowe left the apartment, and proceeded to dress himself for the funeral ceremony.

*   *   *   *   *   *   *

"Mr. Pink," said Gilbert, when he came in, "you are ready, I see, for the funeral."

"Yes, Mr. Paddlebat, I may say I am always ready for anything that comes to me in almost any shape."

"Capital habit that of yours, Pink."

"This?" said Pink, looking at his dingy black, for he was always dressed in black.

"No, I mean your habit of being ready."

"Oh, it's difficult to take a professional man unawares, when he has set his mind to it. I am ready, quite ready, and agreeable to anything in the shape of business."

"Or death," said Rodwell, who was standing by.

Mr. Pink turned pale for a moment, but he recovered himself, as he said, without any smile,—

"Why, death, you see, is a different thing from anything else; you can't trust it as you would any other claim; but I may say, in the ordinary acceptation of the words, I am prepared even for that."

"Well," said Gilbert, "nothing more could be desired; but I will now get ready for the funeral."

Rodwell looked at Gilbert with surprise; for he, too, thought it strange if he should go to the expense of mourning.

But they knew not the sudden resources of Mr. Gilbert Paddlebat, who intended to go to his brother's funeral in a black coat, at all events, since he had found one in turning over the various stores in the house.

"When will all be ready to proceed?" said the undertaker.

"In about half an hour."

"It must not be later, for we shall not have any time to spare, and if we don't get there to a minute, we shall have to come back, for the clergyman will not wait."

"Well, then, we won't be later than that."

"Very good," said the man; "I'll have all in readiness to move from the door in twenty minutes."

"Do so," said Gilbert; and he left the room, as also did Rodwell, to dress himself for the ceremony.

Nicholas Lowe was the first to come down, and he entered the room where the usual refreshments were laid, and where Mr. Pink was regaling himself upon the principle that he was always ready for anything and everything.

He was a mourner by profession, and did it systematically and in a business-like manner, and did not allow it to disturb the flow of his private feelings. He regaled himself with a variety of things, indifferently. Probably he disliked to show any partiality for any one thing over another, and, hence, he ate and drank several.

"Fine day for the ceremony, sir," he said, as Nicholas Lowe here entered the apartment. "Charming weather!"

"It is a fine day."

"Is the churchyard far?"

"I believe not."

"We sha'n't be long in going?"

"I dare say not."

The next who entered the room was Rodwell, and then Gilbert Paddlebat, who had attired himself for the ceremony.

It was with some difficulty they could restrain themselves from exhibiting signs of mirth on an occasion so unsuitable for it; but the cause would have been a sufficient excuse anywhere.

Old Gilbert Paddlebat, in rummaging over the stores of his brother, had found, among other things, an old black coat. This was a treasure to Gilbert, and saved any unpleasant remarks at the funeral; not that Gilbert cared anything about that, on the contrary, he would have braved it out, but having the means at hand, and without expense, to attend his brother's funeral in black, he determined to do so.

"It will do very well," he said; "and just the thing."

Gilbert forgot that the black dress coat of his brother on him was not exactly a fit. He could have buttoned up three men like Gilbert in it; and when he had it on, the tails very nearly swept the earth, and the cuffs he was obliged to turn up; so, altogether, he did present an odd appearance.

Gilbert thought that the whole presented a very decent funeral attire. It was a black coat, and what more would they have?—they couldn't but have a black coat, and as to the peculiar cut, why, all the world knew that depended much upon taste —that is, individual taste.

However, as might have been expected, no remark was made, save among the undertakers, who considered Gilbert an especial object of admiration—an object worthy of their most serious contemplation, and when no one was present, one of the men whispered to the others,—

"I'm d——d if that little old man in the big black coat don't beat Akebo—and he beat the devil, all the world knows. How he'd do for a theyatre!"

And so he would. He would have been a property for the gods; they would have encored his every action.

But to return. All is now ready; nothing remains; the mourners are collected together, and they follow the body, as it precedes them, from the room in which it laid.

Mr. Pink followed side by side with Gilbert Paddlebat, and a pair of exceptions to the human race they certainly were, and served for some remarks among the spectators.

It was a mournful ceremony. There was, however, no other feelings in the breast of old Gilbert than those of a business-like character; he considered it a piece of business; and while he took the slow steps of the funeral procession, he was calculating how he should dispose of much of the money which he held, or should have, of his brother's.

"I will," thought Gilbert Paddlebat, "place it out at interest—good security. All things considered, I shall be able to make a decent thing of it, I have no doubt."

The funeral ceremony was not likely to be one that would be protracted beyond the usual time necessary by any display of great feeling on the part of the heir-at-law, for old Gilbert Paddlebat's feelings were of rather a pleasant character.

It was pleasant to know that he had lived the longest—that he was following his brother, rather than his brother following him ; it was especially pleasant to think, too, of the great profit this death brought him.

"All people's relations are not so profitable to them as mine are," he said ; "but how much better had it been for me if my brother had led a more careful life, and had done more of his own work ; all this would have been increased to double the amount, and then I might have been rich. But, never mind ; we cannot have all we wish or all we ought to have."

By this time they reached within hearing of the bell, as it tolled ; they were now near their journey's end, and they could see, now and then, the vane on the steeple, as they came near the church where he was to be buried.

This was one of those little quiet churchyards, of which there are so many about the city that scarce the inhabitants themselves know anything about them.

It was situated in Basinghall-street, in the midst of a busy and populous neighbourhood, where, indeed, men were passing to and fro every minute, with solid, looking countenances, occupied with their own affairs, and not disturbing themselves about anything they saw, so that it did not help or hinder them.

They entered the old churchyard, and stood in a group ; the minister met them ; a fat man of business was he—one who wasted none of his breath without a substantial reason.

Old Gilbert looked at him all the while he was reading the funeral ceremony, and made a mental calculation as to how many men he must have buried before he could have fattened himself up to that point.

He was evidently fat from good living.

"And a good living it is, too," thought old Gilbert ; "and it will be so, too, as long as people are foolish enough to pay for the unnecessary luxury of lying and putrifying in a damp churchyard."

Nicholas Lowe looked up at the church, at least so much of it as could be seen, and then at the houses on either side of the way, where there were a number of windows, all closed, and, apparently, never cleaned ; not a face was observable among them ; there appeared to be no curiosity among the population of Basinghall-street.

From one window, indeed, there did appear to be one head, and that was a female's.

Yes, from the top attic in one of the houses, whose faces looked into the churchyard, was protruded a female head. She looked down upon the ceremony below with an interest, arising, probably, from the circumstance, that such occurrences were rare—excited only from the fact of the dearth of any novelty in that neighbourhood ; and, to do the female sex justice, there was only that one who knew of it, or they would have been on the *qui vive*.

The funeral ceremony is over, and old Paddlebat, the goldsmith, is placed in his long home.

The black funeral cloak with which old Gilbert was enveloped, hid, it is true, the coat he wore, and, thus, much of his oddity of appearance escaped observation ; but it was quite impossible to hide the man, unless you smothered him ; the hat, ornamented with a band, was a strange, incongruous article of wearing apparel ; indeed, the undertaker turned it about so often as he put it on, that old Gilbert snatched it away, declaring the man should pay for it if he injured it.

The man certainly did say he shouldn't be much out of pocket, if it were fairly valued.

They arrived now at the residence of the late Mr. Paddlebat. Old Gilbert was impatient; he desired to begin instanter.

And very soon after he threw the cloak and band off, and then said to Mr. Pink, in an audible tone,—

" Pink—I say, Pink, now's the time—isn't it?"

" Certainly," said Pink.

" Funeral's over?"

" Certainly," said Pink; " we have just come from it."

" Of course, we have; and they are all together in the parlour—are they not?"

" Yes, all of them."

" Then we'll go in. Come in with me."

Accordingly, they both entered the room in which they were all collected. Gilbert was pleased, yet he did not show anything, save a desire to go over the house, and take possession.

" You are all here," he said.

Mrs. Paddlebat looked as if she couldn't understand the meaning of the words; but she said,—

" Who else do you want?"

" Oh! I want nobody," said Gilbert; " but I ask you all, now you are together, if you have any will to produce, because I am about to take possession in default of any such will, being heir-at-law."

There was a pause.

" I believe there is none," said Mrs. Paddlebat.

" Had we better not make a thorough search?" inquired Rodwell, who had spoken.

" I agree," said old Gilbert, who appeared no ways displeased at this interruption or proposition.

A search was immediately begun, in which all took part; Gilbert Paddlebat, Nicholas Lowe, and Jervis Rodwell. Mrs. Paddlebat shook her head and declined, saying it was useless.

They turned over books and papers most remorselessly; and even old Gilbert was in high glee; he seemed to be touching his own, and in the act of securing it. None were more actively employed than Rodwell.

He looked sharp round the rooms, and over the papers that passed through the hands of old Gilbert. At length he came to a piece of furniture with some drawers, and pulling one of them open, suddenly he seized a parchment, exclaiming,—

" Hilloa!—what have we here?"

Everybody looked round, and beheld the parchment. Old Gilbert turned slowly round, and looked at him; but he trembled from head to hand—rushed a few steps back—a pallid hue overspread his countenance, and he fainted into the arms of Mr. Pink.

———

CHAPTER XXXIV.

THE CONSTERNATION AT THE PADDLEBATS'.—THE READING OF THE DISCOVERED WILL.

THERE certainly was nothing very extraordinary in the fact that the goldsmith should have left a will behind him, nor that such a document should be found in the bureau, where so many of his more important papers were kept; and yet the effect which the actual discovery did produce was most excessive.

Upon the mind of old Gilbert, however, the effect, as we have seen, was quite electrical, and had not his friend and professional adviser, Mr. Pink, been close at hand, there can be no doubt but that the little old man would have fallen to the floor.

He might not have hurt himself, he had so short a distance to fall, on account of his diminutive size; but, at all events, Mr. Pink did save him.

Mrs. Paddlebat looked astonished and anxious. Fanny only seemed pleased to think that now the property of her deceased uncle would, at all events, be distributed in accordance with his own wishes, be those wishes what they might.

Nicholas Lowe was decidedly pleased. That will might produce a desirable change in his prospects; and any change, so far as he was concerned, would be decidedly for the better, inasmuch, as now he had nothing at all to expect, or to look forward to.

It was strange to see how Rodwell trembled as he held that document in his hands which was of so highly important a character.

Perhaps he, too, felt that now there was some hope for him, if before, except through the good feeling of Mrs. Paddlebat towards him, there was none.

A pause of some minutes' duration ensued now, and every one there present appeared to be too busy with their own reflections to make any remark.

It was Mr. Pink who first broke this silence, by saying,—

"Mr. Paddlebat, pray stand up, sir. Perhaps the will leaves you sole legatee."

"You may eat me if it does," groaned old Gilbert, slowly recovering. "I know better—'tis all up, now—all up; and mind, Pink, I pay none of your expenses."

"Hush!" whispered Pink, close to his ear; "hush! Are you mad?"

"Nearly."

"And why? You must dispute this will, and throw the whole concern into chancery. That is the way to meet so very awkward an affair as this."

"Chancery!"

"Hush!—hush!"

"If I go into chancery may I be——never mind."

"Well, ladies and gentlemen," said Rodwell, "this is a most unexpected discovery; but here is the will, and I can only hope that, when it is read, it will prove to be satisfactory to every one here present."

"It's the first," said Mrs. Paddlebat, "ever I heard of Paddlebat making a will. It does seem most astonishing to me that he never mentioned it."

"People often, madam," said Rodwell, "take a foolish pride in keeping their wills secret; but here it is, and I presume that we had better, in order to prevent any cavilling upon the subject, have it read at once."

"Read away—read away," said old Paddlebat, as he flung himself into an arm-chair, amid the ample proportions of which he was nearly lost.

"Ah! Mr. Rodwell," said Mrs. Paddlebat, as she flung herself into another chair, which groaned again beneath her weight. "Read the will—read away —read away! We may as well hear at once what it is all about."

"If such," said Rodwell, "be the general feeling, I shall, of course, gladly respond to it, and read the will of my much-respected deceased employer, and, I may say, friend."

Lowe was silent; but that silence of his seemed very much to annoy Mr. Rodwell, who looked hard at him, as if he much wished that he should make some sort of remark upon what was occurring.

But Lowe was determined to disappoint him, and said not a word. Fanny, too, looked at Lowe, as if she expected some opinion from him as regarded the affair; but even that did not tempt him to speak, although one would have said, of course, with a full knowledge of his feelings towards her, that a silence, when she wished otherwise, was not an easy thing to maintain.

All he would do was to look with a calm and steady countenance upon Rodwell, as if he had thoughts upon the subject which were too deep for utterance, or, at all events, which some principle of prudence induced him, just then, to keep to himself.

"Then, as nobody objects," added Rodwell, "general silence, I presume, gives general consent. I will read the will."

These words were levelled at Nicholas Lowe; but they were as non effective as any that had preceded them.

With a trembling eagerness, that was quite apparent to every one, and which was, perhaps, when we take all things into consideration, excusable enough, Rodwell spread open the sheet of parchment, which purported to contain the last wishes and testamentary intentions of the deceased.

He cleared his throat by a preliminary cough before he commenced ; and then, in a voice which was dreadfully infirm and shaking, he read as follows :—

"I, Joseph Paddlebat, being well in health, and in sound judgment concerning the affairs of this world, hereby make my will ; and I write it myself, because it contains matters of so very simple a nature, that there can be no occasion to trouble the lawyers upon the subject.

"The whole of my property of all kinds whatsoever, and wheresoever, I bequeath to my clerk, named Jervis Rodwell——"

"What!" exclaimed old Gilbert.

"Gracious!" said Mrs. Paddlebat.

Nicholas Lowe smiled.

"I am astounded," said Rodwell ; "and certainly shall not, unless there follow some conditions which will induce me, take advantage of this generous bequest to its full extent. You all hear this declaration. It is made truly, and is one to which I wish firmly to adhere."

"Pray, my good sir, finish the will," said Mr. Pink. "How do you know but what, after all, the property is only left to you in trust for other purposes ?"

A flush of colour came over Rodwell's face, as he said,—

"True—true, Mr. Pink. Perhaps I am premature. I hope and trust, however, that every one here present gives me credit for the best of notions."

Nobody answered this appeal, not even Mrs. Paddlebat, although it came from such a great favourite as Rodwell ; and after waiting a few seconds with the vain hope of some one giving an assent to the self-laudatory profession, he was compelled to go on reading the will without being to that extent gratified.

"My clerk, named Jervis Rodwell, as a consideration for faithful services, provided always, that from the business he pays to my beloved wife a sum which shall exceed in amount by one hundred pounds annually, what her third of my personal estate would have produced her, had such been invested at the rate of five per centum."

"Oh !" said Mrs. Paddlebat.

"So that you perceive, madam," said Rodwell, rather hastily, "that you are by one hundred pounds a year the better for this will, than as if Mr. Paddlebat had died intestate."

"Further, I make it my most particular request to my dear niece, Fanny Leslie, that she marry Jervis Rodwell, who, I know, will make to her a good and a honourable husband ; but if she will not do so, I direct that out of the business likewise, as before mentioned, she be paid the sum of fifty pounds per annum.

"If it shall seem fit and proper to the aforesaid Jervis Rodwell not to carry on my business, he shall be at liberty to dispose of the same, and to convert the whole of my estate into money, from which gross amount he shall be compelled and compellable to invest, in sufficient and ample securities, so much as shall pay to my wife and my niece, what they are each respectively entitled to, under this my will.

"I likewise bequeath, from my general estate, one shilling to my brother, Gilbert Paddlebat, and direct that all my debts be paid.

                                        "JOSIAH PADDLEBAT."

"And your witnesses ?" said Pink.

"Are named here," replied Rodwell. "John Todd and William Johnstone."

"Is that all ?"

"That is all."

"Fury and damnation !" cried old Gilbert.

"My dear sir," said Pink, "will you oblige me by coming away at once ? Mr. Rodwell has to prove the will, and to swear about it, not you, you know. Pray command yourself, if you please, and allow me to remark, that this conduct of yours, and, in fact, any ebullition of feeling upon this occasion, is highly prejudicial."

See page 206.

"Well, but ——"

"Now, now—allow me, I know exactly what you are going to say, and I will say it for you calmly and deliberately. Mr. Rodwell, it is not necessary for our cause that we should have any disguises, but the fact is, we dispute the validity of the will which you have so cleverly produced."

"I produced?"

"Oh, yes, yes. We know all about that."

"My strong impression," said Nicholas Lowe, "is, that he took it from his pocket, and not from the drawer in the bureau at all."

"Say what you please, and do what you can," said Rodwell; "I despise these attacks of petty malice, founded upon disappointed cupidity."

"I am disappointed in nothing," said Lowe. "You will perceive, all of you, that, will or no will, I am in the same position precisely."

No. 25.

"Beware, Nicholas Lowe," said Rodwell. "Beware !"

" I defy you," said Nicholas Lowe. "Rodwell, I tell you now, once and for all, I defy you."

" Well, well ; we shall see. As for you, Mr. Paddlebat, and your attorney, you can take advice, I hope it will be good advice, and do what you can in this matter ; I tell you at once and candidly, I will support my rights and the rights of this lady."

" Will you now, my good sir," said Pink to old Paddlebat, in imploring accents, " come away with me?"

" I will, I will. Confound you all. May every penny-piece of the property prove a curse to you instead of a joy. I leave my malediction upon you all."

" Except Mr. Lowe," murmured Pink, " who will be a witness in our favour, you know, Mr. Paddlebat."

" But," said the old man, " I suppose he's like the rest, looking out for what he can get."

So saying he left the room, shaking with rage, and in a few moments the loud shutting of the street-door betokened his departure from the house.

CHAPTER XXXV.

THE QUARREL.—LOWE'S DEPARTURE FROM THE HOUSE.—THE BOLD STEP OF NICHOLAS LOWE.

THEY were by no means a harmonious set of people that were left together at the goldsmith's, even after the departure of Gilbert.

The last few words which Lowe had uttered to Rodwell, convinced the latter that the hollow peace which had been made between them was at an end, and that consequently nothing was to be got by any further conciliation in that quarter. He accordingly at once assumed the offensive, and said,—

" Mr. Lowe, I hope, after hearing the will of the deceased Mr. Paddlebat read, you will at once see your propriety of leaving this house."

" You are a deeper villain than even I thought you," said Lowe. " I will leave the house, but it shall be to take measures to confound you."

" You are already yourself confounded," said Rodwell. " Stir hand or foot to do me any injury, and I will dash every hope you have, in a quarter to which I need not more particularly allude, to the dust."

" Again I defy you."

" As you please—as you please. I cannot be long ignorant of anything you may say or do, or attempt to do, and then it will be time enough for me to act against you."

" Nicholas Lowe," said Fanny, in imploring accents, " is this a time to quarrel? For my sake—for your own sake, I pray you stop this most unseemly altercation."

" I will and do," said Lowe. " Believe me, it was forced upon me."

" Well, I don't see that," said Mrs. Paddlebat.

" Madam, I regret to say, that you never were my friend."

" And I don't see why I should be."

" Still you might have left me without your enmity. Heaven knows I never did anything to merit it, but of late you have, I fear, had your mind poisoned against me from some source, by some means, and what person can I so aptly accuse of so much baseness as this man, who has all but declared himself to be my uncompromising foe. Yes, this man, Jervis Rodwell."

" I appeal to Mrs. Paddlebat," said Rodwell ; " have I ever said one word to the injury or prejudice of Mr. Lowe?"

" Certainly not," said Mrs. Paddlebat.

" There, sir ; are you now satisfied ?"

" Far from it," said Lowe ; " I believe you to have consummate art enough to impose so fully upon so ingenuous a character as Mrs. Paddlebat, so that even when you seemed to be praising any one, you would really be raising the greatest possible amount of prejudice against them."

" There, Mr. Lowe, you are wrong," said Mrs. Padddlebat; " and if these were the last words I had to speak in the world, I would say so."

" How, madam ?"

" Why, so far from ever saying anything against you, Mr. Rodwell, whenever he has mentioned you to me, has always regretted that there should be anything about you at all suspicious."

" Indeed !"

" Yes ; I can swear to that. He said he pitied you with all his heart; and he really very much hoped that you would so conduct yourself as quite to redeem your character."

" And that," exclaimed Lowe, " is what you call saying nothing to a man's prejudice, do you ?"

" Yes, to be sure."

" Really, Mrs. Paddlebat, you are a greater fool than I thought you."

" Fool !"

" Yes, madam, I speak advisedly, fool. Why, did it never occur to you that the worst cloak which designing villany could ever wear, was candour ?"

" I don't know what you mean."

" Of course, you don't. I was foolish to utter such a sentiment to one who does not comprehend the language in which it was uttered. Jervis Rodwell, you have been fortunate in having to your hand materials upon which to work. You may congratulate yourself; but, remember—remember, I say, that in me there is a witness whose testimony will go far towards proving that the will which you produced is a forgery."

" I call upon all here present," said Rodwell, " to bear witness that this man threatens me with his testimony, and, therefore, it becomes of no value."

" No," said Lowe, " you do not, and you cannot invalidate my testimony. I here say, before Mrs. Paddlebat and Miss Leslie, that nothing in the whole world would induce me for one moment to swerve from the truth ; but I am, from the most conscientious motives, compelled to acknowledge that I have the strongest possible conviction upon my mind, that you, Jervis Rodwell, took that will from your own pocket, instead of from the bureau, where you affected to find it."

" I deny that assertion," said Rodwell. " I deny it in toto. It is either a very great mistake, or a wicked and unfounded calumny."

" And I think so likewise," put in Mrs. Paddlebat.

" And you, Fanny ?" said Lowe.

" I was not observing, and, therefore, can have no opinion upon the subject."

" Now, Mr. Lowe," said Mrs. Paddlebat, " you must be well aware, that, under any circumstances whatever, as you are no party to the disputes now going on, you can have no interest in them."

" Well, madam ?"

" And well, sir. If there is any money owing to you up to now from Mr. Paddlebat, I will pay it to you, and then you can go at once."

Nicholas Lowe felt fully the force of this observation, however uncomfortable a one it was. He knew that in the pending disputes about the will, let whoever would gain the day, he should be repudiated, for he was alike distasteful to all the parties who had any important interest in the affair.

Fanny, who, if Rodwell's will succeeded, would have an annuity of fifty pounds, was the only one towards whom he could have turned with anything like an assurance of a welcome ; but as that was certainly not the time or the place to attempt to commit her to anything, he wisely forbore, and he said, after some moments' pause, to Mrs. Paddlebat,—

" Madam, I regret that, in the natural warmth of a moment, when I found myself most grievously injured, I should have allowed myself to say what my heart, upon calmer reflection, cannot approve. I will, since it is your wish, leave the house ; but I warn you before I do so, to be most especially careful and guarded how you give ear to what Rodwell may say to you as regards the will which he has produced. In that document, it is cunningly sought to win you over to regard it with favourable eyes, because it adds, if substantiated, a paltry couple of pounds per week to your income, an addition which you will never perceive, inasmuch as what you would have without it will be amply sufficient, as well for all your wants, as to surround you with many of the luxuries of life to an extent as great as you have hitherto enjoyed them."

"Oh! indeed."

"Yes, madam."

"Is that all?"

"I should have thought it had been sufficient."

"Then you thought wrong, for it is not sufficient, sir. And now you may go at once, as you have had your say."

"With regard to money matters," added Lowe, "I will make up my account, and send it to the proper quarter, which will be in a short time, most likely, a master in chancery."

"Master who?"

"A master in chancery, madam; and, in consequence of this will of Rodwell's, you, and all persons at all concerned in this affair, may linger out your lives in endless litigation, getting nothing."

Nicholas Lowe was quite willing to alarm Mrs. Paddlebat; but he was wrong in this assumption, and he knew it, for Mrs. Paddlebat happened to be so situated in the affair, that nobody questioned her right to the proceeds of one-third of the estate of the deceased goldsmith. The only question which at all concerned her in the matter was, whether or not she was entitled to one hundred pounds per annum more than that third, or not.

Taking, therefore, such a view of her case as any court of equity would be sure to take, she would be at once allowed a sufficient sum out of the litigated property to support her well, because it would be manifestly and *prima facie* unjust to make her a sufferer, because two other persons chose to enter into law suits.

But Mrs. Paddlebat, not being the clearest reasoner in the world, was alarmed accordingly; and when she heard that the property, through the finding of a will, was at all likely to get into chancery, of which she had, and that was natural enough, rather a dreadful idea, she got horribly frightened at Lowe's words, and exclaimed,—

"Dear me, Mr. Rodwell, really I didn't think of that."

"But you will continue to think of it," said Lowe; "and I rather expect, madam, that I have given you now a subject for meditation, which you will find some difficulty in getting rid of."

"Bless me!"

"You have much need of blessing."

"What trash is this?" said Rodwell.

"Trash, Mr. Rodwell! Do you call it trash," half shrieked Mrs. Paddlebat, "to get into chancery?"

"Trash has been spoken to you."

"Indeed, I don't know; I perfectly recollect once coming home with the late Mr. P., in our *shay*, from Enfield; and seeing a great crowd of people, and a man with two black eyes, and his nose knocked into the middle of his head somewhere, and all his face black and blue."

"Really—really," said Rodwell; "what has that to do with the case in point?"

"A great deal."

"As how, Mrs. Paddlebat?"

"Why, I'll tell you. I heard one man say to another, as we passed on,—'That fellow has had his head in chancery.'"

Lowe, notwithstanding all his feelings of aggravation, could scarcely refrain from laughing aloud at this anecdote, told so innocently, too, as it was, by Mrs. Paddlebat; but he moved towards the door, saying,—

"I shall now bid you farewell, madam, with a sincere hope that you may get clear of the difficulties with which Rodwell, and no one but Rodwell, would surround you, with more ease and satisfaction to yourself than my fears predict."

"Oh, thank you for nothing," said Mrs. Paddlebat.

"Fanny," said Nicholas Lowe, "for the present, I bid you adieu."

"Farewell," said Fanny.

"I'd have you to know," said Mrs. Paddlebat, "you late shopman to the late Mr. P., that the young lady whom you take upon yourself to call Fanny, is Miss Leslie, sir, and my niece, sir; and I think it's like your impudence to call her Fanny."

An angry reply was upon Lowe's lips; but he refrained from uttering it, and at once now left the house.

It was in no very pleasant frame of mind that he walked from the goldsmith's door. There were a number of considerations connected with the very perplexing and unexpected turn which affairs had taken, that, on his part, required the deepest and the most attentive consideration in the world.

He was still in a condition to accuse Rodwell criminally if he chose. Indeed, putting aside the matter concerning the robbery at the goldsmith's, which he, Lowe, had no real doubt whatever concerning, he thought that he had evidence sufficient to substantiate the charge against Rodwell, of attempting his life.

He had some days before ascertained from the chemist, that the white powder which he had submitted to him for analysis, was arsenic, in the usual form in which that drug was kept in the shops.

This, connected with the attempt to shoot him in Wilderness-row, and Susan's evidence about Rodwell coming home, and without a doubt playing tricks with the kitchen clock, made up, certainly, a train of circumstantial evidence against Rodwell, which was amply sufficient to justify Nicholas Lowe in taking proceedings against him even if found not to be sufficient to ensure his conviction upon so serious a charge.

But whether or not it would be politic to take so hostile a step was quite another matter, and one which required no little consideration.

From what had fallen from Rodwell, Lowe felt perfectly sure that he knew something of his, Lowe's, private history, but how much he knew of it, or from what source he had received it, he found it beyond his powers to conjecture.

Of course Lowe felt that the only injury which could be done him now by the most ample disclosures of the episode in his history, which had been a most painful one, would be to at once deprive him of all chance of calling Fanny Leslie his own.

That a girl like Fanny would shrink from an union with a man who had passed through such a scene, was a proposition which he, Lowe, could not for one moment accuse his mind with the idea of doubting.

His feelings were deeply interested in Fanny. He did really love her as much as one who had seen more of life than any one, from his age, would have been warranted in supposing, could love anybody; and about the notion of losing her, there was something which made him feel dreadfully desolate.

"No, no, no," he said; "I cannot now, after nursing the idea so long, consent to give up the idea of losing Fanny Leslie."

Taking, then, such a view of the case, he doubted if he could safely attempt anything against Rodwell.

"The villain," he said, "has it in his power, I am well convinced, to destroy all the trusting confidence which Fanny Leslie has in me, if he pleases; and if I commit any overt act which shall be to his prejudice, no doubt he will do so. But I do not think that he will provoke me to hostilities by commencing such a war."

The more Lowe came to consider the whole of the circumstances in their various bearings and relations one to another, the more he felt convinced that Rodwell would be afraid to provoke him, Lowe, too far. He remembered that, even in his anger, he, Rodwell, had only uttered contingent threats, such as "If you do so-and-so, then I will do so-and-so."

"And, besides," said Lowe to himself, "I cannot fail to know whenever he does succeed in making any impression upon the mind of Fanny Leslie, for I shall at once open a correspondence with her, and the tone in which she conducts it will be amply sufficient always to possess me with what has happened at the house."

It became necessary now that he, Lowe, should look out for some place in which to live ; and, in preference to going to an hotel, which neither his means nor his inclination prompted him to, he looked out for some private and respectable lodging.

In London no one need be long in suiting himself in such a particular, especially a single man.   The amount of accommodation offered in the metropolis to persons so delightfully situated, shows in what appreciation they are held, and how much the good sense and discretion must be valued which has enabled them to remain in a state of such beatitude.

He would not go far from the goldsmith's house, and he had no occasion, for he succeeded in locating himself almost in the immediate vicinity ; and then he considered that the very first step he ought to take was to communicate with Fanny, and let her know where he was to be found, in case of any emergency arising which should induce her to require his advice or assistance.

He sat down to do this, but scarcely had he commenced his task when, to his great surprise, his landlady entered his room, and said,—

" Here is a gentleman, sir, who wishes to see you."

" To see me ?"

" Yes, sir."

" Oh, it is some mistake.   No one of my acquaintances has the least idea that I am living here."

" No, indeed, sir, it's no mistake ; he asked for you by name, and he said his own was Paddlebat."

" Paddlebat ?"

" Yes, sir, and here he is."

Old Gilbert at that moment sidled into the apartment, and, advancing, he, with an odd appearance of cordiality, stretched out his hand, and said,—

" Ah! how do you do, Mr. Lowe ?—how do you do ?   You see I have found you out.   May I hope you are quite well ?   Thank you, ma'am ; that will do, if you please.   All's right.   This is the gentleman."

CHAPTER XXXVI.

GILBERT PADDLEBAT'S SINGULAR PROPOSAL.—A GREAT ALTERATION IN LOWE'S AFFAIRS.—THE FURNISHED HOUSE.

THE astonishment of Nicholas at this most unexpected visit was so great that for some moments he could do nothing but look in the face of old Gilbert Paddlebat in silence.

The landlady left the room, and then, when the door was closed, and they were completely alone, the old miser changed his tone, and no longer affecting the old acquaintanceship with Lowe, which he had put on in the presence of the landlady, he said,—

" Mr. Lowe, no doubt you are surprised enough to see me here, but I am a man of business, and, if I mistake not, you are one too ?"

" Well, sir ?"

" What's o'clock ?"

" Do you come here to ask me so ridiculous a question ?"

" Not merely on that errand, but, as a preliminary step, I merely ask you, in common courtesy, what's o'clock ?"

" Oh, the little old fellow," thought Lowe, " has gone mad upon the loss of the property which he thought to possess himself of so snugly.   I suppose it will be best to humour him, although how he found me out here is to me a profound mystery at present."

Lowe took his watch from his pocket, as he said,—

" Well, sir, if you wish to know what the time is, it is half-past two."

" Precisely ?"

" Within a minute or so."

" That will do. And now to business."

" Mr. Paddlebat, you must excuse me, but I am really not aware of any business which you and I can have together."

" No ; I don't suppose you are."

" Well, then ——"

" Pho !—pho ! Don't waste valuable time, young man, if you please. If you had had business with me, of which I was not aware, you would have come to me. Now, what suppose, by a similarity of reasoning, I have business with you which you were not aware of ?"

" Why, certainly ; then you come to me."

" Very true ; and here I am."

" Well, sir, I will listen patiently to whatever you may have to say, and I have no doubt whatever but that from a gentleman of your well-known business habits, I shall have no difficulty in comprehending exactly what you came about."

" Very well."

" But, in the first place, will you pardon my very natural curiosity in inquiring how it was that you found me out here ?"

" Oh, that is easily answered ; Mr. Pink and I watched you."

" Very well. Now proceed."

" I will at once. A-hem ! I am not a young man, nor a rich one."

Nicholas merely inclined his head.

" Notwithstanding the seeming bad terms I and my brother, the deceased goldsmith, were on, we had a private meeting together about one week before the seizure of illness which has eventually proved so fatal to him—a private meeting at my house, but not so private as that I cannot produce evidence of it having taken place."

" You surprise me."

" Well, never mind. At that interview, my deceased brother entered into a conversation upon a number of family affairs, only interesting to ourselves, but finally he came round to speak of his orphan niece, Fanny Leslie, for whom he expressed as great an amount of affection as he could have done if she had been a very dear child of his own, indeed, and his only one."

" He had such an affection for her," said Lowe.

" I know it. Well, he then and there expressed his full and firm intention of making his will within a few days ; in fact, his words were these :—' Gilbert, I have my own reasons for at once making my will ; I dare say that, to all appearance, I look much as I ordinarily look, but I have a sort of an uncomfortable presentiment of my own that my end is near at hand.' "

All the while he spoke, it was odd to see with what a strange and cunning look the little old man regarded Lowe, as if he would have searched into his very soul to see if he believed what was said to him.

The fact was that Lowe did not believe one word of it, and was only waiting, with all the gravity possible, to know what this exordium was likely to lead to.

" Well, what do you think of that ?" said old Gilbert, as if he could not, from the cool and calm expression of Nicholas Lowe's countenance, make out whether he liked it or not.

" I hear you," said Lowe.

" Oh, very good. Well, of course, I made a suitable reply to my brother. While I endeavoured to combat the nervous feeling which made him think that his end was near, I told him that as to making his will, it was a thing which I would gladly encourage him to do at once."

" Certainly," said Lowe.

" And then, when we had got so far, Mr. Lowe, in our conversation, he said to me, ' Gilbert, tell me now candidly, what you should consider a good and proper sum to leave to Fanny, or in what other way I ought to provide for her ?'

" Upon this question, Mr. Lowe, being propounded to me, I scarcely knew what to say; but after a time I did remark, that—'I thought if, during his life time, he could get her well and comfortably married, it would be about the best and the most satisfactory course that could be pursued.'"

" What did he say to that?" interposed Lowe, who began to be interested in spite of himself, although he really felt convinced, in his own mind, that all the old man was telling him was but a tissue of lies.

" Why, Mr. Lowe, he pondered over that rather, and then he said, 'Gilbert, I did hope that she would have fixed her affections upon one of the young men I have in my employment—Mr. Lowe and Mr. Rodwell; but I am inclined now to think, after some careful inquiry and careful personal watching, that they are neither of them such as I should like to see Fanny Leslie united to for life.'"

Lowe winced a little at this.

" And then he went on," said old Gilbert, " to say, 'My wife, I know, would be glad to see Fanny married to Rodwell; but I like him less than the other, and I am inclined to think that he is a bad young man. If I live he shall leave my employment.'"

" Ah," said Lowe.

" ' As for Lowe,' added Gilbert, 'I have my doubts about him, and I shall watch him; so that so much of the affair being settled, I think, brother, I shall make my will to-morrow or the next day at the farthest, and that in it I shall leave Fanny seven or eight hundred pounds, with full freedom to do what she likes.' Now, Mr. Lowe, I not only firmly believe that such a will is in existence, but I likewise believe that the one which Rodwell has produced is a forgery."

" Do you know," said Lowe, who now began to have a glimmering of what all this was likely to lead to,—" do you know that such a will is in existence, Mr. Paddlebat; because if you do, why not produce it at once, and so settle a matter which is at present in an extremely painful state of doubt?"

" No, no, I do not know it is in existence, but a thorough search in the deceased's house might find it. A search has found one will, dated some time back—why might not another search find another will which would crush it, and place seven or eight hundred pounds in the hands of Fanny Leslie, and consequently in the hands of whoever was so fortunate as to win her for his wife? Can you answer that, Mr. Lowe? Eh, eh, eh?"

Now, indeed, as the phrase is, the intentions of Gilbert Paddlebat were quite evident to your meanest capacity. What he had almost from the first suspected, was now almost, to Nicholas Lowe's apprehension, openly avowed. Old Gilbert wanted him to form a coalition with him against Rodwell, and to fight him with his own weapons.

" You are silent," said the miser. " Say at once that you do not like the idea, and I will go."

" No, no," said Lowe, as old Gilbert half rose from his chair, as if to carry his intention of going into effect. " No, I will think. You have, I confess, startled me a little."

" A-hem!" said the old miser; " I believe I have made no proposition; I have only related a little family scene, which, as I tell you, occurred between myself and my brother."

" I fully understand you. I have no earthly doubt, both from my knowledge of Rodwell, which circumstances have combined to make tolerably extensive, and from the manner in which the pretended will he said he found was produced, that it has been fabricated by him."

" Of course."

" Besides, it precisely suits his own purposes."

" Ah! It would be wonderful if it did not."

" True. The artful manner, too, in which he has secured the good wishes of the weak-minded Mrs. Paddlebat is, to my mind, another convincing proof of the forgery of the will."

" My young friend," cried old Gilbert; " do not combat a shadow any more. That the will which he, Rodwell, has produced, is a forged document, you and I know as well as if we had sat by him and seen him write it. But it is quite another thing when the facts come coldly before a court of law."

"You do not think he will substantiate it?"

"The question entirely depends upon the clearness, or otherwise, with which he has made his arrangements."

"It is a most mortifying conclusion."

"It is; and, therefore, I say, that if another will be found of a date later than the one produced by this man, it will have a better chance, especially as that other will, to all intents and purposes, will appear to all unprejudiced observers, much the most reasonable and proper document of the two."

Now the affair began to appear to Lowe in the most alluring colours. He seemed as if he saw his way clearly in it, and as if there was an opportunity, without danger, of completely getting the better of Rodwell—a consummation, in his mind, most devoutly to be wished.

He looked at old Gilbert inquiringly, as if he would have said,—
" It is better that you should be explicit now at once, than only deal in doubts and hints, and inuendoes." But the old miser was too wary to allow himself to be taken in in such a manner. He had evidently made up his mind that he would not be the first to put the matter into plain English.

" Don't you think," he said, after a pause of some minutes' duration,—" don't you think that you have heard, at some odd times, some hints from the goldsmith, about his having made, or his intention to make, some such a will as that which I have mentioned ?"

Lowe knew that this was a question which, translated, just means,—" You must invent all the likely-looking evidence you can, for the purpose of giving an air of truthfulness to the affair."

He hesitated for about a quarter of a minute, and then he said,—

" Yes."

" Ah," said Gilbert, rubbing his hands together ; " I feel certain that some chance word or another must have dropped from my poor brother, indicative of his intention to make such a will."

" Mr. Gilbert Paddlebat," said Lowe, " I am a young man, and one who has seen enough of the troubles of this life, to feel all the importance of placing myself above its immediate wants and necessities."

" Ah, to be sure."

" Well then ——"

" An old head upon young shoulders. I saw that such was the case from the very first moment that I looked upon you."

" Do not interrupt me, but listen to what I am about to say."

" Well, well."

" It is between us now a piece of needless and mock delicacy to affect that we do not fully and clearly understand each other upon this question. Rodwell and I am sworn foes to each other."

" I know it."

" Miss Leslie and I doubtless might, if circumstances were favourable, marry."

" I know it."

" Therefore a will, such as that which you have mentioned to me, certainly would be one that would tend most particularly and most materially to my advantage. Besides, as you say, it is one that seems, in all respects, more natural than the one which Rodwell has produced, and which leaves him such a large share of the goldsmith's property, and at the same time contains the absurd and extravagant proposition concerning the marriage of Miss Leslie to him."

" Right, my young friend, right."

" Well, sir, and what do you mean to do with Mrs. Paddlebat in that transaction ?"

" What do I mean to do ?"

" Yes, you."

" Really now I do not understand you. I can tell you what my brother told me he meant to do."

" Well, well."

" It was simply this. He meant to leave her two hundred pounds a year over and above the third of his personal estate."

" I see, I see. Rodwell's will propitiates her by leaving her one hundred pounds, and yours further propitiates her by leaving her two hundred pounds."

" A-hem !"

" You then fight him with his own weapons, and enlist Mrs. Paddlebat on your side. And the residue of his property ——"

" Goes to me as his brother, naturally, since he has no children."

Lowe considered for some moments, and then he said, assuming an air of sudden recollection,—

" Now, sir, that I come to think of it, the goldsmith always mentioned, or hinted something about leaving me five hundred pounds for myself as a legacy."

" Did he ?"

"I assure you he did, and it is that circumstance which enables me to recollect a great many pieces of evidence connected with his will, which otherwise would, I fear, slip my memory."

"I'm afraid it is not in the will, Mr. Lowe, and it is better that it should not be there, because the evidence that you will be able to give will come with a much better grace from you if you are not a legatee, than if, by the substantiation of this new will, you got anything. But, my young friend, you need not shake your head and look dubious ; I have so great a respect for my deceased brother's intentions, and so great a reliance upon your word, that if the getting of five hundred pounds will enable you to recollect anything upon the subject that it may be thought desirable should be recollected, as well as to attest the latter will, I myself will give you a check for that amount from my own limited resources."

"Let it be so, then," said Lowe, suddenly, and as if he had made a resolution, which he was then afraid of wavering in. "Let it be so. Let it be so. All ambiguity is now at at end. Give me five hundred pounds down, and shew me that there is a clause in the new will, which secures to Fanny Leslie eight hundred pounds, and I am yours."

"Agreed."

"Agreed."

The shrivelled hand of the old money-broker was clasped in that of the young, vigorous, but, as we perceive, not over-scrupulous Nicholas Lowe, and the iniquitous bargain was concluded.

With some difficulty, for parting with money was always a dreadful idea to Gilbert Paddlebat, Lowe, before they parted, got from him a cheque for one hundred pounds, on account of the five hundred pounds, and then they made their arrangements for forging a will, which should have in it all the clauses they both thought so very desirable.

The remarkable change which had taken place in all his prospects, was enough to confound, and to make him think that some of the events connected with it could scarcely be real.

He paced the apartment agitatedly, as he more than once asked himself,—

"Is all this but a vivid dream, or is it a reality ?"

But this was a frame of mind not likely to last long, and when it had in some measure subsided, he found himself indulging in pleasant dreams of the future, such as his imagination had never before allowed him to paint to himself.

"The skeleton," he muttered, "that haunts me, will be so overpowered by the pleasant incidents of real life, that I shall almost forget its presence, and begin to think that the gloomy philosophy which I have so long adhered to is, after all, at the mercy of circumstances far more than I could ever have imagined."

CHAPTER XXXVII.

NICHOLAS LOWE'S PROCEEDINGS.—THE LETTER TO FANNY LESLIE.

NICHOLAS LOWE on that evening took a long walk in the suburbs of London. He ways had found that when his mind was full of any particular circumstance, and wished to give his judgment the freest scope he could do so most effectively ¹le undergoing a considerable amount of bodily fatigue.

nd the deeper and more correct his thoughts were, the faster he always walked ; s at now he left the great city far behind him, and plunged completely into the co ry, without at all minding in what direction he was going.

leed, it mattered not to him which way he went, or where it might lead him. It the bodily occupation he wanted, in order to get rid of the large amount of nervs restlessness which beset him.

Helt that a crisis had arrived in his fortunes. He told himself that the

" —— Tide in the affairs of man,
Which taken at the flood, leads on to fortune,"

had fchim arrived, and yet, perhaps, a single false step might leave him stranded for evon the beach of poverty.

He resolved, therefore, that nothing should be wanting to enable him to take the full advantage of all the advantageous circumstances that now surrounded him, and it says little for his candour, while it says much for his artifice, that he came to a conclusion which we shall place in his own words before our readers.

"At present," he said, " and with her very indifferent prospects, it will look like an act of generosity to make Fanny my wife. The will under which she will inherit the insignificant sum of fifty pounds per annum, is a litigated document, and may, as she no doubt is well aware, be put aside, so that by now offering her my hand, she must feel that I cannot be actuated by selfish motives. In the most romantic manner I will do so, and with the five hundred pounds which I shall procure from Gilbert Paddlebat, I shall be able to live in great comfort and respectability until the will, which he intends to produce, is fully substantiated, which I have no doubt it will eventually be, for I have an immense reliance upon his tact.

" I will write to her, offering her marriage at once, and imploring her to accede to my wishes. She will consent, for I know she loves me, and I likewise know that her home, now that her best friend, in the person of her uncle, is no more, cannot be a comfortable one.

" From Mrs. Paddlebat she will be enduring continued persecutions, on account of Rodwell's suit, and that she abhors the very sight of him, I am as fully assured of, as I am of her affection for myself."

Having arrived at these conclusions, which to him appeared to be of the most clear and satisfactory nature—and so they were to reflect upon—he turned his face once more towards London, resolved to lose no time in carrying into effect his design, as regarded writing to Fanny Leslie at once, and making her an offer of his hand.

He found, when he came to retrace his steps, that he had got further into the country than he had imagined, and a stage-coach coming up, he was glad to take a seat upon it, and get whirled to town at as rapid a rate as four good horses upon a good road could accomplish the distance.

He repaired at once to his new lodging, and procuring writing materials, he at once set about his letter to Fanny Leslie, from which he hoped such immediate desirable results would ensue.

He had not before, of course, had any occasion to write to her, and he felt a little hesitation now, as to how great an amount of intimacy he might presume upon in addressing her, but he considered that, at all events, to be too cold would be a fault much less excusable than to be too warm ; he determined that no feeling of that sort should affect her when she read the letter, and he therefore wrote it as we now present it to the reader :—

" To Miss Leslie.

" Dearest Fanny—I know not if, in so short a lapse of time from that when we last met, you expected a letter from me, but I will please myself by at all events believing, unless you are so cruel as to contradict the fond delusion, that you have not only expected me to write to you, but that you will be pleased that I have now done so.

" The subject which now engrosses my mind is one which assumes a powerful position. It is this—you cannot be comfortable, or even commonly serene, in the house which you reside in, now that your poor uncle is no more.

" Your aunt, although a woman without a bad motive in the world, is yet a full of weaknesses ; and I much fear that, in Rodwell, she has one of the most ill counsellors that wayward fortune could ever have placed in such a person's way

" You will not be happy, Fanny,—that is one of my propositions ; I love y— that is another ; and from these two I draw the conclusion, which I press wi all the fervour of affection upon your acceptance.

" You know that, from the first moment that I looked upon you, your image warmed my heart. I told myself that I had found my fate, and that in your hands reposed the happiness or the regret of my future life.

" I hope, dear one, that I have not deceived myself when I have thoug that you did not look with an unfavourable eye upon the pure devotion of my h't. I loved you well, truly, and honourably, and my first thought connected with that passion was, that in the face of the whole world, the happiness might be mine of making you my wife, and of feeling that the ties that bound us together were indissoluble.

"Do not, ok! do not therefore blame me, if even at such a juncture as this, when I know that your heart is full of affection, I ask you to be mine.

"True, I am poor, Fanny, but I have a heart, and a hand to shield you from all evils, and an indomitable spirit of industry, which shall find its highest and noblest reward by standing between you and all evils.

"Leave, dear Fanny, all those who are contending about your poor uncle's property to fight with each other how they please, and as they please, their mercenary battles, and do you fly from the sound and the sight of that inglorious contest to the faithful heart of one who loves you well, truly, and who will love you for ever.

"I ask you to be mine—my wife—now at once. A special licence which I will, upon your sanction to such a step, procure, will save delay, and so I shall be able to rescue at once from what now cannot but be a gloomy, solitary home, that only living being to whom my heart clings with the fervour of an honest affection.

"I need not, my dear Fanny, say with what an agony of impatience, so to speak, the answer to this will be looked for by me. Do not, oh, do not, dear one, keep me in suspense. "I am, most devoted,

"NICHOLAS LOWE."

This letter he finished, and carefully folded and sealed. It is not an epistle which we are pleased to have to lay before our readers, as proceeding from Nicholas Lowe, because it is evidently most disingenuous, and we had hoped better things of him. He had talents, unquestionably, but he was eminently selfish.

He feared, so anxious was he that his letter should reach its destination quickly and in safety, to trust it to the post; but when he completed it, late as was the hour, he determined upon taking it personally, and, by the aid of a gratuity, inducing Susan to deliver it to Fanny before she slept that night.

He accordingly left his new humble home, and proceeded in the direction of the goldsmith's house. As he neared it he heard several church clocks strike eleven, but he would not be deterred from prosecuting his enterprise, and with the letter safely in his pocket he reached the goldsmith's door.

He glanced up at the well-known house, but, except in one window, no light was to be seen. That window, however, in which there was a solitary light, he knew to belong to Fanny Leslie's room, and he congratulated himself upon the fact that at all events she had not retired to rest.

Upon the impulse of the moment he said to himself,—

"She may write me an answer, and if she does, it will be an acceptance of my proposal, or, if not fully such, at all events will only use such arguments for delay as may be easily combatted, and which are used but to be so combatted."

He advanced slowly and carefully to the private door, and was just about to push the little iron gate, which, in some measure, protected it from ordinary intrusion, when he saw that the door was about to be opened from within the house.

To start back, and to take up a position within that porch, if it may be so termed, of the shop-door, was the work of a moment, and scarcely had he secured such a temporary and doubtful place of concealment when the private door was opened, and two persons came out of the goldsmith's house.

They paused after the street-door was closed, and then Lowe heard one say in the unmistakable voice of Rodwell,—

"This amounts to a persecution which I will not endure."

"Pho! pho!" said his companion; "persecution, indeed! You give things odd names, but the proposition that I must live, is to me a very strong one; so down with the money I require, or the money's equivalent."

"I cannot, and will not."

"You will not?"

"I have said it, Mr. Johnstone, I have said it. Our bargain is complete."

"So you thought; but I took second thoughts about it, and a more one-sided one I made up my mind could not be."

"One sided?"

"Yes. You have advantages, Rodwell, ten to one of mine."

"No, Johnstone, no."

"But I say yes. Come on. We are talking much too near the house. I will soon open your eyes."

"I cannot comprehend you. Have I not completed my bargain with you fully?"

"Oh! but do you really now think that I look like a fool? Come, come, this won't do, Rodwell. You have the lion's share, as a matter of course, and I don't grudge it to you ; because I consider, that as you found out the game, you are entitled to it ; but let us have fair play. Come on, come on."

They walked on, and their voices died off in the distance ; but Nicholas Lowe had already heard quite enough to convince him that what he had so suddenly and strangely come upon, was no other than the commencement of a conference between Rodwell and a confederate, who, doubtless, had assisted him in the preparation of the will, which had produced so much surprise at the goldsmith's.

"This will," said Lowe, to himself, "be indeed valuable information to Gilbert Paddlebat. I wish I could have heard more, but to follow them would be to bespeak detection, and so to place them at once upon their guard. Enough is known to induce probably old Gilbert to place a watch upon Rodwell."

He then turned his attention more particularly to his own affairs, and with the letter in his hand, which he was anxious should reach Fanny Leslie, he gently rang the bell which communicated with the lower regions of the house.

Susan, fancying that this probably was some visitor of her own, answered it more promptly than she would have done any other appeal for admission to the house.

She ran up the area steps, and Lowe said,—

"Susan, here is a letter," but before he could utter another word, she gave a groan of terror, and bolted down into the kitchen again, as if she had seen some terrible spectre. The kitchen-door was then fastened with a precipitation that not only seemed to Nicholas Lowe to be quite uncalled for by any circumstances of which he was aware, but one of the most inexplicable things in the world.

He waited for some few moments with the hope that this was only some mistake, or perhaps some joke of Susan ; but after a time he become quite convinced that there was no sort of intention to admit him to the house, so, with a feeling of aggravation, exceedingly natural under the circumstances, he gave a loud double knock at the door.

This, he considered, would surely prove effective in obtaining admission for him, but the door remained unanswered for a considerable time, until at last, just as his patience was getting thoroughly exhausted, and he was about, on the suggestion of his anger, to renew his assault upon the knocker, he saw through the fan-light above the reflection of a candle, and in another moment the door was opened, and Fanny Leslie appeared.

It was not at all likely that Nicholas Lowe would object to seeing Fanny Leslie instead of Susan, and the first glance at her beautiful face at once changed all the current of his ideas, and made him forget all his anger at the door being closed against him for so long.

"Dear, dear Fanny."

"Hush!" she replied, "hush! We are listened to now."

"What do you mean?"

"My aunt is dreadfully prejudiced against you."

"By whom?"

" By your enemy, Jervis Rodwell."

" The villain !"

" Villain or not, Nicholas Lowe, he has taught her to believe, in some way, of which I am in complete ignorance, that such a term applies with more force to you."

" And do you, Fanny, believe ——"

" Do I ? nay, do you know so little of me as to ask the question ? Is this kind ?"

" It is not. Pray forgive me for the momentary impulse that prompted me to utter the words. I will doubt Heaven itself, Fanny, before I will doubt you."

" You cannot be received in this house. My aunt has forbidden me to ask you further than the passage, and it is contrary to her strict injunctions that I open the door at all."

" But of what am I accused ?"

" That she will not tell me. She says, in answer to my natural inquiry, that she is bound by a solemn promise to the party who has informed her of some terrible things concerning you, not to reveal them."

" Ah, Fanny, there peeps out that terrific artifice of Jervis Rodwell. Too well can I guess that he is the enemy who has succeeded in taking a thorough advantage of your aunt's predilection for himself and dislike to me, to invent and to pour into her ears some calumny. But knowing it to be such, he dreads that I should know of what it is he accuses me, lest, by so doing, he should enable me at once to rebut the charge."

" All this I have said."

" And you think of me as you thought before ?"

" Yes—yes."

" Then little do I heed the detraction of such a man as Jervis Rodwell, or the weakness of such a woman as Mrs. Paddlebat, which induces her to give ear to it. While you, dear one, think of me as you have thought, I am happy."

" Alas ! Lowe, I know not," said Fanny, with a sigh, " how it is that you have made so desperate an enemy of Rodwell, but without my aunt mentioning his name as that of the party who has made some charge against you, I yet know that he is the man."

" And I too, Fanny ; there can be none other."

" Speak lower. I told you we were overheard, or we should be if we raised our voices."

" By whom ?"

" By Susan, who, I grieve to say, has become the confidante of my aunt. '

" Indeed !"

" Yes. You know that she is a person who cannot do without the companion-ship of some one, and as she found that, as regarded you, I was not disposed to think with her, it seems to me that she has descended to make a friend of Susan."

" Well, Fanny, for your sweet sake I should be content to endure anything. I have some things, as you know, in my room which would enable me to claim to be admitted to this house, but for the present I will waive that right, and all I solicit from you, with all the earnestness in my power, is an answer, as soon as possible, to a note, I have brought for you."

" Can you not tell me now its purport ?"

" No, Fanny, no, I did not think to see you ; but although kind fortune has per-mitted me so to do, I still would rather that you read that note, as it is written, and ponder over it before you answered me."

" Most certainly," said Fanny.

He handed her the letter he had written, in which he had made her a formal offer of his hand ; and then, although he would willingly not so soon have torn himself away from her, turned to leave ; for not only was he keeping her at per-sonal inconvenience, in a cold passage, but he considered that the sooner he left her to the perusal of his letter, upon which he considered hung so much of his future happiness, the sooner he would get a reply."

" I will not, dear Fanny," he said, " keep you here longer. May Heaven guard you."

"Farewell, Nicholas," said Fanny; "and do not suppose that I will, even for one moment, believe ill of you from such insufficient evidence as seems satisfactory to my aunt, who, as regards you, I know well, thinks and acts much from prejudice, which she is not the person easily to shake off."

"It is so, indeed."

"Depend upon an answer to this note."

This was a sweet assurance; but then Fanny's nature was so naturally ingenuous that she never dreamed of one-half of those conventional habits of deceit and distrust in which young ladies are usually brought up, and which seem to be all directed to a studious concealment of every real feeling, and a constant and unvarying system of deceit and hypocrisy.

We do not mean to say, but that men are themselves most to blame for making it necessary that the best, the fairest, and the most loveable portion of creation should be disingenuous, but while we admit so much, we may yet be permitted to regret the fact.

But Fanny Leslie, during the really adventurous life she had led before she reached that house, which had been to her a house of safety, had not had time to acquire the gracious or the artificial habits of life, and she took Lowe's letter as innocently, and with as full an intention of answering it ingenuously, as if it had come from one of her own sex.

A few more words of adieu were spoken, but probably upon Lowe's side they were not so tender as they would have been had he not had the caution which Fanny had given him respecting being overheard by Susan, the domestic spy now and confidante of Mrs. Paddlebat.

When he left the house he rather considered that, taking one circumstance with another, he should yet be able to defeat Rodwell.

But such a consideration as this, however satisfactory it might be to him, was not one which tended to make him feel less indignant against that individual. On the contrary, one-half of his reflections were completely used up in devising some means of accomplishing a revenge against him which should be severe, complete, and enduring.

"The scoundrel!" he said to himself; "he has broken the hollow peace which was patched up between us when last we met. He has no doubt, from a knowledge of the foolish disposition of Mrs. Paddlebat, and a full experience of the fact, that he could make her believe anything to my prejudice, possessed her, along with all such exaggerations as his hatred for me could suggest, with that one episode in my existence which may be told much to my disadvantage."

That this was the case Nicholas Lowe did not doubt, although he most certainly, with all the ingenuity of conjecture he was master of, could not come to the least rational conclusion as regarded the means by which Rodwell had arrived at any of his secret history. But of the fact there could be no doubt.

"What shall I do to crush Rodwell?" was the inquiry which Lowe proposed to himself.

It was one which, as we say, divided his attention from a consideration of the progress of his own fortunes, for in his own mind he fancied that Fanny would at once accept his offer.

How far he was gratified by the facts in thinking that she would do so, we shall see. We do not intend to deny that she loved him, but passion did not with her conquer judgment, so that if the affair be rightly considered, although Lowe had much to hope, he had likewise much to dread.

When he got home again, and thought over what had occurred, he made up his mind that, as in truth he had made now a sort of alliance with Gilbert Paddlebat, for their mutual advantage, it would be as well for him to let that miserly individual know what he had overheard between Rodwell and his confederate.

He felt that it was too late on that evening to do so, but he made up his mind, that at the earliest hour in the morning, when he could expect to find the old man stirring, he would go to him.

"This Gilbert Paddlebat," thought he, as he lay down that night to repose, "has evidently passed a whole life in trickery and chicanery, and although younger, and perhaps of a more vigorous intellect than he is, he may yet be able to tell me what is best to be done with Rodwell."

The morning came most welcomely to Nicholas Lowe, for he had passed a nearly sleepless night ; and when he had succeeded in closing his eyes in slumber, now and then imagination had peopled vacancy with frightful images, and he was glad again to awaken, in order to escape from them.

See p. 220.

He felt that he had arrived at a crisis in his fate—at such an epoch in his destiny that the next few weeks, ay, or even days, perchance, of his existence, might mar or make him for ever.

No wonder, then, that sleep deserted him, or that, when it did come, it came accompanied by the shadows of all his worst anticipations.

By the first streak of daylight he rose, and, dressing himself hurriedly, he went

No. 27.

out, resolved to breakfast somewhere first, and then to proceed to Gilbert Paddlebat's.

This he did, and by about nine o'clock he reached the old man's house, and upon sending in his name, was at once introduced to a dingy, miserable apartment, the whole furnishing of which would have been dear at five shillings. There sat old Gilbert, attired in a dressing-gown which might have been new when he was a boy. It was a world too large for him, and seemed to be folded round him several times, and then pinned so as to keep it together.

Although it was a time in the morning when one might be supposed to see some evidences of breakfast being about to be partaken of, yet not the least vestige of any such meal appeared.

When Lowe appeared, the old man gave him a nod of recognition, and pointed to a chair without a seat to it, saying,—

" You'll find a piece of wood up against the wall there, and if you place it along that chair, you will make yourself a seat."

" Thank you—thank you," said Lowe, as he obeyed the old man's directions ; " I hope I see you well, Mr. Paddlebat ?"—" Well," screamed the old miser, " I'm always well ; I leave being ill to improvident people, who make fools of themselves, and don't take care of their money."

" Nothing can be wiser."—" Ah—ah, so you say."

" And so I think, sir ; but I have come to bring you some news of Rodwell."— " Of Rodwell ? Indeed ! what has he done ?"

" Nothing new that I know of; but I have found out some additional evidence of some of his old doings."—" Say on."

Nicholas Lowe then related to the old miser what he had overheard between Rodwell and his confederate; but he said nothing about the letter containing the offer of marriage which he had given to Fanny, for although he did not conceive that old Gilbert cared one straw whether he married her or not, yet he had a natural disinclination, which the reader, doubtless, has noticed on more than one occasion, to being candid.

" Well ?" said old Gilbert, when he had done.—" Eh ?"

" Well ?"—" Well, that's all."

" Oh, is it ?"—" Yes, and enough too, I think, when you come to consider it."

" I don't see anything to consider in it."—" You do not ?"

" Indeed, I do not. Just ask yourself what there is fresh in it. In the first place, we know that Jervis Rodwell had forged the will he had produced; in the second place, we know that to do so he must have had two accomplices, or else, where were the attesting witnesses to that document? So, you see, your discovery that he has one, is no discovery at all."—" I beg your pardon, Mr. Paddlebat," said Nicholas.

" Granted."—" I was about to say that this evidence of mine would be important, inasmuch as it would go a long way in disproving the genuineness of the will of Rodwell's getting up, and which we are, both of us, so strongly of opinion is a forgery, that we feel ourselves authorised to take the fact for granted."

" But, my young friend, I do not intend for one moment to dispute the will of Rodwell's getting up."—" You do not ?"

" Certainly not. I mean to admit it as a perfectly genuine document. It is dated on the 17th of January, in the present year. Now, just push the bolt you see on the door into its hasp."

Lowe did so, and then looked at the old man with some curiosity, to know what he would do next. He went to a part of the wall which was papered over like the rest, but which, upon a closer inspection, presented what appeared to be the door of a small cupboard. But, when old Gilbert unlocked it, which he did with a massive key, and opened it, Lowe saw that it was an iron safe let into the wall.

From this the miser took a folded parchment, and handed it to Lowe, who read on the outside of it these words,—

" The will and testament of Josiah Paddlebat, goldsmith, of the city of London, dated March 10th."

" There," said old Gilbert, with a chuckle, " do you understand that ? Open it and read it before you make any remark."

Nicholas Lowe did so, eagerly, and he found that the first paragraph ran thus :—

" I, Josiah Paddlebat, do hereby revoke all former wills, or testamentary papers whatever, made by me, and declare this to be my last will and testament, and particularly do I revoke and declare null and void a will made by me on the 17th of January last past, and which I have mislaid."

Then followed a bequest of the whole of his property, wheresoever or whatsoever, to his brother, Gilbert Paddlebat, of the city of London, money-scrivener, in trust for the following purposes :—

" Mrs. Paddlebat to have 200l. per annum more than one-third of the personal estate would bring her; Fanny Leslie to be paid 8,000l., clear of legacy duty; Nicholas Lowe, 500l. ; Jervis Rodwell, a suit of mourning. The whole of the residue to revert to and to belong to Gilbert Paddlebat."

When Nicholas Lowe had read the document, old Gilbert said to him, in a low, chuckling tone of voice,—

" Well, what do say to that? Is that the kind of will which might have been fairly expected from my brother?"—" It will suit me, at all events," said Lowe.

" Ah ! and me."—" The imitation of the signature is one of the most perfect things ever I saw in all my life."

" The what ?"—" The imitation of the signature."

" Mr. Lowe, if you mean to insinuate that I have forged this will, you do me a great injustice, and lay yourself open to a prosecution for libel."—" What folly this is, Mr. Paddlebat, between us," said Lowe. " Why keep up a delusion which can do no good? This is a far more righteous will than the one which was produced by Rodwell."

" Well ?"—" And I look, therefore, upon the moral crime of forging it as of the smallest possible magnitude ; therefore, there need be no delicacy about it."

" I really don't know what you mean, Mr. Lowe. I shall be at my brother's house to-day, at twelve o'clock, and I should strongly advise you to be there likewise."—" I am not welcome."

" Nay, but it is important that you should be there, for all that."—" And what is to be done ?"

" I shall insist upon a further search through all my brother's papers, to see if any testamentary document of a later date than the one produced by Rodwell can be found. You must take this, and place it somewhere where some one else shall find it."—" I understand."

" Now, then, go away. You may use your own judgment about where you place it, as you know the house better than I do ; but if Rodwell objects to the search again through the papers of the deceased, do you suggest that a solicitor should be sent for, unknown to any one of us all, except, perhaps, by name, as a most unexceptionable man, and that the search be left in his hands ; only, take care that this will shall be somewhere where he is likely to stumble over it."—" I will—I will."

" Where will you hide it ?"—" It shall be placed among the last year's ledgers of the business, in the lower part of a cupboard, where other papers of importance, such as agreements, &c., are placed."

" Good. Where is that ?"—" In the counting-house. And I do not see what is to prevent me from going at once. I have some things there in my room, which I can say I am about to remove, but I can be so long removing them, that you will have time to come, provided you make it eleven, instead of twelve o'clock."

" Be it so."

Nicholas Lowe took the forged will, which to him was so much more satisfactory a document than the one which the rascality of Rodwell had produced. In it, old Gilbert had, to the full, kept faith with him ; and, besides, the will, take it altogether, was so much more consistent a document than that which had been produced by Rodwell, that he, Lowe, felt that the latter had no chance against it.

Here, then, if he chose to leave him alone, was ample vengeance against Rodwell, surely ; for not only would he be beaten by his own weapons, but likewise hampered by his confederates in the transaction, who, notwithstanding the failure of the whole scheme, would doubtless harass him to a great extent.

The thought then occurred to him, however, that if any one of those confederates of Rodwell chose to confess the forgery of the will bearing date the 17th of January, it might jeopardise this one of the 10th of March, which acknowledged it.

Full of this idea, he ran off to old Gilbert again, and stated it to him ; but here he found again, that the old man's cunning had not deserted him, for he only smiled, as he said,—

"You are alarmed at a shadow. Although my brother may have executed a will on the 17th of January, it does not follow that the one produced by Rodwell is the document. Does it not state that he could not find the will in the very one you now have in your pocket? Of course I shall say it was found by Rodwell—destroyed, and this one substituted for it, on which he relies."

"Why, then, in that event, Rodwell still stands in a dangerous criminal position, as well as losing all the advantages he pictured to himself."—"He does, he does. Go you and do your part of the business, young man, and be assured that I have well weighed every circumstance connected with the affair, and left no point of difficulty unprovided for. I have greater resources than Jervis Rodwell. Go—go at once, and place the will in the spot you mentioned."

CHAPTER XXXVIII.

RODWELL'S OFFER TO FANNY.—THE ANSWER TO NICHOLAS LOWE'S LETTER.

LITTLE did Rodwell imagine the bitter disappointment which was preparing for him. That there would be a severe legal contest about the will he had produced, he made up his mind, and he considered that it would be with old Gilbert as heir-at-law, that he would have to dispute. But that such a course as that which had been so cunningly got up by the miser, would be pursued, it never for an instant entered into his imagination to conceive.

He cared little about the legal struggle which was at hand, because he relied upon the skill with which he had not only got up the will itself—and it was well done—but he likewise trusted greatly to the handsome manner in which he had behaved to Mrs. Paddlebat.

"I have got her thoroughly and entirely with me," he considered, and the more he thought over that piece of cleverness, the more he looked upon it as one of the most skilful things he had ever been able to do.

Indeed, what with the evident consternation of old Gilbert, when the will was produced, the deep disappointment of Lowe, and the half-and-half sort of satisfaction of Mrs. Paddlebat, he looked upon himself as a prosperous man.

He had succeeded in getting rid of the immediate persecution of Johnstone's demands, so that on the morning after the night on which he had been seen by Nicholas Lowe with that individual, Rodwell wore a very serene and contented aspect.

Now, as regarded Fanny, there can be no doubt but that, in the first instance, when she came to the house, and it became evident what a firm hold her beauty, her innocence, and her affectionate disposition obtained of the goldsmith's heart, he, Rodwell, took an interested view of the case, and eagerly sought to make himself agreeable to Fanny, for the prospective advantage of so doing. Then her beauty had won even upon him, cold-hearted and selfish to a degree as we know he was, and as far as such a man might be supposed to feel such a passion, we may take upon ourselves to say, that he loved Fanny Leslie.

We feel that we profane the word love, while we write it, as regarded such a man as Rodwell ; but such was his feeling, or probably he would not with so much art have placed her name in the will he had manufactured, or sought to induce her to comply with the pretended wish of her deceased uncle with so much real earnestness as he did. Reflection had induced him to wait until the funeral was over, before he made any demonstration of his feelings ; but then he thought it high time to speak out, and he chose that very morning to do so on which such a change was about to take place in the aspect of his affairs.

He consulted with Mrs. Paddlebat, who was certainly favourable to his addresses, as to whether he should himself make a declaration to Fanny of his earnest wish to fulfil the recommendation contained in her uncle's will, or get her, Mrs. Paddlebat, to be so good as take off his hands that delicate task.

But favourite as Rodwell was of the widow's, yet that preference for him was not sufficient to induce her to cast aside all natural feeling towards Fanny, and she replied to him with far more sense and firmness than he had ever given her credit for.

" Why, Mr. Rodwell," she said, " you know I think highly of you, and would be very glad to see you the husband of Fanny, if I thought she would be happy."

" Happy? Oh ! my whole life would be devoted ——"

" Very likely ; but you know all the devotion in the world won't make a young girl so happy as a look, or half a word, provided it comes from the right person."

" But her uncle's wishes."

" Very true—but men don't know anything about those matters ; and when I come to think it over, Mr. Paddlebat certainly ought not to have put in his will any such ridiculous thing."

Rodwell bit his lips.

" But, howsomedever," added Mrs. Paddlebat, " you had better ask her yourself at once, I won't interfere."

" But you will use your influence ?"—" I have none. I did once, and only once, just hint at her marrying you, according to her uncle's will, and the face she made up was quite a sight."

" What did she say ?"—" Oh ! just a piece of nonsense ; she said she no more believed that will was her uncle's, than that it was her's."

" Indeed ?"

" Ah ! and then she walked out of the room like the queen in some tragedy, for all the world."

This was not very encouraging or consolatory information for Rodwell ; but still he determined to essay the matter, and muttering to himself that her fifty pounds per annum was all she should have, if she rejected his addresses, he repaired to the dining-room, where he had previously ascertained Fanny was alone.

And to all appearance she was alone, although she did not feel so, for she had been again and again reading Lowe's letter, and his image filled her breast.

What sort of answer to make to it perplexed her. She at once rejected the idea of so shortly after her uncle's death marrying, but whether to give Lowe a positive promise of her hand at a future period, or not, was the matter which caused her much thought.

That he loved her, and that he loved her sincerely, was a fact to her mind sufficiently established, or she would not have wasted a thought upon his epistle ; but when she had so freely and so candidly promised him an answer, she had not the least idea that the purport of the letter would be so serious as it was.

Well might she, or any young girl, hesitate upon so momentous a subject ; and she was in the midst of these cogitations when Rodwell tapped at the room door, and then opened it, and walked in.

Fanny Leslie rose, and without a word would have left the apartment to him, but he stood between her and the door as he said,—

" Miss Leslie, may I request the favour of a few moments' conversation with you ?"

She paused a moment ere she replied,—

" If only a few moments, Mr. Rodwell, I must request of you to say at once what you may wish to remark, as I am occupied."

" It is shortly said, Miss Leslie. From the first moment that you came to this house, I loved you."—"That is language I cannot listen to."

" Nay, hear me out. I made your uncle acquainted with my passion, and hence, no doubt, did he insert that clause in his will, which has taught me to cherish the dearest hope that ever imagination painted to me."—" What hope, sir?"

" The hope that you would be mine. I now, Miss Leslie, in accordance with the recommendation to you in your venerated and respected uncle's will, beg of you to accept me as your future husband. My whole life shall be devoted to securing your happiness."—" Have you concluded, sir?"

" Ah! upon such a subject when should I conclude, were I to say all that my heart dictates? I love you—I loved you long, and you would indeed look far and wide before you found a heart more devoted to you than mine."—" Have you concluded now?" said Fanny.

Rodwell was silent for a moment or two, during which he looked in the sweet face of the beautiful girl, but he could see nothing now there along with the matchless beauty but an expression of cold determination, which augur ill indeed for the success of the suit he urged.

" I have done," he said, at length. " I will not say all I could say. I have done."—" I reject your offer."

" Think again, Miss Leslie."—" I decline doing so."

" Remember the injunction contained in your uncle's will,—that uncle who to you played the part of a father. Have you so soon, now that the grave has closed over his remains, forgotten him?"

A flash of indignation came from the eyes of Fanny, as she said,—

" Do you imagine that for one moment I was deceived by the shallow trickery to which you have resorted? The will upon which you affect to found this most audacious proposal is, you know well, the concoction of your own hand and heart. I despise, as well as condemn and accuse you!"—" You accuse me?"

" I do. Beware, sir! Let me no more hear from your lips the name of him who is no more, and who would not have dreamt of producing such a document as that under which you seek to enrich yourself. Take all, and take with it the contempt of the good, and the certainty that the time will come when such a man as you are will find that he has mistaken the road to contentment."

Rage took the place of more tender feelings in the breast of Rodwell. He turned as pale as death itself, and, half choked with passion, he said,—

" I expected this. I knew it. Your intrigue with Nicholas Lowe has not passed so entirely unregarded as you think."—" Infamous calumniator!"

" Say what you will, and do what you will, I care not. Go to the beggar, whom you admire, and live, if you can, upon the miserable pittance that will be yours. You will find ample leisure for repenting the girlish folly that now dictates your actions."

" Stand away from the door, sir."—" I will not."

" How dare you oppose my progress?"—" Because it is my will and pleasure. Now you have a reason, make of it what you can. You might have made me your friend, but you would not, and, on the contrary, have chosen to make me your uncompromising enemy. It is your own election."

" If you think to alarm me by your threats, you are mistaken," said Fanny. " Delay me here another moment against my will, and from the streets I will summon assistance; and some one will surely answer the call of a young, unprotected girl, threatened by a cowardly ruffian like yourself."—" You will find me a ruffian of more account to your fortunes than you suppose. I will have your pet, Nicholas Lowe, hanged yet before I have done with him."

" I will endure this no longer," exclaimed Fanny, and she flew to the bell rope, which she pulled violently before Rodwell could prevent her, although he made an effort so to do by stepping forward.

This application to the bell was of so violent a nature, that it brought Mrs. Paddlebat and Susan both to the room, and then Rodwell immediately changed the insolent demeanour with which he had been treating Fanny to one of quite a different character, as he said,—

" Mrs. Paddlebat, I hope you have not been alarmed by the imprudent manner in which Miss Leslie has rung the bell. The fact is, I have been compelled to hear much abuse and vituperation from her."

"Fanny, how could you?" said Mrs. Paddlebat.—"Madame," said Fanny, firmly, "I desire that you now explicitly understand me ; I will not remain beyond to-day in this house, if that man likewise inhabits it. I will, if you will not befriend me in this matter, endeavour to seek some one who will ; but, after the insults I have received at his hands, I will not condescend to reside under the same roof with him."

"You hear her," said Rodwell.—"Lor !" exclaimed Susan.

"Why, what ever is it all about?" said Mrs. Paddlebat.—"It matters not, aunt, what it is about," said Fanny ; "I have stated my determination, and I think you know enough of me to feel that it is one that I shall abide by now."

She walked from the room, leaving Rodwell to make what further explanation he chose regarding the quarrel that had taken place between them, and he was just preparing to do so, when some one knocked at the street-door, and he went to the window to see who it was.

"Nicholas Lowe," he exclaimed.—"Don't let him in," cried Mrs. Paddlebat.

But even as she spoke she heard the street-door opened, and, sinking on a chair, she added,—

"It's Fanny. She has opened the door for him. That girl is really turning so violent that she'll be the death of me. I know she will, so it's no use anybody saying anything to the contrary, because I know she will, and there's an end of that."

CHAPTER XXXIX.

THE RESPECTABLE ATTORNEY.—THE NEW WILL, AND RODWELL'S CONFUSION.

THE unexpected presence of Nicholas Lowe at this juncture, was one of the most annoying things, probably, that could at all happen to Jervis Rodwell. He thought that Lowe would be the last person to come to the house of the goldsmith, and not recollecting, at the moment, that he had some property upon the premises, he thought it a piece of the greatest impudence in the world for Lowe to intrude. Indeed, Rodwell had begun to consider himself as quite the master of the house ; and, by familiarising himself with the contents of the will which he had manufactured, he, like a practised liar, who repeats the same story over and over, till he at last believes in its truth, began to look upon that will as quite a genuine sort of document, and to fancy that he was being extremely liberal in allowing Mrs. Paddlebat and Fanny to remain upon the premises.

He had begun, even for some days previous to the funeral, to show all that petty and contemptible pride which is supposed to develop itself in a beggar when he gets upon horseback.

Nothing was too good for him ; and, in fact, we might say, nothing was good enough. He would have slept in Mr. Paddlebat's bed, but that it had been so recently occupied by the dead that his superstitious feelings peopled both it and the apartment with terrible fancies ; but the goldsmith's easy chair was monopolised by him after dinner, and he familiarised his eyes with the sight of the various costly articles of furniture which adorned the apartments of the house, with a strong feeling that nothing could prevent them becoming his in a due course of law.

Hence the presence of Lowe was a great infliction ; and, but that he was too dignified to do so, he would have gone down stairs to challenge his right to come upon his premises.

Yes ; Rodwell had actually begun to call the goldsmith's house his premises ; and he had in his mind's eye certain alterations which he intended to make to suit his own ideas of comfort, and what he considered elegance.

It was a good thing for Lowe, under the present circumstances, that Rodwell was so inflated with personal vanity as not to be able to come down stairs to quarrel with him, for it gave him, Lowe, an admirable opportunity of executing old Gilbert Paddlebat's instructions.

There must have been some sort of presentiment in the mind of Fanny, perhaps a magnetic principle, which enabled her at once to recognise Lowe's knock at the street door, for scarcely had it reached her ears when she bounded down stairs and opened it.

"Nicholas, Nicholas," she said, "I do not know whether to be glad or sorry that you have come."

"Say nothing, dearest," was Lowe's reply, "unless it be an affirmative to my note."—"No, no; I will write to you upon that subject; but I have been quarrelling with Rodwell, and have threatened to leave the house—a threat which I shall perform unless affairs materially alter."

"Is he within?"—"Yes."

"Then wait here a moment, Fanny; I have something to get from the counting-house that belongs to me, and I do not wish to be dogged in every step that I take by such a man as Rodwell."

Fanny Leslie did think it somewhat strange that Lowe should leave her so abruptly, but she was one more in the habit of drawing kindly inferences than otherwise; so she waited for him patiently in the passage for nearly five minutes.

In the deranged aspect of the affairs connected with the goldsmith's testamentary bequests, it had not been considered expedient to open the shop, so that it was in darkness, and the counting-house, which was immediately behind it, was dimly lighted by a small, dirty skylight above. But to Lowe, every intricacy of the premises was perfectly familiar, and, making what speed he could, he reached the place which he had mentioned to old Gilbert Paddlebat as that where the account-books and vouchers of the past year were kept, as well as other papers useful for reference, and taking hurriedly the will from his pocket, the contents of which promised to be so advantageous to his fortune, he hid it deep among a mass of papers; after which he came back again to the passage as quickly as he could, and rejoined Fanny Leslie.

"Fanny," he said, "I know that I'm not welcome here to any one but yourself, and therefore I will this day remove whatever belongs to me, that is left upon these premises."—"You have a right to do that," she said; "I had forgotten that you possessed so good a claim to enter here."

"Hilloa!" cried the voice of Rodwell, from the top of the stairs; "who's that, I should like to know?"—"It is I," said Lowe; "and I should little trouble this place with my presence were it not necessary that I should come, for the purpose of removing what belongs to me."

"Oh, indeed," said Rodwell. "I think you might have sent some one else upon that errand, with a list of your rubbish."—"Sir," said Lowe, calmly, for he was acting a part, "sir, I admit, that after the will you have produced, as that of my late respected employer, Mr. Paddlebat, I look upon you as the master of this house."

"Oh, you do, do you," said Rodwell, who was more tickled than pleased by this acknowledgment of his supremacy by Lowe than by anything else that had occurred during the whole course of the affair; "you do, do you? And I'll let you and everybody else know that I am the master of the house."—"And so I shall consider you, unless something happens to disprove the will."

"Which I dare say you hope, but you'll find yourself disappointed."—"Very good, sir, I may, and then again, I may not; but in the meantime I trust that no difficulties will be placed in my way when I come merely to take my own property off the premises, where I admit that otherwise I have no business."

"Ha—hem," said Rodwell; "I desire that you be as quick as you can then, in removing your property."

Fanny Leslie was surprised at this pacific and subdued tone of Nicholas Lowe; she could scarcely believe her own ears, and she looked in the face of him who she expected to have shown such a different spirit, for some moments, with unqualified amazement. But as she did look, she fancied she saw a twinkling of the eyes, and the ghost of a smile playing round the lips, which induced her to consider that he, Lowe, was ridiculing rather than submitting to Rodwell.

By a clock that was in the hall it wanted but about five minutes to eleven, and that five minutes Lowe was determined to protract, if he possibly could."

"By-the-bye, after all," he said, "I think I'd better get a truck, or some thing of the sort. Mr. Rodwell, have you any objection to a truck standing opposite to the door?"—"Yes, I have," said Rodwell, "a very great objection. Come, con e, if you don't remove your things at once I shall get a couple of porters and have them thrown into the street."

"But don't you think that would be rather a harsh proceeding?"

Lowe uttered these words in a tone of voice which was quite sufficient to convince Rodwell that he was jesting with him, and in his anger he came down several stairs, and shook his clenched fist, but before he had time to say anything, bang came a knock at the street door, which, though he expected it, startled Lowe himself, and caused Rodwell to run up again to the first floor landing.

Lowe recovered himself immediately, and opened the street door, when in walked Gilbert Paddlebat, rubbing his little thin hands together, and looking as usual the picture of misery.

" You here again !" said Lowe, with well acted surprise.—" Yes, yes, yes," said old Gilbert, " I'm here again. I want to see Mr. Rodwell ; he and I had some words, and a man in a passion says many things that in his cool judgment he wishes unsaid. Is Mr. Rodwell at home ?"

" Well, what now ?" cried Rodwell, from the stair head.—" Oh, my dear sir, is that you ? Ha, ha ! Let me speak to you, and see you. I'll walk up stairs. Come along, Mr. Lowe ; and you, my dear, come along. Ha ! I'm not so old as I look, not by a great deal. But, as you all heard me say some hard things to Mr. Rodwell, when I found myself cut off with a shilling, I think you all ought to hear me say that I don't much mind, and that I wish him joy of his property."

" If that's what you come for," said Rodwell, " you might have done it with a twopenny-post letter ; but, if you came for the shilling that was left you in your brother's will, I'll give it you at once to get rid of you."—" Thank you, thank you," said old Gilbert ; " a shilling's a shilling!" and he held out his hand. " Twenty shillings make a pound. Ha ! a shilling's the interest of twenty shillings in a year. Where is it ?"

" Take it," said Rodwell, with a brutal laugh, as he place it in the old man's palm.—" Thank you."

" Well, ain't you going ?"—" Oh, dear, no ! not yet. He, he !—ha, ha ! I shall sit down in my late brother's chair a little. What a luxurious man he was ! I understand he took a mutton chop for his lunch, always. Waste, waste, waste. I wonder he died leaving anything to anybody."

" What on earth do you want ?" said Rodwell.—" Nothing. But I'll amuse you now ; you shall be amused, Mr. Rodwell, and that'll be some sort of recompense for the injustice I've done you in doubting the will."

" Then you don't doubt it now ?"—" Doubt it, no !"

" You hear that all of you ?" said Rodwell, eagerly. " I shall subpœna you all, if the old man goes to law now. You hear that he don't doubt the will at all.—" I go to law !" exclaimed old Paddlebat ; " I think I see me going to law. The law's better to follow than to meet. But I'll amuse you, I say I'll amuse you, now—now that we're all friends. Ha, ha ! and it can't matter, I'll amuse you !"

Old Gilbert Paddlebat fitted on his spectacles with great accuracy, and then he drew from his pocket what looked like a tolerably thick octavo volume.

" Well," said Rodwell, with a wink at Mrs. Paddlebat—as much as to say, " I'll bring the old boy out !"—" if you can amuse us, do so. What's that you've brought with you ?"—" My diary," said old Gilbert. " Ha, ha ! let me see—my diary. Ah ! February—that's the month. February, the—the—the—fourteenth."

" Valentine's day, as I'm a sinner," exclaimed Mrs. Paddlebat.—" Yes, marm, you're a sinner, there's no mistake about that. February the fourteenth, served Samuel Tomkins with a copy of a writ ; got the better of George Muffum to the extent of seven shillings and sixpence ; passed a bad shilling at a baker's, got elevenpence change and a penny bun ; had previously placed a piece of dirt on the end of my nose—the man in the shop did nothing but look at it, and put the suspicious shilling into the till. Ha ! hum—let me see. Found a pocket-handkerchief a lady dropped ; rather out of breath, and couldn't say anything until she'd turned a corner. Bless me ! where is it ? I shall come to it at last."

" What the deuce do you mean," said Rodwell, " by all that tirade of nonsense ?"—" Oh, ah, to be sure ! hum, ha ! here it is. It wasn't the fourteenth, after all. February fifteenth ; here we are. Brother Josiah called ; wanted something to drink, but objected to pump water."

" Who do you mean ?" said Rodwell.—" Why, your great friend, to be sure, that left you all the property ; my brother Josiah—an extravagant man."

" What of him ?"—" Well, you shall hear. Let me see, where was I ? in some pump water, I think. Oh, ah ! Brother Josiah called ; said he regretted family differences, and wanted to know, if I died, what I'd leave to Fanny Leslie ?

Told him, my blessing and the interest on it; he said, it wasn't enough. Told me, he'd made a will dated the seventeenth of January! Ha, hum!"

"What!" exclaimed Rodwell, with pleasure, "he told you that?"—"Yes."

"And you'll swear to it?"—"Yes; if I get my expenses."

"All's right. Why, that's my will. Why—why, d——d if I can understand it!"—"Yes; that's your will. Ain't you surprised? But you'd better hear it all."

Rodwell turned ghastly pale; he staggered into a chair, and he began to feel that some trick was being played upon him, which would soon develope itself. How could the will, which he had forged only in April, be confirmed by an entry in Gilbert Paddlebat's diary of February? Some deep and desperate move was on the tapis."

"Go on," he said, faintly, "go on. Let's hear it all."—"Oh yes," said old Paddlebat; and he continued to read,—

"Said he'd made a will, dated the seventeenth of January, and that he'd laid it by so carefully, he was d——d if he knew where it was; said he wanted to find it, because he'd altered his mind; said he'd left all his property to Rodwell in it, because he fancied Fanny Leslie would marry him, and they'd be remarkably happy together; said he'd since found out Rodwell was a thundering rogue, and considered himself an old ——"

"What?" said Rodwell.—"Stop a bit till I've wiped my spectacles; it's a long word."

Old Gilbert took off his spectacles and wiped them, all the while twinkling his little grey eyes in the face of Rodwell, and puckering up his curious looking, old parchment face in the oddest way imaginable, and appearing as if he quite doated upon the exhibition of impatience and anxiety that his victim portrayed. •

It was a curious group that that room shewed forth. All eyes were fixed upon the little old miser, who sat in the capacious chair of the deceased Mr. Paddlebat, leaving ample room enough for another ordinary sized person beside him. His knees were poked up to his chin nearly, on which lay the book; and never before, within the memory of any one there present, had old Gilbert Paddlebat looked so jovial as he did that day.

Jervis Rodwell's anxiety, before old Gilbert had thoroughly wiped his spectacles, grew into an agony.

"What the devil," he said, "is the meaning of it all? If you've got anything to say, say it."—"It wasn't me," said old Gilbert, "it was the deceased. Now I'll go on."

"And as quick as you can, for I won't stay here all day to be made sport of by you."—"Humbug!" said old Gilbert.

"What!"—"That's just where I left off. He considered himself a humbug to have made any such will, and intended to make another."

"'Tis false!"—"Very good. Said he intended to make another, and that he wouldn't leave anything but a suit of mourning for Rodwell, because he liked him to be commonly decent; said he meant to leave Fanny Leslie seven or eight thousand pounds."

"Rubbish!"—"Said he meant to leave his respected, handsome, and intelligent partner in life, Mrs. Sarah Paddlebat, the third of his personal estate, and two hundred pounds a-year out of the residue; said he considered her the finest woman in the city of London; said I thought so too."

"Now, can anything," said Rodwell, "be so transparent as this?"—"Nothing!" said the little old man. "Said he'd leave Lowe something; and said he'd leave everything to me in trust to do all this, if I'd take the trust; said I would."

Old Gilbert shut up the book with such a bang, that Mrs. Paddlebat put her elbow through a square of glass.—"Eh?"

"I say, what do you make of all that?"—"Nothing. Good morning. I didn't say I was going to make anything of it—ain't you answered?"

"No; and I look upon you as an old fool."—"Oh, ha! you're a thundering rogue, you know; but, however, if you ain't answered, I can't help it; my only wonder is, ladies and gentlemen, that my brother, after stating to me, on the fifteenth of February, that he would make such a will as I mentioned, should not do so between then and April, up to which month, as you all know, he continued in perfect health, and in the enjoyment of all his faculties."

"But you see he did not make another will!" exclaimed Rodwell.—"Hold!" said Lowe, suddenly, for he felt that the time had come when he was to perform his part in the little drama that had been got up between him and Gilbert Paddlebat, for the confusion of Jervis Rodwell, and the destruction of all his plans and projects. "Hold! it seems to me, Mr. Gilbert Paddlebat, and I speak without an interest in this affair, one way or the other, for I dare say I shall benefit as little by one will as by another, that you ought to consider."

"Who asked you to speak about it," cried Rodwell.—"Nay, nay," said old Gilbert; "let him have his say. Now, my young friend, what horse's nest have you found?"

"Why, look you here," continued Lowe; "your diary, sir, states that your brother mislaid the will dated the 17th of January, and that appears to be the will which was found by Mr. Rodwell, in the search through the papers of the deceased."—"Well?"

"It must, however, be fresh in the recollection of every one of you, that a very natural result followed the finding of that will, which was, that from that moment, the search was discontinued, so that there was no chance of finding another, even if it had been in existence, and bearing a date, which would supersede that under which Mr. Rodwell claims the property."

These words opened Rodwell's eyes at once; he saw in a moment the situation in which he was placed; but how to extricate himself from it seemed to be beyond all human ingenuity. He did not entertain the smallest doubt in the world but that Lowe or old Gilbert had another will in their pockets; and that the result of a renewed search amongst the goldsmith's papers would be, that some sly opportunity would be taken to produce it, as he had produced his, and affect suddenly to have found it.

This, however, he was determined to foil, even with force, if it were necessary. And his first step was, to go to the door and turn the key in the lock, after which, he placed his back against it.

CHAPTER XL.

THE SUCCESSFUL PLAN.—THE EJECTION OF RODWELL.

In a few minutes after Rodwell had taken up this position, he seemed so choked with passion, that he could not speak. When he did, it was in a strange and husky voice, which quite betrayed the amount of his fears.

"I understand all this well enough," he said; "but it won't do; it's clever, I admit that; but I tell you again, it won't do."

"What do you mean?" said old Gilbert; "what won't do?"—"Your scheme, to be sure; you know there are no papers in this room to search for, and no hiding-places where any could be concealed. Mark me! I'm not such a goose as not to be well aware of what you're about. Search as long as you like, but let that search be conducted by persons called in to do it, while you two, if you please, gentlemen, remain here, and I'll keep you company."

"Humph!" said old Gilbert, "you're suspicious."—"And well I may be; I know my company."—"Ha!" said old Gilbert; "it puts me in mind of the old woman who looked for her daughter in the oven--she'd been there herself. Surely, my dear sir, you'll allow Mr. Lowe, who is acquainted with the premises, to search the house."

"Ha! ha!" said Rodwell, "that's it, is it? Why, you're in your second childhood, old man."—"Well, I—I—think I'll go," said old Gilbert.

"No, you won't," cried Rodwell, triumphantly; "you have thrown out this insinuation about there being another will, and I owe it to myself, as well as to the relatives of the deceased Mr. Paddlebat, to prove or disprove that assertion. I will take you at your word ; there shall be a search—a thorough and complete one ; but not by you, or by Mr. Lowe—oh, dear, no ; you will remain here."— " I—I've got an engagement," said old Gilbert.

" And I've got an appointment about a situation I am applying for," remarked Lowe, " so I think we'll both go."—" No, no," said Rodwell ; " we'll have in a couple of the neighbours ; we'll have the house searched from top to toe, while you remain here ; and I don't see why it shouldn't be conducted by Mr. Whiskin, the respectable attorney, opposite."

He sprang to the fire-place, and rang the bell, which was promptly answered by Susan.

" Go," he said, " to Mr. Whiskin, opposite, and ask him to step in here, and get any two of the neighbours you can who have half-an-hour to spare, to do so likewise. Now, Mr. Gilbert Paddlebat, there's such a thing as generalship in the world, I think."

" How remarkably true," cried old Gilbert, and he sat down and pretended to shake a little while ; Lowe put his hands in his pockets and whistled faintly.

Mr. Whiskin, who was really a respectable solicitor, although a slow coach, came over in a few minutes, wondering what was the matter. Two of the neighbours came in, and they were the first that were applied to, for their curiosity prompted them.

Rodwell was great, now, and became quite oratorical.

" Mr. Whiskin and gentlemen," he said, waving his arm, " this is Mr. Gilbert Paddlebat, the brother of the deceased Mr. Paddlebat ; and that's his diary under his arm, gentlemen, and Mr. Whiskin, in it he finds a memorandum, which induces him to think that the deceased, Mr. Paddlebat, has made a will which is somewhere secreted in the house. Now, what I have to request of you, Mr. Whiskin and gentlemen, is, that you will look for it ; and if you find it, I'll eat those fire-irons."

" Well, but," said Mr. Whiskin, " this is irregular."—" Irregular or not, will you look for the will ? I'll accompany you ; you don't expect, my dear Mr. Gilbert, that I'll produce one ; you don't suspect me, eh—do you ?" exclaimed Rodwell.

" Not at all, bless you," said old Gilbert.—" It's decidedly awkward," said Lowe.

" Very, ain't it ?" sneered Rodwell ; " decidedly awkward. Ha, ha ! it's diamond cut diamond, only that the affair's transposed a little. We'll have a bottle of wine afterwards."

" How extravagant !" said old Gilbert. " I can dispense with the wine, provided you will carry out the other promise."

" What is that ?"—" To swallow the fire-irons."

" Ay ; if a will be found trust me for that. You shall see me do it, or I will give you leave to make me, and to call me a fool into the bargain. Now, Mr. Whiskin and gentlemen, you quite understand. After the decease of Mr. Paddlebat, a will executed by him was found—a will certainly advantageous to me, and being so, as you may well suppose, not pleasant to his brother. He, gentlemen, supposes, or says he supposes, that some other will which may be advantageous to him is in the house, and that is why I want you to search, because you being disinterested parties, will do the work faithfully."

" Very good," said Mr. Whiskin ; " of course, as a professional man, you know my time is valuable."—" Oh, you shall be amply paid, sir ; and I cannot help thinking that old Mr. Gilbert Paddlebat here ought to be the man to discharge the bill if you find no wi l."

" I shall not object to anything reasonable," said Gilbert.

While this conversation was proceeding, the two neighbours who had been called in, looked from one to another of the speakers in great astonishment, and thought to themselves what a fine story they would have to tell to their wives and their gossiping acquaintances when they got home, about the strange proceedings at the goldsmith's.

They would not have missed the affair on any account, and they quite wondered that Mr. Whiskin should stay proceedings by making any fuss about payment for his share in that transaction.

"Now, gentlemen," added Rodwell, "we will proceed to business, and in as systematic a way as we can, we will search the whole house."—"Ah," said old Gilbert, " and while you are all gone, I will look again through my diary, and see if there is anything more about it."

Rodwell cast what he considered a withering look upon Nicholas Lowe as he left the room, but Lowe did not return it. On the contrary, he preserved the look of affected mortification which he had, to deceive Rodwell, put on, when first the proposition to call in indifferent people to search the house, had been broached.

How strangely Rodwell had fallen into old Paddlebat's plan. If he had not proposed the neighbours and the solicitor as the proper persons to search the papers of the deceased goldsmith, Lowe would have been compelled to do so, and then Rodwell might have suspected that he was being, as he himself would have said, outgeneralled in some way, instead of fancying, as he now did, that he had completely triumphed over both Lowe and the old miser.

How full of exultation he was, and with what a world of candour he pointed out to Mr. Whiskin and the two neighbours, every possible place where it was likely a will might be concealed.

"But we need not follow them in the search. Let us look at Lowe and old Gilbert, as they were now left alone in the drawing-room. Mrs. Paddlebat and Fanny Leslie had both left the apartment upon the arrival of Mr. Whiskin and the two neighbours ; so that there they were, had they felt inclined fully in a position to speak as confidentially as they chose.

But Gilbert Paddlebat was a man who carried caution a long way indeed. He was not one to throw away the least chance, or to run the least risk, so he only looked at Lowe with a cunning twinkle of his little eyes, and said with a short dry cough,—

"Ahem, Mr. Lowe, I shall be surprised if my brother did not make the will he mentioned to me."—"And so shall I," replied Lowe.

" Ah, well, we are all in the hands of Providence, or chance, or something of that sort, so I shall amuse myself by reading my diary."

The old man said no more aloud, but kept turning over the leaves of his diary, and muttering to himself some particulars of the extraordinary memoranda which he had there put down. Lowe looked at him with a feeling almost approaching to admiration, at the manner in which he had conducted all the affair of the two wills. It could not possibly have been better done. To admit the genuineness of Rodwell's will, was to place him in one of the most perplexing situations as regarded that document, that could be conceived.

The whole of the cleverness which he, Rodwell, had expended upon the production of the forged will which he had produced, would assist in establishing the one which Gilbert Paddlebat thought so much more desirable.

And certainly, although we cannot be accused of any sympathy with the avarice of such a man as Gilbert, yet receiving the matter in all its bearings, we are much more inclined to wish success to the second will than to the first.

Indeed the will which old Gilbert produced was, in some of its provisions, very like what the goldsmith would really have made had he made a will at all ; and, in so far as that it provided handsomely for Fanny Leslie, we are not disposed to quarrel with it.

The happiness of such a being as Fanny was not dependent upon money, and so long as she had sufficient for those legitimate wants which all human beings, in an artificial state of society like our own must have, she was about the last person in the world who would be likely to sigh for more.

The proceeds of her legacy by the will which had been so recently concealed in the house by Nicholas Lowe, would be somewhere about four hundred pounds per annum, and that for her would be amply sufficient, so that we consider Fanny Leslie as done justice to by old Gilbert, and wish success to his will accordingly, without in the least giving him credit for a good motive in so providing for her, because we know it was only done in order to secure the co-operation of Nicholas Lowe.

Not more than half an hour passed in suspense, when suddenly a terrible rushing of feet was heard, and the drawing-room was dashed open by Rodwell, who rushed into the room, looking more like a maniac than a man in the ordinary command of his reason. His hair was dishevelled; his face was ghastly pale; his eyes blood-shot; and he had bit his lower lip, and blood was trickling down his chin, which not a little contributed to give him a terrific aspect.

Lowe, at the sight of Rodwell in so excited a condition, took refuge behind a chair, but old Gilbert never stirred, but screwing up his mouth, he affected to be mightily surprised at the passion of Rodwell.

"Fury!" cried Rodwell. "Damnation!"—"Ah, indeed," said Gilbert.

"Old man, or rather old fiend, you have done this."—"Done what?"—"You know well, but I stake my life upon the venture, you shall not succeed yet. By what devilish art you have so far managed to get the better of me I know not; but by all the furies, you have raised now a devil you will not find it easy to quell again."

"What is the man speaking about?" said Gilbert. "Can you tell me, Mr. Lowe?"—"I cannot hazard a guess."

Mr. Whiskin and the two neighbours entered the room. The former spoke, saying in an indifferent tone,—

"I have to announce that we have found a will among the papers of the deceased. It is dated March the 10th, in the present year."

"Well," said old Gilbert, "I had my hopes. Now, Mr. Rodwell, you may think me superstitious, and, perhaps, I am a little; but if you sit down quietly and comfortably by me, I will tell you a dream I had about this very will."

"D—n your dream and you too," said Rodwell.

Mr. Whiskin looked amazed.

"Really, sir," he said, "this is extraordinary conduct. Here is a will, the contents of which, I presume, all here present are ignorant of."—"Ignorant of!" cried Rodwell—"ignorant of! You are an ass, and don't know what you are talking about. Gilbert Paddlebat knows every word of it, and so does Nicholas Lowe, I'll be bound."

"Sir," said Mr. Whiskin, "you have called me an ass."—"And so you are."

"I'll take counsel's opinion, sir, as to whether that may not be actionable."—"Bah! don't interfere. Mr. Paddlebat, will you grant me a private interview now in another room?"

"Oh no."—"And why not?"—"I have got no secrets. If you have anything to say, Mr. Rodwell, to me, say it at once if you please, and openly; I tell you I want nothing but common justice. If the will which has now just been found, and which I shall propose be left in the hands of the highly respectable professional gentleman now present, leaves you anything which my late brother could call his, I should be the first man to assist you in taking steps to prove the validity of the document."

"Nothing can be fairer," said Mr. Whiskin.—"Hold your tongue, you idiot. Mr. Paddlebat, are you not open to any compromise, sir, in this affair?"

"Open to what?"—"A compromise—an understanding. Come now, sir, I own you have got the better of me—come, now."

"I beg your pardon, you have quite the advantage of me; for hang me if I can understand what you mean about a compromise. I am not aware that you owe me anything, and I am quite sure I owe you nothing."—"Done, by G—d!" said Rodwell; and with a groan he sank upon a couch, looking the very picture of despair.

"Perhaps," said Lowe, "by the time you have eaten the fire-irons, according to your promise, you will feel a little better."

Rodwell cast a savage look upon him, and muttered something which was not very intelligible; but Lowe cared not what the discomfited ruffian said, and old Gilbert cried out aloud, in his odd cracked voice,—

"I don't see why Mr. Whiskin should not at once read the will which he has found, in the presence of these two most respectable gentlemen, who will not only then be witnesses to the finding of it, but likewise to its contents. I propose, too, that Mrs. Paddlebat and Miss Leslie be requested to be present."

Rodwell said nothing, and so this proposition was carried by general consent, and Fanny and her aunt were sent for. When they had come, Mr. Whiskin laid the will upon the table, and said, in a clear voice,—

"Ladies and gentlemen, the document which is endorsed, as the last will and testament of Mr. Paddlebat, was found below, among some books and papers, apparently relating to the business which the deceased gentleman carried on for so many years on these premises, with such great respectability and advantage to himself."

"Ah, very good," said old Gilbert, " very good."—" D——n rubbish," muttered Rodwell.

" The two respectable gentlemen who saw me find this testamentary document," continued the attorney, " will, I have no doubt, attest that fact by their signatures, before they lose sight of it."

Pens and ink were on the table, and this was done at once, during which Rodwell made some hideous grimaces.

" And now, then," added Mr. Whiskin, " we'll read this document, if you please, ladies and gentlemen."—" Ah, yes," said Gilbert, " read it, read it; we may as well know at once what is in it."

The attorney then read the will; but as our readers are already well aware of its contents, we need not trouble them again with a repetition of the various bequests. Mrs. Paddlebat looked bewildered; Fanny preserved her equanimity perfectly; Lowe's countenance wore a triumphant expression, while Rodwell uttered a deep groan.

" Ah," said old Old Gilbert, " that's just what he told me he would do, and what I have got down in my diary."

" Under this document," said Mr. Whiskin, " you, Mr. Gilbert Paddlebat, take possession of everything. It is, I perceive, regularly attested, and seems extremely clearly drawn up, although I do not see an attorney's name to it."—" Indeed!" said Gilbert. " Well, well, I know my deceased brother was a clever man of business, and he, very likely, considered that he could draw his own will as well as it could be drawn for him."

" Stop, stop," said Whiskin, " I am mistaken—there is an attorney's name. Mr. Augustus Crouch, Gray's-inn—to be sure. Well, I really did not see it at first. Oh, Mr. Rod—what's your name—now, sir, can you take upon yourself to insinuate that this most respectable gentleman, Mr. Gilbert Paddlebat, knew anything of this will? Mr. Paddlebat, I would advise you at once to order that young man off these premises."—" So I will. Mr. Rodwell, oblige me by going. We cannot afford to have you here any longer; it's nearly dinner time, and I don't see why you should feed out of the estate of the deceased."

" What!" screamed Mrs. Paddlebat, " order Mr. Rodwell out of the house?"— " Yes, madam."

" Confound you all," said Rodwell, rising. " But hark you;—you, Gilbert Paddlebat, and you, Nicholas Lowe; you both, no doubt, are well aware how much can be done by dint of perseverance, if a person sets about anything in real earnest. Now, I do know enough of you, Nicholas Lowe, to be a dangerous foe; and so you, Gilbert Paddlebat, will find yourself yet leagued with a man who, for his own safety's sake, may think it expedient to sacrifice you."

" Ah," said old Gilbert, tapping his forehead, " it's here he feels it."

" I defy, as much as I despise, the threat," said Lowe. " That you are a villain, and capable of attempting anything, however criminal or desperate, I can well believe; but, beware, yourself, or I may pounce upon the confederate whom you conversed with last night."

" Liar!" said Rodwell.

" Really," interposed Mr. Whiskin, " if this man does not leave the house at once, I should recommend that a constable be sent for."

"Ah, to be sure," said Gilbert; "go for a constable. Susan, will you? we cannot be abused in this manner."

"I will spare you the trouble," said Rodwell; "I am going, but do not flatter yourselves that you have seen the last of me, or that I cannot yet be sufficiently mischievous to confound you all, and blow the forged will to the winds."

"That's decidedly libellous," said Mr. Whiskin. "You have him there, Mr. Paddlebat, and I strongly advise you to bring your action."

See p. 237.

"Oh, poor devil, he is not worth powder and shot, that's the fact. Let him say what he likes."

Rodwell dashed from the room, leaving thus his enemies in complete possession of the field, from which, with his own weapons, he had been so signally driven, and covered with defeat.

That there would be little or no difficulty in establishing the new will is sufficiently evident. The only thing that could at all attack it, would be a voluntary confession on the part of Rodwell that he had forged the previous one ; and that, although it would be a circumstance that might provoke inquiry, and entail upon him serious legal consequences, would be very unlikely to succeed in affecting Gilbert's will, because there could be no possible means of proving that the goldsmith had not executed some will, bearing date, January 17.

And so it appeared, from all the existing state of affairs, that Rodwell was thoroughly beaten ; indeed, in no situation to do, or to attempt to do, anything which was likely even to affect the serenity of the parties who had dislodged him from what he considered his stronghold in the goldsmith's house.

The only person who regretted him was Mrs. Paddlebat ; and her predilections in his favour were so strong, that she looked upon his departure with great regret. What advantage he took of the lady's partiality for him, will in a short time appear, as events, now, are hurrying onwards to a catastrophe as violent as unexpected.

CHAPTER XLI.

FANNY LESLIE'S ANSWER TO LOWE'S LETTER.—THE ACCUSATION.

Now, indeed, Nicholas Lowe felt that something had really been achieved, and that the day of his triumph had come. He looked upon old Gilbert Paddlebat almost with a veneration, for the great tact, discretion, and talent, with which he had conducted the whole affair.

How flourishing did his prospects now look. Five hundred pounds assured to him for himself, one of which he had already in hand for present exigencies ; the love of Fanny Leslie, who was entitled to eight thousand pounds—a sum that, if it could not be called a fortune, was yet amply sufficient to stand between them and all the disagreeables connected with every-day existence, and that struggle to live, which is of so dreadfully depressing a character.

That she would now consent to become his, he did not doubt. Had he not made the offer to her of his hand when he had no knowledge of the good fortune that awaited her? At least, so the circumstance must to her mind appear, she being without a suspicion of the nefarious proceedings connected with the new will ; and, consequently, from what he knew of her disposition, he thought that she was just the person to rejoice at an opportunity of rewarding the generosity of one who would in her poverty have loved her.

He was so well pleased, that, at the moment, he could have forgiven even Mrs. Paddlebat for all that, from time to time, she had done against him, and as he glanced at Fanny, he could not help contrasting his present position with what it was when he was, in a manner of speaking, driven by Rodwell from that house, in which he hoped soon to have a lasting and a substantial footing.

Fanny, however, did not look so pleased or so triumphant as he, Nicholas Lowe, would have liked to see her look. There was an air of great sadness upon her countenance, and he looked upon that token of a mind ill at ease with considerable uneasiness.

He approached her and said, in a low voice,—

"Fanny, you do not seem happy."—"I am not happy," she said ; "and I cannot seem that which I am not."

"Well, but ——"—"Hush! I cannot speak to you here. You shall hear from me in the course of a day or two."

"Shall I remain here?"—"No, no, by no means. Under the present aspect of affairs, you had, for the better, not be in the house. Go, I entreat you to go, and not to come here again, until you hear from me."

This was unpleasant ; but Lowe had no alternative but to obey the mandate, because he felt that the only thing which in any way could have made his stay pleasant there, would have been the smiles of Fanny, even if Gilbert Paddlebat had given him leave to remain as he now, under the new will, might have assumed the favour to do, he, Lowe, would have felt how very indiscreet it was to accept of such leave in the face of an injunction from her whose good opinion was of so much value to him to the contrary.

"I will obey you, Fanny," he said; "you know well that your wishes are laws to me."—"Yes—go—go."

"But when shall I hear from you?"—"In a day or two, at farthest."

"Well, sister," croaked old Gilbert, as he looked scrutinizingly in the face of Mrs. Paddlebat. "Well, sister, you, at all events, seem to be no loser by all these changes and mutations of fortune, eh? You will be pretty comfortable, I'm thinking, after all."

"Sir," said Mrs. Paddlebat, "I desire that you will not address me with so much familiarity."

"Oh, pho—pho! At our age, you know, it don't matter."

"Our age!"

"Yes, you may not be quite so old as I by a trifle; but your chicken days are long past, you know; and now let me give you a word of advice. You will have quite money enough to tempt some blackguard, or some quiet, smooth, silky, sneaking hound to marry you, for there are men who would marry the very devil for money; but don't you do it, Mrs. P.; don't you be such a fool."— "Good God!"

"Ah! as you say, good God! Whenever any such fellow makes you an offer, and tells you that he admires and loves you, go to a looking-glass, and then you will be put in mind that you are a fat, vulgar, old woman, and then you can ask yourself if it's natural, and answer yourself in the negative, after which you had better show the fellow the door."

Mrs. Paddlebat's countenance, during the time that old Gilbert was uttering this dreadful speech, was quite a study, and by the time he had concluded, she had become of a purple colour, like a partially faded copper tea-kettle.

"You old, abominable ape!" she cried.

"Aunt—aunt!" interposed Fanny; "do not condescend to abuse. Can you not see that all that has been just said has been for an express purpose of putting you out of temper? Why will you allow it to succeed?"

"Succeed—succeed!—I out of temper! Oh, dear, no; I despise and look with contempt upon you, you little, ugly, old reprobate. Oh, dear, me; I out of temper—no—no. I'll let you see, you bad-looking old baboon, that you won't succeed in putting me out of temper. I pity you—yes, I pity you; and I don't wonder that you were never married. Where is the woman that would sacrifice herself to a Gipsy mummy? Oh, you'll find me quite calm—very calm."— "Bravo!—bravo!" said old Gilbert.

"Sir," said Fanny, walking up to him, and looking him in the face. "Is this becoming of you in your dead brother's house, to play upon the feelings of one whom he loved, and who has done her duty to him? For shame, sir—for shame! The very intellect that enables you thus to aggravate and taunt one who has done you no harm, ought to have lifted you above the exercise of such a petty exhibition of aimless and vexatious malice."

Oh, what a contrast was there presented between the young and beautiful face of Fanny Leslie, and the old, yellow wrinkled countenance of old Gilbert Paddlebat. He looked at her intently. It might have been her beauty, or it might have been that she brought to his mind some recollection of earlier and happier days; but certain it is, that a wonderful change came over the face of the old miser, and stretching out one of his skinny, shrivelled hands, he held the sweet, white, child-like fingers of Fanny Leslie, for a few moments.

Old Gilbert Paddlebat appeared to be actually within an ace of saying something kind and gentle; but he did not get it out.

"My dear," he said, and then he paused and dropped the hand, merely adding —"Well—well, I have said my say—I have said my say, and am now going—I don't want to stay."

He rose and went to the door, followed by Lowe, at whose movement to leave, he seemed to look with some surprise.

"You can stay," he said.—"No—no," replied Lowe, "I will not intrude."

"Very well—very well; it don't matter to me a jot; settle it among yourselves. I'm off—good day, Fanny Leslie; you are provided for; and—and—I don't grudge it you—no—no."

This was, indeed, saying something wonderful for old Gilbert Paddlebat; and it may be safely concluded, that if he said it with perfect sincerity, that it was the very first time in his life that he had seen any money go by him which might, by any possibility, have reached his own coffers, that he did not grudge most emphatically and enormously.

Nicholas Lowe looked gloomy when they reached the street, which old Paddlebat noticed, and commented upon in his usual waspish manner.

"Well," he said, "what's the matter with you? Have I not kept my word to the very letter?"—"You have, sir. I could not, I do not find fault with you for a moment. It is a coldness on the part of Fanny Leslie, that annoys me."

"Psha! it's always the way with girls. They are taught dissimulation from their very cradles. When they are most pleased, they endeavour to appear most angry. It's always the way. You take a house, set up an establishment, and you will find the wife come to it."

"You think so?"—"Think so? Bah! I know it. Good day."

"Nay—but ——"—Old Gilbert stopped abruptly, and said,—

"Which way are you going?"—"Here, to the right."

"Very well, then, I am going here, to the left."

So saying, he walked away as quickly as his little legs would carry him, leaving Nicholas Lowe not over well pleased with his situation, because it was so beset with doubts as regarded what Fanny Leslie intended to do in the affair which was the nearest and the dearest to his heart. He walked home to his lodgings, feeling extremely unsettled in his plans and projects as regarded the future, and very far from the state of mind into which, for a very brief space of time, he had so pleasurably fallen, before Fanny desired him to leave the house, which was a circumstance that rankled very much in his heart, inasmuch as, had she wished for his society, she had a fair opportunity of procuring it.

———

CHAPTER XLII.

THE LETTER.—THE INTERVIEW WITH MRS. PADDLEBAT.

THE direction which Nicholas Lowe's thoughts took as regarded the coolness of Fanny towards him, was, for a time, very uncertain, until at last they all centered upon the fact that Rodwell must have maligned him in some way.

But how was he to discover that? If he went to Fanny, and asked that question, although he might get a tolerably specific answer to it, yet he could not do so without awakening a strong impression that there was something which Rodwell might know, and which he, Lowe, might wish to conceal.

Then there came across his memory the extraordinary conduct of Susan when he had called at the house. The evident fright which the very sight of him had produced, and the manner in which he could not fail to notice she had regarded him when she was in the room; all these things combined, almost forced upon him the conclusion that something had been said of him by some one, of which she, Susan, as well as Mrs. Paddlebat and Fanny, was aware, and which had filled the mind of the former with horror.

"And who," he asked himself, "could that same one be who had maligned him but Rodwell?" The hint he had let drop about his cognisance of the unhappy episode in the life of Nicholas Lowe, which was but too true, would be quite sufficient on which to found a world of false accusations. He, Lowe, could well imagine how easy it was upon a small and a slender foundation of truth to build up an amazing superstructure, which would borrow an air of probability from the foundation, small as it was, and yet be itself most scandalously false.

He became quite tortured by these apprehensions and feelings, and finding that he could endure such a state of things no longer, he was about, in defiance even of the injunctions of Fanny, to go to the house and ask of her an explanation, when a letter was brought to him by his landlady.

To eagerly tear it open was the work of a minute, for by the handwriting of the direction he judged that it came from her who was so dear to him, and concerning whose thoughts and opinions he was enduring so much intense anxiety. He was not disappointed. The letter did come from Fanny Leslie, and it contained the following words :—

"I did not intend to have written to you for some days, but upon second thoughts I became convinced that it would be doing you an injustice to delay letting you know some things that have very recently occurred here, in which your character and your honour are much compromised. I found that my aunt was possessed, or that she fancied that she was possessed, of some secret connected with you which was very much to your disadvantage.

"I, as soon as I become aware of this fact, took the earliest opportunity of reasoning with her upon the impropriety of keeping such a secret, and finally convinced her that she ought to tell me, which she did fully.

"It appears that Rodwell told her you had been engaged in some transaction which had ended in the death of some very amiable person, and that a male relative of that person came one day to this house to reproach you with the fact, and that you made an appointment with that male relative, from which you came back with a disordered aspect, and blood upon one of your wristbands, which you tore off, and placed in your desk in the counting-house; and this part of the business he has brought forward the servant to substantiate, which she does most unequivocally.

"Is there any truth in all this? Your denial I need not say will relieve my mind from a great burthen of anxiety, and enable me then, which you will perceive that I have not now attempted to do, to answer your former letter to me, as such a letter ought to be answered from you.   "FANNY LESLIE.
"To Mr. Nicholas Lowe."

We cannot say that this epistle took Lowe entirely by surprise, because his previous reflections prepared him to imagine that he had in a supposition of Rodwell's calumnies found an explanation of Fanny's coldness. But yet the letter was so different an one from what might have been expected from a young girl whose affections there could be no manner of doubt had been much compromised, that he trembled to read it, and was for a long time undecided what course to pursue as regarded it.

At length he made up his mind that his first step must be to discover what sort of evidence Rodwell had adduced of his knowledge that there had been any one circumstance in his (Lowe's) life which he might be anxious to conceal. The downright effrontery of saying that it was to him that a man had once insolently come to the goldsmith's counting-house, when, as the reader well knows, it was to Rodwell he came, was just what might be expected from one so utterly destitute of all moral obligations.

But there was Lowe in the unhappy position of not knowing how much could be really proved against him, and fearful, consequently, of contradicting too much, lest a proof of some part what he had contradicted should be forthcoming, and so make, what with truth he could deny, more a false semblance of truth against him. It was for these reasons, then, that he determined upon at once proceeding to the late goldsmith's house.

When he got there, he determined upon first asking to see Mrs. Paddlebat, for he considered that she was more likely to know what sort of evidence Rodwell had produced, or offered to produce, than Fanny; who, had she been cognisant of any, would, in all probability, with the amount of candour which belonged to her, have stated it in her letter.

After some delay, he was shown into the dining-room, and, with an assumption of great dignity, Mrs. Paddlebat made her appearance. Fanny's letter was not one which it was at all necessary to conceal the existence of, so Lowe said at once,—

"Madam, I have received a note from Miss Leslie, which states that you have related to her a communication you have had from Mr. Rodwell, prejudicial to my character, and, knowing that whatever may be your feelings as regards friendship, or the reverse, to different individuals, you would be the last person to commit a real act of injustice, knowing it to be such, I have come to ask you what proof Mr. Rodwell gave you that there was any part of my personal history which I should shrink from having known."

This was a home question; and, after a few moments' delay, Mrs.Paddlebat said, apparently in some little trepidation,—

"Oh! as to proofs, he only said he knew it."

"And that is all?"—"Well, I suppose so."

"Then, madam, I can tell you that it was to Rodwell that a man came one day with threats into your counting-house, and not to me. That it was he, Rodwell, who came home with evidences about him of having been engaged in some mortal struggle, and not I. He has had the assurance to accuse me of his own deeds and that suspicion that I had against him—but which, being only a suspicion, I shrank from saying anything about—he has, with an amount of mendacity, only such as he could be capable of, turned into a charge against me."—"Ah! well I'm sure, I don't know."

"Madam, of course you can only be guided by the weight of evidence which may be produced upon each side. It will be now a duty which I owe to myself to investigate the whole affair thoroughly."—"Very well."

"I will write to Miss Leslie. I fear my feelings would not permit me now to see her calmly upon this question."

So saying, Nicholas Lowe, who thought he could say much more in a letter than he could in an interview, which might have to take place in the presence of Mrs. Paddlebat, for although Fanny was a free agent, and her aunt had no right to exercise any sort of control over her, that was a very difficult thing to say.

Lowe, therefore, at once left the house, and as he did so, he made a solemn declaration that he would leave no stone unturned to convict Rodwell of the crime of murder, which he, Lowe, really believed had been committed, but which, seeing that he had succeeded in obtaining the affection of Fanny, he had not until now thought it worth his while to investigate.

Now, however, he resolved upon bending all his energies to the task, and since Rodwell had thus proclaimed war against him, he was determined that he should find him no passive or insignificant enemy.

"The villain!" he said. "I will bring him to condign punishment, or there shall be indeed some most special reasons to prevent me."

That same evening he wrote to Fanny a general denial of Rodwell's charges, and then only waited for the commencement of a new day, in order to set about his inquiry into any circumstances that might tend to prove Rodwell's guilt.

———

CHAPTER XLIII.

NICHOLAS LOWE'S SEARCH FOR THE MAD WOMAN.—THE RESULT OT AN INTERVIEW, AND THE DEATH.

Now that Lowe was fully assured the antipathy of feeling raised in the breast of Mrs. Paddlebat towards himself was the creation of Jervis Rodwell, who had succeeded in his attempt upon him, and poisoned her mind against him, and that he was endeavouring to effect the same object in Fanny's mind, and that on account of some act of Rodwell's own criminality, he became doubly anxious of discovering the crime, and the author, and to be in a condition to accuse him of the crime, and to bring him to justice.

If he could do this, he would not only relieve himself from all suspicion and unpleasant thoughts upon the subject, he would reinstate himself in the good opinion of both, because they must be conscious they had treated him unjustly, if they regarded him with suspicion, and the reaction of opinion would be more favourable to him, he thought.

Moreover, by such a course, he should remove Jervis Rodwell altogether from the field, and it would be open only to himself; he would have no rival, and be himself the point on which all events turned.

Nicholas determined to make the attempt, and that, too, in a careful, diligent manner, and to omit nothing that would give him a chance of success, for he felt morally convinced that there was no doubt but that murder had been committed by Rodwell.

The very circumstances that were intended to turn to the disadvantage of him, Lowe, were, in his mind, a sufficient proof of the fact against Rodwell, because Lowe had seen them as they occurred, and therefore knew well how far they bore upon Jervis's guilt, and in what way.

The first thing that he had to do, was to endeavour to find out who it was that had been murdered; that was his grand object, but it was one of difficult attainment, as will be seen. To effect this, however, he quitted the house, and proceeded towards the public-house at which the inquest was held, there to make some inquiries, the result of which would, he hoped, give him some clue to proceed upon, in search of the individual's friends who had been murdered, and among whom he thought he could make a few useful inquiries, and ascertain matters that, in his hands, would bring to light the facts he desired to learn, and to gain what proofs he could.

Nicholas Lowe made for this place, as being the first at which he ought to call, and at which he expected to learn the nature of the first link in his chain of evidence, that he thought he could collect against Jervis Rodwell, who was endeavouring to ruin him in the eyes of her he loved most, in a manner that was at once treacherous and cowardly.

"However," he muttered, "he shall reap what he sows. He had better have left this alone; it will do him but little service, but me much; however, as he has had the temerity to father upon me his acts, I will endeavour to prove who the father is to such a child, and Master Jervis Rodwell's triumph shall be but short lived."

As these thoughts crossed his brain, he traversed the steets of London, and at the same time he endeavoured to ascertain whatever might be going on around him, for something might happen so purely accidentally to put information in his way, that he could hardly believe it otherwise than designed; and however miraculous these things might seem, since they did often happen, he would not refuse the guidance of a directing hand, merely because he did not know whence it came.

"However, nothing happened of this character, neither did he meet with anybody whom he knew as acquaintances of Jervis Rodwell, and of whom he could have made any inquiry relative to the absence of any one in particular.

He met with nothing of the sort, but arrived quietly at the house where the inquest had been held. Here he determined to walk in, and seeing no one in the bar, he entered the parlour, and, as the readiest way to get information and attention, he ordered some refreshment.

It was a waiter that came in—a dapper little man, who seemed to imagine that the whole essence of gentility was concentrated in his own person, and in reply to Lowe's orders, replied instantly with a sudden " yes, sir," which was ejected from his lips almost in one syllable; certainly with only one effort or impulse.

" Do you remember some time since —— ?"—" Yes, sir."

" What ?" said Lowe.—" What were you going to say, sir ?"

" Do you know ?"—" Oh! no, sir."

" Oh! I see," said Lowe; " do you remember an inquest being held here on the body of —— ?"—" Yes, sir."

" Who ?"—" Don't know, sir."

" It was on the body of a man who had been murdered."—" I do, sir."

" There was but one, I believe ?"—" That's all, sir. We haven't had an inquest besides upon anybody at all," said the waiter.

" And what verdict did they return ?"—" An open verdiet, sir."

" But what was it ?"—" An open verdict."

" And you don't know what it was in terms, then ?"—" No, sir, it was an open verdict, which means, you see, as anybody may be taken up and hanged, if so be they can be caught, and found guilty of the murder."

" I understand."—" Yes, sir ; though I cannot help thinking it would have been just as easy to hang a man for murder without, as with a coroner's inquest."

" So it would ; but I want to ascertain who this man was," said Lowe ; " his name, or connections, or anything connected with him."—" Ah! that I don't know, sir."

" Is your master within ?"—" Yes, sir."

" Send him in to me."—" Yes, sir."

The waiter departed, and in a few moments more the landlord himself entered the parlour, and begged to know what it was he desired to say to him. Lowe did not expect much, after what the waiter said to him, and he therefore merely said,—

" I wished to obtain some information respecting the man who was murdered some short time back, and an inquest was held upon him here. Can you tell me who he was ?"—" I cannot, for no information was obtained at all of him. Nobody knew him, and he was not identified."

" Then there is no trace of him at all ?"—" None."

" Nor any suspicion as to who was his murderer ?"—" No ; for if we had any, it might serve as some clue as to whom he was ; we might have made inquiries ; but as it was, all the conclusion we could come to was, that a man had been murdered by somebody, but by whom there was no evidence to show, and a verdict was given accordingly."

" I am much obliged to you. I was particularly anxious to make some discovery respecting another party, and therefore intend to make inquiries in all quarters, without distinction."—" Very right, sir ; you may, while upon one matter, suddenly come upon some facts that may tend to throw light upon some other, and bring some delinquent to justice."

" That is very true, sir," said Lowe ; " and now, perhaps, you will answer me one question—do you know anything of an old beggar woman, who is supported upon the charity of the frequenters of the city ?"—" Oh, yes, I know whom you mean ; I think she was seen on the day of the funeral."

" She was ?"—" Oh, yes, I have seen her about often enough."

" But have you seen her lately ?"—" Not for a day or two."

" Where does she live ?"—" I cannot tell ; nobody knows—indeed, nobody cares. Who should, for an old beggar woman ?"

" No one, certainly."—" Exactly ; not because she is not worth caring for herself, but because she has no claim upon any one, and only seen or known because she has been for some time in one locality."

" True ; where can I hear of her ?"—" That's more than I can tell."

" I should be glad to find her out."—" I cannot tell you, I am sure."

" I think l can, sir," said the waiter.—" Can you ?" said Lowe.

" Yes, sir."—" Where ?"

" Do you know a tall black man, who carries a board about the city ?" said the waiter.—" I recollect having seen such a person."

" Well, he knows."—" But how do you know that ?"

" Because I have seen them walking about, and talking together, and drinking together ; so I think he may know where to find her."

" That is all very true ; but where am I to find this perambulating board-supporter ?" said Lowe.—" Lately he has changed his profession ; from stress of times, or from choice, or from expectation of greater profit, or from ——"

" There, there, James, that will do ; condescend to mention the fact the gentleman is desirous of knowing, and do not meddle and lose youself in so many suppositions."—" Well, sir, I had just come to the last when you stopped me, and in less time than this you would have known all I know."

"Well, what is it?"—"That he now uses a broom instead of carrying a board, and cleans a crossing," said James.

"But where?"—"At the bottom of the lane, opposite."

"Oh, I see; and he's to be found there?"—"He was there at eight o'clock this morning," said James, "and I expect he's there now; or if not, I can't tell where he's gone to; but he stays there till late in the evening, which he goes and spends at some favourite crib, where he is a great man."

"Shall I send for him, sir?" said the landlord.—"It will be giving you great trouble."

"Oh, none at all; I will send a boy to bring him to you."—"Thank you."

The landlord quitted the room, and in a few minutes more a boy was dispatched at full speed to ascertain the whereabouts of the black man, who, in his own circle, was denominated a gentleman of colour, and sometimes a foreigner.

It was not long before the animated trunk of a poplar or sycamore tree came slowly walking after the lad, who was endeavouring to urge him on by several inducements, especially by the application of undeserved epithets, as,—

"Come now, snow-ball, move your stumps. Now then, old chalk-pit, you can't move faster than a haystack. Now then, young whitewash, do move ahead;" and sundry other matters; but no, the man of colour was not to be thus unduly urged—he took all in good part, and kept rather a good look out, but betrayed no anger. Suddenly, however, the boy forgot to keep a look out, and thus the black man stole a march upon him; and in an instant one of his long arms was stretched out, and he seized the culprit by the ear, which he rang with such force and vigour, that he produced such a series of shouts that alarmed the whole neighbourhood.

"Sarves him right," said the waiter; "that boy is a nuisance in the house, and most woeful sarsy."

"Is he?"—"Ah, dreadful, sir; nobody can manage him, sir; but I'll warrant the black man has given him something to remember."

In another moment the black man entered the parlour.

"Here he is, sir."—"Ah," said Lowe, as he looked upon the man; "I remember very well that countenance. Come in."

"Yes, sar," said the black man. —"I want to ask you a few questions."

"Berry well, sir."

"Will you answer truly?"—"Dat I will—only try."

"I don't want you to do it for nothing; I will reward you for your trouble," said Lowe, anxious to get at the truth.—"As many as you please, sar."

"But I may want you to do more, perhaps, afterwards; so tell me truly what I shall ask of you."—"Berry well, sar," said the black man, with a long bow.

"You know an old woman, who walks about and sweeps crossings, and begs of people?"—"She only asks, sar."

"Oh, well, asks, then. I want to know where I can see her; I want to speak to her."—"Yes, sar."

"Do you know where she lives?"—"Yes, sar."

"Where?"—"I cannot tell you, sar."

"Not tell me?"—"No, sar: cause the place has no name."

"Can you show me the way, and bring me to speak to her," said Nicholas Lowe, "as I want to see her?"—"I can."

"Will you undertake to conduct me to her place of abode, where I can see and speak with her?"—"But I shall hab to leab my shop."

"Your shop?"—"He means his crossing," said James.

"Oh, you want to be paid for your trouble, I suppose; that's what you mean by leaving your shop?"—"Yes, sar."

"Well, I will take care and reward you for your trouble."—"Thank you, sar; I will be berry glad to come wid you, go where you will," said the black man, with a leer.

"Where is she?"—"I can't tell, only show that, sar; me no know de name of de place; I no think it hab name at all—it neber be baptized—it no Christian place at all."

"Oh, it will do, I dare say, for all that."—"Oh, yes, massa," replied the black; "are you ready?"

"Quite. Is it far?"—"Yes."

"In the city?"—"No, massa, a long way off in de country," said the black man, swinging about his arms and legs in a singular manner: "a long way, ob where de trees and de fields grow."

"Oh, very well. How long will it be before we can get there? how long will it take in walking?"—"About two hours," said the black man.

"Then we will go at once."—"How is it," inquired the waiter, "that the old woman should go out of London; I thought she never went out of the city?"

"No, sar; but she goes sometimes on a country excursion, and when she comes back, she says she's been ill; and she sometimes makes a berry good thing ob it, I assure you, sar."

" I dare say; but it is upon such an excursion she has gone now, I suppose?" inquired Lowe.—" Yes, sar."

" And how can you be sure of finding her?"—" Because she hab been taken ill, and cannot go any furder, and I think she will die."

" Why?"—" She is berry old," said the black man, shaking his head ominously as he looked upon Nicholas Lowe.

" Well, well, then, there is more need of haste," said Lowe, as he ran and gave the landlord the reckoning; and, having given the black man something to begin with, in the shape of drink, they both left the house.

Nicholas Lowe found that there was one inconvenience attached to walking in company with his long companion—and that was the slowness of his motions; for he was indeed an awful slow coach. Do what he would, he could not induce him to increase his gait; one long see saw of a walk it was, that made it inexpressibly tedious and tiresome to Nicholas Lowe.

True it was, the walk was one that was pleasing in the extreme, for it was a very fine day. The sun shone beautifully, and the birds sang cheerfully in the hedge-rows; the fields looked a beautiful green, and the diversity of hill and dale in the vicinity of London always renders the scenery much more pleasant and beautiful to the sight.

He walked slowly enough to note every inch of the ground, had he been so minded; but his thoughts were otherwise employed, and he thought of other matters, while his eyes wandered over the landscape, unconscious that there was anything that might attract the sight.

" How much farther?" he asked of his guide.—" About two miles more, sar."

" I wish you would walk a little faster."—" I am walking, massa."

" But faster."—" I walk fast enough, massa."

" You walk slow—very slow."—" Berry good pace, sar."

" Yes, at a funeral."—" Funeral! Do you mean to insult me? Funeral, indeed; and dat's all because I am coloured."

" No, no; I wasn't thinking of your colour, only of your slow movements, which are a dreadful thing to wait for."—" Berry good movement, massa; can't go quicker —never did go quicker—me no run away."

" I think not; for if you were to run away, I think I could forgive you, for it seems so me impossible."—" Impossible!—what's dat?"

" A thing that can't be done."—" What, you say I no run?"

" Yes, you could not."—" I'll show you I can, massa."

With this the black man bounded away in the most grotesque and singular style of progression imaginable, and, withal, at such a rate as would have done credit to one practising a race.

When he had got about three or four hundred yards, he turned round, and waited the approach of Nicholas Lowe, who had been left some few score yards behind; and when he came up, he said, exultingly,—

" Ah, massa, you no run like me; you berry good at a walk, but you no use at a run at all."

Lowe was compelled to admit he was no use at such a run as the one he had just seen, for he could not run in such a manner as the black man did.

They had not much further to go now, for they came to a place where they saw many small houses, built all together and anyhow. It is singular how many houses hold together. They are built of all materials, and supported in their places by some mysterious dispensation of Providence, for it is entirely hidden from man.

The materials are old, and stick in their places, it is presumed, from custom; and they often seem to have fallen into their places, since they have, at best, but been piled up without order or regularity, and, in many places, there seems to have been a singular fall in the level, for one end of a room often fell a foot and a half below the other.

How this came about, without the whole fabric coming down, is very difficult to say; but certain it is, that such things often happen, as any person well knows who may happen to travel occasionally out of town for some ten or twelve miles.

Nicholas Lowe gazed up at these places in some astonishment, and wondered how people would trust their lives in them ; they, however, do so, and will, though they were to see them tumbling down, year after year. People seem to imagine that so long as a house stands that it will stand, and, to a certain extent, they are right, for it does stand until it falls, and that is often after it has become dangerous.

From among these houses branched a narrow lane, and down this apparently little frequented pathway the black man went, and Nicholas Lowe followed him close.

"Does she live here ?"—"Yes, massa."

"Is she alone ?"—"Don't know, massa."

Not finding he could extract much information from his black companion, he followed in silence his footsteps, until they came to a miserable hovel, built half of boards, bricks, and stones, with an additional patch of mud to stop some gap, and as for glass there was none—it was all dark.

The only sign of life that he could see about the hovel was some smoke curling out of the chimney.

"Is this the place," inquired Nicholas Lowe of his companion, "where the old mad woman lives ?"—"Yes, massa," said the black man. "My errand done now ; I hope you are satisfied ?"

"Quite. Won't you go in and speak to her, and see if I can speak to her; she may not like a stranger to walk in unannounced."

The black man's wide lips parted, and displayed a formidable row of teeth, as he grinned all the while that Nicholas Lowe was speaking, and when he ceased, he said,—

"Gor-a-massy ! She neber heard ob all dat. We go in at de door, and out ob de door, and you can do de same, massa, if you like ; no hindrance. Me 'greed to bring you here, but not to go in as well. Oh, no ; me no do dat."

"And why not ?"—"Why not, eh ?"

"Yes, why can you not ?"—"Oh, I could, if I liked. I have my private objection. I no go in dere, massa, for any money."

"Well, then, will that satisfy you ?" inquired Lowe, as he gave him some money, which was enough for the purpose.—"Yes, massa, me berry satisfied ; but, sar, me be more satisfied with anoder sixpence."

This was given, and the black man was dismissed on his travels homeward ; and Nicholas Lowe, hearing no sound within, he knocked at the cottage door, but waited awhile before he entered, but no sound was returned. A thought rushed to his mind that gave him no agreeable feeling.

"Surely," he thought, "the black man hasn't played me false, and brought me all this way for nothing, and left me to make my way into an empty house, having played the fool with me."

He was somewhat angry at the thought, and at once opened the door, which was rather awkward, since it stuck in some places, and not in others, which caused it to stick, and cling, and double half over, as though it had gone into pieces.

However, with a little humouring, he at length opened it, and entered the hovel. A hovel it was, in every sense of the word. It was but of one apartment—a room, in which there were but few articles of furniture, and those of the most wretched description.

The floor was composed of the earth itself, which had been well grimed in with ashes from the grate, or fire-place ; it would be a difficulty to tell which.

A table of a primitive character stood in one corner, and in another was the fire-place ; and, in almost total darkness, was a quantity of straw, which had been laid there very recently, and upon it Nicholas Lowe saw, when his eyes became used to the place, the object of his search lying extended on her back.

Nicholas Lowe paused at this scene of misery and poverty. It was one of those dark, damp, and dismal holes, of which not a few are to be found among the rural districts. Altogether, Lowe had never seen the equal of this place ; there was little light, save what came in between some bushes that had been thrust into the orifice that had once been a window, but which had apparently, for some time past, been a mere gap.

There was, to be sure, a few smouldering embers of a wood fire, but the heat they gave was scarcely perceptible, while the light they shed was little more than what sufficed the spectators to gaze upon them, and no more.

He turned towards the straw, and saw the woman lying so still and so motionless that he thought she was dead; he, therefore, stepped up beside her, and saw that her eyes were shut, and it was some seconds before he felt assured she yet breathed; but she was either insensible or she slept.

Drawing a stool near him, which was the only article he could sit down upon, he sat and watched her. This was suggestive of many thoughts, and, among others, brought to his mind the condition before death of some who had at one time been dear to him, but who were now clay-cold, and rotting in their graves, forgotten by all. How long the old mad woman would have slept, he could not form a notion; perhaps she never would have awoke again; but he began to think the day was wearing away, and he had better make some effort to attract her attention.

He took her hand and lifted it up. It was mere bone and shrivelled skin, and looked ghastly and shrivelled-like. Lowe let the limb fall on the straw instantly, so great an effect had the shock upon him.

"Good Heaven!" he said to himself; "and can humanity come to this pass? Horrible! horrible!"

The action woke the old woman up, and she turned her head slowly towards the side where Lowe sat, and said, in a low, weak voice, as she gazed upon him,—

"Who is it that disturbs the dying? You come not with the intention of smoothing the pillow of one who has but a very short time to breathe the breath of life?"—"I am a stranger to you, my good woman," said Lowe, who felt at a loss how to proceed.

"Yes, yes; the death chamber of the poor is not sacred to them, but must be invaded by those who are desirous to found a tale, or amuse themselves with the manners of the destitute and wretched. But are all worlds alike, and are the inhabitants gifted with the same wretched feelings that find place in the breast of human nature in this much vaunted world?"—"I am none such as you describe."

"Come you with charitable intents, then? Do you come, indeed, with the hope of prolonging life, or smoothing the pillow of the dying poor, who have none to care for them?"—"I do not."

"You do not," said the mad woman, "you do not; and wherefore come you? Ah, ah! You come to satisfy your curiosity, then? That is often the strongest motive with the rich to do good, or even justice."—"My errand," said Nicholas Lowe, "is one of justice."

"Ay?"—"It relates to justice."

"Then wherefore come ye to me? I have no power. I cannot dispense the attribute. Who should but your licensed dealers in the article?—who have their own order and their own fancy to please. Infringe upon either, and the Bridewell opens for you."—"I come not upon so poor an errand as to seek aught of you but what you have to give."

"And what may you imagine I can have to give? I am dying, and have not one atom I can part with."—"That which will cost you only the trouble of uttering: words, mere words," said Lowe.

"And very few of them," said the beggar woman.—"But they may enable me to overtake the guilty and punish those who now escape with impunity."

"Has any one done you some damage, then? Have you lost as much as would be valued at a few pence, and desire to punish some starving wretch, because his necessities drove him to the deed? Man, man, ye are more careful of your beasts than you are of your fellow-creatures. Men must live; but you would punish them if they took aught of yours to sustain their existence. You would punish them sorely."—"I want nothing of the kind," said Lowe. "I want to injure no one because he may have taken what necessity compelled him to take; but I wish for something else."

"And what do you desire?"—"That justice should be done to the murderer!"

"Can I aid in such a thing?"—"You can."

The old beggar woman shook her head slowly; she seemed unable to comprehend the exact meaning of what Nicholas Lowe said. At length she said, in a calmer tone,—

"Speak, speak, and tell me what you require. My lease of life is nearly out; tell me what you desire."—"I would know who was the murderer of the man whose body rested at the door of Mr. Paddlebat, a short time since?"

"Ah!" said the mad woman, "who are you that ask it?"—"One who is like to become calumniated, and one who is in danger of being accused of another man's crime."

"Ah!"

"You accused Jervis Rodwell."—"I did."

"And was that accusation true?"—"It was."

"But how know you this?"—"I cannot give you the proof, though I know it is as certain as any truth in heaven."

"How can you prove it?"—"I cannot. I am poor, and did not see the deed done; and, had I done so, it would not have mattered; they would not believe the mad beggar woman—no one would heed her accusations. Besides, I should not live to make it : the sand of life is nearly run out."

"But cannot you afford me information that may enable me to be certain in my own mind (as, indeed, I am) that he is the murderer, and then I should feel myself justified in following him, and overtaking him, and using every means in my power to obtain evidence of the deed I believe he has committed?"—"He has committed the deed."

"I believe it."—"Then I will tell you all about it that I know."

The old woman paused a few moments, as though she were endeavouring to recollect the past with greater clearness and precision.

"In that niche," she said, pointing to a hole in the thatch, "is a small phial; give it me."

Nicholas Lowe rose and walked to the spot indicated, but he could not see nor feel what she described.

"Where is it?" he said.—"Beneath that projecting piece of wood."

"I can't see even that."—"The place is dark to you; but I can see it very well from this place. There, put your arm higher and you will feel it."

Lowe did as he was desired, and found the phial, which he handed to the old woman.

"I am sinking," she said, "and this cordial may revive me for a time, and enable me to tell you all I wish."—"Do not hurry."

"There is no time to spare," said the old woman.

She placed the phial to her mouth, and drank the contents off very slowly indeed, and, when done, she cast the phial away, saying,—

"That will never more be used for me. I have been in need of that for many hours; but there was no kind hand to administer restoratives to the poor and miserable."

"Have you had no one to see you this morning?"—"None."

"Indeed!"—"None," said the old woman, "since last night, early."

"And you have had nothing since?"—"Not so much as a draught of water."

"Good Heaven! what neglect."—"You forget I am poor."

"But that is no excuse for neglect, when in extremity."—"It is."

"Indeed! I never heard it alleged before; least of all should I expect to hear it from one in your condition."

"It is the only one that we can give why it is done. But enough; my time for complaining of others has gone by. I am likely soon to find my home in another world. And now about Jervis Rodwell."

"Yes," said Lowe; "it is of him I would hear."

" And the murdered man ?"—" Yes, yes."

" You may know something of the acquaintances of Rodwell; and, if so, you may remember one who appeared to be one of those men who set society at defiance, and whose chief pleasure lay in his acquaintance with taverns and houses of public entertainment."—" I do recollect such a person."

" A careless, dissolute person."—" Yes ; I remember such an one."

" He is the murdered man !"—" Ah !" said Lowe; " I know whom you mean ; but I know nothing more of him. I knew not whom he was."

" But you shall hear enough presently that will satisfy you whom he was from his nature. It is now many years ago since he and Rodwell became acquainted together. They were strangers ; but accident more than design brought them together."

" Did you know them ?"—" Yes."

" What, this man ?"—" Yes."

" And how came you to be thus acquainted with them?" said Lowe, with some curiosity.—" That cannot affect you. My acquaintance with these people and my knowledge of them is great ; but it can matter to you very little how it came about."

" That is true," said Lowe. " Proceed."

" Jervis Rodwell and this man became acquainted many years ago in a somewhat singular manner. Rodwell was, at that particular juncture, very poor, and wanted a friend to help him on. Jervis Rodwell's notions of what belonged to himself, and what to other people, were no doubt just ; but experience proved that this knowledge did not prevent his appropriating anything that could be safely secured without exposing himself to hazard."

" Indeed !"

" It is true. Listen : It may now be seven or eight years ago when these two men first met. It was on a wet evening, and both of them entered a small gambling house : a place where small sums were ventured, and he who had the most to venture frequently lost the most. Rodwell saw his friend there, and saw him play ; but he was always lucky in winning when he was most desirous of doing so, and when the largest stake was to be had.

This, in Rodwell produced a suspicion that all was not quite right, and finding that he was not doing quite so well himself, he coveted the means of holding his luck in his hand, to pounce upon any stake that would be useful to him.

One evening he saw him perform some trick which told him palpably that he did not win fairly, and he waited until the game was over before he said a word to him ; but then he called him out, and spoke to him in private. At first he denied it, and then, after some strong asseverations on the part of Rodwell, and a declaration that he desired to share with him in the secret, so that he might make it profitable, he admitted that he had used sleight of hand, and promised Rodwell that he would let him into the secret. This was done, and Rodwell became an accomplice of the man whom he has now murdered.

In a year after that there were a few more successful gamblers, on a smaller scale than Jervis Rodwell and this man ; but their success was so great that it created a suspicion; and, they in turn, were both watched, discovered, and turned out, and then they were compelled to resort to some other mode of getting money.

In a small town they determined to make an effort of some kind or other to put money into their pockets. It was determined they should take the town hall, and give a grand musical festival. Cards were issued, and every attempt made to draw an audience, which was eminently successful, and the number of tickets was immense. They pocketed a handsome sum on that occasion, and the night before the festival they walked through the town, and a short distance beyond.

" Rodwell," said he, " we had better not go back any more."

" Go back no more ?"—" No."

" Why not ?"—" We had better take the coach that goes on to London, which will pass in a short time."

" But our baggage ?"—" Is not worth altogether five pounds."

" Well ?"—" We had better leave it, and take care of ourselves."

" There will be time enough to allow of our going back, and obtaining our baggage."—" It would excite suspicion."

" And if it were," said Rodwell,—"'if it were we could pay our tavern bill, and take our luggage in spite of them."—" And they could take us to he cage in spite of us."

" The cage ?" said Rodwell.—" Yes."

" And wherefore? The time for the festival is not come yet."—" That may be ; but we may be taken upon suspicion, and detained, especially as we are known to have a good sum of money, and they would detain us in a minute."

" Would they ?"—" I know they would : besides, I have seen a man that I do not like in the town. I do not think he saw me, though it is not impossible that he should ; but he would in a moment grab me. We had better be off."

" Very well," said Rodwell.—" Here comes the coach."

In a few more moments the coach came, and the man inquired of the guard if he had places for two.—" Yes," said the guard,—" outside."

" Yes."—" Get up."

In less than two minutes more they were in full career for London, leaving the little quiet town to grow excited and noisy, the next evening being that of the festival as advertised. Whatever happened cannot be well told, but they got to London safe, and were successful.

Several schemes of this sort were perpetrated between them, and they were in funds for some time. It sometimes happened that they were rich, and sometimes very poor ; and thus they fluctuated between the two extremes for some time. Any one dishonest trick and success never lasted them long ; they spent what they got rapidly, and in all kinds of excesses, which feverish kind of life they called enjoyment. Then again they were sometimes reduced to beggary.

From this state they would rise again by some swindling transaction, which would enable them to appear like persons of property, and thus again enable them to carry on their schemes against the public in general, and individuals in particular.

They took a large house, and ordered an upholsterer to furnish it, which he did, at an expense of eighteen hundred pounds ; in less than a week it was all sold for the eight hundred, and they were not seen again. It is impossible to say how the landlord got into his house again, but it was a very vexatious job for him.

Rodwell and his friend ran through a number of adventures of this description ; but, by some good fortune, they always escaped their deserts, and were never had up, even for a charge of any kind, though they ran some fearful risks.

Their whole course represents shifty, mean, and petty criminality. However, time and impunity made them bold, and they determined to attempt some more dangerous and profitable crimes.

Their first attempt was upon a merchant in the city, who required momentary accommodation of a loan of money, when they obtained his bill ; but he never got bill or money back again, but was compelled to pay it when it came due. Once in this line, they went on for some time.

It was singular that Rodwell always contrived not to be seen in these affairs, while his companion was hardy and careless, and never hesitated upon taking all the dangerous part upon himself, and he did so.

" Rodwell," said his companion, one night.—" Well," he replied

" I have a new scheme in my head."—" Have you ?"

" Yes."—" Is it good ?"

" Very good ; and plenty of money."—" That is the thing," said Rodwell.

" But you must do your part."—" I always do."

" No, no, I have hitherto done all the work ; but in this affair I cannot, or I would. I don't care ; luck's all, you know, Rodwell, and we can't be hanged before our time."—" Hanged ?"

" Yes ; don't you understand, Rodwell ?"

"I think I do; but I don't like such joking; it ain't pleasant. But go on with your scheme."—"You can write well?"

"Yes, yes, I can."—"And you can imitate well?"

"Yes, pretty well."—"I have seen you do it very well."

"I believe I can," said Rodwell; "but what has that to do with your scheme for getting money?"—"This much—you can sign a cheque or a bill for somebody else, can you not?"

"And be hanged."—"Oh no, only run your risk of being hanged; nothing more."

"And enough, too."—"Well, but you can well imitate hand-writings, especially signatures. Now, we have exhausted nearly all the sources by which we can procure money."

"We have."—"And a new one must be had recourse to."

"If it can be done without hanging."—"Exactly; that's not pleasant. Now, you know Messrs. Wilkinson in the city, merchants?"

"Yes."—"Well, their bills are as good as money."

"They are."—"Well, you could draw and accept a few of his bills—push them into circulation—realise a large amount of money—have a swinging cheque ready—and then bolt."

"It is very dangerous—too dangerous."—"Not a bit. We shall not be required to do much more. We shall have much money, which will give us the opportunity of residing in some other country, where we shall be ever free from all alarm or danger."

Rodwell pondered over the plan, and considered the probabilities, one way or another, and weighed the chances of impunity well in his own mind, and thus familiarized himself to the contemplation of the crime; and then, after a day or two, he said—

"Get me a number of Wilkinson's signatures, both on bills and on cheques, by any means you can."

This was done, and how matters not; they were stolen, I believe, said the old woman. In a few days more some bills were ready, and between them they endeavoured to pass off upon merchants and others, who readily took them, and gave their proper sums for them.

This emboldened Rodwell, who now forged several, and eventually a cheque, which he presented, and he obtained the money for it. A short time afterwards the whole affair was blown, and they had to conceal themselves.

It was after that that Rodwell came to Mr. Paddlebat's; he was thoroughly frightened, and determined to make some attempt to shake off the connection, and earn a living by another and less dangerous manner. He did so, as you know, and this man being nearly destitute, and unable to work, came upon him for sums to support himself with; he was a drain upon Rodwell, and haunted him about, for Rodwell was fearful of the exposure, as there was a reward offered for the apprehension of the principal, and a pardon for an accomplice—so he could drain the resources of his companion at will.

One day they met; their conversation was angry, and a fierce struggle ensued, commenced by Rodwell, who had made up his mind that he would rid himself of this man, which he did by murdering him, and then flying from the spot.

"What proof have you?"—"I—I— have ——"

She endeavoured to speak, but a rattle came from her throat; she could not articulate her words, but an indistinct murmur came from her lips; and with her mouth wide open, her eyes starting from their sockets, she remained motionless.

For several minutes Lowe gazed upon her, expecting to hear her make some effort to speak, some fresh attempts, even if a failure, and he listened to catch the slightest sound, so as to distinguish it, and draw information from it, but all in vain. He stooped down and listened; she did not breathe. He placed his hand upon her heart, but there was no motion, no pulsation. The old beggar woman was dead.

Nicholas Lowe rose, and after gazing upon her form for some minutes, he muttered to himself—

"Her troubles are over. She will bear no more witness to the deeds of men; but she confirmed me in my opinion of the guilt of Jervis Rodwell, but I am as far off as ever from the proof. I am sure of it, yet I cannot openly accuse him of the crime."

He turned away, and quitted the cottage, and made the best of his way towards London, filled with many thoughts and speculations upon the scene he had just gone through.

CHAPTER XLIV.

FANNY'S REFLECTIONS.—THE ANONYMOUS LETTER.—THE AGITATING INTERVIEW.

NICHOLAS LOWE could scarcely congratulate himself upon this partial success which he had achieved in discovering so much as he had done of a detrimental character regarding Rodwell. True, he had confirmed some of his worst suspicions and placed himself personally in such a position that he could accuse Rodwell with all the boldness of a man confident that he is right in his accusation, but substantial or legal proof he had none; and if he ventured upon speaking aloud upon what he really himself knew, and then were asked to prove his words, he would find himself in the uncomfortable position of one who had brought forward a charge of which he lacked the power to substantiate.

He was placed in a most peculiarly awkward position, one of those positions of dread, doubt, and difficulty in which a man feels that he is inimical to certain charges, and that his only chance of steering clear of their consequences is the poor one of blackening the character of his accuser.

Well did he, Lowe, know that there was an episode in his life which would not stand the test of examination; and although among men of the world, and what are termed free spirits, he might, if the affair were alluded to or known, pass it off as a piece of gallantry, rather more to his credit than to his disgrace, yet most acutely did he feel that, to such a mind as Fanny Leslie's, the circumstance would bear all the character of heartless profligacy.

For well he knew, with all her simplicity and all her girlish innocence, she had reason and reflection enough to call things by their right names; and the very last person was she to be deceived by the conventionality of custom into calling that gallant and meritorious which was nothing but heartless and deceptive.

We do not purpose to make any mystery of this event in Nicholas Lowe's career, it was one of those which unhappily are too common. There was confiding innocence on one side, and admiring libertinism on the other. One of nature's happiest and best creatures fell a victim to his evil passions; and although he really loved the beautiful being whom he had decoyed from virtue, he then, with a strange inconsistency, blamed her, and considered her unworthy to become his wife because she had yielded to become his mistress.

Then had followed a series of events which, by the reader, may be well conceived, and need not by me be described.

The poor victim of delusion felt herself betrayed; she felt that the firmest promises of him alone she had loved, not wisely, but too well, were as naught balanced against his selfish passions.

And he, Nicholas Lowe, perhaps not worse than a thousand others, contented himself with the notion that the affair would wear off, and that, after a few stormy and angry scenes with his victim, all would be over, and the intrigue would reckon, as one of the things gone by, leaving no consequence behind.

But he was mistaken; the barb had sunk deeper into the heart of her whom he had taught to love him than he had imagined. He might, but she could not forget, and she became doomed to afford another illustration of the poet's lines—

> " Man's love is of his life a thing apart,
> 'Tis woman's whole existence."

The stormy scenes he looked forward to did not ensue, but sorrow, remorse, and the heart's desolation, did their dreadful work, and, when too late, he became terrified at the ruin he had made, and would, at the altar's foot, have gladly repaired all. He found that the bright star of his first affection was clouded for ever— the mind had given way—his victim became a hopeless lunatic—the queen of a fantastic realm, in which strange images of disjointed things alone found a place.

And this was Nicholas Lowe's skeleton. No wonder it haunted him—abroad, or at home, in chamber, or in hall; and most probably it was the reason, the sole inducing reason, why he got up the strange, the true, but the gloomy piece of philosophy, by which he became so famous among all who knew him, or even conversed with him upon such a subject.

It is saying little then for us to assert that he did all he could do to alleviate the natural distress of his victim—that is to say he supported her in a lunatic asylum.

This was done at the sacrifice of half his income, and long and grievous did the burden become to him until death closed her eyes, and he attended at her nearly lonely funeral at the dead hour of night. These were the circumstances to which Jervis Rodwell had alluded, but how he became possessed of them was perfectly mysterious to Lowe, since he would have been the last man whom he would at all have taken into his confidence, and he could not imagine by what combination of circumstances he could have become possessed of the secret.

But possessed he was of it, for to know anything at all of it was probably to know all; and most keenly did Nicholas Lowe feel that if, as a consequence of this early adventure, he and Fanny Leslie became separated, he would have suffered a retribution which, in his own mind, he had ever scoffed at the possibility of.

But thus it is that men's evil deeds come round upon them. Lowe thought, when he saw his poor victim placed in the low and silent grave, that he had done with her for ever, and little dreamt he that she had left behind her even in the memory of her wrongs, an avenging spirit, which was yet to work him a world of mischief.

Now, the only way in which he could stop further inquiry into the particulars of this tale, would be by overwhelming Rodwell with odium and disgrace, so that for him to assert anything, would be at once to exonerate any one from imputed crime.

And what a glorious thing it would be to fix upon him the stigma of murder—to bring down upon his head all the consequences of a crime the greatest of which human nature is capable, and to show him that in his attempt to do an injury, he had only brought down upon himself an amount of destruction of a most sweeping and terrific character.

But here was a failure. Nicholas Lowe felt that he could not do so much, and, after the death of the mysterious female, whose living would have been of such great importance to the accomplishment of his wishes, he feared that he might look long indeed for any other evidence of an available character against Rodwell.

The eight thousand pounds which by old Gilbert Paddlebat's will was left to Fanny Leslie, seemed gradually slipping through Nicholas Lowe's grasp, and if that will were established, all he was likely to get appeared to be the five hundred pounds, which he was promised, and some of which he had already fingered, as a bonus for his co-operation in the forgery.

And, beside, there is no doubt that he loved Fanny Leslie about as much as he could love any person. Perhaps he loved her the more now because he thought there was a chance of losing her ; and, what with his dread of the forgery being found out, and his being implicated in it, combined with the dread of losing his reward, for being a party to its commission, he got into such a state of feverish anxiety, that he could scarcely contain himself, but more than once madly thought of attempting something of a personal character against Rodwell, which should put him and his evidence alike out of the world for ever.

But Nicholas was fully alive to the danger of such an attempt, and as often as it suggested itself to him, he rejected it, rather choosing to fall back upon what he considered the strong affection which Fanny Leslie had for him, and which he thought would surely get her over any little temporary suspicion that might attach to his name and fame.

But there he was wrong. There was such a sense of rectitude about the mind of that beautiful and intelligent girl, that she would not have wedded an emperor, had he a stain upon his honour ; and so Lowe was in a more frightful dilemma than he fancied himself, unless he contented himself with the five hundred pounds, and gave up the chase after the eight thousand pounds, with the beautiful girl into the bargain.

But let us see what Fanny's opinions are upon the matter. She loves Nicholas Lowe, certainly, there can be no doubt about that—but she loves with judgment and discretion ; she does not allow the passion wholly to overwhelm her reason.

"I will not," she said, "upon mere vague suspicion, cast aside an affection which I have cherished ; I will demand proof of the accuser, and I will have proof before I yield credence to an accusation ; but before that proof is yielded, for a reasonable time, at least, Lowe must stand to me in the position of one placed upon his trial, and, consequently, with whom I can hold no sort of intercourse which would commit me in my future conduct."

Perseverance, too, in any course will achieve wonders ; and we know that Mrs. Paddlebat was no friend of Nicholas Lowe's ; he had offended her in a way in which no woman like her is more easily offended—that is to say, in her personal vanity.

Now, we do not mean to assert, that anything Mrs. Paddlebat would say could have much effect upon such a mind as Fanny Leslie's, but as we are well aware it has grown into a proverb, that the accurate waterdrop will drill a hole through adamant. It is not to be supposed, that even Fanny Leslie was quite proof against this continual harping upon the same string which her aunt indulged in.

If it got up no other feelings, it got up one, consisting of a nervous anxiety that Lowe should come out of the ordeal quite perfect ; and, as a consequence of the accusations which were insinuated against him, she was likely to be far more particular with regard to his moral position than under any other circumstances she would have been.

"Ask him, my dear," was Mrs. Paddlebat's continual expression, "ask him to his face if he be guilty of ever betraying the affections of any one, and then if he deny the imputation, it is, of course, for Mr. Rodwell to prove that he actually has done so."

This was reasonable enough, and by being often reiterated, Fanny got so tortured that she resolved on having a scene upon the occasion, and, if possible, confronting Lowe with his accuser. She had come to this determination just about the time that Lowe had finished the inquiries which had achieved only so unsatisfactory a result, and she was thinking of writing to him on the evening of that day when Mrs. Paddlebat came into the room with considerable agitation of manner, carrying in her hand an open letter, which had just arrived to her by post.

Whatever might be the contents of the letter, it was evident that they much discomposed her, for her face had assumed that coppery hue which was incidental to her on great occasions, and she trembled from head to foot.

"Aunt what is the matter?" said Fanny ; " you look agitated."—"Agitated, my dear, I may well look agitated—I am agitated. Do you see this letter ?"

" Yes ; what is it about? Heaven knows we have enough evil now, without any one adding to it."—"Yes, indeed, so I say ; but, howsomever, it's not to be helped —the truth's the truth, you know, and there's an end of that."

"But, aunt, you've not told me what it's about."—" You shall hear, my dear ; I'll read it to you at full length, and then you shall judge for yourself, as you ought to do ; and as it's high time you should do, what wretches the men are."

Fanny Leslie had a suspicion rankling in her breast, that this was something concerning Nicholas Lowe, and she was scarcely less agitated than her aunt, although she exhibited it by paleness, instead of a furious red colour, as she sat down to listen to what that good lady might have to say.

"Now you shall hear," said Mrs. Paddlebat. " I've only just now received this dreadful letter, and I shall read it to you at once, just as it comes, so here goes ; now listen to every word of it."—"I shall attend to it, aunt, most certainly. I only hope that it does not concern me."

"Ah, but it does though ; and this is it."

Mrs. Paddlebat sat down, and fitted on her spectacles, for she had taken to those adornments, and then, in a voice of the most indignant pathos, she read the letter as follows,—

"Madam,—Although a stranger to you, I presume to address you, having been on excellent terms with your late husband, and feeling a great interest in everything that appertains to you. I should be extremely sorry if any unhappiness should fall upon you, or any which are allied to you, which it was in my power to avert, and I omitted to use the proper exertions so to do. I understand, madam, that you have a niece who is at once beautiful and confiding, and that there is every reason to suppose that she has given, or is about to give, her affections to one Nicholas Lowe. If this be so, I feel it to be my duty to inform you that he is anything but such a character as you would wish to be introduced into your family. If he can deny that he has committed a systematic and a cruel seduction, he has a greater amount of self-confidence than even I give him credit for. I do hope, therefore, that before any further proceedings be taken, the question will be put to him in such a manner that he will either admit it or deny it. If he do the former, you know what course to pursue yourselves; and if the latter, why, then, the proof of his villany will, perhaps, be forthcoming when he least expects it.

"I am, madam, yours,
"A WELL-WISHER."

"What!" exclaimed Fanny Leslie, as she sprang to her feet; "and have I, after all this, been listening to an anonymous letter?"—"A synominous what?" said Mrs. Paddlebat.

"An anonymous letter. That letter has no name to it; and what faith, then, can be placed in the charge it conveys?"—"No name!" said Mrs. Paddlebat; "yes, it has a name; it comes from a well-wisher, don't you see?—and a very good name, too. Really, Miss Fanny, it strikes me as being particularly remarkable how you can say it is without a name."

"But it is, aunt, without such a name as we can substantiate. Don't you perceive that it is so? An anonymous letter affords the readiest means for inflicting an injury that can be imagined; it is a kind of mental assassination, which should be repudiated by every one."—"Well, I'm sure the letter says that Mr. Lowe's done something very bad; and, what's more, he has, for all you know—he really may."

"He, aunt, or any one, may; but not upon the faith of such an epistle as this. Throw it from you, aunt, and repudiate its contents as you would repudiate its author, for nothing can be more despicable than to make any charge anonymously." —"Well, I don't know that, exactly," said Mrs. Paddlebat; "you may want to place somebody upon their guard, and yet you may not wish to have your name mixed up in the matter."

There was a silence of some moments, after which Fanny spoke, and she spoke decidedly.

"Aunt," she said, "this letter has made no change in my feelings, or in my opinion. I am quite aware, as you know, that such a charge has been insinuated, or, I may say, made by Rodwell already, against Mr. Lowe. I'm likewise perfectly aware that he has failed to substantiate it."—"Well, but, my dear, it may be true for all that."

"But a man, aunt, is not to be condemned because a thing may be true against him. It must be, and should be, true before we are authorised in treating him as if he were guilty."—"Well, you are too particular, it strikes me; and if you're so very nice about it as all that, you'll never succeed in bringing Mr. Lowe to book."

"Heaven forbid, aunt, that I should succeed in anything of the sort; but, as I was telling you, I had made a determination what to do before this letter made its appearance."

"And, pray, what does that determination come to?"—"It was to ask Mr. Lowe himself to admit or to deny the charge."

"And can you be such a ninny as to suppose that any man will admit such a thing against himself?"—"Yes, aunt, I can believe that there are circumstances under which people will criminate themselves."

" Well, you can try it. For my part, I go a great deal by people's looks, and if you'll let me be present, I'll watch him all the while."—" Nay, aunt, I do not go by people's looks in cases of accusation. It by no means follows that the most innocent persons have the strongest nerves, and many a cheek will blanch at an accusation although the heart knows its guiltlessness of it."

" Well, my dear, that may or may not be ; all I can say is, that if you go to the theatre, you'll know the ruffian in a moment, and that when they say at the end of the play ' Seize the villain !' he steps forward, and owns himself the villain at once, and never makes the least opposition. That may do at the play, aunt, but it will not do in the drama of real life."

" Here's Mr. Nicholas Lowe, ma'am," announced the servant at this moment.

CHAPTER XLV.

THE QUESTION AND ANSWER.—LOWE TEMPORARILY DEFEATED.

" Bless us and save us !" said Mrs. Paddlebat; " talk of the thingumery, and he's sure to be at hand. What's to be done, my dear? do you mean to see him or not ?"—" I will see him. Vague and indistinct as are the charges brought against him, I do not feel myself authorised to deny him my presence, and, therefore, I will see him."

" Well, then, my dear, I hope you mean to ask him what he's got to say for himself ; and I hope you won't forget all that Susan has said about the bit of shirt wristband covered with blood, that he had in his desk. Ah ! that speaks five volumes against him, in my mind. Show Mr. Lowe up, Susan. I'll stay with you. Heaven knows what he might try to make you believe."

Fanny made no objection to her aunt remaining ; indeed, she would rather of the two that she would, for, without showing any violent amount of partisanship in favour of Lowe, she did hope and believe that he would be able to clear himself, fully and entirely, from what was imputed to him, and so shine out with redoubled lustre from the temporary cloud in which his reputation had been enshrouded.

When Lowe entered the room, he could see, by the countenances of both, that something unusual had occurred, and he guessed that, in all probability, he had been the subject of discussion. He bowed, and then looked from one to the other in silence ; after which Fanny said, in a voice which trembled slightly with emotion, but which she endeavoured to make as firm as possible,—

" Mr. Lowe, you have been the subject of conversation in this house—of conversation which, I grieve to say, has not been to your advantage. I need not say how much I regret this, and that it becomes necessary for me to say more than I have already said of an accusatory character."

" Of what am I accused?" said Lowe. " Need I say that an accusation from those lips carries with it a sting which no other circumstances could impart to it."
—" You are accused of being a betrayer of innocence ; can you lay your hand upon your heart, Nicholas Lowe, and say that this is untrue ?"

Nicholas started and turned pale, and a visible emotion pervaded his whole system.

" There, there—look at him !" said Mrs. Paddlebat ; " how white his lips are ! ain't his looks enough to hang him ?"—" Is this generous ?" said Fanny, turning a reproachful look upon her aunt.

" Is it just ?" said Lowe, trying to rally from the state of confusion into which he had been thrown. " Oh, Fanny, Fanny ! if I am shocked at this question being put to me, it is not for its own sake, but because it comes from you. I did hope that you knew me better, and appreciated me better, than to consider it necessary to ask of me such a question."—" Oh, a cock and a bull, and a roasted soldier !" said Mrs. Paddlebat.

" Nicholas Lowe," said Fanny, mournfully, " I might say that I wonder you do not appreciate the motive which actuates me in asking such a question. It is not hat for myself I doubt you so much, as that I wish your utter innocence and purity of purpose to appear clear and manifest to the whole world ; so that not the least taint or reproach should reach you, or the slightest breath of scandal sully the purity of a name which I would have surrounded with nothing but honourable associations."—" I do understand you," said Lowe ; " and I feel grateful."

" Then I will not regret questioning you."—" I know my enemy well. It is Rodwell ; he has all but accused me of a murder, which I am certain he has committed himself. As I have before remarked to you, Fanny, from the first moment I set foot in this house, that man has been my most implacable foe ; but a day of retribution will come, when ——"

" Fiddlededee !" said Mrs. Paddlebat ; " that's all very fine, you know, Mr. Lowe ; but you haven't said you did nothing of the sort, for all that."—" Madam," said Lowe, again evading the question, " I regret exceedingly to have become aware that you have imbibed some prejudices against me."

" But you have not answered, Nicholas," said Fanny.—" Then I will answer," said Lowe ; but he shook as he spoke—" I will answer, and I say I did no such thing. Let him prove it if he can. Now, Mrs. Paddlebat, what have you to say against that ? Let him prove it, if he can ; and if he don't prove it, and fully too, I have a right to demand a verdict of acquittal at your hands."

" I rejoice to hear you speak in such a strain," said Fanny ; " it now becomes only the duty of him who has accused you to substantiate his charge, or, failing to do so, to labour under that worst of stigmas, the having made a false accusation."—" Yes, yes," said Lowe, " I dare him to the proof."

" Well, then, he'll come forward," said Mrs. Paddlebat ; " he's told me he would, a hundred times : and now that it's come to this point, the sooner it's settled the better."—" As soon as you please, for my part," said Lowe ; " but I know from whence all this rancour arises. Rodwell was not long in discovering where my best affections were fixed, and when once he had made that discovery, and along with it the mortifying one that I was a rival to himself, he became my deadliest and most implacable foe."

" Do not enter into that subject," said Fanny ; " I beg of you, let that rest. One can hardly suppose any one so criminal or so weak as to attempt, by such means as he has resorted to, to accomplish his purpose."—" You do not understand, Fanny," said Lowe, " such a man as Rodwell ; the next desirable thing that appears to his mind when he cannot accomplish his own purposes, is to effect the ruin of his opponent ; and he would find a gloomy and misanthropical happiness in knowing that I was unhappy, although by such a thing he advanced no one object of his own existence. I know myself that he is a murderer, although, if I were put upon the proof that such was the fact, I should fail in tendering it, because the only person who could prove it is no more."

" A murderer !" said Fanny ; " does, indeed, your suspicion go so far as that ?"

" Nay, suspicion is a mild term to apply to the feeling ; it amounts to a certainty."

" But do not you, Lowe, fall into the same error that he has, and make a charge which possibly you lack the power of substantiating ; it is a grievous thing to do, and should be most specially avoided."

" I will avoid it, and yet, if I were to go upon Mrs. Paddlebat's maxim, and seek to condemn people by their looks, I doubt not but that Jervis Rodwell's would sufficiently intelligibly accuse him of the crime which I know him to be guilty of."

" But we will have no such experiments ; and now, aunt, I call upon you, since you have so strenuously taken the part of Rodwell in all these affairs—I call upon you to vindicate him from the stigma which must otherwise fall upon him of making a charge that he shrinks from."

" Why, what do you mean ?"

" I mean, aunt, that you ought to bring him forward, and make him prove his words."

" Well, then, I will bring him forward ; and any day and any time you like to name, I'm quite certain that Mr. Rodwell shall be here to meet you."

" Be it to-morrow, then," said Fanny, " at this hour."

"Agreed," said Lowe, and he took from his pocket a note, which he handed to Fanny at the same moment, but she would not receive it, only waving her hand, and saying,—

"After to-morrow—after to-morrow, Mr. Lowe; there is a gulph at present between us which neither of us must leap; after to-morrow I hope that we may meet without the shadow of a reproval even from my aunt."

"Indeed," said Mrs. Paddlebat; "you may meet as often as you like for aught I care."

Lowe's temper very nearly got the better of him, and he turned fiercely to the lady, but Fanny interposed, saying,—

"Hush! Nicholas, hush! go in peace; remember still that this is a house of mourning, if you please, and do not desecrate it by the least exhibition of passion."

"I will not," said Lowe; "farewell, Fanny, your wishes are my laws—believe me, dearest, all will be well at last—the calumnies of disappointed malice shall melt away like mists before the morning sun, and you shall only be dearer to me for the candour which you have this day exhibited, than as if, from mere motives of affection, you had chosen to absolve me from all censure whatever without inquiry."

Fanny said nothing, but she looked her approbation of this speech, and as Lowe saw that that was the case, he thought it was better to take his leave at once, since he could do so with so good a grace. He therefore bowed and left the room, being assured that in the quarter where he most wished it he left behind him a favourable impression, and caring little what Mrs. Paddlebat might say or think, since he knew that Fanny was as well aware as he was of the many prejudices which she entertained with regard to him, and which could never be eradicated.

———

CHAPTER XLVI.

LOWE CONSULTS OLD GILBERT AND FINDS HIM IN A FRIGHT AND ABOUT TO REMOVE.

NICHOLAS LOWE felt now that he had fairly thrown down the gauntlet to Rodwell by thus daring him to the proof of what he had insinuated. The fact is that Lowe had quite sense enough to see that he was completely pushed up into a corner, and that his only chance was in Rodwell's insufficient information.

If he had declined answering as he had done, and we have seen that he rather shuffled over it, the consequence, unquestionably, would have been a presumption of the truth of what Jervis Rodwell had asserted.

But there was the chance that Rodwell's information upon the subject only amounted to some dim and uncertain guess, and that when actually brought to the proof, he would not be able to substantiate in any way whatever his charge, if charge it could be called.

Conscious guilt had hitherto kept Lowe back from meeting the charge with sufficient boldness to give himself this chance of escaping from it. But now, like many animals who will escape from a foe if they can, but who, when fairly pushed into a corner, borrow a courage which ordinarily does not belong to them, and turn upon their opponent, he, now that he, in a manner of speaking, fancied himself at bay, was resolved to dare the very worst and Rodwell defy to the proof.

If he, Rodwell, should fail, Lowe's position in the eyes of Fanny Leslie would be wonderfully bettered, because nothing could tend to advance him more in the estimation of so kind and just-minded a creature, than having been the victim of an unjust aspersion against his character.

The more, then, Nicholas Lowe now thought over the change which had taken place in his affairs, the more he felt that it was by no means for the worse.

Still he felt extremely anxious to have some better advice than he could give himself, as regarded the propriety of doing something in the matter of the strange confession which had been made to him regarding Rodwell's delinquency.

He was well aware of the extreme danger of making a charge against Rodwell which he could not support; but still he was most anxious, at all events, to make use of, in some way, the information he had acquired with so much difficulty.

At first he thought of going to some solicitor, and intrusting to him the affair; but, upon second thoughts, he justly enough considered that all a professional man could or would say to him upon such a subject would be, that as he had no evidence, it would be the height of imprudence to stir in the matter at all.

Now, Nicholas Lowe knew that much well enough himself; but what he wanted was some cunning advice as to how to do Rodwell some damage with the least possible chance of risk.

After some considerable time spent in reflection upon the subject, it occurred to him, that from all he had seen of old Gilbert Paddlebat, he was just the sort of man to advise him on such an emergency. Besides, from the circumstances in which they were together involved, he felt that he had some sort of claim upon old Gilbert's consideration, and doubtless he, Gilbert, would likewise think so, and give him the best advice in his power.

This idea had not taken possession of Nicholas Lowe's mind many minutes before he proceeded to carry it into execution : it, at all events, had one recommendation about it, which was, that if it did no good, it could not possibly do any harm.

The distance was short to Gilbert Paddlebat's house—that identical house where he had lived so long, and where so strange an episode in his existence had occurred with respect to his superannuated old partner.

Lowe entered the dingy office, and inquired for Mr. Paddlebat; in reply to which he was informed that Mr. Paddlebat, not feeling very well, was up stairs and lying down, but that he, Lowe, should be announced if he wished it.

"Thank you," he said ; "I do want to see Mr. Paddlebat, but as I am a friend, I do not think you need trouble yourself to announce me ; I will go up."

At this moment there came the sound of a bell upon his ears, and it must have been a bell, too, of no ordinary size, for it made noise enough, although the sound of it was muffled, as if coming from a considerable distance.

"What bell is that ?" said Lowe.

"Mr. Paddlebat's bell, sir," said the wretched clerk, in reply. "Somehow I think he has got a little nervous, for he sent out this morning to borrow a bell, and now and then he rings it, and when I go up, he only looks at me in an odd, scared kind of way, and says, ' Yes, yes—something human. That will do, that will—I do not want anything, but be sure you come when I ring again.'"

Before the miserable man, whom old Gilbert Paddlebat called his clerk, had finished these words, the bell rang again, and off he went as quickly as his age, for he, too, was old, would let him, to answer the summons.

"What new freak," thought Lowe to himself, while he was left alone, "can this be ? Is the old man going mad at last?"

In a very few moments the clerk returned to say that Mr. Paddlebat would be glad to see Mr. Lowe, if he would walk up stairs, and push open the door to the right, when he got upon the first landing. This Lowe did, and made his way into the miser's room, which has before been presented to our readers.

He found old Gilbert dressed, but lying upon that wretched truckle bed, which the veriest beggar would have scorned to occupy. There was an odd look upon the old man's face. His eyes looked preternaturally bright, and wide open ; and, altogether, had Nicholas Lowe been asked to define what he considered the prevailing characteristic of his face, he would certainly have said that "fright" was the word which came the nearest to a description of it.

It will be seen that he was not far wrong.

"Good day, Mr. Paddlebat," he said ; "I am very sorry to hear that you are not so well as you usually are, or as I would wish you."

The old man fixed his keen, glistening eyes upon Nicholas Lowe's face, as he said, in strange, suppressed accents,—

"I am quite well, quite well. Bodily indisposition is my excuse to the busy, meddling world, for what I really suffer. Shut the door ; I do not mind having the door shut, when something human, however bad it may be, is with me."

Nicholas Lowe took no notice of this very equivocal compliment, but he did as the miser directed, and closed the door of the room.

"Now bring yourself a chair," added Gilbert ; "there is one there, and you will find a piece of wood in the corner over there by the window, which you can place upon it, since it is a little out of repair, I think." The chair had no seat at all.

"Mind the bell, mind the bell," added Gilbert, as Nicholas brought the chair to the bedside, and with his foot accidentally struck a large bell which was there, and within convenient distance of old Gilbert Paddlebat's hand.

"The bell," said Lowe, as he looked down ; "what do you have such a bell as that for ? Why, it's about the size of a postman's bell."

"All the better, all the better. I had to send all over the neighbourhood before I could find one at all, but at last this one was lent me. It once, they say, belonged to a ship. Well, well, it don't matter to me, whether the ship was lost or saved ; I have the use of the bell for nothing."

" But what do you want it for ?"—" Why, to ring, to be sure."

" Yes ; but there are quieter means, surely, of making your wants known, than ringing such a ponderous bell as this."—" All of which cost money ; but you, I know, are reckless and extravagant. Tell me, young man, did you ever see— see ——."

" See what ?"—" It is not a what, it's a him. Did you ever see my late partner, Sheepy ?"

As old Gilbert asked this question, he shook so, that the bed creaked again, and cast around him such terrified glances, that Nicholas Lowe felt some amount of nervousness stealing over him, as, after a few moments' pause of wonder at the question, he replied,—

" No, no ; I never was here during the lifetime of that person, although I certainly have heard of him frequently. He died from some accident, did he not ?"

" Hush ! hush ! Don't speak so loud. You don't know Sheepy by sight. Ah ! l wish that I was in a similar blessed state ; I know him too well by sight— too well. I don't usually make large pecuniary offers, but I would give fifty— or—a—twenty—or, at all events, five pounds, never to see Sheepy again, or not to know him if I did see him."

" See him again ! Why, good God, Mr. Paddlebat, he is dead, is he not ?"

" Yes, yes. And that it is which makes it so horrible, so very horrible. I will never again—no, no, never again have two chairs in a room."

" What do you mean by that ?"

" If you are inclined to know, listen, and I will tell you what has happened. I shall have to move away from here. Alas ! alas ! I did make some preparations to do so, but somehow I altered my mind, and stayed. I wish I had not. Do you believe, Mr. Lowe, that the spirits of the dead have power, at their own caprice,—if there be spirits of the dead, and if they have caprice,—to come and torture the living with a sight of features we supposed rotting in the grave?"

" It is a subject which has been one of discussion," said Lowe, " since first man began to reason ; but, for my own part, I am an unbeliever."

" You are ? you are ? And why ? Tell me why ?"

" Because I think that if such things were, the occasions of their appearance would be much more frequent than they are ; so the subject would be placed beyond the shadow of a doubt."

" Ah ! a good argument, but still not conclusive."

" Tell me, Mr. Paddlebat, if you please, what it is that has so discomposed you, and given your mind this superstitious turn ?"

" It may be superstition ; yes, it may be superstition. I will not say it is not so, but you shall hear. As you have yourself said, Mr. Sheepy met with his death by an accident in this very house. The stairs fell down, and he with them. He was not materially hurt, they said ; but the shock killed him, and ever since then I have had a sort of dislike to the place, and often thought of leaving it, which now I will, most assuredly. But yet nothing occurred of a particular nature, and the chill feeling that sometimes used to creep over me at night, was, I thought, slowly wearing away."

" Time always achieves wonders in such matters."

" Yes, yes ; and I began to have some hopes of forgetting. I am not a young man, you know, Mr. Lowe, neither am I so old but that I may yet look forward to many years of life yet—ah ! many years. But it would be horrible to be haunted."

" Haunted, Mr. Paddlebat?"

" Yes—yes ; last night, only last night,—it was rather late, but I had some accounts to make up, you see, and I made up some of them down stairs ; but feeling chilly there, as I think the ground floor always is more chilly than those above, I took the book which I was attending to in my hands, and came up here with it."

" Yes, yes. Go on, sir."

" Well, there were two chairs in the room, one of which you are now sitting on, and one which I have had since removed. Yon table I drew near to the bed, and sat down myself on one of the chairs. It was mere accident that the other happened to be just opposite to me, and so placed at the table as if waiting for some unexpected guest. The clocks about the neighbourhood had struck eleven some time; but I knew that the accounts were rather complicated, and required careful revising. It was on account of some money which had been lent on mortgage, and which ran back several years."

"Not a subject calculated, Mr. Paddlebat, to direct the imagination to the immaterial world," remarked Nicholas Lowe.

"No—no; quite the reverse. I went on with the accounts, until I came to several pages, which were in the handwriting of Sheepy. He was as blind as a bat, and yet would always insist upon making entries in the books. I could not make out what one-half of it meant, and I got vexed enough. Well, Mr. Lowe, after I had tried in vain for some time, it struck twelve o'clock by some church clock in the immediate neighbourhood. I counted the strokes, and then, vexed and irritated at finding I had been so long making out an account, which, had it been properly kept, would not have taken a quarter of the time, I took off my spectacles, and said,—what do you think now I said?"

"It is quite impossible for me to guess, Mr. Paddlebat."

"Well, I said, 'd—n Sheepy; I wish he would come and tell me which, in his account, meant three, and which five, for I cannot distinguish one from the other.'

"The words were no sooner past my lips, Mr. Lowe, when, casting my eyes across the table, I saw him sitting on the chair, immediately opposite to me."

"Indeed!"

"Yes, indeed. There he was, with his white, chalk-like looking face, and his eyes fixed upon me, as if he would look me through with that horrible glassy stare."

"And what did you do?"

"What did I do? What would any man have done? I felt the blood curdle in my veins, and the cold dew fell drop by drop from my brow, upon the pages of the book that was before me."

"Did the vision speak?"

"No—no—nor I—nor I. Perhaps if I had, it might. I do not know; they say that such appearances must first be addressed by those whom they visit, before they have power to utter an articulate sound. It may be so. If you once receive the idea that such things may be, you may as well receive, at the same time, every superstition connected with it."

"And how did all this result?"

"Thus: either the vision slowly faded away before my eyes, or I, becoming insensible, lost gradually the power to observe it, for I knew no more until the morning light was glaring into the room, and I found myself lying upon the floor."

"Was all as you had left on the preceding night?"

"Yes, there were the two chairs, and there was the book, the bit of candle at which I had been sitting had burnt out, and there was not the least appearance of any one but myself having been present in this apartment."

"But, really, Mr. Paddlebat, I should have supposed, that, upon reflection, you would have felt that what you supposed you saw, was but the result of imagination."

"I have told myself all that. I have striven hard to convince myself of that philosophy; and yet the horrible fear clings to me in one shape, which I cannot shake off, let me do what I will, in my endeavours to rid myself of it."

"What shape is that?"

"It will come again."

"Likely enough, now that your imagination is in such a state of intense excitement upon the subject; but, in a short time, you will be able, I hope, successfully to fight up against such impulses; and, after all, the most reasonable view to take of such matters is, that if it be strictly true, in every respect, that really we need not care; because an immaterial spirit can have no real power of injuring us, and as for the soul, that, as Hamlet says,—

'Is a thing immortal as itself.'

Yes; you can reason; you can philosophise upon what you have not been called upon yourself to endure; but I cannot—I cannot. I think I see him now always. Sometimes at my bedside, sometimes at its foot. Then, again, looking in at the window, and sometimes gliding along one of the walls of the room, as he used to walk in life, feeling his way as he went, on account of his partial blindness."

"What do you do, then?"

"Why, then, I seize this bell, and ring it, and some one comes to me. At the sight of a human face the hideous vision vanishes again!"

"Which ought to convince you, that, after all, Mr. Paddlebat, it is nothing but imagination; and you are, in my opinion, by shutting yourself up here without society, going the very way to foster such impressions. You should mingle with the world."

"What, and spend more money than all the society of all the knaves and fools with which the world abounds, is worth? No—no—no."

"Well, then, if you will lead the life of a solitary, you must expect the invariable consequence of such a state of things; namely, a diseased imagination; and you will, now that you have once commenced doing so, soon people solitude with all sorts of hideous phantoms, by which, at last, you may destroy your very reason, and be incapable of ever freeing yourself from such a state of mental distress. While it is time, Mr. Paddlebat, let me advise you now to use some portion of that wealth which you possess, in surrounding yourself with the comforts and the elegancies of existence. By such means, you will soon shake off these disturbed fancies; but, in your present mode of life, you may depend that they will grow upon you."

"Ah!" said the old man, "the old story, the old story."

"What old story?"

"Why, I never yet found anybody who gave me a word of advice upon any subject that it did not point to some expense."

Lowe did not press the matter, but he told the old man what he came about, which old Gilbert answered by scouting the idea of any girl giving up a husband on any such grounds.

"You pursue all your original arrangements," he said, "as if nothing was amiss, and you will find that, let Rodwell prove what he may, you will have, if you like, Fanny Leslie for a wife."

———

CHAPTER XLVII.

THE MEETING AT THE PADDLEBATS'.—RODWELL'S DEFEAT, AND LOWE'S WEDDING-DAY FIXED.

OLD Gilbert Paddlebat's common and foolish idea of women was borrowed from what he had read in the works of cynical authors, who, failing in finding any female who would waste a second thought upon them, take their revenge by reviling a whole sex, of which they really know little, or, indeed, we may say nothing.

Nor was Lowe quite free from entertaining a degrading opinion of those fairest creatures of creation, so that when old Gilbert advised him to go on with all his arrangements, as if nothing had happened, and to rely upon it, that if Fanny Leslie loved him, love him she would, in spite of all that Rodwell could do or say, he thought there might be a good deal of truth in so comprehensive an opinion.

"It may be so," he said to himself, "after all; and, in my imagination, I may have been making by far too much of this affair, so I will even take Gilbert

Paddlebat's advice, and set about at once procuring such a home for Fanny Leslie as she cannot but be delighted with when she comes to be the mistress of it."

He amused himself by wandering about till he saw a house to let, which he thought would suit him well; and, upon inquiry, the rental was much less than he expected it would have been, so that he all but took it, and that evening found great pleasure in making out a long list of elegancies with which he intended to adorn it.

This was quite a delightful employment, and contributed so much to withdraw Nicholas Lowe's mind from anything which was uncomfortable in his situation, that he passed a better night than he had done for a considerable time, and dreamt of all kinds of splendour and enjoyment in his new home that was to be.

The morning, however, brought with it some reflections with regard to the coming interview with Rodwell, at the house of the late goldsmith; and again and again did he, Lowe, puzzle himself to think how it was possible Rodwell could have gathered the least hint of the melancholy affair which had terminated in the death of the seduced at the lunatic asylum.

The whole affair, however, defied conjecture, and all he hoped was that something would arise in the course of the proceedings at the Paddlebats' that would enlighten him upon that point.

And it was a very important one for him to be enlightened upon; for if he but once had any clue to the source of Rodwell's information, he would very likely be able to ascertain, with some amount of correctness, the extent of his danger.

Twelve o'clock was the hour which had been named, and a little before that time he reached the well-known door of the goldsmith's house.

But what a strange, altered, and sombre aspect did the closed shop present to what it had worn in the days of its proprietor, when all was activity and life. It was, indeed, a melancholy commentary upon the uncertainty of worldly things.

Susan admitted Lowe, and conducted him to the drawing-room, where, in a few moments, he was joined by Mrs. Paddlebat and Fanny.

The former had put on a remarkably dignified face, as she no doubt thought, for the occasion; and only condescended, when she entered the room, to make a sort of congee, that it required a quick eye to take any notice of at all.

Fanny looked pale, and, from the appearance of her eyes, Nicholas Lowe thought either she had been weeping, or had passed a sleepless night.

She spoke to Lowe, and her voice had a touch of sorrow in it.

"I hope you are well?" she said.

"Yes," he replied; "yes, I am quite well, and far from anxious on this occasion, because I come here to prove my innocence."

"Thank Heaven!" said Fanny.

There was a knock at the street door, and Mrs. Paddlebat, as she looked triumphantly at the clock over the mantleshelf, exclaimed,—

"That's him. I knew he would come. To be sure. True as the needle to a pole."

"Mr. Rodwell," announced Susan, and Jervis Rodwell entered the room.

His appearance was anything but in his favour. His eyes were bloodshot, and there was an unhealthy flush upon his face, which betokened to the experienced glance of Lowe the consequences of an over night's debauch.

"Good morning, Mr. Rodwell," said Mrs. Paddlebat; "good morning. You got my note, of course?"

"Yes, madam; and am here in consequence of it. I do not know the meaning of this meeting, since the note merely required that I should be here at twelve o'clock, without fail. I did not expect to see Mr. Lowe. I hope you are well, Miss Leslie."

Fanny made no reply, and Rodwell bit his lips with vexation.

"I dare say you did not expect o see me," said Lowe; "and I dare say I may go further and say that my presence here is to you full as unwelcome as it is unexpected."

"Well, sir."

"You have the grace to acknowledge so much, at all events. Mrs. Paddlebat, shall I or will you open these proceedings?"

Mrs. Paddlebat gave a toss of her head as she said,—

"You may do as you like."

"Then I will. Jervis Rodwell, you have made some accusation against me, which I am here now, in the presence of one who has heard these charges, and whose good opinion is of importance to me—demand you to prove or to retract."

"Indeed! and that is what has brought me here."

"That is it. Now I want your answer."

"What answer? State the charges that I have brought against you."

"No, I will not. It is not for me, who am accused, to take any such initiative step. I demand of you now, face to face, to say, if you have anything to state to my prejudice. If you have not, then the affair is at an end."

Rodwell was silent for a few moments: he seemed to be considering deeply; and, Nicholas almost hoped that he would be prudent enough to decline making any charge, and so clear him in the eyes of Fanny.

Rodwell might possibly have adopted this course, had it not been that he had a character to support with Mrs. Paddlebat. He knew well that she felt deeply interested, in consequence of her dislike to Lowe, in the fray, and therefore he determined to do what damage he could to him.

"There are many things," he said, "which one man knows about another, which it is far from prudent for him to talk about; but, when we find that any individual arrogates to himself any superior virtue, we are tempted to inquire upon what grounds he does so."

"Ah! to be sure," said Mrs. Paddlebat, "that's the point."

"Really, aunt," remarked Fanny, "I cannot see any point in it."

"Mr. Nicholas Lowe," continued Rodwell, "I accuse of a seduction."

"There, there," cried Mrs. Paddlebat; "now, Mr. Lowe, I believe you are answered."

"Answered, madam, I am," said Lowe, "but I am not yet convicted. I have yet to learn that a mere accusation carries with it at once the condemnation of the accused. Now I deny the charge, and declare it to be false and calumnious."

"You do?"

"Yes! and I here demand of Rodwell the proof of the statement."

"Here," said Rodwell.

Nicholas Lowe turned of a death-like paleness, and he staggered a little as Rodwell took from his breast a pocket book, and commenced rummaging over the contents of it, as if in search of some damnatory document which should at once confute Nicholas Lowe, and carry his condemnation on the face of it.

It was a very anxious pause that, for all persons concerned; Fanny, by great good luck, so far as Lowe's prospects were concerned, kept her eyes fixed upon Rodwell's movements, or she must have seen how powerfully agitated he was, and have drawn a conclusion from it unfavourable to him, notwithstanding all her wish not to do so.

Perhaps, on the part of Rodwell it was a little bit of malice; but he certainly was an uncommonly long time in finding whatever it was he wanted to find in that pocket book of his. At length however he did produce what looked like a letter.

"Here," he said, "is my proof. This is a letter addressed to Nicholas Lowe, and which he must have dropped, as I picked it up in the counting-house some time ago."

Lowe still looked pale and agitated, while Rodwell, in a voice which shewed how much stress he placed upon the document, read as follows:—

"Sir,—I have to inform you that a very serious change for the worse is taking place in her whom we need not name to you. She raves continually and calls upon you as her seducer, so that I think it would be prudent for you to come down here and try what you can do to pacify her, I am sir,

Your's obediently,

"To Mr. Nicholas Lowe.   "JAMES WORTHINGTON."

"Then," said Rodwell, when he had finished, "there is my proof."

The eyes of both Fanny and Mrs. Paddlebat were turned upon Nicholas Lowe, who now, drawing himself up to his full height, like a man who has suddenly got rid of a heavy burden, glanced with a look of ineffable scorn at Rodwell, as he said—

"And do you imagine that, by such a flimsy contrivance as that, any man's character is to be blasted for ever? Villain, you have come prepared with that forged document, in order to do me what mischief you could; but who would convict a cat even of petty larceny on such grounds, I should like to know?"

"Do you deny the letter, Nicholas?" said Fanny.—"I do."

"You say that it is a forgery—that it was never written to you?"—"I do."

"Then, Rodwell, you will be troubled to go to some other proof before the accusation can be presumed to be substantial."—"There are none so blind," said Rodwell, "as those who will not see."

"Yes, to be sure," exclaimed Mrs. Paddlebat, "I am convinced."—"Madam," said Lowe, "you were convinced before without any evidence at all; you must recollect, therefore, what you say now is of very little consequence. I demand further proof, and I denounce that letter as a rank forgery."

"From where is it dated?" quickly asked Fanny.—"There is no date to it, or place mentioned from whence it came," said Rodwell.

"Of course not," cried Lowe. "If there had been, immediate inquiry might have been made, and the falsehood of the mock letter proved at once, without the shadow of a doubt. There being no place mentioned in it, of course stifles inquiry."

"Is there no post mark?" said Fanny.—"There is not; it seems to have slipped out of an envelope."

"Shallow, most shallow," said Lowe. "Convicted libeller, I look upon you with the scorn you so richly deserve. But be assured that you shall not wholly escape some punishment for this attempt to cast a stain upon my honour. What the law can do for me, I will call upon it to do.—"Enough, enough," said Fanny; "it is sufficient."

"And you wo'n't," said Mrs. Paddlebat, "you wo'n't, my dear, have anything further to say to Nicholas Lowe, after this, I presume."—"You mistake me much," said Fanny; "it is in his innocence that I believe fully and entirely. There is no evidence whatever which makes the least impression now in my mind of a contrary tendency."

"The girl is mad, the girl is mad. It wasn't so with young girls in my days; then they would no more think of thinking for themselves, and picking and choosing who they would have, and who they would not, than of flying over the moon; but things are changed indeed."—"And, I think, for the better, madam," said Nicholas Lowe. "Fanny, this is the happiest moment I have known for a very long time indeed."

He took her hand, which she permitted him to do unresistingly, and then she said—

"Nicholas, you must promise to grant me a favour."—"Call it not a favour," he said; "you have, Fanny, but to name any wish of yours to ensure my immediate and cheerful compliance with it."

"You will, then, promise to take no proceedings against James Rodwell. Let it suffice that his malice is defeated; leave him to God and to his own conscience."—"Be it so," said Nicholas Lowe. "You owe your safety and impunity, Rodwell, to this beautiful being, who takes but too lenient a view of your iniquity."

Rodwell, while all this was going on, looked from one to the other, like a man bewildered. Indeed, on after consideration, Lowe was inclined to think that he was far from recovered from the preceding night's intoxication when he came that morning to the Paddlebat's.

"Never you mind, Mr. Rodwell," said Mrs. Paddlebat; "you have done your duty; and, instead of reviling you, Miss Fanny Leslie there ought to be obliged to you for endeavouring to put her upon her guard."—"Aunt," said Fanny, "I cannot be obliged to a man who would make me unhappy if it were in his power to do so. And as for that letter which he affects to found his accusation upon, if it were true that Mr. Lowe had dropped it, which it is not; but if it were true, I say, nothing could be more unworthy than for him, Rodwell, thinking it belonged to Mr. Lowe, to retain possession of it."

"Go on," said Rodwell, "go on; say what you like. As for you, Miss Fanny Leslie, you will live to repent taking the side you have taken to day. You are wrong; and perhaps I shall yet be able to call such another meeting as this, with some better proof than I can at present tender to you. Till then, farewell. You are, I see, resolved upon making that man your husband. I wish you joy of him; but you will remember my words now, 'You are about to wed one who has already committed more crimes than you will ever be aware of, and who only now takes you because you are entitled to eight thousand pounds by the will which he and old Gilbert Paddlebat, the miser, have manufactured between them.'"

So saying, he at once left the room, and in a few moments the violent bang of the street-door proclaimed that he had left the house.

CHAPTER XLVIII.

RODWELL AT HOME.—HIS DESPAIR.—THE HAPPY THOUGHT.

RODWELL, when he left the goldsmith's house, did so, as may well be supposed, under the influence of the most violent feelings against Lowe and Fanny, and with an accession of gall and bitterness in his disposition, consequent upon his defeat which was sufficient to prompt him to any act of desperation. He almost wished for the presence and company of that man who had, in consequence of becoming possessed of some of his secrets, acquired so strong a power over him; but that uncommonly clever individual had been pounced upon by Dame Justice at last, and for some offence, solely unconnected with any of his present proceedings, he was in gaol, awaiting what he, and every one else, well knew would be a sentence of transportation for life.

It was a wonder that he had not sufficient bad feeling to bring Rodwell into some trouble, but he did not. Probably some few visits of mock sympathy which Rodwell paid him softened even his heart, accompanied, too, as each visit was, by various coins of a pleasant jingling sound.

Rodwell, therefore, was free of this man, who might have been a most dangerous incumbrance to him through life; but, like most persons steeped in iniquity, he, Rodwell, felt most grievously the loss of, or rather the want of, some associate, to whom he could speak freely, and advise with, upon his iniquities.

But, then, Rodwell wanted such a confidential person who should be no expense to him. He, by no means, liked the idea of paying anything for such an associate; and thus it was that, in all human likelihood, he had found, to his mind, ample reason to imbrue his hands in the blood of the man, concerning whom Lowe really felt that he knew so much, while he could prove so little.

Rodwell, had he been well—certainly he was not perfectly sober—would have cut a better figure at the Paddlebats' than he did; and, probably, had he been a little more intoxicated, it would have been all the better for him; but, in reality, he was in that state of mental and bodily prostration which arises from excesses of the preceding evening, from which the system has by no means recovered, although all the exciting and exhilarating effects have completely gone off.

It was this reason that made him cut so very tame a figure, indeed, in the transaction, and, in a manner of speaking, actually sneak out of the house, without scarcely making an effort to vindicate himself from all the aspersions which were cast upon him.

Deep hatred, and a burning thirst for revenge, were, however, in his heart; and when he left the Paddlebats, he went to the poor and solitary home that he had provided himself with, determined to give some hours' deep and anxious consideration to the whole subject.

This house of his was a single room over a third rate coffee-shop, in a low neighbourhood, so that it was by no means one of the most inviting that could be conceived; nevertheless, he felt that his prospects were in so very frail a condition that economy was necessary; that is to say, when he was sober, he felt and told himself all this, and then, as morning approached, old habits would assume their supremacy, and he would sally out to spend more money in public-houses than would have sufficed to have supported him in an extremely comfortable and respectable style for the whole of the day.

Then would follow the morning's headache, and consequent repentance—a drunkard's repentance, which is as short lived as his pain, and the evening would again find him at his orgies.

"What shall I do to be revenged on Nicholas Lowe?" was the question which he now asked himself. He threw himself upon his not very inviting couch, and shutting his eyes, so that external objects should not interfere with a shady train of thought, he gave himself up, as completely as he could, to the task of contriving a satisfactory answer to the query.

He found that it was a question much easier to be asked than answered ; and, while he is thinking, we may as well show how much he actually did know of that episode in Nicholas Lowe's life, which, if he had known the whole of it, would have at once sufficed to separate him from Fanny Leslie, and destroy at once, fell swoop, all his most fondly cherished hopes.

What he, Rodwell, knew, then, was just what the letter contained, and no more. For once in his life, he had spoken the pure truth, without retraction or exaggeration. He had picked up, just as he stated, that letter in the counting-house, without its envelope.

In consequence of its having been addressed in the cover inside to Nicholas Lowe, he found that it was he who must have dropped it ; and, by reasoning with himself over every word of it, he found that it must relate to some intrigue in which Nicholas Lowe had been engaged.

This opinion he was, of course, confirmed in by Lowe's own conduct, when he, Rodwell, gave a hint of such a thing only ; and he found he possessed a power which, so long as it was not particularly scrutinised, might be exercised fully enough. Now, however, that Lowe had had the boldness to question it, and to bring it to the test, it was quite another affair ; and, like some unsubstantial vision of the mind, which, while shunned, possesses wondrous powers of mischief, but which, when boldly met, vanishes into thin vapour, so did this fancied power which Rodwell had over Lowe disappear at the least touch of real opposition to it.

This was mortifying—doubly mortifying, under the circumstances ; because, not only did it place him, Rodwell, in a contemptible position, but it was highly beneficial to Lowe, inasmuch as it gave him possession of the hand and the fortune of Fanny Leslie. Again and again he said to himself,—

"What shall I do to be revenged upon Nicholas Lowe?" and the answer appeared to be us far off as ever, and he was completely baffled in all his mental inquiries.

He then rose, and procured the letter which he had exhibited at the Paddlebats', and read and re-read it over and over again, with the hope of extracting something from it which should help him to an opinion in his present state of difficulty. He pondered over every word of it, slowly and carefully, but he could make nothing of it, and, in the midst of his cogitations, he was startled by a knock at his room door.

There were certainly some few persons, and but very few, to whom he had intrusted the secret of where he resided. It might be one of those, and he approached the door, inquiring,—

"Who is there?"—"It's me," said the voice of a young man, whom he knew, and upon whose pocket he had frequently drawn for his current resources.

"Oh, come in," said Rodwell. "How are you, old fellow? You must excuse being brought to such a place as this ; but, really, taking one thing with another, I find it the most independent way of living, and you see there are no responsibilities."

—"So I should say," replied his young friend, whose name was Green. "So I should say ; but what are you going to do to-night—eh?"

"Well, I really have not thought of that, yet. Have you anything to propose?"
—"No ; you know I always leave all that to you."

"Oh, you know as well, if not better than I do, where amusement is to be got, I'm sure ; so you shall make your own choice, and that will suit me well. By-the-bye, Green, I know you are a clever fellow, so just oblige me by reading this letter."
—"This letter?"

" Yes, I want your opinion concerning it."—" In what way?"

" Why, without me telling you anything about it, suppose you had picked it up, and knew that the person to whom it was addressed at the corner was a young man of not very scrupulous morality, what conclusion should you come to?"— " Oh, very good ; I'll read it. Let me see; oh, something wrong here."

Mr. Green read the letter, and when he had finished, Rodwell said to him,—

" Well, what, now, is your opinion regarding the affair which is hinted at in that letter. Speak at once, now, anything that comes uppermost to your mind, and never care whether it seems to you at all probable or not."—"Well," said Green, putting on a wise look, " you know I don't know, really, anything of the circumstances at all ; and, therefore, to the best of my judgment ——"

" Yes, yes."—" I really must say that, upon the whole, and taking it roughly into consideration, I don't know what to think upon the subject."

" Psha! you are jesting with me, Green. You are not such a fool as you pretend to be. Ah! you deep dog; you will always have your joke."—" Joke! I don't see any joke in it at all. But what is it really all about now, Rodwell? One would almost think that this Mr. Lowe had seduced some girl, and then put her in a madhouse."

" A madhouse! D—n it, that's it ; a thousand circumstances rush to my mind to confirm it. A lucky thought, Green. This letter comes from the keeper of some madhouse. Well do I remember, now, that one evening, when the conversation turned on the causes of lunacy, Lowe started up and left the house. His conscience touched him. You are right ; I have a clue at last."

" A clue to what?"—" Why, to this letter, to be sure ; about which I have endured more anxiety than enough. I will not leave a lunatic asylum in London or its neighbourhood now unvisited, until I find which it is that has contained the person alluded to in this letter."

" That's a mighty pleasant sort of job you have set out for yourself," said Green.

" I trust it will be so. I have a great object in view, and now feel twice the man that I was before. I will not commence to-day, for it is too far advanced ; but from the proper quarter I will get the names and addresses of every private asylum within ten miles of London. Far off it cannot have been; for when Lowe was occasionally absent, it was never, altogether, above half a day."

" Ah, well!" said Green, with a yawn ; "that's your business, not mine. I want to know what you are going to do in the way of amusement to-night, you know."—" Come out, then, and we will talk it over. I want something to eat, for nothing in that way has passed my lips to-day ; and now I begin to feel a little hungry, which, I suppose, is a good sign."

———

CHAPTER XLIX.

NICHOLAS LOWE'S NEW HOUSE.—THE PREPARATIONS FOR THE MARRIAGE.—THE DOUBLE ANNOUNCEMENT.

LOWE's contentment was further increased by the receipt of the following letter from Fanny Leslie. When he first looked upon the handwriting, it was with a feeling of pleasure and joy quite new to him, and filled his heart with a feeling so new and so light, that he would not have exchanged his situation with that of a monarch.

" I shall have a triumph," he said, " despite all that can be done. I shall triumph over my enemies, and I shall win her and wear her. I feel it is so."

He then tore open the letter, and read as follows :—

" DEAR NICHOLAS,—I may call you so now, without any impropriety, I presume. You expected a promise, and a promise I must give you ; but do not expect too much, do not expect I can give you an immediate acquiescence.

" Dear Nicholas, let the day be this day month ; on that day I suppose I must consent to the change of life I seem destined to make ; and on that day I resign my liberty into your hands. Be careful of it, and be ___, what you have often promised, kind-hearted and faithful. Do this, and I hope for a happy life, or, believe me, the promise I now give would never be wrung from me.

"You may put up the banns at some quiet, out-of-the-way country church, where we shall attract but little attention from the people. I must leave all arrangements to you, Nicholas; you will do what you think fitting. I shall be content with whatever you may do for the best, for our comfort and happiness.

"Ever yours, sincerely,
FANNY LESLIE."

Lowe was, indeed, well pleased with this letter, which spoke so much for the pure simple-mindedness and ingenuousness of Fanny. Her letter, too, had another trait in it that spoke well, and that was the frankness with which she had placed herself in his hands, and trusting all to his efforts to make her happy.

"And she shall be happy, too," exclaimed Lowe. "If man can make her happy, I will make her happy; I will try. She shall not find less of future hope and joy than she expects. I will seek out the means of placing her in a position that will make her feel she did right by confiding in me. I will take a handsome house, it shall be well furnished with all the appliances of elegance and comfort."

Nicholas Lowe was well satisfied with the smooth course events were now taking; happiness seemed to beam before him, and seldom, indeed, did he give one thought of the past; that was buried in oblivion, only to be recalled upon some extraordinary occasion, that would strike a responsive chord in his breast, and produce the images of the past.

    *   *   *   *   *   *

He came to the determination that he would procure a house well situated, and furnish it in such a style as should be a surprise, and a pleasing one, too, to Fanny Leslie, when she came to her new home; and she should feel a delight in it, a pride in being its mistress.

This was a feeling very pardonable in Lowe; it was praiseworthy, and, with the utmost diligence, he procured a house in a good and handsome situation, which he determined to furnish handsomely; and to do that he would employ some of the best upholsterers, and at the same time he would exercise his own judgment in the choice of furniture.

The decorations were not forgotten, and, from the basement to the attics, there was an air of uniformity about it, that gave it a really beautiful appearance.

Unity of design is a great thing, and when perfect, without that mere dead uniformity of livery about it which some houses have, which makes it appear as if it were necessary to recognise the furniture again, has a very pleasing effect.

Such was the house and furniture of Nicholas Lowe, and he was well pleased with it; it was well chosen, and well appointed; each part was well and amply furnished for its object, and with all the appliances that were required.

"Surely," thought Lowe, "this, at all events, will be satisfactory. I know and feel it will; it will have her approbation who is the sole cause of my doing it. Fanny Leslie is not so hard to please; but this will content her. I have done my utmost, and I really think, now I look at it, that it deserves her commendation."

"And now," thought Lowe, as he looked at the letter, "now for the banns; that must be done. Notice must be given, and then, when the time runs on, we shall then be married. It will be a happy day."

But where to go to was a matter of more than ordinary perplexity. He began by enumerating the different places with which he was acquainted, but could find none of them in which he could discover the exact description that accorded with the letter of Fanny Leslie.

"They have all congregations," he said, "who come from London, people who live there, and transact their business in town, and then fly out there for the sake of a country residence. No, no, they will not do; I must go somewhere else; people go to these churches of a Sunday, to see, and be seen by others, and they wouldn't miss such an opportunity of staring about for a trifle; on that day. I must go about and endeavour to ascertain what place will most likely answer such a description, and one that so well suits my own feelings."

It was some time before he could think of what course he could pursue, which way he could go, for all places near at hand he believed to be occupied by citizens who had established themselves in country houses. After some puzzling over the matter, and an inspection of the map, he suddenly exclaimed,—

"It must be somewhere in Essex. Yes, yes, Essex must be the place ; people are not much of Londoners there, nor do people run from London down there. That place is not much desecrated in that manner. Walthamstow—Low Layton—Ah! that's the Newmarket road," he said, as he looked at the map, and placed his finger on each place as he named it. "Ah! Tottenham's in Middlesex, but that would be no objection ; only Tottenham is full of Londoners, and it is fearfully evangelical, and a power of Quakers reside there also."

He paused for a moment or two.

"Yes, yes ; there's Walthamstow. I'll try there. I'll go and see what kind of place it is, and ascertain if it be a quiet place, and such a one as I can take her to. I do not know much of Walthamstow, but it seems an ancient place, if I may judge from the name, and one well calculated for my purpose. There is a church, and the number of inhabitants does not seem very great, and it is a quiet place, with little trade ; that shews it is within itself."

After some further self communing, he determined to go down that very day. It was then very early ; in fact, it was breakfast-time. He was examining the map at the moment, which lay before him.

"To-day, I will take the Walthamstow coach, or I can go to the Flower-pot, in Bishopsgate-street, and ride down. Let me see. Ah! I can take the Tottenham coach, and get down at the Seven Sisters ; there seems to be a way clean up to Walthamstow that way, and I will go there."

In about an hour afterwards he was ready, and walking through the streets sharply towards the coach-office in Bishopsgate-street, where he arrived in good time.

"Tottenham coach, sir," said a man, who was standing about ; "yes, sir, one starts in five minutes, sir. In five minutes, sir, and no more."—"Very well ; I'll get in," said Lowe, "and take my place at once, and so secure it."

"You can't, sir."—"I cannot ? But why not ?"

"Because you see, sir, it ain't come yet. It ain't come ; it won't be five minutes, though."—"Why, you said it would start in five minutes."

"Ay, sir, so it will, when it once comes ; that is, you see, only a short time to wait."

"Is there no other that goes that road ?"—"Not for an hour or two, sir. Will you walk into the ' Pot,' and wait a few minutes ?"

"Walk into what pot ?"—"The Flower-pot, I mean, sir ; the sign of the house. Shall I give you a call when it comes ?"

"Yes," said Lowe, who thought that it would be a tiresome task to wait about for the coach ; so he did go into the "Pot," as the man called it, but not with any good will ; only a kind of necessity that seemed to exist, that he should sit down somewhere and wait.

In about half an hour the coach was ready to start, and Nicholas Lowe had secured his place ; and then, indeed, in five minutes the machine did start, making good the man's words that it would start in five minutes, meaning five minutes after it came to the door of the Flower-pot. The morning was fine, and the drive a pretty one. The Newington road was interesting, and from Stamford-hill, some pretty views were seen.

From the summit of the hill to the Seven Sisters the scenery was pretty. To the left there are fine views towards Hornsey and Muswell-hill, and on the descent into the hollow just before you get to the Seven Sisters, is the coldest spot between London and York. To the right lay the marshes of Tottenham and Walthamstow.

Having arrived at his destination, he got down and walked towards the Hall, where he there saw a collection of small houses or cottages, where the humble classes lived, and chiefly those who worked at the mills.

Passing through this place, and then down a road that led to the bridge thrown over the barge cut, he proceeded along a place or road, that was called a street, though why, it is difficult to say, save that it wasn't a street.

It was only a continuation of this road that enabled him to reach a place called Chapel-end. When there, he walked into the only house that seemed to offer accommodation for strangers, known at that time as the Crooked Billet.

"Which is Walthamstow church?" he inquired of the landlord.—"At no great distance, sir; you can see it, if you take the trouble to come a few yards, sir."

"I will presently," said Lowe, "after I have rested awhile. What sort of place have you got here—a gay part of the world—is there a very crowded neighbourhood?"—"Not very. There's about what there was many years ago. People don't seem to increase fast in these parts, and if they do, why, they don't stay long here."

"Ah! I see."—"But, else, other things go on much the same as in other places, for all I can see to the contrary. Births, marriages, and deaths go on much in the same way they did in the time of Alfred the Great, and don't seem to increase much."

"Is your church here an old one?"—"Yes, sir, it is; and though I don't go there myself, yet I have been there; and you may take my word for it, it's an old simple looking place, ay, as you could wish to see."

"I'm fond of old churches."—"Ay, you'll say you like it when you have seen it; not because of Jack Sheppard, or any other noted highwayman, pickpocket, or thief, being buried there."

"You are right," said Lowe, "in saying I should like it, notwithstanding it was not hallowed by such popular remains as those you have alluded to."—"You should see the old church, sir, at Christmas time, and then you'd say there was something worth seeing."

"Why?"—"Because when it is crammed with holly and ivy, the red berries and dark green leaves appeared to be a living emblem of the time of year; indeed, our old minister seems to be more like an owl in an ivy bush."

"Then I'll certainly take a walk to the church. Where does the sexton live?"

"Not far from the church, sir."

"I'll call upon him."—"There's no need, sir; he is in the tap-room, and will be ready to take you there, if you be minded to go, whenever you please."

"Then in a quarter of an hour, tell him; I'll go with him as soon as he can get ready after that time."—"Very well, sir," said mine host, who disappeared.

After some thoughts upon the matter, he could not help thinking that this would be the best place in the world for the purpose he desired it.

He rested about an hour, for it was full that before Lowe started, for he found that his walk had fatigued him, and he sat in deep thought gazing out of the window of the Crooked Billet, watching the flight of the birds.

"Are you ready, sir?" inquired a voice.

Lowe turned round and beheld a little old man; little he could be hardly called, because he was, or had been, a big, hard-featured man. Age, however, had shrunk him up, and his avocations had caused him to contract a stooping posture, so that he appeared a small man.

"What do you mean?" inquired Lowe.—"Please, sir, I be the sexton of Walthamstow church, and heard you wanted to go over the church."

"Oh, yes, I am quite ready," said Lowe, "quite ready. Well, I forgot all about it."—"I thought you had, sir; but here I be, and if you have a wish to go, why, say the word."

"I will; I am ready," said Lowe, and he rose up and followed the sexton out of the Crooked Billet towards Walthamstow churchyard, where, in due time, they arrived.

The old church was certainly picturesque, standing alone as it did, in a well wooded district, where it was embedded in trees and woods.

" You have a quiet place here," said Lowe.—" Yes, reasonably quiet," said the old man, " for a country place like this, you know, sir ; we don't often hear carriage wheels, or see any great disturbance."

" Well, there's no great loss there, I suppose ?"—" None, as I know on," said the sexton.   " Yet there are some people who couldn't do without them, and who would sooner be buried than walk to church."

See p. 275.

" Indeed ; they must have a queer taste, they must," said Lowe ; " but I think there are not many who would do so."—" Why," said the old man, " there are many who would do so, I believe, or they think they would, until the moment of choice come, and then, I reckon, life would be sweet."

" So it would," said Lowe ; " but whose tomb is that, yonder ?"—" Oh, one of our parishioners, a Mr. Constable."

" Who was he ?"—" Why, a very great man in his day, and a very good man too; he had the parish pound repaired at his own expense, which was, they say, public spirit."

" Indeed, they have notions of public spirit in Walthamstow, at all events."

" Yes, sir, they know what's what in this place, as well as anywhere else."

" Do you have a full congregation here on a Sunday?" inquired Nicholas Lowe.

" Pretty fairish, in fine weather."

"Indeed; many visitors in the week, eh? have you many strangers here?"— " Very few."

" Once in a week?"—" Not once in a month," said the sexton, shaking his head doubtfully. " No, very few people come here."

" You don't often have marriages performed at this church; you don't trouble yourself about the registry?"—" I does all that myself; but that, as you say, don't trouble me much; we have very few marriages here, save those of the country people about."

" How do you account for that?"—" I can't tell, unless it is we are not known, and people don't visit us much; we lay out of the way, too, and that's another reason," said the sexton.

" Then if you'll conduct me to your place of abode, I'll give you a notice and promise of marriage in a few weeks."

" Eh?" said the old sexton.—" I will give you notice to put up the banns next Sunday in this church."

" You will?"—" Yes, I will."

" God bless your honour, it will do the heart of the sexton good; now, if they would but ring the bells, I should believe I could live another ten years at least."— " Well, they shall ring the bells, too, since you desire it," said Lowe, and he and the old sexton left the churchyard.

" It's a pretty quiet place, certainly," said Lowe; " and one that lays out of the way."—" Yes, sir, it's very retired and quiet; there ain't one person in twenty as would ever think of a marriage being performed here; even the parson himself will be surprised."

" So he may; but I hold the opinion I have always held, and that is, there is no place so fit for happiness as that which is retired, quiet, and unfrequented."— " So it is, sir."

They now arrived at the old sexton's house, when notice of banns was duly given with a fee, and then Nicholas Lowe trod his way back to Chapel End, and then to Tottenham, where he waited for the coach that was to come by, and then he reached London towards the evening. Thus Nicholas Lowe had done so much towards the approaching marriage between himself and Fanny Leslie.

To prevent any possibility of any mistake taking place, he determined that he would attend the church on Sunday morning to hear the banns read by the clerk, so that there should be no mistake or blunder. If it were so to happen that one was made, why, he was then on the spot, and could immediately after the service was over, correct the mistake.

*   *   *   *   *

That morning Nicholas Lowe went down early to Walthamstow, and breakfasted at the Crooked Billet, and awaited the signal for going to church by the ringing of the church bells.

Then Nicholas Lowe walked towards the church across the fields, out of the common tract, so that he might escape the scrutiny of the congregation, who are usually very curious on those occasions.

He came, however, and slipping a shilling into the hands of the pew opener, she placed him in an unoccupied seat, where there was a curtain which he could draw around him, and isolate himself from the congregation, who appeared to be inclined to scrutinize him pretty closely.

He listened to the names that were read over, and heard, with a joy that beamed in his countenance, his own and Fanny Leslie's name coupled and asked for the first time.

But there was a surprise for him—he came there to hear his own and Fanny's name announced, but he did not anticipate that he should hear of any one else's that he knew ; judge, therefore, his intense astonishment when he heard the names of James Rodwell and —— Paddlebat, widow.

He could hardly believe his ears, and yet he was convinced that it was so. He could hardly forbear to smile at the incongruous match that had been made between them. Of course Rodwell's motive was the money. It was strange that they should have chosen this place, probably from the same motive that induced him to do so, on account of its being so retired and out of the way.

CHAPTER L.

NICHOLAS LOWE ASKS HIMSELF WHAT HE SHALL DO.—HE FINDS THAT A FINE BED-CHAMBER DOES NOT INSURE REPOSE.

NICHOLAS LOWE was so much astonished at the news which he had obtained by going to the suburban church, that on his road home he could think of nothing else ; and even when he reached his new and really handsome house, not the novelty of its decorations and furnishing could withdraw his mind from the fact of Rodwell's projected marriage with Mrs. Paddlebat.

Full of folly, as he certainly had always thought that lady, he never for one moment could have imagined that she would sincerely think of marrying again, and if she did, that she would like such a man Rodwell, concerning whose loose mode of life she must know a great deal, notwithstanding she always chose, when he was attacked in any way, to become his champion.

Besides, too, it seemed most monstrous for her to marry so soon after old Mr. Paddlebat's death. At her time of life, too, when, as Hamlet remarks of his anything but respectable mother—

"——The heyday in the blood is tame
And waits upon the judgment ;"

or, at all events, should so wait whether it does or not.

Had any one told him of such a coming event, he would have doubted the accuracy of the information, but he had actually with his own ears heard the announcement, and therefore, so far as that part of the preliminaries to the marriage between Rodwell and Mrs. Paddlebat went, there could be no mistake whatever.

He then, as he came to think the matter over, considered, and justly, too, that it would be rather awkward for him and Fanny Leslie to arrive at the same hour to be married, as Rodwell and his somewhat portly bride. That such a state of things would ensue unless he, Nicholas Lowe, changed them in some way, he could not doubt, for as his had been, so had been the banns published between the other persons, announced to be the first time of asking.

With a pang of vexation, he came to the conclusion that he should have to go somewhere else, and put up the banns, and so lose a week, unless he chose to purchase a special licence, which he, when the thought struck him, made up his mind that he would do.

"Yes," he said, "yes ; I will that way foil this stroke of evil fortune. I will write to Fanny upon the subject, informing her of this *contretemps*."

He dreaded that some one might have been at the church on Rodwell's account, who, if such were the case, would assuredly go and let him know the same amount of intelligence concerning him, Lowe and Fanny, which the banns had proclaimed of him, Rodwell and Mrs. Paddlebat.

This was a most especially provoking idea, and one which haunted Lowe's mind so, that let him do what he would to busy and engage himself differently during that Sunday, he could not forget it.

That Rodwell himself was not there, he felt well enough assured, but still some one from him might be present, as people, Nicholas Lowe knew well, when they put up the banns of matrimony at any particular church, generally take the precaution to go or send on the first Sunday, in order that there may be no mistake when the fatal day comes.

"Well, well," said Lowe, "at all events, if such be the case that Rodwell does become aware of my intention and of Fanny's acquiescence in it, he cannot prevent me, and he can only go with his news to Mrs. Paddlebat, which, after all, is no great harm."

Thus he endeavoured to console himself for the unlucky circumstance, and he wrote to Fanny a note, in which he explained what had occurred, and soliciting her leave to get a special licence, and be united at an earlier period than the one which she had consented should be fixed.

When he had finished and sent off this note, he felt much better satisfied, and he told himself that should she consent, which in all probability she would, to the special licence being procured, he might after all steal a march upon Rodwell, and secure the hand of Fanny before the tedious fortnight had expired, which would embrace the three Sundays on which the banns would have to be published.

"I will not forbid," he remarked to himself, "the continued operations at the church. Let them each Sunday make the announcement, I need not be married there, or at all, for all that."

Thus, then, he reconciled himself to the circumstance which at first had given him so much uneasiness, and he only now regretted that it had never struck him or old Gilbert Paddlebat to insert a clause in the will to the effect that Mrs. Paddlebat, if she married again, should lose the property bequeathed to her.

This, of course, could have been easily done while the will was being manufactured, and of course, likewise, it would have prevented so obvious a mercenary marriage, as that which Rodwell was going to effect with the vain old woman, who ought to have known better, and who amply deserves all the consequences which may accrue from so ill assorted an union.

But when are the ladies old enough to know better upon such a subject?—fearful questions only, we presume, to be solved along with the riddle of the sphinx.

Nicholas Lowe now tried to find amusing occupation in looking over and suggesting to his own mind alterations in his new house, to which he expected so shortly to be able to introduce a mistress. This was likely enough to be a charming occupation, and it did for some hours beguile the day of its extreme weariness, and, when we consider what a dreary blank sort of a day Sunday in England and more particularly in London is, we cannot wonder that it hung upon Lowe's hands.

As a day of rest out of seven, we consider that the Sunday has numerous claims to our consideration; but, why it should not be as well one of recreation to those, who, during the whole week, have been constantly engaged in fatiguing or monotonous employments, we must confess we cannot see, and still less can we say, why it should be converted into a day of gloom, as the saints would fain make it, a day on which everybody was expected to groan, and pull an extraordinary long face, God knows for what.

Nicholas Lowe had always a great objection to going out on a Sunday, an objection which is shared in by numbers of persons who differ as to the manner in which that day should be observed; so, after fatiguing himself as much as he could in looking over his house, he retired to bed. But it is one thing to retire to bed, and another to sleep, which Nicholas Lowe found out. For hours he could get no repose, and at length, when, just at the turn of midnight, he dropped off into sleep, horrible dreams haunted him.

He kept fancying that Rodwell was murdering him, and that he had not strength to move a limb to resist him, although the mind was fully alert to the danger he was in.

This occurred twice, and then he was compelled, unless he chose to risk so much mental suffering a third time, to rise.

He paced his chamber for some time, and glanced at the rich hangings of his bed, as he thought of Shakspere's words,—

> " Then happy low lie down,
> Uneasy lies the head that wears a crown."

Troublesome thoughts of the past began to haunt him, and, to escape them, he seized upon a book, and, to a certain extent, lost a perception of his uneasiness in the following narration.

    *   *   *   *   *   *   *

The impressions of early life seldom or never leave the mind, the more especially where that impression occurs from any important event in life. Those that have been caused by our being saved from impending calamity or evils, hardly ever become banished from the sensitive mind.

This is the most remarkable when we come to consider the number of impressions events must make upon the mind, each one making encroachments upon the other.

In the family of a deceased friend, a circumstance occurred that was not divulged in life; but, after death, it was found related on paper, as will appear from the following.

We may premise that the lady is since dead, and she bore, while living, one of the best characters a lady could desire. She was a kind and affectionate wife, and a good mother; a sincere friend, and died regretted by all who knew her.

We feel it necessary to say this much, because the manuscript describes that which few women would ever have left any memorial of, though it was well known to him whom she left behind—an attached husband. It ran thus:—

I was but a giddy girl, when about seventeen. I was considered very beautiful. I state it, because, I heard it so repeatedly, and at last began to believe it. It was so, and there's an end of it. But I was considered more than beautiful; that was nothing strange—I was lovely, very lovely, and so I was.

My friends had great fears for me. They all thought that my volatile disposition would be my ruin, and, perhaps, my disgrace. Why they should think so I cannot imagine; not because I was too romantic—oh, dear, no, not at all.

And yet, I was very susceptible; nothing could be done that was at all likely to injure another, whether by accident or not, but my sympathies were sure to be wrung, and my heart was in my eyes, and I could not check my tears, they would flow. I was as susceptible as I was lively. My parents were, however, indulgent; they loved me, and could not bear the idea of checking any of my fancies, however absurd and extravagant they might be.

I had many lovers, as any young girl in my situation was like to have; for I had expectations sufficient to afford a very comfortable independence to any moderate pretensions and desires. It was, therefore, with the utmost anxiety that my parents watched over my childhood, and the change from girlhood to womanhood, or the few years approaching the latter period, with the greatest care, a care I can never repay, and which now I am able to appreciate, but which then I could not even comprehend.

Every girl is capable of taking care of herself, so she will tell you; and in justice it must be admitted, that they believe it, and hence it is the more dangerous fallacy, because it is not known as such to them.

But, alas! for feminine nature, they know not what they have to encounter or what to escape; they do not imagine the perils they sometimes escape without knowing it; for this is sometimes the case, and yet the escape is never apparent, and hence no experience can be gained from it.

There was, at that time, a very gay neighbourhood in the vicinity of my father's house. I mean, we were all on good terms; my father being a man of property, and much liked, did not hesitate to join in the round of pleasure that was offered by others to him, and to give balls and parties in return. But it must be remembered, that that was in the country, and not in London; our neighbours were all at home, they had their houses and estates all around them, their families and their friends occasionally, too, were present.

What could be more delightful than this? You might have more splendour and more people in a given compass in town, but here you knew every one whom you saw, and that to me was a great charm.

I was at home go where I would; we were emphatically all friends, and therefore we feel the greater pleasure and freedom in such society. Once I remember meeting with a cousin of one of my young friends; he was the handsomest man I think I ever saw, and was all that a young girl, just entering into life, could for a moment desire.

He belonged to the army; he was scarcely twenty—a cornet, but he had many advantages, and his promotion was expected to prove speedy. However, when I first saw him, I felt that I could love that man; he it was, I thought, that was doomed to make me happy or miserable.

Well do I remember the first time we met; he was then in undress, blue frock-coat, braided, with sword and sash. He did not see me at first; he looked grave and calm, but not severe. When he saw me he rose, and greeted me with much dignity and some frankness. I was confused, and scarce knew what I said or did; but I got through that interview.

When alone with my young friend, Laura Grange, I said to her in a whisper,—

"Whom have you got at your house now, Laura? I am sure you never mentioned to me that you expected such a visitor as this in your house."—"No, I did not," she replied.

"Who is he?"—"My cousin. Did I not tell you that when I introduced you to him."

"You might have done so," said I; "for I really know nothing that was said on the occasion. I was so confused."—"Oh, fie!"

"Nay; I may be excused, I am sure. Did you never feel flurried when you had a handsome man introduced to you suddenly, without any preparation?"—"I never saw any."

"Do you not mean to say that this gentleman is not a handsome man?"—"Well, he's not an ugly one, certainly."

"Not only not ugly, but really and positively handsome. You cannot deny it."—"Well, well, be that as it may, I see he has made a decided impression upon you."

"Yes, he flurried me."—"Ay, to be sure. We know what follows. But I will keep your secret," said Laura.

"My secret!" I replied.—"Yes, your secret."

"If I have any, it is more than I know of, and if you know of it, you know more than I do."—"That may be, my dear," said Laura, "because we are not the best observers of ourselves, while others can look at us, and see what we feel."

"Very good, Laura; go on again."—"I have more to say. You must be very careful of this gay and handsome man, my cousin."

"And why, good Laura?"—"Because he belongs to a profession the members of which are gay deceivers by profession and reputation, and yet there are some good, I know, among them; but, at the same time, they are all till they meet the one destined to enchain them."

"Ah! I see you are reading a lecture."—"No; only this gentleman is particularly gay, and has had as many sweethearts as I cannot bear to think of."

"Have you been one?"—"You might as well have asked me if I were not at this moment," replied Laura.

"Then explain. Are you touched by his good qualities, and would not have others think as warmly of him as yourself? if so, let me know, and I will not see him again."—"I am not stricken with my cousin, and, if you must know, I have hopes and fears in another quarter."

"Indeed!"—"Yes; but I tell you to beware of my cousin, Charles Neville; he is one you ought to shun, if you love, for I am convinced he has a life of gaiety to go through."

"Indeed!"—"Yes; he is young, lively, and gay; he has no home tastes, and his opinions are too free to make him a desirable acquaintance at all to a young lady."

"So you prohibit my visits, or my receiving any attention whatever from him, because he is a handsome man? Well, now, I must say that is as strange as anything can well be. But I cannot understand you, save you think I am particularly liable to fall into any gentleman's arms who may open them for me."—"Now you grow angry, and I will say no more; but believe me I have said no more to you than I would have wished said to myself under the circumstances."

"Well, well," said I, "we won't quarrel about a young man whom nobody knows or cares about, as yet; but really, at first, I thought you intended to keep him to yourself."—"No; as I said before, I have other hopes and expectations."

"You said fears before."—"I did. But more of that some other time."

I will not relate more of our conversation on that occasion, but merely say that it caused no diminution of admiration for this young gentleman on my part. Indeed, the character she gave me of him was by no means such as to make me dread him.

I was by far too self-sufficient for that, but at once determined to enter into a flirtation with him; and for this purpose, or rather with this view, I dressed myself in the most becoming style, and thought that when I had attracted his notice and attention I was making a conquest.

I forgot that all this while he was paying me merely those attentions that are due to a pretty flirt, over whom he would take the first advantage that presented itself.

There was no opportunity which offered itself that he did not take of offering me all the attention he well could, without attracting too much notice from others. This did not please me, for I had sense enough to see that he did not claim me before others; he did not seem desirous that the world should understand he had chosen me from all others, but that he paid me the full measure of his attention when we were alone.

Little did I think that he was quietly planning my ruin; and yet, in private, he was swearing all the vows of love, though at times I could not but suspect that something was wrong in the affair, and that I should only be disgraced by the termination.

Disgraced I never could be, because my conduct would place me far above that; but I should get no credit for suffering the attentions of a professed libertine.

I lost my mother about this time. I felt her loss much, and it made me very unhappy. She had been a most kind, valuable parent to me. She loved me sincerely, and was indulgent. Could I do less than deeply deplore such a parent? It was a loss never supplied, and never hoped to be so.

One day I was alone, weeping at the remembrance of her who had gone from me, when my lover, for so I called him, entered my apartment.

"Eliza," he said, "ah! do I see you weeping? refrain, dearest, from shedding those pearls. I know they are caused by grief, and hence my concern to see you thus."—"Can I mourn such a parent as I have had too much? She has been what I never shall see again. Alas! alas! she was not old, either."

"No, no; she deserves all your sympathy and all your sorrow. I can well grieve, too, for it brings to my mind the loss I have myself sustained some time since."

"Have you lost a mother, too?"—"I have; but my loss is not a recent deprivation; it has been my misfortune, for some time now, to know what the loss of a mother is."

"And you can allow for my grief?"—"I can, I can; but, Eliza, I know the effect of inordinate grief, and, believe me, the injury you do yourself while you indulge in it, at the same time though it may, and does, show an excess of feeling, yet it never can benefit the deceased, or render your sorrow more complete."

"I cannot help it."—"I share your feelings; but have some love for those who live. Do not love those that are dead only; recollect that there are some who only live but for you."

"Ah, that may be pleasing to hear," said I; "but it is but lip love, it comes not from the heart."—"Indeed it does, by Heaven!" said he.

"Hush!"—"Nay, I will swear ——"

"Swear not at all; besides, you have sworn enough to have made certain the whole world, because one asseveration cannot be made more binding."—"I admit it, and yet I cannot hesitate to swear again what I have once sworn to."

"Granted."—"And the more one repeats that which one says, the more one feels inclined to repeat it as emphatically and as warmly; do not think, therefore, that my asseverations are of less value because I do not hesitate to utter them afresh, whenever I speak of my hopes and love."

"And yet you never yet spoke before another; you seem to talk to me, and yet none know, save myself, that your attentions to me are even honourable."—"I have refrained from letting the world know what my object is, because I had ample reasons."

"Name them."—"You may think I am wrong—very wrong, but I will tell you the whole truth."

"Nothing less," I replied, "will let us be friends."—"I expect to be condemned, but there are circumstances that plead for me; I have many expectations in the world."

"You have."—"And I have some friends whom I must not, dare not disoblige," he said, in a candid tone.

"I would not desire you should do so for me."—"And some few more, whom I must not disappoint in my career towards fame."

"Right, sir."—"I see you grow angry, but I am not deserving of it. You have heard how much I have of expectation in promotion to the influence of some friends."

"I have heard something of the sort."—"Well, that expectation is based upon some circumstances which will hardly admit of any explanation to female ears."

"Indeed!"—"Yes. I labour under some difficulty and liability to misconstruction: and, even after my explanation, I feel I should be placed in no better situation by doing so."

"You can choose," I said, "whether you will give me any or not; I care not exactly."—"Well, well, I will be candid, but judge me leniently; the fact is this: in a certain family of distinction and influence there are several daughters, one of whom fancies that because I have availed myself of their influence, or rather intend doing so, that, in return, I am to take one of the younger ones off their hands."

"Indeed!"—"Yes, indeed, such is the presumption, I know; though, why it should be so, I cannot conceive; but, by conferring an obligation, they imagine that I am bound to them."

"I see."—"It seems just to them, no doubt, that if they use their influence to help me to a fortune, that I should help one of them to one likewise; that is, in plain words, that I should take one of the younger daughters in marriage."

"'Tis very strange," I said, "but not only strange, but unnatural, that such bargains should be made."—"Do not think that such a bargain has been made, or even hinted at."

"Then how know you that it is even expected?"—"Because I know such things are done daily; and the business-like manner in which my application for his influence in my favour, and the incidental intimation that his daughters are growing up, and would be an acquisition to any gentleman; that though they had not what was called a fortune, yet family connections were useful to men in need of promotion."

"Did a father say that?"—"Yes; and I was invited there constantly, and thrown much in their way."

"Are they beautiful?"—"Some say so. I must not do them an injustice—I must act honestly, and say they are handsome."

"And how came you not to attach yourself to one of them, all things following?"—"I had no taste for a connection so begun, and certainly not one to be so connected; besides, the lady was not to my liking; and, though she might be handsome, yet there wanted a few other traits as well to secure my heart."

See page 281.

"Your fancy is truant."—"Hardly so; but we all know we pass by estimable persons before we find the one to whom we find ourselves irresistibly drawn, despite all endeavours to the contrary. I need not tell you of the irresistible power of love; look at me, Eliza, and see it."

He fixed an ardent and affectionate gaze upon me; I felt my prudence give way, I felt there was no man that I would love but him; he was all in all to me. I loved him, and I was almost tempted to say so.

"Eliza," he said, "we are both under age; we have yet the world to know. Believe me, I feel what I speak; we are made for each other; say you love me, and we will take the earliest and quickest way we can of uniting ourselves; and then, when the deed is done, when no envious mind can part us, then we will avow before the world what has been done—that we loved each other, and have united our fates."

I gave him my hand.

"Surely," said I, "you cannot mean wrong when you say this; more cannot be done."—"More! no dearest girl, we can but be made one by those laws which are sanctioned by Heaven and man."

"And yet there are those who would say you did not even mean so much as that."—"I mean no less, dearest. Come, now; nothing hinders us; I have a vehicle at the door; we shall very soon be across the border, and in another country."

"Cannot we go by two routes?"—"What should hinder us going together? besides, I shall have you by my side, and I shall know you are safe; and, by my side, we shall both be the happier."

"I would prefer going by myself."—"Nay, dearest! the chances of detection are double; you see that one or the other of us is sure to be overtaken. No, no, dearest, let us go together."

"I yield," I said, and I almost fainted in his arms.

At that moment a film seemed to be lifted off my eyes, and I thought I saw my mother coming towards me with an expression of grief and sorrow on her countenance. She seemed to forbid my leaving my father's home with my lover. She frowned—she seemed to entreat—and then tears gushed to her eyes; the sight was too much for me.

"Mother!" I exclaimed, "mother, forgive me! I will not go—I will to my father and tell him all; I will tell ——"—"Well," said my friend, "what's the matter with you, Eliza?"

"Laura! where am I?"—"Why, you are in my room, to be sure; and a pretty flirt you are, to be sure, to play with the count as you did."

"Oh, I see it all now—it's a dream!"

*   *   *   *   *   *   *

I had sat down in my friend's room and fallen asleep, but I never afterwards forgot the dream—it was real to my faculties. I never saw the cornet afterwards.

Nicholas Lowe looked up. The dawn was breaking; a faint gentle light was shining into that really handsome chamber of his, and gently bringing into existence, as it were, the ornaments with which it was so profusely decorated.

"Now," he said, "I think that, before the bustle of the day commences, it is more than likely I shall be able to get some repose."

He threw himself again upon the bed, nor was he now disappointed. By the little work of fiction he had read, his mind had been withdrawn from too close a consideration of his own circumstances, and amid a chaos of strange images that kept floating through his brain, he fell into a profound slumber, which lasted several hours.

CHAPTER LI.

OLD GILBERT PADDLEBAT CHANGES HIS RESIDENCE.—THE HOUSE IN CHANCERY.

IF that night was to Nicholas Lowe one of some disquietude, what was it to Gilbert Paddlebat? His mind, once filled with the idea, that the spirit of old Sheepy had obtained leave, as some folks think it necessary, from the authorities of another world to wait upon him, would continue to do so, was almost certain to fulfil its own predictions.

In the daytime he might succeed, to a certain extent, in shaking off his terrors. Besides the various calls of business, and the chances of profit from such transactions as were likely to come under his notice, all tended, together with the consciousness that whenever he felt unusually nervous, he could ring the great bell which he had provided himself with, to make matters a little more endurable.

But, when night came, what was he to do? How was he to shake off the terrors that beset him? Who was there then to answer his bell? He might ring it, but when the old clerk had gone away, of what avail would it be to do so?

As the day advanced, all these feelings and terrors came most vividly across his mind, and at length, towards sunset, he had quite come to a conclusion, that he could not, that he dared not, attempt to sleep another night beneath that roof, lest his wits should forsake him, with terror, during the dreary lapse of time before the hours should come round again to bring him some one whom he could summon to his aid.

"Here's an exposure," he groaned; "I shall have to go somewhere now, and actually hire a bed. I shall be ruined. The ghost of old Sheepy is determined upon my absolute ruin. I must go out and inquire what is the lowest possible price at which a bed can be procured.

When he got to this determination, and he did so with very great reluctance, his next step was to attire himself in his curious garments, those garments which were made for a boy, but which, on account of their cheapness, he bought, and managed to get into and proceed down stairs, in order to ask the ancient clerk if he knew of any place where a cheap bed was to be had.

"Where do you live?" he said.—"Where do I live, Mr. Paddlebat; why—why, I'm so asthmatic lately that I sha'n't live anywhere long, I'm thinking."

"What do I care whether you are asthmatic or not? I say, where do you live, and what does it cost you for a bed at night?"—"Why, sir, I really can't, be said to live; I haven't enough to live upon, you see, sir."

"You'll have less presently," said old Gilbert, "for I'll discharge you, unless you answer me a plain question, and that pretty quickly, too. I want to know what a bed can be got for."

"What it can be got for, sir? oh, it can be got for threepence."—"Indeed?"

"Yes, sir. They have a large room, and they stretch some ropes a little way above the floor, and lay down a lot of old flock beds on them, and you pay threepence."—"It's cheap. Ha! that is to say, nothing is cheap."

"Ha! ha!" laughed the old clerk, and then he nearly choked himself by the effort. "I never heard you say anything was cheap before, Mr. Paddlebat; never—never."—"Didn't you? It's no matter to you, I suppose, whether I say anything is cheap or not. Humph! Shall I, or shall I not go to that place he mentions?"

"Please, sir," said the old clerk, interrupting his meditations, "here's been a man here to-day, sir, who wanted to know if we knew anything about that very house we were talking about the other day."—"What house?"

"The house near Queen's-square, sir, that's been in Chancery so many years, and locked up, you know, sir, all the while. What a sad thing—what a sad thing to think of, to be sure; and I'd be so glad of it."—"You?—you?"

"Yes, sir; I pay, I can assure you, as I am a living man, and only get nine shillings a-week from you—a matter of one shilling-and-threepence for half an attic. Only consider, sir, half an attic. And the old woman in the other half, stops her nose up every night when she goes to bed, with snuff, so that she makes the most horrible noise in breathing, that you can imagine."—"Bah!" cried old Gilbert, "I don't want to hear what you give."

He walked up to his own room again; and, when he got there, he seemed for a time in deep thought, and then he muttered,—

"It's a good idea that. The house that's in chancery. Ah! what's to hinder me from taking possession of it myself. Quite quietly, of course. It's a very good idea. It's a—a—famous idea, indeed—an uncommonly famous idea, that it is. Nothing to pay—no rent, no taxes,—a nice quiet life,—retired and pleasant. I don't want any furniture. Not I; no, no, no. And then, as for my business—my discount business. Ah, ah. What's to prevent me doing it all on the Royal Exchange, or in coffee-houses where the party who wants any cash will have to take me and pay for anything that's ordered as well, so that I shall live quite free, too!"

Old Gilbert very nearly laughed, but not quite. He made a strange sort or sound, which almost alarmed himself, and then he rubbed his hands together, as he added,—

"It's a capital idea, and I'll do it. It's a precious idea. I have the key, and I'll go at once. I'll discharge the old fool below, and so save his nine shillings—actually nine shillings a-week. Let me see, 52 times 9—9 times 2 is 18, put down 8 and carry 1; 9 times 5 is 45, and 1 46—468 shillings. Actually who would have thought he cost me 23l. 8s., which is nearly, actually, good God! 2½ per cent upon 1,000l. I wonder I ain't ruined. I'm too liberal; I always suspected I was too liberal. He only comes at seven in the morning, and stays till ten at night. The wretch, and I've good reason to believe, too, that in spite of all that, he is not satisfied."

This became now a settled point with old Gilbert. The clerk had made a most unlucky speech when he mentioned the house that was in chancery. It had procured him his own discharge, and the poor wretch, on account of extreme age, was not likely again to get even nine shillings a-week from any one, although, on account of his intimate acquaintance with all old Gilbert Paddlebat's customers, he served his turn well enough.

"If," he went on reasoning with himself—"if now I could get into the house, I should save the threepence, which, I suppose, is the lowest price at which I could get a bed, and that would be something; threepence a-day comes to a large sum in a year. Well, well, I don't know what's to hinder me. I have the key which was left here as long as twenty-six years ago."

He went to a hook on the wall, where hung a number of old keys, to each of which was appended a small parchment label, announcing to what door it belonged; and from among these he at length selected one which he believed to be the key of the house in question.

"I will go," he said, "as soon as it gets a little darker. I will go, then, and obtain an entrance to the house. I will take with me the means of getting a light, and what is to hinder me from there and then remaining until the morning?"

He did, upon consideration, think that it would be a hard case to have nothing in the shape of a bed to lie down upon; but, after a time, his ingenuity and habits of contrivance got him rid of that difficulty altogether, and he decided upon carrying on his back his miserable flock bed, on which he had slept many years, and choosing his opportunity when no one was looking to take it into the house where he intended to fix his abode.

"It will be perilous," he said. "It may be perilous, because some one may see me; but still I will do it. Only consider; to save rent, taxes, and nine shillings a-week, besides. A fortune! a fortune!"

He slipped away from hence, taking the key with him, and repaired to the street in which the house that had so been long in chancery was situated.

It was not at any time a great thoroughfare, that street, and so he could not have much difficulty in finding an opportunity of slipping up the steps, and laying the key where no one would be likely to observe him in the act of so doing.

Several persons went past the door while he lingered upon the spot; but at length, although he looked each way, he saw no one approaching, and he at once ascended the steps, of which there were several, and tried the key in the lock.

To his chagrin he found, that though, to all appearance, the key fitted the lock well, yet, from long disuse, the rusty wards would not act, and all his strength was in vain.

While he was striving to do all in his power to open the door, he heard the footsteps of several persons approaching, and was compelled to desist from the attempt, lest he should be seen; but he carried the key away with him, which, by a vigorous effort, he succeeded in wrenching from the lock.

He did manage just to escape detection, and he heard one man who was passing the house, say to his companion,—

"What a time that house has been shut up."—"Yes," said the other, " t's in chancery, they say; and what's more, they say it is haunted, so that shut up, I presume, it is likely to remain."

"I should think so. And yet I——"

The sound of the voices died away as they walked on, and old Gilbert Paddlebat staggered against the iron rails of the area, as he said to himself,—

"Haunted—haunted—haunted! why, I am leaving my own house for such a reason. Haunted by what—by whom? What care I so that it be not haunted by old Sheepy. What is it to me? I will not be deterred by such an idle tale. Not I, not I."

But how to procure admittance, that was the question, and he held the rusty key up to the light as he told himself that some oil upon it might enable him to open the door with it. But how was he to get oil? Pay for it he certainly would not. That was completely out of the question. At last he thought of a scheme.

He went to an oil shop, and demanded the price of the best sperm oil per hogshead. The shopkeeper told him and showed him a specimen, which he took to the door, pretending to look at it, and surreptitiously dipped the key in it.

"Ah," said old Gilbert, "I'll call again to-morrow, and I dare say buy some."

Another attempt at the door succeeded. The lock yielded to the oiled key. The rusty hinges creaked for the first time for many a year, and old Gilbert Paddlebat found himself in the passage of the house, which, in imagination, he began to look upon as almost his own.

CHAPTER LII.

GILBERT PADDLEBAT'S FIRST NIGHT IN THE HOUSE IN CHANCERY.—HIS ADVENTURE WITH THE MADMAN.

OLD Gilbert Paddlebat cautiously closed the door after him, and listened for a while, as he stood in the hall of the empty house—not that he anticipated that any sounds would disturb the stillness of the place, yet Gilbert was a cautious man, and never acted precipitately; besides, the place was so lonely; it had been so long uninhabited; and, taking all things into consideration, it was a strange and dismal place to come to.

The very smell of the house was enough to tell one that no human being had inhabited that house for many a year; it was damp and desolate. There was a kind of feeling about Gilbert that he could not ascribe to any other source than the dampness of the place and the peculiar mustiness of the air.

"Dear me," muttered Gilbert Paddlebat, "what a place! how musty! the very dust must have gotten mouldy, and the very walls seem clammy and moist to the touch."

There was no sound in that place that Gilbert heard. It was all silent as the grave; and yet, how many joyous shouts and songs, and Christmas revelry, had at one time been heard within those walls. But what cared Gilbert Paddlebat for that? "It was better as it was," he would have said; because it was about to become his lodging, and at a low rent.

Yes; it was Gilbert's home. He had it at a low figure, a very low figure, indeed; even Gilbert Paddlebat admitted the rent was low and the lodging cheap; for there being no recognised or ostensible owner, he paid nothing.

That was the payment Gilbert liked of all others to make; but he did not like receiving in the same denomination; he required an additional coin.

"There's nobody here," said Gilbert to himself; "nobody at all; I didn't expect anybody here; it would have been a trespass, that's all; but I have the key; that's lawful possession, at any rate; and I'll keep it till they serve me with a notice of ejectment; but I dare say there's neither bell nor knocker, and, therefore, it's no matter; it will be long before they serve it on me."

Pleased with the whimsical conceit, which he thought a good joke, he slowly walked along the passage, until he came to the foot of the stairs.

Here again old Gilbert paused and listened. He turned his head to one side, as though he wished to incline one ear and one eye towards the upper part, and one towards the lower.

Thus divided as his attention was, yet he could do nothing in the way of detecting any sound or disturbance of the stillness of that dismal place.

True it was, that thrice since he had been in that passage, he had heard the tramp of a passenger's footsteps as they neared the house and then receded from it. At first he was inclined to believe that the noise was in the house; but he was speedily convinced that it was not, by the nature of the sound, its gradual approach, and its alike gradual disappearance.

"Ah! it's nothing," muttered old Gilbert; "who should hear sounds in an empty house? Ha! ha! ha! God bless me!" he said, as he heard the sounds of his own voice. He stopped short in his laughter. The cachination sounded so strange and unnatural in that house; it had such a disagreeable, echo, too; it seemed a senseless repetition, as if somebody had laughed with evil intent.

"Ah! there'll be no want of conversation here," muttered old Gilbert, in an undertone; at all events, not while I speak out, for I shall have an answer from above."

Old Gilbert was half inclined to be facetious, but stopped his mirth from gaining any outlet by means of his lips, lest he should again awake the dismal echo above stairs, and set the house in a noise.

Old Gilbert looked at the flock-bed he had brought in with him. It was a small one, a very small one; but then Gilbert was a diminutive man, and it fitted him very well; to be sure, when you came to place it upon the boards, it was not soft. But here, again, old Gilbert had the advantage of other men.

He lived lightly; there was no grossness about Gilbert; he was very light, bodily, and the tiny bits of flock, of which the bed was composed, did not suffer much compression by the weight of his body as he lay on it.

This was a subject of great gratulation with Gilbert.

"Now," he muttered "some men pride themselves upon being big men; fine men they call it; but I call it grossness; but every one to their trade. Now, if I had been a fine man, what would it not have cost me in eating and drinking, not to mention clothes? Then, let me see. It might cost me, goodness knows how much more a week to live; quite as much again, quite as much again."

Gilbert was lost in mental arithmetic; he was adding up unknown quantities, and then multiplying them by the days in the year, and dividing the amount by pounds, shillings and pence, and trying to find a definite expression for the result.

This, however, would have defied the calculating powers of the youth Bidden, the calculating boy; and it is no slur upon the arithmetical character of old Gilbert Paddlebat to say it defied his efforts to arrive at a definite and precise result from such data. This, however, Gilbert attributed to the vastness of the sum concerned, and not to the insufficiency of the information.

"Dear me, dear me, it exceeds all belief and calculation. A large man loses by being big and overgrown. I always thought so; but now it exceeds even what I had imagined; and when you come to add interest and compound interest, there would be no figures in the language to express it."

Gilbert was now quite satisfied with the result of his own calculation. He was a small man; and if Gilbert were disposed to thank anybody, he would have thanked Providence for making him one, though, at the same time, he congratulated himself upon the happy fact that he was so.

There lay the flock-bed and a blanket, and a something else, an indescribable wrapper of some sort, in both of which the bed was tied up; and Gilbert wiped his brow, for he was heated with the exertion he had undergone in carrying his bed to the uninhabited house.

"Come," muttered Gilbert to himself, "say what one will, this will be a cheap lodging."

This pleased Gilbert; and a something, approaching a smile of satisfaction, crossed his lips, as he muttered,—

" Yes ; cheap, very cheap ; I wish I could live upon the same sum ; I might then hope for some good ; I might expect, that is, in time, to be a rich man."

Thus Gilbert consumed the few minutes he stood at the foot of the stairs in the hall, alternately listening and chattering to himself ; and then, after a pause, he muttered,—

" Well, now, where shall I make up my bed? where shall I sleep? in what apartment shall I take up my abode? I must make an inspection of the premises ; yes, that must be the mode of procedure, and the snuggest room I can find, one with the most glass and fewest draughts, must be the room for me. That shall be, Gilbert Paddlebat. Lord, what a fool my brother was ! but that's neither here nor there ; the folly of one man doesn't taint another. I am free, thank God !"

Gilbert thanked God because it was a form of speech, for he immediately turned to his bed, as he was about to walk up stairs, and muttered,—

" That will be safe here. Oh, yes ! I can't afford to lose it ; oh, no ! But I am sure it is safe here. Nobody can come in but myself ; I have the key."

Having satisfied himself by feeling for the key in his pocket, he again turned towards the stairs, and slowly ascended the great staircase, which, by the way, was a double one, leading to another part of the hall. It was a large house, and most of the rooms led one into another, and then into the passages and galleries, so that to walk over it was a task.

What could be done? Gilbert walked manfully up. He saw the house was a large one—that he knew before—but, with only himself in it, caused him to look up, and the house looked all the larger.

" How the dust has accumulated," muttered Gilbert ; " it is as thick as a carpet."

This was the fact. Layer after layer of dust had fallen ; and, what with damp and the lapse of time, it had become a fabric, almost woven ; and, had it not been so short, it would not have moved from the floor by the action of any substance passing over it.

As it was, however, it was much about the same, save in colour, to a person passing over a light fall of snow, which sticks to the feet, leaving the impression of the feet on the floor. But, in this instance, it was much more plain and perceptible.

" Well," muttered Gilbert, as he pushed open the door of the drawing-room, " this is a fine place ; what a size the rooms are, to be sure. What fools people are to part with their money thus ! Locked up in chancery, eh? Well, I'd as lief be locked up in chancery myself as have my money laid out in such a place, with such a seal to secure it."

Gilbert, however, thought that he got the house cheap, and that though it was folly to build such places, and greater to live in them, yet, upon the terms he took possession of it, he deemed it not unreasonable.

" In fact," said Gilbert, arguing the question with himself, " mine is decidedly a beneficial occupancy."

There was no denying the truth of this ; it was a clencher, and had he had a doubt about the propriety of the step he was taking, this would have settled the matter ; but Gilbert had no such thoughts or scruples at all ; he intended to occupy it. Besides, if he had thought of the matter, he would have insisted that he was benefiting the house, because his sleeping and living there must have tended to air it.

How many Gilbert Paddlebats it would have taken to air a mansion like that, would have been a curious inquiry indeed ; it might have been compared, in effect, to a farthing candle placed in the midst of Milton's Pandemonium. It would have been something to look at by those who were favourably situated, and blessed with good eyesight.

" What's that?" muttered Gilbert Paddlebat, as he stopped at the door of the room in which he had been carrying on a very careful examination.

Gilbert was great at the finding of cupboards, and greater in turning over their contents. He had already discovered a moth-eaten flannel, a duster full of holes, and a brush without any hairs, when his attention was aroused by some ominous sounds that came from below.

We may now mention, as a fact not known before, and that was, that the house was the resort of another person, who slept there unknown to Gilbert Paddlebat. This individual was one of an unfortunate class whose brains are not manufactured in the same manner as other people's, or they had been differently used, or misused, or something of the sort, and the consequence was he was what society has deemed proper to term a maniac.

This individual had walked about till he was tired, and now, from some motive or other, thought proper to return to his domicile, there to sleep away the fatigue of his erratic perambulations.

According to custom, the maniac was very cunning; he did not choose that any one should see his mode of entrance, which was an unusual one. Having satisfied himself on this head, he scrambled rapidly over the railings, and, by means of some complicated process of falling or scrambling down, he got into the area safe, and without any bruise or blow.

"Ah!" muttered the maniac, "that's well done. I know it by heart now. Jumping down an area is quite an art. I wonder if the man in the moon could do such a thing."

After this inquiry, he turned to the place called a scullery, beneath the flag-stones that went over the doorway, and took a vaulting jump through the orifice that had once been a window, but which had now departed for some time, and bore a great resemblance now to a hole made for a dust bin.

Having alighted on his feet, he ran into the passage, and then pushed the door to; but this went swinging with a bang that re-echoed through the house.

This was the sound that startled old Gilbert Paddlebat, and who stood listening some minutes before he spoke again.

"Ah!" said Gilbert, "there are some of the doors open, and the windows are out of repair, and a good current of air goes through the house, banging all the doors. I wonder if that was the first idea of the Eolian harp? it was a funny one, certainly, but it might have been. Not that I ever saw such a thing, or cared to do so; but it might have happened for all that. I have heard of such things. I must go down and shut these doors," he muttered, after another pause, during which he thought he heard the sound of a footstep. "No; it's outside in the street. I'll go down and shut the place up, and have no more of this rattling."

So saying, old Gilbert Paddlebat quitted the room he was in, and walked down stairs, and, having arrived in the hall, he paused again, for more sounds met his ear.

"God bless me!" he muttered; "what can be the meaning of all this? Let me see; there is my bed all right. Ah! it's all imagination, I see. I'll go down and see what's the matter. Sounds multiply in a large, empty house like this."

He turned to the kitchen stairs, and had descended about two or three stairs, fwhen he was petrified at hearing and seeing the maniac walk up the like number rom below.

"Hilloa!" the maniac cried, in a loud, deep voice, that made old Gilbert Paddlebat tremble.

He made no answer, but opened his eyes very wide, and shook violently.

"Hilloa!" repeated the maniac; "where's the great khan of Tartary, —where's Ho Fang?"

Gilbert Paddlebat was most emphatically stupified. It is quite questionable if ever, in the whole course of his existence, he met with a case in which he was so utterly confounded, thunder-stricken, and confused, as he was in this instance. He could not go back; he was equally unable to move forward, for if he did, he must have gone into the arms of the maniac, who stood with a dubious kind of expression, watching him.

"Well," he said, "so you've no express from Kintale; nor have brought any eels from the Orkneys? What's to be done, now? I'm hr y—very —quite ravenous."

As the maniac spoke, he made a motion as if he intended satisfying his crav-

See p. 288.

ings by a demolition of the material composing his, Gilbert Paddlebat's body. No sooner, however, did the latter see the other make a demonstration of this nature, than the spell which bound him was broken, and he, in an instant, turned and fled with all the precipitancy he was capable of.

The maniac was not prepared for this; but he no sooner saw Gilbert take to flight, than he joined in the chase with a loud hilloa, that added greatly to Gilbert's terror, and hurried him onwards. He made a desperate rush to the door; but he was defeated in his object by his own bed.

Yes, there lay the flock bed, rolled and tied up, which Gilbert, in his terror, had not seen, and over this impediment he made a desperate rush, but was thrown down in the dust that lay so thick in the passage.

The maniac was close after him; but he, too, met with the same fate, and measured his length on the floor, while Gilbert, feeling that he could not reach the door, scrambled up on his hands and feet up the staircase, and then went up at a cat-like gallop, till he got to the landing.

Here he paused for several moments, groaned, and drew his breath, for what between terror and exertion, Gilbert Paddlebat was completely out of that necessary article.

In another moment, however, the maniac was up; and when he arose, he looked up, exclaiming,—

"Well, here's for an Ethiopian chase; by the beard of a Mussulman if I catch him, there will be more music than will be found in the ocean."

Suddenly, he darted up stairs, taking two or three steps at a time, and quite confounding Gilbert, who had only time to rush into the room, to save himself from the grasp of the maniac, who seemed to grow furious, for he hilloaed and shouted in a manner that quite terrified him, so that he knew not what he did; but somehow or other, instinct taught him what to do.

For some time he found himself dodging backward and forward behind the doors in the drawing-rooms. There were several doors and several rooms, and in turns Gilbert honoured them both; but he was driven from them all.

On one occasion, he attempted to shut one of the doors, and keep the maniac out; but this was a vain task; the maniac was much more powerful than he, and with one effort, he rushed against the door, throwing it open despite all Gilbert's attempts to keep him out.

Gilbert Paddlebat was thrown backward by the concussion, and his enemy was projected across the room before he could stay himself, of which the other took advantage, and passed through the door as quick as his terrified limbs could carry him.

"The lord—have—mercy!" ejaculated Gilbert, in a very queer, jerking manner. "I—I—I'm nearly done for. I—I—I—can't breathe—my—head g—g—goes into my heart."

Poor Gilbert hurried about, and looked like a hen with the croup, tormented while at the last gasp, and trying to escape from some dreadful object of terror.

Gilbert was forced to commence the dodging system again around the doors.

"Ah!" exclaimed the maniac, suddenly; "do you hear?"—"Hear," said Gilbert, in a shrill, trembling, treble voice.

"Yes, hear—hark—do you not hear it? God! I hear it as plainly as I did at my mother's death. Ha! ha! ha! Do you not hear it?"—"No; I beg your pardon, I only hear you."

"I mean the bell," said the maniac.—"The bells!"

"The bells; no—no; the bell; the passing bell; it tolls for some one not yet dead."

Gilbert Paddlebat trembled; he could not speak, or he would have said the bell never tolled but for such as were dead, and never for the living. But he was too terrified to speak; he watched the motions of the maniac with jealousy; his whole soul was concentrated in that one effort.

"Monster!" suddenly exclaimed the maniac, who had paused a moment or two, as if he were intently listening. "Monster! that you are; you destroyed her, and I will destroy you."

As he spoke he rushed at Gilbert, who adroitly avoided him, and doubled; but in doing so slipped down, and lost the advantage the action gave him, and he found the maniac so close upon him, that he had no other chance than sheer speed.

Away he went; but this time could not get far enough away to permit him to turn, and dodge his pursuer. Thus for several minutes the race continued; the maniac making several ineffectual grasps at the coat of Gilbert, who, by some eel-like twist, got clear; but at length he made a dart down stairs.

How Gilbert stepped down—he didn't count the steps. Ah! no; he had forgotten all about arithmetic, or even tumbling. He made a desperate attempt to get down the kitchen-stairs ; they were stone ; he slipped, and fell terrified in a heap, almost insensible ; when he was aroused by a violent kick, and, in another moment, the maniac, who couldn't stop himself, was thrown over, and fell several yards.

All was still. Gilbert looked up, trembled excessively, and wiped his face—looked around and saw the maniac lying on his back, his head nearest him.

The fact was, in falling over, he had been precipitated some yards down, with the top of his head in contact with the edge of a step, and killed him instantly ; he was thrown there on his back a complete somerset.

Gilbert Paddlebat approached the body cautiously, and by degrees he became acquainted with the foregoing facts, and then passed a deep internal consultation as to what was to be done. Gilbert never once opened his lips—not a sound escaped him ; you could not have heard him breathe, so still and terrified was he.

He searched about, and found a kind of pantry or cellar, with a lock and key to it. He then approached the body, and dragged it towards the door. He dragged it very slowly, for he was not a strong man ; moreover, he had suffered much from terror and exertion. However, by much perseverance and exertion, Gilbert Paddlebat drew the dead body into the place, and then shut the door, locking and double locking it, and taking the key out.

CHAPTER LIII.

THE INTERVIEW BETWEEN LOWE AND FANNY LESLIE ABOUT THE MARRIAGE.—
THE APPARENT VEXATION OF RODWELL.—THE WAGER.

SITUATIONS of suspense are certainly among the most trying, if not of themselves the most trying, to which human nature can be subjected ; and we may well imagine, knowing so much as we know of the character of Nicholas Lowe, how much he must have felt the circumstances in which he was placed.

He had the consciousness continually now haunting him, that, as regarded Fanny Leslie, he stood upon a mine, which each moment might explode beneath him, burying at once all his prospects in one gust of ruin. Well he knew that, even if the fact of the episode in his existence, of which the reader is aware, did not seem to Fanny's perception a sufficient reason for casting him off for ever from her affections, yet his disingenuousness in not telling her of it, would be sufficient.

The manner in which he had braved Jervis Rodwell, and dared him to the proof of anything of an injurious character to him, Lowe, was what Fanny never could forgive, if once she became aware that it was all duplicity, and that such an amount of virtuous indignation was all based upon the presumption that he would not be found out.

Pure-minded as she was, and full of the noblest and most honourable feelings, it was not in her nature to affect to love a man who could have acted so profoundly hypocritical a part.

All this he knew, and hence he became in a state of mind almost bordering upon distraction, to get the marriage over as speedily as possible.

He felt upon what a slender thread hung all his fortunes. The five hundred pounds to which the forged will entitled him, he well knew would not support his new establishment for more than one twelve months ; and should he, therefore, fail in getting Fanny's money, he trembled at the idea of the inevitable ruin that awaited him.

He had not even the resource of applying to old Gilbert Paddlebat, because, if he, in any way, made an endeavour, from disappointment or revenge, to implicate him in the forgery of the will, to do so at all effectually, he must proclaim the share that he took in that transaction, and so criminate himself to a fearful extent.

"No, no," he said ; "I must make Fanny Leslie mine, and that at once, too. A special licence, to which I must get her consent, will be far better than going to that suburban church, to be wedded on the same day that Mrs. Paddlebat has consented to bestow her hand upon Jervis Rodwell."

Much as he disliked going to the house where Fanny was, he decided still upon doing so, to ask her if she would be a party to his making every exertion to procure the licence, and the wedding taking place with as little delay as possible.

He did not know either, but what some one might have been at the church on Rodwell's account, and so heard the banns published between him, Lowe, and Fanny Leslie, in the same manner as he had those between Mrs. Paddlebat and Rodwell, and this was a possible contingency which induced Lowe at once to see Fanny.

Let us, however, just look for a moment at what is now passing in the house of the departed goldsmith. We shall find, by something that is there occurring, that Nicholas Lowe's enemies were fearfully active.

Mrs. Paddlebat is alone, and she is reading a note from Jervis Rodwell, a part of which runs thus :—

" I have found out enough about Lowe, to convince me that I shall find out a great deal more. Indeed, I am now quite certain, that if the contemplated marriage between him and Fanny can but be delayed, I can stop it altogether, by giving her such proofs of his immorality as shall convince her of the double-dealing nature of his disposition. What I leave to you to do, is to put off the possibility of Lowe's persuading her to be married by special licence suddenly, somewhere. Do that in any way you think most expedient, knowing as you do, all the circumstances, and that he has put up the banns at the same church to which I unadvisedly or unluckily went."

Now, Mrs. Paddlebat, without at all being anything of a conjuror, had that sort of woman's wit about her, which enabled her to come to a very good opinion with regard to how this was to be accomplished.

She knew enough of Fanny, to find that it was not a very easy matter to deceive her, and that if anything at all were to be accomplished with her, it was through her feelings there was the greatest chance of doing it. After, then, some consideration she went to Fanny, and said,—

" My dear, you and I have not understood each other, I am sure, so well as we ought to do. Now, you have consented to marry Mr. Lowe. Well and good. May I ask of you a favour?"—" If the favour, aunt," said Fanny, "be to forego my intentions, I ——"

" Oh! no, no, no," interrupted Mrs. Paddlebat; "what could put that into your head? You would rather now, I am sure, for the sake of the memory of your poor dear uncle, who is dead and gone, marry with my consent, than without it."—" I would, indeed, aunt."

" Well, then, all I ask of you is, that you will not be married secretly from me. Do you promise me so much?"—" Truly, I dislike secresy of any kind or description, aunt, and am always better pleased with any action which can be done openly, as I am more in love with any opinion which is avowed candidly."

" That's just, Fanny, what I fully expected you to say, and now I am satisfied. Who's that, I wonder? there's a knock at the door."

" Mr. Lowe, ma'am," answered the servant; " he says he wants to see Miss Leslie, ma'am."

" Well, Fanny," said Mrs. Paddlebat, " if you wish to see him, you can, you know; don't let me be any hindrance on any account. Only as you have made me a promise, I shall rely upon your keeping it."

" Aunt, did you ever know me break a promise, that you think such a warning necessary?"—" Oh, dear, no, no, not on any account. I'll go up stairs, for I know the sight of me is as bad as poison to him."

Mrs. Paddlebat sailed majestically out of the room, so that if Lowe could have persuaded Fanny by any arguments, he certainly had a fair stage to act on, without any interference from any one.

We need not pursue the interview which took place; suffice it to say, that Fanny finally arranged with him as follow,—

" I will meet you," she said, " at the door of the church, precisely at 10 o'clock in the morning, when the publication of the banns has expired, and I pray you to say no more about a special licence."

This was too positive to admit of dispute. Lowe could not but see that she had completely made up her mind, and then he said, rather foolishly, for it was awakening suspicion,—

" Well, Fanny, be it so; and now let me implore you to believe nothing of me; to listen to nothing concerning me, except what comes from my own lips; for you know I have enemies, and those most serious ones, too, who would scruple at nothing whatever to interrupt my happiness."

" And can you, Lowe," she said, " can you for one moment imagine that I would lend a greedy ear to anything that might come from your enemies to your prejudice? Do you still know so little of me as to suppose that any assertion merely could affect me? No; if anything is broached against you, I shall, with what calmness I can, demand the proofs of the accusation."

Lowe winced a little at this, for it was not exactly what he liked, and he, after a moment's pause, said,—

" Would it not be better, Fanny, to listen not at all. Why should you be made anxious and uncomfortable? Turn a deaf ear to all that can be said upon the subject. That is the course that I should advise you to pursue. Apparent proofs, you know, may be forged, so as to seem like truth."

" They may, Lowe; but do not apprehend anything. Let a consciouness of your own innocence of any wrong doing, support you. Well! you know that the more active and energetic Jervis Rodwell makes himself in inquiring into your past life, the more severe will be his disappointment at finding nothing to compensate him for his trouble."

" Yes, to be sure. Oh, certainly. There is nothing like a consciousness of one's own entire innocence. But do you really think he is so foolish as to be making any such inquiries?"

" Yes. The last time he was here, I heard him say that he had made a wager with himself; that is to say, his ruin against yours."—" The villain!"

" I can echo that opinion, Nicholas. But, after all, how far are you above all those shafts of petty malice! They ought not—nay, I would not allow them, were I you, to wring from me even a hasty interjectional expression. What need you care for the enmity of such a man as Rodwell, or for what he can find out, when all that he does so find he will keep sedulously secret, because it must and will redound to your honour?"

A cold sensation crept for a few moments over Nicholas Lowe's heart, as he said to himself,—

" Good God! does she know anything? and is this a refined kind of irony, that she is only indulging in at my expense?"

A second thought, however, sufficed to chase this idea from his mind; for Fanny Leslie was just about the last person in the whole world who would ever dream of adopting such a course.

But for Nicholas Lowe to think so, even for one brief minute, most clearly showed how the consciousness of guilt overcame him, and how conscience, that inward monitor, would occasionally be heard, and fill him with alarm.

" Yes, yes; oh, of course," he said, hurriedly; " but still it is annoying to have the feeling that any one is raking up all one's private history, supposing there be nothing in it which one would not cheerfully enough own to."

" It is that, Nicholas; and the more especially when the motive which actuates the inquiries is a bad one."—" Yes, yes; that is how I look at it."

He was, on the whole, rather glad when this interview was over; and now that he saw there really was no other resource but to wait patiently until the day should come round on which he could make Fanny Leslie his own, without her having power to recall the act, he strove to comfort himself with the assurance that Rodwell could find out nothing.

We shall see.

———

CHAPTER LIV.

THE WEDDING MORNING.—LOWE'S COSTUME.—THE CARRIAGE.—THE VISITOR.

THE long expected, anxiously longed-for day has come at last. Yes, that morning has arrived on which Nicholas Lowe is to lead the beautiful, and very probably blushing Fanny Leslie to the altar, and on which Jervis Rodwell is to perform the same ceremony as regards the portly, and not at all blushing widow of the jeweller.

Oh! folly! folly! thy name is an old woman! What on earth, Mrs. Paddlebat, could induce you to dream of trusting your future contentment, to put the stronger term of happiness out of the question, to such a man as Rodwell?

Did your glass not tell you you were old and fat? Did you not remember that the apparently luxuriant crop of auburn hair that hung down each side of that purple-looking face, owed their existence to the ingenuity of a neighbouring barber—we beg his pardon, *artiste de cheveux?*

Mrs. P., Mrs. P., you ought to have known better.

Did Nicholas Lowe sleep that night? Did he feel happy that morning, which is the happiest in a man's life? To the first question, no. To the second likewise, most decidedly, no.

He arose—for he had gone through the farce of going to bed, and had wanted energy to get up again before the morning,—fevered, anxious, and nervous, to an excess, which made it the remark of his own servants.

He could take no breakfast. The mind's deep anxiety destroyed the appetite, as it generally does, and oh, how he wished for that day to be over!

Yet over and over again he asked himself what he had to fear? How could Rodwell find out anything about him? He had no clue, that was quite clear, and all accidents were against him. Besides, was not she who only could be a damning evidence against him, already numbered with the dead—swept away from the face of the earth, and all that concerned her and her story long since consigned to the safe keeping of the silent tomb?

"What have I to fear?" he asked himself; and even as he did so he trembled with an undefined terror, he knew not why.

Nicholas Lowe, Nicholas Lowe, you have somehow missed the right road to happiness, and chosen instead a crooked and a tortuous path, which already you find to be full of thorns and briers.

But there is nothing in all the world which men so much persevere in as in the wrong; it is an idiosyncrasy in human nature, that where there exists a positive perception that a particular path is being pursued, that cannot but end in bitterness and disappointment, people will not turn back.

There is not one man in a million who will retrace his steps to safety, although he sees destruction looming darkly in the perspective before him on the road which he has chosen to traverse.

The thought of making a full, free, and unreserved confidence with Fanny, as the best way of counteracting all the exertions of Rodwell against him, could not but have occurred over and over again to Lowe, and yet he did not do it. Such a plan had everything to recommend it. He could, for there were two ways of telling any story, have taken care to tell his in the way which was least to his disadvantage; and then, had he thrown himself upon her mercy and her affection, ten to one he would have been forgiven.

But now that course was too late; it could not be done now, and he had no resource but to go through with the matter as best he could, trusting to Rodwell having been unsuccessful.

It was at a very early hour that Lowe rose; for although he intended to start from home at nine o'clock, in order to keep his appointment with Fanny Leslie at the church-door, he need not have risen until two hours later than he did.

And how frightfully heavy he found the time lagging upon his hands! How fearfully slow each moment seemed to pass. That three hours, for it was three, seemed lengthened into three days of tormenting anxiety.

After the mockery of sitting down to breakfast, for that was what it was, he went to his room to dress in some extremely handsome apparel, which he had ordered for the occasion.

Nicholas Lowe, take him all in all, was not a bad looking young man, and, despite his extreme anxiety, he could not help casting an approving glance at himself in a glass when he had finished his toilette.

But that was only for a moment. Personal vanity has immense power; but it could not for more than such a space of time check the current of uncomfortable thoughts which, in full tide, had set in upon the brain of that most melancholy and unhappy of all bridegrooms.

A great thing, too, which tended to make him feel more bitterly all the worst chances that might befall him, consisted in the fact that he had no friend with him who would have made an attempt to wean him from some of his anxiety.

And this did not arise from the fact that Nicholas Lowe knew no one on whom he could call for such aid on such an occasion; but he had deliberately secluded himself from any one since the forgery of the will. He had a dread that by some inadvertent expression he should betray himself, and feel compelled to make a confidence which might, even if all else went well, be the bane of his future peace.

He had, therefore, determined upon going alone to the church, and trusting to some of the officials who might be then present, to act in the capacity of father to the bride.

This he knew was a common enough thing for them to do, so it did not cost him a second thought to adopt that resolution at the time when it was adopted; but now that the morning had actually come, he most terribly felt his own loneliness, and almost wished that he had so far trusted some one as to take him to the church with him.

At about half-past eight o'clock, agreeable to arrangement, a handsome carriage drawn by four grey horses drove up to the door of Lowe's house, and then it became apparent to all the neighbourhood that a marriage was on the tapis, and the usual throng of idlers collected on the spot, anxious to obtain a glimpse of the bride or of the bridegroom, as the case might be.

But it would be madness to think of going so soon;—for to have to wait at the village church half-an-hour would be worse than waiting within his own house, so Lowe, with his watch laid before him, waited for the minutes to pass.

Nicholas Lowe had passed some uncomfortable half hours in his life—who has not?--but never one like that. It seemed absolutely interminable.

He sat in his drawing-room. It was a splendid apartment, replete with all that taste could adorn it with, and on a side table ample refreshments were placed, for Lowe intended, after the marriage ceremony had been performed, to bring his wife at once home with him, instead of going through the absurdity of rushing out of town for a month, as people usually do.

He had, therefore, provided a *dejeuner* of a costly character, which he hoped to be able to partake of with his bride when he returned, with something like an appetite. And that return, if all went smoothly off, would be about eleven o'clock. He was to meet Fanny at the church at ten. The ceremony was, by arrangement, to be performed at once, and that, all the world knows, occupies the space of about seven minutes, so that they could then get into the carriage again, and be whisked off to London, fully in time for anything like a fashionable breakfast.

This, then, was the arrangement, and a very good one it was of its kind, and reflected some credit upon Lowe's tact and discrimination.

Time and tide wait for no man, however long a man may be waiting for them; but slowly—surely, though slowly—those moments, which were anything but happy ones, passed, and it came to be within six or seven minutes of the time when Lowe thought of starting, with a conviction that without putting the horses beyond a gentle trot, he should reach the church about five or six minutes only before the time arranged between himself and Fanny.

Strange to say, now a feeling of sudden confidence came over him, and he breathed more freely, as he said,—

"How foolish I have been to allow myself to be made the victim of so many terrors! What have I really to dread? I am as one who makes himself unhappy about the possibilities of existence, when all the probabilities are in his favour, and on the side of happiness. Now I am safe. Another hour and a-half, now, and I can laugh at Rodwell's utmost extent of malice. Let him then find out what he may. The wife will find out that she must excuse what, as the unwedded girl, she need not, unless she willed it."

He swallowed now hastily a couple of glasses of rich wine. He could not eat, but he felt that he required a stimulant. The invigorating liquor danced through his veins like fire, and he laughed at the state of nervousness which now only became a thing of recollection.

He rang the bell, and ordered the carriage to be close to the door, and in instant readiness. Then he wrapped around him a handsome cloak, as well probably to conceal the gaiety of his apparel, as to guard against a certain amount of chilliness which was in the morning air.

All was ready. He had his hat in his hand. He cast a glance of satisfaction round the room, and then he suddenly heard the sound of hasty footsteps on the staircase.

There was a confusion of voices, some apparently in threatening tone, and some in expostulation. Then the drawing-room door was thrown open, and his heart sank within him, as he saw upon the threshold Jervis Rodwell.

CHAPTER LV.

THE LAST INTERVIEW BETWEEN LOWE AND RODWELL.

HAD Nicholas Lowe, some hour or so before, sat down to think what extraordinary circumstance could possibly happen of a character to transcend all probability, he might have said that he could think of none half so extravagant as a visit to him from Jervis Rodwell.

With such a feeling, then, it cannot be wondered at that the sudden entrance of that man, of all others, into his room, staggered almost every faculty of his mind, and for a time deprived him almost of the power of protesting against what was indeed so abominable an intrusion.

At such a time, too, and on such a day, it was doubly, trebly obnoxious. There cannot be a reasonable doubt, but that had Lowe at the moment been possessed of any death-dealing weapon, that moment would certainly have been Jervis Rodwell's last.

They glared at each other, those two rivals in everything, for some few moments in silence, and Lowe could perceive that there was upon the detestable face of Rodwell a look of ill-concealed triumph, which, he imagined, boded him no good.

It was Rodwell who first spoke, but ere he did so, he cautiously closed the drawing-room door behind him, and locking it, he cast the key into the centre of the apartment.

"Now, Nicholas Lowe," he said, "now you will find out, however, at the eleventh hour, it is in my power to foil you."

The thought flashed across Lowe's mind, that now the two insidious attempts to murder him, which Rodwell had made, were about to resolve themselves into a third, which should have all the chances of success about it, on account of the boldness with which it was conceived.

"Villain," he said, "I understand you, but beware. You will find me no easy victim."

"Pho, pho," said Rodwell; "you do not understand me at all. You fancy I come intent upon some plan against your life; but you are much mistaken, I am only the bearer of a little note."

As he spoke, he advanced to the table and threw down before Nicholas Lowe a sealed packet.

Then, folding his arms across his breast, he waited silently for him to read it, while such a smile of devilish exultation sat upon his features, that Lowe, without reading it at all, might well have been sure that it contained a something most damaging to his peace.

He took up the letter with a face as pale as death—he broke the seal, and the envelope in which it was confined fell at his feet.

For a moment the words of the writing seemed to swim before his eyes, and h-was utterly incapable of reading them; then, however, all became in another instant fearfully and frightfully distinct.

The note ran as follows :—

"Nicholas Lowe, you have deceived me. I have but one wish with regard to you—it is that you should forget me.   "FANNY LESLIE."

Lowe uttered a faint groan, and the letter dropped at his feet. He understood it all now—his worst fears were realised. Fanny Leslie had cast him off at once and for ever.

He staggered along the room till he came to a seat, upon which he sank quite unnerved, and with no more strength, at the moment, left him, than might have belonged to a child.

Oh! was not this sport for Jervis Rodwell! He could not conceal his exultation. He clapped his hands together, and he laughed aloud.

"Bravo!" he cried; "bravo!"

"All lost!" groaned Lowe; "all lost!"

"Yes," said Rodwell; "all lost. This is famous. Why, now, as you are more in the listening than in the talking mood, I don't mind telling you how it was I have found out all that you took such pains to keep concealed. The keeper of the lunatic asylum, for a bribe, told me all, and so I kept the matter safe and snug until last night late, when all the proofs of your former intrigue were laid before Fanny Leslie. Behold the result."

Nicholas Lowe look at him as he spoke, as if he only half comprehended what he said.

"Do you understand me?" added Rodwell. "You poor devil, what will become of you now? Ha! ha! Your carriage is at the door—why do you not get into it and drive to the church? Ha! ha!"

Still Lowe said nothing. A strange kind of stupor seemed to have come over him, in which all his faculties were completely engulphed.

"Do you hear?" said Rodwell.

"Oh, yes, yes!"

"Well; and as I have got the better of you now, I will give you a word or two of advice what to do."

"Thank you," said Lowe, with a horrid sort of calmness.

"Ah, but, first of all, let me tell you what Fanny Leslie said."

"Yes, do."

"She said, 'If he had told me all that I now know, himself, from the first, I would have forgiven him.'"

"Did she, indeed?"

"Yes; and so you see how you have outwitted yourself, Nicholas Lowe. What a poor shallow-witted fellow you really are. Ha! ha! ha! It's enough to make any one laugh. Upon my soul, you are well lodged here, too, and smartly dressed as well. Wine as well, at hand! Why, what a merry life you intended to lead, Nicholas Lowe, and what a change it will be to you. Ha! ha! ha!"

"A great change," said Lowe, "for both of us. And so you found out all this affair, which at the last moment has been my destruction."

"I did!"

"And, with a devilish perseverance, you have hunted me to despair."

"I have. You crossed me and my views, so what could you expect? I drink to your better judgment for the future."

With an amount of insolence that only such a man of coarse tastes and habits like Jervis Rodwell could at all have compassed, he poured out some of Nicholas Lowe's wine, and raised the glass to his lips.

"Capital," he said; "capital," as he tossed off the generous liquor, "really capital. Won't you drink?—Well, then, I must do double duty; and now, the toast shall be, better luck to you next time, for I am satisfied."

"And I," said Lowe.

He rose as he spoke, and before Rodwell could have the least idea of what his intention was, he took a long sharp knife from the side table, and buried it up to the very hilt in the right side of his tormentor.

The glass dropped from the palsied hand of Rodwell. He gave a gasping sob, and clutched wildly at the air. Then he sank to the floor, strangely doubled up, and twice he uttered the words,—

"Oh! God—oh! God!"

Nicholas Lowe laid down the knife which he had committed the dreadful deed with on the table from whence he had taken it; and any one who had seen him do so would have thought that he was as calm and as collected as any human being could be who was engaged in some of the most ordinary affairs of life.

He then sat down upon the chair from whence he had risen, and, folding his arms across his breast, even as Rodwell had done a short time before, he looked on, apparently all unmoved, at the struggles of his victim.

And there was Rodwell, writhing in the agonies of a dreadful death, even at that moment when he had considered himself as triumphing over one whom he had chosen to consider his worst foe.

It was a dreadful spectacle. The knife had gone deep into his lungs, and so, whenever he attempted to speak or to scream, for no doubt he essayed the latter, the result only was, that a deluge of blood came from his mouth, and he was nearly choked.

He made the most frantic and terrible efforts to rise, and his struggles upon the floor were of such a dreadful character, that they were heard all over the house—so much so, that a servant came and tapped with his knuckles on the panel of the drawing-room door, thinking that something was the matter.

" All's right," said Nicholas Lowe, in an assumed cheerful tone; " I am not ready yet."

" Thank you, sir," said the servant; " I beg your pardon;" and away he went.

Oh! what a terrific effort Rodwell, during that brief colloquy, made to utter some sound indicative of the fact of his dreadful state. Again the blood came from his mouth in a horrible, sickening gush.

Now he did struggle on to his knees, and he clasped his hands, and held them up, while, with an expression of imploring agony upon his countenance, he looked in Lowe's face, as if beseeching for that mercy he had not himself shown.

But Lowe surely was at that time labouring under some temporary insanity. He sat as calm and still as a statue, and looked on like some old play-goer at a drama of the terrific cast, which affects him not, because he has seen too much of stage delusions, and only looks on with a critical eye to see how artistically the thing is done by the actor.

This was, however, a state of things which could not last long. Rodwell was a murdered man, and the loss of blood he had suffered was momentarily reducing his strength,—he could not last many moments longer. Now, without making any effort to speak, he began to vomit blood from the gorged lungs. Slowly he dropped his hands—his eyes assumed a strange glassy look, and he fell back with a deep and awful groan.

" He is dead," said Lowe, and he rose from the chair on which he had been sitting; " he is dead!"

He stepped into a pool of hot blood. The very atmosphere of that magnificent apartment was now reeking with the horrible effluvium. Blood was everywhere. It lay upon the gaudy carpet—it was splashed upon the silken hangings, and still now it welled forth from the lips of Rodwell, as though it would never cease, but took its source from some fount which was inexhaustible.

Then Nicholas Lowe shuddered, and he reeled like a drunken man as he approached one of the windows of the magnificent drawing-room, and looked into the street.

He knew not why he did so, but there he saw the gay carriage which had been now waiting for so long, to carry him to the church, which he should, he felt convinced, never now look upon again.

There was the idle throng of persons waiting to see him come forth, and the horses were pawing the ground with impatience, while, ever and anon, the postillions would look up towards the house as if wondering at the delay.

Something was said by some one in the throng which produced a general laugh, and Lowe laughed likewise—a strange hideous kind of laugh; and then he withdrew from the window.

His eyes fell upon the corpse. There it lay, its clothing soaking up some of the ensanguined pool in which it reposed. The key of the door, where was that —where was the key?

It took Nicholas Lowe some time to find it, and when at length he did descry it, he found that it lay in the blood almost covered up. But, revolting as the task was, he must lift it from the ground, and he did so. He wiped it and his hands carefully on the rich table cover which was over the centre table, and then he walked to the door, looking askance as he did so upon the horrible spectacle before him.

He turned the key in the lock, and then he took it out, and passing from that room of terror, he carefully locked the door on the outer side, and placed the key in his pocket.

A costly mat was outside the door, and upon that he wiped the blood from his shoes, after which, with a calmness that only the temporary kind of mental hallucination which he must have been in could have given him courage to assume, he descended to the dining-room of the house, which was immediately below the apartment now the receptacle of so harrowing and sickening a spectacle.

"William," he said to a servant whom he met in the passage, "go and discharge the carriage; I shall not want it to-day."

"Not—not want the carriage, sir!"

"Go and discharge the carriage; I shall not want it to-day. Do I not speak plainly?"—"Yes, sir—I—I ——"

"Do as I bid you, and when you have done so, come to me."—"Yes, sir."

Away went the astonished servant to obey his master's orders. There was a great shout in the street when the carriage drove off—a shout which reached the ears of Nicholas Lowe, as he opened an escritoir in the room where he sat, and took from it a check-book of the banking-house where he had placed the money that he had already obtained from old Gilbert, on account.

In another minute William came into the room, and stood waiting the further orders of his master.

"William," said Lowe, "how did I engage you?"—"A month's notice, sir, or a month's money."

"And the other servants you engaged for me, I presume, upon the same terms?" —"Yes, sir."

"Well, then, William, a change has taken place, which induces me to keep no servants. I will pay you all up to-day, and give you two months' wages, provided that within half an hour you are all out of the house."

William looked perfectly amazed, as well he might, and he continued for some few minutes to stare at his master without making any reply.

"Do you not comprehend me?" said Lowe.—"Why, yes, sir, I do, I hope we haven't all of us, or any of us, done anything to make you send us all off in such a way?"

"Had that been the reason," said Lowe, "I should hardly go out of my way to give each of you an extra month's wages as a gratuity."

This was an unanswerable argument, so William ran out of the room to carry the odd news to the rest of the establishment, and he came back in about five minutes, to say that they would all be gone in half an hour.

Of course the impression among them was, that at the last moment the lady to whom Lowe had been about to be married, had turned fickle, and that, as he was to have money with her, he could not carry on the establishment he had so imprudently commenced.

Lowe drew checks for the wages, and one by one the servants left, but William said to another, as they passed through the hall,—

"I say, Thomas, did you shew that gentleman out that came to see master about an hour ago?"—"No; didn't you?"

"Not I."—"Well, that's odd enough, because, you know, you nor I never left the door for a moment, because we expected every minute that master would come down to get into the carriage."

"Well, that's odd. What suppose he's here yet?"—"Then, if he is, he's in the drawing-room. I tried the door as I came down stairs just now, and found it locked."

"You did?"—"Yes; I thought a glass of that old port that was decanted this morning, and what you and I so much approved of, might do me some good."

"And he'd locked it up—well, that was mean! He's a shabby wretch, after all, only to give us two months' wages, when he might as well have made it three, and then it would have looked handsome, being a quarter of a year, you know."

"Ah! to be sure; but I thought what he would turn out. A disagreeable wretch! I'm glad I'm leaving him."—"And so am I."

That was all the good which Nicholas Lowe got for his generosity, in giving a month's more wages than he needed to have done to his servants. In another minute Nicholas Lowe was alone with the dead.

CHAPTER LVI.

THE HIDING OF THE DEAD BODY.—THE FRIGHTFUL TASK.—THE RESOLUTION.

He sat in that parlour, or dining-room as it might more properly be called, absorbed in thought, while such a wrapt stillness reigned throughout the house, that one might have thought that he too belonged to the existences which had been, rather than occupying a place as he still did among living beings.

Oh! who shall hope to tell—what imagination shall conceive, or what pen describe the thoughts of Nicholas Lowe during the two hours which succeeded the departure of his servants, and his being left alone in that house, with the knowledge of the dreadful sight that was in the room above.

How fearfully then did he feel that a retribution of the most terrific character had overtaken him, for the fault he had committed in destroying the happiness of that one being who now slept the calm sleep of death.

What had not that led to! To murder! Yes; he was now a murderer. He had shed man's blood, and he knew the penalty. By man would his blood be shed, if a knowledge of the dreadful deed that he had committed should ever come to light.

He had likewise lost all that he counted upon—all that to him would have invested life with its choicest charms. Oh! what a miserable game had he now played. He had lost her whom he had really loved, and he had lost all his hopes of fortune.

What was to become of him? And how—for that was the most startling question of all—how was he effectually to conceal his crime—that crime which would, if discovered, condemn him to a hideous death upon a scaffold? And soon the mode and manner in which he was to conceal the evidences of the deed which he had done, became his prominent thought.

It cannot be said that at any one moment during all his painful reflections, he felt any actual regret for the death of Rodwell, except in so far as it compromised his own safety. He did certainly wish that he had not done the deed, because he could not but feel what a hazardous one it was for himself; but on Rodwell's account he had no qualms of conscience whatever.

The day wore on, and still Lowe sat thinking—drearily, gloomily thinking over the past, and in deep and anxious reflection for the future.

"The body must be hidden or destroyed," was the repeated assertion he made in a low voice to himself; and then he added, "But how? But how?"

Fearful question. Difficult as well as terrifying to answer; for no scheme suggested itself which did not comprise some actual personal contact with that ensanguined corpse; and Heaven knows how he shrank from that.

But what else could be done? There was no resource. It must be hidden somewhere, and he must hide it. To trust an accomplice—to make any one cognisant of the affair, who, from unscrupulousness and greediness of reward, would help him, would be, in all probability, to entail upon himself, at no distant period, the necessity of another murder, in order to free himself from the danger attending having a confidant in such a matter of vast importance even to his very life.

"No, no," he said, as this idea crossed his mind; "I must trust no one. Horrible as the task may be, I must do it all myself."

He felt conscious, too, that the longer he delayed doing that which ought to be done, if he would preserve now his own existence, the more dangerous would be his situation, and the more revolting would be his task.

"Let there be the slightest whisper that he has been here," thought Lowe, "and then, of course, I shall have the house searched, and what a dreadful discovery will there be made. I must guard against that, and quickly, too."

He rose with a half formed resolution, and walked some distance up the staircase, but his heart failed him, and he descended again, and sat down in the parlour with a deep groan, while a sensation of great sickness and exhaustion came over him.

He found in the escrutoire some powerful spirits, of which he drank enough to have produced intoxication, had he been in an ordinary frame of mind; but it had little effect upon him beyond getting rid of that faintness which he had began to feel, and which, in a short time, had he not counteracted it, would probably have completely made him ill.

Feeling now much more capable of taking some step in the dreadful business than he was before, he first of all carefully fastened the street-door, and closed the dining-room shutters partially, so as to give, without excluding all the light, an impression as much as possible that the house was empty.

Then once more he, with the key—the wards of which were still encrusted with blood—in his hand, slowly ascended the drawing-room stairs.

He stood upon the landing, on that mat on which he had with such elaborate care wiped his blood-stained shoes, and there for more than ten minutes he hesitated, before he could muster courage to turn the key in the lock.

And strange to say, he placed his ear to the door, and listened attentively, before he could open it, as if he feared that the dead might be stirring, or that something evil might be holding revel in that apartment of death.

At length, mustering with some difficulty the necessary amount of nerve to do so, he slowly turned the key, and then, as he opened the door, he drew hastily back, as if he feared a something, he knew not what, might rush out upon him, and clasp him in a hideous embrace.

All was still. A more than natural repose seemed to reign throughout the house. The very stillness of the grave appeared to have taken possession of that place which had become the abode of the dead. It looked as if the very presence of that body of the murdered man had a subduing effect even upon the noise made by the wheels of the vehicles, which now and then rolled past the house.

With quite a desperate sort of energy it was that Nicholas Lowe crossed the threshold of the room, and then he again looked upon all that remained of Jervis Rodwell.

The body lay upon its back, as it had last fallen over. One leg was doubled up under him, for he had, it will be recollected, been upon his knees when the death pang came upon him.

The hands were stretched out as far as the arms would permit, and upon the face, which, somehow or another, caught a glare of white reflected light from a mirror, there was a horrible expression of agony. One of the eyes had partially closed, but that circumstance only seemed to impart a more horrible expression to the other, which appeared to be looking in the face of Lowe, as he stood by the body, with a horrid and altogether indescribable expression.

"Good God—good God!" was all that, for many minutes, Nicholas Lowe could say, and then he looked down at his feet, and found that the blood, which had flowed about in such abundance, had, as it had cooled, become thick and coagulated, and was sticking to his feet as he there stood.

"Horrible—horrible!" he groaned, and he tottered to a chair, upon which he sank in a perfect agony of horror.

But he could not, for one moment, take his eyes off the dreadful spectacle—no, not for one moment. Any one, to have seen the manner in which he regarded it, would have thought he must have had lingering in his mind some supposition that, if he withdrew his eyes, even for a moment, it might rise, dabbled with gore as it was, and spring upon him for vengeance.

Now he began to wonder if any of the opposite windows, belonging to the houses of his neighbours, commanded a view into that drawing-room. It was something most full of apprehension to think of the possibility of such a danger, and it almost enabled him to withdraw his eyes a moment from the dead body.

With a sidelong motion, he approached the windows one by one, and pulled down the holland blinds, which, of course, effectually excluded any prying eyes from discovering what he was about.

Then he glanced around the room, to think of how he was to carry out the halfformed plan for the concealment of the body of Rodwell, which had found a place in his imagination while he was seated in the room below.

This plan was a strange one. He had fully considered the difficulty, as well as the dreadful nature of the task of taking up the dead body and carrying it anywhere down to the lower part of the house to conceal it ; and, therefore, he had thought over the possibility of hiding it in the very room where the deed had been committed.

The only way he considered in which this could be done, was to pull up one or two of the floor boards, and cram it in between the roof of the room below and the joists that supported it.

This scheme had the one recommendation, at all events, that it avoided the necessity of removing the body, and hence it presented itself to his mind in something like attractive colours, and he resolved to attempt it.

He moved the centre table up into a corner of the large and handsome apartment, and then he commenced at one of the walls, dragging up the costly carpet, which was now so completely, to the greater part of its extent, soaked in gore. This he succeeded in doing, and rolled it up for some distance ; but the most difficult part of the task was to raise the floor boards.

To accomplish this he was compelled to leave the room, in search of some tool which would enable him to do it, and he crept down the staircase with all the caution and noiselessness, as if he were really afraid of awakening some one.

He had reached the hall, and was about to turn an angle of the staircase, so as to go to the kitchen, where he thought he should likely find something to answer his purpose in taking up the floor boards, when a heavy knock at the street door startled him, by its suddenness, to such an extent, that he gave a loud cry of alarm, and had to clutch the balustrades for support.

"What shall I do?" he said—"what shall I do? Who can that be? Good Heaven! am I discovered? Has any one suspected what has happened?"

Again the knock came, and this time it was promptly followed by a ring at the area bell, which jarred as painfully upon the nerves of Nicholas Lowe as the knock had previously done. Had he really wished to proceed at once to the door and open it, he could not, at the moment, have commanded physical energy sufficient to enable him to do so, and the knock and the ring came a third time, before he thought of what he was to do. Then he went down to the kitchen, and opening the door which led into the area, he walked out and looked up.

There was a man upon the door-step, and Lowe, after looking at him well, in order to come to some opinion as to whether or not he was a police-officer in disguise, called to him, saying,—

"What is it—what do you want here?"

"Oh, you have come, have you?" said the man. " I want to know if you are provided here with a milkman? because, if you ain't, there's my card, and I can only say that the best article at the ——The devil! what a rage he's in. Gone in again, has he? Well, it's quite clear after this, that I shall get no custom here ; so d—n me, here goes !"

The infuriated milkman executed such a peal of knocks upon the door, that the whole street was alarmed, and then he rung the bell till the house echoed again with the sound.

What a desire for vengeance against that man came over the heart of Nicholas Lowe, as he was thus gratuitously rendered dreadfully nervous, and felt conscious that the attention of every one who happened to be passing, as well as of the whole street, must be directed to his house. And yet, what could he do? There he was, compelled to endure any amount of insolence, because of the dreadful circumstances in which he happened to be placed.

He waited until the noise had subsided, and then, with all his nerves more shaken than before by this accident, he once more searched for some implement with which to complete his up-stairs piece of work. He found a saw, a hammer, and a long chisel, so that he was well enough provided, and then again he returned to the scene of blood.

He found that, before he could succeed in getting up any of the flooring of the room, it would be necessary to remove the skirting-board next to the wall, and he found that, by the aid of his chisel, he could easily do so. A long piece of it came away with a very small amount of force, and in another minute he had wrenched up one of the floor boards. The first step in this case was all the difficulty; another and another quickly followed, and he found that there was space enough in which, with a little cramming, he could surely hide the body of Rodwell.

And now came the horrible task of dragging the loathsome remains of his enemy to the receptacle he had prepared for them, and he sickened and shook, like one wrestling with death, as he stooped over the noxious object, and laid a hand upon part of the clothing. The weight of the corpse, though, was almost too much to allow it to be thus dragged along, and he was compelled to go to the other side of it, and, with his foot, propel it towards the place where he intended it should henceforward remain.

When he afterwards thought of the dreadful proceedings of that day, how much he wondered that he had been ever able to go through them, and more particularly that part which he was now about.

There is many a man who can take a life, but few who, with nerves not unstrung, can, after death has claimed his victim, visit and handle the sad remains of him whom they have hurried to eternity. And so, indeed, most truly did Nicholas Lowe feel that it was easier by far to murder Jervis Rodwell, than it was to hide the ghastly and terrific evidences of the deed of blood.

Nothing in the world but a strong conviction that it was absolutely necessary for his own safety that the dead body should be immediately removed, could have nerved him with power to execute the dreadful task.

And now slowly the horrid mass of blood and death rolled over, and fell partially into the hollow between the joists. But the space was too narrow, and much of the body projected above the level of the flooring.

Nicholas Lowe hesitated for a moment, and then he pressed it down with his foot. He could do the deed in no other way. He must use feet or hands to the troublesome task, and much he preferred, consequently, the former to the latter.

And now all was accomplished, except replacing the floor boards, and that part of the operation he was quite willing to do with all possible celerity, inasmuch as they hid the terrible spectacle that was beneath.

A few moments sufficed to cover up the dead. He replaced the long piece of skirting-board which he had been compelled to remove, and then once again he dragged the heavy, rich carpet into its place. The table, too, was slowly rolled upon its castors over the spot where lay the body, and then Nicholas Lowe, as he wiped from his brow the heavy drops of perspiration, felt some sensation of comparative ease.

He glanced at himself in the costly glass that occupied the whole of one end of the apartment, and then he started to observe the awful change which the agony and the anxiety of the last six hours had made upon him. Ten years of ordinary existence could not have produced so great an effect. He looked, positively, old, pale, and ghastly.

"Can this be possible," he muttered, "that in so short a space of time the mind can exercise such an influence upon the body? or is this only the effect of temporary fatigue and temporary excitement, and, as such, calculated to wear away again?"

Again he glanced around that costly and luxurious apartment, and it was with a shudder that he noted those objects which, at their first appearance there, had so delighted him by their richness and their beauty.

"How hateful," he said, "will all this place be to me now, and how full of horrible recollections. Already the rich gilding seems tainted with the colour of blood, and I shall always scent gore in the very atmosphere of the place."

He remained for some time in deep thought, and then, suddenly, he spoke again

"Yes—yes," he said; "I am decided. The house I dare not leave, because, if I were to do so, any new occupant would soon discover what a ghastly and terrific guest shared it with them. The remains would be recognised, and the scaffold would be prepared for me. No—no; I dare not, now, leave here. I must remain to keep my lonely watch upon the dead, at all events, so long as until I can assure myself that decomposition has sufficiently done its work to render my position not so hazardous. What, now, if I were to burn down the house?"

This was an idea which, when first it struck him, seemed to be one feasible enough, but, the more he considered it, the more he shrunk from it as uncertain in its effect, and full of danger. It was not likely, if he set fire to the place, that the existence of the conflagration could be for many minutes kept a secret; and then, what if the exertions which were made to subdue the flames should be successful? Of course, that would be his destruction; for would not strange people rush into the house, and might not all be discovered?

"No, no," he muttered, "that will not do. It might suffice, if I were sure of the annihilation of the whole structure. If I could make certain of the house being burnt down to its very foundation, and all within it reduced to ashes; but, upon such a result I dare not attempt to calculate."

There was, then, positively no other resource but to remain and watch the place, so as to prevent the possibillity of any one else becoming possessed of it. But still, why need he, if he even keep watch and ward in the house for a year or more, ever terrify his imagination by visiting that room? There certainly could be no occasion for his doing so, not the least.

"I will close the door of this apartment," he said to himself; "it shall be carefully locked, so that there shall be no chance of any one visiting it; and, as I am not likely to do so, the key can be hidden in some place of security known only to myself."

This resolution was decided upon the moment it occurred to him. It was too much in accordance with the then state of his feelings to be long hesitated about, so he at once proceeded to the windows, and closed and barred the shutters.

Then he left the apartment, and double-locking the door on the outside, he said,—

"Farewell, Rodwell, I hope for ever."

He crept softly up stairs to his bed-room, and then it took him an hour, or more, to wash carefully from his boots and hands all traces of blood. The water he carried to the lower part of the house, and poured it down a sink, so that, except in that room which he had closed, there were no evidences of the dreadful deed that had been done.

It was getting dusk, now, and Lowe felt fearfully nervous at the idea of the night setting in. He thought that if he could get over the first night, all would be well, and that he should be able to endure, with more composure, the time that was to come.

But he certainly did view, with a shrinking horror, the idea of lying down to sleep alone in that house with the man whom he had murdered.

And yet, what else could he do? Was it likely that his apprehensions would allow him to sleep anywhere else?

"No, no," he groaned, "terrific as my sufferings may be here, they would be far greater elsewhere, for I should never be free for one moment from the apprehension that some one was breaking into this house, and making a discovery of that which I have taken such pains to hide."

We cannot but give Lowe some credit for a great amount of courage and resolution in passing the night at all there. It is not enough to enable a man to do any particular act, that he feels the necessity of it; and although Nicholas Lowe might be fully aware that, beyond all question, his best plan was to remain in the house, he might have been very far, indeed, from able to do so.

But he did. He went to the kitchen, and he collected all the candles he could find, and set half a dozen of them up in the dining-room. There was some sort of safety and consolation to his mind in having plenty of light.

And there he sat with wine before him, of which he drank liberally, although, in the still excited state of his feelings, it seemed as if it would have been impossible, let him take what quantity he might, to have produced the ordinary effects of intoxication.

There are sudden mental shocks which have been known to sober men in a moment; and no doubt there are states of mind which prevent wine from producing its wonted effects upon the system.

How these mysterious sympathies between the mind and the body are produced, it would be foreign to our object to inquire, suffice it, that there can be no doubt, from abundance of experience, that they do exist.

Lowe drank at first cautiously, for he dreaded taking too much, and so, perchance, inducing some indiscretion that might be fatal to him; but when he found that the liquor took very little effect upon him, but slightly warmed the life blood in his veins, he partook of it more freely, and likewise got from the lower part of the house some refreshment of a solid kind, of which he partook, endeavouring all the while, as much as he could, to withdraw his mind from a too minute consideration of the proceedings of the day.

And yet, was it likely, or possible, that the important matters which that day of expectation, of horror, and of bitterness, had given rise to, could, for one moment, be absent from his imagination?

No, no; he felt that he had now objects of contemplation presented to his mind's eye while he lived. He felt that, let his future career be as successful or as varied as it might, he should ever have present to him the proceedings of that dreadful day.

And now he thought of Fanny Leslie, who was lost to him for ever; and, for the first time, he told himself that he had really loved her.

"Oh, what a fate is mine!" he groaned; "unhappy in the only two attachments I ever made; the second avenging to the full upon me the first. Why did I ever dream or hope to emerge from the plodding state to which fortune appeared to have consigned me? Why did I assist that man Gilbert Paddlebat to grasp at wealth, so small a moiety of which has reached me?"

He leant his head upon his hands, and reviewed with that rapidity with which the mind can recal the busy scenes of the past, the whole of his life. Every incident marshalled itself before him, in the plainest colours, until he came to the consideration that Rodwell had twice attempted his life.

That remembrance came like balm over his wounded soul, and he said,—

"I have but killed the man who would have done as much for me; nay, who tried his utmost, in the most cold-blooded and deliberate manner, to take my life. It is but self-defence—it is but self-defence, after all."

This was a poor argument to justify a murder, but yet, to a man in Lowe's position, any slight argument—like a straw to the drowning wretch who has nothing more tangible to grasp at—was sure to afford some relief.

He felt that if he could now thoroughly convince himself that it was only in self-defence—that most sacred right of human nature—that he had slain Rodwell, he should be restored to his serenity; but the task of imposing upon himself so shallow an argument, he found most wonderfully difficult, and soon he relapsed into his former state of despondency.

He thought that if he sat up until downright weariness took possession of him without his making the least attempt to go to sleep until that state of things should ensue, he should have a better chance of tasting the sweets of repose, than as if he courted it before such bodily exhaustion brought the feeling on him.

And so he sat in that dining-room another hour or two, listening now and then to the chance footfall of some passenger who passed the house, and more than once going to the door of the dining-room to listen if all was still within the precincts of the mansion.

What did he expect to be moving there? Had he been asked the question, he must have answered that he did not know; and yet he could no more have got rid of the feeling, than he could of the memory of the deed he had committed. He sat at a table which was near to the window, while the large dining-table that was in the centre of the apartment had upon it the wine and refreshment which he had provided himself with, as well as several of the candles which he had lighted.

A chandelier depended from the ceiling of this apartment, and the candles that were on the table below it caused it to cast strange and grotesque shadows upon the walls and the ceiling.

All was as still as the very grave, and Nicholas Lowe thought that he would lean back in the capacious easy chair in which he sat, and, perchance, go to sleep, when a noise attracted his attention, and in an instant awakened every faculty to the utmost stretch. It came upon his ears so suddenly, and was over again so quickly, that it had not a sufficiently defined character about it to enable him to come to any hypothesis concerning it. That it was in the room, he could not doubt. It seemed as if some one had given the table which occupied the centre of the apartment, a slight tap with a finger nail.

Nicholas Lowe had sprung to his feet the moment the sound reached him, and he glared around the room with terror-stricken eyes, while he trembled in every limb, and felt as if his life was going from him.

"What—what," he gasped; "what was that?"

The sound of his voice died away again, and all was still. He drew a long breath, and, after a few moments more of fearful observation of the apartment, he sank into the chair again, as he muttered,—

"Nothing—nothing. It was nothing—only imagination. I might have been on the verge of sleep, and so imagined the sound, which had no real existence. And besides, it is common for furniture to make such sounds, as alteration of temperature takes place. How foolish of me to be alarmed at such a trifle."

But still he was alarmed, and very much alarmed, too, for all that. He did, now and then, close his eyes, but it was only for a moment. A dread of something being in the room caused him to open them again, and look around him with a scared expression. Oh, what a night of exquisite misery that was to Nicholas Lowe!

About a quarter of an hour, or so, might have elapsed, and he had got rid of much of his terror, when suddenly, just as he had closed his eyes, and actual sleep was stealing over him, the mysterious tap upon the table came again. As before, it thrilled through every nerve of his system; and, as before, he sprung to his feet on the instant.

There could be no mistake now. Twice, imagination could not play him such a trick. The sound was a reality, let it be what it might. And yet he saw nothing; all, as before, was profoundly still. He, and he alone, was the occupant of that apartment; at least, as he told himself, he was the only visible occupant of it.

Sleep now was completely out of the question, and he was thrown fearfully back upon his imagination, to find a solution for the mysterious sound that had now twice disturbed his repose.

"God of heaven!" he moaned; "what can it be?"

It was not like the sort of sound caused by the creaking of furniture; but it was a clear, distinct tap upon the dining-table; ay, as defined and clear as if he had deliberately himself walked up to it, and done it with one of his fingers.

The dreadful thought came across him, that he should never be permitted to sleep again; but that, whenever he attempted to do so, he should be aroused by that strange sound, and so that his life would become a burthen to him.

We cannot wonder, situated as he, Nicholas Lowe, then was, and having passed through what he had, that he should be affected with such a strange fancy. It was a terrible one to think of; but he knew himself a murderer, and how could he tell what form Heaven's vengeance might take?

Now, he made up his mind that he would not make the least attempt to speak; but that he would carefully watch for a renewal of the sound. He accordingly laid his watch down on the table before him, and being thoroughly aroused, he kept his eye on the alert, so that not the shadow of anything could move without his detecting it.

A quarter of an hour or rather more, again elapsed, and then tap came the sound again upon the dining-table, but he could see nothing. By a great effort, he walked to that part of the table from which the sound proceeded, and then he found a horrible solution of the mystery.

Immediately beneath the lowest point of the ornaments that adorned the chandelier, there was a little pool of blood upon the table. The gore from the body of Rodwell, which was just above, had found its way through the ceiling, and trickling in a hideous stream down the chandelier, was now falling drop by drop with that terrifying sound, upon the hard-polished surface of the table.

Nicholas Lowe saw that this was the state of the case in a moment. What to do he knew not, and after, with a bewildered aspect, regarding the effect for some moments, he blew out all the candles but one, and snatching that up, he rushed from the room, nor stopped until he gained his own chamber on the second floor of the house, in which he immediately locked himself.

"Haunted—haunted!" he said. "I am every way now haunted by blood! Oh! who would have supposed, that, in any human being, there resided such an enormous amount of that dreadful fluid!"

Sleep now, for some time, was out of the question. He flung himself upon a chair, and seizing the book which he had before found a temporary relief from the perusal of, he did to some extent succeed in withdrawing his mind from the fearful realities of his life, by plunging into the realms of fiction.

He read as follows :—

The loud howling of the wind, and the roar of the terrific thunder claps that every now and then sounded through he heavens, making the welkin ring with horrible sounds, caused the earth to feel as though it vibrated with the shock of the contending elements, which seemed as though on this night, they would destroy the space they occupied.

Occasionally, broad and bright flashes of lightning spread through the dark masses of clouds that hung over the south, and showed for a moment the scene that was below. The country for miles round might be seen with great distinctness for a moment, and then all was again enveloped in the most complete darkness.

It was during one of these momentary flashes, which, for an instant, illumined the earth for miles, that a traveller, attended by one servant, could be seen travelling along the road, which here led within a short distance of the river, the banks of which were rocky and precipitous, and ran in some places to a great height, and even mountainous.

The noise of the rushing waters, too, came upon the ear, and added to the horrors of the scene, which nothing could surpass. The tumult was indescribable; to have seen the water would have caused any one to shrink back, as the bubbling and boiling mass rushed forward, with the white foam hurrying and eddying onwards with the sound of a cataract.

The rocky sides of the current every now and then were washed by an accumulated mass of water or waves, with a sound that made the traveller think the river had broken bounds, and was about to sweep all away before it.

Then the thunder which followed each flash, came leaping and cracking through the air, as though the vaults of heaven would split by the tremendous report that followed.

On the one hand was the open country, laid out in vineyards and much wood; while, on the other hand, were the precipitous rocks that formed the banks of the river, while, on the summit of these, stood an ancient and solid pile of buildings known as the Castle.

This building, at once strong and extensive, was owned by the descendant of a long line of barons; the whole race had been warriors of some note in their day, and even now the present baron had been engaged in more than one feud, though, at the same time, he had also led his vassals to the battle-field, where he had earned both favour and renown; but it was well known that he was fierce and lawless.

It was towards the castle occupied by this baron, that the traveller and servant were making their way as well as they could, and now the rain fell in torrents. A sudden flash of lightning now showed them they were on the rocky road, close to the bank of the river, and that close at their feet ran the furious torrent of water. For a moment the traveller drew his bridle and paused; he was almost blinded by the vividness of the flash, that showed him the danger below.

"Fritz," he said, after a pause, as the servant rode up to his side. "Fritz—Fritz."—"I am here, captain," said the servant, touching his hat in a military salute.

"This is a dark and dismal night. I never remember such a night as this."—"I have seen one such, and only one, captain; but what do you intend to do, not remain here all night, I suppose, nor travel till we find our way into the river?"

"Do you know the road, Fritz?"—"Yes, captain, I do know the road, and a very beautiful road it is usually considered by those who travel by daylight in good company, and in the summer months."

"But now, Fritz, that is the question; what kind of travelling are we likely to encounter, between this and the next house, where we can put up for the night?"

"It is near, or, perhaps, more than two hours' riding to the next place where we can stop, captain, and even when we get there, I doubt if they will take us in at such an hour at night."

"Indeed, our case is desperate, unless we can obtain shelter before we reach there. Suppose we try the castle, yonder, which the lightning showed us not a minute since."

"As you please, captain; it is only necessary to give your orders, and Fritz is here to obey them."

"I know you are a faithful, tried servant, and can trust you implicitly; but you know more of these parts than I do, and can best say what chance of shelter we may find, if we apply at yoncastle."

"They say the old baron is a churlish customer; but he would not refuse you the rights of hospitality. But there are two things it is as well to avoid in the company of hese barons on the river banks."

"And what are they, Fritz?" inquired the captain.

"Not to play with them, nor appear to have any jewels or money, for they are avaricious, and care but little for cutting a man's head off provided they have a reason for so doing in the shape of valuables."

"Then I am safe upon that score; for you know I have but very little in purse or in prospect. However, we will push on, for hark, how the rain falls, and the river rushes! It makes one quite chilly to listen to it."

They now rode on at a brisk pace on a hard road, as they could tell by the sound of their horses' hoofs as they struck the rocky soil.

"The road now narrows," said Fritz; "but one can go abreast here, sir, and the road has been made so on purpose, because the way should be more difficult of approach than it would otherwise be. This road is commanded by the towers that are built on either side of this path at its end."

"How do we enter the castle?"

"Under a large gateway, guarded by a drawbridge, and portcullis. The castle is considered to be perfectly impregnable when well garrisoned; as but one man can approach it at once, and he can be knocked over from the castle with ease and safety to the defenders."

"That is but a poor consolation at all events; but the place must be worth looking at. Push on, Fritz. Diable! what a deluge of rain! I will dismount, or I shall be blown over, horse and all. I have no mind to feed the fishes, and shall take care of myself."

"The precaution is a good one," said Fritz. "I have known a man blown over before to-day. Poor fellow, he's been dead and gone many a day."

Fritz himself dismounted, and led the way, until they came to the drawbridge, when Fritz stopped, but could not speak for some time, such a horrible noise did the thunder, wind, and dashing stream below create, that he could not make himself heard, and when he did, he said,—

"Do not move, the drawbridge is up, captain, and there is a hole that will let you down some three or four hundred feet in the shallow water, and on the sharp broken rocks, forming the bed of the river."

It may be imagined that the traveller required no further caution, but stood still enough. There was, however, a horn hung within reach to a post, and this Fritz unhung, and applied it to his lips, at the same time he produced a loud and discordant tone, that sounded dismally in the storm, but was soon swept away.

"Do you think that will reach the warder's tower?" inquired his master.—"I can hardly say, but I strongly suspect it will not; but I'll wait until there is a lull in the wind, or a partial lull, at all events."

"That will not be yet awhile, Fritz," said the captain; "for I never stood in such a wind, or such a storm before."—"I have, sir."

"So you said but a short while since. On what occasion was that, eh, Fritz?" —"I will tell you, sir, while we wait here; but first I'll give another wind before I begin."

He did wind the horn, and this time produced a shriller note, which seemed to fill the air, and before Fritz could begin, a light appeared at the watch tower. A gateway was thrown open, and the warder appeared, and called out in a hoarse voice to know who wound the horn.

"A traveller," replied Fritz, "begs the hospitality of the castle on such a night as this."

"It is a fierce night," replied the warder. "How many are there? Will you tell me?"—"Two: a traveller, and his servant."

"I will return in a short while, when I have acquainted my master of your wants."

So saying he went in, and they were left to themselves, standing in a somewhat perilous position, for the pathway that ran up to the castle was on a point of the rock near the drawbridge, higher, and more exposed than any other part about it, save on the turrets of the castle; and the wind was so powerful that they could hardly stand, neither could they see, it was so dark.

Indeed, when the lightning came, they could for a short time see all around them. But the brilliant illumination showed them but the accumulated horrors that surrounded them, and the dangers they were exposed to.

"By Jupiter, Fritz, I'd much sooner mount a breach, or lead the hope, than stand here for two hours."—"It's much worse, in my opinion, than an eight hours' drill," said Fritz. "But I hope we may not have to travel back again. It would be better to lie down, and take our chance till daylight."

"Don't speak of it—it would be truly diabolical! It would require superhuman strength to endure it! But there, the door opens, and the warder is coming to us. What does he mean by going there?"

"He's going to let the drawbridge down; that is a sign that we shall get in, sir, and warm quarters too, I hope, for I am like a rat that's been just pulled out of the river."

"Ay, Fritz; I am just as bad. But stand clear, down comes the drawbridge a dreadful bang. Why, if you were too near it would brain you."—"And leave me food for crows in the morning."

All further conversation was stayed by the lowering of the drawbridge, and then the warder shouted to them to come across. This invitation was joyfully obeyed, and they were soon safely within the shelter of the castle walls; their horses were taken from them, and they were desired to enter the guard-room, where they found a large and blazing fire—a most welcome sight to them.

"Well, comrade," said one of the guard, who were lounging about, "come near the fire. You'll have need of it, I expect. I never saw such a night as this before."

"Nor I," said Fritz, "but once ; and never wish to see such another.   I shall never forget it."

"You knew another such a night as this? and pray when was that ?   You don't seem to be a very old man—much younger than I am—and yet I cannot remember the time when such a night as this ever happened."—"I was serving against the Turks, comrade, and ——"

"Against the Turks! did you serve against them?" inquired the man, in surprise. —"Yes, I did ; and there I remember such a night as this, or rather worse. You see I was on duty, as sentinel, on the castle walls.   There were double sentinels posted that night, it was so dark, and so many sounds were heard, that it was difficult to say what they were.

"I and my comrade walked backwards and forwards on our post for some time. We tried to converse, but we could only do so by shouting, and then we left off. The wind howled and blew, and the lightning flashed, whilst the heavens seemed to be rent, and the reverberation of the thunder sounded so terrifically, that we could feel the shock.

"Then came a sudden gush of wind, so strong, so furious, that I never saw anything like it.   I was on about a yard before my comrade, when I heard a cry.   I had just reached an angle of the wall, which sheltered me.   I turned round, and saw him whirled through the air like a piece of straw, and carried some hundreds of yards away."

"It was a fearful night, comrade."

"So it was ; and that night had been chosen by the Turks to make an assault upon the place, and to endeavour to carry it.   Now my comrade was thrown upon an advancing column of men, who were not a little surprised at this kind of missile being employed.

"However, the first moments of surprise over, on they came, and revealed their forms to me in the next flash of lightning that came, and I gave the alarm."

"Did they succeed in the assault, comrade?"

"No ; we were prepared for them, and that they did not expect ; for they had not heard our movements and they came on in perfect security, and were nearly all destroyed."

There was now some stir, and after the traveller had changed his wet garments for others, the captain was invited to the baron's table, to which he was conducted, and then introduced under the designation of Captain Frederick von Herbon.

"Welcome Captain von Herbon," said the baron, with a condescending familiarity.   "Brave men are always welcome in the castle, and I only regret that I have not accommodations befitting them ; but such as are here you are heartily welcome to, as long as you please to stay."

"Thanks, baron. A far less comfortable and hospitable shelter would be welcome on such a night as this.   It is truly terrific ; I never saw its fellow."—"I never heard one like it," said the baron, "save one."

"Save one?" said the captain,—"Yes; and that was five-and-thirty years ago ; but that is a legend connected with the only apartment that can be prepared for your reception."

"Never mind that," said the captain.   "I wear a sword, and I have worn it on the battle-field.   I fear no mortal foe, and as for the others, I have no faith in them. But first may I crave of you the favour, that, as I have to be at a particular hour on parade, I may leave the castle one hour before daylight, as duty and not inclination compels me."

"I will excuse you, captain.   I know that duty—military duty—is imperative. —"It is imperative, and I set my troop an example of it. Were it otherwise, I could but with an ill grace exact it from them."

"That is true ; but now to supper, and my daughter will grace the board, and make you welcome."

The lovely Geraldine now came in.   She greeted the traveller with embarrassed courtesy, and blushed.   The captain was polite and easy ; but when their eyes met, there was a greater degree of intelligence beamed therefrom than might reasonably have been expected in strangers. The table groaned beneath the cheer of the baron, who was anxious to tell his story; and when the cloth was cleared, and the hock placed on, he began :—

"I was about to tell you of a singular occurrence that happened full five and thirty years ago—it occurred to my unfortunate grandmother."

"She was a very beautiful woman, and an amiable one too, which made her loss the more sensibly felt. The room where you will sleep in, formed the

extreme angle of a wall, on which she used to walk, and view the course of the river for many miles around; here she would sit for hours, to enjoy the beauties of the landscape."

"Well, one day, the sun-set was very beautiful, but portentous; he sat in a mass of deep heavy clouds, that came up with surprising quickness; the glories of the sun-set were quickly eclipsed, and my grandmother sat watching the effect of the clouds; when, suddenly, arose such a hurricane, that it swept her over the wall, into the foaming torrent below, where she was dashed to pieces, upon the pointed rocks in the bed of the river."

" Poor lady !" said the captain.

" Yes, she was suddenly cut off in her prime. I would that she had never sat there, but it was her fate, and, poor lady, she suffered."

" And the room ?"

" Was built over the spot, a sort of guard-room ; which was always kept as a sleeping apartment, in case any sudden emergency should arise—such as the present—as that is always kept ready for immediate use."

" Was the lady's body recovered ?" inquired the captain.

" Never. She was searched for in vain by the baron, down the stream for many miles ; and the river was examined by boats ; every hole explored and dragged ; but all to no purpose, the body was not found."

" It is said," remarked the baron, with some hesitation, " it is said, that during the raging of such storms as these, she sometimes visits these walls, especially the part where they have built this room."

" Then she may come on such a night as this," remarked the captain, thoughtfully.

" She may, but I never saw her, though some pretend to have done so," replied the baron.

" Well, should I do so," replied the captain, " I shall not fear the presence of the gentle spirit of such a lady, I shall believe myself the more favoured."

The baron made no reply, but pushed the bottle round, and drank deep himself. Conversation assumed a general tone, until at length the captain said :—

" Baron, I have to quit your hospitable roof an hour before day-break, will you permit me to retire ? Time wears away ; I thank you for your hospitality.

" It is welcome, especially so, to such as you ; to those who defend their country's tegrity against a foreign foe. You have my good wishes, captain."

Bidding adieu to the baron and his lovely daughter, the captain retired to a handsome apartment which had been built to commemorate such a sad event of which the baron had spoken. When he reached his room he sat down, but not to sleep, and when Fritz came to him, he said :—

" I have seen her, Fritz."

" And so have I, sir ; and she remembered me, for she gave me this letter to give to you."

The captain snatched it out of his hands, and read the contents ; and then he said :—

" Which is the western tower, Fritz ?"

" The one at the end of this wall, and there is a door opening into it ;" said Fritz.

" Then I must go there and see her—she wishes to speak with me—I was sure of it ; she never could have forgotten her promise, and this confirms me."

" Lord ! captain," said Fritz, " you'll never go."

" And why not, Fritz ?"

" Because I am told the ghost of a lady rides upon the storm, and sweeps people off."

" You cannot believe such stuff, surely."

" I can, and do, captain ; and, moreover, I know the wind is strong enough to carry any man off the wall, for well I remember it was just such a night as this when my comrade was blown over on the sands."

" Ah, well, blown over or not, Fritz—ghost or no ghost—meet Geraldine I must."

" Well, captain, as you please ; I'll do what you order me, captain."

" Do you fear to follow me, and help the lady along, for I intend quitting the castle before day-break."

" It will be difficult on such a night as this, but I am ready at all times to face danger in obedience to orders."

The captain and Fritz proceeded along the wall until they came to the door in the house. On the outside Fritz remained stationed, to see that no one approached, and to give notice if they did; while his master went in to meet the lady whose love he had won.

What took place has never been ascertained; but in less than an hour they came out, wrapped up ready for travelling, and the captain had her secured by passing his arms round her waist; and when he came out, he said to Fritz :—

" Fritz, take hold of me, and stand on the other side of the lady; our united weight will render it impossible to be blown over the wall. It will make us more secure, and there is a lull in the wind, now, if we can get over quickly."

They immediately moved swiftly along the wall, until they had gone over nearly two-thirds of the distance, when the wind again arose; and, with it a shriek so piercing and shrill, that it pierced their ears and caused them involuntarily to stop; and, in a moment afterwards the form of a female became visible to them with her long dishevelled hair streaming on the wind, her temples all bedaubed with blood, and her long robes flowing around her.

" Oh, God! 'tis the spirit of the storm—my great grandmother; we are lost, we are lost ! "

In the confusion of the moment they relaxed their holds of each other. The wind came on again with increased fury, and they were swept away, with shrieks so piercing, that the whole of the inhabitants of the castle were woke up.

     *   *   *   *   *

There was, some years afterwards, to be seen in the city of Cologne, a cripple; he had been a soldier; but, how no one knew—he had every limb in his body broken, and set awry. This was Fritz, the only one who escaped total annihilaton on that awful night. He had crawled away, and got cured at a peasant's.

Lowe laid down the book with a deep sigh, and reclining partly upon his bed, while he still sat upon the chair, which was close to the side of it, sleep closed his eye-lids, and for a time, he did forget that ever such a man as Rodwell had lived and died.

Happy would it have been for him, Lowe, if that sleep could have been changed during its continuance, into the sleep which knows no waking. But it was not so to be. He has yet a part of some importance to play in the busy drama of existence. Yet, has Nicholas Lowe something to do which shall paint a moral, and adorn a tale.

CHAPTER LVII.

MRS. PADDLEBAT'S DISAPPOINTMENT.—THE CONDUCT OF FANNY LESLIE.—WOMAN'S DEVOTIONS.—THE LETTER TO NICHOLAS LOWE.

WE may now leave Nicholas Lowe with some degree of feeling, for the situation into which he has plunged himself; a situation which, while it entails upon him abundance of pains and penalties, we cannot help to some extent, pitying.

You may, for he fears our exertions in any way to attempt to palliate the dreadful crime of which he has been guilty. Murder is, at the best, most foul, but even in that crime, hideous as it is under any circumstances whatever to contemplate, there are degrees of comparison; for example, Lowe's murder of Rodwell, impulsively as the deed was done, was not one half so bad as would have been the murder of Lowe by Rodwell, in the cold-blooded, systematic, deliberate manner in which he, with the air-gun, had endeavoured to accomplish that deed. For some one can truly and safely say, that the thought to do the deed, and the execution of it, occupied the same space of time, so that it could not be called a deliberate murder, and we may, from our knowledge of the manner in which he was goaded to the act, gather a still further palliation of the deed. Yet still a murder it is, and even while we pity we cannot but condemn.

And now for the situations and the prospects of some of the other personages who occupy an important place in our tale.

There can be no doubt, but, that what Rodwell had said to Lowe, in the few minutes conversation he had with him immediately preceding his decease, was correct. After the idea had once occurred to him, Rodwell, that he might at some lunatic asylum get the information which would confound Lowe, he had but a straightforward course to pursue. He was, by the foolish liberality of Mrs. Paddlebat, provided with ample funds, and as he got a list of lunatic establishments, he had but to go from one to the other, and by dint of bribery effect his object. That he succeeded, and succeeded easily too, there can be no doubt; and then, that he kept his information back until almost the last moment, for the sake of achieving a greater amount of vengeance against Lowe, we can readily imagine. But as we are in possession of the facts of the case, we may as well detail what he actually did. On the evening, then, before the day when the two marriages were to take place, Rodwell went to the house of the deceased, Mr. Paddlebat, and there he detailed to that lady the whole of the information which he had received from one of the attendants at the lunatic asylum, with regard to that episode in Lowe's life which he had always been so anxious to conceal from every one, but most of all from Fanny Leslie. Mrs. Paddlebat heard him with amazement, not unmingled with a large share of gratification, for Lowe had so repeatedly wounded her vanity that she hated him with a hatred to the full extent of what her mind was capable of feeling towards any human being.

"Then Jervis," she said, "you may depend upon it that Fanny will no more think of marrying him than of marrying the pope of Rome. If she does, after this disclosure and resistance, I shall be somewhat surprised and have much mistaken her character. Take my word for it she won't, I know she's careful, but if once she thinks any one has deceived her, she will never trust them again. He has no more chance of marrying her than you have."

"My dear Mrs. P., do you for one moment believe, now that I am blessed with an assurance of your esteem, that I wish for any chance of marrying anybody but you." "Well, I don't say you do, of course, Jervis, but I was only saying so in manner of speaking."

"Alas, Mrs. P. you know well, that from the first moment that she found out how much I preferred you to her, she took a hatred against me." "Well, I believe she did Jervis."

"You know she did, my dear Mrs. P." "Pray don't call me Mrs. P., cannot you, since we are so sure to be united, call me Mrs R."

"And will you really permit me to do so?" "Oh, yes, you insinuating man."

"Nay, it is you who are insinuating; of course while old P. was alive, I could not venture to tell you how much I loved you." "No, certainly. Ah, he was a troublesome man, and yet, now that he is dead, I feel as if I ought to forgive him."

"Amiable soul! There is not one person in a thousand that could utter such a sentiment as that; oh, I am not deceived in my judgment of character, when I said to myself, 'if there be goodness on a large scale, it is to be found in Mrs. P.—' Mrs. R. I beg your pardon, I meant to say Mrs. R." "Ah, you false man."

"No—no, upon my soul no. But had we not better tell Fanny, what we now know of the fellow Lowe. I have abundant proofs so that she cannot doubt, for a moment, the accuracy of the statement; and if she does, I can bring her the very man who saw some of the friends of the young girl whom he had actually seduced, and then, no doubt, as I hear the story, driven her mad by his cruelties toward her."

"There is no doubt in the world but that that was just what he did, and yet he comes here playing the hypocrite, and pretending to find fault with everybody else. Oh, I have no patience with such a fellow." "Nor I, nor I."

"Come at once into the drawing-room; Fanny is there, I'll be bound, for she always gets out of your way, you know, since she finds that there is no chance of getting you all to herself, and we will just let her know now what a beauty it is she thinks of being foolish enough to marry." "A beauty, indeed, my dear madam, a beauty, indeed, as you say. If this affair does not open her eyes I don't know what will."

Mrs. Paddlebat conducted Rodwell to the drawing-room, where sure enough was Fanny; because, by a kind of tacit agreement, whenever Rodwell called, Mrs. Paddlebat saw him in the dining-room, while Fanny occupied the drawing-room, and so neither party intruded upon the other on these interesting occasions.

Fanny Leslie was, consequently, a little surprised, but a little indignant at this interruption ; and she expressed both those feelings in her manner and countenance when she rose, as the unexpected visitor made his appearance.

Rodwell saw, that if he did not something to detain her, she would in another moment have left the room, so he spoke at once, saying—

" Knowing of course, Miss Leslie, how very unwelcome my appearance is to you, I have but to apologise for intruding upon you, and then state my excuse for so doing."

" Both, sir," said Fanny, " will, I hope, be as brief as possible; and both I can readily dispense with rather than hear."

" Of that I can have no doubt, but I appeal, Miss Leslie, to your sense of justice, and in that sacred name I beg of you to listen to me."

Thus abjured, Fanny paused, and slightly inclined her head, as much as to say, " go on." Rodwell took the tacit permission so granted to him, and proceeded—

" It must be fresh in your remembrance, Miss Leslie, that I have made certain undefined charges against Nicholas Lowe. It was very imprudent of me to make those charges, because I was unprovided with proof to substantiate them; and, consequently, I became subject to many reproaches from Nicholas Lowe, much injury and contempt, all of which I was compelled to endure as best I might."

" Well, sir, what can all this have to do with my sense of justice?" said Fanny.

" You shall hear, Miss Leslie. When a man is so situated, it of course becomes in him a strong wish to justify himself. I own that I did pant for those proofs which would turn the tables upon my adversary. My excuse for this intrusion upon you to-day is, that I have, with no little labour, at length procured them."

" No, no, no," cried Fanny.

" Yes, Miss Leslie, I have procured them, and there is but one alloy to my satisfaction, which is, that they distress you."

" You will not make me believe," said Fanny, " that that consideration is any alloy to your satisfaction." " As you please, Miss Leslie—as you please ; I have proofs here that Nicholas Lowe, far from being the pure and the immaculate character which he has represented himself to you, is a systematic seducer. I have proofs of one case in which the victim of his unbridled passions found death in the cells of a madhouse and a grave, unknown and unbedewed by the eye of pity."

" I will not believe so much," said Fanny, faintly. " But, my dear," said Mrs. Paddlebat, " if you did have proved to you all that, in such a way that it would be impossible to doubt it."—

" Then, aunt, I would tear his image from my heart, even though it broke in the effort ; but it is not, it cannot be true."

" These papers are the proofs," said Rodwell; " I have here notes in the handwriting of Nicholas Lowe, with which, no doubt, you are sufficiently familiar to enable you to judge if they be genuine or not, addressed to the keeper of the madhouse, as well as to his victim in happier times, when despair had not quite overthrown her reason."

" He could not." " He has. Here is one note which, even in her madness, she has preserved, and which was found by one of the attendants after her death, and given to me. Here is another, written to the keeper of the asylum, begging him to keep the affair secret, as, if it transpired, it would ruin his, Lowe's, prospects."

Rodwell laid these documents before the trembling Fanny, who, as she read them, found all the airy palace of her happiness crumble to dust. One of the notes ran thus :—

" You ask me to fulfil my promise, and to make you my wife ; but, really, that promise upon which you build so much I cannot recollect to have ever seriously passed my lips, nor could you for one moment ever have believed me to mean it when I made it. Can you not be satisfied with my affection, my most devoted love, and allow me to make, which, doubtless, I shall be able to do, some matrimonial alliance that will provide me with abundance of means both for your exigencies and my own."

This was sickening; and Fanny could read no more, although there was much else in the same strain. The other letters merely contained the following words:—

"Dear Sir,—You will pardon me for again writing to you, to be extremely strict in cautioning your establishment not to answer any inquiries concerning me. I am about, I expect, to make a matrimonial alliance of consequence as regards my pecuniary resources, and the little affair of which you, and some members of your establishment, are now only cognizant, might, if it come to light, do me a most material injury. I am thus particular, because I know there are parties who will spare no pains to do me an injury.—I am, dear Sir, your's faithfully,
                                                    "NICHOLAS LOWE."

This was conclusive. Fanny Leslie said nothing before Rodwell; indeed, she could have done nothing but weep, for her heart was too full for speech, but she slowly left the room and repaired to her own chamber.

"What do you think she will do?" inquired Rodwell of Mrs. Paddlebat. "There, I cannot take upon myself to say that I have the least idea."

"She will not look over it?" "Oh! dear no, she is a world too proud for that."

"Then I am satisfied." "Do you wait here Jervis, and I will go to her and speak to her kindly about it, and get from her what she really thinks."

This proposition was agreed to, and Rodwell sat down to a bottle of choice wine in the drawing room, while Mrs. Paddlebat proceeded to Fanny's bed room, at which she knocked gently for admittance. In a moment the door was opened to her by Fanny, who said with a subdued aspect of great calmness—

"I was going to ask for you aunt. Here is a note which I want forwarded at once to Nicholas Lowe. I can see what question you would ask me, and think you ought to have an answer. It is this, if he had told me all that I know now, himself, I think I might have forgiven it, but now he never shall be mine."

"And a very proper idea too," said Mrs. Paddlebat, "I could not have thought of anything more to the purpose myself, my dear. You may depend upon it, you are quite right, and won't repent acting in such a spirited manner."

"Enough, enough," said Fanny, "spare me any remarks, aunt, and let me beg one favour at your hands."

"Certainly, my dear. What is it?" "That you will never again mention to me the name of Nicholas Lowe."

"Well, my dear, if you wish, I won't. Oh, I feel for you! the wretch! the oderous monster!"

In spite of Fanny's resistance, Mrs. Paddlebat would insist upon enfolding her for about half a minute—another half minute would have smothered her—in her capacious embrace; and then she left her, and went trembling down stairs to Rodwell.

"It's all right," she said, "Fanny has written him his dismissal, and here's the letter." "Bravo!" exclaimed Rodwell, "give it to me, and I'll take care it shall be delivered to him in time; and remember, my dear, we must be at the church to-morrow at twelve o'clock. You will be punctual?"

"Heigho!" said Mrs. Paddlebat, "I really suppose I must."

CHAPTER LVIII.

MRS. PADDLEBAT WAITS IN VAIN FOR THE BRIDEGROOM.

"No hand but mine," said Rodwell, "shall deliver this letter to Nicholas Lowe," and he kept his word as we well know.

Nothing, of course, could have been easier than at once to have transmitted Fanny

Leslie's note to its destination, but he preferred himself delivering it, that he might have the satisfaction of noting the dismay with which it would be received. He felt, that now he was more fully avenged upon Nicholas Lowe, than by any other means he could ever have hoped to be. That the new will that had been produced, and which left Fanny the five thousand pounds was a forgery, he, Rodwell knew, as well as if he himself had concocted it ; and that Nicholas Lowe had but himself to thank, on account of making so sure of wedding Fanny. That it was the same thing as bequeathing the five thousand pounds to himself he likewise, knew." But now, how bitter must be Lowe's disappointment, to find that he had taken all the risk, and all the trouble of such a transaction, to miss the large prize which he looked to as its consequence. What was the five hundred pounds which had been left to Nicholas Lowe, according to the terms of that will, which had been so cleverly concocted by him and old Gilbert Paddlebat, when placed in competition with a sum of ten times that amount, that he had now missed ?

"Oh! it will go near to kill him," said Rodwell to himself; "I would not for ever so much lose the pleasure of seeing him read that letter. It will be a positive piece of pleasure to me to look at his countenance while he does so. He will go mad."

Little, little indeed, did Rodwell suspect what was to be the awful result to himself of this indulgence in the pleasure of seeing Nicholas Lowe read these few words, which were the extinction of all his hopes. Little did he dream of the awful price he would be called upon to pay for that poor gratification. That Lowe would attempt such an act, never for one half moment crossed his imagination. That some personal violence in the shape, perhaps, of a blow might result, he thought to be sure was altogether improbable ; but then he had a strong impression that he was the more powerful man of the two, and that the consequence of such a step on the part of Lowe, would only be to add a thrashing to his mental chagrin. All that evening therefore, Rodwell kept congratulating himself upon the pleasure he should have in the morning by going to Nicholas Lowe's new house, and handing to him Fanny's brief—but very much to the purpose—note.

And Rodwell could not make up his mind to remain in ignorance of what was actually in that epistle, so when he was quite quiet, and by himself, without the fear of any interception, he imitated some of Sir James Graham's tricks, and actually opened and perused the epistle.

Its contents delighted him. They were just what of all others, he and lovers wished. Fanny had said enough to extinguish all hope in Lowe's breast for ever. There was no loop-hole by which he could escape the accusation which she brought against him. It was not upon the merits of the case that she dismissed him, for they might have become subject-matters of inquiry, but she gave him his congé, simply, on the fact, that he had decived her—a fact, which admitted of no possible dispute.

Never, perhaps, did Rodwell pass so pleasant a night, as on that which preceded his death.

He was full of deep congratulation. He had conquered and secured Lowe, and by his marriage with Mrs. Paddlebat on the morrow, he was about to supply himself with the means of living in that luxurious style, which so much accorded with his habits and taste.

He rose early. A very small amount of perseverance, in the way of inquiry, had enabled him to discover exactly what Nicholas Lowe was about. He knew that he was to meet Fanny Leslie at the church, at a very early hour, in order, no doubt, to avoid a collision with him and Mrs. Paddlebat.

Taking, therefore, a hasty breakfast, Rodwell walked off to Lowe's house, and when he reached it, he could hardly conceal his satisfaction to see the carriage at the door, and to feel convinced from that circumstance, how confident Lowe was of all proceeding right according to arrangement.

By making an inquiry of the servants in the hall, he ascertained—for servants are always inclined to be communicative on such subjects—that Lowe was coming down at a particular hour, and so he waited, as we know, until that hour had nearly arrived, and then he made his appearance.

What followed, we are well aware of; and, therefore, we will give a glance at Mrs. Paddlebat.

That lady, if she congratulated herself upon getting, so soon, a second husband, was doomed to become an illustration of the proverb, which remarks upon the number of slips between the cup and the lip.

Who would have supposed, now, that any disappointment could possibly occur in Mrs. Paddlebat's matrimonial arrangements? All was setted with the greatest precision. She was to be at the church by twelve o'clock, to meet the bridegroom, and if an angel from heaven had come to her, and told her that he would not be there, she would have said,—

"Sir," or, "Madam," as the case may be, "you are misinformed."

And yet, unless Rodwell rose up from the dead, Mrs. Paddlebat was doomed to all the bitterness of disappointment. At about nine o'clock, that lady commenced the task of arraying herself, in becoming costume, for the occasion. The widow's weeds were laid aside, and she came out strong, in white muslin, sprigged with roses. The most elaborate cap that ever woman wore, was placed upon her head, and the most natural false hair, that ever peruquier contrived, shaded those cheeks, which, if they had outlived the natural roses that may once have bloomed upon them, had a tolerable shape of artificial roseate hue, in the shape of carmine, upon them, to make up for nature's unkind withdrawal of support in that line. And a most gorgeous, and, we have no doubt, to many people's perception, fine looking object, did Mrs. Paddlebat become. Fine, in everything else but in woman, means fine, but in that application, coarse; for we never see a reputed fine woman, but we find, that she owes all that reputation to her dimensions being of an Amozonian character.

Alas, poor Fanny Leslie! She never left her room on that eventful morning, but there she remained alone, and making such efforts to conquer the sad and melancholy thoughts that would come across—as never heroine made—to achieve a reputation that should last for ages. But there are more heroines in private life, than people suppose, and Fanny Leslie was one of them!

To be sure, Mrs. Paddlebat thought it very unkind of Fanny, as she had no grand toilette of her own to make, that she did not come and assist her, and she told her so, but Fanny begged to be left alone, in a tone and manner, which showed that she really meant it, so that Mrs. Paddlebat did not persecute her, but put up with the assistance of the servant. And that personage did really, under the circumstances, much better than Fanny, because she burst, every few minutes, into rapturous expressions of delight, as each article of exclusive finery was put on by her mistress: and that was just what suited Mrs. Paddlebat's mind.

"Oh, mem, well, you do look lovely!"

"Now, don't you be foolish, Susan. You know, you don't mean it, and are only saying so to flatter me."

"Always begging your pardon, mem, I ain't doing no such thing; and whether you are offended or not, mem, I will say what I think, and that is, as you do look lovely, mem. If you was to give me this moment a month's notice, mem, I'd go on saying."

"Oh, you are a foolish girl."

"Oh, mem, how all the men will eye Mr. Rodwell, mem, when they see you agoing along."

"Do you think they will?"

"Think they will, mem! I knows as they will! I haven't lived as long as I have, mem, not to know what men is."

"Well, well. Susan, hand me the cap."

"Yes, mem. Here's the cap. It is a pity —"

"What's a pity?"

"That you can't decide yourself, mem."

"Why so?"

"Because I know as well, as if I was in their insides, as there will be a many sad heart to-night, all on account o' their being no hope or chance of having you, mem; I've seen people look at you, as they passed the shop, many a time."

"People loo   at me, Susan?"

"Yes mem; it was but the other day as two gentlemen—oh, real gentlemen! mem, came by, as they saw you, and one of 'em says to the other, says he, 'Good Lord!' says he, 'Look there!'"

"Did he really?"

"Yes, mem, and then the other looks and he says, says he, 'oh, come along, a glance, says he, is a dose, says he.' And then away they went, walking as fast as they could, and why, mem? why, I asks, mem, why?"

"Well, I don't know, Susan, why."

"Why then, mem, 'cos most likely they were both married men, and so couldn't think of you, that's why!"

" Ah, Susan, you have seen a deal of the world ; and really, I will say, that you are very observing, Susan."

" I believe you—I is, mem."

" What do you think of me now, Susan ; move the glass a little so that I may see the flounces ; there, that will do."

" What do I think on you now? I'm afeard to thnk"

" Well, I think I shall do."

" Oh, you will do, mem ; Mr. Rodwell is a happy man this moment."

That moment Rodwell lay a corpse.

" I dare say he is all impatience, and will be at the church hours before he need. Well, well, that will look all the better if he is, won't it, Susan ? "

" In course, mem."

" And now I really think I may call myself ready."

" Except your gloves, mem."

" Oh, I will not put them on till the last moment ; one's hands are apt to get wet and—and—"

" Perspiry, mem ? "

" Well, a little, and so I will not put on the gloves yet, Susan ; oh, gracious ! I hear the sound of wheels."

" It's the carriage, mem, it's the carriage ! " said Susan, making a wild rush to the window ; " Yes—oh, yes, here they are, white bows, mem, with fresh nosegays stuck in their bosoms."

" Oh dear—oh dear ! "

" And such a crowd of people gathering like bricks, mem ; there, there's some-one has throwed something at the footman, and he's a swearing."

" Susan, I think I'll go at once, is there a great crowd ?"

" Yes, mem."

" And that odious being, Finick, who was to have had the honor of being my bridesmaid, hasn't come."

" There's a hackney coach, mem, it is—no—yes—no—oh ! yes, it is Miss Finick, mem.   White silk, mem, as I'm a sinner, and hope to be a sinner."

" White silk and flounces ?"

" There mem, there ! "

" She wants to cut me out, I know she does."

" Cut you out, mem ! I'd like to see the mortal bean' as could cut you out ! oh dear, no, if Miss Finick was to begin with flounces at the nape of her neck, mem, and go on with them till she came to the pint of her heels, she couldn't cut you out, mem ; shall l run down and open the door for her."

" Yes, Susan, yes."

Susan run down stairs, and admitted Miss Finick, oh ! the duplicity of human nature ! Susan's first remark was :—

" Well, you do look lovely, Miss Finick, and between you and me, you cannot think what a odious old fright missus looks."

" Well, I should suppose she does."

" Everybody will be taking you for the bride, Miss Finick, and I shouldn't wonder that the people will be so aggravated when they find as it isn't so, that some gentleman there will insist upon marrying whether you will or not."

" Oh Susan ! how can you say so ?"

" Oh, Miss Finick, how can you sleep in your bed of a night ? I don't know, when you must be aware how many people's hearts you have broken."

" Well, I'm sure, Susan," said the delighted Miss Finick, " You pretend to know a great deal, but there's half-a-crown."

" Thank you, miss.   Half-a-crown," added Susan to herself ; " soft soap goes a much larger way than folks think, it would only have been a shilling now, I'll be bound, if l hadn't lathered her down so."

The meeting between Miss Finick and Mrs. Paddlebat was as cordial and radiant with smiles, as a meeting between two women who hated and envied each other amazingly could well be.   The fact was, that each had just what the other wanted.

Miss Finick had youth, that is to say, comparatively with Mrs. Paddlebat; for if the dreadful tale must be told, Miss Finick was no chicken.   But Mrs. Paddlebt had money and that Miss Finick had not, so they mutually called each other 'dear' and 'love,' while envy held high court in each of their heads.

"Now it's really cruel of you, Mrs. Paddlebat," said Miss Finick.

"What's cruel, my dear?"

"To make yourself look so fascinating."

"Oh, you flatter."

"No, dear, no, upon my word, no; now I appeal to Susan."   And the unblushing Susan undeniably responded to the appeal, by saying :—

"A angel! a angel! bang out of heaven, that's what she looks like, or I've on sort of conscience, whatsumdever."

We have no doubt that our readers will accept the alternative and agree that Susan had no sort of conscience whatever, rather than, that Mrs. Paddlebat was an angel.

But the time had come—it was necessary to start, and down stairs with a great fluster went Mrs. Paddlebat, closely followed by Miss Finick.

"Oh, dear me," said Mrs. P., when she crossed the passage, "what a flutter I am in to be sure, my dear; you go first, Susan, are there many people?"

"A good many, mem."

"Oh gracious, what a dreadful thing! I'm afraid of my nerves."

"Think of what you did many years ago, my dear," said Miss Finick, 'you know this would be more trying to a younger or less experienced person."

"Would it really, I often wonder that you never had an offer, but men now-a-days I think are cleverer than they used to be, and know a woman's temper the moment they look in her face, my love."

"Really, lovers are not so clever though, Mr. Rodwell must be rather behind the age."

Susan became positively alarmed, she felt that if the present style of dialogue continued much longer, affairs would grow serious, so she put a stop to it by flinging the door wide open, when a shout from the mob reached the ears of both the ladies, and put an end to the vexatious controversy.

Miss Finick walked out first, and the ungracious remark of some one in the mob was—

"She's a rum un to look at, ain't she?"

Vulgar wretches, thought Miss Finick, as she seated herself in the carriage.

Then came Mrs. Paddlebat, and she was saluted first with a roar of laughter, and then many such ungracious remarks, as "there goes the old un; fat and fifty; mind how you go old lady; sit down easy, or else you'll break the springs; my eye what a whopper; &c."

Mrs. Paddlebat was highly exasperated, and drew up the glasses of the carriage which nearly broke them.

The postillion cracked his whip, and amid another roar of derisive laughter, off they went.   It was a good quarter of an hour before Mrs. Paddlebat recovered her equanimity, but having a tolerable share of self-conceit to fall back upon, she did at length get the better of her chagrin.   Moreover, both ladies had now had a little time for reflection, and they thought how very absurd it was to be at war with each other, so by mutual tacit consent, the former contentions were allowed to drop and they talked together very lovingly all the way.   The horses went at a good pace, and the village church at length came in sight.   At the appearance of the coach with the postillion, and the white bow upon his breast, everybody of course knew, or thought they knew, what was going to happen.

"A wedding! a wedding!" was the shout, and by the time the carriage drew up at the church porch, the whole population was on the alert.   The steps were let down, and out got Mrs. Paddlebat, and Miss Finilck; a glance, and it was one of anger, told her that Rodwell was not there, as of course he ought to be to hand her out.

"Not come," she exclaimed, "God bless me!—"

"Don't be alarmed," whispered Miss Finick, "something may have detained him' and I think we are a little early."

Mrs. Paddlebat was accomodated with a seat in the vestry, and there she waited, yes, there she waited in vain for the dead. Minutes grew into quarters of hours; quarters into halfs, and halfs into hours, still he came not; the parson went home, the clerk went home, the crowd got angry and impatient, and the beadle glared at Mrs. Paddlebat, and thought it yet possible she was hoaxing him, and keeping him out of his dinner. But we may say, what the parson did and thought; and what the clerk did and thought; and what the beadle thought, and did not do; we may talk of Miss Finick, and of the crowd without, of the houses, of the carriage, and of the postillions, but how shall we speak of Mrs. Paddlebat.

Rage, shame, and terror, kept up a constant war in her breast; she got at length desperate, and just as the beadle said—

"Pray, mam, may I make bold to ask you, how long you think of waiting," she gave a groan, and fainted away, almost demolishing Miss Finick, who made a vain attempt to support her.

———

CHAPTER LIX.

GILBERT PADDLEBAT DREAMS THAT ALL THE BANKS BREAK.—THE ATTEMPTED ROBBERY, AND THE DEATH OF THE HOUSE-BREAKER.—HE SEES SHEEPEY'S GHOST AGAIN.

GILBERT PADDLEBAT, when he had dragged the body of the maniac into the cellar, or pantry, felt and turned the key upon him, wiped his forehead with what he termed his handkerchief; for the exertion and fear he had experienced, had even caused the carcass of the miser to expend some moisture—and considering that it was Gilbert Paddlebat, he had perspired profusely. He sat down upon the steps, and wiped his head and face, and he coughed terribly. That cough of his was a nuisance, it made a noise, besides Gilbert at all times disliked a cough, it seemed as if it caused some reminisence of church yards, grave stones, coffins, and a variety of other things inimical to human life. However he had undergone more fear this last hour, than he had ever before felt; there was scarce another hope left for him, when his tormentor fell forwards and killed himself by accident.

"Yes," said Gilbert, "I didn't do it that's plain, not but what it served him right, what business had he here disturbing me, but nobody will know anythinof the matter, there"s nobody comes here that's one thing, the lodgings are cheap, and they suit me, I shall remain."

Gilbert Paddlebat could not conceive the idea of quitting the old house, merely because the dead body of a man is locked up in one part of it. Oh no, that was not to weigh against the answering benefit of gratuitous lodgings. He made up his mind to that, and refused all inducements which he made himself, to quit the place, because of the dead body.

"Nobody knows it but me, and nobody will know it, I'll take care nobody does know it; and if they did, they can't say I did it, and the wounds will prove how he died, so there's no fear, besides he might have died long before I came here, nobody can tell when I came here, so there is in fact nothing to fear, and everything to gain."

"One thing is certain," muttered Gilbert Paddlebat, "and that is, no one will ever come before morning, for who would expect to find the current coin of the realm, in a house like this; that's the great point—persuade people you can do much, but you aint rich; that you can get money, if you are sure they will pay, or that you have ample security; then you may go to work, borrow further, but never admit that you are rich, that's the whole art of lending money."

"A friend comes to me and says, 'Gilbert, can you lend me this sum, and that sum, you know me,—I'll repay it—I am a man of my word at all times.'

' Certainly,' says I ; 'I know you are, but I haven't got it ; but, as you are a man of your word and a friend, I will get it for you, or borrow it somewhere.' "

" Then you'll want security?"

" Yes, I shall—that does the business; the man of his word, and my friend, often says no more about it, or he gives what is required. There is another way of doing business, too, that I find successful sometimes, and that is, when the question is put to me. Yes, I have money; but it is placed in my hands for investment—an orphan's, or child under age, or something of the kind—infant, anything that will take the entire ownership off my shoulders—there, I shall be able to get security, there's nothing like security in all money transactions."

Old Gilbert Paddlebat paused in his cogitations; he had struck upon a theme which, in his mind, found many a responsive chord. Suddenly, however, he seemed to have an idea strike him which caused him some uneasiness.

" I have often thought of this," he muttered, " very often, indeed ; and it strikes me strongly that some of these days the banks will fail."

Gilbert arose, and walked into a room above stairs : it was a small room, and there was a seat in it—a low seat, and upon that he sat down and began to think upon the same subject that he had before been employing himself upon. He had seemingly, for the time, entirely forgotten the presence of the dead body in the house, or he did not heed it.

" Yes, that has more than once struck me," he muttered ; " but never so strongly as it does now. What's to hinder a bank from breaking, I should like to know? nothing, and everything why it should ; I am sure they must do some-times—all have ; the principals live in splendour. Ah ! that's all very well, but they spend as fast as it comes ; that's not my way, and there are my means locked up at a banker's, and supporting such luxury and extravagance—abominable ! I am sure they will bring me to ruin. There was there the firm of Thistleton, Bushell, and Peck, broke the other day ; and a few days afterwards it was ascertained that another firm, Penton, Rush, and Bramble, were great losers by them, and they became bankrupts too, and the creditors in either case were lucky in getting two and sixpence in the pound ; then who may not suffer by these two?—then, perhaps, another breaks, upon which two or three more are involved, and the end of it is nobody knows where. I am sure that one or two accidents of this sort would, in a short time, ruin the whole country; the securities never come up to what they state. What could I have been thinking of to have left my money in the hands of men who give me no security at all ! I wouldn't lend without security, and why should I deposit large sums without the same ? It comes to the same thing in the end ; if I must lose anything, I had better lose interest than principal, I had much better be my own banker than receive a dividend of two and sixpence in the pound, paid at indefinite periods, and in the meantime I should come to beggary."

The old miser rubbed his dry hands together, and rocked himself to and fro on his seat. It seemed a dismal reflection to his mind that there was even a chance of his losing money ; and when the state of the country seemed so to him, as it did, then he felt most acutely the necessity of incurring some loss—a loss of profit at the least. That was a reflection that gave him much pain—to lose at all was a rub he had never learned to conjugate in the first person at all. Singular or plural, he never said, ' I lose,' or ' we lose.' That was not in Gilbert Paddle-bat's vocabulary ; but now, with a bad grace, he was compelled to say he should lose, and take the necessary steps to do so, this was making bad worse, but there was no help for it.

" If one bank breaks," he said, " another may do so too ; and it is more than usual that another does. I may say it's a general rule ; however, I must admit, in peculiar cases, there may be a solitary case, but they are very few. Well, if one bank breaks it causes another to break; if that break too, then they may cause several more; and their influence is felt by many more, and the more that are breaking the worse. Certain is it that the evil will spread far and wide—yes, yes ! I see it now, I see it now !"

He had made up his mind that he would have his money out of the hands of the bankers since there was so much danger; and, since the prosperity o the country was to be thus threatened, and probably ruin brought upon thousands, he was resolved he would not be involved in the general misfortune that was to come upon all.

I am not to be ruined in that manner—no—Gilbert Paddlebat must serve his own, I wonder why it has never occurred to others that they leave no security; why lending your money on bad security, is surely better than none. There you have your interest and a certainty of the greater part of the principle, and yet in a banker's hands you have nothing for your money but the cashier's signature."

"Dear me! who could have invented such a system, so fraught with danger and delusion—they must have been fools."

With their consolatory expression of opinion, Gilbert Paddlebat arose and went over the house, and looked about in every hole and corner, and secured as many places as were capable of being secured, and those that were not—he left in the state he found them. Then he carried his bed into the small room and placed it in one corner—in the snuggest corner—where there were fewest draughts of cold air.

"Here," he said, "I can sleep sound and undisturbed, and when I get up I shall begin my plan of withdrawing all my money from fictitious investment for such bankings."

"Why, man," said Gilbert, as he rolled himself over and over, to get the quilt thoroughly wrapped round him. "Why now I shouldn't wonder if some of those banks do not pay dividends—interests out of their capital—and when the telling-day comes, that is, perhaps, if they are fortunate, get a shilling in the pound."

*   *   *   *

Gilbert Paddlebat lay down to sleep. He had gone through unwonted personal fatigue that day, and despite a calculation he had just begun of the amount his money would produce at interest, so that he might be fully alive to the fact of how much he was about to lose—he fell asleep and that spoilt a fine specimen of mental arithmetic. It was late before Gilbert arose, and when he did so, he rubbed his eyes and stared about him, and it was some few minutes before he could well remember where he was.

"Ah! I was tired last night," he said, "I remember very well the man that wanted to murder me, but killed himself; I shut him up in the butler's pantry, I think they call it."

He got up and walked about awhile, and then examined the house as to its capabilities for concealment, that is for the concealment of cash, or anything of that bulk.

"Yes, yes," he muttered, "there is plenty of places here, plenty of places, and shall do very well. I will persevere in my intention, for if I am to be ruined—robbed of my money—I should never be right again."

There was much truth in all this—for the probability was that poor Gilbert Paddlebat would have gone raving mad and spent the remainder of his days in a mad-house. Out, therefore, Gilbert went, and first of all he obtained a cheap breakfast, for the miser seemed not to have an appetite for anything that was not cheap, unlike the rest of mankind who long for what is usually most difficult to procure; but then Gilbert himself was greedy enough where he could take them without cost to himself, it was money that spoilt his tastes. After some hours spent in the city, and when darkness was again on the earth, Gilbert returned to his abode in the empty house, he entered it and listened if all were right, and soon found that everything was as still as death itself. Now and then a passenger's footstep could be heard as he passed the door, but that was all, and Gilbert crept along the passage as carefully as though he had feared to be surprised by some maniac or concealed foe, and then he came to the little room which he opened and examined every corner most carefully.

"Well, there's nobody been here—that's certain—I didn't expect they would, but then who's to know what may happen, I'm sure I can't tell.

However, he searched the whole house, and then deposited in one corner several bags, which as they touched the floor, at once told that they were gold.

"There," said Gilbert, sitting down and contemplating the heap—" there—I am safe so far—yes, quite safe, but I must go pretty often before I shall have got through all my wealth. I shall have a score journeys—I am sure I cannot carry more at once than I have to-day. What a weight gold is to be sure, I must make another journey to-night."

Having secured the door, he went out again, but did not return for nearly an hour, and then he came in loaded with more gold, for the old man had carried a heavier burden than before, and he could not move under it well.

"There," he said, "there, no banks will be the cause of my losing that produce of my industry."

The old miser took extra pains this night in securing the doors and means of access to the house, and bestowed his gold in many odd places—all safe places—of course, places where Gilbert Paddlebat could, of course, find them, but nobody else, that was certain, he knew that. His sleep was not, that night, so sound as the previous night's, he was fatigued then, and now he was anxious, that did not seem as if there was any comfort in the once possession of money ; for, certainly, Gilbert Paddlebat, possessed a much less pleasant night than the previous one The next day he arose and did not go out till it was late, he busied himself about the place and ran from room to room, with a cautious noiseless step, and when he did go out he waited for an opportunity to go out when no one was near at the moment, so that he was not seen. However, he returned two or three times that day and added more gold to his store and went out again cautiously—yes ; very cautiously —and then, when he did return, he brought a few things in with him to serve him in this mode of life. After he had been out, for the last time, he went down stairs and established himself in the kitchen, where he lit a small candle and began to pull several things out of his basket ; for instance, some bread, a knife, and a cold half of a sanguinary James, which he had purchased after a long battle, but a successful one, with the mistress of a tripe shop. This was a feast—Gilbert Paddlebat never indulged in such a feast as this, not once in three months—there was enough meat on the bone to have sufficient to make three meals, and he had magnanimously resolved that he would devour the whole at one sitting. " It is gluttony, I am sure, but I have worked very hard all day and I forgot my dinner and tea ; I never thought of it, so I may reasonably conclude, I am entitled to a little more than is usual, especially at this hour, when I could go to sleep and forget all and sleep till morning. I don't know how it is," he muttered, " I hope its no forerunner of ruin, but, I begin to think, a little of eating so much at once. Here am I about to devour that ha'porth of meat at once, and that at my own cost." This was a dreadful reflection, and for some moments, he could not carry on the process of mastication, so heinous did the crime appear in his eyes, but the mutton looked tempting and he had been hard at work and had, moreover, an appetite, he cut off a slice and began to eat.

"This sheep's head," said Gilbert, " is worth more than I gave for it, two-pence half-penny is what was demanded, but I got it two-fifths of that sum less."

This was a gratifying reflection and he set to it with some zest, and after he had eaten half of it, he said :—

" Well, if I do finish it, I shan't want any breakfast that's clear. No, no, such a quantity of meat will preclude the necessity of a breakfast at all."

Again he went, until at length he had finished the whole, and was looking narrowly about the little corners near the eye, and to see if there had not been some little piece, that had escaped the sharp pointed knife Gilbert used.

" Well," he said, it is done now and there's no use recalling it, and that is the truth, though I begin to regret having given way to one's own animal propensities in the matters of eating and drinking ; but then it was cheap and the day's expences won't upon the whole be more than the average."

With this consolatory reflection he put the last mouthful of bread into his mouth, and was bending the point of the sharp knife against the dresser, by the side of which he sat. Suddenly, his attention was attracted by a noise near the railing, which increased rather than diminished, and sounded as if somebody was getting out.

"What's that," muttered Gilbert Paddlebat, turning dreadfully pale, "what is that I wonder !"

It was soon explained, by the sound of feet, as if some one had fallen or jumped down into the area. Paddlebat trembled, for he remembered the maniac who had given him so much trouble and from whom he had only been delivered by an accident, such as he couldn't hope for again—much less experience. There was a descent into the area and Gilbert Paddlebat heard the door attempted; and then some more vulnerable point was assailed, and presently a man entered the kitchen. Gilbert was making himself up less—in one corner—than he was naturally, which was quite unnecessary; but the man saw him at once and beckoned him out.

"Come here little 'un," he said, with a familiar air, "come here, I want to speak to you,"

"W-w-what do you want with me," stammered Gilbert Paddlebat, woefully alarmed, for his gold was in the house, and he thought he was a ruined man.

"Oh, I dare say you would have done a great deal of good if you had had money; but as I happen to know that you have some thousands of pounds, I will have some too. I tell you what I will do with you. I will lock you up in the butler's pantry, and there secure you while I look over the place, and search for what you have hidden."

"I have hidden nothing; I have not, indeed;" said old Gilbert, who dreaded to be locked up more than anything else, save and except of course the finding of the money, and he began to asseverate with the utmost earnestness that he had nothing about the house.

"Well, well, I shall try the other plan, and give you a little choking; the cord is the thing after all—there is a good staple there—bethink you. Come, come, now no noise or nonsense, or I shall be compelled to knock you on the head at once."

"Mercy, mercy, for God's sake have mercy upon me, and let me go away—indeed, indeed, you are mistaken. I have no money; there is none here."

"I know more about that than you are willing to acknowledge. I have long known you for a miser, and have waited for an opportuniny of catching you when there was a good bag of the needful at hand."

"I have no money," said Gilbert, doggedly.

"Come, now, don't be obstinate; I know better. Come, you my as wel do at first what you will be obliged to do at last. I know you will do it, but it will be after you have had to suffer some pain, and put me to some trouble and bother."

"Mercy, gentle sir, have mercy. I have no power to help myself. You would not crush a worm like me."

"I would crush a much less worm than you are, when there is a few bags of gold to be had by doing so."

"Merciful heaven, help me! Oh! spare me! Spare!" almost shrieked Gilbert Paddlebat, as he fell upon his knees in a supplicating attitude, as the man advanced towards him, with the cord in his hand.

"Come, come, none of that squealing, if you please, or I shall be obliged to squeeze your throat with my hand, or knock out your eyes with my thumb nails."

"Mercy, mercy," whispered Gilbert. "Oh! have mercy upon me—I am not worthy of your anger."

There was something so truly ludicrous in the attitude and appearance of Gilbert Paddlebat when compared to himself, that the robber indulged in fits of laughter and merriment. The shattered form and hard-featured hatchet-face of old Gilbert, was the very impersonation of terrified avarice; but there was something in his expressions that amused the robber greatly, and he laughed loud and long, and when he ceased he wiped the tears from out of his eyes, and said—

"Well, well, that will never do; business afore pleasure, as the executioner said when he left his pipe and pint to hang a man; I must settle with you and laugh afterwards."

Gilbert supplicated most earnestly for mercy—begged and prayed in all the terms he could think of; but it was no use, the man was inexorable, and made an attempt to seize him; but Gilbert eluded him, and dodged about until the other got angry, and, with a sweep of the arm, gave him such an awful swinging hit on the ear that made him reel several yards, to the great amusement of the robber.

"He, he, he," he said! "well, I never saw such a game as that; who would have believed there was half the fun to be had here? I shouldn't."

"Mercy, mercy!"

"You dog, if you don't be quiet, and let me catch you comfortably, I'll squeeze you in two."

Again he dodged the robber, who muttered a curse, and said,—

"Well, I never came near such a pig; there's no catching you. I declare if you ain't as awkward as a pig to catch; but I'll certainly take your teeth out one by one if you don't be quiet—that is, all those that are left : you haven't many, I'm sure ; you are too old."

Again Gilbert was seized, but it was only slightly, and he succeeded in escaping, by making a sudden bolt through the other's legs, and getting out behind.

" He, he, he ! Well, who would have thought of that ? Why it's as good as a play. Now, you little parched pea, I shall have you now. I have you up in a corner ; your life and your money-bags are mine."

" Mercy ! do not kill me. I am a poor old man, a poor old man, a poor old man."

And so Gilbert Paddlebat kept repeating the words, " A poor old man !" so rapidly and repeatedly, that the man could hardly refrain from shouting with merriment, so extreme was his terror that he could make no further attempts to escape, but remained on his knees, shaking dreadfully as if he had an ague.

The man seized Gilbert Paddlebat by the throat with one hand, and effectually stopped all his supplications for mercy, and then he with the other hand placed the noose over the head of the wretched miser, and began to draw it tight.

Gilbert saw his case was desperate, and plunged and kicked with fearful violence, but the man held him off until he was tired with struggling.

" You infernal little hornet," he exclaimed, " you have kicked me in a very tender part of my shin. Now, I'll break your leg across the dresser."

The robber had drawn Gilbert closer to him, and then he suddenly let go, and reeled backwards and fell to the earth saying, as he did so, " I'm done for ! I'm a dead man !"

There was no more said : the robber fell back and expired with a groan.

The fact was Gilbert had retained in his hand the sharp-pointed dinner-knife, which he had used for his supper. It had been a green ivory-handled knife that had been worn to a point by cleaning and sharpening—he in his terror had never thought of it, never dreamed of using it, till he felt the cord tighten round his neck, and the pressure of his thumb against his throat, and then he, with a sudden effort, plunged the knife in between his ribs.

This was a sudden and unexpected deliverance, and Gilbert sank upon his knees and gasped for breath, and when he was a little recovered he tottered to the chair, and sat down in it with a look that seemed to say he could not have stood another minute to save a fall.

It was some minutes before Gilbert was so far recovered as to meditate upon what was to be done.

" This makes two of them," he muttered.—" two dead men ; what shall I do ?"

This was a consideration which was not very easy to answer, and he paused as many great men do in their discourse, but, as is usually the case, none came.

At length he resolved that, as he had one dead body in one cellar, he could see no reason why he should not place the other in another, where he could lock it up and have no more trouble with it.

Gilbert Paddlebat, when he made up his mind what he would do, went to the water-butt and took an invigorating draught of water ; and then, having taken the cord off his own neck, he tied it round the dead body, and with an infinity of exertion and trouble dragged it to the cellar.

It would have been a strange sight to have seen old Gilbert, thus employed, straining every nerve to drag the body after him, with the cord over his shoulder, just as if he had been employed by the parish to do piece-work.

Then, when the body was disposed of and huddled up in a damp corner of the cellar, there was the kitchen to restore to its former state, which took some time to effect, so that Gilbert Paddlebat did not go to bed that night till after midnight considerably.

*   *   *   *   *   *   *

That was an eventful night, for not only had Gilbert rid himself of a dangerous assailant, but, somehow or other, he had contrived to recall old Sheepy's ghost from the realms of darkness, for again did the spirit of his late partner appear to him.

"Well," muttered Gilbert to himself, when he arose in the morning, "it's of no use to fight against ghosts. What can't be cured must be endured; and, as for old Sheepy, why, there's no getting rid of him. I hate to be stared at by him in that manner, but it can't be helped."

After he had considered awhile, he came to the conclusion that it was useless to attempt to escape from the ghost; it seemed to follow him about from place to place; and, as that was a good place and a cheap place, he would remain in it.

"If old Sheepy will come," argued old Gilbert, "he may as well come here as anywhere else. I shall not budge: I am sure this is to be a lasting place for me—I feel it is, and I shall stop here for a long time; and, feeling so, I am sure my money is much safer here than anywhere else."

"It is very cheap, airy, and convenient," he said, looking around him, "and besides it is safe, for I have had more danger and trouble here than ever I had before, which ought to exempt it, for the future, from any more."

CHAPTER LX.

FANNY LESLIE WRITES A REPENTANT LETTER TO LOWE.—MRS. PADDLEBAT
PAYS HIM A VISIT.

FROM our knowledge of Fanny Leslie we do not suppose that she can be altogether at ease; we cannot think that, after having once permitted affections for any human being to find a home in her breast, she is of that nature that can readily and easily warn the tender passion from such a haven of rest.

No; she must be suffering, and that acutely indeed; and the pride of virtue which belongs to such a character had induced her, at the moment of discovering that she had been so much deceived by Nicholas Lowe, to write to him in the style she had—apparently for ever dismissing him from her heart and thoughts. But this was only apparent: it was the indignant act of an offended girl, who felt that where she trusted she had been deceived. Would it—was it likely to stand well the test of calm and patient reflection?

Alas! poor Fanny Leslie, we can pity you!

She retired to her own chamber; and there, with her fair head resting on those small and exquisitely formed hands, she gave herself up to all the bitterness of painful thought.

"Oh! Nicholas Lowe, Nicholas Lowe," she said, "why did you not disarm your enemies of the weapon which you knew they had to wield against you, by telling me all? I might have found excuses for you. There may be many circumstances of extenuation that are not and never would be mentioned of you by those who have told the tale of your falsehood to me, but you might have made apparently easy many things, if you had trusted me!"

Tears flowed from her eyes, and she felt that having once loved, and loved in vain, she never again should be able to feel the light of joy in her heart, or nourish a nobler passion at all its equal in beauty and intensity.

"Ah! no," she said; "the best and most beautiful dream of my existence is over. But ought I to do no more? Ought I to say no more—but thus so coldly and so abruptly cast him from me whom I was prepared to swear to love?"

Fanny was yielding. Unhappy, wretched Nicholas Lowe! but for that dreadful deed of blood which you have stained your soul with you might yet be happy!

Some time longer she remained in sad and conflicting thoughts, and then she drew towards her the little desk which contained all her gentle secrets, and she wrote the following epistle to Nicholas Lowe.

It was too late—much too late—now. The dye was cast. Nicholas Lowe had himself raised up a barrier between himself and Fanny that he dared not cross. Could he, calculating and unconscientious as we are free to admit he really was—could he, with the consciousness of the dreadful act he had committed ever to his mind, dare to make any one so wretched as to link their fate with his?

No, no; Nicholas Lowe was bad enough, but he was not so bad as that. He loved himself well—but yet he loved Fanny Leslie sufficiently to enable him not wholly to sacrifice her to such a wretch as he had now become.

But let her letter speak the feelings of her mind, and from it we shall gather what sort of struggle Nicholas Lowe was forced to hold with himself.

It was this—the original lies before us :—

"NICHOLAS LOWE,—You have heard already from me ; and, perchance, did not expect to hear again. Had I only listened to the suggestions of pride, that brief epistle which I wrote to you would have ended all communication between us, but I cannot quite yet forget what we might have been to each other, even in the fact of what we are now. You know that I am justified in what I have done, Nicholas. You know that you have deceived me. Had you trusted me, the case might have been different. I am not one who looks for, or who dreams of perfection in human nature. And one who loves, and loves truly, can forgive much—anything but want of confidence. There, Nicholas, you have foiled me, and in that one point which of all others, surely, is the very pith and substance of true affection : you have foiled me there. You would not trust me, Nicholas, and the result has been that I have heard from another that which ought to have come from your lips, and which had it so come affection might have looked over—but which now pride cannot. Oh, Nicholas, why have you placed yourself thus in the way of my happiness? I yet fondly believed me your own to fear, and cannot doubt that you loved me—so there be anything you can say or do that shall excuse you. I do not wish to judge hastily—perhaps I may have done so.

"FANNY LESLIE."

What was there not to hope from such a note as this? Oh! had Nicholas Lowe but been free to go to her and to say—

"Fanny Leslie, I love you. Let the past be buried in oblivion—and the reason why I told you not of that sad episode in my existence was, that I feared to lose one whom I loved so well. Will you—can you now forgive me?" Our readers, without being conjurers, can imagine a very probable result as ensuing.

But he could not. He was a murderer, and he dared not look again in the face such a character of virtue and goodness as Fanny Leslie.

He was sitting gloomily, alone, of course, when the letter came. Oh! with what a pang he read and re-read it through and through!

"God bless me!" he said; "ha! ha! What right have I to call on God to help me? I a murderer! Oh! what shall I do? What shall I say? Why did I stain my soul with the blood of that man who lived my enemy—but who, in dying, has left me a curse that will cling to me for ever? I have indeed now a gigantic skeleton to think of."

He struggled long with himself as to what he should do. At one moment he thought of trying to put on an outward show of composure, and going to Fanny and making her yet his wife—" but again," he asked himself, " what am I to do with the dead? Am I to bring her—my wife, home—open that door which leads into the apartment, odorous with blood ; dare I this from here? No—no—it is part of the retribution which is exacted of me for my dreadful crimes that I am doomed to remain here a solitary sentinel over its damning evidences." He gave up in despair all idea of altering his situation; he dared not leave the house any more than he dared bring any one home to it ; for, in either case, he ran the risk —a risk which almost amounted to a certainty, of the dead body of Rodwell being discovered, in which case his accusation of the murder and condemnation for the deed must be events repeatedly succeeding the one upon the other.—" No ; I am doomed," he groaned, " I am doomed ; and yet I must answer this note from her who even now would forgive and forget all. Oh, could I but have supposed for one brief moment that she really loved me, I know—I know too well, and fatally she does—how absolutely unconscious would all the words of Rodwell have fallen on my ears! But, I was mad—I was mad—and it was a dreadful deed done in a dreadful moment of passion." He sat down to answer Fanny's epistle, which he, after much painful thought, succeeded in doing, in the following lines:

"DEAREST AND BEST,—Leave me to my fate. You have already decided, and decided wisely, too. I am unworthy of your love : there are more causes than you can imagine. I have but one wish, but one hope now, and that is, that you'll quickly chase from your bosom all thought of the unhappy

"NICHOLAS LOWE."

This note he at once dispatched, in answer to the one which he had received; and after this act of firmness and justice, for it partook of the character of both, he felt a little calmer, and looked forward to a life of never-ceasing regret with as serene a feeling as it was possible that any human being could do. The night had passed away; the morning came, bright and beautiful, and Lowe began now to think of what means he could find to live. He made an accurate estimate of the amount that it would take him to keep the house and himself quite alone in it. He considered that he could get rid of some of the costly articles from the walls, always excepting that one apartment, into which, he hoped, never again to have the necessity of treading.

"No, no," he said; "if my subsistence depended upon anything that was to be got from them, I could not open the door of that apartment."

But, with all his calculations, he found that it would be absolutely necessary that he should think of some kind of profitable industry, or he would not be able to pay the heavy rental and taxes of the house, putting aside altogether the question of his own support, which he calculated he could manage upon a very trifle indeed. These considerations gave him great uneasiness; for although it would, at first sight, appear that in London there were numberless resources for an educated man, yet such is not the fact, for every channel of industry is so filled up by persons possessed of recommendation, or other advantages beyond others, that it is next thing to a miracle for one the best qualified to get employment. Moreover, the sort of employment that Nicholas Lowe wanted was something that would not take him often from his watch upon the dead. He did not like to leave the house long, for fear some attempt at successful robbery should result in a discovery of that dreadful fact which he had devoted his very existence to conceal.

Old Gilbert Paddlebat seemed to him to be his only resource, and he made up his mind to hold a consultation with him, without telling him the real cause of his wishing to keep so expensive a house over his head.

"He cannot refuse me some help," thought Lowe, "and he ought not. He will soon, by the will, which I could, if I chose, destroy all the effect of—although, to do so, would be to inflict upon myself much injury—come into a large sum of money, and being rich besides he need have no scruple about assisting me."

At this moment there came a violent knock at the street door, which so startled him that he actually screamed out in the excitement of the moment. He flew to a window, and a glance told him it was Mrs. Paddlebat. She had a female with her whom he did not know. We do, however; it was the bridesmaid—Miss Finick.

CHAPTER LXI.

THE DREADED QUESTION.—MRS. PADDLEBAT'S SUSPICIONS OF LOWE, AND HER THREATS.

"WHAT can Mrs. Paddlebat want here," thought Lowe; "and what can she suspect, that she has brought another with her? No doubt to listen, and depose afterwards to what I may say. I must be doubly cautious."

He hesitated for some time, indeed, whether or not he should receive Mrs.

Paddlebat and her companion at all, and probably, had he not felt that his conscience was corrupted with deep guilt, he would have adopted that bold and determined course, and refused the ladies admission altogether. But he was so full of apprehensions of one sort and another, and so dreaded to incur the enmity of any one, that he could not make up his mind to act so independent a part as, in good truth, he might really have done, with the most perfect safety. On the contrary, he appeared to be fast emerging into a state of mind when he would become the slave of any one who chose to tyrannise over him; so he crept to the street-door, and opened it for Mrs. Paddlebat and Miss Finick.

So little did the former-named lady expect that Nicholas Lowe would himself answer her summons for admission, that she had prepared herself to ask if he were within; so, immediately that the door was opened, the words, "Is Mr. Lowe at home?" came from her lips, whether she would or no, and then she immediately added,—"Oh, I beg your pardon; I'm sure I didn't know it was you."

"You see, madam, that it is I."

"Well, now, should I suppose you were going to open the door youself? Ahem! it shows people's bringings up, though."

"What do you want with me," said Lowe, who was determined that, unless there was no help for it—and he felt quite convinced it would be for the best—that he would not quarrel with Mrs. Paddlebat.

"Perhaps, sir," said the indignant lady, "if you was to say, 'walk in,' it would be only a civil thing, always remembering as you have walked in pretty often to a house of mine, Mr. Nicholas Lowe."

"Walk in," he said, with a strange, subdued tone of voice, that almost frightened Mrs. Paddlebat from availing herself of the offer; but being impelled by Miss Finick, she did walk in, and was shown by Lowe into the parlour.

By the manner in which Mrs. Paddlebat looked around her at the furniture and the decorations of that apartment, anyone would have supposed she had an intention of making an offer for it, or that she had merely come out of curiosity to see how Nicholas Lowe was lodged.

He had hoped that the latter feeling had more to do with her visit than anything else; but upon that point she quickly undeceived him, by saying, in a tone of voice which, to his mind, implied something suspicious, or some foreknowledge, he could not tell which,—

"And pray, Mr. Lowe, may I make so bold, sir, as to ask you when you last saw Mr. Rodwell?"

Mrs. Paddlebat looked him hard in the face as she spoke, and it was wonderful how well Lowe had schooled himself to withstand such an examination. He had told himself that such questions would be asked him, and he had arranged how he was to look. After a moment or two of pause, as if he was really then considering when it was that he last saw Rodwell, he said:—

"Really, I don't know."

"You don't know, Mr. Lowe!"

"No, madam. I think it was at your house, when some rather unpleasant conversation took place between us, that I saw him last; and I can assure you, if you come with any message from him, that, although I have discarded all idea of bearing him any malice from my heart, I decline having anything to do with him, or to say to him."

"Oh!" said Mrs. Paddlebat.

"And I hope," added Nicholas Lowe, with great sincerity, "I hope that I shall never look upon his face again."

"You do, do you? Oh, my poor heart! I did think, Mr. Lowe, that you might have known something of him, for nobody else does."

"What!" exclaimed Lowe, with well-acted surprise, "nobody know anything of him! Oh, madam, you have come to have a jest at my expense, now that you are recovered. By-the-by, allow me to offer you my congratulations upon that auspicious event."

" You wretch !"

" You—you wretch !" chimed in Miss Finick ; " you know well that this dear, sensitive creature is not recovered, and that Mr. Rodwell has disappeared, and nobody knows nothing about him."

" Disappeared !"

" Yes, gone, gone !" added Mrs. Paddlebat ; " I dreamt he was murdered."

" What an odd dream !" said Lowe.

" Was it an odd dream, Mr. Lowe ? Perhaps not so odd after all, for who knows but he may be murdered ?"

" Ah, who knows ?"

" And by somebody who hated him, too. Oh, I have my suspicions."

" Have you, really ?" said Lowe.

" Sir, you are enough to aggravate a saint, you are ; but I'll find out if you have seen Mr. Rodwell or not. I suspect, but I won't say what I suspect. I'll make inquiry. If I have another dream, I shall feel quite sure. Oh, you think you are very fine in your house, I know, with your new furniture. Ah ! I wonder while you were about it you did'nt see that stain in the roof. A nice look it gives the room ; but this is the first time, and it's the last, I'll ever set foot in your place ; and I know, as well as if you had told me yourself, that you have had a hand in getting Mr. Rodwell out of the way."

" Madam, you are quite at liberty," said Lowe, " to remain as long as you please, for it really makes no difference to me. Being a single man myself, and residing here all alone, you may well imagine how pleased and flattered I am at this visit from two ladies."

" He's a monster," said Miss Finick ; " come away dear."

" I'm coming, I'm coming ; You are flattered are you? oh ! I hate you ; that's not flattery ; at all events. There's one thing I am glad of, and that is, that you are disappointed. So Mr. Rodwell found you out at last, with all your cunning."

" Yes, madam."

" Oh ! I wouldn't have your conscience for the world—not I—I hate and despise you, and look upon you as covered with odium and contempt."

" Exactly, madam and as for conscience ; and the troubles of the mind, you know that I have often asserted, that there'a a skeleton in every house."

" Oh ! is there ? I only hope you will find one that will frighten you out of your wits. Come along, Miss Finick."

The ladies moved towards the door, and Lowe preceded them, and opened it for them. He said nothing, but merely bowed as they went out, although he could see that Mrs. Paddlebat was ready to burst with vexation, that she could not put him out of temper, which she would have gloried in, for no doubt, she came there to have a downright bully, which kind intention was completely thwarted by the quiet calmness of Lowe, who, as the reader will have perceived, kept his temper admirably well. When they were fairly gone, he breathed more freely, and felt if a great weight was taken off his heart.

" They know nothing," he said, " it is all suspicion : they know nothing, and I have warded off, by my manner, I think, even suspicion. That trial is over now. Oh ! what have I not already gone through on account of this dreadful deed?"

He sat down in the dining-room, and looked up at the palpable and increasing stain in the ceiling, to which Mrs. Paddlebat had alluded.

" How little," he said, " did she suspect what that dreadful stain was, when she was asking me for Rodwell ; how little, with all her cunning, did she suspect she was so very near to him !"

Lowe shuddered, and looked more intently at the dark stains in the ceiling.

" Let it be," he said, " age will deface it of its colour, I can do nothing with it, I have now done all that I dare do, I cannot do more—no, no, I cannot do more. If that stain excite suspicion and inquiry, I have but one resource, and that, is the moment I find out that inquiry is being made, to take the best measures I can to burn down the house at night, with the whole of its contents, it must be nothing more than idle superstition, which says that the body of a murdered person will repel the flames."

But Lowe was in that state of mind as to feel far from satisfied that it was only an idle speculation, and he looked forward to burning his house down as a scheme by which he might possibly ward off danger, but which was still attended with too many risks to be easily undertaken.

And what did Mrs. Paddlebat really think of her interview with Nicholas Lowe? Did she have her suspicions increased? No; she was made very angry, but the cool, matter-of-fact way in which Lowe had received her, had shaken her much in any idea she might beforehand have had of his guilty knowledge of anything concerning Rodwell. To her vulgar perceptions, a man who knew himself to be guilty of a murder, ought to do as they do on the stage of the theatre, when ' the acknowledged heroine of the common-place and nasty' is performing, cry, "Ah, my guilty soul! &c. &c." But, as Nicholas Lowe did none of these things, she went away from his house with, in her own mind, a presumption of his innocence.

" And did you really dream a dream," said Miss Finick, " that Mr. Rodwell was murdered?"

" No, but I thought it was as well to say so, just to see how Lowe looked."

" Oh, he's a downright wretch! and not at all good-looking to my mind; he aint a personable man, not he."

" No; what Fanny could ever see in him gets the better of me altogether."

" Ah, some girls are so foolish; now, I don't like him at all."

" But then your age?" said Mrs. Paddlebat, who could not refrain from giving her dear friend a sly rub on that subject; " your age you know, dear, enables you to judge better."

" Yes, dear," said Miss Finick; " but what a judge you must be, if age is to be the criterion of judgment."

" Oh yes, oh yes—(wretch)!"

" Certainly, my dear Mrs. Paddlebat—(old cat)!"

The ladies parted with mutual protestations of regret, while each hated the other with that sort of hatred which can only arise between two extremely vain women who have made sharp speeches to each other.

That danger, then, so far as regarded Mrs. Paddlebat's suspicions of Nicholas Lowe, might be said to be over, although he could not so well tell what kind of impression he had produced by the line of conduct he had pursued. That it was the best he could pursue under the circumstances he still thought, for he had done nothing, and said nothing, that could be construed into defiance, or that in the least might be tortured into a strengthening of the suspicious circumstances, that Mrs. Paddlebat had pretended to see in the whole transaction.

And so he sat thinking, and looking at the stains on the ceiling in the drawing-room.

CHAPTER LXII.

LOWE IS ALARMED AT THE NIGHT.—A GUILTY CONSCIENCE NEEDS NO ACCUSER.

SATISFACTORILY, to a certain extent, as he had got rid of Mrs. Paddlebat's troublesome inquiries, Lowe felt anything but at his ease upon the subject.

The well-known enmity that had existed between him and Rodwell, he was aware, would, if mentioned to the police, have a great effect in inducing them to think that he knew something more of the disappearance of that individual than he chose to divulge to anyone.

How far Mrs. Paddlebat's suspicions might carry her, he had no notion; only he knew that he had much more to dread from her as an opponent in the transaction than as if any man had taken it up—for a woman can say and do things upon the vaguest surmises which a man would shrink from, knowing the legal consequences of so doing, and that those legal consequences would be enforced against him, where they would not against a female however bad the enemies against which she acted might have been.

Hence, then, Lowe sat himself to work mentally to find out some mode, if he could, of effectually silencing the suspicions of Mrs. Paddlebat. He had better, however, probably left the affair alone, but it is one of the most frequent blunders of human nature not to know when to leave well alone.

He could well guess what a struggle must have taken place in the mind of Mrs. Paddlebat, between her idea that something serious had happened to Rodwell, to prevent him from keeping his engagement with her, and the lingering suspicion that was seen to find a place in her mind, to the effect that, at the last moment, not even all the money she had was sufficient to induce him to marry a woman old enough to be his grandmother.

There could be no doubt, we say, that such a struggle must have taken place in Mrs. Paddlebat's mind between these two agonising suggestions: the one so little flattering to her vanity, and the other so alarming to her fears, and calculated to awaken all her suspicions of Nicholas Lowe.

Now, that the latter of these notions was the one to which Mrs. Paddlebat the most pertinaciously clung to, was sufficiently indicated by her visit to Lowe's house, but he thought it would be possible enough to fan the smouldering spark of the other feeling into a tolerable flame in the lady's breast if the full means were adopted for doing so.

He spent some hours thinking of how he could accomplish such a result, and at last he thought the only way which lay open to him would be to write to Mrs. Paddlebat a letter, purporting to come from Rodwell, in which he should say that at the last moment he had repented him of the promise he had given to marry her, Mrs. Paddlebat; that he wished her all sorts of happiness with somebody, but that, so far as he was concerned, he declined the alliance. At all events, Lowe considered that if a note of this complexion did no good, it would do no harm; and that he could imitate the hand-writing of Rodwell easily he knew, because, in the course of business, he had seen so much of it. He accordingly produced, with some pains, the following epistle:—

"Madam,—I can assure you that no one can feel more acutely than I do the dreadful and painful necessity that forces me to write the words which herein will meet your eye. The fact is, that from the first I may as well be candid. From the first, then, it was Fanny Leslie to whom I felt inclined to pay my addresses, and, even when Mr. Paddlebat died, I had no more idea of making you my wife than of marrying Susan the cook. But I found, that what with one piece of juggle and another connected with the will I was to have eventually nothing at all, and, therefore, I became desperate. I found, too, that Fanny and Lowe had made up matters completely, so there was no chance for me in that quarter, and then I thought that I would marry you, and make off afterwards as soon as I could, with as much of your money as I could put in my pocket. Only the evening, however, before the ceremony was to take place, I received information that a relative had died abroad intestate, and that advertisements had appeared inviting his heirs-at-law to come at once forward: so I bid adieu to you, and make no doubt but that with the means you have at your disposal you will soon be able to purchase some man, who will as willingly as I would have done sell himself to one whom he cannot love, but can surround him with the solid comforts of life.

"Wishing you all manner of success, and bidding you adieu for ever,
"I am, Madam,
"To Mrs. Paddlebat.   "Jervis Rodwell."

Now, certainly, if anything in the world was likely to stir up all the bile in the disposition of the disaffected lady, this was what we would suppose capable of producing such a result. The imitation of the hand-writing of Rodwell, in which Lowe produced the letter, was so perfect, that it was almost certain to defy any attempt by comparison, to cast a doubt upon, so that he was quite sanguine of the success of his plan.

He crept out of his house by the area, carefully locking after him the kitchen-door, as well as the area-gate, and tossed the letter some distance from his house, and then returned to it again, with a feeling of some satisfaction that, at all events, he had made an attempt to ward off from his head any impending evil that might be consequent upon Mrs. Paddlebat's suspicions.

To retire to rest was now with Nicholas Lowe a process that made him tremble. He had a dread of what might occur in the course of the night, while he was all alone in that now gloomy house, in which there was so ghastly an evidence of the guilt with which his soul was stained. He took some laudanum, as he had done before, with the hope that that insidious drug would smother some of the pangs of conscience, and caring little if the habit of taking narcotics were to grow upon him or not; but it not unfrequently happens that remedies of this description for a vitiated imagination take quite a contrary effect from what might be expected to ensue from their use, and only increase for a time the evils they were intended to remedy. And so it was in this case, with Lowe. He certainly went to sleep, but in lieu either of a dreamless repose, or one only filled with pleasant fancies, everything that was horrible haunted his sleep, and he passed some hours in an agony of mind that beggars all possibility of description.

He was still sleeping; but he thought that he was suddenly awakened by hearing a loud noise in the house, and he sprang up to listen to it. It seemed like a heavy footstep coming up the staircase: he could count the treads. Up it came, until it reached his chamber door, at which some one knocked, and a deep, hollow voice said—

"Rouse yourself, Nicholas Lowe; rouse yourself. James Rodwell is now making great exertions to get out from under the flooring: rouse yourself nd go to him, or he will succeed."

Absurd as this idea was to him, his reason was not sufficiently awake to detect it; and with a feeling of such horrible terror that his tongue clave to the roof of his mouth, and his knees smote each other, he made his way down the staircase to the much-dreaded drawing-room, where the supposed danger was, and within which he heard the most horrible noises. He had not the key, nor could he recollect at the moment where he had hidden it; and all the while that he wrung his hands in the agony of supposing that Rodwell would get out from beneath the floor, a hideous, grinning, fiend-like shape sat upon the staircase which he had so recently descended, pointing at him with a long skinny-looking finger, as if enjoying the mental agony he was enduring. Suddenly he felt a sensation of pain at his foot, and that awakened him. He had trodden upon a nail; and he found that he had risen from his bed under the powerful influence of his dream, and was actually standing by the drawing-room door. A few moments sufficed him to reach his bed-room again; and there he lay for hours in a state of the most dreadful fear at the thought that, should he once get into the habit of walking in his sleep, he might do something—perhaps leave the house, and utter some words, that might proclaim to all the world the guilt that was at his heart.

CHAPTER LXIII.

THE ILLNESS OF FANNY LESLIE.—THE PAINFUL INTERVIEW.

THE illness of Fanny Leslie, which was consequent upon the change of demeanour in Nicholas Lowe, was severe and long, and at length induced the full belief that she was dying. This was the effect of a long serious indulgence in grief, which had so preyed upon her spirits, and brought her to a bed of sickness, from which she never expected to rise more. The sorrow and sadness that sat so heavily at her heart that it soon showed itself in her wasted and enfeebled form. There was no longer the joyous sparkle of the eye, the smile, the intelligent look, the vivacity of spirit, and the ardent temperament by which she had been distinguished before the events that have been recorded in these pages had happened to chequer her life. She lay now pale, and emaciated, wholly confined to her bed, without any hope of a recovery from this sad and reduced state; she had no hope nor expectation. She did not wish to do so—her desire for life was fled; indeed, she had no motive to induce a wish for life. Her heart had once felt the pleasure of love, and now bereaved, for such she considered it, of the object of her first and only passion, she now sickened and lay but for the last stroke of the grim visitant of humanity, who leaves none, who spares none but for a season, and, if some escape longer than others, it is but to be cut off at last from the face of the earth from among the few who are left to mourn the aged, who sink to their lonely graves alone.

This was not the case with Fanny Leslie: she was certainly nearly alone—that is, she had not the many relatives that some have—no mother, or sister, or brother—none of these had she to tender the nutritious draught, or to soothe the pang she felt; no tender and affectionate relatives had she who would watch and smooth the pillow for her weary head; at the same time, he who was to have been to her what these would have been, and more than all these, now deserted her.

He who was to have stood between her and the world was now wanting, and deserted the charge he had undertaken, and that, too, at a moment when he had taken from her all self-dependence—when he had so far secured her affections, that the greatest evil she could suffer was a slight at his hands, and this she had received in a form that gave her the greatest cause for grief and heart-breaking disappointment.

She lay on her couch of sickness, and the thoughts of the past, and the love that Nicholas Lowe had so often professed for her, and the change that had come over the spirit of her dream,—her prospects had of late changed, and what appeared to be a long life of happiness and ease, was suddenly cut short, and an almost sudden death became her fate. She knew she must die, and believed that the moment was not far distant when all earthly matters would be alike indifferent to her, and she felt that she could not die easy, unless she once more saw Nicholas Lowe, and to him confide her last wishes and hopes for his welfare, and at the same time to tell him that she forgave him the end he had thus brought her to.

"He shall not say I died with any ill-feeling towards himself, or any one, least of all would I do so with him; he must have some reason for doing this; he must be well persuaded that he has a justification in his own heart all cogent enough, but with which he does not choose to acquaint me. I have no right to complain—it may be for the best."

The tears broke from her eyes, when thoughts that she was bereft of his love and confidence crossed her—the thoughts of her own sad case, and her abandonment by him she loved so dearly.

"I will send for him," she muttered; "I feel I am dying—I feel I have not long to live, and then, when I have bidden farewell—a long and last farewell—I shall be resigned to the fate that awaits me,—sink into the grave that yawns for me, and then bid a long farewell to all the earth contains."

She still lay thinking on the past—she now thought of the present; that could not be absent from her mind, and of the future, there was so little of it for her that it was not to be thought of—she would pass through it, and each moment would bring its own event with it, be that much or little important, or of no moment whatever: be as it would, she could not fail to see they were to her all-in-all, for they were the sum of her existence, and therefore the measure of life.

"I will send," she said, aloud; "I will send—I cannot die in peace, unless I once again see him and hear his voice, and tell him I forgive him, receive his last farewell, and hear him say he loves, although he abandons me; then I can die in peace, for all will be accomplished that remains to be accomplished."

She turned on her pillow and called her attendant, to whom she gave instructions relative to the sending of a message to Nicholas Lowe, expressing her desire to see him.

* * * * * * *

Nicholas Lowe was within when the message of Fanny Leslie reached him. The motives that induced him to decide upon acting in the manner he had, were, he felt convinced, right and proper, and yet he knew in what a light he must be held by Fanny Leslie, and he heard her desire to see him with something more than a foreboding of what was to happen.

"She must hate and despise me," he muttered; "but she cannot think worse of me than I know of myself. Heaven seems to will that I should be tormented, and suffer in life all the pangs that are fabled for the departed."

He received a letter, and then he said to the messenger—

"Go, tell her I will come speedily—I will see her, as she desires it. Heaven help her in this extremity!"

The messenger left, and Nicholas Lowe was a prey to grief both deep and bitter, for well he knew that he was the cause of all the evil that befel the unfortunate Fanny—to him she could look and say, I never should have suffered these pangs but for you. All I endure and all I lose is owing to you, and came from no act or part of my own." This was a bitter reflection; and though he had been, and was the author of all this, yet there were none who could feel more deeply the wrong he had done, or more sincerely repent it, or who could more strive to avoid it. However, it was useless to speculate upon the causes of the evils that now were in being. It was of no use repenting; but he must hasten to utter the few words of comfort that yet remained to be said, and they were few enough, to her who yet lay on what, for aught he knew, was her death-bed. Full of gloomy anticipations, with a breast overcharged with sorrow, and a spirit bowed down by the sense of his own iniquity, Nicholas Lowe sought the abode of her whom he yet loved, but of whom he had proved the utter destruction. There was no mistaking the sources of Fanny's troubles, and they could not remain a doubtful point one moment—alas! he knew too well.

"I have my skeleton, not figuratively alone," he muttered, "but mentally and bodily."

The next moment he slipped up to the door of the house in which Fanny lived, and knocked at it. He was almost instantly admitted, for his presence was looked and waited for with something like impatience. A few brief words with the attendant sufficed to tell him her state. He sighed and compressed his lips.

"Alas! sir, she is," said the good woman, putting the corner of her apron to her eyes, "very bad, and I fear there is no hope left."

"No hope," he muttered to himself, as he entered the sick room of Fanny, "no hope—no hope!"

He entered, and there saw the pale, wan visage of Fanny, as she lay propped up by pillows, with a smile, a faint smile, upon her almost bloodless lips. She held out her hand to him, which he took in silence, and sat down by the bed-side; but he dared not look in her face.

"It is kind," she said, "Nicholas, that you should come to me when I sent for you thus to the sick-bed of one who no longer holds the same place in your heart; she needn't say it is kind, Nicholas, of you."

"Fanny," he said, with a faltering tongue, "I came at your bidding; if you will, you have an unquestionable right to blame me—to upbraid me."

"I mean it not."

"Nay, your sorrow, sadness—nay, illness—is a reproach of itself to me, and yet you cannot know nor believe the unutterable sorrow and anguish I feel."

"And yet Nicholas, and yet——"

"And yet, you would say," he hastily interrupted; "and yet, why have I acted the part I have?—why have I stopped short in the course I was pursuing?—why, in fact, should my affection abate at a moment when it was about to be crowned with the success it sought? I know, Fanny, all this; but yet I have a motive, and a sufficient one, for what I have done, though it has produced effects I would a thousand times have rather had visited upon my own person."

"Nay, Nicholas, as I before said, I do not blame you—I do not even ask your confidence."

"It is impossible to grant it."

"I do not desire it—I am satisfied with knowing you believe it to be sufficient; that is enough for me. I am well aware you have a motive for what you have done, and have no intention to draw from you an acknowledgment of what it is, or whom it might affect."

"The motive I cannot, dare not disclose; but be satisfied, Fanny: if you can place any confidence in what I assert, I solemnly tell you, you would as readily assent to the truth of my assertion, that it is not only sufficient, but highly necessary; indeed, I have done nothing that I could avoid."

"I am willing to believe you have done nothing but what you deem necessary, and I regret that it should be so, but it cannot now be avoided."

"The motive I have does not rest or remain with you—it is entirely caused by myself; 'tis I who am to blame; you are blameless and innocent of all, Fanny—of all; there is not one thing in your conduct that I would have had otherwise than what it is: I would I could say as much for myself."

"Say no more, Nicholas. I do not, as I before said, upbraid you, or harbour one unkindly thought ; I do not believe you would willingly act unjustly ; but I am about to quit this life for, I hope, a better."

" Oh, Fanny, say not this ; it carries a pang to my bosom that you even little dream of—a pang you cannot conceive. I—I know well that I am the cause of all this. I have wrecked your happiness and my own ; henceforth I shall look upon myself as one that deserves the death a thousand times over, that I have brought you to the brink of the grave."

" I freely forgive you, Nicholas. I have now no earthly wishes or fears ; my mind is made up ; the last sad hour is come ; we must part, and part for ever, and it is well it is so—Heaven's will be done !"

" Amen, Fanny ! but not to so melancholy a catastrophe as that which you allude to. I hope yet to see you happy, and forgetting him who once brought you to such a pass as this, and who sorrows deeply in his own—too deeply ever to feel aught else than grief. Nay, you speak too, by far too despondingly."

" No ; I am dying !"

Nicholas Lowe felt that there was something more of truth in what she said than is usually to be found in the predictions sorrowing and illness had given rise to ; he saw she was brought down to the lowest ebb of human strength that it was possible to say or speak with.

Here was a pause of some moments. Fanny was weak and completely exhausted, and Lowe had so much on his mind that his heart was too full to speak, and tears found their way to his eyes when he ventured to gaze upon the wasted form and features of the once happy Fanny Leslie.

How great was the change that had taken place—how great was the sin he had committed that had produced such a result—he saw, he felt it was very great and could never be repaired ; hope was fled, and nothing but despair remained to him, and a sense of his own iniquities.

He strove to make it plain to her that he yet loved her ; that he was not one whit the less her admirer than he had been, and certainly there was no other object that he had in view than to save her pain and future sorrow.

" For me, Fanny," he said, " I can never now be a happy man ; the time is past, my fate is fixed, and Heaven above knows that the happiness I once had so fair a promise of is now denied me, because I am unworthy—because I should render your whole life one of extreme bitterness and regret."

It was with some tears that Fanny listened to him, and endeavoured to believe that there was some secret at the bottom of all that caused so much unhappiness to him and her, but of such a character that destroyed their hopes for ever, and which he could not reveal to her.

" It matters not now," she said to herself, " it is all one ; I could not now reap the advantage, if any could accrue from the knowledge of it. I am about to leave this life and all that belongs to it—may Heaven pardon my sins !"

" Nicholas Lowe," she said, once more extending her hand with a faint smile, " I bid you farewell, my strength is scarce equal to the task of saying so much ; but, since it is my last effort, I shall not deem it ill-spent."

Lowe grasped her hand in silence.

" You have my dying wishes for your welfare ; may you be happy—I die in peace with all, especially with you, Nicholas, for I am persuaded you have sufficient cause for what you have done ; I accuse you of no wrong, and believe you would do none ; farewell—farewell !"

It was with a heart charged with sorrow that Nicholas Lowe took his last affecting farewell of Fanny Leslie. He knew not what he said, for full sorely he felt the state of misery and wretchedness he had reduced her to, and he knew, also, the great extent of mischief he had done.

The interview was over, and he left Fanny insensible ; she had exerted herself to a greater extent than she could bear, and had fainted away. Remorse and sorrow so preyed upon him that he could not stay when every word and deed reminded him of the iniquities he had committed and which had occurred only through himself ; he, and he alone, was the only person who had done all this mischief.

CHAPTER LXIV.

NICHOLAS LOWE'S VISITOR.—THE MEDITATED CRIME.

NICHOLAS LOWE went back to his own home with a heart more filled with sadness and grief than, perhaps, it had yet experienced ; for he felt most acutely the state to which he had reduced Fanny Leslie, and he could not but see clearly enough that it was all of his own doing, and that a course of circumstances over which he appeared to have little or no control, had hurried him into the commission of acts which he could never recover.

There was an air of indescribable grief about him when he threw himself into a chair, and sat in moody meditation upon the present situation of affairs, when he was suddenly startled from his reverie by a solitary heavy knock at the street-door.

Nicholas Lowe did start—for the knock was unexpected and so singular—it jarred every feeling he had within him, all he could do would not tend to raise himself up to walk and see who it was.

"Surely," he muttered, "my nerves are unstrung, and every little incident alarms, or rather excites me ! Who can it be that comes here ? Some stranger, perhaps, or maybe some one who has wares to sell ; I'll not trouble myself about it."

But these words were hardly uttered, when another fierce rap came at the door.

"There, there—again," muttered Lowe, who now rose and crossed the room, and endeavoured, by peeping through the windows, to see who it was at the door ; but this he could not, for the person there had possibly anticipated that manœuvre, and, dreading the fate that would await him if seen, he removed behind the door so close that Lowe could not catch a glimpse of him.

There was no help for him—go to the door he must ; he would hear some remarks made by others, and, perhaps, cause some disturbance in the street : upon that score he determined to open the door, and walked there with an unsteady step, until he came within a few yards of the door, when the door was again assailed by more knocks so loud and sharp that it seemed that the man had become somewhat impatient of waiting any longer at the door.

Nicholas looked aghast, and at once opened the door, and there stood before him a young man in a somewhat-the-worse-for-wear suit of clothes. Lowe remembered the features, but, at the moment, he could not well remember where he had seen him, nor who he was.

"Mr. Lowe !" said the man, looking at him very hard.

"Yes," said Lowe, "that is my name."

"You do not, perhaps, recollect me ?" and the man looked at Lowe more fixedly than ever.

"I have seen you before, certainly ; but I do not now remember very well."

"If you have a few moments to spare," said the man, stepping inside the passage and shutting the door, the latch of which was in the hand of Lowe, but he pulled it together, nevertheless, and then he said to him :—

"Since you do not remember me, I must act as my own master of the ceremonies, and inform you who I am."

"The sooner the better," said Lowe sharply, "for I do not understand what you want."

"When I last saw you, Mr. Lowe, you came in this house—just been disappointed of being married."

Lowe started as though an adder stung him.

"And then the establishment you had just set a-foot was as suddenly abandoned, to the surprise of all those engaged. I was one of your domestics."

"Oh ! I now remember you," said Lowe.

"I thought you would," said the man, "I thought you would ; but, let me tell you, I have been in some trouble since I last saw you. I think this is an unlucky house, for ever since I got my discharge I have been unlucky."

"Well," said Lowe, "what do you want with me? I paid you at the time, and have, therefore, nothing more to say or do with you !"

"Oh, yes, you have," said the man.

"Have I? Just inform me, then, of a matter which I am really so ignorant that I cannot even understand it."

"You shall even know it, then, since you desire it. I am, as I said before, in distress."

"I am sorry for it," said Lowe.

"Exactly !" replied the man; "but that, you know, is not the means by which a man becomes any better for his misfortunes ; now, I have some better hopes of you. I think you will relieve the distresses of one, who is certainly only the victim of the ill-luck that seems to infect me from your house."

"This is another—a curious claim—and upon equally curious grounds. I never heard or such before—they are something to remember; but say what you have to say, for I have something else to occupy my time than this."

"The sooner the better," said the man; "I come to you for money, that is the long and the short of it."

"For money !" echoed Lowe.

"Yes, for money. Did I not tell you I was in distress, Mr. Lowe? and is not that a very good pretext for asking your aid in a small way, especially as I know you can afford it very well? So, now, I beg you will not waste your own time, but proceed at once to business."

"My good man," said Lowe, his visage darkening as he spoke, "my good man, though I am aware your distress may move you to ask—yet it cannot do so much with me as to induce me to comply."

"Indeed," said the man, "I had hoped otherwise."

"It is hardly to be expected. Distress, you see, is very common ; and we can only afford help to some few whom we know well enough; but to any one else it would be beyond one's means, and a means of encouraging extortion."

"Very like," said the man, coolly.

"So, my friend, as you have come with a somewhat indifferent plea, you must go away again as you came."

"Oh, very well !" said the man; "I see I can't expect much sympathy from you ; but I like to hear after old acquaintances—pray, how is Mr. Rodwell, old Lowe ?"

This was put in rather a pointed manner, and Lowe was much unnerved by the question, though he exhibited no change of demeanour to the eyes of the stranger, who awaited his reply in silence, and Lowe took time before he did reply, and seemed to await until he recovered himself, or it might be to consider his answer.

"What !" he said, "have you not heard, then, that he is missing, and has been so for some time ?"

"Yes, I have heard as much, but I thought you might know a little of his whereabouts."

"I know nothing of him."

"And yet the last place he was seen in was in your house, Mr. Lowe. I saw him that you know very well. I saw him go in, but never saw him go out."

"Indeed ! I dare say that may often happen, for it is a very common occurrence for people to be seen entering a house and not to be noticed when they go out again —there's nothing very singular in that."

"Neither do I mean to say there is, Mr. Lowe. I do not mean to say that you know more about the matter than I do ; but at the same time, you must admit it was a very strange thing that you should deny it."

"I said, leave suddenly."

"Yes, you, when you were questioned concerning him, you denied having seen him at all, or that he has been at your place at all. Now, I have never mentioned this to any one, but it is time I did do so. It may not matter to you, it may not affect you, I do not say it will; but you must know I shall get my expenses as a witness—they are little enough."

"Yes, yes."

"And anything more besides that may be coming in consequence, but at the same time I was in hopes you would make a better thing of it, for me to hold my tongue and give you no trouble about the matter."

"Why, as to that," said Nicholas Lowe, in a tone that seemed to betray a knowledge that he might have much mischief done him by the story that the other possessed if it was made known to others—"I do not care if I do not hear any more of it; but at the same time, I care not if I do—I have no reason to dread your tale."

"Oh, I do not mean to say you have; it's only to save trouble that I speak; it's not that you fear inquiry, that I thought you would wish the matter to be hushed up, but at the same time I thought you might not like the trouble."

"Well, I should not like the trouble," said Lowe, "that is very true; I have a disinclination to trouble—my breath is not good, and I cannot bear fatigue."

"So I thought; well, if you will lend me a few pounds now and then, you understand, why we may get on very well together, and I promise you to be discreet, and not meddle or interfere in other people's affairs."

"Very good," said Nicholas Lowe, and he pulled out his purse and gave the man ten pounds, saying,—

"I give you this now, because you are in distress; but mind you remember the fable of the fool, who put his hand into the pitcher, and grasping at its contents, could not withdraw it without destroying the source of his riches."

"Oh yes," said the man, "I know that very well, and I will not forget the lesson, as I will take care to draw out the contents only by degrees and not all at once, and so I shall avoid the extent of folly alluded to, and the consequences likewise."

The fellow placed the gold in his pocket with a significant look, as much as to say, 'I am your man, whether it's at a table or at a scamping trick—I am not to be done only by a better man than myself, and you are not he.'

There was a pause when the man turned to depart, but he suddenly stopped and said,—

"By the by, I may as well ask you to name your own hours and days, on which I may see you without putting you to any inconvenience or annoyance, for as you are about to act as a gentleman, why, I will do the same by you, and take the signal from you."

"I would sooner come to you," said Lowe.

"As you please; but you take more trouble than I wish to give you; I wish to save trouble."

"I would rather you did not come to my house at all, and you may be assured of my being punctual, unless something arises which will render it impossible; otherwise, you know where I am, and, if I come not, you can come to me then; but I prefer coming to you in some place where I shall not be liable to be recognised."

"Oh, that is easily done."

"What is easily done?" inquired Nicholas Lowe.

"Why, to tell you of a place where you can see me; you will find me," said the man, "near the fields between Kentish-town and Camden-town."

"I know the place."

"Here," said the man, "is my address; I have it written down, as it often happens, at least now and then, I am not able to find my way home; only, if anybody finds me, they can pack me off home without any troubling of the watch-houses and other places of confinement."

"If you get intoxicated, you may."

"Hush, hold! intoxicated? I never get intoxicated at all; whoever saw me drunk?"

"I don't know, but at all events, if such a thing should happen, you are likely to spoil your own opportunities, besides doing mischief against others."

"Not I," replied the man, "good day, Mr. Lowe, I'll see you in a fortnight, I dare say."

"In a fortnight!"

"Yes, I don't want to be intrusive, but the fact is I have to lay some of this out upon immediate necessaries, so you see I shall be in distress again, eh?"

"Very well, but be cautious, else the same trouble you want to save me from, may come upon you."

"In that case I am content," said the man, "to abide by it, but I shall give too wide a care for anything in the shape of a trouble, that it won't happen."

So saying, he opened the door, and then walking out of the house, he said as he was leaving—

"Well, good bye, Master Lowe, I shall be sure of seeing you, what a beautiful day it is! good bye!"

Lowe made no reply; he was too much disgusted at the manner of the man, and his matter, which raised up other thoughts in his mind, and he shut the door with a compressed lip; but yet he showed some want of firmness.

"No, no," he muttered, "I must not resort to such a scene again, and yet what am I to do in such an emergency? this fellow will make but a tool of me, I shall never have one shilling of my own, and never know quiet or repose; he will haunt me, my wealth will be his, and all I hold dear will be his if he demand it. If I have wealth in my possession, it will be but to hold it as his trustee; there is no denying it; he will ruin me and then he will betray me; at least I should have some little money I might keep back from him."

As he spoke he walked hastily back to the parlour, and then in the broad daylight bethought over the matter, until he had come to some resolve, but it seemed no easy task.

"This much must be settled in my own mind, that I must submit at once, or force him out, and how to do that I hardly know; the fact is, any corroborative evidence at all will cause a search, and then—and then I am lost."

He paused a moment or two, and gazed at the closed blinds that were placed between the windows and himself, but they were dull and dingy, and scarce able to help him to an idea, while he threw himself upon the couch that was there to consider what to do.

CHAPTER LXV.

GILBERT PADDLEBAT'S ADVICE.—THE DEATH OF THE WITNESS.

"I HAVE it," he murmured after a pause of some length, "I have it; I cannot do this matter myself; I must get rid of this fellow, and yet it is another crime heaped upon my shoulders. What is to be done? Were I to destroy him I should run another risk, another chance of doing a deed that might bring destruction as its consequent; that, indeed, may come without any fresh accession of crime, for does this man not already know too much? I will go to old Gilbert Paddlebat, he can advise me, I can make a confidant of him, though he is an avaricious man—a miser in fact; I know with whom I deal when I speak to him, that is one advantage. He is cool and collected, and will advise me better than I can advise myself, as well and perhaps more successfully. However, whatever his advice may be, I'll go and hear it, and I am determined this time not to do anything that may be hasty and hurried; I will away to Gilbert Paddlebat at once, and hear what he says of the matter. With that Nicholas Lowe rose, and paced the room for a few moments, as though he would have deliberated yet more on the project, before he even consulted so efficient a counsellor as Gilbert. Having made up his mind, Lowe put on his hat and cloak, left the house, and made for the house of Gilbert, who yet lived in the empty mansion, where he had two dead men, locked up in two different cellars. This seemed no impediment to Gilbert's enjoyment of his home, such as it was, if such a place could deserve the name, but yet it had all the attractions to Gilbert that the most joyous fire-side could have to another person. Had it not the one great, and, to him, invaluable quality of being cheap—very cheap, and, moreover, it had the great merit of not in any way exposing his way of life.

Nothing to pay, plenty of room, and an airy abode, are things not often met with between four walls; however, it was so in Gilbert's place, and moreover, it had the additional advantage of being capable of being turned into a burial-ground, or a vault for the dead, as Gilbert Paddlebat had already used it on two different occasions.

Lowe's thoughts as he came along were not of the deepest and most mournful that could be imagined, far from it; he was much excited by the last interview he had had; indeed, deep as was his self-reproach and accusation on account of the unfortunate result of his love for Fanny Leslie, he had returned to his own desolate abode to ponder and mourn over the fate of one so young and so lovely, whose only misfortune was her love for him ; when this last occurrence drove the remembrances of the former from him, and made him think upon the more immediate matter of self-preservation.

When he arrived at Gilbert Paddlebat's, he found some difficulty in making that w thy hear, as was, indeed, very natural, seeing Gilbert had gone out some little way o or erform a necessary act, but at the same time, one which he did with very extreme reluctance—it was the purchasing of food and some few necessaries of life. Gilbert could not bear the idea of being compelled to lay out money at all, and it was always a sore point with him, and caused him to heave many a deep sigh.

"Well," said Gilbert, as he came up the steps, "you here, Mr. Lowe, you here ? I didn't expect to see you. Do you want me ? I was not at home you see."

"I perceive it," said Lowe, "and that accounts for the fact that I could not make you hear."

"Exactly ; nothing more natural."

"I do want to speak to you, Mr. Paddlebat, and ask your advice upon a matter connected with myself, if you have a few moments to spare me."

"Oh, yes, come in ; my place aint particularly well furnished, but it's enough for a single man ; bachelors aint over particular, I believe ? We can find a seat of some sort, if it were on the stairs—eh ?"

The old miser chuckled at the witticism, unseen to any but himself, and rubbed his hands in glee.

"Yes," said Lowe, "that will do well enough ; we can converse well enough there, as anywhere else, if we are alone, that is all I care about."

"Then, we are alone as much as two living men can be," responded Gilbert ; "come this way, and tell me what you desire to consult me about."

"You shall hear," said Lowe, as he followed Gilbert down the kitchen stairs, and thence into the kitchen.

Gilbert Paddlebat here disburdened himself of several small articles, which he carefully placed in a small drawer, and then coolly turning to Nicholas, he said—

"Now, Mr. Lowe, sit down and tell me what you have to say ; we can talk as well in the twilight as we can if we had a candle."

"It would be quite superfluous," said Lowe.

"So it would, so it would," said Gilbert ; "and now proceed to the business which brought you here, for the purpose of consulting with me and asking my advice, I suppose."

"Yes, that is my object, you know," said Lowe, speaking in a slow tone, and suppressed voice. "You know the relative position in which I and Miss Leslie stood to each other ?"

"Yes, yes ; you were upon the point of being married, and somehow or other the match has been broken off ; I couldn't understand it, but I suppose you had some good reason behind which you were loth to make common by using it too often in every body's ears."

"You shall judge for yourself," said Lowe, "as to how far my motives were correct. You also recollect, no doubt, very well, Jervis Rodwell ?"

"Yes, yes."

"Well, he came to my house· You knew he was missing, and hadn't been heard of ?"

"I do, very well ; go on," said Gilbert, very coolly, who seemed to expect the at astrophe, and without any peculiar degree of disgust and fear."

"Well, he came to my house ; we had words, and in the heat of the altercation we seized each other, and I being the strongest, or the most fortunate, overcame him, and deprived him of life, and he lay a dead man before me."

"Oh, you murdered him ; well—eh ?"

Nicholas Lowe paused and started at the words of Gilbert, and was a little though not much amazed at his coolness ; but it must be remembered that Lowe did not calculate much upon any squeamishness on Gilbert Paddlebat's part, and had he known that at that very moment there were two dead men in the cellar, he wou l hardly have thought that his own case was so severe a one as he believed it.

" Yes," said Lowe, " I suppose that is what the world would call the crime."

" You may depend upon it that it would do so," said Gilbert Paddlebat ; " they would call it murder, and not only do that, but attach the penalty of hanging to the commission. Don't be alarmed, you know me—I am speaking in confidence."

" And I to you," said Lowe ; " you will not betray me, I know. I have told you this, and now you know the motives that induced me to break off my engagement with Fanny Leslie."

" Yes, yes—I see ; but what of all this ? you have not told me so much without having some object in view ?"

" No, I did not.".

" Well, to the point—to the point !"

" It is this," said Lowe : " there was one man, and one man only, who ever saw Rodwell come to my house ; he saw him go in, but not come out again."

" Truly, that cannot be a very strange occurrence in a place like London ? But who—what is this man that you speak of ?" said Gilbert.

" I will tell you," said the other, " I will tell you. You remember I have given up the whole establishment I then engaged, as soon as I had taken the step of breaking off the connexion with Fanny Leslie."

" Aye, the servants—but not the house."

" Exactly—I did so. Thus far I discharged all the servants, and retained the house, because I was afraid to part with the house for certain good reasons—there had been a murder committed there, and I was not anxious that the trace of it should be discovered."

" I see," said Gilbert ; " very right—go on."

" Well, one of these servants—a man—wittnessed the coming to my house— and he is sure, at least, he does not say so, but I can see what he means—that Rodwell never went away again."

" Well, that's no harm."

" Yes, this much I positively denied that he came to my house at all, and no one could contradict me. But now, up starts this man, and tells me beware ! therefore I am in some danger from him," said Lowe.

" I understand—he wants money of you. He will make you his bank, in fact, while you have friends—"

" That is the exact state of the case," said Lowe ; " he has had one small sum, but that will be repeated as often as he believes I have the means of paying his demands upon my purse, and that will continue as long as I have a shilling to satisfy his wants."

" Of course," said Gilbert, gravely, " of course it will ; and then when you are quite ruined, out of revenge, he'll give all the information he can to your enemies— and, if possible, ruin you ; and this will then be more easy—because the fact will come out that you have paid him to be quiet."

" So I feared !"

" You have nothing to expect from such a person," said Gilbert ; " when he has got all he can—when he has pumped you dry—he will destroy the well."

" So I feared ! But what can I do ? I wished to consult with you—to give me a hint of what you thought most advisable to do in such a case."

" That is a difficult matter," said old Gilbert ; " but I do think that when time and opportunity served, I should have him quietly put out the way—that is, if it could be done without being found out, if it were safe."

" Exactly. Well, I must admit I have a strong thought that way myself. I do believe there will be no rest so long as he lives ; when I have no means of purchasing my life of him, I must lose it."

" To be sure you must ; and it becomes a matter of self-defence in you to put a stop altogether to his claims and his power to do mischief from the first.

" It does," said Lowe.

There was a pause of some moments, as if Lowe was pondering in his own mind as to the practicability of the advice ; but he resumed the conversation, and spoke more freely upon the subject, and Gilbert Pattlebat had no objection whatever to broadly advocate the putting to death of the witness who was inclined first to enrich himself at Lowe's expense, as the only means of saving himself and his property.

With this advice, he afterwards quitted old Gilbert, and returned to his own desolate dreary mansion, which might, like the one he had just left, be called a charnel-house, for both had their dead within them.

*   *   *   *   *   *   *

Nicholas Lowe had made up his mind that the deed must be done—that there could be no other cause was evident to his own sense, as neither threats nor entreaties could in any way affect the purpose of the man who thus held the rein on Lowe himself, and could at any moment consign him to a common jail.

The thing was not to be thought of, and he hastened towards the abode of the man whom he once employed as his servant, but who was now, in fact, his master.

The evening was dark and a drizzling rain fell, while a cold blast swept up the streets, and made everything cheerless and miserable, cold, wet, and windy.

The hours crept on : it was near ten o'clock when Nicholas Lowe, after having endured the weather for some time, now came to the abode of him whom he believed to be his enemy ; he entered the house, the door of which stood open, and went up stairs to the room in which he had been taught to expect the man lived or slept, according to his written direction.

Here was an impediment, but it gave way to gentle force, and not much trouble was required to make an entrance into the room where he expected to find his enemy. He did find him—he was sitting, or rather reclining upon the bed, with a table by his side, on which stood a candle and a bottle and some glasses, which showed he had been engaged in a debauch and had fallen asleep over it.

Nicholas Lowe overturned one of the glasses as he approached the bed, and was compelled to draw back to avoid detection, but the man opening his eyes, recognised him.

"Ah! Mr. Lowe," he said, " glad you are come; I've finished what you gave me, and, therefore, yours is an angel's visit, one that has spared me a walk. I should have been with you to-night, only it was so wet, and I got credit and made a night of it.   Sit down, we'll have some wine."

As he spoke he sat up in the bed, yawned, and then rubbed his eyes as if he couldn't see.

At that moment Lowe raised his hand above his head and struck him a terrific blow on the skull with a loaded life-protector—the effect was instantaneous—the man fell back and without a single convulsion expired.

To make matters more sure Lowe repeated the blow, but it produced no effect at all, and then, after a moment's pause to look upon the corse, he turned and left the house muttering to himself as he went along—

"'Tis done and well done—I have left no traces within—it is well done, and that ensures success—because now I can boast of being free from any apprehension from that quarter."

CHAPTER LXVI.

THE TWO PICTURES.—THE INTERVAL.—THE MELANCHOLY MAN.

And now, how fared Nicholas Lowe?   Had he purchased for himself any more contentment by his new crime—alas! alas! no—was he the happier? fearful questions to a man who now never knew what it was to know a moment's peace.

And yet there are people who will fancy that to escape the most obvious and worldly consequences of crime, that is to say, the punishment which human laws have appended it, is to escape wholly.

Alas! into what a fatal error do they fall. It is not the man who is overtaken by human laws, and to whom is meted out the amount of punishment proportioned to his offence, by those social institutions which he has outraged, who suffers most.

So strange and enigmatical as the doctrine may sound, it is he who escapes who suffers by far the greatest pangs.

He has all the suffering contingent upon a thousand terrors and sighs of anguish which the deluded criminal escapes, by the very fact of his detection. Have our readers not heard frequently how, the night after his trial, the apprehended murderer has often slept so long and so serenely, that we might well wonder how aught human could enjoy so blissful a repose with blood upon its soul, crying aloud to Heaven for vengeance.

But it is the re-action of the mind which has produced that seeming security for a time—the absolute rest of the imagination—the apprehended man knows the worst—he no longer shrinks appalled from any one who approaches him— his ears are no longer familiarly alive to the last sound—no longer does he look distrustfully in the countenance of any one he sees to note if there be any appearance of suspicion.

No, he has passed through that period of terrific suspense and watchfulness, and the new state into which he falls is grateful to every sense.

But Nicholas Lowe, with a fervid imagination, suffered all these terrors, living too alone, as he did, with the knowledge of the continual presence of the dreadful evidence of his guilt, no wonder that his fancy peopled even vacancy with terrors, and made him as miserable a wretch as ever trod the earth.

The bright sunshine had no charms for him—he saw no beauty in earth or in air—he cared not for what other men delighted in—his whole soul was wrapped up, as it were, in the consciousness of his own guilt, and his whole thoughts and anticipations were directed to the means of escaping that detection which really, perhaps, would have been the happiest thing that could have befallen him.

And, if any evidence were wanting of the fact, that crime begets crime with the most frightful facility, surely we should find it in the career of Nicholas Lowe. At first he had committed that offence which, among those who consider themselves quite as choice spirits, and men of the world, is thought a meritorious thing ; that is to say, he had succeeded in trampling over the trusting innocence of one who had

"Loved him not wisely, but too well."

That was his first great offence ; but when his victim had gone to the grave, he at least thought that he was free from its consequences ; but, alas ! how little knew he of the cause of human events, and in what a hidden chain they hang together, link by link ; the one essential to the continuity of the whole fabric as n o he. The murder of Rodwell was as direct a result of the seduction of the innocent creature, who had surrendered up her spirit to her Maker in the cell of a mad-house, as any one human event could possibly be said to follow another in the most easy and natural order of things. And then came the most calculating and cold-blooded crime of all. The last murder he had committed, which had no passion to extenuate it—which could not be said to be done under the strong influence of human feeling which blinded him to the nature of the deed, but which was done coolly and calculatingly, merely to save himself from the consequences of his heinous great enormities. Let us look at him now as he sits, three days after that deed, alone, as usual, in his house. A chair—a large arm-chair is placed against the wall in his dining-room, and there he sits. His eyes are fixed upon the chandelier that depends from the ceiling—that chandelier from which has come the drops of blood from the dead above, that the reader will recollect excited such lively horror in Lowe. Ever since that time, when he first heard those gloomy taps upon the table, and became aware of the cause of them, after passing through so much of the misery of conjectures, he had kept his eyes, when in that apartment, upon the chandelier. Probably he, in the fever of his imagination, expected again to see some such frightful evidence of that which was concealed above. And the dark and hideous-looking stain in the ceiling, the cause of which he knew well, but which no one else of the few who had seen it had guessed it —that had grown larger and more palpable.

Many a time he thought of attempting to do something which should remove such an object of suspicion from before his eyes ; but he shuddered at the idea of interfering himself with it ; and, as for calling in any workmen to whiten the ceiilng afresh, it was a thing he could not think of for a moment : so that the hideous evidence remained.

And how much Nicholas Lowe was altered! The period of time since we first introduced him to the notice of the reader is comparatively insignificant ; and yet, to look at him, one would fairly enough suppose that the hard wear and tear of a quarter of a century had passed over him. His cheeks were hollow and sunken, his frame bent, and the wild, restless aspect of his eyes too surely betrayed a mind ill at ease. Alas! for him there was no hope, nor expectation of any joy. The past was nothing but a gloomy retrospection ; the present, a frightful source of misery ; and for the future, what could he hope, but for that estimation which he could not flatter himself he would really achieve?

There he sits! He has not tasted food for hours ; but his gazes still upon the chandelier and the stain in the ceiling, even as if his whole soul was drinking-in some dream of beauty, from which he could not turn his mortal eyes.

* * * * * * *

And now let us look at Fanny Leslie. She, at that same time when we have indulged ourselves with this peep at Nicholas Lowe in his solitary home, was likewise sitting alone—alone in the room in which she had at one time, in her reveries, filled with pleasant images of the future, in each of which Nicholas Lowe had held his place. Her head is resting upon her hands, she knows not where she is, and she sees nothing. Let us listen. Are those sobs that come from her depressed heart? Yes !—she is weeping—she whose life, if her fate had been consistent with her deserts, ought to have been one dream of glorious happiness. We cannot, without the deepest of human sympathies being roused, think of the poor, desolate Fanny Leslie! She sobs as though her heart would break. Some sudden revulsion of feeling has come over which she cannot control ; and knowing that she is alone, and likely to be alone for a considerable time—for Mrs. Paddlebat has gone out to pay a visit—she has given way to it, and is now relieving her heart by shedding those long-pent-up tears, which the destruction of all her better hopes in this world has generated in her heart.

For more than half an hour she so remained. She did not speak during the whole of that time, but no doubt if one could have looked upon her face, that tablet of unutterable thought, there would have been found abundant food for speculation.

But that sweet countenance was concealed partly by her hands, and partly by the long and glossy ringlets of her hair, which in native and disordered beauty streamed around her.

But suddenly something moves her. There is a low wailing sound, and she looks up. The faithful dog is by her side. His face, almost human in its sympathies, is turned towards her.

"My poor dog," she sobbed ; "you, at least, are faithful to me yet."

At the sound of her voice the huge creature testifies its joy ; it licks the small, gentle hand that is extended towards it ; and for a moment Fanny Leslie finds some consolation in the affection of her dumb favourite.

But soon the train of thought which had been thus interrupted resumes its sway again ; and, in a voice of moaning anguish, she said, "Farewell to all happiness—a long farewell. Oh! Nicholas Lowe, Nicholas Lowe, what has happened to separate us thus for ever?"

To Fanny Leslie, of course—for it was not at all likely that Lowe would make her a confidant of the real cause of their separation—his conduct was most inexplicable. She had often and often exhausted every possible conjecture upon the subject, but could arrive at no satisfactory or even probable conclusion. Well might she exclaim,—

" What have I done that I should be thus repudiated by one who, with all the seeming fervour he was capable of, sought my love !"

But so it was. There was the fact, and nothing but the fact: Nicholas Lowe had himself repudiated her, for it was folly to say or to think for a moment that any resentment arising from that note of hers, which in a moment of excited anger and jealous feelings she had written, and which had cost Rodwell his life to deliver, could have been sufficient to account for Lowe's conduct. Oh! no; she knew better by far the workings of the human heart than to believe that that was the cause of the

separation. And now again, shutting out external objects from her eyes, she strove, for the hundredth time, to think of some feasible explanation of his conduct. But all was in vain; she exhausted every hypothesis upon the subject— nothing could be done; as, even now, as has been the case always before, she was compelled to tell herself that the whole affair baffled and confounded all conjecture.

And she, too, was much altered. To be sure, her beauty still remained to her but it had lost its joyous tone of feeling.   There was a look of care upon her face which too plainly showed that she had her miseries.

Most truly was that strange and gloomy philosophy of Nicholas Lowe's, that there was a skeleton in every house, exemplified with regard to all our characters, the good and the evil.

Not one escaped the ban.   Lowe truly had his, gigantic and terrific—Fanny Leslie had hers, too.   She surely ought to have been spared.   And Mrs. Paddlebat had hers, for the sudden and mysterious disappearance of Jervis Rodwell was by no means made more palpable to her by the letter which Nicholas Lowe had, with such abundance of art, manufactured and sent to her, as if from her bridegroom that was to be.

So the lady, although perhaps she acquitted Lowe in her own mind of participating in the mysterious disappearance of Rodwell, had her skeleton for all that.

And, probably, old Gilbert Paddlebat would have freely enough declared that he had his skeleton, and he might have concluded that his was the worst, and possibly it was so, if we put Lowe out of the calculation.

As for Fanny Leslie, it would have been a good thing if she could have continued to shake off entirely all thoughts of Lowe—if she could have brought herself to believe that he was unworthy of her; but that was what she, of all living beings, was the least adapted to do.   She did not even make the effort, from a conviction of how vain a one it would be.

But Fanny's retrospections were brought to a close by the return home of Mrs. Paddlebat, who really seemed to be in such excellent spirits that no one would have supposed for a moment that she had any skeleton to trouble her.

Her face was radiant with satisfaction ; and when Mrs. Paddlebat's face became radiant with anything, it was a tolerably conspicuous object.

Fanny, from the moment that she heard her aunt's voice, became well aware that something must have happened of a nature to give her great satisfaction, so she endeavoured, as well as she could, to stifle her own griefs by putting on an appearance of composure which, alas ! had now for some time been a stranger to her heart.

Mrs. Paddlebat was quite in a fluster to get off what she called her things. And as Fanny helped her it was evident that the good lady was almost bursting with some piece of intelligence which was quite of a congratulatory and agreeable character.

Mrs. Paddlebat had been to a party which was given by a married friend of Miss Finick's ; and, as the events which there occurred are certainly of a deeply interesting character, we feel ourselves quite in a position to bestow a chapter upon them.

And the reader will bear in mind that we do not do so half so much out of any reverence for Mrs. Paddlebat—whom with all her faults we do not love—as for the events themselves—events which were doomed to exercise so marked an influence upon the future destinies of both Mrs. Paddlebat and Fanny Leslie.

But first we may as well, in order to clear the way as we go, state that the forged will which had been got up so cleverly between Nicholas Lowe and old Gilbert Paddlebat, had thriven well, and that all had gone on swimmingly.

Perhaps the absence of the plotting intriguing Rodwell from the scene of action contributed not a little to the ease with which that part of the business was conducted. But, be that as it may, it certainly was conducted easily and comfortably.

The will was duly proved ; Mr. Paddlebat's stock was disposed of, all his debts paid, and likewise all owing to him called in.

Then an arrangement was made with Mrs. Paddlebat, by which old Gilbert handed her in cash what she was entitled, and Fanny's five thousand pounds were duly invested in her name ; while Nicholas Lowe got the balance of his five hundred.

But Mrs. Paddlebat, although now she had ample means of doing what she liked, would not, like a prudent woman as she was, leave the house in the City until it was let, because, as she said—"What can be the use of paying rent some-where else, when a house of one's own is actually untenanted."

This was an argument which nobody attempted to contradict, because the real fact was, that nobody cared one straw whether she lived there or anywhere else.

Fanny was offered by her aunt a home with her, which she accepted on condition that out of her own means—for her five thousand pounds brought her in nearly two hundred per annum, she should be permitted for independence-sake to pay for her board.

This was a proposition which, from all our readers know of Mrs. Paddlebat, she was not likely to object to, so the affair was settled.

To be sure, Mrs. Paddlebat did make an effort to get rid of Leo, the dog, but finding Fanny quite firm upon that point she soon gave it up, and everything to all outward appearance went on smoothly enough.

And now for the party at which Mrs. Paddlebat had encountered an adventure which had so much pleased her, as to bring her home in such abundance of spirits to Fanny, and with the radiant face we have before made mention of.

CHAPTER LXVII.

THE ENTERTAINMENT AT CLAPHAM.—THE GENTLEMANLY MAN, AND THE LION OF THE PARTY.——MRS. PADDLEBAT'S PREDILECTION.—THE CONSERVATORY, AND THE SUDDEN DECLARATION.—THE INVITATION.

MR. and MRS. LANDELLS, and the Masters Landells, and the Misses Landells, had all retired from Cannon-street in the City, to luxuriate at Clapham Rise, in what the whole family joined unanimously in calling " The WILLA."

Mr. Landells had for a period of forty years been engaged in putting salt herrings into casks and taking them out again, by which means he had realised a consider-ble sum of money, so that he at length listened to the intreaties of his family and set up the genteel.

Cannon-street was forgotten. Such a thing as a salt herring very probably would have been met by a vacant stare on the part of any of the young Landells, and a shake of the head, implying an utter want of knowledge of the name of the fish. In fact, they became mighty genteel.

This then was the family to which Mrs. Paddlebat went to dine. Fanny Leslie had been invited likewise, but she had got clear of the invitation on the usual plea of indisposition, for she did feel herself quite unequal to the task of going into company.

But, as Mrs. Paddlebat remarked, what is the use of cooping oneself up when surely something may be done? What can be the use of making oneself miserable and never going out, when one has the means of going out respectable?

What Mrs. Paddlebat called going out respectable, was carrying half a mercer's shop upon her back, and glittering with all the resplendent glories of a jeweller's ditto.

But Fanny was proof against such fascinations, and go she would not, so Mrs. Paddlebat, to the dismay of the younger branches of the Landells, arrived alone.

And well might they be dismayed, for Mrs. Paddlebat was just about the size of three of them put together ; and, whenever she sat, she was almost certain entirely to hide and eclipse some of the family.

Moreover, Master Tom Landells had seen Fanny Leslie, and, to use his own language, he thought her a devilish nice gal, by Jove. Whether his admiration would have carried him any further we cannot say, but we can assert that her own avowal was a great disappointment to that promising youth, who looked, forthwith, all the indignation he felt.

"Damn it," he said ; " here's the old one come alone."

"My dear," said his mother ; " you really should not—hush ! How do you do,

Mrs. Paddlebat? we really are all delighted to see you, and Tom has only just said, we shall be all as comfortable as we wish, for there is Mrs. P.—Ahem!"

Mrs. Landells was in such a habit of fibbing in a small way, that somehow she said ahem! always after one of her little romances, as if by such means she cleared her throat and her conscience at the same time.

"Oh! you are very good," said Mrs. Paddlebat, "aint it disgusting, that—"

Tom Landells turned his eyes up to the ceiling and pretended to be shocked. Poor devil! he was one of those who see the mote in the eye of another, without being at all able to detect the beam in his own.

"We had Miss Fanny's note," added Mrs. Landells, after acquiescing in the remark concerning the heat, "but we did hope she would be well enough to come."

"Ah," said Mrs. Paddlebat, with a tremulous motion of her head, and then she whispered in the ear of Mrs. Landells, "she's still thinking of that odious fellow."

"You don't say so, Mrs. P. surely; well, I did think that was all over."

"Ha—ha—ha! I know what I know. Oh dear me! yes, but mum is the word, of course; ah! it is a sad thing when we throw ourselves away."

"Very—very. But, bless me, here is Mr. Arrowdale, and he's brought with him his cousin Horace—oh, such a nice young man, Mrs. Paddlebat; but I must introduce you at once."

A gentlemanly-looking man, decidedly on the shady side of forty, made his appearance now in the gaudy drawing-room, where this conversation had been carried on, and he bowed with a manner that had in it much to gratify the ladies. He was followed by a much younger man, about whom there was considerable intellectuality of expression. His face was pale—

"With the high caste of thought;"

and no one could look upon him twice, without feeling that he certainly ranked above every-day people.

There was something provincial about his general appearance, and his dress hardly reminded one of London. At all events he was an extremely different looking man from his relative, Mr. Arrowdale, who preceded him into the apartment of the Landells.

"Allow me the pleasure," said Mrs. Landells, "of introducing you to Mrs. Paddlebat, my dear sir. Mrs. Paddlebat, this is Mr. Arrowdale."

The gentleman started, and then placing his hand upon his waistcoat he bowed low, after which he said in a low voice, so that it was not likely to be heard by any but the two ladies :—

"Madam, I have longed so much for this pleasure, that—that— pardon me, I know not what I am saying; Mrs. Landells, pray oblige me by explaining to Mrs. Paddlebat, that I looked forward to seeing her here with the greatest pleasure."

"And so you did, Mr. Arrowdale," said Mrs. Landells; "that I can answer for."

"I was not aware," said Mrs. Paddlebat, making a great effort to assume a tone and manner of extreme juvenility; "I really was not aware that we had ever met before, sir."

"I have, certainly," said Mr. Arrowdale, "never had the satisfaction of meeting you before, but—but—"

"But what, sir?"

"I have seen you at a time when to attempt to forget was virtue; when—when—oh, what am I saying? ladies, forgive me, I am not master of myself."

He retired abruptly and cast himself into a seat in the recess of a window, leaving Mrs. Paddlebat in a state of astonishment difficult indeed to be described.

"My dear Mrs. Landells, what does he mean?"

"Hush! not so loud, Mrs. Paddlebat, I cannot help it; he has told me—he has made me his confidant. . I really cannot help it, nor had I the heart to tell him he should not come here to-day, it would have killed him."

"You alarm me!"

"Hush! step this way, Mrs. P."

" Yes, yes."

" Mr. Arrowdale loves you. Yes, you may start, but he does ; he has told me so. He loves you ; before Mr. P. died, he loved you, but then he had no hope ; now, he says he has. There's no accounting, you know, for tastes, but I do believe he loves you, and loves you sincerely."

" Oh, good gracious, Mrs. Landells, how could you, knowing of such a circumstance, be so cruel as to ask me here to-day? You ought not, oh, indeed you ought not."

" If you would rather go, there is an omnibus to town in half-an-hour."

" No, no. As I am here, I think I will remain ; it would look so odd to go now, and it would make him think, too, that you had told me the secret, which I would not have him know for worlds."

" Oh, of course not ; but still it was only proper that I should let you know, because, you see, it put you on your guard."

" Yes. Oh, yes. What is the creature ?"

" A stockbroker."

" Indeed ! I pity him, of course. He is not a bad-looking man altogether ; but I fear all I can do is to pity him. I am much afraid, do you know, Mrs. Landells, that I can really do no more than pity him. I'm sure I—"

" Dinner on table !" announced a fat-looking boy, who did duty as page.

Before the echo of the always welcome announcement had passed away, Mrs. Paddlebat heard a voice whisper to her—

" May I hope for the pleasure of handing you down stairs Oh ! forgive me for so much presumption."

It was Mr. Arrowdale. Yes, it was the amorous stockbroker—the man who had been smitten by fat, fair, and fifty-five. What could Mrs. Paddlebat do ? Was she to doom him to some rash act, perhaps to suicide, by refusing such a simple act of courtesy ? Oh! no, she could not do so. She ought not ; so she faintly faltered " Yes," and they brought up the rear of the string of guests who descended from the drawing-room, according to established custom, arm-in-arm, that being of course the most awkward way of two people getting down stairs together that can be conceived to the dining-room.

Nothing was more natural than that they should sit together, and oh ! the thousand little polite attentions which Mr. Arrowdale contrived to bestow upon Mrs. Paddlebat.

Did she want a little more gravy, who but he got it for her? A slice of the brown from a roast duck—oh, yes, in an instant ! And then how delicately he drank wine with her—with what mandarin-like gravity he gave the accustomed nod of the head.

" Really," as Mrs. Paddlebat said to Mrs. Landells afterwards, " he was quite the gentleman, and came nearer to her ideas of George IV. than anybody she had ever seen."

Probably she was quite right there.

But the largest and prosiest dinner must at last have an end, and so had this at the willa of the Landells'. The ladies rose to go, and the door of the dining-room was obsequiously held open by Mr. Arrowdale.

During the dinner, Mrs. Paddlebat had purloined from an epergné a rose, and she wore it at her breast. As she passed out of the dining-room, Mr. Arrowdale, with an air of desperation, snatched it from her. She was rather alarmed at first, but in a moment she understood the motive—she knew that that rose would find a place beneath his pillow at night. And now, the gentlemen are left alone—yes, alone— and, somehow, Mr. Arrowdale crushed the rose into his pocket, and sitting down, said—yes, he actually said, unromantic as it may appear—he said, in the most natural manner in the world,—

" Now that we have got rid of the women, let's be jolly !"

Yes, he, the romantic, sentimental Arrowdale, said this ; and then he poured out a glass of old Landells' best port, and gave a toast, and a sentiment after it ; and, altogether, looked as unlike a man deep in love as any very jolly sort of person could well do. Oh! the duplicity of human nature!   And this is the man who had so longed to see you, Mrs. Paddlebat, and who, when he did see you, was almost too overpowered to speak—this is the man who almost died of the pleasure of being allowed to hand you down stairs—who was so attentive during the dinner—who snatched from your bosom the rose after it.   Yes, this is the man too, who, with a thank-God sort of an expression, talked of being jolly after getting rid of the women. It was really too bad—a great deal too bad. Mrs. P., look to your three per Cents!   We cannot satisfy ourselves as to what share in this transaction Mrs. Landells had.   Perhaps, it was nothing more than the general love of match-making, which forms part of the very nature of some ladies—perhaps, she was deceived herself completely by that most artful Mr. Arrowdale ; or, perhaps —— but we really don't know.

Mrs. Paddlebat got Mrs. Landells into a corner of the drawing-room, and then and there she told her of the conduct of Mr. Arrowdale—how very polite he had been—what tasteful compliments he had paid her during the dinner ; and, finally, she detailed to her the story of the rose.

" Well, really," replied Mrs. Landells. " I must say, the man seems remarkably serious ; of course, Mrs. Paddlebat, it is for you to judge."

" Oh ! yes, of course ; he is quite the gentleman."

" Oh ! yes, that he is, and I assure you he is used to the very best society y. ;

" Is—is—he rich ?"

" I don't know, but I suppose he is well off ; at all events, he must be by his habits and his manners, Mrs. P."

" No doubt, no doubt.   Ah me! why will the men go on so? oh dear, oh dear, it's a dreadful thing to be so persecuted."

" Persecuted, my dear Mrs. P.   I really hardly know what you mean, you don't think that at your age the men are at all inclined to persecute you."

" My age, Mrs. Landells ! I really think if some people would mind what they are about, and not make themselves so very ridiculous to some other people, some people would behave themselves with more discretion."

" Do you, indeed ?"

There was a prospect of a serious dispute between the ladies, for when that most dreadful subject age comes to be discussed, there really is no knowing how far it will carry them ; but Mrs. Landells, who certainly had shot the first shaft, began to see the necessity of saying no more upon the subject, for, in addition to Mrs. Paddlebat being her guest, which should have the effect of most certainly stopping her mouth, she was open to the same dreadful reproach—the ladies themselves have made it one—of not being quite so young as she once was.

" My dear Mrs. P.," she said, " you know I was only joking. I am quite aware that Mr. Arrowdale admires you very much, and it is for you to consider what kind of encouragement, or the reverse, you choose to give him."

This carried, a long speech was duly accepted as a peace-offering by the injured lady, who at once smiled beningnly, and replied—

" Really you know, Mrs. Landells, one don't know what to say to the men."

" Well, it is difficult, sometimes."

" Oh, very—but I think you might bring him to a tea-party at my house."

" If I do then, let me bring his quiet cousin Horace with him, and then the thing won't look at all particular, you know."

" Exactly.   You are a clever woman, Mrs. Landells."

" And you are very kind and complimentary, Mrs. Paddlebat."

" Oh, don't mention it.   Really now, when I come to think of it, your idea of asking the cousin is just the very thing, because he can engage Fanny's attention, you know, while Mr. Arrowdale is paying me those delicate attentions which, no doubt he will, judging from the state of feeling, feel inclined to do."

" Exactly, Mrs. P.   That was part of my idea in the matter, and who knows but Horace Arrowdale may take a fancy to her and she to him ; so that, as I am sure nothing could give you more pleasure, than to see her comfortably settled, that is just what might result from the whole affair, you see."

" Yes, of course ; well, then, Mrs. Landells, when shall it be ?"

" When you please, of course."

" Would the day after to-morrow do ?"

" Quite well ; but I will take care to ascertain if Mr. Arrowdale and his cousin Horace are disengaged on that day or not, before I give them your invitation ; so that, if they are engaged, there will be an opportunity of altering the day without seeming to do so purposely—for then, you know, Mrs. P."

" You are quite a jewel, Mrs. Landells, that you are."

The conference of the ladies was broken up by the arrival of the gentlemen into the drawing-room ; for they had sat a much shorter time over their wine than might, from the first commencement of their sitting, have been expected.

Mr. Arrowdale became devoted to Mrs. Paddlebat, so that she had some difficulty in preventing him from rendering the flirtation too evident, while his cousin Horace, after an ineffectual attempt to do the agreeable to some of the young ladies present—an attempt which failed because he was a gentleman and said things they did not at all understand—took up a book and retired into the recess of a window to amuse himself.

But now there came a fresh animal, who was welcomed by the beaming looks of almost the whole of the party. He was a Mr. Smyrke, and was about as great a dandy as ever stepped. But he was quite the man for such a collection of people as were there present, with one or two exceptions. He dressed outrageously, wore an enormous flowered waistcoat, in the manufacture of which some shining metallic threads had been introduced ; so that, as he turned about, with his thumbs stuck into the arm-holes of the aforesaid waistcoat, he looked as if he had some extraordinary Brummagem cuirass on. Then he had an enormous wide mouth, and he laughed a great idiotic kind of laugh that was enough to stun any body. And he tried to say sweet things, and nobody could possibly mistake when he said a sweet thing, because he always laughed at it first, and that was a signal to all his admirers to go and do so likewise, and they did accordingly.

There are people in society who somehow manage to be so intrusive that when they are in a room you see scarcely anybody or anything but them. They are perpetually in the way, and seem to monopolise, in some extraordinary manner, the space which ought to be at the service of, at least, half a dozen persons.

How they manage this we are quite at a loss to discover, but it is a great fact for all that.

Now this Mr. Smyrke was just one of these people, and, turn which way you would, there was Mr. Smyrke's great offensive-looking face before, or his back within an inch of your eyes, while his hyena-like laugh was the principal sound that fell upon your ears. And, like many sorry farce-writers, who cannot be witty legitimately, he tried to make a laugh out of mal-pronunciations.

To be sure Horace, the quiet cousin of Mr. Arrowdale, suspected that this was a piece of art to cover real deficiencies, as some persons, when they are writing a letter and come to a word not convenient to spell, blur over it, making a blot so as to deceive the reader into a belief that, but for it, would have been all right enough.

And this is the sort of animal who is permitted to be a great man at parties, among people too who, we have no sort of hesitation in saying, ought to know better. This is the sort of brute who puts modest men into the shade, and becomes the observed of all observers—a fellow who cannot string together words to form one tolerable sentence—and, as for ideas, he is as deficient in such a commodity as a pig is of political economy.

Horace Arrowdale laid down his book and watched this man as he would have done the manœuvres of some animal, new and strange, which, for the purposes of exhibition, had been brought over to England from some far-off land. But, as for in any way interfering with him, that was completely out of the question.

" Mr. Arrowdale," said Mrs. Landells, approaching the stock-broker and holding up the expanded fingers of her left hand while she counted off the words she spoke with her right, " Mr. Arrowdale, are you disengaged for the day after to-morrow ? "

" The day after to-morrow," said Mr. Arrowdale, rubbing up his hair as if with a painful effort to remember, " the day after to-morrow—let me see—yes, I am."

" You are disengaged ?"

" Certainly, madam, certainly."

" Then do you happen to know if Mr. Horace, your cousin, be disengaged ?"

" Well, really, I don't know ; but the fact is he goes out so little that I should say it was a hundred chances to one against his being engaged. But he is just in that window-recess, we can ask him at once. Horace—Horace !"

Mr. Horace Arrowdale slowly advanced, and to him, then, Mrs. Landells put the question as to whether he was engaged or not on the day after the morrow? and as he really was not, Horace very innocently answered in the negative, for it was such a novel way of giving an invitation that he was thrown off his guard.

" Then," said Mrs. Landells, " I want you both to be knight-*errands*."

" Knight what, madam ?" said Horace.

Mrs. Landells felt a little fidgetty, for she fancied she had not said the thing that was perfectly correct, so she hastened to get over the difficulty, by adding,—

" I want you both to escort me to tea at Mrs. Paddlebat's."

" Oh, with great pleasure !" exclaimed Mr. Arrowdale. " Certainly we will ; I am certain I can speak for Horace."

" Yes," said Horace ; " but the heroines of romance, madam, used to be content with one knight."

" Ah ! but," interposed Mr. Arrowdale, " Mrs. Landells has altered all that, and requires two, so we won't hear any objection, Horace. Don't be captious ; come now, say—handsomely, at once—that you are much pleased, as I know you are, to go."

What could Horace do but bow and smile in acquiescence at this ? for whatever infliction this tea-drinking might be to him, he could not now possibly—without a roughness which was foreign to his nature—get out of it.

And so Mrs. Landells carried the point for Mrs. Paddlebat, who felt proportionably gratified, and the hour was fixed and everything arranged, consequent upon the invitation—which, Mr. Arrowdale took care to inform Mrs. Paddlebat in the course of the evening, gave him so much pleasure to think upon, that he scarcely knew what he said or did, and that he was quite certain it would be a useless ceremony his going to bed that night ; for that, when his mind was intensely occupied, he never could sleep.

Mrs. Paddlebat tried to laugh away this gallant speech, but she thought it was very nice for all that ; and probably never had she enjoyed a day so much since the death of her late husband, as she did that which was spent in such delightful society at the Landells' Willa, at Clapham Rise, from whence were to arise more important consequences than even she calculated upon, taking her dreams of possibilities and probabilities at their greatest amount.

And hence did she come home in so agreeable and delightful a frame of mind, astonishing Fanny Leslie by her extraordinary urbanity and the freshness of her appearance. Rodwell was forgotten. Mrs. Paddlebat now cared little whether he was murdered or not, and had anyone called upon her with the news that he was hanged she might have said " dear me," or some such expression, but it is very doubtful if the intelligence would have half so much occupied her mind as did the image of the gallant and highly eligible Mr. Arrowdale.

CHAPTER LXVIII.

THE TEA-DRINKING AT MRS. PADDLEBAT'S.—THE CONVERSATION BETWEEN HORACE
AND FANNY.—THE MUTUAL CONFESSION.—THE OFFER OF MR. ARROWDALE.—SUDDEN
EVENTS.

MRS. PADDLEBAT debated within herself gravely, on the following morning,
whether or not she should make a confidant of Fanny, but, upon giving the subject
mature consideration, she decided that she would not ; for, as she told herself, Fanny
had a number of prejudices upon different subjects, which might interfere.

"No," she said, "I will have her to find out the devoted attachment of Mr
Arrowdale for me, as best she may. She will soon see it Ah, poor man, as he tol
me himself, he finds the effort to conceal it far greater than any he is capable o
making."
Having come to this conclusion, all Mrs. Paddlebat said, was—

"My dear Fanny, I have a few quiet pleasant people—only three, to tea to morrow, and you will do me a great favour if you will join us."

When the thing was put to Fanny in this way, it was not likely she would refuse, so she said at once, of course, supposing that the visitors mentioned were ladies—

"Oh yes, aunt, certainly; you know that I am very bad company, but such as I am, you are welcome to me."

Thank you, my dear—thank you; I am not going to make the least fuss, you must know, just a quiet evening, and something nice for supper, so now, mind you don't go out, or be moping in your room and fancying yourself ill, or any nonsense of that sort."

"Oh no, you may depend upon me; I have given you my promise, and therefore most certainly I shall keep it."

This point then was very satisfactorily settled, and Mrs. Paddlebat, being determined that the first impression which the gallant stockbroker should have of her at her own house, should not by any means be one inimical to her hospitality, provided a small but a most expensive supper, which, if Fanny had been at all in the habit, which she was not, of noticing what took place around her, in the way of domestic matters, must have excited her suspicions that there was something more in this matter than met the understanding.

But she knew nothing about it whatever, and when the hour came, and the guests had made their appearance, she had not made even the least alteration in her ordinary costume. Mrs. Paddlebat left the lady, Mrs. Landells, for a moment, to run into Fanny's room, and engage her to come down. And oh! how gorgeous was Mrs. Paddlebat. Talk of a macaw, with all its brilliant plumage; it was nothing to her! She was a mountain of different-coloured satins, and the jewellery upon her must, by its weight, have made itself sensibly felt.

"Fanny," she said, "do put on something, and come down."

"Put on something, aunt! I have got on something, I hope."

"Yes, that black silk, which is all very well in its way, you know, of course, but you really have, you know, handsomer things than that."

"I have finer things, certainly, aunt; but I had no idea you wanted me to dress for this affair—none in the least, I assure you, or of course I should have done so to consult your wishes. Allow me, however, if it will not make any serious difference, and I cannot see that it will, to go down stairs as I am."

"Very well. Oh, it don't matter to me a bit, I'm sure. Come as you are, by all means, if you prefer it."

Upon the whole, Mrs. Paddlebat did not dislike the idea of Fanny making herself so great a foil for her, and instead of supposing that the simplicity of Fanny's costume would have the pleasantest effect to the eye, by being contrasted with her own gorgeousness, she considered the subject quite the other way, and said to herself,—

"It's as well as it is, certainly. If she had been dressed, of course it must have taken a something from me; but now she cannot, and my costume and jewels will show all the more on that account."

And she was right enough as regarded their showing all the more; for they did do that with a vengeance.

Fanny walked down the stair-case, and entered the drawing-room after her aunt, with all that graceful ease which only an intuitive sense of good taste can enable any one to exhibit; and much surprised was she to find that, of the party of three, two were gentlemen.

This surprise, too, was a little coupled with indignation, because she felt that her aunt had purposely left such a fact a secret from her, lest she should therefore object to joining the party at all, which would have been highly probable.

But Fanny did not exhibit either of those feelings, for she thought that, after all, the visitors could have had no part in the deceit; and, as they were there, they were duly entitled, as a matter of course, to her utmost courtesy.

And how they both looked to see the sweet, modest, beautiful-looking Fanny

Leslie glide into the apartment without a single ornament upon her after her gorgeously attired aunt, who made such a flaming appearance.

"Allow me, gentlemen," said Mrs. Paddlebat, "to introduce to you my niece, Miss Leslie. My dear, that is Mr. Arrowdale, and that is Mr. Horace Arrowdale."

The gentlemen both bowed, and Fanny did so likewise, and then she glided to a seat, while, as far as good breeding would allow him to do so, Horace kept his eyes riveted upon her face.

He had come with reluctance; but now with what a world of reluctance would he have left. How amply did he feel repaid now for accompanying his cousin to the great fat woman's house, for so he called Mrs. Paddlebat. But then, how was he beforehand to guess that it contained such a treasure as it did?

And now, before proceeding further, we will put the reader right as regards the relative position of these two persons.

Horace Arrowdale knew so little of his cousin, the stockbroker, that if we were to say he knew nothing but that there was such a personage, we should be almost near enough to accuracy. The facts of their connexions were simply these—

Horace's mother and the stockbroker had been sister and brother, and he (Horace) being left by the death of both his parents friendless, but still perhaps with the best friend of all—a tolerable sum of money in the public funds—had come to London to take the necessary steps to have the affairs re-arranged, so that what belonged to him should stand in his own name.

Knowing, then, that his mother had a brother who was a stockbroker, he sought him out, and allowed him to conduct the business concerning his (Horace's) funded property.

He was aware that this Mr. Arrowdale had done something or another which had alienated from him his relatives, but what it was he hardly knew; and although it might so far influence him that he might feel himself inclined to become very intimate with Mr. Arrowdale, yet he did not feel that it interposed any great obstacle in the way of his (Horace) allowing him to transact business for him on the Stock Exchange.

But rascals such as Arrowdale are generally extremely specious and plausible, and what are called good company, so that by degrees the stockbroker converted a slight acquaintance with his cousin Horace into a sufficient intimacy, that, at all events, he could invite him to Mrs. Paddlebat's.

Certainly Horace had come rather listlessly to the party, little supposing that he would meet one there who would be so likely to charm him as Fanny Leslie, or who suddenly would make so strong a sensation of affection rise at his heart.

But from the first moment that he looked upon her, the feeling came over him that she was part of his destiny; and that through life, let his fortune be what it might, and let what might occur to him, he should never forget the form of that gentle girl who, in all her beauty, beamed upon him so unexpectedly in that house, where he least of all expected to find anything that he could admire, to say nothing of actual love.

And often, aye, very often, Horace had held arguments with persons who had told him that love was a passion of rapid growth, and that it would burst forth, bud, and blossom, in an instant. But now he felt the full truth of such an assertion; for had he at that moment been put upon his confession, that is to say, after he had spent half-an-hour in the society of Fanny Leslie, he must have said that he loved her.

And what shall we say of her feelings towards him? Did she feel anything of the electric shock which is said to thrill through the nerves when the predestined object of our fondest affections first appear before us? or did she yet remember sufficient of Nicholas Lowe to deprive her of that natural sensibility which must have made her acknowledge how highly Nature had favoured Horace in personal appearance, and how every word he uttered bespoke the man of talent, feeling, and all that romance of genius which she most admired?

She could not be insensible to the fact that Horace was all that she could have wished in one with whom she would have chosen to go through life's pilgrimage.

But she did not ask herself the question if she loved or not. She did not ask herself if she had yet a place in her heart for a new attachment, or if the shadow, or even something of the substance of her first passion, lingered there to the exclusion of all others.

And yet why should not Fanny Leslie love again? Love is a sentiment arising from certain causes, and the same qualities which bespoke her admiration in one case must naturally bespeak it in another; and it would have been monstrous indeed if, because Lowe had turned out to be unworthy, she was for ever to shut her heart against all affection, and live on cherishing a regret for the remainder of her days, which it was her duty as well as the greatest wisdom to forget.

One can easily imagine how Mrs. Paddlebat comported herself on this emergency—in what a perpetual state of smiling bustle she was, and how she very nearly made everybody dreadfully uncomfortable, for fear they should not be quite the reverse.

It would have required but a very small allowance indeed of worldly wisdom for any one to have observed that she had made up her mind no ordinary difficulties should prevent her from becoming Mrs. Arrowdale.

Like the Irishman in the play who wanted to marry a heiress and considered himself half-way towards that object, because he had given his own consent, any one could have seen that she was half-way towards being Mrs. Arrowdale in a similar manner.

Indeed, she was far too occupied with her own thoughts and felicitation, to pay any attention to what Fanny was doing, and as we happen to know that the stockbroker entertained such serious thoughts of uniting himself to Mrs. Paddlebat, three per cents. with her as an incumbrance, we cannot be surprised that during that eventful evening, Fanny Leslie and Horace were thrown much together.

And hers was such a pure child-like-spirit that when she found any one who had feelings and thoughts in common with her, she could not avoid throwing her whole soul into the conversation, and if she had made a previous impression in her favour, she was then certain to convert it into warm admiration.

It takes but a very short time indeed for kindred spirits to find out that they really are such, and by the time Fanny and Horace had had an hour's conversation upon music, poetry, and painting, they had both made the discovery that it was the luckiest chance in the world that had brought them together.

" I own," said Horace, with a smile, " that I am sufficiently shy of company to have actually come here with reluctance, little expecting the pleasure I should experience when I did reach this place, or that I should find any one who would tolerate my romantic notions upon many subjects."

" Tolerate !" said Fanny, with a slight tone of reproach, " I assure you, sir, it is a long while since I have found any one—"

She paused, for she feared she might be saying almost too much to a comparative stranger and he was too bashful and diffident to urge her further upon such a subject, so that the conversation which, up to this point, had flowed so freely, became a little constrained between them.

But this was not the case with Mr. Arrowdale and Mrs. Paddlebat, and the wily stockbroker, whose affairs were quite sufficiently desperate to induce him to entertain an urgent wish to better them by the assistance of Mrs. Paddlebat's thousands in the Funds, and he had no minor scruples, but took care to press his suit with all the energy he was master of.

" My dear madam," he whispered, " how melancholy and dull you must feel alone, accustomed as you have been to be the life and soul of society. It is really shocking that so much sweetness—"

" Really, Mr. Arrowdale," said the lady, with a simper that looked uncommonly odd upon her rather extensive physiognomy, " really, Mr. Arrowdale, you must excuse me."

" Nay, madam, nay, I am a plain man, and say what I mean. I was going to say sweetness and beauty when you interrupted me, and I feel that it would be unjust to you if I did not say it now."

" You are so very complimentary, Mr. Arrowdale, that really one doesn't know what to say to you."

" You need say nothing," whispered the enamoured stockbroker, " you need say nothing, madam, but only cast upon me one of those bewitching glances which you know so well how to use, and I shall be the happiest of men."

Could an evening do otherwise than pass off pleasantly, under such circumstances as these ? for all parties were well pleased, and although the vivacity of Fanny Leslie had received a slight check, she felt that she could go on talking to Horace for ever without tiring.

When the party broke up, it was to the regret of all those four persons. Fanny had never spent so pleasant an evening since the death of her poor uncle ; and as to Horace, while he was talking to her he forgot all the world beside, and every care that he had ever known vanished like mist before the sunbeams.

Mrs. Paddlebat felt that she was going a long way towards getting a husband, and that husband, too, vastly superior to Rodwell in all respects ; so that she considered now that her escape from marrying that individual was really quite a providential thing, and, far from being to be deplored, was to be considered one of the happiest things in her life.

The stockbroker went away contented, because he made up his mind that he was already as good as married to the goldsmith's rich widow.

But he was rather shy of Horace in the transaction, because he felt that his motive was seen through ; and from that evening, without one word being spoken upon the subject, there was a distance between Horace and the stockbroker which effectually precluded the possibility of anything like confidential discourse.

Mrs. Paddlebat, considering that she had netted her prey, was of course tolerably anxious to bring it to shore ; so that within the next fortnight she got up two other parties, at each of which were the stockbroker and Horace ; and it was from the very acquiescence of Fanny in these domestic arrangements, that Mrs. Paddlebat began to guess there was something more than merely a desire to oblige her in the matter, and a vigilant watching, upon the last occasion, soon convinced her of the mutual attachment that had sprung up between her niece and Horace ; and the idea struck her that the way to arrive at the truth would be to confess to Fanny the soft impeachment under which her own affections laboured.

But here Mrs. Paddlebat made a great mistake ; and her vanity had been so tickled by the many compliments which Mr. Arrowdale had paid her, that she quite began to believe herself an engaging creature, and lost sight altogether of any suspicion that it was her money that the stockbroker attacked.

" My dear," she said to Fanny, as the latter with a laugh had just declared that she could not drag her aunt's stay-lace any tighter, notwithstanding Mrs. Paddlebat seemed to have an idea that she was infinitely compressible. " My dear, have you noticed anything particular in Mr. Arrowdale's attention to me ?"

" I regret to say I have, aunt," was Fanny's very serious reply ; " and it shows a great want of principle in him to affect affection for you, when it is quite evident it must be your money he wants."

Mrs. Paddlebat turned almost purple, she was in such a rage.

" Miss Fanny Leslie," she said, " the insolence of that remark is scarcely what I ought to have expected, after the manner in which I gave you a home here when you were a pauper."

" If there had been any obligation of the kind, aunt," said Fanny, " those words would have cancelled it, but it was to my uncle that I owe that debt of gratitude, an uncle who has now left me independent."

" Well, I'm sure !" cried Mrs. Paddlebat, " beggars on horseback cut strange capers, but I know what it is—because Mr. Arrowdale has not preferred you, it must be my money that he wants, but that's the way of the world ; and now you don't suppose that I am so blind as not to see you are setting your cap at Mr. Horace, and here a little while ago you were going to be married all in a hurry to that wretch, Nicholas Lowe ; but that goes off, oh dear, yes, that goes off ; and now it is to be Mr. Horace Arrowdale. I am disgusted, I really am quite disgusted.

Fanny made no answer, for she knew from experience that anything in the shape of argument from her aunt was completely out of the question, and that when once she began upon such a strain as the present, it was quite impossible for any human being to say when she would stop.

After finding, therefore, that she had it all her own way for some time, Mrs. Paddlebat walked down stairs, highly indignant, and presently left the house, for she seemed to have some appointment.

CHAPTER LXIX.

THE PROPOSAL AND ITS ACCEPTANCE, AND THE NOTICE TO QUIT.

ALTHOUGH Fanny had preserved a silence when her aunt reproached her so bitterly, she was none the less touched at that unkindness, and walking down into the drawing-room for the purpose of endeavouring to wean her mind from a recollection of it, by the soothing charms of music, she sat down by the piano-forte, but the effort was too much for her, and leaning her face on the instrument she burst into tears.

How long she remained in grief she knew not exactly, but she was aroused from it by feeling a hand gently touch her, and, looking up with startled surprise, she beheld Horace Arrowdale.

"Pardon me, Miss Leslie," he said, "and believe me that this intrusion was accidental, although I cannot regret any circumstances that give me the pelasure of seeing you. Your servant told me you were in your dressing-room but that you would be down shortly, and asked me to take a seat in the drawing-room."

"'Tis I alone am to blame," said Fanny.

"You are in grief, Miss Leslie? Oh! that you had known me long enough, or trusted me well enough, to give me the privilege of a friend, in inquiring the cause of your affliction! Nay, do not leave the apartment, or I shall think you are offended with me, and I scarcely yet dare tell you how essential your opinion is to happiness."

Fanny was moving towards the door, but a second thought told her how unjust it would be to blame him for an intrusion of which he was really so guiltless, and she paused, as she said in a tone of subdued sorrow,—

"Pardon me, Mr. Arrowdale, for my apparent rudeness to you, but when grief oppresses the judgment —"

"Grief!" he exclaimed, "what grief ought to hang its heavy mantle upon so fair a brow? Oh, Miss Leslie! a kind of desperation seizes me, as if at this moment a crisis in my fate had arrived which I could not resist, and forgetting all caution, and forgetting all those suggestions of my mind which made me think that I would try and make you know me better before I spoke, I cannot help saying now that I love you."

"Oh, forbear—forbear, Mr. Horace!"

"Nay, Miss Leslie, this is no boy's passion, having the fleeting existence of a moment, but it has become part of my very nature, and I will even own to you that I have tried to suppress the passion—but all in vain."

"I have one answer," said Fanny, tremblingly, "which will enable you to do so, I am unworthy of you."

"I would not hear another utter such a word."

"Nay, hear me out, Mr. Horace, and I know when I tell you that I have loved another you will shrink from me."

"Never, never!" he cried; "I, too, have loved another; and deceived by the litter of beauty, I plucked from my own fancy many virtues in which to array my eart's idol, but I found she was unworthy, and never again has her name passed ny lips. But that love was not like the love I bear to you; that was the infatuated adoration of a boy, but this is a sentiment arising from the deep settled conviction of a man—a sentiment which will cling to me while life exists. Oh, Miss Leslie! if you think that even serenity—greater serenity than you at present enjoy—can be yours by an union with one who will appreciate you as I shall, let me have a hope that I may call you mine?"

There was a deep and honest fervour in the words, and the manner in which they were uttered by Horace, that went to the heart of Fanny, and when he had ceased talking, and she saw by his countenance how much he had thrown his whole soul into the words he had uttered, a gush of mingled feelings came across her heart, and she was unable to answer him.

Before she could collect her scattered senses, a tremendous knock at the street-door announced an arrival, and Fanny knew that it was her aunt, for of late that good lady had thought it fashionable and great to imitate a footman in appeal for admission in her own house.

"We are interrupted," said Horace. "Oh, Miss Leslie, before I go, grant me but one word of hope; say that you will not, for the audacity of my proposal, banish me from your presence."

Fanny held out her hand to him, and a smile struggled through her tears.

He pressed it to his lips for one moment, and murmuring a blessing upon her, he turned, and, darting down the staircase, he passed Mrs. Paddlebat with such velocity, that she gave a scream of terror, and then into the street he took his way, without uttering one word to her.

"Gracious Providence!" exclaimed Mrs. Paddlebat, "what low ruffian was that! There's thieves, and I suppose, I shall be murdered next in my own house."

"It was only Mr. Horace Arrowdale, mum," said the servant; "but he certainly did go out, mum, like a bum-shell and two sky rockets; and I think, mum, that he and Miss Fanny have had some words, for she has just flewed up to her room, wiping her eyes."

"Indeed," said Mrs. Paddlebat, rising from the stairs, on which she had sat down in her fright. "I'll soon find that out, and, Susan, I shall give you a new dress next week, and you may have my tuscany, with the feathers, for I shall not wear it any longer. I am going to be married."

"Married, mum. Lor! that accounts for my dream, for I thought I saw five black beetles in a desert plate, and that one of them asked the cat what o'clock it was, and the cat said ask my tail; and if that didn't mean a marriage in the family, I don't know what it did mean."

Mrs. Paddlebat bounced into Fanny's room, and commenced at once, saying—

"Miss Leslie, when you send your fellows down stairs, just ask them to say, below there, will you, before they come down like iron hoops and sacks of nails, smashing people to death in their own passages; and what's more, I am going to tell you, that I am going to be married this day week—special licence—lots of coaches—a large party, and *dejeuner-a-forke*, as they say in French, at 12 o'clock, and Mr. Arrowdale and me have been considering, and we rather think it will be inconvenient for you to stay here any longer, because I shall want your room for my own maid—you understand—my own maid."

"I will leave," said Fanny, very quietly "before this day week."

"You need not put yourself in any passion now, for there is not the slightest occasion for that, I can tell you; for although you have quarrelled with your fellow, it appears, and sent him down stairs like an Egyptian mummy fired out of a pop-gun, I am not going to stand the brunt of it."

"I am in no passion," said Fanny, "and as I have accepted an offer from Mr. Horace, I dare say I can leave very comfortably in a day or two."

"Accepted an offer! why you—you—you—don't mean that? Susan told me you had quarrelled, and that was the reason he went down stairs so quick, like a cock with a flat iron on his back."

"We do not take Susan into our confidence," said Fanny, "and while I am here, as I pay for it, I should feel obliged if you will allow me the privilege of my own apartment."

This was meeting Mrs. Paddlebat in a style which she did not at all expect; but it subdued her, and she left Fanny very shortly to her own reflections.

———

CHAPTER LXX.

THE MARRIAGE, AND MRS. PADDLEBAT'S LITTLE DISAPPOINTMENT.

AFTER this one can well imagine what sort of note it was that on that evening Fanny Leslie directed to Horace Arrowdale, and with what rapture it was received by him. A better couple to come together under circumstances more likely to assure happiness, could scarcely have been found. Equal in fortune as they were, and with only that disparity in age which gives the husband a little more extensive experience in life than the wife, and with a wonderful similarity of taste and habit, it would indeed be something strange if they did not sip of all the felicity which wedded life could bestow; and while Mrs. Paddlebat was up to her elbows, aye, up to her ears, and running about, as Susan said, like a mad bull, in making preparations of the most showy and expensive character for her approaching nuptials, Horace and Fanny pitched upon a little quiet retired country church to which, having procured a special licence, they went in a plain chariot, and were quietly married. The old, venerable, white-headed clerk of the parish gave the bride away, so that no one knew anything about it who could at all be a trouble or annoyance to them. But how different indeed were Mrs. Paddlebat's arrangements. Her state of excitement was prodigious—there were visiting cards—a new carriage—a great footman in yellow livery, and such a number of persons invited, that, if poor old Mr. Paddlebat had looked up from his grave, as Susan remarked, he would have said, " Lor' bless me."

The old house, to use a popular phrase, was turned out of the window, and up to the very morning when the ceremony was to be performed the upholsters were finishing off the decorations. And there was one piece of malice in particular, for there were a great many of a minor character which Mrs. Paddlebat could not refrain from doing, and that was to send a letter of invitation, with a card tied round with embossed silk, to poor, miserable, old Gilbert Paddlebat.

But what was her surprise and consternation when a note came back to say, that he, Gilbert, would certainly come, for that was what she did not expect at all; and she considered that if he did come; a more serious blot upon the brilliancy of the day's proceedings could not have been imagined.

But there was no help for it now she had sent the invitation; and named the day and hour; so come he would, if he said so; and she quite dreaded to see his little monkey-like carcase wrapped up in its usual rags among her gaily attended guests.

This fretted her exceedingly; but, when another note came to say that he not only meant to come, but that he hoped to have the honour of giving away the bride, and that he meant to make her a present of something handsome on the occasion, she could scarcely believe in the evidence of her own senses; but she shewed the correspondence to Mr. Arrowdale, who said—

"Oh, let the old man come, by all means. I know he is amazingly rich, and there is no saying what these eccentric old fellows take it into their heads to do. For all we know, he may give you three or four thousand pounds—or perhaps ten thousand pounds—for ten thousand pounds would be nothing to him; and if he comes like an old guy, we can explain to everybody that he is supposed to be worth a million of money, and that will settle the business."

With this they reconciled themselves to the appearance of old Gilbert to the wedding; but when he did come, their astonishment knew no bounds.

Gilbert was in full dress. Yes, actually, Gilbert Paddlebat had on a pair of nankeen tights, silk stockings and pumps, a blue coat with brass buttons, and a yellow waistcoat which reached down to his knees.

"Mrs. Paddlebat," he said, " I do hope that all differences that have existed between us will now be considered at an end; for Mr. Arrowdale, your intended husband, must be the most disinterested of all men, and you the most single-minded and generous of women. I won't say what I am going to give you till after the ceremony."

Mrs. Paddlebat did not see anything in this speech beyond a great amount of civility. She replied to it accordingly, that all disagreements had ceased, and she looked upon him, Mr. Paddlebat, in a most amicable light.

As for the stockbroker, he was quite profuse in his acknowledgments of the honour he derived from Mr. Gilbert Paddlebat's presence, and thus loaded with compliments, they went to St. George's, Hanover-square, and were married—old Gilbert actually giving away the bride, and performing his part to a miracle;

after which the party returned to the house to the breakfast, which was certainly laid out in most magnificent style, and at a cost of so much that even the stockbroker shrunk from calculating it.

The guests got seated, amid some bustle and confusion ; and amid the gay and noisy clatter of knives and forks, and the buzz of animated conversation, the champagne corks began to fly about quite wonderfully.

Scarcely was there ever known such a delightful party ; and everything up to then, too, had gone off so well, no cross accident whatever had happened to her ; and the nuptials of Mrs Paddlebat, now Mrs. Arrowdale, seemed to promise everything that could be expected from the most happy espousal.   And animated by the champagne, too, those who had been silent before grew eloquent, and as for the eloquent, they outshone themselves.   And how red in the face Mrs. Paddlebat got ! but that was an infirmity ; she couldn't help it ; and we beg her pardon, likewise, for calling her Mrs. Paddlebat when she ought unquestionably to be called Mrs Arrowdale.

Hams, tongues, chickens, turkeys, and all sorts of confectionery, disappeared as if by magic ; and not the least astonishing part of the business was to see how old Gilbert, as the stockbroker remarked, pitched into everything, and drank more wine than any one would have thought his physical corporeality could have held.

And not the least delightful thing was to hear the tongues of the ladies, which, somehow or another, the champagne had let loose, while here and there, in odd corners, little quiet flirtations were going on ; and it seemed as if the marriage of Mrs. Paddlebat would have a good chance of being productive of a few more matches, just in consequence of people seeing how pleasantly everything of that sort might be done if set properly about.

But it was when the cloth was removed that the really interesting part of the business commenced.   Then it was, when the decanters were placed before each of the guests, and the travelling carriage in which Mr and Mrs Arrowdale were to go galloping off in an another hour could be seen from the windows, that the feast of wine and flow of soul really commenced, and everybody looked as happy as so many crowned heads.

Old Gilbert had not said much, hitherto ; but now a kind of expression came over his face, which made the person who sat next to him think that he was going to make a speech ; and that person said—

" Shall I call for silence for you, sir."

" Not yet," said old Gilbert.   " But I shall have a toast to propose before we separate."

" The bride, of course."

" What a conjuror you are !   I'm annoyed at your penetration, I am, quite. Really you must be some conjuror, you must."

The guest did not know exactly what to say to this, for he could not come to an exact conclusion as to whether old Gilbert was laughing at him or not ; so he contented himself by turning to his neighbour and paying no more attention to him.

Things went on now very lively and well, indeed, for another half hour, at the end of which time there was a slight kind of pause, during which old Gilbert Paddlebat rose to his feet, and attracted everybody's attention by saying—

" Ahem !" with such vehemence that several of the guests doffed their knives and forks in sudden terror at the shock.

" Ladies and gentlemen," said old Gilbert, " I rise—"

Loud acclamations greeted him, and for some moments he was not allowed to proceed ; but when silence was restored he continued—

" Ladies and gentlemen, I rise to propose a toast—an admirable toast, I assure you—such a toast as you will be all delighted to drink in bumpers, gentlemen."

" Hear, hear, hear !"

" Yes, gentlemen," added Gilbert, " I have a toast to propose to you.'"

This announcement was a perfectly natural one, of course, on such an occasion for any guest to make, only, no doubt, it was extremely amusing to see old Gilbert Paddlebat rise to make it, inasmuch as no one, to look at him, would have for one moment supposed, that there was in him anything approaching to good feeling or conviviality. He looked the very antipodes of anything of the sort, and, indeed, so he was; but the reader, who has a guess of that which old Gilbert is about to announce, can more easily understand than can the guests who hailed the appearance of the old miser, the reasons that induced him, of all people in the world, to make such an announcement.

There was a great clattering of glasses on the table, and loud cries of " Hear, hear—very good—Mr. Paddlebat's toast !"

When this clamorous reception had subsided sufficiently for him to be heard, the cunning old money-lender proceeded—

" Ladies and gentlemen,—When I see around me so much youth, and beauty, and fashion, I cannot help congratulating myself, that virtue and disinterestedness have after all in this world, so many ardent admirers."

" Loud applause." " Hear, hear !"

'Gentlemen,—I thank you for the cordial approbation with which you hear me. It is seldom that I speak in this way, very seldom, and I am rather surprised that my cough has not prevented me ; but perhaps, on this delightful occasion, it is content to leave me alone. I can ascribe it to no other cause, ladies and gentlemen."

" Capital, capital !"

" And now, I dare say that there is not an individual in all this assembly who does not guess the health which I am about to propose should be drunk by us all, with all the honours that we can afford to such a toast. Of course, I cannot but allude to the late Mrs. Paddlebat, the present Mrs. Arrowdale."

The cheers became deafening, and Mrs. Paddlebat asked herself,—" Have I been in a dream all this time, about old Gilbert? Have I mistaken his character, or has he so strangely and suddenly altered ? Why, he's quite a different being."

And so old Gilbert was. The pleasure he felt at the successful piece of villany he was about to play off, had for the time, to his perceptions, taken the weight of twenty years from his head, and he felt quite vigorous and strong. Pleasure sparkled in his little grey eyes, and he showed the delight he experienced by the tones of his voice.

To get the better so fully, as he knew he had, of Mrs. Paddlebat, whom he detested as much as any one human being could possibly detest another, was a treat of no ordinary kind to old Gilbert ; and no wonder then, that, quite *cona more*, he made that speech, which never was forgotten by any one who had heard it.

" Ladies and gentlemen," he continued, " it rejoices me to hear how cheerfully you all respond to that toast, which I have risen, so inefficiently,—yet with a sincerity, in which I will yield to no man—to propose. I have known that lady long, and have had many opportunities of studying her character; ladies and gentlemen, she is the most amiable person I know."

(" Hear, hear.") " What a limited acquaintance he must have," whispered one person to his next neighbour. " Very."

" We all know she is beautiful," added Gilbert.

"Oh, really now, you are joking, Mr. P.," said the bride.

" Joking, madam! joking—I should like to see the man who could joke upon such a subject ; and, I say, ladies and gentlemen, we all know that she is beautiful and amiable, and I now assert, that it was for that beauty and that amiability, that Mr. Arrowdale sought her hand, and not from any other reasons whatever. I appeal to that gentleman."

Mr. Arrowdale, when thus appealed to, laid his hand upon his waistcoat, and bowing his head until nobody saw anything but the extreme top of it, he said—

" Most certainly—of course. He is no friend of mine who doubts it. What to me is money ? and where my affections are fixed I am happy."

There were loud cries of " hear, hear," and one voice shouted " gammon," but nobody took any notice of the very unpolite piece of candour. Suppose it was gammon, as of course it was, what business had that censorious individual to say so. If all the gammon that was uttered in the world, was declared to be such, at the moment of its appearance in society, Good God!—what should we do? It was very wrong, socially and morally wrong, of anyone to call out in such an unhesitating manner, "Gammon!"

"I am satisfied," continued Gilbert; "my good friend Mr. Arrowdale has just said what I knew he would say, and he does honour to his head and to his heart, I am proud, gentlemen,—I am proud, ladies, to find that I am even distantly and collaterally now connected with that gentleman; it is a great honour, and I feel it as such."

"Oh, the honour is all the other way," said Arrowdale.

"No, no. I insist and I shall now, ladies and gentlemen, prove to you what a love-match this is; I shall prove to you, what a noble, disinterested affair it has been from first to last, and I shall, in consequence of what I am about to tell you, make you all feel that generosity, disinterestedness, and virtue, go hand-in-hand with a Paddlebat and an Arrowdale."

"What the devil is he at," thought the stockbroker; "damn it, he is never such an old fool as to fancy I yoked myself to an old fat woman, for anything short of the ten thousand pounds she has in the Three per Cents? If he does, he is in his second childhood, that's quite clear, and if he don't what can he be about?"

"He must be out of his senses," thought Mrs. Arrowdale. "What can he be going to say next?"

"There was, of course, abundance of applause, when old Gilbert made the last point in his address to the guests, and he was not allowed to proceed for some moments; but at length, by mute appeals to them, he did obtain silence.

"Ladies and gentlemen, allow me to explain. I will show you, in a few words, how true and how sincere must have been the affection of Mr. Arrowdale for Mrs. Paddlebat; and I will show you how deep must have been her trust in him. You are all aware that my poor departed brother was not poor in the ordinary sense of the term. He showed the estimation in which he held his amiable partner, Mrs. Paddlebat, by leaving her well to do—in fact, quite independent, ladies and gentlemen."

There was no applause; for Gilbert's manner was now so odd, that people felt certain that something was coming that they would not put off the chance of hearing quickly by any delay which applause of the orator might have occasioned.

"I presume, ladies and gentlemen, that your glasses are all charged with bumpers; and therefore, without detaining you any longer, I shall propose to you, with three times three, the health of Mrs. Arrowdale, who, with the most noble disinterestedness, has consigned everything for the man of her choice."

"Hurrah, hurrah! Mrs. Paddlebat. Hip, hip, hip! Hurrah, hurrah, hurrah!"

The toast was drank; and Mr. Arrowdale, coming forward, said to old Gilbert,

"I beg your pardon; but, instead of saying *for* the man of her choice, you should have said *to* the man of her choice. There has been no settlement whatever."

"I beg your pardon, Mr. Arrowdale—I am quite correct. I think she resigns all for the man of her choice.—that's you; and as for a settlement, unless you made one, there could be nothing of the kind, of course."

"Nothing of the kind, eh?"

"No."

"What do you mean, Mr. Gilbert?" said Mrs. Arrowdale.

"Now, really," said old Gilbert, "this is a joke. I know you neither of you think anything of it—I know you don't care one straw. But I will explain to the ladies and gentlemen present what I mean; and you shall neither of you, although I know you fain would do so, escape the just encomiums which your conduct so truly deserves. I will explain."

"Oh, he's mad!" whispered Arrowdale to the person who sat next to him; "the old man is out of his senses, or else he has taken too much wine—for I really, upon my word, don't know what he is about."

"Hush! we shall hear."

Old Gilbert pretended to be seized with a violent cough; but, when he had mastered that, he spoke, clearly and distinctly enough, to the intense surprise of all, and the intense gratification of some.

"Ladies and gentlemen, I am quite sure you will excuse the infirmities of age, and allow me to plead them as my apology for keeping you so long out of the information which redounds so much to the credit of Mrs. Paddlebat that was, and her husband, that you ought to know it. The fact is, as perhaps most of you are aware, my late brother, from a well-placed admiration of the many noble qualities of his wife, left her a most ample provision, which might or might not be taken out of the business; but Mrs. Paddlebat preferred that the business should be sold, and that she should get all that she was entitled to in cash. Well, ladies and gentleman, as executor, I did not oppose that mode of settling the affair; and accordingly the sum of ten thousand pounds was made over to that lady."

"Yes, yes," said Mr. Arrowdale, "ten thousand pounds, Three per Cents, now being done at 102."

"Exactly," said old Gilbert.

"Go on, sir, go on."

"I am going on, Mr. Arrowdale, if you will permit me. Now, ladies and gentlemen, I am, at once about to silence for ever the tongue of malevolence. I am at once about to convince all of you that nothing but the purest and the most heartfelt, and the most genuine affection could subsist between that lady, whom I hope I may call my illustrious relative, and Mr. Arrowdale, for by that happy marriage we have this day assembled to celebrate, Mrs. Arrowdale, as she now is, gives up the whole of that money."

There was a general start of surprise; and Mr. Arrowdale, turning of an ashy paleness, sprang to his feet.

"What!" he said; "what, old man, what do you mean—are you mad?"

"Not that I know know of."

"Give up the Three per Cents, give up the money!"

"To you, of course," suggested some one. Mr. Arrowdale sank into his seat again with a sigh of exquisite relief.

"Oh! ah! to be sure, to me. Oh! yes, to me—to her husband, of course."

"But," said old Gilbert, "you do not mean to tell us that if what I had said was to have been taken in its literal sense you would have felt your affection less for the charming being whom you have taken to your heart?"

"Perish the thought!" exclaimed Mr. Arrowdale, who felt that, as he had very nearly committed himself, it was highly necessary that he should say something to undo the impression he might have made. "Perish the thought! Mrs. Arrowdale would be as dear to me without one farthing as she now is with all her stock."

"Bravo!" cried old Gilbert; "what a relief it is to me to hear you say so, for, after all, I really meant what I say, and I am really much surprised that you should be in ignorance of the little circumstance to which I allude."

"Little circumstance, sir."

"Yes, oh, a mere trifle, when we come to consider the real state of your feelings. the merest trifle in life, nothing worth speaking of, I assure you.—a mere bagatelle. But I must own you gave me something of a shock at first. Have you really not seen Mr. Paddlebat's will?"

"Good God, no!

"Well, I am sorry for that, rather."

"You old wretch!" shrieked Mrs. Arrowdale, who could now no longer restrain her feelings. "You old odious wretch, what do you mean? What do you mean, I say?"

"Bless me, this is too bad when you are praising people to the skies. What I mean is simply this, there house is a codicil to the will of Mr. Paddlebat which says, that if his widow should marry again the whole of what he leaves her shall revert again to the general estate, and as I am the person to whom the general estate belongs, why it comes to me."

"Damnation," cried the stockbroker.

Mrs. Arrowdale gave a loud scream.

The greatest possible amount of confusion reigned among the guests; some rose and appealed to old Gilbert to say he was only joking. Some were anxious to go to spread the news about among their friends and acquaintance, and others were absolutely terrified.

".You old villian—you old ape," cried Mr Arrowdale, why in the name of all that is damnable, did you not tell me this before?"

" I tell you. Oh, you knew it."

" I did not know it."

" I tell you, you did. You must have known it. A man like you not to know a fact that so nearly concerned him. Phoo, Phoo! Don't tell me such nonsense. I say you did know it, and you are now only having a bit of fun with us all."

" Fun! fun!"

" Yes, fun. Why don't you all laugh, ladies and gentlemen! Don't he do it well now? anybody to look at that man who did not know him so well as I do would really think that he was quite in a rage at the thought of not being the possessor of the very money that he gave up voluntarily, and with such a perfect good grace."

" Monstrous devil," cried Arrowdale, "let me get at him, I'll have his life, I'll kill him, I cannot permit such a fiend to live."

" Hold him, hold him," said old i l bert, "hold him."

" The guests threw themselves between the enraged Arrowdale and the delighted old Gilbert Paddlebat, or fit is just possible that in the bitterness and the agony of his disappointment, the stockbroker might have completely annihilated the miser, and qualified himself for a place in Newgate. His rage was of the most wild and desperate character that can be imagined, and it took the united exertions of two or three gentlemen present to keep him from actually getting across the table to old Gilbert."

" Really now, my dear friend," said Gilbert, " you have carried the joke too far almost, you will make yourself ill."

" Do you mean to tell me that, Mrs. Paddlebat—"

" Arrowdale, if you please, Arrowdale; really now, the unpoliteness of a married man calling his wife by any other name than that which he has just bestowed upon her, is too bad."

" Do you mean to say that she has no money?" roared the stockbroker.

" Certainly I do, it all reverts to me."

" But you do not intend to—to take it."

" I do not care one straw for the money, not a jot; what do I want with it?'"

Here was a hope. Mrs. Arrowdale gave some symptoms of recovery, and said faintly, for she had thought it prudent from the first moment that the dreadful announcement had been made, to lapse into a sort of insensibility.

" Where is Mr. Gilbert, oh, where is he? let me see him, he is so kind and generous."

" I am here, madam," said old Gilbert, "pray console yourself."

" Oh, my dear sir," said the stockbroker, "best of men, do you really mean to say you do not care for the money because—because—we do?"

" When I say I do not care for the money," said old Gilbert, " I speak the genuine sentiments of my heart, I assure you; what is such a sum of money to an old wretch?"

" Nay, nay."

" I say nay to an old ape, a monster; what can such an amount be to me, and I here before all these ladies and gentlemen renounce it, as regards my own feelings, but—but—respect for my brother's memory, a respect which I can only show by adhering rigidly to his intentions, forces upon me the cruel necessity of taking the whole of it."

The stockbroker looked livid with rage, and turning to Mrs. Arrowdale, he said—

" And you knew this?"

" No, on my soul I did not."

" Curse you all! damnation! does anybody here imagine for one moment that I should have been such a besotted idiot as to match myself with an old fat hog of a woman for nothing ?"

Mrs. Arrowdale gave a shriek, and then in her turn she cried—

"And does anybody suppose that I would have given up my fortune for a wretch like this ?"

"Really," said Gilbert, "there must be some strange mistake here. I am quite astounded, for I thought, of course, you both knew all about the will; I can hardly believe my own senses, when I hear you talk in the way you do, and I still think you may be joking, and that it will all end in a good laugh."

There was now a silence of some few minutes' duration. The fact was h at nobody knew very well what to say, but there was not one soul present in that room who thought the affair a joke. No, no, they had seen good acting in ther lives, but this was nature itself—they had no doubt whatever but that the unfortunate stockbroker was jilted.

But how it was that he of all men should not know it, was the mystery : a man of business well known for being such almost to absolute sharpness—a man who, some people said, did not scruple ever to take an advantage if he could keep to the windward of the law—that he, as the greatest speculation of his life, should be so completely taken in, really appeared to be positively incredible. They were confounded, and looked at each other to gather opinions, being each afraid single-handed to come to a conclusion upon the subject. Then Mr. Arrowdale rose and walked towards Mrs. Arrowdale.

"Madam," he said, "will you allow me three minutes' conversation in private?"

She hesitated a moment, as if she thought it possible that he meant, now that he was so much disappointed in the fruits of the alliance he had made, to murder her, but still she did not like absolutely to refuse, and she rose and followed him from the room. The guests were puzzled whether to stay or go. Some of the most modest and quietest took their departure at once, but intense curiosity to know what would next happen, we are sorry to say, kept the remainder in the house.

Old Gilbert laughed, rubbed his hands, and sat down.

But what could Mr. Arrowdale now have to say to his wife, after the very uncourteous expressions he had used towards her ? We shall see. The moment they were alone, he said almost fiercely—

"Madam, can you look me in the face, and say you did not know of this?"

"I had not the least idea of it," said the terrified Mrs. Arrowdale, "and what's more, I don't believe one word of it."

"You—you don't?"

"I do not ; I know old Gilbert Paddlebat well. For the mere pleasure of getting up such a scene as that in which you have so committed yourself, that we shall both be the laughing-stocks of the whole city, he would have said all that he has said."

"Is that possible ? If it be so, I shall never have done cursing my own folly ; but to business. Your money is in the Three per-Cents ; give me now and at once a writ'en authority to sell out my portion of it, and I will go and do so ; it will be a shorter process that, than setting about proving my claim to it, by virtue of being your husband."

"Anything, anything," said Mrs. Arrowdale, "to convince you that I did not know of it, I will write what you like, only tell me what it is to be."

Mr. Arrowdale dictated to his wife a note, which was quite sufficient to give him full power to sell out the whole of the ten thousand pounds stock, and then he said—

"Is there any way by which I can get out of the house without being seen by those who are in it?"

"No ; but you can slip down stairs—nobody will notice you."

"I will ; and now, Mr. Gilbert Paddlebat, you will find that possession is nine points out of ten in law ; and you will find some difficulty, I'm thinking, in getting your ten thousand pounds out of my hands."

cautiously he stepped down the stairs, and out at the door. To be sure some people, who were waiting for the bride and the bridegroom to come out, gave a shout when they saw him in the gay attire, which at once bespoke him as belonging to the marriage throng, but he soon gave them the slip, and as fast as he could he hurried to the Stock Exchange.

Mr. Arrowdale, you may be a very clever man in your way, but old Gilbert Paddlebat is one too many for you. Could you believe it possible that he had committed such an error, as to allow you the best chance of playing him such a trick?

No; when Mr. Arrowdale reached the city and made an effort to sell out the ten thousand pounds stock, that stood in the name of Mrs. Paddlebat, he was duly informed that the process of law, called a distringas, had aleady been gone through, which would suffice to stop a private banker from giving up money until some disputed claim to it is settled.

This was a severe blow, and it almost prostrated Mr. Arrowdale completely. He reeled again when the intelligence was given him, and a friend, who was near at hand, that is to say, a fellow stockbroker, asked him, " what was the matter?"

"Nothing—oh, nothing," he said; "only I am a fool—an idiot—an ass. That's all—good day—good day!"

The other stockbroker looked after him in amazement, and then, with a toss of the head, he said—

"Something wrong in the cranium I should say, and no mistake. I'd lay a new hat with anybody now, that we shall hear of Arrowdale doing something desperate by-and-by."

"Whether or not the stockbroker was in a mood to do anything desperate or not, we shall soon perceive; but while that subject remains undecided, we may as well take a peep at the guests at Mrs. Arrowdale's, and see what they are about."

When the bridegroom had left, the lady asked herself what she should do, and after some time she hit upon what was certainly the most prudent plan to adopt. She retired to her bed-room above, and from there sent a message to the guests that she was too unwell to come down stairs, even to bid them adieu, and hoped they would excuse her. Thus she succeeded in clearing the house, and then she dismissed the carriage which was to have conveyed the happy pair to Brighton, and she awaited, with no small amount of impatience, the return of Arrowdale.

Hour after hour passed away, and he came not; until at last, wearied out both in mind and body, and as miserable as any human being could well be, poor Mrs. Arrowdale took off some of her bridal finery, and, throwing herself upon a couch, she gave herself up to some of the most painful and most agonising reflections that her situation presented to her, and Heaven knows it was one likely enough to be prolific in such matters.

And now we will take a peep at Nicholas Lowe, and see what he is about while these strange events are taking place among persons whom he knew so well.

CHAPTER LXXI.

NICHOLAS LOWE FINDS OUT HOW MUCH HE STILL LOVES FANNY LESLIE.—HIS DETERMINATION.

SINCE the moment that he (Lowe) had been made acquainted, which he was by old Gilbert, with the fact of the approaching marriage of Fanny Leslie, he had suffered all the pangs which a blighted affection was capable of inflicting upon him.

He had fondly imagined that since the death of Rodwell, which had induced him to take the most commendable step he had ever taken in his life—namely, a determination not to make, under such circumstances, the young and beautiful Fanny his wife—that he had schooled his mind to hear with calmness the news, which he was quite sure would one day come upon him, that she was another's.

But in so fancying, he had given himself credit for a strength of mind which he did not possess, and he found that when the actual intelligence did come to him, that she was about to become a wife, he was wretched—most wretched.

Then for the first time, probably, he was able to define to his mind how much he loved her. Then he found that all the

"Pangs of cankerous jealousy,"

might yet be awakened in his heart, and that far from forgetting the love that had warmed his bosom for her, the passion had only slumbered, and that the thought of her becoming another's was the spark which again roused it to activity.

But what could he do? Had he not voluntarily cast from him the glorious possession? Had he not already waged war with passion, and had he not gained a glorious triumph for principle? Alas, he found that that triumph only subsisted while Fanny Leslie remained as she was, but that at the first breath of information that she was about to unite herself to another, he was nearly maddened.

Now, indeed, came some of the retribution which he, Nicholas Lowe, was condemned to for the deed of blood which he had done. Now, indeed, he felt that he was alike ruined in his love as in every other hope of his existence.

He could not retire to rest on the night preceding that day on which Fanny Leslie was to pronounce those words that would make her Horace Arrowdale's, and which would banish from her imagination all thought of affection that she might have formerly felt for him, Nicholas Lowe.

"Oh, this is agony, indeed," he exclaimed, as he flung himself upon a couch, and hiding the light from his eyes, he mentally went back again to all the scenes that had passed between him and Fanny, and pictured to himself her every look, and heard again, amid the stillness that surrounded him, her soft, sweet voice talking to him in the fond accents of affection. And what was he now? Who now would speak to him one word of love. What was he but a moral blight upon the face of nature. A pestilence to be avoided—one on whom the vengeful heavens had set the seal of reprobation—the murderer—the slayer of God's image ; he, who had taken that precious life which no human art could restore.

He pictured her to his mind's eye as he had first seen her, when she arrived so desolate at the old Goldsmith's house, with no companion, no friend, that then she knew of, and the affection of whom she could count upon, but the dog who had travelled with her so many miles by sea and land.

Then, with what a vivid and distinct impression came her sweet voice over him as he thought again he heard her thank him for the books that he had lent her !

Oh, such thoughts as these were severe agony.

He remembered, too, the thrill of joy that pervaded his whole frame when he had the first time pressed his lips upon her cheek, and kissed away a tear that at some sad remembrance had hung there like some rich gem. He remembered well, how she had told him she would be his, and with what a noble confidence she had placed her small, soft hand in his, and hoped with a smile, that spoke more of certainty than of hope, that he would always love her well.

The night was waning, and he could not sleep. To attempt it would be futile. And, besides, of what materials would his dreams be likely to be composed of? Would he not see her, perchance, at the very altar's feet with another, and then awaken to more agony, to find that she was so utterly lost to him for ever? oh, yes—yes. He dared not sleep.

And more than once he now regretted that he had cast her from him, even although he was a murderer. He thought that surely they might in some other land have found that peace, which in this he, at least, could not hope for. But then, again, what excuse but the true one, could he have made to Fanny for such an act of expatiation ? What could he have told her that would have been sufficient to induce her to see the necessity of such a proceeding, but that he was a murderer?

And then, what would she have said, and what would she have done ? Would she not have shrunk from him with horror? Oh, yes—yes.

Thus tortured by thick-coming fancies, had Nicholas Lowe, whom at times we cannot help pitying, notwithstanding the great crime of which he has been guilty, takes him almost without the pale of that feeling, passed some dreadful and weary hours.

Midnight had come and gone. The still hours of the night were speeding onwards, and Nicholas Lowe began to feel that if he continued much longer in such a train of thought, he would in all human likelihood, drive himself to madness.

"No, no," he said, "I dare not thus indulge the bitterness of fancy, I must find some resource—something that will withdraw me from the pain of thought."

He reached himself a book, and trimming the light, which was burning in the room, he banished altogether the idea of attempting to seek repose, at all events, until daylight, and made an effort to withdraw himself from the terrors of real life, by plunging into the realms of fiction. He read as follows:—

Beneath the walls of Belcroft Castle crept the figure of a man who, in an ample cloak, enveloped his person so completely, that it would be impossible to discern his figure, and save that the plume in his bonnet denoted him a person of distinction, he would have been unknown to any human being, even though he had been his own brother. He slowly moved forward in the shadow of the high towers that stood up high in the flooding moonlight, that danced on many a glittering stream, and silvered many a trembling leaflet.

No soul was nigh, and yet the figure moved cautiously until it came to some ivy-crowned wall, and there, by means of the plant and the ruggedness of the stone surface of the walls, he climbed up the wall until he stood on the ramparts of the castle.

Pursuing his way along, in the shadow of the towers, he suddenly came upon a sentinel, who was leaning on his partisan and looking over the wall upon the sylvan scenery around, when the man hearing a slight noise turned his head to ascertain the cause, and the figure, spreading out his arms, and the ample cloak that wrapped him up so comfortably was spread open, and then a sight presented itself to his eyes that made him stagger.

The features of the stranger were skeleton-like, but there was a likeness to the living—to one, who had been living, that could not be mistaken—but the body was that of a complete skeleton; the long boney limbs—the ribs—the whole structure indeed were too plain to be mistaken.

"Holy Virgin!" exclaimed the sentinel, "Santa Maria!"

But his ejaculations were cut short by the figure advancing on him, and when within about a foot of him, the trembling and chattering soldier fell to the earth in a swoon.

The figure passed on and was seen to enter a small door that opened into one of the towers, and there it was lost.

That same night the baron of Belcroft, who had newly come into the estates, upon the death of his brother and the failure of his heir, who had died abroad, sat in his chamber; he had been but a few weeks in possession of the place and now he proceeded to con over, in his own mind, the various projects which engaged his attention. It will be as well to let him speak.

"For a younger brother," he muttered, as if speaking to himself and counting off on his fingers the various facts that he stated, "for a younger brother, I have, I think, done very well, from another John of Lackland I have become possessor of a kingdom, from an acreless boy I have grown into a good baron and owner of many a broad vale, many a stream, and many a wood.

"Dear and roe, fish and fowl, are mine; and yet how have I acquired them? aye, that is the question : why, it has been done by the force of my own character, by my own policy and cunning, and when that has failed me there have been means that have not failed me. If men are perverse and will live they may yet be made to die despite all that they may say about its justifiableness.

"I have the whole of my brother's inheritance; he was killed, accidently, and, moreover, his heir has disappeared, nobody knew how; his body was found too mangled to be recognised; I saw that but didn't do it; oh no, I didn't do it.

"But once again there's my brother's ward; aye, the gentle Gertrude, who is as gentle as she is beautiful, my very good nephew's intended bride; aye, my brother had an eye to her fortune, which is immense, and, moreover, my nephew had an eye to her beauty—then why should not I?

"Certes, there can be no objection to my looking at her fortune and coveting it, or being enamoured of her person. I like both, and, by the Holy Virgin, I will have both!"

As he spoke he lifted his eyes from the contemplation of his slipper to the ceiling, but in doing so he encountered the gaze of a pair of eyes that caused him to tremble, and with a shaking hand he sought the help of his sword.

"Who are you?" he exclaimed.

The figure that stood opposite to him had on a bonnet or slouched hat, with a drooping funeral plume that seemed to overshadow his face, and an ample cloak over, enshrouded his person.

"Who are you, and what do you do here?" again demanded the baron in great perturbation.

The figure slowly nodded his waving plumes, and then gradually extending his arm, opened the cloak—lifted off the plumed bonnet, and revealed its horrific form.

It was that of a mere skeleton—bones—nothing but bones, save in the face, where there was a marked likeness to a large portrait that hung in the room; but it was so pale—so ashy pale, while the eyes shone with lustrous fire.

The baron shrank up in a corner of the huge chair in which he sat, trembling and unable to speak; and at length covered his face with his hands as if he feared to look upon the form that stood before him; he was as one in an ague fit.

The figure replaced the hat, and re-enveloped itself in the cloak, and once more he slowly left the apartment by a sliding panel in the wall, but so quietly that he was not heard.

*   *   *   *   *

It might have been an hour ere the baron dared lift his head to see if the awful apparition had yet disappeared; he shrunk from encountering the gaze of those eyes—he dared not look upon those well-remembered features, and that bony structure, too, told a tale too horrible to be remembered without emotion—it spoke more than any wordy reproach—more than any human ingenuity could inflict.

At length he did gradually remove his hands, and open his eyes to look about him; he saw the figure was not there—he looked around him and yet saw it not.

"Gone!" he ejaculated; "gone!"

He paused some moments, and sat up in his chair; his face was ashy pale and bedewed with perspiration—cold and clammy, caused by the fearful emotion he had undergone.

"Gone!" he again repeated at an interval of some minutes, and he arose to his feet and gazed all around.

It was marvellous to see the great change that had been so suddenly effected in a strong man—a man capable of exerting himself for his own safety, with success, were he to battle for it, against odds.

He seemed to breathe more freely now, and somewhat reassured as each moment passed by without the appearance of the much-dreaded figure.

"God of Heaven!" he exclaimed, "is it a dream—a mere fancy? Surely it must be—it has left no stamp of its reality, save on the soul—and there, indeed, I do feel it. But what is it after all, a phantom? I dare say some momentary mental disorder seized upon my brain, and converted the whole into a false shadow of the past."

"A false shadow!" he muttered to himself, "that—that could not be—and yet it need not be. What has been my cast? A shadow on the brain, which in mental disease may sometimes suddenly be reproduced, and seem real. That is what I have suffered."

This reasoning in a great measure composed him, and he continued his former strain of reasoning.

"Now let me see. Aye, there's gentle Gertrude, as I call her—aye, I might as well call her beautiful—most beautiful; indeed, I know none so well qualified as she is, to be the queen of beauty; but that is only an accidental qualification—because were she as ugly as the portress of purgatory, I would marry her—that is, if she had the same broad lands as she has—not else—not else.

Riches I want. If I had riches, I would have beauty—but not beauty alone—I prefer the means. The end can always be attained when you have them.

"Enough of this to-night, I will to my bed, and to-morrow's dawn shall not sink before I have opened this matter to her. She must see the many motives I have for such an alliance; and gifted as she is, she cannot fail to acquiesce."

Thus having settled in his own mind the course he would take on the morrow, he retired to his couch.

*   *   *   *   *   *

The gentle Gertrude that evening was more pensive than usual; she had long heard of her lover's death, his uncle had told her of it, and she had grieved sadly, or it; but no consolation appeared. Little was said how he had died, and nothing was said by him about her; she could not but feel that she had lost one who loved her; of that she was very sure, and one whom she loved too.

He had been dead now more than a year, and she remained in the castle with his uncle, who had been so immersed in his own affairs that she knew little of him, and that little did not please her; and yet she could not but admit that he paid her every attention she could wish, and desired to make himself agreeable to her.

"And yet he is nothing like Robert of Belcroft, who was as brave and fearless as he was handsome;" she would say; "alas, for him! that he should be cut off thus early in youth! he was following the footsteps of his gallant father, but, alas! —"

The lady suddenly started. She saw something that caused her to rise from her seat, as though a serpent had coiled itself up before her and was ready to spring.

She stood mute with astonishment, perhaps terror had no little share in her feelings; she gazed upon a small table that stood by her side.

On this table—which was more ornamental than of any utility—lay a silk scarf, such as ladies wrought when their knights left them for some journey or joust; she knew it again—it was one she had herself embroidered, and gave to Robert of Belcroft before he left England, and which he promised never to part with.

"Holy Virgin! what means this?" she exclaimed as she seized upon the scarf; "what brought this here? who can have done this thing? Oh, God! have mercy—there is blood!"

She dropped the scarf upon the floor, and stepped back a pace or two, as though she feared to step upon it.

"It is blood—Robert's blood! God of Heaven! how came it here? and wherefore was it brought?"

The scarf lay on the floor; she stooped and picked it up as though it would have been dangerous to handle it. There were two large holes in it, as if a sword or dagger had been thrust through, and those parts were especially bloody. The blood was now dry and hard, and the silk stiff from that cause alone.

"Wherefore came it here?" she muttered; "surely, surely, he has died an unfair death. Oh! Robert, Robert, never will I forget thee—never absent from my mind—I will never love another but thee! and, be the end what it may, I will never wed for thy sake! I will keep this scarf I gave thee—which is now stained with thy precious blood — in remembrance of thee and in memorial of this promise; and, moreover, it may assist to bring those to justice who have done thee wrong."

As these words passed her lips, a soft and melodious strain of music, not unlike some solemn dirge, passed through the apartment and continued for a minute or two, and then ceased altogether.

Gertrude sat and listened to it in silence, and with a strange desire to hear it continued; it was perfectly enchanting; but when it ceased she sank back in her chair, and rapid thoughts passed through her mind, she knew not what to imagine.

The occurrences that seemed to be taking place around her seemed suddenly to have changed their character. She began by examining her own position and that of the dead, and then that of the living, but there was nothing as yet tangible —she could only come to the very common-place conclusion, that what was— was; and what was, in course of change, would be.

She had no means of drawing conclusions from bare facts, because there appeared no predicates among them.

That was a matter that would have to grow into being, as after events grow out of former ones, and enabled her to trace a relationship between them, and thus arrive at their source, and then a conclusion could be come at respecting motives, and sometimes the knowledge of the latter led to a knowledge of the authors.

*   *   *   *   *   *   *

The next morning the Baron of Belcroft sat down to his morning meal with a clouded brow. He did not seem to be the same wily and crafty man; he was too much absorbed and too shifty, and looked too much at the doors when any of them opened.

At length a retainer came towards the table, and stood at a distance. He saw there was something in the man's appearance that denoted disquiet and disorder.

"How now, Hugh Bolton; what would you have with us this morning? Tell me, did aught strange come in the castle last night?"

"Aught strange, my lord," repeated the man, opening his mouth and eyes very wide indeed.

"Yes; is there much that is strange in my question?"

"No, my lord, but—"

"But me no buts; tell me at once, varlet, what has happened in the night, or I'll have your fool's ears grace the armoury wall. Did any strange thing or appearance find its way within the castle walls?"

"Then it is true, my lord."

"Now, by the holy rood, if this aint enough to exhaust all patience; but I will hear thee first and punish thee afterwards. I will tell thee what, if you speak not out at once, thou shalt remember thy folly if thou livest after it; tell me what you mean?"

"Why, Gilbert," said my lord; "that—that—"

"Gilbert," shouted the baron in a rage, as he dashed a large goblet at Hugh Bolton, in a frenzy of passion.

Gilbert stood forward, not without much tremor and dread, but he had less fear of speaking his mind out when desired to do so.

"What is the meaning of all this? You heard my questions to Hugh. Answer them and take his place.

"An please you, my lord, I was doing duty as sentinel on the ramparts, where I was looking over the country for some distance; an please you, my lord, it was quite moonlight. I had walked up and down my watch often enough, and stood there a few moments. I then turned to move on again, when I saw something suddenly standing close by my side.

"You believe, an please you, my lord, I was rather scared at this—but, I asked who was there, or something like it, when it opened a cloak, and showed me its body and face."

"Well, well," exclaimed the baron, impatiently, but almost out of breath from the excitement he felt.

"Yes, an please you, my lord, I saw he was only bones; yes, only bones, an please you, my lord: and then—and then—"

"And what then?" exclaimed the baron, in voice of thunder that made the retainers all start. "What then?"

"Why, then, an please you, my lord, he had the face of—of—"

"Of whom?" roared the baron.

"Of—of—the late baron, your brother, an please you, my lord,' whined the miserable retainer in an almost cry of despair; "and, and—"

"And what?"

"I fell down in a fit," he gasped out.

The man ceased to speak. He was almost on his knees by the time he had done; and an ashen hue came across the face of the baron, whose haughty pride, however, caused him to dissemble the fit of terror that he could not dispel, and cause his own confusion by violent gestures and a loud tone.

"Away, away," he said; "trouble me not with these old wives' tales. I will not hear them. My castle shall not be the receptacle for frighted hinds who dare not keep watch and ward, lest some shadow should flit across the room.

The retainers shrunk back aghast and ashamed. They knew not what to do. They must believe their comrade had been terrified, or, what was not a very improbable matter, that he had taken more than the guard-room allowance of ale.

No more was said, but some few saw that the baron himself was not in the usual state of equanimity. He appeared to be more than usually thoughtful, and that he was somewhat apprehensive, and was continually looking around him with the air of a man who fears to see some unwelcome sight each moment that he turns himself.

This was painful, and he tried all he could to conceal it, and fortunately he succeeded. However, the Lady Gertrude appeared to watch the turn of events, and she could not help thinking there was a great alteration in the baron's manners, as if a load of care had suddenly have added to his years.

After the breakfast had passed off, he said to her suddenly—

"I hope, Gertrude, that these silly tales of these men, who are frightened at their own shadow, this will not, I trust, abridge your walks on the ramparts."

"Not at all," replied the Lady Gertrude; "I am not so silly as to believe every idle tale, though I have by no means a mind that rejects all warnings or supernatural visitations."

"A very prudent resolve. When you are at leisure this morning, I shall be glad to see you upon some important matter, upon which I wish to speak to you about."

"I shall be at leisure whenever it may suit you to speak to me," replied the wondering Gertrude.

"By mid-day I will pay my respects to you," said the baron; and he arose and left the hall.

* * * * * * *

At mid-day the baron sought the bower of the young and beautiful Gertrude—she was to his imagination more beautiful than ever—it seemed as if at that moment every trait of loveliness shone forth with much more than its ordinary strength and refulgence.

"Lady Gertrude," said the baron, "I have sought this interview with you that I may explain and make evident to you the propriety of my wishes, and the reasons that I hope may insure you to consent to their completion."

"Well, my lord?"

"You know well I am wealthy."

"You are my lord."

"And so are you," continued the baron, "you are very wealthy also."

"So I understand, my lord."

"Yes, yes, no doubt you will be so in time to come, if—if no untoward accident happens. Now when so much property lies at the disposal of single persons they are liable to all the evils of flatterers."

"You, my lord?"

"I mean we," said the baron, somewhat hastily, and then he added, "My object in this matter is to render two persons of equal rank and fortune happy."

"No doubt."

Nor have I. I shall make a very good husband, a very good, quiet ruler of a wife and a castle. I lay my life and my wealth at your feet, my dear lady Gertrude, and hope the want of ceremony and shortness of the courtship will be no bar to our happiness."

"Certainly not," returned Gertrude; "for it can have no effect upon me, for I don't intend to marry."

"My lady—"

"Nay, do not interrupt me. I am only telling you what I have long since made up my mind about, my lord. I will not marry under any circumstances whatever at present, until I am of age at the least; when I am free then I may make a choice, but not before under any circumstances whatever."

"Nay, lady, you must make no such cruel resolve."

"I have said," replied the lady Gertrude, "and I am not so much of a spoilt child that I must re-say what I have said."

"I am far from implying you are, when I hope such a resolve will not be persisted in. Little do I desire to wed for the sake of property. I have enough to gild a life; and I could leave my widow a splendid dowry."

" I seek it not."

" No, no, fair Gertrude, "you are a fortune in yourself. I seek you—I love you—do not look cold on me. Do not reject a suitor because he is too honest and proud to pour strings of silly compliments and flatteries in your ear! Do not reject me because I have ceased to be thoughtless and silly!"

" I do not ; but I will not marry."

" I will leave you," said the baron, " to reconsider your resolve—to make some change in your determination. I will say no more, lady—I will say no more. Shall I say you will keep your apartment till you have made up your mind ?"

" As you please. If I must be a prisoner, I must ; but when I cease to be a maid, I shall, I hope, be free."

" Nay, you are free to choose. Say nothing, therefore, but what is strictly true. I sue you not as a boy, but as a titled man. I am one unused to sue in vain."

" You must in this case," replied the Lady Gertrude ; "for marry the uncle of the man I loved I never will."

" The boy is dead !"

" I know he is ; I had evidence of the fact ; his blood was shed, I have the proof."

" You have the proof," said the baron, growing somewhat pale, but perfectly self-possessed. " Then you have no doubt about the truth of what I say, and the impossibility of his ever returning. Do not grieve, fair Gertrude : another may supply his place."

" Another never can nor shall supply his place," said the gentle Gertrude ; " I will remain unwedded as long as he whose blood stains this scarf shall live in my remembrance."

Gertrude, as she spoke, threw the bloody and torn scarf before the baron ; who no sooner saw it than he started back in great horror, and gazed at it without uttering a word ; and then he arose, after a while, saying, as he bowed low, to the Lady Gertrude.

" I well remember that scarf : it belonged to my unfortunate nephew, and recalled him most forcibly to my memory. How you came by that scarf I know not ; but it had a great effect upon me. I will renew this conversation when I have recovered the shock that garment has given me."

So saying he arose, and left the apartment. The Lady Gertrude, being unable to understand, from his conduct, whether it was purely sorrow or guilt that caused so sudden a change to come over the baron. She was in great perplexity, and resolved, at all events, she would not marry him, but remain single.

The baron retired to his own apartment ; and, when he got there, he threw himself into a large chair, when he began to reflect upon what has happened. He could not, however, prevent unpleasant thoughts, which, however, took but little shape. He could not tell in what way danger might lurk. There was no tangible shape—nothing that could, in any way, assist him in doing what he most desired—understanding the " signs of the times."

" At all events," muttered the baron to himself, " there can be little or no danger —save from some lurking enemy, who desires to frighten me. I will, however, secure myself, and marry the Lady Gertrude. Her great estates will become mine —of which I cannot by any means whatever be deprived. Yes, yes!—money is the word, and marry I will. Who said he ever heard me retract?—or, who is there that ever knew me to fail, in one attempt, when seriously set about. She must be mine—either by fair means or foul."

The baron had one more interview with the Lady Gertrude, but was unable to shake her determination, and he accordingly confined her to her apartment, a small room, where there was no chance of escape from his safe custody. The next morning there was evident signs of consternation among the retainers, every one of them seemed terrified and the baron scarcely knew what to do, but he resolved to ask no questions, but chose a solitary walk on the ramparts. That evening he resolved to visit Gertrude in her imprisonment, for such it was. As he walked along the passage that led to the apartment, he heard some sounds that alarmed him, he looked up, and found himself face to face with the horrible figure that had before alarmed him ; he staggered back, and well did he remember the features of his nephew, for he pulled aside his cloak and showed a dagger—a dagger he well knew, for it had been his own, sticking in his fleshless ribs. This was more than he could bear, and he sank on the floor with a deep groan, his light went out, and he was left alone.

How long he remained there was not known, but when the baron recovered from his swoon, he found himself in the hands of his attendants, who were exerting themselves to recover him, when he was conscious he inquired what had happened.

"We heard a groan, my lord, and on going to the place where we thought it came from, you were lying insensible upon the floor, we brought you here and that is all."

"Saw you anything?"

There was a dead silence of some minutes duration, and none spoke or dared to speak.

"Saw you anything else?—speak," thundered out the baron.

" The same apparition has appeared to us that we saw before on several occasions, and more than one amongst us have seen it, we have seen it in the castle."

" Where is the lady, Gertrude ?"

" In her chamber,' replied the servant.

" Send her to me—stay, tell her I will be with her, as I wish to speak with her, presently."

The men departed upon their errand, for there were none bold enough to traverse the castle after dark ; indeed, they all went about by twos and threes, so as to help one another.

The men returned, and stood gaping at the baron, but feared to speak—inexpressibly alarmed himself, for his nerves had been greatly shaken by the strange events that had happened.

" What have you seen now ?" inquired the baron, after a pause.

" Nothing," was the reply.

" Then why stand gaping there like idiots ?" exclaimed the baron. " Had you seen anything to alarm you, there would have been some excuse, but now, there is none—men cannot surely be frightened at nothing."

" But the lady Gertrude, my lord."

" Ah! what of her ? speak at once," exclaimed the baron, in some agitation.

" She is no where to be found, my lord. We found her door unlocked, and on entering it, found the room empty,"

The baron immediately put his hand to his belt, and found the key was gone. He had had it there before he swooned, and now it was gone. The retainers, however, presented one to him ; he looked at it, and immediately recognised it as the one he had had but a few minutes before he fainted.

" Strange," he muttered—" strange—what can all this mean ?—who could have taken the key from me ? The vassals dared not have done so—they would never have ventured upon it ; besides, they had no object in doing so."

He remained some time in deep thought, and when he awoke from it, he ordered the castle to be thoroughly searched, from one end to the other, and he superintended the search in person.

It was evident that the lady could not have got out of the castle by any ordinary means, they were all too palpable, and the sentinels declared, she had not passed them. She could not have done so, without they knew she had done so.

Strangely perplexed, and much terrified himself, he knew not what to do, and he resolved that he would not prosecute the search for her that night, but begin the next morning, and take horse with a couple of score of his retainers, and see if he could not overtake her, wherever she might be gone to, and this was done by day-break.

The pursuit was a vain one ; and, after two days' exhaustion, he was unable to secure his object. She had left no traces behind, as to where she had gone to.

He returned to the castle, and entered the court-yard with his retainers ; when suddenly the draw-bridge was pulled up and the portcullis fell with violence, and the retainers appeared in arms.

" What means this ?" inquired the baron.

At that moment, a knight, dressed in plain armour, but whose long, drooping plume and haughty mien told he was of gentle birth, stepped forward, and by his side stood a lady, wrapped in a large mantle. The knight took the mantle off, and the Lady Gertrude stood before him in a bridal dress, and the knight removed at once his helmet, and exhibited the well known features of Robert of Belcroft.

The baron shook to and fro in his saddle, as one that was drunk ; but he contrived to say—

" What is the meaning of all this ? "

" It means, false knight and murderer," said the knight, " that you have now got into the lion's mouth. You are now arrested, in the king's name, of the crimes of fratricide and attempted murder. My father died by your hand, and, but for accident, I had shared the same fate. Now surrender yourself. You will be sent to the Tower of London, murderer."

"Liar!" shouted the baron; "I will prove it with my sword."

As he spoke, he attempted to draw his sword, but rocked to and fro in his saddle more than ever, and, before any one could come to his assistance, he fell to the earth, and never moved more.

He was picked up; he was dead; he had pitched upon his head; and, what with the weight of his armour, and the roughness of the stones he had fractured the bones of his skull,

Little had he anticipated such an end.

Loud were the shouts of the vassals at the return of Robert of Belcroft, and the air was rent with the sounds. That day the castle gates were thrown open to all; for it was the nuptials of the knight with the gentle Gertrude. All was joy and felicity, and a prelude to many years of happiness.

A faint streak of daylight came into the apartment, and Lowe laid down the book, feeling himself at least, from the conflict of ideas which he had got up in his mind, more capable of coming to some definite conclusion as to what he was to do; for by some means he seemed, from the first moment that he had heard of Fanny's marriage, to consider that he was called upon to do something, although what it was, he knew not.

Strange to say it did not strike him that really he had nothing whatever now to do with the proceedings of Fanny Leslie, any more than as if she had been the most perfect stranger to him; but, on the contrary, he still thought that there was a something which wove, as it were, their fates together, and that it behoved him consequently to take some step on this the occasion of her marriage. That this step should be one that should have a tendency to let her know that he still entertained for her the tenderest regard, he adopted as a principle; and, when the morning's light brought better thoughts and calmer reasoning, he thought that he owed it to Fanny Leslie now to do a something which should let her know that he felt and considered he had created the chasm that had divided them. She shall not think, he said to himself, that I entertain any feeling of resentment for what has passed. I should rather like to see her, and to tell her that it was because I considered myself as not worthy to possess such a treasure that I shrunk from calling her mine, than that I entertained any doubt of the value of the possession. This thought now slowly grew upon him, until it assumed so strange a shape that he could not shake it off, and the desire to see Fanny once again became an impulse which could not be resisted. Old Gilbert had informed Nicholas Lowe where the ceremony was to be performed that was to unite Fanny to one so every way worthy of her, for he had taken quite interest enough in the affairs of the Paddlebat family generally to be well aware by some means or another of whatever was about to take place.

Nicholas Lowe then had no difficulty in knowing what to do to enable himself to see Fanny Leslie if he choose; and he, towards eight o'clock in the morning thoroughly made up his mind that he would leave for a longer period of time than he had ever yet done, his house, and proceed to Wilsden. He meant to walk the distance for he was familiar enough with the road, and he thought that the quiet serenity of the country lanes, which lead from the Edgeware Road to the pretty and seldom visited hamlet, would prepare his mind for the scene he had to go through. He took a frugal breakfast, and then, after going over his house to ascertain that all was secure, he locked it up and departed. Before he went though, he had from habit taken a long and earnest look at the stain in the roof of the dining-room, which was immediately below where the dead body of Rodwell lay, as he, Nicholas Lowe, hoped, rotting. Day by day he had looked at that stain of blood; and yet, although so considerable a space of time had now elapsed, strange to say, it had not much altered in its colour, but had at all events, to the eyes of Nicholas Lowe, an appearance of hideous freshness that much perplexed him to account for; while, at the same time, it added greatly to his fears of a discovery of the dreadful deed; that there lay the mute but terrified evidences of those evidences, which he had for the remainder of his existence compelled himself to keep a lonely and a gloomy watch and ward over.

"'Tis strange and terrible," he said to himself, as he walked in the direction that would lead him to the village he wished to reach; "'tis strange and terrible that no change seemed to take place in that mark of blood. They do say that murder will out: it may be so—it may be so. Heaven help me if it be."

He had a hundred times told himself that the place which he had chosen as the resting-place of the dead body of Rodwell was just about the worst he could have picked out; but, as to any idea of removing it—that was completely out of the question.

And when we—as, of course, we must—agree in the proposition, that almost anywhere would have been better and safer, as a place of concealment for a dead body, than where he had put it, we must not forget, in reasoning upon such a subject that he was the murderer—that not only were his faculties, at the time, in a state of the utmost confusion and horror—but he could not then have brought himself to touch the corpse of the man whom he had thus suddenly sent to his long account, on any consideration whatever. So that, taking these things into consideration, we cannot altogether say that the place was the worst that was available for him.

True—he might certainly have taken it up and carried it down stairs; but what an awful task would that have been for him to accomplish. That dead, limp corpse —yet warm and dabbled in blood! No, no!—he could not have done it, although such an act would have saved him shame from all chance of any pains and penalties that might otherwise come to him in this world.

And having now, more as it will be recollected by the aid of his feet than his hands, succeeded, at all events, in placing the body out of sight, he could not think again of making an effort to look upon the ghastly spectacle.

He pursued his way to Wilsden now, quickly; for it was his earnest wish to get there before there was any likelihood of Fanny and her intended husband reaching the spot. It was two hours' walk, he knew; so he calculated upon being there by about ten. He was right enough; for, as he came within sight of the little old Norman tower of the church, the clock struck ten.

A glance sufficed to show him that no preparations were going on at all indicative that the nuptials of any one were in progress; but he knew too well the simple tastes and habits of Fanny Leslie to conclude at once, from that circumstance, that he had been misinformed by old Gilbert; and, with a confidence in the fact that he was right, he walked onwards.

The church door was open, and a man and woman were cleansing the interior, both of whom respectfully saluted Nicholas Lowe as he came up.

"Is there to be a marriage here to-day?" he asked.

"Well, sir, they say as there be," replied the man, "but it aint a regular thing, you know, sir, with the banns, but a license affair, from all as I can hear."

"Very well, I thank you; may I wait in the church?"

"Yes, sir, if you please; but you'd better wait a little, sir, or else you'll be smothered, for we haven't swept it out yet."

"Oh, certainly. It is an ancient church."

"Very sir—very. Them as built it won't have the head-ache any more, I'm thinking, you may be bound, sir; they say it's a matter of fourteen hundred years old."

"Doubtless it is so. I will walk about the old grave-yard until you have swept out the church, and then I will remain in it till the parties come; and hark, you, my man, here is a crown, I am a friend of the parties who are coming here this day to be married, but for reasons of my own, I do not wish them to know that I am here, until I choose to declare myself to them. Do you understand me in that particular?"

"Truly, sir,—truly," said the man, as he pocketed the five shilling piece which Lowe handed to him, "your honour, sir, knows how to make things quite clear to poor folks."

"That will do, I thank you."

Nicholas Lowe, until the church was ready for his reception, amused himself by trolling about the precincts of the old grave-yard, where in the simple inscription on some of the tombs, and the pompous statements upon others, he found ample food for meditation. After about half-an hour the man came to tell him that the church was quite ready, and Lowe accordingly walked into the calm, cool precincts of that ancient temple.

"If you please, sir," said the man, with a doubtful air, "I think we shall have, do you know, sir, to lock you in; the curate tells us not to leave the church unlocked, and I'm forced to go somewhere, so that if it's all the same to you, which as you are going to wait, I should say it was, sir, you won't mind having the key turned upon you."

"Not at all," said Lowe, "not at all. Do as you please in that respect, it makes no difference to me at all."

"Thank you, sir, very much obliged. There's nothing for a gentleman like you to be afraid on, sir, here; it's not as if somebody as had done a murder was locked up in a church, all alone, to think of his wickedness."

"Hold—hold!" cried Lowe, "upon reflection, I—"

He spoke too late; the door was closed, and Nicholas Lowe found himself alone with God in the temple dedicated to his holy worship."

Oh, what an awful accidental suggestion was that which the man had made, and how little he suspected it was so frightfully a home-thrust at the visitor who had treated the being locked in at first so lightly, but who now, from those few foolish superstitious words that had been uttered by an ignorant man, had a train of thought awakened of the most painful character.

Yes, it was nothing to one whose soul was untainted with crime to be locked in a church; nothing whatever, but it was everything to him who had committed one of the most henious offences against God's holiest ordinances. He had not thought of that before; but now, as the cold dew of perspiration sat upon his brow, he looked fearfully around him, and shrunk from the sound of his own footsteps.

"Alone, alone," he said; alone with my own dreadful thoughts, in a place where I should have shrunk from entering at all. What have I now to do with churches and with religion? I, who if the latter be true, can surely hope for no mercy, even although it is said that 'Heaven's mercy is infinite.' Alone, alone; surely some fate has dragged me here for an especial purpose that will be achieved to, perchance, the destruction of my reason.

He turned twice completely round upon his heels, as if he could not satisfy himself entirely that there was no sight there present which might turn his heart to stone to look upon. There was nothing of a living form that he could see, either of this world or another but himself, and yet he shuddered, he knew not why.

There was a strange, holy calm around him, speaking of that rest which is eternal, but which, alas, he feared he should never be entitled to be a sharer in. The very spirit of God seemed to be in the still atmosphere of that little ancient church; and, as Nicholas Lowe gazed about him he clasped his hands, saying, in tones of the most agonised description—

"And I am a murderer!"

There was a faint echo about the spot, and the word "murderer," after a moment's pause, came with a strange murmuring sound to his ears.

"Yes," he exclaimed, for at the instant he fully believed that some spirit from heaven spake the accusation; "Yes, I am a murderer! Curse me, ye avenging angels. Look upon me with eyes of horror. Condemn me—condemn the murderer who has ventured before his God in that temple which should be ever one of peace."

The word peace came back to his ears even as that of murderer had done, and then he sunk on the steps of the altar.

"Oh, if I could—if I could but pray," he gasped.

"Pray," sighed the echo in the old church.

Nicholas Lowe started at the sound; he clasped his hands, and while he trembled from head to foot, and betrayed all the outward appearance of one suffering the most intense mental anguish, he strove to address himself to that heaven whose behests he had so greatly outraged.

He tried to remember, but the effort was a futile one, some simple prayer of long-forgotten childhood. He could not summon up from memory's depths, the blessing he had learnt to crave for, when a child he had knelt at his mother's knee.

"If I could," he faltered; "oh, if I could but remember that old prayer, I think the repetition of its simple words in this place, would bestow some peace upon me."

The effort was a vain one, and now resting his head upon his hand, he sat there a miserable man, and a dreadful specimen of the consequences of unbridled passions.

If any one wished to be revenged on Nicholas Lowe—if any one hated him so much, that they would have rejoiced in his unhappiness, their revenge and their hatred might surely now be both satiated, for a more wretched object than he presented could not be conceived.

The worst enemy he ever had, would surely have been moved to pity, to see him thus bowed down by affliction, and so utterly prostrated by the recollection of a crime, certainly a great one we admit, but yet accompanied by circumstances of extenuation, that enforces a kind of pity from our heart.

For about half an hour he remained in this state, and Heaven can only know what a world of misery he endured in that comparatively short space of time.

And what is half an hour to the happy, passed amid the ringing laughter of those whom they love, while the jest and the song, and perchance the sparkling wine cup, all lend the magic of their charms to make existence beautiful? What is half an hour to him who can calmly think upon the past, and find nothing that shall impart a pang to memory's revelations. But hold! are there in the whole wide word such an one?

No, no, not one—not one solitary instance. We must, whether inclination go with us or not—we must revert to the gloomy, but alas, the too true philosophy of Nicholas Lowe himself—a philosophy, which in gayer moments than he can ever know again, he had often spoken of, "There is a skeleton in every house—a skeleton in every bosom!"

But few have such a skeleton as Lowe to contend with. Few indeed can have made up anything so gaunt and terrific to the imagination, as the skeleton which now haunted him. The philosophy that perplex human hearts with such fancies of deep regret remains the same, but in its manifestations the varieties are immense. Little did he, Nicholas Lowe, ever imagine that he was doomed to be so powerful an example of his own philosophy.

And now with trembling steps he rose, and crept slowly and silently to one of the old pews, in which he sat down, looking so pale, so wan, and agitated, that any one would think he had come there to die, after witnessing the nuptials of her whom he found, now too late, was most dear to him, but who he never could call his own.

CHAPTER LXXII.

THE MARRIAGE OF FANNY AT WILSDEN.—A HAPPY DAY.—A CONTRAST.—THE SUDDEN APPEARANCE OF NICHOLAS LOWE AND THE NOBLE CONDUCT OF HORACE ARROWDALE.

WHILE these proceedings were taking place at St. George's, Hanover-square' a more unpretending ceremony, but quite as solemn, was taking place at Wilsden There Horace Arrowdale had met by appointment Fanny Leslie. She, too, wa true to the hour, and their hearts were long united before their hands.

The morning sun shone with unwonted splendour over the fields, and the quie roads about Wilsden gave no signs of commotion. The very dust lay undisturbed on the paths, and now and then, when a gig or a cart past, a cloud was raised that whitened the leaves on the hedge rows. The very birds seemed gay, and fluttered about from branch to branch.

"All nature is gay," said Horace; "it seems as though our happiness was showered down in animated nature. I know not if it be that I am now inclined to look upon things with a partial eye; but Heaven itself never, to my mind, looked half so beautiful."

"The fields certainly appear lovely," replied Fanny. "I never experienced the air more balmy."

"Or the heavens more serene," added Horace. "See, Fanny, yonder stands the old church; 'tis a very old one, as you may perceive, but it is a pretty and picturesque church."

"The rooks build their nests in the trees around."

"They do, and long time has given them impunity. They fear not the approach of man, though they fly up when you approach; but they continue their cawing and fly round in eddying circles, and settle upon the trees as before."

They reached along the road and admired the many pretty and respectable-looking places; the fields, too, the Wilsden paddocks, all looked most beautiful, being some of the finest near London.

The old church reared its head among the trees, looking quiet and simple enough. The morning sun threw a strong glare into the ancient edifice.

There were a few persons about—some from curiosity, some because they had heard that a wedding was about to be solemnised, and others because they were concerned in the church in some way or other, no matter how, that enabled them to take a pew for some object, or under some pretence.

Some have said this is a fee-taking country, and it must have been a fee-going country—go where you will—if it be only to make use of your eyes, it is sufficient reason to extract a charge from it—anything is done for a fee; no public place, be it of what sort it may, exists without some such privilege being given to it, that is, the attendant or owner in fact; it would be an anomaly to see a place where there was no fee in this country.

However, Horace Arrowdale and Fanny Leslie walked into the church-yard, and gazed upon the tombs.

"These are unpretending enough," remarked Horace, "what a contrast between this and some of the church-yards in town, where the tomb-stones are carved, monuments erected, and anything done that could be to gild the ensigns of death."

There was a feeling of quiet happiness throughout their minds, and Horace and Fanny strolled around into the lane behind the church, then round until they again came to the church again.

"Now," said Horace, "we may go in—the time is just at hand, and if the minister be not at hand, they will send for him—we may as well go in."

"As you please, Horace," said Fanny, who hung on his arm; and he entered the church-door, and then the body of the edifice. It was plain and unpretending enough, and a few moments sufficed to tell them the extent and nature of the interior.

Horace led the way to the small room, termed a vestry, and there saw the clerk of the church, to him he addressed himself—

"Is the minister present?" he said.

"No, sir; do you want him?"

"Yes, I have an appointment with him here at this hour."

"He will be here immediately; see, yonder, he comes; now, sir, you will be able to speak to him."

They turned their heads, and could see through the opened door a venerable looking man—that is to say, one on whom good living had not been thrown away.

He came, and entered the church, and then the vestry, and then Horace and Fanny saw no more of him for some minutes. However, he did not keep them long, but soon returned, and led the way to the altar, when he turned round and faced them.

Then the clerk, with the assistance of some others, placed them in due order before the curate, who commenced the ceremony.

The mysteries of Hymen are pretty well known to the public now, having endured ever since the world began, and that of the Christians these eighteen centuries and a-half, therefore the reader is presumed to be pretty well acquainted with so notorious a matter as the marriage ceremony.

It was ended, the registration effected, and the fees paid, which is a very important part of the ceremony.

They spoke but little, their hearts were too enraptured to waste their feelings in words they could not condescend to speak those feelings before others, for their greedy ears to drink in all that they might say.

Horace paid the fees, and gave some handsome gratuities, which were unexpected, seeing there was no parade or show. They left the church by a side door, not the usual entrance, when an old man said something to Horace, and held out his hand towards him.

"Eh?" said Horace, hearing only partially what was said; "shake hands with you—certainly."

As he said this, he took the paralytic old man's hand, and gave it a hearty shake.

"Sixpence!" roared out the old man, somewhat angry at being so used, and being unable, perhaps, to comprehend that a mistake had been made, and thinking himself ill-used.

"Oh," said Horace, "I understand you now; will that satisfy you," and as he spoke, he put some silver in the man's hand.

This was apparently highly satisfactory to the old man's palate, for he smiled, and said something nobody paid any attention to whatever.

Before, however, they left the church, there was one object that attracted their attention, which was some person in one of the pews, who had, until the ceremony had concluded concealed himself, but he slowly came forward and revealed himself to them.

This was no other than Nicholas Lowe.

Fanny could not devise why he had come there, and certainly felt her happiness somewhat clouded by his appearance; but, as he neared them, she saw there was melancholy resignation upon his countenance that banished all fear or apprehension.

Horace Arrowdale had now led Fanny into the church-yard; and Fanny looked back and saw Nicholas Lowe following them, and Horace looked back too."

"Do you see that person following," said Fanny.

"That melancholy looking man?"

"Yes. That is Nicholas Lowe. I cannot imagine why he should come here to-day; but I fancy he must intend to speak, else he would not walk this way."

"We will stop and see," said Horace. "He may wish to say something to us; at all events we may as well see."

As Nicholas Lowe came up, he touched his hat slightly to Horace Arrowdale, and said, turning to Fanny—

"Forgive me, for one moment, in intruding upon you; but I come to witness your happiness, and to wish you a life of that joy I now can never know. I come too to tell you I am glad this has happened, and to hope that the last lingering regret for the past, if you have one, will pass away."

Fanny scarce knew what to say. She looked at Horace, and then said in a low tone—

"This is Mr. Nicholas Lowe, Horace."

"Sir," said Horace, civilly to Lowe, "your congratulations are welcome; and, from what I have heard of the past, they are the more so as they must cost you some pain to give them."

"Not pain," said Nicholas Lowe. "And yet I hardly know how to characterise my own feelings. A sorrow and regret for the past I do and must ever feel, and the love I once bore I feel now and ever shall; but there are circumstances connected with myself that made it impossible that Fanny ever could be mine—circumstances of which I alone am cognizable."

"I have heard as much," replied Horace.

"I cannot, however, avoid saying that I am glad, I am comparatively happy, to see her so. I would not for any selfish motive of my own have it on my conscience to say that I feel a jealous pang when I see and hear she is happy. It might have been otherwise, had I not created the chasm that separated us; but much as I regret the necessity, I cannot repent of what I have done; neither do I repine that she is blessed by the affections of one most willing and able to protect her. Before I bid you farewell, allow me, Mr. Arrowdale, to congratulate you upon the event, and to hope your joys will be unceasing."

For a moment Arrowdale paused, and gazed upon the features of Lowe, who appeared to express his wishes with fervour, that his pale features were lit up with a momentary gleam that made him look animated and handsome, and he thought he saw much self-devotion and denial in him, and, upon the impulse of the moment, held out his hand, saying—

" Allow me, Lowe," he said, " to thank you for your warm wishes, and to hope you will not object to pass the afternoon with us. Believe me, it will give me great pleasure if you will do so." ·

Lowe took his proffered hand, which he shook, but said gravely—

" I cannot do what you would ask—this much has not been accomplished without a task, and had I possessed less unbounded admiration for her every virtue, I should not have been here to-day ; but she is what you will find in no one else—she is perfection without alloy. Farewell to you both !"

" Cannot I persuade you ?"

·" No," said Lowe ; "it must be as I say—again farewell. Peace and joy be with you—my wishes are with you !"

So saying Nicholas Lowe left the churchyard in an opposite direction to that in which Fanny and Horace Arrowdale were about to leave the church.

It was some minutes before either spoke, and they had watched Nicholas Lowe quite out of sight before they turned away and left the place.

" I am sorry," said Horace, " that he seems unhappy, and is so, no doubt. I wonder what cause of secret sorrow preys upon his heart, and causes him to appear thus sad and melancholy."

" I have no idea ; in fact, I know nothing beyond what you now know. Some secret cause there must be, but that is all. I cannot even form a guess or suspicion of what it is ; but be it what it may, it was of a sudden existence."

" Indeed ! how do you know that ?"

" Because his behaviour changed suddenly ; that is the only thing about it that I know at all."

They now left the churchyard at Wilsden, and as there were several heads out to gaze upon the newly-married pair, they resolved to quit the locality.

In the meanwhile Nicholas Lowe, completely exhausted by his own efforts to keep up an appearance of equanimity, no sooner left the churchyard, and felt that he was at a safe distance—that he was no longer seen by those he had just left—than he felt what he had gone through had cost him an effort too great to be carried off lightly.

He staggered, and would have fallen, but that he came to a gate, across which he supported himself for several minutes.

" It is done," he said, in a tone that seemed more like a groan than anything appertaining to human speech, but which told the depth of the emotion that caused it—" it is done, and I have seen the last of one who would have made me happy, but for the foul blot that stains my soul—a dye so deep a red that it can never be washed out. But I will return. I must quit this place, and in solitude indulge in grief."

Then rising from his leaning posture he walked slowly away, and sought the nearest route to the Edgeware-road, where he was fortunate enough to find the Watford coach, and he got upon that and rode to town. The reflections of the unhappy man were sorrowful to a degree. He could not but look upon Fanny in the arms of another man as the acmé of his misfortunes—misfortunes which appeared never to have any end to them ; for they were permanently engraven on his heart.

He could not have wished it otherwise now, and yet he felt an anguish at his heart which he could not dispel, by telling himself it was all for Fanny's happiness. This was a consolation, it was true, and he knew it was such ; yet it was difficult to feel happy, because another now occupied the place he should have held himself.

He hurried home to his lone, solitary home, where no human face ever shone in kindness and sympathy upon his own. Here gloomy sorrow sat and reigned alone, and as Lowe staggered up the steps the place looked more gloomy and melancholy than ever.

The door opened, and Nicholas Lowe stepped in. He closed it after him, and the whole house reverberated with the sound. There was a dismal hollowness about the place that struck upon his senses with a chill and blighting effect.

"There are none to welcome me," he said; "none who smile to greet me. I am banished for ever from happiness." He struck his head with his hand, and then sank, overpowered by his emotions, senseless on the cold marble pavement in the hall.

CHAPTER LXXIII.

LOWE'S HOUSE IS BROKEN INTO, AND HE MAKES A FRIEND.—THE STOCKBROKER LEAVES MRS. PADDLEBAT A SECOND TIME WIDOWED.

NICHOLAS LOWE told himself that he never could make a friend while he lived; but we shall see how he did so.

The evenings were passed by Nicholas in melancholy meditations, and he would sit and listen to the howling of the wind and the roaring in the chimneys, which were in consonance with the musings of his soul.

One evening in particular, when the wind blew fierce and roared among the tall tops of the houses, and the windows shook throughout the whole house, there was not a room that had not its own peculiar echoes, that were awoke by the storm.

"Ah!" said Lowe, as he paced through the rooms, "howl on!—let your tones be as loud and hollow as you can! Little do I heed such sounds, though they assimilate to my own feelings and thoughts. Lonely and alone, I am ever likely to be the sole tenant of this abode.

"Never can I know the many delights that other men know; but I know wholly what they can never know, that is, the heart's desolation, *that* I feel. Neither love nor friendship can by any accident have charms for me, save such as the recollection of a once well-beloved face—one that we have seen, never to meet again.

"God! what a life have I not to live!—a continued scene of wretchedness and misery! Nothing can be more abject and sorrowful than my way of life, and yet there is no prospect of an alteration."

Nicholas Lowe was indeed wretched—more so, perhaps, than any human being in London. He dared not form a friendship with any one, because he feared that any one should set their feet in the house where was concealed that direful secret—the murdered body of Jervis Rodwell. There was no getting over that. The body was concealed, and might by some prying eyes be detected, and then he would have to meet that awful doom which he feared to meet, and which had so many terrors.

The storm increased, the wind howled, and the rain came pattering down with all the force it could receive. The war of the elements without was not more melancholy than the thoughts of Lowe, who listened to each gust of wind that blew, and the fall of the rain, as it came in dashing showers against the windows.

These sounds were but sorrowful and sad. The hours, too, could be heard from he neighbouring steeples, when the wind blew and startled the dull monotony of the night.

Now and then, too, the sound of a footstep fell upon the ear of Nicholas Lowe, who listened to it, as it approached and departed from the locality; he could count the steps and speculate upon the sounds, until they ceased to come upon the ear.

How little thought the hapless passengers of the wretchedness that dwelt in the house, as they passed by it. Such persons might have looked up and thought how happy must they be who could afford to live in such a large house; that they must have the elements of happiness about them ; and why should they not have more—why should they not have happiness itself?

These were questions easily asked, but no one attempted a solution of them, because no one was acquainted with the facts of the case, nor are they ever, and hence how it is we are apt to over or under-estimate our neighbour's happiness and means of enjoyment.

Nicholas Lowe listened to the beating of the rain, and the sudden sullen dashes that the wind brought with it against the side of the house, but he heard them with indifference, for he had that within him that could not be equalled in sadness, and therefore the efforts of the elements were more in unison to his feelings, than running counter to them. He seemed wearied, and yet he sat late, listening to these sounds.

"What do I do here?" he muttered : "I have no comfort in reflection, no hope in the future ; wherefore should I think about it? and yet I cannot control my thoughts, they are free and independent of me."

Thus it is people are chained down sometimes to the consideration of some subject from which they would release themselves if they could, but they are unable to do so at all with them. The hour was growing late, and Lowe determined he would retire for the night as he felt wearied with the day ; his mind had been more than usually busy in recalling to it the recollections of the past ; his old friendships were all severed, and his love for ever lost ; he was alone and without any human sympathy. He felt this more than usually acute, and threw himself on his bed with something akin in feeling to a reproach of fate, for the necessity that seemed to surround him to isolate himself from society.

As he lay thinking in bed, he thought he heard other sounds besides those of the storm ; it seemed to him as if there was an attempt somewhere in the house to force the place—to make an entry—which could not be done unless some persons were about it ; thieves might expect to find a booty, and yet, who could have known that house and expect to find anything there in the way of costly moveables, such a solitary and secluded life as the owner led?

The more Nicholas Lowe listened the more he thought that some one was getting in, or endeavouring to break in ; but the noise of the storm continued, and he thought it was more than probable that he had been mistaken.

He arose, and dressing himself, he walked to the door of the room and listened attentively for some minutes, and thought he could hear more distinctly than ever the sounds of some one endeavouring to force their way into the house by means of breaking through the doors and shutters.

"Surely," he muttered, "they would not break into this house! But I will search and find out the cause of this, if there be any at all."

So saying, he procured a light, and, taking a pair of pistols with him, he crept cautiously down stairs, examining every room as he went through the house, and shutting the doors after him, until he got to the landing, when he again listened to the sounds that were now plain enough, and they appeared to proceed from the kitchen.

Upon that Lowe descended the stairs and entered the kitchen, but he could see nothing whatever ; and having examined the place, he thought he must have been disturbed by some freak of his imagination, which was more than usually active upon this evening.

He, accordingly, having seen to all the fastenings, left the lower stories, and again searched the upper, but finding no signs of anything, he returned to his bed-room, where he laid down to endeavour to sleep, for he was wearied and tired with the fatigue of thought.

His thoughts again tormented him : he thought he could see Fanny Leslie now reposing in quietness and happiness in the arms of another—that other he himself might have been, had not things happened to prevent it. How happy he might have been was evident, and how miserable he was, was no less evident, for he felt the latter, and was daily experiencing the truth of it.

What a life to lead ! What unhappiness! What wretchedness for one man to live in—to exist in. And yet, Nicholas Lowe had all this to contend with; but still he did not go mad or destroy himself; and yet men with less provocation have done so.

Poor Lowe! for with all his crimes there is something about him that shows he would have been otherwise; had not circumstances led him on, his part would have become a better destiny.

He lay thinking for some time, till weariness overcame him, and he fell into a sound slumber, from which he was suddenly aroused by a strange noise that he could not understand.

He sat up some moments to listen, when he heard the same sound repeated; and he jumped up, plainly hearing that some one was making no child's play with the knocker of his door.

"What can it mean?" said Lowe to himself. "What can be the cause of it? Some one knocks—what can they want? I have nothing to do with any one—I have not any communication with any one. It might be Gilbert Paddlebat, and yet what could he want at such an hour?"

Nicholas Lowe's heart smote him as he thought of the only thing that was probable, and that was caused by the disappearance of Rodwell; and yet, how could that be, who knew now anything about it save himself?—the dead could tell no tales.

However, the knocking was again repeated, and Nicholas Lowe got up, and having dressed himself, he descended the stairs; he came to the door just as the noise was again repeated.

"Who is there?" demanded Lowe.

"Open the door!" replied a voice, to which he was an entire stranger.

"What do you want?" demanded Lowe.

"I have just seen some men skulking about the area, and having attempted to break in, or they have got in, I don't know which," replied the voice, "I thought I would alarm you."

"I will open the door," said Lowe, "in a moment."

In another minute the street-door was opened by Lowe, and the form of a young man stood before him. He was dressed as a gentleman, and had all the external marks of being one.

"I would not have disturbed you," he said, "but I saw several men in your area, in what I thought to be an attempt to break in. Shall I fetch assistance from the station-house?"

"No," said Lowe, hastily, "do not do that."

"You will not let them escape? If you had aid you might secure them—there is aid close at hand."

"Nay, nay," said Lowe, "I am sure they cannot have had much time to do any mischief; do not call any one. If you will aid me, I am sure we can frighten them off."

"Well, just as you please," said the gentleman. "I am willing to assist you, if you prefer doing this business by yourself."

"Thank you," said Lowe, "I do; while you are gone for assistance these fellows would overpower me, being alone, and then hurry off before I could obtain any relief."

"It might be so; but are you all alone?"

"Yes, I am. I am a solitary, you see, and hence I remain here by myself; but come, I will lead the way to the kitchen."

As Lowe spoke he walked to the stairs, followed by the stranger who had thus disturbed his slumbers; but he had scarcely set foot on the stairs when he heard the sound of feet at the bottom, and a rush towards the back door.

"They have got in, then," said the stranger. "I thought they were getting in; take care of yourself, sir, else you will get into mischief."

"I see the scoundrels," said Lowe; "they appear to be making out towards the back; we shall be close upon them."

As Lowe spoke he rushed in the direction which they had taken, and seized one, who was the hindmost of the three men, who were making off in the direction of the back of the house, but he contrived to slip away and get into the back yard, when they all jumped over, and such was their haste that they tumbled over each other and fell on the other side, and were seen then to make off.

"They are gone now," said the stranger.

"Yes; I am obliged to you for that," said Lowe; "but for the trouble you have taken, I should, ere this, have been robbed, and probably suffered from the violence of such men as these."

"They do not stand upon trifles, I believe, when they are interfered with; when they feel certain they can overcome you, they do not care to stop short of murder."

"They will not," said Lowe. "Will you walk in here and sit down a few minutes and rest yourself?" said Lowe, opening the parlour door.

"Thank you, but I am detaining you; you will be glad to retire to rest, I dare say—it is very late."

"It is late; but now, I dare say, I should not sleep if I were to attempt to do so, which I shall not do, and a glass of wine will not be anything too much after the excitement and trouble of such an affair."

He entered the parlour, and Lowe produced a couple of bottles of wine, which he placed upon the table, and a couple of glasses; and then sitting down opposite the stranger, he desired he would help himself, saying—

"The occasion of our meeting is a strange one, but not less so than the hour; however, I am the favoured by both, and, but for your kindness, I might by this time have been a murdered man."

"Why," returned the stranger, "I am out later than usual, though it is no unusual thing for a student to keep late hours. I have been dining with some friends, and they detained me till late, and as I was coming by this house on my way home, I saw these fellows lurking in your area, and I thought I had better give the alarm."

"You have acted very considerately, and I cannot express to you my thanks," said Lowe; "I hope you like the wine."

"I do, I have seldom tasted better; but I have already had a fair share, and that makes me spare it now."

"As you please; you say you are a student—are you studying the law?"

"No," replied the stranger, "I am studying medicine; my name is Ross, Robert Ross, a student of medicine. I have now been some time such, and I look forward to the day when I shall be emancipated from the toilsome path of learning to the more profitable one of practice."

"I dare say; I hope it may be a speedy and profitable one. It requires something like perseverance and energy to get over the troubles of scholarship in any walk of life."

"It is so," replied Mr. Ross; "but the hour grows late, and as I have to attend to some matters connected with my profession, I must now take my leave of you."

"May I hope to see you again, sir?" said Lowe; "the favour you have done me makes me desirous to know if I can at any time return the obligation; I would do so willingly, if the occasion should offer itself."

"You are very good, but I do not desire it; it was purely an accident that enabled me to call on you, so that I deserve no credit, at all events I have received more than a reward; however, I shall be happy to see you again—there is my address—it is but a student's lodging."

"Yes, yes," said Lowe.

"And if you will give me a call there I shall be most happy to see you, and spend an evening together."

"I will accept the invitation at once with pleasure," said Lowe, "and trust you will do so with mine."

Ross arose, and wishing Lowe good night, took his departure, at the same time Lowe saw him to the door and saw him depart, and when gone Lowe returned in deep thought, as if he had for once obtained some new idea that forced itself upon his mind.

"It is strange," said Lowe, "that I, who have suffered from my fellow-men, and I who have declined friendship and eschewed society, and even marriage, because the presence of another might be fatal to me, should now be making friendships and inviting another home to me!"

And now that we have shown how Nicholas Lowe, even in the midst of his most gloomy and depressed condition, was able to find some one to whom he could cling with an idea of friendship, we will take a glance at Mrs. Arrowdale's situation; that is to say, the Mrs. Arrowdale with whom we have not abundance of sympathy, and not Fanny, towards whom our feelings are of a widely different character.

The rage of the stockbroker when he found that old Gilbert had taken the legal step, which at once prevented him from selling out the Three per Cent stock belonging to Mrs. Paddlebat, was so great as to be beyond all power of description. He felt that degree of enmity against old Gilbert that, had he come across him, some serious affair might, and indeed must have resulted; and he likewise, as many men do when they are foiled in their designs, looked upon himself as one of the most ill-used persons in existence, as if he had been specially marked out for all the evil fates to expend their bitterest shafts upon.

He did not go back to his wife—not he, on the contrary, he sat down in a quiet corner of the Royal Exchange, and gave himself up alternately to rage and to reflection. What was he to do, he asked himself, to get rid now of the unwelcome trammels that surrounded him? Was he to be persecuted with the society of an old woman, without any real or prospective advantage arising therefrom? Certainly not. But how was he to escape? His wife was now, by the same act that had made her such, absolutely beggared, and of course the law would force him to support, if it could not force him to bestow upon her his society. Such thoughts were maddening, and after a while the stockbroker retired to one of the coffee-houses which abound in that neighbourhood, and sat himself down with pens, ink, and paper.

His object was to ascertain carefully his exact position—to find out how he stood as regards pounds, shillings, and pence, and to make up his mind as to what would be the best course for him to pursue for the future.

The task was one that consumed the better part of an hour, and at its conclusion Mr. Arrowdale arrived at the opinion that he was so surrounded with difficulties, that when it came to be known to those to whom the knowledge was of importance, how completely he had failed in his matrimonial speculation, he would be prostrated at once.

Then, like a skilful general, he made up his mind that he must make as dignified a retreat as possible, and his notion consisted in getting away with as much money in his pocket as he could get there placed.

And now we have to record an act of Mr. Arrowdale's, which is really too bad. He had power, for the mere understood financial purpose of profiting by the changes in the value of the funds, of selling out and buying in for Horace to the amount of the £5,000, which constituted the whole of his worldly possessions, and with a deliberate villany he at once proceeded to the Stock Exchange and converted that amount of stock into money.

"Now," he said to himself exultingly, "now I shall be off, and Mrs. Paddlebat may amuse her guests as best she can, for she will wait in vain for me to come and assist her so to do."

He ordered a post-chaise at once, and having arranged some few little matters, by slipping a note or two into the nearest post-office, he amused himself by writing the following note to Mrs. Paddlebat, while the chaise was getting ready:—

"MADAM,—The best of us will sometimes commit the most egregious follies. But it does not happen always, madam, that when men fall into such uncomfortable circumstances as those which now surround me, that they have sufficient energy to escape from them.

"My object in writing to you this epistle, madam, is to assure you, that I have that amount of energy, and that I freely and unhesitatingly intend to avail myself of its advantages.

" You wanted a husband, and I wanted money; therefore, as far as that went, the bargain and sale was properly and equitably conducted between us. But, although I, the husband, have in no way altered the conditions of the transaction, it appears that the money is not forthcoming, and therefore I have the necessity of bidding you at once adieu, as I think a little continental tour will be advantageous to my health after what has occurred.

" Very much regretting that such should be the case,

" Believe me to be, madam, your most obedient servant,

" CHARLES ARROWDALE."

"Damn her," said the stockbroker, as he sealed this insulting letter, " I think that will choke her off tolerably well, if anything will. Confound her, I hate the very idea of her—she is gall and wormwood to me !"

By the time Mr. Arrowdale had finished his epistle, the post-chaise was ready, and he, in five minutes more, bade adieu to London, as he thought for ever, with Horace Arrowdale's five thousand pounds in gold, safely secured in a carpet bag, that was the only article of luggage he took with him.

Poor Mrs. Paddlebat! we can really hardly help pitying her, for, after all, ignorance and folly have more to do with her conduct than any thing in the shape of real censurable feeling. What a wretched state was she now reduced to ! Where was she to look for succour or for assistance?—where was she to look for sympathy, now having, as she had done, carried everything with so positively high a hand, that she could not say she had one real friend in the wide world to whom she could turn with anything like a chance of obtaining the comfort of a few kind words of genuine pity or commiseration. She waited hours alone for the return of the stockbroker, but, alas ! he came not ; and, when at last that cruel explanation of his absence, in the shape of the insulting letter, which we have laid before our readers, reached her, Mrs. Paddlebat might, with the hero of antiquity, although from different motives, have said, " Now let me lie down and die."

Had she not, in a manner of speaking, cast away from her the only heart that really would have clung to her under all circumstances ? Had she not done her utmost to turn Fanny from her? and could she, now that the clouds of misfortune had dimmed the brightness of that sky, which she deemed before too luxurious to permit Fanny to dwell under, appeal to her? And who else was there? No one. Mrs. Paddlebat could not name one whom she could really call a friend, now that the time had arrived when friends might have been of great service. In the time of prosperity, there were some who would have owned to the title, at all events.

" Yes," she said, as she sat with the stockbroker's letter in her hand ; " yes, I must send for Fanny, that is my only resource—it must be so—I have no one else who will speak one word of comfort or consolation to me, I am certain."

And then she burst into tears, and wept more bitterly than she had ever done in all her life before.

CHAPTER LXXIV.

FANNY RECEIVES A NOTE FROM HER AUNT.—THE KIND REPLY.—THE FATE
OF HORACE.

IT was not long after these occurrences that an incident occurred which brings Mrs. Arrowdale, late Mrs. Paddlebat, again before our readers. Her troubles were drawing to a close, that is, they were getting worse and more urgent in their character.

Fanny received a letter from her aunt. She and Horace Arrowdale were seated at breakfast one morning, when the servant entered the room and presented a letter to her.

"From my aunt!" said Fanny, as she looked at the handwriting; "I can always tell her letters at the first glance. What is the nature of her communication, I wonder?"

"Nothing cheering. Poor soul," said Horace, "she is full of trouble; I dare say her second marriage is not likely to prove so happy as the first."

Fanny opened the letter, and read as follows:—

"My DEAR NIECE,—Had your dear uncle, the late Mr. Paddlebat, been alive, I never should have been reduced to the state of distress I am now placed in. He, good man, never permitted things to come to such a pass; he loved his home and kept a home—a good home! But there, it's no use of thinking of the past, it won't mend the present, though I can't help recollecting what has been.

" Here I am, my dear niece, up to my eyes in trouble. It's really strange how the world expects more of you than you have got to give them.

" The tradesmen hereabout want their money; it may be very true, but if I haven't got it to give them, what can I do? What they have done you shall know.

" My dear niece, I have all my goods seized for rent. Think of that! Your aunt is reduced to distress, nay, to poverty—I can hardly speak the word. Believe me, I never could have dreamed such things could come to pass.

" Who could have believed that Mrs. Paddlebat, the late goldsmith's wife, would come to have a distress in her house and to want a shilling? Oh! my dear niece, you cannot imagine what a dreadful state I am reduced to.

" Will you and Horace assist me? I ask you, and yet I hardly think it is necessary to do so, to such a nature as yours. You will, I am sure. I am in distress, not only in pocket but in mind. Things are not as they used to be, and yet I sometimes think I am too old now to become used to a change, but Heaven's will be done! Write to me, my dear niece, and believe me,

" Your ever affectionate aunt (in distress and tribulation),
                                        "—— ARROWDALE."

" Well," said Horace, " poor soul, she is in great distress: I don't see what we can do for her, save to invite her here to remain with us."

" The very thing of all others I would wish to offer her," said Fanny; " you know not, Horace, how kind she will take such an offer from us : it will be so much better than merely relieving her wants and putting her into a lodging."

" It would only induce her creditors to follow her, and take from her what we had given her."

" Exactly."

" Then write to her, Fanny, and tell her we shall be glad to see her here immediately, if she will come at once, without any further preparation than putting on her bonnet."

" I will do so immediately."

And on the instant Fanny sat down to a small table, on which was placed writing materials, and wrote as follows., in reply to her aunt's note :

"MY DEAR AUNT,—I with sorrow read the note you sent me. I regret to hear your misfortunes, but am glad to have the means of offering you some consolation in the way of help.

" If you will come to us we shall be most happy to see you. We shall be glad to see you take up your abode with us, as I did once with you.

" Do not hesitate a moment; come at once—never mind how, so you leave your troubles behind you. Let your creditors take what they have seized, and do you come to us ; we shall be happy with your company.

" Believe me, my dear aunt, we sympathise with you, and feel sorrow for your change of fortune ; therefore come, where I hope the troubles you have will be forgotten—at least it shall be Horace's and my endeavour to make you forget them.
                    " I remain, dear aunt, your affectionate niece,
                                        " FANNY ARROWDALE."

" There, Horace," said Fanny, as she finished reading the epistle, " will that do for her? I wish it to be kind ; have I succeeded in being so? you can best tell me."

" I can, Fanny : but I suppose you want a compliment, since you ask me ; however, I must say you have succeeded, and it is strange to me if it does not bring your aunt here before night."

" I hope it may, for it must be very uncomfortable to be in the state she describes."

" Yes, her case is to be pitied. She never anticipated such a decline of life as hers is like to be."

" No. My poor uncle was a man well to do, and would never lose sight of what he called the main chance, though a most liberal and kind-hearted man, and one whose heart was ever overflowing towards those in trouble."

" The change she now experiences must be doubly bitter, since she has brought it on by her second marriage," said Horace. " Do you know, Fanny, I do not think a second marriage is at all likely to be happy."

" Perhaps not, though I have heard of such things."

" So have I, but I never saw one."

* * * * * * *

It was not many hours after this that Mrs. Arrowdale (late Mrs. Paddlebat) arrived, but Horace and Fanny were out ; they had gone out for an hour or two to enjoy the morning, and to see the various sights and make such calls as they deemed necessary and proper.

And it was not until they were on their road back that they thought of the arrival of Mrs. Arrowdale.

" I wonder," said Fanny, as they stopped at the door, " if my aunt has arrived."

" She may," said Horace, " though I hope not, until we are prepared to receive her. She will deem it so unkind if we are not present to receive her, just at such a juncture, too."

They entered the house, and the first person they saw in the drawing-room was her aunt herself, seated before the fire, apparently in deep thought.

" My dear aunt," said Fanny, " I am sorry we were not at home to receive you, but we did not know at what hour to expect you, and, of course, we could not tell when you might come ; but now you are here I hope you will make yourself happy."

" I will try, my dear niece, to be so, though you cannot but see how hard it is to forget what I have been, to what I have come to at last."

" You have come to one whom you have been kind to, and whose duty it is to be kind to you in return."

Many kind words passed between them, and they all formed a very comfortable family party. Mrs. Arrowdale related the whole length and breadth of her misfortunes, interspersed with many curious reflections, somewhat at variance with each other occasionally ; but that was no matter ; it made up the sum-total of the conversation, which passed off agreeably enough.

Horace was well pleased with Mrs. Arrowdale, though she every now and then made a reflection upon the past to the disparagement of the present, at the same time she referred to the exaltation of the past.

Certainly her day lay in the past, and hence it being her best days, she naturally judged it to be the best of all others. This is possibly the reason why people are always disposed to look upon the past as having an advantage over the present. Our best feelings and our strongest passions are most in play, and hence all may appear as though looked at through a better medium, giving it an undue preference over the present. However that may be, Mrs. Arrowdale was gratified with her reception by Horace and her niece Fanny, both of whom did their best to make her forget her misfortunes and distress and at the same time to enjoy the present, and feel herself at home.

One unacquainted with the rascality of Mr. Arrowdale might have supposed that, at all events, now, after the severe lesson misfortune had taught to Mrs. Paddlebat, she would have had some period of repose, brief though it might be, after the many storms and troubles she had gone through since her husband's death.

Knowing as we do all the good feelings of Fanny Leslie, and feeling convinced that if any one could make allowances for the oddity of her aunt's disposition, she would be that person, we should unhesitatingly say, but for one circumstance, that Mrs. Arrowdale would experience as much contentment as her relatives were capable of bestowing upon her.

But the circumstance known to the reader as well as to ourselves, which interferes with such a presumption, consists of the most alarming fact, viz., that Arrowdale, before his departure from this country, had taken with him the whole of Horace's fortune.

This dreadful circumstance (for really a dreadful one it is) Horace and his wife were in complete ignorance of.

He received the dividend arising from his five thousand pounds in the Funds half-yearly, and as it wanted at least five or six weeks to the next period of payment, his villanous relative had calculated upon that period, at least of impunity, from the consequences of his criminality.

But we, who know the impending ruin that is hanging over poor Horace and his amiable wife, whose fortunes we have narrated thus far, cannot, but with a gloomy and regretful feeling, listen to their anticipations of the future, unaccompanied as they were by the remotest notion of the catastrophe that had taken place.

Little did they suspect that they were actually then spending the last few guineas they could call their own.

They sat together on the evening after Mrs. Paddlebat—for she deserves that name better than Arrowdale, and we think we had better call her by it—had arrived.

"There is a great change," said Horace, "in your aunt, Fanny—a very great change; she is one of those persons that show best under the cloud of misfortune. Prosperity she cannot stand; she becomes arrogant, vain, and full of what she considers worldly wisdom; whereas now, when she really is suffering under the pangs of misfortune, she is reasonable and almost amiable."

"I know that you are not censorious, Horace," said Fanny, "and that you merely mention this as a trait in my aunt's character, which you have observed; but there is another period likewise at which her better nature peeps out, and that is when she is really called upon to behave kindly or sympathisingly to any one in distress. She is fully capable of such behaviour, and, in point of fact, I am certain that if it were not for personal vanity, which is her besetting sin, and has so frequently made her the tool of the designing, she would be one of the most amiable of women."

"And you say that, Fanny, in the face of her having asked you to leave the house?"

"Yes, but then she knew I was not destitute. By-the-by, I suppose, Horace, you have allowed your cousin to invest my money for me, or rather your money, Horace, since I have bestowed myself upon you and all that belongs to me."

"Yes, I believe him to be a skilful financier. Your thousands are along with my thousands in the Three per Cents., where, as we are not ambitious, we will let them remain, and give ourselves no trouble about the world and all its speculations."

"Your wishes are my wishes, Horace. You know that I shall be content."

"And I, and so will your aunt, after a time, when she finds that she has all the comforts of a home about her, and forgets her present disappointments. It was very cruel for Arrowdale to desert her after he married her."

"It was, indeed; it seems a cruel act; and yet, perhaps after all, may be the kindest he can perform; for, just imagine what a sad life she must have led with one who could have no affection for her, and who would be continually telling her of the bitter disappointment he had experienced. You may depend, Horace, it is far better that he should be gone, and that my aunt is well rid of him."

"Well, well, you are right; and now I hope, Fanny, that your troubles are over, and that the stormy period, which sooner or later will occur with every one's existence, has passed away, giving place to the sunshine of uninterrupted felicity."

"Can I be otherwise than happy now?"

"It shall be my greatest pleasure, Fanny, to believe in the impossibility of your being otherwise than happy; and perhaps after all at times, when I must be absent from my home, you will find it agreeable for your aunt to be here, and that in her society you will pass a few hours occasionally with less weariness than you otherwise would."

We will pass over now some length of time until one morning, when Horace said to Fanny, with a smile,—

"I suppose you have scarcely a notion of how poor we are?"

"Poor, Horace!"

"I do not mean in happiness—I do not mean in affection; but I do mean in money, and I may almost say,

"Who steals my purse steals trash;"

for there is really very little in it."

Fanny looked serious.

"Nay," said Horace, laughing, "it's of little consequence; for if I must make such remarks, give me this day, of all others, to make them in."

"This day, Horace; and why this day?"

"Because I go to the City to receive a half-year's dividends of your money and my own; so that, although I am poor at present, a few hours makes me wealthy."

Now it was Fanny's turn to smile, and she said,—

"You quite alarmed me, Horace, for the moment; for there are some little debts which have accumulated, which I wish to pay to-day; and, moreover, I want to make my aunt a little present, for I cannot forget that she did behave kindly to me when I came a destitute orphan to my uncle's house."

"Consult your own feelings and disposition, Fanny, in anything of that kind. You know well that all is at your disposal, and that you can do nothing which will not give me pleasure."

The breakfast was despatched, and with a light heart Horace went to the City, in order to possess himself of the few hundreds which his own and Fanny's funded property would yield.

Not the least notion of any impending evil came across him, and he pleased himself with the idea of carrying home some costly little remembrance which he could purchase, as he returned, for Fanny.

He knew that there was a Mr. Anderson on the Stock Exchange, who had been intimate with Mr. Arrowdale, and "Ahem!" he called out to him,—

"How do you do, Mr. Anderson?" he said; "I want to trouble you to transact a little business for me, now that my cousin has taken himself off, and is not in a condition to transact business for anybody."

"Certainly, sir; I recollect you very well. That was a strange affair of your cousin, Mr. Arrowdale, going off. He was a defaulter to a considerable extent."

"I dare say he might have been," said Horace; "but I am really so ignorant of financial matters, and what is called the money-market, that I understand little about it."

"Well, it is of course quite a business of itself; but what can I do for you?"

"Why, you must know, that hitherto my cousin has put me in the way of transacting my business, and receiving my dividends. I am so ignorant of the necessary forms, that I must get you to put me in the way of securing the proceeds of the stock that is in my name."

"I hope your cousin did not victimise you."

"How victimise me?"

"Why, he had a power of attorney to sell and buy for you; and I suppose you are aware he got, after some difficulty, your wife's money transferred to your account."

"Well, you know that was all the same."

"Very good, come with me, and we will see what stock is standing in your name, and get your dividend."

Mr. Anderson took him to the proper office, to get a warrant for the dividend, and, upon stating the name and the amount, a clerk, in a business-like manner, turned to a book, and after a search of about a minute and a half, he said—

"Why, what's the meaning of this coming here about stock, which has been sold out by power of attorney a long time ago?"

"Sold out!" said Horace.

"Come away, come away," said the stockbroker. "It's of no use saying a word here, my dear sir.   You have had your answer, and you may depend it is a correct one.   Your cousin Arrowdale has served you, as he served everybody else, I presume, for whom he had power to act.   He has taken your money, and gone off with it.   I hope the amount will not seriously inconvenience you?"

Horace did not speak a word.   The calmness that sat upon his countenance had something positively frightful about it, and Mr. Anderson, as he looked at him, became seriously alarmed at the possible effect which the sudden announcement of the loss of so large a sum of money might have.

"Come, come, Mr. Arrowdale," he said, "you must bear this as well as you can; I can assure you that you are not the only sufferer by the delinquencies of your cousin, to a serious extent; so come, sir, it is a great loss, I admit, but perhaps a little retrenchment and expenses, and so on, may put it all to rights again."

Still Horace spoke not a word, but when he reached the street he placed his hands upon his head and gave a deep groan, and fell upon the pavement as though he had been shot.

Mr. Anderson was much alarmed, and called upon the bystanders to assist him.

A crowd soon collected, and several lifted the insensible form of Horace from the pavement.   Some suggested one thing and some another, but Mr. Anderson most positively insisted that he should be conveyed immediately to a surgeon's, and he was carried into a shop of a chemist close to the Royal Exchange.

Then with great difficulty the door was closed against all but Mr. Anderson, and those who had helped to convey poor Horace into the shop.

A dense crowd remained outside, and those who were the nearest, as usual, flattened their noses against the glass of the window, and shaded their eyes with their hands, in an eager but vain endeavour to see what was going on inside.

The surgeon, who likewise kept this retail chemist's shop, was a man of experience and judgment.   A very serious expression crossed his face when he looked at Horace, who was supported in a chair by Mr. Anderson.

"How did it happen?" said the surgeon.

"It was the sudden effect of bad news.   I was with him, he gave a groan and dropped at once."

The surgeon tore open Horace's waistcoat and shirt, and placed his ear close over the region of the heart.   He listened attentively for several minutes, and then getting up from his stooping posture, he looked at those around him, who were waiting with great anxiety to hear what might be his opinion of the case, and said—

"He is quite dead.   It's of no use trying to do anything, for he is quite dead. He has ruptured a vessel of the heart, and death has been instantaneous.

Those who were present looked at each other in silence, as if the information which had just reached them had completely paralysed all their faculties.

CHAPTER LXXV.

FANNY AT HOME.—THE OMEN.

In the mean time Fanny, with a heart as light as any bird's in the sweet summer time, when it thinks of nothing but of sunshine and flowers, sat at home wileing away the time as best she might until Horace should return to her.

Mrs. Paddlebat, with a wish to make herself useful, had stepped out a short distance to purchase some articles for the house, so that Fanny was alone.

Yes, she was alone in person, but the spirit of affection and happiness was about her, and she had abundant food for pleasant and happy thoughts in the sweet future, which seemed to be dawning upon her.

"I will seize this opportunity," she said, "to finish the working of this purse of silver beads, which I intend for Horace; he shall not see it until finished, and well I know he will prize the slender gift, because it comes from me."

She sat down opposite to a half-length portrait of Horace, which hung in the apartment. It was one of those pictures, the eyes of which ever seemed to be looking into your own, and by some strange fascination, such as she had never before experienced, Fanny could scarce withdraw her eyes from a fixed contemplation of the painted face. And as she looked she fancied that the eyes of the portrait bore a mournful expression, as if they were fixed upon her in deep sorrow, such as she had never yet noticed in them.

"This is nervousness," she said, "and the effect of an excited imagination. Now, when Horace is out, that portrait, instead of being a consolation to me, as it ought to be, will become a great annoyance. I ought not to sit opposite to it, and then I could not look at it, and it could not seem, as it does, to return my gaze with such deep pathos."

This was a wise determination if she had carried it out, which she did not, for although she strove to direct all her attention to the piece of work she had in hand, her eyes, still despite all her wishes to the contrary, would wander to the face of the portrait, and there fix themselves with an earnest and scrutinizing gaze.

"How sad it looks," she said; "how very strangely sad—surely, surely, it never before wore that most strange and singular expression!"

Again she looked down, and tried to work at the purse she was knitting, but only for a few moments could she pursue that occupation, when the silk and the beads again hung listlessly from her hands, and her eyes were again fixed upon the portrait.

"I wish that Horace would come home," she said. "This strange species of nervousness never before came over me. Oh! that he would come home, and laugh me out of my imaginary terrors. Terrors! said I? Why should I be terrified—what is there to terrify me?"

She rose from her seat, and slowly paced the apartment for some few minutes in silence, but she could not shake off the impression that had stolen over her; and once again she seated herself opposite the portrait, and looked upon it with a marked and fixed attention.

Still to her imagination it wore that strange look of sadness and glooom, and the more she looked the more her eyes seemed to gaze with a melancholy reality upon her.

Suddenly then the blood retreated to her heart with a frightful gush, for she saw that the face actually moved, and terror chained her to the spot.

This was no delusion of the imagination, for the hook which held the cord by which the picture was suspended, gradually relaxed its hold in the wall, and allowed the cord to slip off it.

The picture fell with a crash upon the floor—it stood for a moment on the edge of the frame, and then leaning forward fell upon its face.

Fanny was so overcome at this circumstance, really trifling as it may appear, that a sudden faintness came over her, and she never in her life was so near lapsing into perfect insensibility, without that state actually occurring, as upon that occasion.

It was a fortunate thing that at the moment Mrs. Paddlebat, who had returned from shopping, entered the apartment full of exultation at having achieved some wonderful bargain, but when she saw Fanny half upon the ground, and half upon the chair only, she gave a scream of terror, and it was a minute or two before she could come to her assistance.

"Why, Fanny!" she exclaimed, "what has happened? Good gracious! and the picture's fallen too! Why, who's been here? Speak to me at once, or else I am certain I shall go off in my old hysterics. I am positive I shall; so don't keep me in suspense. Gracious; what's happened! has she fainted?"

It was a considerable time before Fanny could recover herself sufficiently to return anything like a rational answer to her aunt; but when she was able to speak and saw who was with her, she clung to her with pertinacity, exclaiming—

"Oh! aunt, aunt! I have been frightfully alarmed, and yet so foolishly so the

I cannot tell you why; my mind has been full of all sorts of dreads; the thoughts of some impending evil seem to have come over me, and almost to drive me distracted."

" But what evil, my dear?"

" That I cannot tell you. I know nothing but that I have been in a state of agony and distress; and, in the middle of it, Horace's portrait fell from the wall, and I suppose I fainted, or nearly so."

" But, my dear," said Mrs. Paddlebat, " how very foolish it is of you to give way to such sort of feelings; you ought to fight out against them, indeed you ought. Just because Horace is gone to the City to receive his money, you are to put yourself in a fume and a fever about nothing. I wonder he has not come back!"

" Oh! I wish he had, for even now I cannot shake off from my mind a presentiment of much evil. I am certain, quite certain, that something dreadful has occurred."

" Dreadful!" said Mrs. Paddlebat, as she dropped into her chair. " What could occur, Fanny? Horace, you know, is not a child that's likely to get run over, and, as for not coming back from the City soon, I recollect when poor Mr. Paddlebat, who is now dead and gone, rest his soul! used to go to the Bank, he always called in at a place in Threadneedle-street, where they sold some particular kind of soup he fancied, and he never got home for two hours."

" But you know, aunt, Horace would not do that, and so the delay in his coming home is rather serious."

Then came a tap at the room-door, and a servant came in to say that a Mr. Bull had come for his little account.

" Well, how vexatious!" said Mrs. Paddlebat; " you can tell him that Mr. Arrowdale is gone to the Bank; and, as soon as he comes back, we will send to him. How provoking, to be sure, to have people dunning one when there is really lots of money, only one can't lay one's hand upon it, of course, all of a minute. It's really provoking; but, you make yourself comfortable, Fanny, and depend upon it he will soon be back, and when he does come you will find he has been to the soup-shop."

" No, no, aunt, certainly not. Horace has no fancy that way; and he would go to the City a hundred times without thinking of soup."

" Well, my dear, if he did, it's natural enough, so make yourself comfortable."

It was easy to say to poor Fanny, make yourself comfortable; it was easy to tell her never to mind; but all that had no effect in assuaging her fears, or in inducing her to think that Horace's absence was not most uncomfortably and unaccountably long.

And as hour after hour passed away, Fanny's fears increased; and the consolations of Mrs. Paddlebat diminished, for she was not one who would fight against circumstances at all, and when she said never mind, it was because she did not mind herself; but when she got alarmed, she was much more likely to increase Fanny's fears beyond a reasonable limit, than to allay them.

There could be no question that Horace had been absent twice the time necessary to proceed to the City, and transact all his business there; and as Mrs. Paddlebat admitted herself this fact, hinting, too, that even her supposition of the soup-shop must now fail, inasmuch as he could not have been so long in consuming that gelatinous compound, Fanny's alarm got to such a height, that she rose and determined to go in pursuit of her husband.

Her aunt at length complied with the proposition, and then not liking her to go alone, she insisted upon accompanying her, and they both started for the City together.

That was a most anxious walk—one full of dread and trouble, and after all, when they got there what could they do? for totally ignorant as they were of business transactions, they had no idea of where to make any inquiry. But still it was something to go to the neighbourhood where they knew he had been to, and where, at all events, there was a possibility of acquiring some information.

As they neared the Bank, and passed down a narrow street in its immediate vicinity, they perceived several small knots of persons conversing together, and apparently deeply interested in the theme of their conversation.

Fanny was not at all curious, and under ordinary circumstances would have been the last person in the world to attend to any subject of public gossip, but a something impelled her, she knew not what, to pause for a moment and listen to what a woman was saying, who seemed to be expatiating upon some subject with great energy of manner.

"Well," she said, "it's a shocking thing of course, but my first husband, who, though I say it, was as fine a looking a man as you would see on a summer's day, went just in that way. We was setting at tea—black with a dash of green in it—when he says to me, Susan, says he, I'm agoing, and with that down he comes, smashes the Britannia metal tea-pot, and dies like a lamb."

"Really!" said another.

"Yes, marm, and a coroner's inquest sat upon him for three hours and a quarter, and they brought it in that nobody could help it, and it was a vis.cation, and after that I married Mr. Crumples, the shoemaker."

"Well, it's one comfort," said another woman, "that the gentleman that fell down dead at the bank did not look like a married man."

"Good heavens!" cried Fanny, "what do I hear? Aunt, aunt, did you attend to what she said? speak again, tell me of that some of you, do not let me expire of suspense, but tell me at once, I implore you, who and what he was."

As she spoke she burst in among the throng of astonished women with her hands clasped, and such an expression of desperate agony upon her countenance, that they were terrified, and for some few seconds could return no reply to her anxious questions.

At length one of them spoke, saying—

"Why marm, we were talking of a gentleman as fell down dead at the bank or thereabouts."

"Yes, yes, and his name."

"Why, marm, as regards his name nobody seems to know; leastways, if they know his name, they don't know where he lives, and they have taken the corpse to the workhouse."

"No," said another woman, "they have taken it to the public-house."

"I beg your pardon," said a third; "but the wery doctor as lives under the Royal Exchange has got him, and if them as he belongs to don't look sharp he will be made an anatomy of as sure as eggs is eggs."

"Now, really," said the first person, "didn't I see him with my own eyes took away in a shell from the doctor's to the workhouse—seeing is believing I think."

"Now you speak to me," said Fanny, "you can describe what you saw—speak, speak to me, and be accurate."

"It had black nails?"

"What, what? It is of him who died I speak."

"Oh! I didn't see nothing but the coffin, leastwise I seed the men as took it away, and I seed Mr. Ragget, the beadle; but you seem ill, marm, I hope you don't know nothing of the gentleman."

"I am distracted," said Fanny, "have pity upon me some of you, and show me at once to where the surgeon lives, of whom you make mention."

This was easily done, the shop was pointed out from the very spot on which they stood, and Fanny, bearing upon the arm of the terrified and bewildered Mrs. Paddlebat, made her way towards it with a feeling of agony at her heart, and distraction in her brain, that it was a wonder she was able to move or to preserve her intellect sufficiently clear for its most ordinary exercise.

Once or twice she wrung her hands and said, in half-choked accents—

"Oh! aunt! aunt! something tells me it is Horace—something tells me it must be he. Heaven help me! Heaven help me now!"

"Something," said Mrs. Paddlebat, taking Fanny's words in their literal sense, and looking all round her; "something tells you, I don't see anything, but I am in such a fright I don't know what I do see, and what I don't. I don't know whether I'm on my head or my heels."

"On, on," said Fanny, as she urged her aunt forward towards the chemist's shop; "on, on, oh! quicker, quicker, I have a dreadful question to ask, a question, the answer to which will make or mar my peace for ever."

They reached the shop door, Fanny had to place both hands upon the lock to open it, and then she trembled so that she could scarcely accomplish her purpose, it was only by a great effort that she succeeded, and in another moment she stood at the surgeon's counter, where he had been summoned by a bell, which the opening of the door was made to ring.

He looked at her with evident surprise, for the expression of her countenance was quite sufficient to convince him that she was in the most painful state of doubt and infirmity. And now, at that moment, her voice seemed to forsake her, and it was a full minute before she could command utterance.

Indeed the chemist had to speak to her first ere she could speak to him. He perceived that from some cause or other his visitor was completely overcome, and unable to utter a word. He therefore spoke, and spoke kindly, saying—

"Madam, if there be any service I can render to you—pray command me, allow me to offer you a seat, I hope that it is only a little indisposition which produces this agitation."

"Tell me," said Fanny, "tell me," and her voice was indicative of agitation, ' tell me the name of the gentleman who died on the threshold of the bank."

The truth seemed to strike the surgeon, that in this young and interesting girl—for a girl she still looked, although a wife—he saw one nearly allied by the ties of kindred or of affection to the gentleman who had been brought to his shop, and upon whom he had been compelled to pronounce the irrevocable fiat of death.

He was silent. Oh, how fearfully eloquent to the heart of Fanny was that silence.

"You, you need not speak," she gasped. "I read the fatal truth in your eyes."

She clutched at the counter for support; her yielding figure slid from off its polished surface, and she fell despite a remonstrance from the surgeon to Mrs. Paddlebat, who certainly ought to have assisted her, but who herself was really too much affected by the incident to be able to render aid to any one.

As soon as he could he rushed round the counter, exclaiming—

"Good God, madam, why did you not support her, you must have seen she was fainting? and you're big enough, God knows."

Mrs. Paddlebat's face had the infirmity of getting red, when her feelings were strongly affected, and the contrast with the pale countenance of Fanny was so great, that really it was no wonder the medical man looked upon her as a great, fat, indifferent looking person, who had from sheer inhumanity or stupidity, allowed a small fragile creature like Fanny Arrowdale to fall to the floor without making an effort to assist her in her extremity.

The surgeon himself helped Fanny from the floor, and carried her into a little parlour at the back of the shop, as tenderly as if she had been a child of his own. Indeed, a tear glistened in his eye as he carefully deposited his lovely burden upon a couch ; and then he stood for a minute gazing upon her pallid features as he said—

"Poor thing! poor thing! your'e happier now than you will be when I have done my duty and recovered you from this state of physical prostration. I know not what may be the tie of affection that binds you to him who is now no more ; but it must be a strong one to move you thus. Gracious Heavens ! what noise is that ?"

Mrs. Paddlebat had not sufficiently recovered to give expression to her feelings, and she was what she called crying, which consisted of what may be called a despairing howl, perfectly dreadful to hear, and which the medical man for a few moments could scarcely believe to be human.

CHAPTER LXXVI.

SHOWS WHAT BECAME OF ARROWDALE, THE STOCK BROKER, ABROAD.

It is worth while to trace what became of Arrowdale abroad.

The first place he made for on arriving on the continent, was to push on to Paris ; there he could enjoy life to perfection ; he had plenty of money, and he being a very sharp man, could do more in the way of making money go a long way than a great many men, he had come lightly by it, and moreover, he could add to it by means best known to sharp practitioners.

After spending about a fortnight or three weeks in Paris, just to get a little acquainted with a few matters he deemed desirable, and wear off the rough edge off himself as far as regarded cultivated manners and acquaintance with Parisian matters.

Then he started off upon a grand tour to visit all the continental cities, that is to say, such of them as were the capital of their respective kingdoms.

He went to Berlin, and their mixed with the society that place afforded, and found out more than one gaming house; he bought experience here, and paid for it five hundred pounds, which sum he lost at the gambling table.

However, there can be no manner of doubt but he secured a little caution for the money, and learned how to guard against a trick or two, and then he hoped to be able to practice that elsewhere, and make more by it.

Afterwards he proceeded to Leipzig, and there he made a stay of five weeks in this quiet, but ancient capital. Here, however, he found that a man with money could find plenty of occasion to employ his time at the gaming-table.

It is astonishing the amount of money may be got rid of, and how many gaming-tables are to be found all over the continent, and even at Leipzig—there he found there were some new means of disposing of his money.

At the hotel were he lodged, one morning a gentleman entered the room, and bowing to him, remarked that he had seen him at a certain place the night before.

This was said in so casual away that Arrowdale did not attempt to deny it, but at once admitted he was at the place indicated.

" Then," said the stranger, " you must be beware that you have subjected yourself to a heavy fine and some months' imprisonment."

" You are liable to the same," said Arrowdale, sharply, " since you were there too."

" I am employed by the police."

" You ?'

" Yes, I ; now I may as well pocket a little extra myself, and let you off the imprisonment."

" What do you mean by that ?" inquired Arrowdale.

" This much; if you will hand me the fine I will say nothing about the matter; whereas, on the other hand you will pay the same fine, half of which I shall have, and you, in addition, will have to suffer eight weeks imprisonment for infringing the regulations of the city."

Arrowdale knew so much that gambling was illegal, and therefore after many inward curses paid the money and left Leipsic, and determined at once to traverse onwards until he came to Venice, where he resolved to remain a few weeks.

Here he fell in love with a dark-eyed Venetian beauty, but their connexion did not last long; but it was curious—it was as follows :—

One evening as he was walking on the bridge that crossed the grand canal—there were few persons present—and as he loitered about a mask came up to him, and after looking around to see no one was near at hand,

" Signor," she said, " bright eyes have looked upon you; one of the fairest in Venice from her window has seen you; you are a favoured man, Signor."

" What do you mean ?" inquired Arrowdale, who had listened to this in amazement.

" Follow me, signor, and you shall know more about what I say in a less public place."

The mask then turned away abruptly, leaving the spot, and Arrowdale followed much wondering what was going to happen, and if he were acting wisely in following so great a stranger upon so strange an errand. However, there he was, and he must go on now, though he would have his own choice of how far he would go, and that was all he need care for.

Suddenly the mask turned round and said,—

" Signor, a lady loves you, and if you deserve all the happiness you are likely to receive, you ought to be generous. Your personal appearance, you air, and mien, have done it all ; but the lady would regret seeing you if she thought you would deem the step she has taken an improper one."

"No, no," said Arrowdale, "certainly not; I am honoured by her choice—I am, indeed."

"Then follow me."

As the mask spoke he turned away and led through several streets till he came to a low garden wall, and then he gave a low whistle as he stopped at a small door. The whistle was answered by the door opening, and the mask beckoned him to enter.

Arrowdale saw a handsome garden.

"It is all right, sure enough," said Arrowdale to himself, "it is a real adventure and no sham."

He entered the garden, which had the appearance of being laid out expressly for the accommodation of lovers, as there were many long winding walks, but at the same time they were all impervious to the sight.

He was led through some of these, and then he entered a house, one that was handsomely furnished. He walked on tiptoe, and so did his conductor, but after a little while he paused at a door, at which he tapped, and then a fat old woman came out and stood on the mat outside.

"Well, signora, I have done your bidding; here is the gentleman; he is generous, he has received me."

"'Tis well; you have no more to do, but you may remain in readiness in the garden if you please."

"I will, signora."

"Will you come this way? Ah, signor, what a happy man you are; but though you are happy, you could not be so cruel. Well, well, go in, and you will see Donna Isabel."

Putting a piece of money in the hand of old Duenna (a piece of gold) he went into the room. It was handsome, hung round with tapestry, and not a sound met the ear. A gentle light came through the blinds, and shed a subdued light upon a young and handsome female, about the age of seventeen.

Arrowdale was perfectly enraptured; he had never seen so beautiful a creature, and he bowed to her with the air of a lover, and approached her.

"Signora," he said, "this happiness is more than mortal. You have made me blush."

"I feared, signor," she replied, "I feared you would deem me wrong in acting thus, but I was unable to let my sentiments be known to you unless I sent a messenger to you."

"Certainly, signora; nor should I have had this felicity had it not been for your doing so. I could not even have known you, for I am a stranger in this country."

"I am very glad of it, Signor, for I may be of service to you, for I am sorry to say there are in Venice many unprincipled persons who would not hesitate to take advantage of any one they found means to do so."

"You are kind. I shall be glad to learn experience in your hands, Signora," said Arrowdale.

"Ah! Virgin Mary! Holy mother! What shall I do—what shall I do? I am ruined, undone for ever."

"Eh?" said Arrowdale, putting his arm round her waist, and endeavouring to take her beautiful hand; "eh? what does this mean? I have not frightened you, I hope?"

"No, no; I—I—I—"

"Eh? what? what were you about to say?"

"My husband, my husband."

"Your husband, dearest; I did not know you had one. You really must not flurry yourself; I am here."

"And so am I," said a gruff, powerful voice beside him.

Arrowdale, petrified, looked slowly round, and beheld a tall, dark-looking Venetian, with a sharp, glittering stiletto in his hand; he, however, could not speak.

"Shall I sacrifice the worthless foreigner to my injured honour, to my just indignation, to my revenge? Yes, yes—blood, blood, must be spilt."

As he spoke he played with the glittering blade as if anticipating the deed he was about to commit. Arrowdale was terrified to a degree, but he was incapable of moving or speaking till a dreadful kick in the stomach laid him on his back, and after a little time he gathered breath enough to say—

"Mercy! mercy! I haven't done anything; there's no harm done. Have mercy—spare my life."

"What compensation can I have for my wounded honour?"

"I have not hurt your honour, on my soul."

"Peace, fool; and you, madam, you must prepare to die."

"Mercy, mercy, have mercy upon me; I am sure the stranger will do anything reasonable either to save me or himself from death, and, worse than death, dishonour."

"Oh! yes," said Arrowdale, "anything in reason;" and he looked at the weeping beauty by his side, and then at the dark and jealous Venetian who stood eyeing him with a sinister countenance, and playing with the bright blade of his long keen stiletto.

"You make compensation," said the man. "Let me hear what it can be that will stay the passage of my dagger to your heart; it longs to be there."

"For God's sake say what it is you want to let me out without being touched by that dreadful weapon."

"A thousand pounds," said the Venetian.

"I haven't got the hundredth part of that sum," he replied at once.

"Well, well, I will not be delayed," and as he spoke he threw off his cloak, and preparing to stab him—

"Stay, stay, husband," said the lady, throwing herself between Arrowdale and the infuriated husband; "stay—the stranger will do half what you ask him for my sake, since I must say it, though not for his own;" and then, turning to Arrowdale, she gave him an imploring look, which seemed to say—

"You see what terms I have made for you. Do not sacrifice me for the sake of money."

He thought there was no escape whatever, and fearing his body might be made acquainted with the stiletto, he gave in in an agony of terror, and agreed to give the sum required. However, he had but a small portion of that sum about him, upon which the Venetian declared that he would make him a prisoner until he had the money sent him.

There were many excuses made, but the tall Venetian overruled all, and it was astonishing to observe how cool he was.

The end of it was—the money was paid, and he departed in safety, swearing he would never engage in another adventure, nor even stop in Venice another hour; but set off straight for Paris, where he arrived in great joy.

Here he gave way to excess for a short time, and made a serious inroad into his funds at the gaming table. This he determined upon repairing in the same manner as it had been occasioned—namely, at the gaming table.

This was for him a very unfortunate resolution, for he had informed an intimate friend of what he was about to do, and the result was his bosom friend knew one or two more bosom friends to whom he communicated the same, and a small party was formed to enrich themselves at the expense of the silly foreigner, who had so much money by him, and tried to make more of it at the gaming table.

Arrowdale was accordingly met, and play was carried on skillfully, and without any attempt to draw him in for many days, until, at length, however, it set in, and after playing for some few nights with alternate success, until Arrowdale, with for or five sharpers, sat up one night, during the whole of which they carried on their game at a determined pace.

Arrowdale was losing, as could be seen by his feverish and anxious countenance. He lost game after game until the last stake was made, and then, with a feverish and excited brain, he sat down and lost it.

He arose and quitted the gaming-table to be a ruined man. All his hopes were gone. The thought that he was not able to return to England was a pang. However he walked through the streets to his lodging, and the sun shone upon him brightly and beautifully. It was broad day. There was he in Paris with only a ten franc piece in his pocket, and heaven knows what he could do to live when that was gone.

CHAPTER LXXVII.

WHAT OCCURRED TO FANNY AT THE CHEMIST'S, AND HOW SHE LEFT HOME.

WE left Fanny in the kind-hearted surgeon's study, just at the critical moment, too, when Mrs. Paddlebat had become sufficiently conscious of what had happened to give strange and inarticulated expression to her feelings, much to the discomfiture of the surgeon, who, although a good-hearted man, was one of rather a nervous and fidgetty temperament.

"My dear madam," he said, "let me implore you to go into the streets if you are going to do that. Don't go into the Royal Exchange, for you'll impede business; but, any rate go where you will, I can't have that noise in my shop."

Mrs. Paddlebat stopped the torrent of her grief, and muttered something about some people having no consideration for other people's feelings, which the surgeon could not understand at all; but commenced taking measures for the restoration of Fanny to consciousness.

"There a gentleman," he said to Mrs. Paddlebat, "there was a gentleman who had dropped down dead somewhere about the threshhold of the Bank of England, and who was brought in here. I am sorry to think that this young lady must be related to him."

"Oh! what was his name?" said Mrs. Paddlebat. "What was his name,"

"His name was Arrowdale."

"You've hit it," said Mrs. Paddlebat, and she staggered back upsetting a large white jar full of leeches.

"Damn it, madam," said the surgeon, "what are you about? You first of all terrify me so by howling in an extraordinary manner that I can hardly attend to this young lady, and then you want to destroy my stock in trade."

"Bless us and save us," said Mrs. Paddlebat, "are they black beetles?"

The surgeon was rather furious, but he collected the leeches, popped them into another vessel, and then, darting a look at Mrs. Paddlebat, which, if he had possessed the power of the Fabled Gorgon, would certainly have turned her into a corpulent stone statue, he continued his active exertions for the restoration of Fanny to consciousness.

"Ah! dear, dear," said Mrs. Paddlebat, as she sat down upon an extremely small chair, which her voluminous garments hid entirely. "Ah! dear, has it come to this?—poor Mr. Arrowdale! and so there's an end of him. Ah me! ah me! there's nothing but misfortune in this world—when you think you're most safe, you aint."

Crack went the chair and Mrs. Paddlebat came down on the surgery floor with a bounce that shook every bottle in the place, and at that moment Fanny opened her eyes.

The despairing look that was upon her countenance was sufficient to have melted the most obdurate heart; and the chemist, although he had, in the course of his profession, seen many a scene of woe, thought that he had never looked upon a countenance so sad and so mournful as that which now was before him.

He paid no attention to Mrs. Paddlebat, who he really cared not whether she broke his chairs or not, but to the broken-hearted Fanny he devoted all his skill; and by dint of persuasion induced her to swallow a restorative which he prepared for her. She was now able to speak, and when she did so, it was not what she said that brought with it the agonising consciousness that she would never know peace of mind again, as much as it was fears she had in which she spoke, that such a catastrophe was to be concluded.

Indeed, as regarded the words that came from her lips, it was evident that one of those strange and unnatural accessions of calmness had come over her which are common enough when the heart is overcharged by some gigantic grief, which defies the power of ordinary language to express it.

The chemist was not deceived into any idea, that Mrs. Horace Arrowdale was receiving her misfortune with indifference, because she did not rave about it, although Mrs. Paddlebut was. We find after all that we must call that lady Mrs. Paddlebat.

He at once advised that Fanny should go home; and turning to her after giving that advice to Mrs. Paddlebat, he said in a tone of solicitude and kindness,—

"You now know the full extent of your misfortune, and you must endeavour to summon to your aid what amount of fortitude you can, always bearing in mind there is nothing for you yet to know which, in the slightest degree, can tend to dress the affair in any more terrors to the imagination, than simple death possesses. A more calm, placid, and painless cessation of the faculties of life, could not possibly take place.

Fanny looked at him as if she scarcely comprehended the meaning of the words he uttered, and then, with a shudder she said,—

"Yes, as you say—calm and placid the colours of death!—the horrible placidity of the grave."

"My dear," said Mrs. Paddlebat, who had gathered herself up from the ruins of the chemist's chair; "my dear, let me beg of you to come home at once."

"Home!—home!! God! what home have I?"

"Alas, alas!" replied Mrs. Paddlebat, "poor thing. What now if this was to affect her wits. Dear, dear, what a world we do live in, to be sure."

"Never mind that," said the chemist; "but do you get her home as quickly as as you can, madam, for I can tell you that this calmness which appears at present to have complete possession of her, is a deceptive feeling, and but the prelude to a more violent exhibition of grief, which had far better take place in her own home, than anywhere else."

"Gracious! you don't say so."

"I do say so, madam, and I think so likewise. Do go and get a coach, and take the poor young creature home. I pity her from my soul, but this is not a case for which medicine can do anything."

Thus urged, Mrs. Paddlebat left the shop, in order to carry out the chemist's suggestion; and when she was gone, Fanny spoke again in the same strange altered tone which had before struck so painfully upon his ears, and which he knew betokened that dreadful apathetic state of mind which, for many hours sometimes follows some great shock.

"You will tell me all she said some other time before I die."

"Die! oh you must not think of that. Time will do much towards, I will not say reconciling you to the great misfortune which has befallen you, but it will do much towards softening its effect; and when you come to take into your consideration, how frail a thing human life is, and how we are, the best of us, the sport of the merest accidents, you will be able, I hope, to look with more philosophy, upon this most sad matter."

"Philosophy—oh Heavens! when did Philosophy ever heal such a wound?"

"You will," continued the surgeon, "learn, in course of time, to look back with a calm and a patient regret upon this sad day, and to wait with resignation that period when you and I, and all of us, shall, in the natural order of things, go down to the grave and be rgotten,"

To a contemplative and thoughtful mind like Fanny's this was certainly the course of argumentation most likely to produce some beneficial result, but it came too soon. The mental shock she had received, had too completely overwhelmed all her faculties to enable her rightly to feel the truth and force of what was said to her, and the sad, vacant way in which she said "yes," convinced the chemist that although she heard the mere words he uttered, they reached no further, and brought to her mind no corresponding ideas.

Mrs. Paddlebat now returned with a coach, and while it waited at the door, she

came into the shop again, and seeing Fanny, as she thought, looking so calm and quiet, and the medical man talking to her, she could not but believe that she was taking her loss with abundance of philosophy and resignation, and was much rejoiced to see that such was the case.

"Come home, my dear," she said. "Come home, at once, and have a rest, and then you will be able to lie down, you know. Oh! I remember quite well when poor Paddlebat went off like a lamb as he did, I am sure I was not myself again for weeks and weeks, and I can tell you, Mr. ——, what's your name that what with one thing and another, I suffered a martyrdom."

" I don't doubt it, madam, in the least. You look, even now, as if you had fallen away."

" Do you really think so, sir ?"

" I do, indeed, madam."

" Well, do you know, sir, some people will try to make out as it's quite the reverse, and that I am what may be called positively stout. I can't see it myself, I'm, sure."

" Nor I, nor I. But allow me to hand this young lady to the coach, and if you will give me your address, I will call, for I should not be much surprised at some illness succeeding this days' proceedings, and, do not mistake me, madam, I wish to call as a friend."

" Indeed, that very kind of you, sir. The address is on that card, and I can only say that we shall be very glad to see you to take a cup of tea, at any time, and, I dare say, although it is really quite a shocking affair, that my niece, after a time, will come round again, and be a little more reconciled than she is now.

" I hope so—I hope so."

Fanny was handed into the coach by the chemist, and then Mrs. Paddlebat got in to the great hazard of the springs of the vehicle, which, however, by some miracle, recovered from the shock which her weight gave them, and thus the coach, after all the preliminary jolting and groaning, and swinging from side to side, fairly got away. The chemist shook his head as he stood at his door watching its progress, and said to himself,—

" Poor young thing, she has not yet awakened to the full feeling which, I fear, before many hours are past, will come over her. These great afflictions are like great physical injuries, at first so overpowering and stunning, that they do not produce the amount of pain, which, when the nerves resume their action, and the system becomes more composed, is certain to ensue. If I do not greatly mistake that poor young creature will astonish her aunt yet by some exhibition of grief which she will not be prepared for."

Fanny sat with a countenance as pale and motionless as that of a statue, in the coach. Her very smiles seemed to be rigid, and the only evidence she gave of existence was now and then by a very slight convulsive movement of her lips, as if she were on the point of uttering something, which, however, died away before it could be made at all articulate.

As for Mrs. Paddlebat she went on talking, and as long as she could hear her own voice she was quite satisfied, although, to her justice, we will say that all she did talk about was intended to be of a consolatory nature to poor Fanny.

" Ah !" she said. " That's the way. We are all nothing but grass, and the hay season comes, and then, death, like an Irish labourer, comes and mows us down. It's the way with all things, great and small, and there's no help for it, that's a fact, so you see, my dear, you are only like hundreds and thousands of other people, a young creature, and only think of me how cruelly I have been treated. Haven't I had troubles enough I'm sure to make any one get headforemost into the water ? but, of course, I have, and nobody knows that as well as you do, my dear, and, as what with one thing and another, and putting this and that together, you perceive that, after all, matters may not be so bad as they look."

CHAPTER LXXVIII.

NICHOLAS LOWE ENDEAVOURS TO SET HIS HOUSE ON FIRE.

It was while these event were taking place, as regarded Fanny Arrowdale, that Nicholas Lowe began seriously to ask himself if he could not derive some means of getting out of the house, which may be said to have hung like a millstone round his neck for so long, and to which he had been confined by the horrible and constant dread that some new occupant of it would discover the corpse of Rodwell.

Perhaps no human laws could possibly have inflicted upon him the amount of punishment which the necessity of residing constantly beneath the same roof with that ghastly remnant of the man, who had been his mortal enemy, gave him.

For how many weary and sad hours had he sat looking at the dark stain in the roof of the dining-room, just above the chandeliers, and which he knew so well was produced by the blood, and by the process of decomposition of the body of James Rodwell. Could human ingenuity have contrived anything more horrible than that? coupled as it was, too, with the continued dread that, what was so well known to him would be suspected by others, and that he knew not a moment in the day or night when he might hear the words,

" Come forth, Nicholas Lowe, the murderer, and meet your doom !"

But, now, that so long a time had elapsed, a new hope sprung up in his heart— a hope which he long pondered upon, and, which, when once he began to think it pointed to a probability, never left him. That hope was, that the juice of the dead body would be, by that time, sufficiently dried up, that fire would consume it entirely.

Long before that time he would have taken measures to burn down his house, and obliterate all traces of the deed that he had done, but he dreaded to find that, instead of being a mere idle superstition, it was but too true, that fire would not consume a murdered body, and, although he told himself, that the reason it would not was the same reason that made it a matter almost of impossibility to destroy any corpse in such a way; yet, there was a possibility in that case, and no wonder, some superstitious feeling mingled with it, or he shrunk always, until now, from making the trial.

" I know he told himself that the difficulty of consuming a dead body is because the many juices and fluid portions of it quench the flames. But surely by this time the corpse of Rodwell cannot present such a difficulty; and if I could but succeed in burning the house down and all its contents, I should draw a more free breath than I have done for many a day."

As he made these reflections, he would stand beneath that dark stain in the roof of the dining room, and examine it most critically, to satisfy himself that it was hard and dry; and so, a criterion of the state of the dead body above, which he so much panted to destroy.

" Surely, surely," he said, "I should succeed were I now to take my measures so as to fire the house, and so arrange that no amount of officious zeal should suffice to extinguish the conflagration. What an exquisite relief it would then be to me to know that the only damning piece of evidence that the world could produce against me would be completely and for ever destroyed. When I shall see the friendly flame bursting through the roof, and when I shall feel that the whole fabric is involved in destruction, carrying with it the ghastly remains of that man who drove me to do the deed I did, I shall be content, and then each moment of my future existence I shall devote to the task of trying to forget."

Nicholas Lowe might well say trying to forget ; for even as he said it, he felt the impossibility of succeding in forgetting, that, although he might get rid of all the evidence that would suffice to convict him before a mortal tribunal, he never could release his imagination from a full and complete remembrance of all that had taken place on that dreadful occasion, when he had done the deed of blood, and afterwards been compelled to take the steps he did to hide its terrific and accursing results.

But with all this, the idea of firing the house still clung to him, until it became one of those fixed resolves which were not likely ever to depart from his mind until he had at least made some efforts to carry it out into active execution ; and it afforded him, perhaps, more satisfaction than he had been able to experience for a long time, to think over the best and safest means of accomplishing his object.

It was indeed a positive mental relaxation to do so, and in the solitude of his home he would now sit for hours together, thinking and planning how it was to be done; and although he had, as we are aware, made an acquaintance with whom his intimacy was rather upon the increase than otherwise, he never for a moment thought of making him a confidant; and indeed very seldom received him at his house, but met him abroad frequently, and passed some hours in his company, during which, at times, he would forget the perplexities that surrounded him, and almost fancy himself as once he was, with the world before him, and free to exercise what talent he possessed in the advancement of his fortune.

And this friend, for it seemed to be a natural feeling of good taste, forbore to ask Nicholas Lowe any questions regarding his former life, so that Lowe was not placed in the awkward position which some persons of less gentlemanly habits would have placed him in, of either insisting what was not true, or of admitting that he had dangerous secrets, which he meant to keep to himself.

At length Nicholas Lowe really thought that he had matured a plan, which he hoped would enable him to set fire to the house, and get that fire sufficiently complete and furious to resist all efforts to extinguish it that might be made when it should be discovered.

That plan consisted in the placing a number of dry combustible matters in such positions that flames would rapidly and easily communicate from one to the other without producing a good quantity of smoke, which was a thing he wished most to avoid, inasmuch as so long as he could keep any evidences of fire from showing themselves to persons in the street, so much the better would the chance be of the complete destruction of the house, which, of course, was the thing he aimed at.

He thought that if he managed to close all the shutters very carefully, both back and front, of the house, and to shut up as well all air passages that might be in the roof, he should be able to let the conflagration, from being confined, get into a considerable extent without stopping, and that then, when he found the place too hot for him, he could easily open the doors, and go out, giving the alarm himself.

He considered from the fact that he had effected no insurance upon the goods he had in the house, that he would, from the absence of any ascertainable notice to commit the deed, never be suspected of having done it himself, inasmuch as he would, by the destruction of whatever he had in the house, be a great loser.

Whenever this plan was in his mind fully arranged, he set about the carrying it into effect with what skill he could bring to bear upon the subject, and more than that, he told himself, that it would materially advance the probabilities of success if he were to lodge in the drawing-room some of the highly inflammable materials which he intended should so much assist him in the matter.

But although reason told him that there was nothing to dread, and that now by going into that room there was nothing to meet his eyes, he yet, from a feeling which he could not get over, dreaded to do so; and notwithstanding he several times fancied he had sufficiently got over his fear, and actually went to the door of the drawing-room for the express purpose of opening it, he as often drew back again trembling, and gave up the attempt in despair.

"No, no," he said, "anything but that. I cannot, dare not, go into that apartment. It will be full of the odours of blood, or I shall fancy it so, which, in effect, is the same to me, so I cannot take that step, although I do feel its importance."

He now took long walks to strange out of the way and remote districts of the metropolis for the purpose of purchasing by degress the combustible materials he wanted, and which he always brought home himself, so that, in the course of about a couple of weeks, he had a stock of such matters, which, if he had purchased all at once anywhere, might have materially furnished food for future suspicion.

At length all was ready, and having made up his mind that if any one should knock at the door, which, however, was so rare an occurrence that it was not to be expected, he would not open it, he commenced the arrangement of the inflammable matters which were so materially to assist him in the destruction of the house.

It was night when he fairly began this operation, and he intended, if he should get anything like a complete arrangement made before the morning, that he would not run the risk of leaving affairs in such a state, but would set fire to it all at once, and stand or fall by the success or failure of the scheme.

It is endless for me to take up time in describing with what ingenuity he placed the various substances in connexion with the wood inside of the house; but, suffice it to say, that he managed so to place them that a light applied to one would be the means rapidly of kindling them all, so that there would a complete range of fire from the lower to the upper portion of the house, which surely could not fail of producing the result he wished and anticipated.

By the time he had done all this it was about two o'clock in the morning, and the night a profoundly dull one. He closed with great care the various shutters, which he could get at. As for those on the first floor, he knew that they were closed, and likewise that the windows were so completely covered with dirt, that it afforded of itself quite a sufficient screen for that part of the building.

Then he looked out into the street, and was gratified to perceive that not the least glimmer of light came from any of the the windows far or near, which convinced him that if any hour more than another was well calculated for his scheme to be successful in, it was that in which everybody had gone to repose, and all was profoundly still, and perhaps when not even a foot passenger might pass the street once in a quarter of an hour.

He closed his street-door after making these observations, and then came an anxious moment, and he sat down upon the staircase once more to ask himself if he was quite certain of the wisdom of what he was about.

For more than half an hour he gave the subject the most anxious thought; and although he was fully alive to the much worse position in which he would place himself in case of failure, he was resolved to make the attempt, which he flattered himself could but be successful after the admirable manner in which he had arranged all the preliminaries.

He crept down into the kitchen and procured a light, and then, once more, seeing that all the fastenings were secure, so that even when an alarm should be given, there might be still a little delay in getting in, as when he left he could close the shut door as if by accident he returned to the passage where he intended that the first attempt to ignite the inflammable substance should be made.

" Now," he said, " now for an act which will make me or mar me—now for an act which will enable me to feel myself free from the dreadful companionship which has been mine for so long, or which shall—but no, I will not anticipate, and I will think of nothing but success, because I believe that success will come."

In another moment he applied the light, he carried, to some of the combustibles, and a bright flame began to spread itself along the passage, room, and up the staircase as well, emitting an amount of heat which he could hardly have believed it possible would have arisen from so small an amount of flame. But he had not long to complain that the amount of flame was small, for in a few minutes he began to hear—and it was a welcome sound to him—the crackling of some of the wood work in the dining-room, and he had the pleasure of believing that shortly the fire would have got a hold of the principal beams of the house, from which would be impossible to dislodge it.

But now, in consequence of the top of the house having been made by him so secure, no smoke could there get out, and it came down the staircase again in immense volumes, so that Lowe felt that, without a strong chance of suffocation, he should not be able for many seconds longer, to hold out against such an amount of suffocating vapour. It was only, indeed, by stooping low down, and by that means getting into a purer draught of air, that he could at all manage to breathe without inhaling the effluvium of the inflammable material he had himself so artfully arranged·

He was, at length, just upon the point of crawling towards the street door, and opening it, which, of course, would have given an astonishing impulse to the flames, when he heard a tremendous rolling of wheels, and then, before he could ask himself what it meant, there came upon his ears the loud terrific shriek of " Fire !—fire !—fire ! "

With a little imprecaution, Nicholas Lowe dashed into the street, and there he saw the first engine, and several firemen, with a rapidly increasing mob of disorderly persons, among whom was a boy fanning himself with his hat, who, the moment Nicholas Lowe made his appearance, ran up to him exclaiming with a voice and manner of great triumph :—

" It was me, sir, it was me : I was passing by and saw the light in the passage, so I ran and fetched the engine. Nobody would have seen it, sir, if it had'nt been for me : I did'nt say anything, sir, but I ran and fetched the engine. I hope you'll remember me, sir.

Nicholas Lowe, if he could have done so with any degree of safety, or consistency, would have remembered the boy with a knock on the head, that would, doubtless, have had the effect of not making him so anxious of running for an engine upon another occasion ; but it was impossible he could show any resentment, before other people, so he merely said :—

" Oh ! I am much obliged, but I think it's a mistake."

" Hurrah ! here's the plug out," cried the boy ; and as he spoke, up bubbled the water from the nearest plug hole, and commenced flooding the street, until two firemen made their way into the house, frantically followed by Lowe, who, to his surprise, when he got in, found it was much clearer of smoke than before, and that there was certainly no appearance of anything like an extensive conflagration going on.

" You see," he said, " it is all a mistake—there is no fire : I was merely burning some old letters and some things I did not want. There is no fire. Cannot I have a light in the iron pan of this stove, that is in the passage, without the alarm of a fire being given ; and if that boy, instead of being so handy as to run away for you, had knocked at the door, he would have found out what it was, and spared you trouble for nothing."

It was quite clear to Nicholas Lowe himself, as he spoke, that the plan had failed, owing to the inflammable matter he had procured burning out much too quickly to enable the flame to get a hold of more than a small portion of the wood work in the dining-room, and the firemen were even convinced that there was nothing like a house on fire, nor was there the least indication of even a chimney being in a state of blaze.

" I hope you are satisfied," said Lowe.

The principal fireman said nothing, but he walked out of the house and said aloud :

" Hulloa ! where s the lad that brought us the news ? "

" Here I am," said the boy ; " here I am : I hope you won't forget me."

" No, and I'll take good care that you shan't forget me. Hark you, young fellow, the next time you fancy you have caught a house on fire, take care it don't turn out to be a mare's nest instead. You wanted to grab a reward for fetching the engines first, and for all you cared everybody in the house might have been burnt in their beds, always provided you had got the engine first, and that was why you could'nt think of making any alarm."

" Let me go, will you."

" Not yet ; I'll just teach you *something* that you won't forget ; and when you fancy a house is on fire another time, just say so, and don't be so avaricious as to think of nothing but the five-shillings, for calling at the engine-house."

" Hit one of your own size, will you."

" Oh, I ain't going to hit, but I think it's a pity the plug is up for nothing, so here goes to give you a taste of it."

As he spoke, the fireman, who was naturally enough indignant at being made, as it were, such a catspaw of to put a few shillings in the pocket of the amazingly cunning lad, took up that ingenious youth by the back of the neck with one hand and the largest portion of his unmentionables with the other, and so completely soused him in the bubbling stream from the plug, that astonishment and cold water together quite rendered him dumb and submissive.

The fireman was not satisfied with drenching the upper portion of his physical formation with the water, sat him down in it next, and then rolled him well over, so that by the time the ingenious youth could get breath to cry murder, he was as saturated with moisture as he could possibly be.

" Oh, murder! murder! Let me alone. Murder!" he shouted.

" Ah, that's the way to do it," said the fireman, as he let go of him, " that's the way to call out, my man, and not the way you did when you came sneaking off to the engine-house and left a house on fire, as you thought, behind you. Be off with you now, and thank your stars you have gathered a little experience."

Nicholas Lowe was not at all sorry to see this act of retributive justice overtake the boy, who certainly, independent of the provoking manner in which he had behaved to him, Lowe, certainly deserved, in accordance with the arguments the fireman had used, some justice.

The engine, to the great mortification of the men who had come with it, was dragged away, and Nicholas Lowe, after fastening his street door, walked with a dejected air into the dining-room, which he had hoped never to see again, and flinging himself into a seat he fixed his eyes upon the stain in the ceiling, which was just beginning to be visible by the faint light of early dawn, and said, with a groan of mental anguish,—

" Yes, yes, it is my fate—it is my destiny. I cannot avoid it. I am doomed to be a living exemplification of my own theory, that there is a skeleton in every house, and in vain, alas! all in vain, do I struggle to rid myself of that one which now for so long has been my bane! Oh, Jervis Rodwell! Jervis Rodwell! living, you were to me a thing of hatred and a constant source of disquietude and annoyance ; but dead, you are to me a curse, indeed !"

CHAPTER LXXVIII.

THE GRIEF OF FANNY.—THE FUNERAL OF ARROWDALE, AND THE UNEXPECTED MOURNER.

THE surgeon in the City was quite correct when he prognosticated that before long Fanny would awaken to a full consciousness of the dreadful loss she had experienced, and that when she did so awaken that it would be to a violence of grief of which Mrs. Paddlebat had as yet no conception.

The strange kind of apathy which her aunt, perhaps pardonably enough, mistook for the composure of philosophy, lasted until she reached her own house, and for some time longer indeed ; but suddenly, when she, Mrs. Paddlebat, least of all expected any outburst of grief, Fanny shrieked out—

" Horace, Horace! come back to me!" and burst into such a violent paroxysm of despair that the good lady was as much alarmed as she was astonished, and stood for some moments quite petrified and unable to afford any assistance or any consolation to the poor bereaved heart which now fully felt the agony of destitution

" Oh, Horace, Horace! where are you? Why did you teach me to love you but to leave me to despair! God help—God help me now! Help me to the grave quickly ; it is the only boon I ask! Death! death !"

" Gracious me !" exclaimed Mrs. Paddlebat ; " I'm *petrified*, and I to think she was taking it so well. Oh, my good gracious! Fanny, what do you mean by going on in that way?"

" Give him back to me! Let me look upon the face which has so often beamed with kindness upon me. If in death even let me look upon it! Why, oh! why am I not with him ?"

Mrs. Paddlebat held up her hand, but before she could say anything, Fanny commenced sobbing so bitterly that even to her aunt, who we know was not exactly gifted with the most romantic sensibilities, it was a perfect pain and a terror to hear her, and she tried in vain to stop that torrent of grief, which, even if she could have controlled it, would have been a thousand pities to do so; for it probably was the only thing that saved poor Fanny from positive phrenzy.

"My dear, my dear!" cried Mrs. Paddlebat; "what have you thought of all of a sudden that has made you so bad? Really, Fanny, you have nearly frightened me out of my wits."

She only sobbed still with that dreadful bitterness of anguish which is so awful when it comes from an adult, and which, let the circumstances be what they may that produce it, is calculated to shake the stoutest nerves.

"I declare," added Mrs. Paddlebat, "that I am all of a tremble."

"Leave me!" sobbed Fanny. "Leave me, oh! leave me."

"What! leave you, and you in such a sad state as you are, I could not think of it. Do you think, Fanny, that I am a stock or a stone I should like to know? Leave you, indeed! No, Fanny; if I were a wild beast in a caravan I might leave you, but not while my name is Paddlebat."

"Yes, yes; leave me to Heaven and to my own bruised and saddened heart!"

"Well, but now, Fanny, don't you see, my dear, what a sad thing it is of you to give way in such a manner. All the tears in the world, you know, won't bring anything into life again. Look at me; you don't see me weeping, although, heaven knows, I ——"

"Oh! aunt, do not speak to me," said Fanny, and rising she passed out of the room and into her own chamber, the door of which she locked on the inside, leaving Mrs. Paddlebat a prey to the most agonizing fear; for the idea took possession of her that Fanny was just in a fit state of mind to commit suicide, and she did not know whether to call in the police or not.

But nothing was farther from the intention of the pure minded and beautiful being whose griefs it gives us such pain to record, than to hurry from this world uncalled for by that Creator who alone should be permitted to hold human life and death at his disposal. No; when she was alone, her first action was to cast herself upon her knees and to pray that heaven would grant her fortitude and support to bear up against the grievous trials she had to pass through, and that she might be endued with strength enough yet to perform whatever duties the wisdom and the justice of God designed for her.

Let people's religious opinions be what they may, there still cannot be any question but that prayer, when spontaneously it rushes from the heart as it did in this instance from poor Fanny's, is one of the greatest elements of consolation that can be afforded to suffering human nature. And she found it so; for when she had finished her simply fervent and eloquent appeal, she felt a peaceful, holy kind of calm pervade her breast to which before it was a stranger, and burying her face in her hands she strove to school herself to the many trials she must now endure.

But, alas! she as yet knew not how wholly destitute she was left.

She had yet to learn the cause of the dreadful catastrophe which had made her a widow so young, and despoiled life to her of all its charms. She had yet to discover that it was the sudden rush of painful thought, which, on her account came over him, that had produced the death of poor Horace.

If she had, however, just at that moment been told, that she was as regarded pecuniary means destitute, the news would have fallen but flatly on her ears, and she would, perhaps, have told the author of it, that the one weighty grief, with which her heart was full, completely and entirely absorbed all minor ones.

When she emerged from her bed-room, there was a death-like paleness upon her countenance; but yet, it was not convulsed with grief as it had been. Her solitary meditations, and her prayers to Heaven, had done something for her; and, although she did not feel the loss—her sad bereavement, she was able to bear more calmly, to outward showing, with the loss, which to her was indeed a loss of all, at one fell swoop.

She spoke to her aunt in a quiet, calm, subdued tone; and it was evident that those words that she now felt there was a necessity should be uttered, cost her a painful struggle to speak.

"There is much," she said, " that will have to be done in the shape of duties to the dead; and let me ask of you that between this time and that when he shall

be placed in the tomb, I shall know nothing of those details that—that might once again, if I were to be involved in them, drive me to that despair from which, with Heaven's help, I have now, to some extent, emerged."

"Yes, my dear," said Mrs. Paddlebat; " I quite understand you; I will do everything. You remind me of myself when poor P. died. I said to Mr. Blinks, the undertaker, 'Now, Blinks,' I said, 'just don't trouble me about anything, but do it all yourself; and when it's done, tell me, that's all!'"

Mrs. Paddlebat went about the thing in earnest, and soon found out all the circumstances connected with poor Horace's death. And, indeed, although the very knowledge that such a thing had taken place was carefully kept from Fanny, an inquest ensued as a matter of course, at which it was given in evidence that the shock from the sudden knowledge of the reverse of fortune that had come over him, in consequence of the rascality of his cousin, had produced his death from an affection of the heart, although there was no real disease.

A verdict was entered of " Died from natural causes ;" and Mrs. Paddlebat, with a judgment one would hardly have expected from her, had the corpse conveyed at once to an undertaker's instead of the house of Fanny, and she did hope that she should be able to persuade her to forego an intention, which once she had expressed since the death, to see the body before it was committed to the earth.

" My dear," she said, when she came from the inquest, " let me advise you to remain perfectly quiet now, and not at all to interfere in what is done or doing."

" They have not yet," said Fanny, " consigned him to the tomb, surely ?"

" No, oh ! no."

" Then, there is yet time, and I shall yet be able once more to look upon his face, even in death though it be. You must take me to see him, aunt. I can perceive by your looks that you object to this, and that you are disposed to reason me out of it, but let me pray you not to do so."

" But, my dear, only consider for a moment—just think."

" Aunt, aunt, I have considered and thought until both processes have become painful. Do not urge me, I pray you, to do so now, I have made up my mind that I must see him ; and recollect, that when the grave has once closed over him, I cannot do so. Do not, therefore, I pray you—do not oppose me."

There was no resisting an appeal like this, so Mrs. Paddlebat was fain to give the matter up and agree that she could go to the place where the body was lying, although she really dreaded the consequences of taking such a step.

" If you have, Fanny," she said, " as you tell me you have, thoroughly made up your mind to that, you must go, but I do wish you would consider it. Don't be angry with me for saying so, because I know it would be for your good to stay away, but still, as I say, if you will go, of course you shall."

" Yes, yes, it may and will be a pang to me at the time, but afterwards it will be a consolation, and if I were not to see him before he is placed in the tomb, I should, I am certain, live to regret it."

" Well, then, in that case you may as well go. And as you are to go, in my opinion, the sooner you do go, and it's all over, the better it will be."

This was an opinion in which Fanny herself coincided, so it was duly arranged that on that evening she was to accompany her aunt to the undertaker's, where lay the sad remains of him whom she would have given her own life to have preserved.

By this time, as the reader may well suppose, Fanny had become acquainted with the extent of her pecuniary loss, but upon that subject she scarcely made a remark. It did not at all seem to come home to her, or to present itself in a tangible or understandable shape. Time, and the consequences of being left so utterly without resources, could alone now, in her state of mind, awaken her to the importance of that circumstance.

Mrs. Paddlebat, before the hour came at which she had promised to take Fanny to see the dead body of Horace, went herself to the undertaker's where it was lying, in order to inform him that the widow would come on such a melancholy errand, so that there might be no more disagreeables attendant upon the matter than were absolutely necessary on the occasion.

The undertaker promised to be quite ready for her at eight o'clock in the evening, and he assured Mrs. Paddlebat that everything should be so arranged, beyond the mournful spectacle itself, *that* of course he could not deprive by any artificial means of any of its sad and mournful interest.

With this Mrs. Paddlebat returned to Fanny, and at about a quarter past seven, which gave them ample time to get to the undertaker's in the city, they both started on foot on one of the most melancholy and heartrending expeditions that could possibly be undertaken.

Fanny was silent, for her heart and brain seemed too full of the one subject that occupied all her thoughts, to enable her to speak upon any other, and as regarded that, she felt that her aunt, however well meaning she might be, was not qualified to converse with her.

And so scarcely exchanging any conversation, except now and then an occasional remark from Mrs. Paddlebat, gently answered by Fanny, they at length reached the undertaker's door, the first signal of having arrived at which consisted of their ears being saluted by the tap, tap, tap, of the hammers as they were employed in putting those rows of nails which by some means or another are considered necessary to the jackets of foot-boys and coffins.

The undertaker knew Mrs. Paddlebat at once, but he had not yet seen Fanny, and even his sympathies, accustomed, as he was, to be as it were continually dabbling in death, were sensibly touched, as he looked upon the beautiful young creature who thus came so pale and wan to look upon all she had loved on earth.

"Pray, madam," he said, "be seated. This is a sad piece of business you know, madam, but we must all go some day, you should bear that in mind. It's a common fate, and I can assure you, that a handsomer corpse than poor Mr. Arrowdale I have not seen for many a long day."

The undertaker meant well, although, if he had spouted a couple of Greek verses, Fanny would have paid just about as much attention to what he said. She however, seemed to listen, although her thoughts were with the dead ; and, after she had by an inclination of her head acknowledged the courtesy of the undertaker, she turned to her aunt, and whispered,—

"I do not see him—I do not see him."

The undertaker heard the question, and replied for Mrs. Paddlebat, saying,—

"If you will step with me, madam, I will show you the body. This way, if you please, madam—this way."

He took a light from the table, and preceded Fanny and Mrs. Paddlebat to an outbuilding, in the yard of his house, which was always used on similar occasions, and in the centre of which, supported by tressels, was a coffin, over which had been hastily thown a velvet pall, which certainly added much to the solemnity of the object and the place.

Fanny tottered in and stood by the side of the coffin, but she had not strength to lift aside the covering, and the undertaker advancing, just turned the pall away from the face of the dead, and there, in the repose of that death which is eternal, Fanny beheld the face of him to whom she had plighted her faith, and who had taught her to love him so sincerely.

Oh ! that was a moment of agony—such a moment as ought not to occur above once in any life-time—a moment sufficient almost to shake reason on its throne, and to drive the poor blighted heart to some mad and desperate violence, that an eternity of repentance could scarce atone for.

Mrs. Paddlebat fully expected a burst of grief, as did the undertaker, but they were both disappointed. All the sound that at the moment came from Fanny's lips, was a kind of half-choked sob. Then she stooped, and kissed the pale brow.

"Horace, Horace !" she gasped, and in another moment she fell insensible upon the floor.

The undertaker rushed forward and picked her up.

"Ah, poor thing !" he said, "it's too much for her—a great deal too much. She ought not to have come at all. Take the light, ma'am, if you please, and I'll carry her into my parlour. My missus will soon bring her round, I dare say. Poor young creature! It's a sad thing, you know, when you come to think of it."

Mrs. Paddlebat trembled so, that she could scarcely hold the light, but she did manage to carry it into the parlour, closely followed by the undertaker, bearing the insensible form of Fanny. He laid her gently upon a sofa, and then resigned her to the care of his wife, who, with much gentleness and commiseration, tended her.

A very few minutes more, and she had recovered, and the first words she uttered were,—

"God of Heaven, what a dreadful dream!"

But even as she uttered these words, recollection came fully back again, and she knew that it was a sad reality that she had gazed upon, and that had so strongly affected her.

"My dear," said Mrs. Paddlebat, "you see you had better not have come here after all."

"Oh! yes, yes! but I will now go. Horace, Horace, farewell for ever in this world. I do but sigh for that time, when we shall meet again to part no more. Take me away now, aunt—I am willing to go—I am willing to go at once. My sad mission is accomplished."

It was quite out of the question that Fanny should walk now, so one of the undertaker's men was sent for a coach, in which the heartbroken young creature was taken home.

She said nothing all the way, even in answer to Mrs. Paddlebat, who thought it her duty to go on talking, for the purpose, as she thought, of withdrawing Fanny's mind from too painful a retrospection of the past. Alas! could any human eloquence have sufficed for one moment to drown the remembrance of what the bereaved one had that night seen?"

When she reached home she did say a few words to her aunt, thanking her for her kindness, and then she announced her intention of retiring for the night, which she did at once. Heaven and herself only knew in what anguish that night was passed, but certainly in the morning Fanny presented a calmer and a more resigned aspect, and she even made a remark or two upon indifferent matters, although the tone of voice in which they were uttered showed the effort it cost her.

CHAPTER LXXIX.

THE RESOLUTION OF NICHOLAS LOWE.—NEW THOUGHTS, AND A VERY VAGUE HOPE IN THE MURDERER'S HEART.

FOR the whole of the weary night succeeding his abortive attempt to set fire to his house, did Nicholas Lowe sit up in deep and painful meditation over his situation. He began to think now that when he said, as frequently he did, "that it was his destiny to live with the corpse of Rodwell," and that no circumstances would ever occur to free him from such a terrible companionship, that they were no idle words that fell from his tongue, but the expression of a fact.

"It must be so," he muttered, "and this is the way in which Heaven is making me feel that retribution which, it is said, ever comes over him who commits murder. I have escaped hitherto the penalty which human laws affix to my crime, and this companionship with the dead body of my victim is the way Heaven has punished me for my deep iniquity."

As he made these remarks, he became conscious of the approaching daylight, for he could now, although only a small portion of one of the shutters of the dining-room was open, could see the dark stain of blood upon the roof quite plainly—that stain which he had hoped never to see again, and which he had so confidently expected would by this time have been entirely lost and consumed in the flames.

"There it is," he muttered, "and there it will ever remain, to tell me of the dreadful object which has produced it. Oh, why was I so besotted as to hide the corpse there, of all places in the house, when the smallest exertion would have surely sufficed to place it, not only out of my own sight, but almost beyond the possibility of being discovered by anyone else?"

He ran over in his mind all the excellent hiding-places which the house really afforded, quite forgetting, as he did so, that his horror of touching the corpse of

Rodwell at the time had been the grand cause of his placing it where he did, instead of in a place of far greater safety and security.

"A board or two," he said, "taken up in the kitchen flooring would have made a grave for it, that would not only have been out of sight, but would, by its contact with the earth, have much facilitated the progress of decay, so that if it had been found at any future time, a few yellow, rotten bones would have been all that could be seen."

He rose, and paced that large, handsome dining-room with hurried steps, and then he exclaimed,—

"Oh, fool that I have been, first to do a deed, involving such fearful consequences, and secondly to adopt such weak and puerile measures as regards the hiding it from observation!"

He walked to the window and unclosed one of the shutters. It was broad daylight, and people were hurrying to and fro, intent on business or pleasure, while he felt that he was a stranger to both, and had no interest in the great world or its concerns—to feel that there he was an isolated being, with no hopes, desires, or wishes, in common with human nature. He seemed not to belong to the world, although he still inhabited it, but to be a kind of connecting link between this life and eternity—a sad spectator of what was going on, more than an actor in the busy turmoil of existence.

"Oh, that I were dead," he said, "nothing but death could now relieve me, nothing but death, and if it were not that I do tremble to make, uninvited, my visit to

'————————That undiscovered country,
That bourne from whence no traveller returns,'

I would soon end this horrible existence, and by my own hand put an end to the beating of this saddened heart, and the painful throbbing of this distempered brain."

Suddenly he started in alarm, for the area bell of his house was rung.

"What's that?" he cried, "what's that? who is that? Hush—hush! Be still! Who—who can that be?"

"Pa—per," bawled a voice, and then something was dropped into the area.

Nicholas Lowe drew a long breath of infinite relief as he said,—

"Oh! I had forgotten. How foolish of me! It is the newspaper I have daily. How confused must my mind be this morning, that I should completely now forget that circumstance which is one of daily occurrence at this house! Yes! I see the newspaper because it satisfies me that as yet there are no suspicions entertained—no meddling fool has gone before a magistrate to say that he thought me a murderer. Let me see; will there be anything about the false alarm of fire here? Not so soon, surely; not so soon, if at all."

He walked down to the area and picked up the newspaper, with which he repaired to the dining-room again, and almost the first article that met his eyes was this :—

"AWFULLY SUDDEN DEATH.—Yesterday an instance of the uncertain limit of human existence was painfully witnessed by a number of persons in the city. A gentleman of the name of Arrowdale, upon going to the Bank to receive the dividends upon his property, found to his horror that the whole of his funded money had been made away with by the stock-broker whom he had entrusted with power to sell and purchase for him, and the sudden shock of the discovery caused his instant death. The body awaits a coroner's inquest, which will be held to-day at the Marquis of Granby Tavern, near the Royal Exchange."

Nicholas Lowe read this paragraph twice, and then the newspaper fell from his hands, and he uttered a deep groan. He knew well that the paragraph must have relation to the husband of poor Fanny, for not only was the name an uncommon one, but the circumstances, all of which he had taken some pains to make himself acquainted with before, tallied with what he knew, and he at once understood the whole affair.

" I see it all," he said ; " the villain who married Mrs. Paddlebat, and then, upon finding, in consequence of the contrivance of old Gilbert that he was to get no money, absconded, has robbed his cousin Horace, the husband of Fanny, of all, and not only now is she a widow, but she is destitute likewise."

Nicholas Lowe leant his head upon the table, and remained for a time in deep thought. His mind was evidently much disturbed, and he was full of conjecture concerning what possible consequences might ensue from what had happened. At length he spoke, and the words he used, although in some instances following as they did the wayward nature of his thoughts, were not well connected, will yet suffice to show something of the nature of these thoughts:—

" Shall I make an effort to see her? Ought I, after all that has happened, to do so ? No—no ; and yet she shall not want ; nothing in the shape of destitution shall approach her while I possess the means of warding it off. And I have now those means. Yes, I will bless now the money I have been despising, and which has been accumulating, because it will enable me to place her in a position far above want. But will she accept it at my hands after what has passed ? That is the question ; and something seems to tell me that she will not."

He was now silent for a time, and when he spoke again it was evident that a new idea had found a place in his brain, and he said, in a tone of more animation and excitement than he had used for many a day,—

" Oh, would it be possible to revive in her heart any of those emotions which once inhabited it for me ? Dare I now have a hope, however vague and distant, that she would join her fortunes to mine, and fly with me to some other land, pass by some other name, and so for ever be out of the recollection of all who knew us. But dare I tell her why I must so fly ? Why I must change my name, and seek under other skies for that safety I cannot know here? No, no, I can picture to myself the look of horror with which we regard the murderer."

Despair now took possession of him at the thought that not only would Fanny refuse any pecuniary assistance from him, but she would, if she knew his real guilt —guilt which perhaps she already suspected—shrink with loathing from him.

It was strange, too, that now that he knew she was free, all his former tender· ness and affection, which seemed to have been quite submerged in other matters of more fearful interest, returned, and once again Nicholas Lowe pictured to his heart the Fanny Leslie of his early affection, and he loved her as he had loved her before his hands were stained with the blood of a fellow-creature, and his soul tainted with the crime of murder.

Unable, then, any longer to control his impatience, he left his house, taking care to secure all the means of ingress to it, and hastened to the city, in order to ascertain beyond the shadow of a doubt that he was right in identifying Mr. Arrowdale, who had dropped down, as the husband of Fanny, and then he soon learnt sufficient particulars to make perfectly sure of the fact.

It was placed in his mind beyond dispute, and he was present at the inquest, where the whole of the circumstances were fully detailed, and when some severe remarks were made by the coroner regarding Arrowdale, the stockbroker, whose villanous conduct had been the direct cause of all that had taken place.

But how was he to get an interview with Fanny, for an interview was what he wanted unquestionably ; and he decided that if he were to call and have himself announced, that she would at once refuse to see him, perhaps mistaking altogether the object of his visit.

" She will think," he said, " that I take the opportunity, now that her husband is dead, and before he is laid in his grave, to persecute her with new addresses, and I shall be refused an interview and have her contempt, as well as perhaps her suspicion and dislike, to contest against. No, no; I dare not call upon her."

Having come to this resolution, which, under the circumstances, was a natural enough one, he had no other resource than to wait until he was favoured by some opportunity of seeing her, when she could not avoid him until he had explained the object of his intrusion.

"Surely," he thought, "when I tell her that I love her as before, beyond being able to place in her hands the means of ample support, if she refuse such aid from me she will refuse it kindly and gently, and I shall not have the bitterness of thinking that she rejects it because she despises the donor. That would be too much even for me to bear."

A little diligent inquiry, and a little money liberally dispersed, enabled him to ascertain, not only when the unfortunate Horace Arrowdale was to be buried, but the exact day and hour on which the ceremony was to be performed; and although he did not think it very probable, he did think it quite possible, that Fanny, who he knew was a person not bound down by many of the cold conventional rules of society, might be present at the funeral.

With this hope he made up his mind that, at all events, he would be there, and should he find that she had followed to the grave her husband, there could not be a better opportunity of speaking to her than on that occasion, when her heart would be softened, and when all her sensibilities would be most acute.

He waited therefore patiently until that day week, on which it was appointed that the funeral was to take place at the little churchyard of Willesden, although why that suburban place of interment had been chosen he had no means of guessing, nor could the undertaker's man, from whom he gathered some of his information, tell him, although he had no difficulty in at once assuring him of the fact that Willesden-churchyard was the place pitched upon, for he (the man) had been sent there to make the necessary arrangements with the parish authorities of that village.

There could be no doubt upon the subject after such information, so Nicholas Lowe did not trouble himself to make any further inquiries, but quietly waited for the day to come.

Fanny had pitched upon Willesden-churchyard to be the last resting-place of poor Horace, because she remembered that once, as they were strolling through it, he had jestingly himself said,—

"This seems to be a quiet, snug sort of place, and I think I shall choose it at once, to save further trouble, as the place in which I will be buried."

She had at the time chidden him for an allusion to a subject full of painful reflections and suggestions, and which she little then thought was really so close at hand as it was; but now that he was gone from her, those few words that he had spoken came back to her memory, and she told her aunt, who had a sort of super-stitious reverence for burying people where they had themselves chosen, and who not only acquiesced in the idea of conveying the remains there, but was really urging it as a step which came almost under the denomination of an absolute necessity.

. The undertaker was duly informed of this determination to have the deceased buried at Willesden, and as everything which tended to increase the expense was to him a subject of congratulation, he of course said that he considered it to be quite right always to recollect where the persons had said they wished to be interred.

And so it was definitively arranged.

Nicholas Lowe, too, turned out to be quite right in his conjecture that Fanny might take it in her head to attend the funeral, although it was not usual so to do, for she said to her aunt, on the evening before the mournful ceremony was to take place, as they were sitting together,—

"I should suffer so much by remaining here to-morrow while the sad scene was enacting at Willesden, that I have made up my mind to go there to-morrow."

"Oh, don't think of it."

"Nay, aunt, I have not only thought of it, but I have determined upon it, so do not seek to dissuade me. I do not say that I will make an exhibition of my grief, but I will be there; and my intention is to remain in the church while the sad last offices of religion are paid to him, and then beneath that ancient, sacred roof, I can join in prayer to the Almighty as well that I may soon myself be called from this world of woe as for him who is no more."

Upon this, Mrs. Paddlebat thought it was better to give way, for she really had nothing to oppose to the wish of Fanny, but merely that it was not the fashion for females to attend funerals, except among the very lower orders of society, and she knew enough of Fanny to be well aware that was not an argument that would be very likely to deter her.

"Well, my dear," she said, "of course if you go, I will go with you; because it would be a sad thing for you to be alone, and I only hope you will be able to command your feelings."

"Do not fear for that. All violent exhibitions of grief have passed away, leaving behind it that settled melancholy, which will remain so long as I remain in being."

Mrs. Paddlebat said nothing; but she thought to herself that time would do much towards assuaging that grief which at present so completely possessed Fanny; for she, in common with every one who has lived long enough in the world to see deaths occur and the grief of survivors, knew well that there is no species of mental depression which so soon and so marvellously yields to the healing influence of time, as grief for the dead.

And well it is that it should be so, or the whole world would be a place of lamentation and mourning; for who is there who has not some loved object to lament the loss of?

CHAPTER LXXX.

THE STRANGE INTERVIEW IN THE OLD CHURCH AT WILLESDEN BETWEEN LOWE AND FANNY.

It was indeed a sad morning that on which Fanny rose for the purpose of proceeding to Willesden church-yard, to pay her last homage to the memory of him whom she had held so dear, but who had now gone from her for ever into the cold apathy of death.

Never again would she hear the sound of that voice, which to her was melody itself; never again would she gaze upon that face, which to her had always presented an aspect of kindness. All had now passed away, and he could only live in her recollection like the dim vestige of a dream.

And now that death had taken him from her, and she could no longer hear the sound of his voice, how deeply she regretted that she had left many things unsaid which now she would have given worlds to say! How she blamed herself for not upon particular occasions, which came upon her memory, saying kinder things than she had said.

But these are regrets that alway follow the dead to the tomb, and perhaps there never was a living being who ought, from her uniform kindness and gentleness of demeanour, to have had fewer of them than Fanny.

Mrs. Paddlebat hoped almost to the last that Fanny would change her determination, and after all not go to Willesden on such a melancholy errand as she contemplated, but when she saw her making actual preparation for the journey, that hope at once vanished, and she said nothing about it.

"I shall go at once," said Fanny, "and wait in the church until the arrival of the sad *cortege*. But do not, if you feel any disinclination so to do, do not come with me."

"Do you think, now, that I would leave you to go alone?"

"No, no, I do not think that! I believe you have said you would come with me, but at the same time I cannot but feel that it is solely on my account that you do so, and therefore it is that I urge you to let me go alone, if you feel any repugnance to the step."

"Say no more about it," remarked Mrs. Paddlebat, "I mean to go of course! A likely thing, indeed, that I should leave you to a parcel of men, and not myself take any care of you, or pains with you. Oh dear no! I shall go on purpose to protect you, and take care of you. And although you say you think you can manage to control your feelings, I don't know that you will be able, and what if you were to get unwell, and faint away, and find nobody but the undertaker's man or the beadle of the parish to look to you?"

"Well, well," said Fanny, "if you will come with me, of course I shall be much pleased, very much pleased, and shall thank you, aunt; but all I wished was to give you the option of staying away, if you thought fit."

"Oh, fiddle-de-dee, about option of staying away, I am ready as soon as you please, Fanny."

We cannot say but that Fanny was truly grateful for the company of Mrs. Paddlebat, notwithstanding there was so little in common as regards feeling and sentiment between them, for it was certainly an awkward thing for her to think of going quite alone.

The funeral was to take place—that is to say, the ceremony of actual interment, at twelve o'clock, but, without reference to that hour, Fanny and Mrs. Paddlebat started a little after ten and reached Willesden about twenty minutes before twelve; that there was some time to wait before the procession, which, after all, was a simple one, and only to consist of a hearse and one mourning coach, could reach the grave yard.

The mourners consisted of the chemist, the gentleman who had been with Horace when he died, and two old friends of the Paddlebat family, who had volunteered their services on the occasion, upon being called upon by Mrs. Paddlebat, and asked to do so.

"There is time enough, aunt," said Fanny. "We have come too early, but I cannot regret it; we can see in what quarter of the church-yard they have dug the grave."

"But little consolation as that may be," said Mrs. Paddlebat, "yet it is some to know where they have laid him. Indeed, I don't know but the knowledge is absolutely proper, not that I know it can make any difference, only it's as well to be able to say where one's relatives are, in case one should marry again."

Fanny smiled at the idea that her aunt had expressed, and looked upon her with some mournfulness. Her aunt, however, interpreted her feelings and continued—

"Ah! it's all very well now, but you may have another mind some of these days. You don't know what you may feel and think. I thought so too at one time, and then I altered my mind, not but what I have made an error of judgment, yet that aint everybody's lot."

"Certainly not," said Fanny, "certainly not; but we may not all feel the same. We may have different prospects, hopes, and enjoyments, all which you see make a great difference in one's conduct through life, and the sum of it too."

"Well," said Mrs. Arrowdale, "well, I dare say that it's all right enough, and, at the same time, I must say I can't see anything wrong, or, indeed, any impropriety in marrying again."

"None. It must rest with the mind and affections."

"Certainly," said Mrs. Paddlebat, "certainly," and she gave a sympathetic sigh, though, poor lady, she had not much idea of the precise meaning of what was said.

"It is a simple but ancient looking building," said Fanny, looking up at the church.

"Yes," said Mrs. Paddlebat;" I like it very much, but that nasty caw-cawing of the rooks."

"Don't you like it, aunt?"

"Like it, indeed, my dear! There's no music in that terrible noise. I have often heard people talk of the noise of a rookery, as if it were really something pleasing."

"And do you not think there is something very pleasing in the sound of the rookery?"

"None that I can see, my dear. How can anybody dream of it? You should admire the croaking of frogs if you admire that. I am only amazed they allow them to remain here disturbing the quiet of the dead."

"Indeed, aunt, I think you are too harsh with the poor rooks. Their presence is a sign that there is little disturbance in this quiet and calm spot."

"I dare say not, my dear, though the neighbourhood is well supplied with public-houses, and there is the accompaniment, the cage and the pound."

"The church-yard contains but a few obscure graves—a monument or two of modest pretensions. Alas! it is a quiet and obscure corner to sleep in."

"What matters, my dear? it is as good as any other for such a purpose. Besides, it has some advantages over others—had it not, it would not have been chosen."

"Certainly not, aunt. You are right there, at all events. Yonder is the grave—the sexton is standing idly by."

"Shall we go up and see it, my dear?" inquired Mrs. Paddlebat, directing Fanny's attention to the spot where the grave had been dug, and where that functionary stood.

"No, no," said Fanny, "no, do not go there. I cannot bear to look upon it.

It reminds me too strongly of the end we must all come to, not that that can be anything one ought to shrink from, but at such a moment the yawning grave is terrible to look at and makes me shudder."

" We may as well go in, my dear. See, the hour is close at hand, and I think I can hear the sound of carriage wheels at a distance."

Fanny and Mrs. Paddlebat left the grave-yard and entered the deserted and empty church, and sought one of the pews, into which they entered and sat down, close by the pulpit, and not far from the communion table.

They could now hear the sounds of carriage wheels, and, as the hearse came up to the door, the church clock struck the mid-day hour, and its notes re-echoed for some moments, and the trembling tones vibrated in the air.

"They are punctual," said Mrs. Paddlebat, whose good nature on the occasion manifested itself in making her endeavour to occupy Fanny's attention as well as she could, so that she should not dwell more than possible upon the melancholy occasion. Indeed, she thought it was better to say anything than nothing."

" Yes," replied Fanny, "they are here ; but I do not think of leaving the church during the ceremony."

" No, no, my dear, I would not think of it upon any account; you can do no good whatever, and you may do yourself much harm. I am sure you have done quite enough."

" Sorrow does not consist in the observance of any strict etiquette or ceremony," said Fanny.

" No, my dear, if it did it would be very easy to be sorrowful, and it wouldn't affect our health, and we could soon be very sorrowful indeed, and it would cost but little trouble—but there is the clergyman in his surplice."

" Will they bring the body into the church ?"

" I believe the clergyman will meet the body, and walk with it to the grave, himself in advance."

There was some little delay in getting the body out of the hearse, and then it was brought into the church. The usual ceremonies were gone through, and the clergyman, with the four gentlemen, went to the grave.

About ten minutes or a quarter of an hour was consumed in the reading of the burial service, and that was then followed by lowering the body, and then the earth was thrown over it.

The mourners stopped to witness this last part of the ceremony performed—to see the earth closed over the body of the unfortunate deceased.

The feelings of Fanny it would be difficult to describe under the circumstances. There always is a heart-sickening sensation only to be understood by those who have felt it under similar circumstances. She did not faint away at the time, but a worse feeling came over her. She, however, strove to maintain all the calmness and decorum that could be shown or expected upon such an occasion.

The chief mourners—that is those who followed the body—came up and spoke some words of consolation and comfort to her, but she could only regard them as the effusions of kindliness and good-nature, and she could but thank them for such attention and friendship as they had shown her.

Then again they left the place ; the hearse left the churchyard gate and proceeded to one of the houses in the neighbourhood, where the men were regaling themselves, while the mourning-coach proceeded homewards with a quicker step than that in which it came to Willesden.

There was something in the air of the place that brought with it a host of recollections, which weighed upon her imagination and oppressed her mind, that she leaned her head upon the pew as she recalled to her memory the fact that she was now alone, and if not pennyless, yet she was destitute, without means, and she knew of no way in which she could improve her condition.

This reflection was brought on by the melancholy and sorrowful train of thoughts she was at that moment too likely to indulge in. She was not selfish, but these thoughts were natural consequences of the position in which she was placed.

" Shall we now return to town, my dear?" said Mrs. Paddlebat. " I think you have been here long enough—you will only get more mopish than you are—and it is quite unnecessary that you should do so. Come away, my dear."

" In a few moments, aunt," she replied, " I will follow; only a few moments, leave me alone, and I will not fail to follow you—I shall be better then."

" You will be made worse."

" Indeed I shall not, aunt—believe me."

" Well, well, my dear, I'll come back in a few moments, if I don't see you before—though I really do not know that I ought to let you be by yourself."

Mrs. Paddlebat however did leave the church, and left Fanny, who kneeled forward on the hassock and prayed for the rest of the soul of the departed, and for strength to meet her own fate, which did not appear in the brightest colours—at the same time she felt relieved in her mind.

Somewhat lightened in her breast, she arose, and was about to quit the church, when another form appeared rising from one of the principal pews in the church.

She turned, and at once recognised the form and features of Nicholas Lowe, who was advancing towards her, and when he came near enough he held out his hand, saying,—

" Fanny, I can condole with you on your loss; believe me I am sincere, Sorrow is too well known to me to be a stranger to my heart: but for you 'tis hard."

" Hard as it is," she replied sorrowfully, " it must be borne; but your presence, Nicholas Lowe, is unlooked for here, and on such an occasion too."

" The occasion is," he replied, " the cause of it. You are unfortunate; the misfortune you have now experienced does not end here, Fanny."

Fanny shook her head.

" That misfortune I would make lighter, and the moments you would spend in needless pain I could shorten."

" This is kind of you, Lowe, and yet I cannot well see what all this tends to."

" To this, Fanny—Heaven itself is a witness that my motives are pure towards you, and I would be looked upon as a friend upon whom you could call to stand between you and misfortune; if ever man loved—hopelessly I know—"

" No more on this head, Lowe; the time for such thoughts has long since passed, when I could listen to this—I trust I shall not want for friends."

" I hope not, Fanny; and yet, by the remembrance of the past, let me conjure you to look upon me as a brother, as one on whom you can look in the hour of adversity—nay, I know you are now left without protection or means, let me press upon you my assistance. My purse you may command, and such a mark of confidence in me will be the most gratifying reward I can meet with."

" No, Lowe, I am not in such need as that; I hope, however, that Heaven will aid me."

" But, Fanny, remember what we once were to each other—that we have loved—that I still love."

" Nicholas Lowe !"

" Forgive me, Fanny, for speaking of the past. 'Tis past, and I would only allude to it now for the purpose of impressing upon your mind the little ceremony there need be between us, and, believe me, your happiness is even now one of the chief objects of my wishes. Accept it as coming from one who loves you—from—a brother, Fanny, from a brother."

" There can be but little in common between us. Do not think I have any churlish feelings. I thank you for your intended kindness, but at the same time I cannot accept of it; and now, farewell !"

" Nay, Fanny, one moment more."

" I have expressed my determination; seek not to destroy it, I am resolved."

" But, Fanny, do not forget the past; do not for one act, and that act the most painful one in my life, turn from me and refuse that which is offered in all honesty and honour."

" I do not doubt it, Lowe; I do not doubt your faith, but I cannot accept it—

once for all I cannot accept your offer. I would sooner endure any toil or privation than be beholden to you for pecuniary aid. Farewell !"

As she spoke she turned from him to leave the church, and slowly paced the short aisle and reached the door, while Lowe stood in an attitude of despair.

" Ah ! my dear Fanny," said Mrs. Paddlebat, " I thought you wouldn't come, and so I came to bring you away. It is time to go to town ; we must return. It will do you no good to remain ; take my arm, my dear."

They disappeared from the door, and Lowe remained standing alone in the church for some minutes, gazing after her without changing his attitude ; until, at length, he clenched his hand and struck the edge of the pew, muttering,—

" By Heavens ! she shall never want. I will follow her and watch over her, and she shall not be overtaken by want and misery ; all I have shall be expended in preventing her from being distressed, or from suffering any of those miseries which those who are destitute and so little able to meet the exigencies of life as she is, suffer."

As he muttered these words he seemed aroused to a sense of his situation ; he took his hat, which lay on a seat beside him, and left the church.

CHAPTER LXXXI.

LOWE AGAIN URGES FANNY TO ACCEPT ASSISTANCE FROM HIM.—THE REFUSAL BY MRS. PADDLEBAT.—OLD GILBERT CALLS UPON LOWE WITH A PLAN FOR MAKING MORE MONEY.

THIS interview between Nicholas Lowe and Fanny was equally sad to both parties, bringing back, as it did, those recollections of the past which had far better have been for ever buried in oblivion.

The circumstance altogether stirred up so many recollections in his mind that he was doubly unhappy in comparison to what he had been for a long period before. Time had, to a great extent, healed up some of the wounds which his deep disappointment as regarded an union with Fanny had made at his heart, and so many considerations concerning his own personal safety had always been present to him, that he had gradually took a fine sense of his deprivation.

But now that he had seen Fanny once again—now that he had conversed with her, and heard the sounds of her voice ringing in his ears—all his old feelings seemed to have revived ; and he could, as he covered his eyes with his hands, and sighed deeply in the solitude of his home, have almost fancied himself back again at old Mr. Paddlebat's, the goldsmith, and that all the events that had since then passed were but the visions of some vexatious dream.

Oh, if he could but have awakened to a perfect consciousness that such was the case. If he could but have once more restored himself to his state of comparative innocence, what a wonderful revulsion of feeling would have been his, and how differently would he have regarded all things and all occurrences !

But, alas ! that was impossible. The circumstances were too vividly real. He had but to look up to the ceiling of the room in which he sat, and there, in that blood-stained mark, he would see abundant evidences of what had really taken place. There was no such thing as getting over that mute evidence of the dreadful deed that had been done above.

" All is real," he said, " all is real—it is no delusion. I might have been happy, but am a murderer ; and the only consolation I can give to myself is, that I was not wicked enough to entangle, as I might have done, in my future destiny, so fair a being as Fanny Leslie, but that I did spare her from becoming the wife of one whom the penal laws of this country might have snatched from her arms to place on the scaffold."

We cannot wonder at Nicholas Lowe taking some credit to himself for not pursuing his marriage with Fanny, even after the terrible death of Rodwell, for most unquestionably he might have done so; and it did show some feeling of compunction, and some indication of a better nature in him, that he forbore to take advantage of her ignorance of what he was, and make her unhappy for life, by an after confidence which he would have been compelled to make with her.

"Thank God!" he often exclaimed, amid the silence of his home; "thank God that I did not wed with her. Could I have borne the one look of reproach that she must have cast upon me? What reply could I have made to her when she should say to me, 'Nicholas Lowe, if you were such a thing of guilt as you know yourself, you should at least have spared me an association with so much terrific criminality?'"

Lowe was right, for whether or not Fanny would have put to him such a question, she was, at all events, fully entitled to do so, and he had a perfect right to expect she would.

There was now one thing, however, which began sensibly to annoy him the more he reflected upon the scene in the church at Willesden, and that was the fact that he had forgotten his caution, and forgotten his resolve, so far as to allow himself to be for a short time betrayed into the language of love.

Yes, he had not confined his offer of assistance merely to an offer of money, but he had yielded to his recollections of the past, and had spoken to Fanny in a tone which had made her think, that, combined with that offer, and contingent, most certainly, upon its acceptance, there were some hopes of still making her his.

The more he thought over what he had said, and what she had replied to him, the more he felt convinced that such must be the case; and now that he could reason upon the matter alone, and in cool and sober judgment, without having his imagination led away by a knowledge that she was close to him, he deeply and bitterly regretted that such should have been the case.

To regret such a circumstance was certainly the next thing to endeavouring to think of some means by which so grievous an error, for a grievous error it was, could be repaired.

But how was that to be accomplished? Were circumstances likely again to throw Fanny in his way, as they had done? How was he again to meet and let her know that the temporary excitement of the moment had passed, and that although he loved her, and although the same reasons existed for his preferring, even if she were willing, not to link her fate with his, he meant to place at her disposal what pecuniary means he possessed.

He could not again hope to meet her in such a quiet contemplative spot as that old church where they had met, and where he had had such abundant opportunity of talking to her. Call upon her, he felt that he dared not, and ought not now, more especially at such a period of mourning, but, he began to consider that most if not all these objections might be got over by letter, and accordingly he determined to write to Fanny.

It was no easy task to write to one with whom he had been upon such kind and tender terms—it was no easy task so to frame the sentences as to make her feel that his offer of assistance was purely disinterested, and at the same time that he fully repudiated the most distant thought of urging her acceptance of his hand, to convince her that it was from demerits of his own he came to that conclusion, while his old admiration and his old affection for her remained intact, as it was long, long ago.

But it was to be done; and Nicholas Lowe set about it with a good spirit, to do it as best he might, fully aware of the difficulties, but resolved, if possible, to conquer them.

After really much labour he produced the following epistle, and our readers will judge for themselves how far he succeeded in conveying the sentiments he wished.

"To Mrs. Arrowdale.

"Madam,—Do not fancy, from the formality of this address, Fanny, that my heart follows the dictates of that custom, which, by placing us apart, as we are, compels me so to address you, for in all honesty of purpose, and in all deep and true sincerity, I love you still.

"Yes, I love you still, as I have ever loved you from the first, and do not believe that this is a confession made for the purpose of contributing to your annoyance, for on the contrary, strange and inexplicable as it may seem,—it is uttered but to be repudiated, as regards any result beyond its mere utterance.

"It is needless and it would be painful for me to say why I know myself to be unworthy of you, but I am so. There is a secret which, although I know I could confide to you, it would be most ungenerous to do so,—a secret which has altered the whole complexion of my life, and which has made me the wretch I am.

"But misfortune has come upon you,—you who I thought so under the special protection of Heaven as being one of its purest and choicest works, that you would be saved those shocks of common life that beset others. This, however, I grieve to know has not been the case, and you have suffered.

"And now, Fanny, that I have told you that I love you—now that I have told you that although loving you, I urge no suit, let me implore you to give to me the only satisfaction that I can now hope for, namely, that of using gold, otherwise to me most useless, in providing for your exigencies.

"Do not, I implore you, refuse me this request, but frankly take what is frankly offered to you from one who—when he says he will not presume upon the fact that you have accepted assistance at his hands, speaks nothing but the sacred truth—a sacred truth he will adhere to while he lives. This from your unhappy,

"Nicholas Lowe."

This epistle he duly sealed and addressed to Fanny by the name of Arrowdale, which it was really to Lowe a great effort to write, although he felt the propriety of doing so.

"Arrowdale," he repeated. "How strange it sounds for me to call her by such a name, and what a pang, at one time, it would have brought to my heart to do so, bringing with it as it would the conviction that she was another's!"

Being loth to entrust his letter to the post, and still more loth to entrust it to any messenger, who might make some mistake in its delivery, he resolved himself to take it to the house in which Fanny resided, and, without asking to see her, deliver it into the hands of some one who would promise that she should have it.

Night was the most favourable time for such a purpose, as he did not wish of course that he should be seen, and accordingly, when the shade of evening had wrapped all things in its sombre mantle, Nicholas Lowe, with his letter in his pocket, sought the house in which Fanny had passed some of the happiest, and now some of the most miserable, hours of her existence—the most miserable it was likely she could ever know.

Oh, what a sad and sombre aspect that house now wore, to what it had done when he who had given life and animation to it was alive! The shutters were closed—some neglected plants hung in the balcony, and a cage, in which had been a wild bird, which Fanny by gentle arts had been training, was now vacant.

She had given the little prisoner his liberty, for she had no heart now to trifle with it.

Lowe crossed to the other side of the way and stood in a door-way for a time, giving himself up to melancholy and bitter reflection.

"Alas, alas,!" he said "misery appears to fall alike in this sad world upon the innocent and upon the guilty. My habitation scarcely presents such a melancholy spectacle as this, and yet death has been there too, and death under its most terrific form. Why should you suffer any pang, such as I suffer Fanny,—you who are innocence, and so near akin to Heaven, that when you join the angelic throne they will welcome you at once as a dear kindred spirit."

So completely absorbed was Lowe in these sad thoughts and reminiscences that he for a time quite forgot the errand he had come upon, and was only aroused by seeing a light appear in one of the rooms.

The blind was closely drawn, but he could observe the shadow of some one clearly defined upon it, and so distinct was that shadow that he knew it was that of Fanny, and he could see that the attitude she was in was one of deep grief and dejection.

"Oh that I had the right," he cried, "to wipe away those tears—Oh that it was my province—"

"I beg your pardon, sir," said a voice behind him, "but if you will give me leave to get out of my house I shall be very much obliged to you indeed."

Lowe immediately turned and saw that he had been blocking up somebody's door-way most completely, so, making some slight apology, he at once crossed the road, and walked up to the door of Fanny's house, at which he knocked gently and somewhat timidly, for he rather dreaded who would answer the summons.

Perhaps if his knock had been a bolder one Mrs. Paddlebat would have replied to it, but as it was the servant answered him, to whom he said—

"Is Mrs. Arrowdale within?"

"Yes, sir," was the reply, "but unless your business is very particular, I am sure she would rather not see any one."

I know—know—I do not want to intrude upon her, if you will be so good as to give that letter into her own hands as soon as possible, for it is important."

"Oh certainly, and shall I say who called?"

"No, no, thank you!"

Nicholas Lowe walked away well satisfied that at all events Fanny would be certain to get his letter, and with a great hope, although scarcely a confident expectation, that she would, send him an answer to it, but what that answer would be he dreaded to think, for, in all probability he could not help feeling that it would surely be a refusal.

"Well, well," he said, "I must take my; chance I have done all I can, and if she now refuses my aid, I can but watch her and do by stealth, so that she shall not know from whom the assistance comes, what she will not permit me to do openly."

It would most unquestionably have been now, perhaps, the greatest pleasure which Nicholas Lowe was capable of feeling, if Fanny would have accepted his assistance.

He would have felt that he was in a small way making up to her something of the evil he had done in inducing her to love him once, and then himself committing an act which imperatively forced a separation from her.

"She is surely too kind and gentle," he said to himself, as he proceeded homewards, "not to answer me. She surely, even if she refuses, will couch her refusal in some kind words which will be to me a treasure—a great treasure."

We will now leave Nicholas Lowe to wait for the chances of an answer to his note to Fanny, while we step into the interior of that house of mourning, and see how Fanny herself is employed.

After she came home from the funeral she fell in a state of dreadful dejection—a dejection which the interview she had so very unexpectedly had with Lowe in the church, had by no means tended to dissipate.

She was quite incapable of conversing with Mrs. Paddlebat, and she prayed to be left alone so earnestly, that that lady did so, and for many hours Fanny shut herself up in a darkened room of the house, making an almost vain endeavour to reason herself into some sort of composure.

The mere fact, that she did make such an effort, of itself is sufficient to prove that she was likely to be able to present some outward show of resignation, whatever real sad feelings might hold an undivided empire in her secret thoughts.

While she was thus occupied, she was surprised at the number of knocks at the door that came, and finally, when she did emerge from the apartment in which she had passed those solitary hours, and asked Mrs. Paddlebat what was the meaning of the numerous appeals for admission, that lady shook her head and heaved a deep sigh.

This was not very explanatory to Fanny, and she was about to ask for some information of a more conclusive and understandable character, when the door of the drawing-room in which they now were suddenly opened, and two rough-looking men made, to Fanny's great surprise, their appearance.

One of these men kept just a little in the rear of the other, while a certain vulgar air of finery about the one in advance, seemed to say that he was the master, and that the other, who was so much dirtier and shabbier, was the man. The former carried in his hand a book and pen, while there dangled from one of the button-holes of his coat a little ink bottle.

Without taking the least notice of Fanny, he commenced looking around him, and speaking in a hurried tone with a monotonous cadence—

"One chimney-glass, curtains with poles, &c. complete for three windows; Brussels carpet and rug to match; one small fender and fire irons."

"What is the meaning of this?" said Fanny.

" One loo table, rosewood; James, look what maker's name is on that piano : twelve rosewood chairs, covered with crimson velvet ; one couch, ditto, ditto."

" My dear," said Mrs. Paddlebat to Fanny, in a whisper, " this—this—person (all Mrs. Paddlebat's politeness could not call him a gentleman, or even a gent.), has come to seize the goods for rent."

" I understand—I understand now—of course, we owe money, and have none to pay with—alas, alas! what will become of us now ?"

" Six occasional chairs," said the broker.

" Yes," replied Mrs. Paddlebat, " and all those people that knocked at the door came with their bills, and made such a riot about being paid as never was known. I could hardly get rid of some of them : I assure you, they would scarcely take any excuse, not even when I told them what a sad day this had been.

" Two card tables," said the broker, "covered with crimson velvet ; an ottoman ;— are those glasses between the windows fixtures, ma'am, or furniture belonging to the tenant ? "

" Oh, don't ask me any questions, you wretch !" said Mrs. Paddlebat, " I hate the sight of you."

" I must seize, ma'am, when I have instruction to do so. It's all in the way of business, you know."

" Seize yourself then, and don't trouble me ; I won't answer anything, so you need not expect I should : and now you have your answer, you ill-looking puppy."

" Come away, come away," said Fanny; " had we not better, aunt, leave this place at once ? We can do nothing here. I will give up the trifle I have in my possession, in the shape of money, and I can do no more, unless in course of time my industry will enable me to pay everybody, which, Heaven knows, I wish to do if I possibly can."

The broker, finding he was not likely to get anything but hard words from Mrs. Pabblebat. forbore to make any further inquiries of her, but went on with his inventory, and finally left his man in possession of the goods, who forthwith flung himself at full length upon one of the sofas, and seemed to enjoy his situation amazingly.

Fanny, not without some difficulty, however, persuaded her aunt not to interfere with him, but to let him do as he pleased; and then they both seriously consulted as to what was to be done for the future ; and in that consultation not the slightest idea crossed Fanny's mind of accepting the offer of Lowe to assist her, for she considered that that offer had been as definitively made as it had been upon her part definitively rejected.

Mrs. Paddlebat made a sort of calculation, which ended in her saying,—

" My dear, we need not be under no apprehension for some months, for both you and I have clothes and trinkets enough to spare that will produce enough to last us, I dare say, comfortably, half a year, and who knows what may turn up in that time : you know it is a great length of time to look forward to—six months—twenty-four weeks, you know."

Mrs. Paddlebat certainly seemed to think that she made the time longer by this species of arithmetic, and an evil which was so far off as six months, even to Fanny, did not certainly seem immediately pressing.

" It must be so then," said Fanny, " anything but being beholden to any one, if we can help it. I do not—cannot think that I am wholly destitute of the means of doing something for myself: there is surely abundance of employment in such a great city as this, connected with the arts, of which I have some knowledge, for those who are willing to undertake it."

" Ah !" said Mrs. Paddlebat, " there is abundance of work, but I'm afraid there's abundance of people to do it too ; but, however, it's time enough, my dear, to think of all that when we cannot help doing so, and in the meantime don't you trouble your mind about it at all."

" I have only one request to make to you, aunt."

"And what may that be?"

"It is that you will make arrangements so that we may leave here to-morrow."

"I will, for I assure you I don't like seeing people that come after money when we haven't the money to give them—people that you owe anything to, are always as civil as possible, till you tell them there's any difficulty in paying, and then they all of a sudden turn into so many raging lions."

"I have no doubt, aunt, of that, and therefore, I urge you to take measures for our departure to-morrow to somewhere where, at least, we shall be in quiet, and I shall have an opportunity of endeavouring to renew the tone of my mind."

"A little way out of town it shall be, my dear ; I will go out and find some place in the morning, and to-morrow night I do hope we shall sleep somewhere else."

This was a comforting assurance to Fanny, for now no place could be so full of sad and melancholy recollections as that in which she had passed such happy hours as to make the present, by contrast, most frightfully miserable.

CHAPTER LXXXII.

THE RECEPTION OF LOWE'S LETTER, AND MRS. PADDLEBAT'S STEP IN THE BUSINESS.—LOWE'S FRIGHT.

In the evening of that day, and when Fanny was left more to herself, in consequence of Mrs. Paddlebat going in and out for the purpose of getting rid of some of her own superfluous jewellery, she at times felt such sudden accessions of grief that it was with the greatest difficulty she could subdue them.

She could not help at times remembering some kind thing which Horace had done, or some affectionate words that he had spoken to her, perhaps at times when she now thought she had been a little wayward and capricious; and whenever one of these reminiscences of the past came across her, she felt such a rising in her throat that she had to summon all her resolution to her aid to prevent herself from falling into a complete paroxysm of woe.

It was on one of these occasions that Nicholas Lowe had seen her from the opposite side of the way resting her head upon her hands in her own room, when he concluded, and concluded justly, that she was in an attitude of profound grief, and was brooding over her loss.

Then there came a loud tap at her chamber door, and she started to her feet. It was the servant with a letter in her hand, which she handed to her mistress, saying :—

"If you please, madam, here is a letter. I should not have disturbed you, but the gentleman who left it was particular that it should be given into your own hands, and I think, from what he said, that it is important."

"Thank you, thank you," said Fanny, "leave it."

The girl laid it down upon the dressing table, and Fanny did not cast her eyes upon it for some time, for who was there now in all the world from whom she cared to receive any communication ?

At length it was by mere accident that she cast her eyes upon the superscription, and saw that it was from Nicholas Lowe, for there was a peculiarity in his hand which she knew well, but it showed how great events completely overpower all minor feelings, that she scarcely felt the least emotion at opening that note from one to whom she had once given her affections, so completely and so entirely was her mind engrossed by the gigantic grief which she felt for the sad loss she had sustained.

She read the letter attentively, and when she had finished its perusal, she breathed a sigh, as she said :—

"No, no, no! I cannot accept of assistance from such a quarter, even proffered thus. I cannot, and will not. We must either be as once we were, or utter strangers. It is all in vain, Nicholas Lowe. Heaven only knows what is the secret to which you refer, but we have both changed now, and the feelings which once were ours can never be restored."

Whether or not to answer the letter was a question which did not agitate her, because there was certainly nothing in the epistle which should deprive it of the courtesy of an answer; but while she considered that she was bound to reply to him, she resolved to do so as shortly as it was possibly so to do.

"I will answer him," she said, "and I will answer him with a decision that shall put a stop to the possibility of his thinking that my resolution can be at all shaken."

While she was considering of these matters Mrs. Paddlebat came in, and Fanny showed her the letter, saying:—

"You see what Nicholas Lowe says, aunt, and I am sure you will approve of my resolution to refuse entirely anything in the shape of aid from such a quarter. I cannot come into contact with Lowe, without reviving in his mind the past, and therefore it is for the better that we should continue entirely separate."

"Ah! my dear, you know your own feelings in the affair better than any body else, of course, and I think it's entirely in your own hands to settle how you like. All I can say is, that I have a great curiosity to know what the secret is that he talks about. I must own I should like very much to know that. I really wonder what it can possibly be now. It's a very strange thing, and the more you think about it, somehow the more you get puzzled."

"It cannot matter to us, aunt."

"No, of course not. But there was always a something about that Nicholas Lowe that I did not like; and do you recollect that odd notion of his, about a skeleton being in every house?"

"Alas! that was but too true a thing. There is a skeleton in every house, as you, aunt, have ample reason to know. What human being is there in the whole world, who can lay his or her hand upon their heart, and say, that there is nothing t regret, nothing to dread?"

"Why yes, to be sure. But then one don' want always to be reminded of disagreebles; I am sure, as you say, I have had my share of troubles, for ever since poor Mr. P. departed this life, I have had nothing else but trouble."

"Then the philosophy of Nicholas Lowe, you acknowledge to be correct?"

"Why, so far."

"And that is as far as it went."

"But do you mean to answer his letter?"

"To-morrow, I cannot do so to-night. In the daylight, I shall be better able, but at present, I am too weak and nervous to do so. It deserves an answer, and a kind one too, for God knows what he may suffer, or how much he may be injured by the secret that he avows exists."

Mrs. Paddlebat said no more upon the subject, but she had her own thoughts, and those thoughts shortly grew into intentions, which we shall speedily see the execution of, and which all arose from her desire to know what was the secret to which Nicholas Lowe alluded.

"Could there be," thought Mrs. Paddlebat, "a better opportunity of getting the secret from him than this? He is monstrously anxious to assist Fanny, because, as he says, he loves her still; and what if I were to go to him and tell him, that, unless he tells me the secret, I will persuade her, might and main, to have nothing to say to him; but, if he does tell me, I will take his part, and get her, if I can, which I know I cannot, but that makes no difference, to see him again, and take some of his money."

As Mrs. Paddlebat spoke, she put her bonnet on, which betrayed a tolerably conclusive decision in her mind that she really meant to go on this errand to Nicholas Lowe.

In the course of a few minutes more she was in the street, and fully determined upon an expedition which it would have given Fanny great pain to have known of, and which would have convinced her what a dangerous thing it was to take such a person as her aunt into her confidence, under any circumstances as there was no such thing as knowing what she would do.

"I hope I shall find him at home," thought Mrs. Paddlebat, as she walked along towards Nicholas Lowe's house, as fast as her size would permit her—"I hope I shall find him at home, for it's getting rather late than otherwise, and to-morrow I know I shall not have time and leisure ; and besides, Fanny will have written to him, and that would spoil all."

Mrs. Paddlebat did not start with an intention of saying to Lowe that she came as a messenger from Fanny, but she had no objection to his inferring that much if he chose to do, and provided she got his secret from him, which, the reader will agree with us, was not very likely, as she did not particularly care what mistakes he made with regard to ambassadorial powers.

The distance was rather considerable for a lady of Mrs. Paddlebat's girth, and by the time she reached Nicholas Lowe's door, she was as nearly tired as she could very well be, and she could not but remark to herself what a dreadful, vexatious thing it would be if she should now fail in her errand.

The cold, dark, dismal, sombre appearance of the house, made her pause a moment or two before she could muster courage to knock at the door ; but at length she did so, although what style of knock to call it would have puzzled the greatest connoisseur in knocks that ever breathed.

There was no answer, after several minutes' waiting, and with a growing conviction that Lowe was not at home, she was about to execute a more vigorous appeal to the knocker, when a voice so close to her, that it made her nearly jump off the step, said,—

"Who are you?"

"Oh, gracious," said Mrs. Paddlebat, "who are you, and where do you come from I should like to know? I don't see you."

"I am here," said the voice, whom she now recognised as that of Nicholas Lowe, "and I find that you are Mrs. Paddlebat, or Arrowdale, I suppose, as now you ought to be called."

"Oh, I see you now. You have got a ladder actually from the area to the step, I perceive. Is that the way you answer your visitors?"

"Yes," said Nicholas Lowe ; "and if your visit here be on your own account, or merely for idle curiosity, you had better go away again, for you will most assuredly be disappointed."

Mrs. Paddlebat thought that this, as a commencement, was not very promising, but she was not inclined, since she had come so far, to give up the matter quite so easy, so she replied :

"Well, Mr. Lowe, I'm sure you are not such a remarkably pleasant person that I should come to you unless I had some business to come upon, and if you write letters I suppose you expect answers."

"Ah!" said Lowe, "you bring me an answer from—from Fanny."

"Really, Mr. Lowe, that's a very cool way you have of speaking of a married lady though she is a widow. Oh, he's gone. I suppose he will open the door now, and a fine rage he will be in when he finds I have no letter for him at all. But what do I care about his rage. it's nothing to me, and I'll give him as good as he gives any day. Oh, I hate the wretch! He called me a corpulent old woman— I shall not forget that in a hurry. I wish one of the skeletons that he says is in every house was crammed down his throat, the vile, ugly, thin, odious, disagreeable—oh, here he is."

Lowe opened the door at this moment, and cut short the interpositions of Mrs. Paddlebat, who forthwith entered the house, and was guided by its melancholy occupier to the dining-room, in which he usually saw the very few people, indeed, whom he was compelled to admit to that sad and solitary mansion.

"Be seated, madam," he said, in a voice of some emotion, "be seated. Even you on this occasion are welcome."

"Oh, am I? I'm very much obliged, indeed—really am I. Well, if you, Mr.

Lowe, had come so far to see me, I'd have asked you to have a drop of something."

" I do not want to be deficient in hospitality, madam. You will find the water-butt down stairs nearly full, and you are welcome to drink it all, if you like, for a fresh supply will come in to-morrow."

" Well, I'm sure, was there ever such horrid stinginess ? But I don't want to be beholden to you for nothing, no, not I, so I'll just say at once what I came about. You wrote a letter to my niece ?"

" Yes, yes."

" Well, you say in that letter that you have a secret, and what I come here about is to say that, if you don't tell that secret, she won't have nothing to do with you, so now you know what you have to expect, and why I came to you at this time in the evening too, walking all the way, and then to get offered nothing in the world but a water-butt full of cold water."

" Do you mean to tell me," said Lowe, " that Fanny commissioned you to come to me with this request ?"

" Well, I'm sure you are wonderfully particular, Mr. Lowe. It speaks for itself, I think, that I am here. A likely thing, indeed, that I should come unless I was particular."

" You have not answered my question, Mrs. Paddlebat, but fenced with it. What I ask you explicitly is, did Mrs. Horace Arrowdale, your niece, send you here to ask me what my secret was ?"

" Did she send me ? I am not exactly my niece's servant, and I can come or not come, as I like, I suppose, and I can tell you that there is not the least chance for you, if you do not at once tell me what the secret is."

" I am sufficiently answered," said Lowe. " This visit is merely on your account, I premise, and is an idle piece of curiosity, and nothing more. How could you from what you know of me suppose but that it would be a most signal failure ? I am surprised at your presence here, and can only strongly advise you to go away again as quickly as you can."

This was about as decidedly unpleasant a speech as Nicholas Lowe could possibly have made to Mrs. Paddlebat, and it at once obliterated the faintest notion that her scheme would be effective, and convinced her, without the shadow of a doubt, that she had taken all her journey and all her trouble literally for nothing.

" Very well, Mr. Lowe," she said, " very well, sir, very well. That's your idea, is it ? Very well, I say."

" I say very well," replied Lowe ; " and it will be better still if you go at once, in which case I shall be inclined to look over this intrusion."

" You look over this, wretch! I'll tell you a bit of my mind now that I'm here. I believe you have done something that will hang you some day—that's what I believe."

" Do you ?" said Lowe, while a slight accession of colour tinged his usually pale cheek, " do you ? You are quite welcome, madam, to any opinion you may form of me that will best suit your inclination. It matters to me not a jot what you think or what you say ; but if you will not, when I request it, leave my house, I shall leave you this room to yourself, in which you may wait to your heart's content, only I lock my door just about now, so that you will have to stay all night till it suits me to open them again in the morning."

This threat had the desired effect, and Mrs. Paddlebat rose, for there was a calm sort of determination about Nicholas Lowe which she had never before remarked in him ; but, before she went, she longed to be as annoying as possible, and she looked round the room to see what she could lay hold of as the subject of a remark.

" Oh," she said, " so you have not got rid of that ugly mark in your ceiling, which looks, for all the world, as if there was a dead body in the room above and some of the blood had come through ?"

It was a wonderful piece of determination and self-command that enabled Lowe to reply in a tolerably firm and clear tone of voice to this—

"Indeed! does it? Well, madam, you are quite welcome, as far as I am concerned, to the enjoyment of that opinion."

"I suppose I am. I'll enjoy what opinion I like, you mean scrub, and no thanks to you. I suppose you will light me out."

"With the greatest pleasure, madam, I assure you; and I consider that that last remark of yours is the best you have yet made since you have been here. This way, if you please."

"Ah! It will be something wonderfully particular that gets me to come within your doors again, I think; and as for your supposing that Fanny will have anything to say to you, you may get rid of that idea, I can tell you, for I'll give her your character in a very few words indeed, so you may consider that as settled."

"Very good," said Lowe. "Here is the door."

"I see it, you hyena, and look upon you as a rhinoceros, I do."

"Yes."

"A—a—a—bad-looking rattlesnake, and I leave your house disgusted. Do you hear? disgusted!"

"Yes."

"And when you are hung, which, of course, some day you will be, I'll come and see you—I will, and enjoy it and laugh. Do you hear that? I'll laugh while you kick, and be glad to see you kick for a quarter of an hour at least."

"Yes."

"I—I—don't know exactly what I'll do. Murder! fire! oh gracious, what's that? I've rolled over some animal."

Nicholas had opened the street-door, and, as Mrs. Paddlebat had been much more intent upon abusing him than upon looking where she was going, she tumbled over somebody or something, which was crouched down upon the door-step, and rolled into the street. In a moment afterwards a low, chuckling laugh came upon her ears, and she heard the detested voice of no other than little old Gilbert Paddlebat say—

"Ha! ha! I think I had you there, sister-in-law. Oh! oh! why don't you look before you leap? Why, Nicholas Lowe, you must be quite a gallant man to be letting a lady out of your house at such a time of night, and you a bachelor too. Oh! oh! oh! sister-in-law, I'm ashamed of you!"

CHAPTER LXXXIII.

THE CUNNING PROPOSAL OF OLD GILBERT, AND ITS REJECTION BY LOWE.

NOBODY could be more surprised than was Nicholas Lowe at a visit from old Gilbert, for they had now for some time so completely ceased to have any sort of communication together, that he had certainly not again expected to see the old man.

If, however, his mind had been at all inclined to anything of a risible tendency, he must have laughed at the singular manner in which Mrs. Paddlebat had come in contact with the miser, presenting, as they did, the most remarkable difference in personal appearance that any two people could, for at a very moderate computation, Mrs. Paddlebat had certainly the absolute material of at least four Gilbert Paddlebats in her composition.

As for the little old man, it was hard to say whether he was cunning enough to have noticed Mrs. Paddlebat coming out, and so place himself wifully in her way, or had set down to rest himself, as he was occasionally wont to do, upon the step of a door, and so been tumbled over by the lady.

As it was, however, he rose much more quickly than she could, and rushed into Lowe's passage, where he stood laughing in his own peculiar manner, and evidently, although he was a little bruised, enjoying the joke.

"Shut the door, Lowe," he cried, "shut the door, as, when she does rise, she will slaughter me. I know her of old—oh! I know her well. Oh! oh! oh! she has—has broken her back, I hope—that's to say, her neck. Wouldn't it be a pity if dear Mrs. Paddlebat was to break her neck, now?"

"Mrs. Paddlebat," said Lowe, as he closed his door, "I do not see that you are entitled to any assistance or courtesy from me after the opprobrious terms which you have used towards me, and if I were to render you any assistance it would be practically to give you the lie, and it would become an insult of the first magnitude."

So saying, he closed the door completely, to the great enjoyment of old Gilbert, who laughed thereat amazingly, and tried to knock Lowe upon the back as he said—

"Bravo! bravo! so she has been abusing you, has she? Well, well, there she lies in the kennel, for which you ought to be grateful to me, for it was my work to do so—all my work. What did she come to you for?"

"I know not, except out of curiosity, and to abuse me. But I am glad to see you."

"Are you really—are you? That's not what many people say."

"Then it must be your own fault, Gilbert Paddlebat, for you have the means of purchasing abundance of blessings."

"Abundance of what?"

"Blessings, by the free use of that wealth which you possess."

"You don't mean that as a joke, do you?"

"Certainly not. Heaven has given you abundance, and you may, if you choose, make it a means of diffusing a great amount of happiness around you."

"I beg your pardon, Nicholas Lowe. Heaven never, that I knew of, gave me anything but the rheumatism; and as for any money, I think I can safely say that, in one way or another, I earned it all myself. It's all very well for a man to be told that Heaven has given him abundance, when he has been abused through a long life for the means he has himself taken to increase his store. I am, and have been all my life an usurer, I know it. I admit it fully and completely, and what has Heaven to do with my money, I should like to know? Master Nicholas Lowe."

"Well, well, I do not want to argue that point with you, Gilbert, but walk into the dining-room and I will tell you, at all events, why it is that I am glad to see you."

"Ah! I am curious to know; but I wonder how my charming old friend Mrs. Paddlebat gets on in the kennel?"

These words had scarcely passed from old Gilbert's lips, before there came such a tremendous knocking at the door of the house, that one might have imagined that twelve twopenny postmen, at the least, had gone mad, and all resolved to wreak their wild vengeance on that particular door.

"Ah," said old Gilbert, with great coolness, "that's the lady, but I would not by any means advise you to let her in."

"I don't intend."

Bang! bang! bang! bang! rat-tat-tat-tat! bang! bang! went the knocker, and then there came a terrific ring at a bell by the side of the door, which she seemed to have but just discovered, and immediately then there was a loud shriek, for the wire broke, and away went Mrs. Paddlebat for the second time that night into the kennel, carrying with her the bell-handle, and a long straggling bit of wire hanging to it.

"Good again," said old Gilbert, "good again. If she don't do herself some deadly bodily injury this time it will be a thousand pities, for, you see, nobody can be blamed for it, as nobody asked her to ring your bell, in that maniacal sort of way."

They both now waited in silence for some time, but as no further evidences of the presence of Mrs. Paddlebat were exhibited, they concluded that she was tired of the affair, and had gathered herself up and gone away.

"Tell me now, then," said Gilbert, "why it is you are glad to see me?"

"I am glad to see you," said Nicholas Lowe, "because I can tell you of a thing you ought to do, and of a thing you can do, easily. In consequence of the means by which you deprived Mrs. Paddlebat of her fortune, you are aware that her husband Arrowdale the stock-broker fled, and in the most rascally manner too."

"Well, well, what is that to me, you don't want me to marry her, do you?"

"No, I propose to you something much easier to do. He not only ran away with all the money belonging to strangers he could lay his hands upon, but he took with him the entire fortune of Fanny Leslie, as well as all that belonged to her husband, who, you may have heard, died of the shock."

"Oh, ah, well!"

"What I propose to you then, is to replace Fanny's fortune."

"Who? I?"

"Yes, with your great wealth you will not feel it, and when you come to consider that it was, really, you know, through you, that Arrowdale the stock-broker absconded, taking her small property with him, I think you ought to do so, and even then you are an immense gainer by your brother's death."

"Well," said old Gilbert, as he drew a long breath, "I suppose Mr. Lowe you fancy I have taken leave of my senses? How long is it since you have entertained the idea, that I was a likely man to make good other people's defalcations, eh? Mr. Lowe?"

"Enough, enough. You refuse. That is sufficient."

"I should think it was. I don't want to come to the workhouse in my old age, hardly. Oh dear no—no—I—I—may live a few years yet, and I don't want to come to want."

"Say no more. If you do not yourself, now that I have stated the circumstances to you, see the almost obvious propriety of such a step, nothing that I can say, I am certain, will have any effect in the way of convincing you. But I did hope that when you heard that that niece of your brother's, for whom he was so anxious to provide, was destitute, and when you knew you had so much of his money, you would have loosened your purse-strings, and for once in your life have done a generous and commendable action."

"Well," said Gilbert, "upon my word, that's good."

"It would have been good, had you done it. But since you will not, say no more, for it becomes an idle as well as a painful theme."

"Does it, Master Lowe? Let me ask, since you are so very anxious about this affair, why don't you, from your means, do a something for her, eh?"

"I have offered my all."

"You have: then what need I do anything? Does she want two fortunes for one that she has lost?"

"No—but she refuses assistance from me because she cannot forget that once I said I loved her, and that we parted for ever."

"How funny!"

"What?"

"I said 'how funny,' because I begin to see now really what you meant, and don't think you half such a fool as I did: oh dear, no—it's—it's on the contrary, rather good, that it is. You thought that if you got five thousand pounds out of me, you would, now that she is a widow, marry her yourself. Not a bad plan either—not a bad plan either!"

"Can you think me so base?"

"Base? I call it decidely clever. Base indeed! It's a very business-like transaction to my mind."

"I perceive, Gilbert Paddlebat, that it is of no use talking to you of feeling. You know nothing—understand nothing—you care for nothing but how to get money."

"Just so," said Gilbert; "you never said anything truer in all your life, Nicholas Lowe; and I have come here now to tell you how to make two thousand pounds, you know."

"Go on, go on!—I will listen to you; but I don't want money."

"Oh yes, you do. Don't tell me you do not want money, because I know better. All the world wants money, that's a fact; and all the world is striving after money, and you among the rest: so don't try to tell me any such nonsense as that you despise money."

"If," said Lowe, "I could get Fanny to take it, I would be glad to hear of any plan by which the sum you mentioned could be placed at her disposal."

"Oh, you may dispose of it how you like! If the thing succeeds, as I think it will, your share will be two thousand pounds."

"And yours!"

"Mine will be three thousand pounds: and little enough too, considering that I shall have a great deal of trouble in managing the affair. I want you to insure your life for five thousand pounds, and then to die."

"To what?"

"To—to die. I think it may be managed well, do you know, with a little caution; so that you may seem to die—you understand, comfortably. Here you live alone, and no one in the place knows you hardly by sight;—well, what so easy as for you and I to get a dead body and place it some night quietly in your bed, while you get out of the way?   Well, things go on just as usual, till the neighbours begin to miss you."

" Well?"

" Then they smell the body."

Lowe started.

" By-the-by," continued Gilbert, " I have fancied there was always an odd smell in the house.   I—I smell it now,—a kind of a putrid-blood sort of a smell. Are you not conscious of it? I can assure you, when you come in out of the open air, it is quite strong ."

"Is it ?"

" Is it? why, have you no nose that you ask is it?   The more you sniff the more you have of it; it's a continuous smell : I wonder what it can be!"

" You had better not come here, if it offend you.   I daresay it is a drain, but that owing to my living here so long I am unconscious of it, and do not smell it."

" Ah well, that may be it, but what do you say to my plan? you know there is nothing wrong in it, because it's all in the way of business, if it can be managed at all, you know;   I don't think that there's any risk by-the-way in which I would manage it at all, and, on the contrary, I think it is the safest way I know of to nett two thousand pounds."

" I decline."

"You decline? Decline did you say? Oh, you don't mean that, Lowe? Why do you decline?"

" I decline the thing upon its merits entirely.   It is of no use coming to me with such schemes—no use at all.   My path in life now is too fixed and melancholy a one ;   I would scarcely give myself twenty-four hours' trouble for two thousand pounds, as far as I am myself concerned, and I am inclined to think that, as regards Fanny, the spirit of independence is too strong within her for to accept anything from me, so I have no motive."

" Oh, he's out of his senses," said Gilbert, " he is quite out of his senses. There was a time, Lowe, when you would not have been so very scrupulous. There was a time when you would have—"

" What? "

" Taken a life for a smaller motive than to put two thousand pounds in your pocket.   Come now, what has become of Jervis Rodwell?   You know, and nobody else does.   You cannot deceive me—I say you know—you know well. Ha! I can see it in your looks now I move the candle on one side; and I repeat my question—' what has become of Jervis Rodwell ? ' "

" Idiot! " exclaimed Nicholas Lowe, as he sprang upon the old man, and seized him by the throat, " I suppose you are tired of your life, but have not yourself courage enough to rid yourself of it, so you came to tempt me to do the deed."

"Murder !—murder !—what do you mean ? "

" Just what I have said."

" Murder ? "

" Yes, murder : you are a dead man, Gilbert Paddlebat, and if you can remember any prayer you had better now utter it, for you have but little time to spare in which to do so.   Fool, to come and brave a tiger in his lair ! better had you done so, for the beast, unless hungred, might have let such a paltry wretch go ; but you have awakened a demon in my breast you cannot quell—again your hour has come."

" Have mercy on me ! " gasped the miser, as he writhed in the grasp of Nicholas Lowe; " have mercy on me.   I—I will do anything you please.   I—I only ask for my life."

Lowe's passion as promptly evaporated as it had been kindled.   It was lucky for old Gilbert that he had no weapon in his hand at the moment, for in that case nothing could have saved him ; but before he could execute the deed of vengeance Nicholas Lowe had time to recover from the sudden storm of passion that the incautious words of Gilbert had awakened in his breast, and he let him go.

The old man was not long in availing himself of his liberty, for before Lowe could speak a word, he ran out of the room, opened the street door with all the wonderful celerity as if he had been used to it for many years, and made his way into the street, where he was, of course, comparatively in safety.

CHAPTER LXXXIV.

THE REMOVAL OF FANNY AND HER AUNT.—THE DISTRESS OF BOTH.—THE CREDITOR.— SECOND REMOVAL.

FANNY was still intent that the removal should take place on the following day. She urged Mrs. Paddlebat again to go on an expedition in search of some new abode, which, as regards cost, should be more consistent with their means than the one they at present occupied, and while she did so, and indeed during the whole of the morning meal, she could not but wonder at the absence of mind manifested by her aunt.

Occasionally Mrs. Paddlebat would shake her two clenched hands above her head, and mutter something which sounded like vowing some great vengeance against somebody, and when Fanny asked her who she meant, she only nodded her head a great number of times, and said in a very mysterious, and at the same time a menacing tone of voice,—

"Never mind—never mind."

"I regret, aunt," said Fanny, "to see you so much disturbed, and fear some one has been annoying you."

"Annoying me," almost shrieked Mrs. Paddlebat, "you said annoying; but never mind."

"Well, of course, aunt, I have no right to intrude upon your confidence, but I hope that to-day you will be able to think of some place where we may go and reside, which, in addition to being more economical than this, will present the features of novelty, and not continually remind one of the past."

"Oh, yes," said Mrs. Paddlebat, "I'll do that; you may make yourself easy about that, but only just let me find either of them—that's all—only let me come across either of them."

"Either of whom, aunt?"

"Never mind."

Fanny was compelled to put up with this most ambiguous answer, for it was quite clear that unless she pressed her aunt much more than was consistent with her ideas and opinions to do, she was not likely to obtain any further information upon the matter. We cannot say for certain, but perhaps Mrs. Paddlebat would have been glad to be so much pressed that she could have had a fair excuse for saying,—

"Well, since you will know what it is that has so much distracted me, it is just this," &c.

But if such really was her wish, and if she really threw out all these hints as so many baits to Fanny to press her to a disclosure of her source of annoyance, she was doomed to be disappointed, for Fanny said no more about it.

Mrs. Paddlebat upon this made a great fuss in attiring herself for out of doors, and sallied forth to seek for a new home for herself and Fanny, while the latter retired to her own room to answer what she thought she now ought to do, the note which Nicholas Lowe had sent to her.

Twice she had sat down on the preceding evening to answer that letter, but as often had she risen from the task, feeling her inability to execute it, and that she could not, satisfactorily to herself, indite such an epistle as should be sufficiently kind as an acknowledgment of the offer of assistance he had made to her, and at the same time, be sufficiently cold to convince him there was no hope whatever of her accepting such assistance.

But still, with all its difficulties, that answer had to be written. She felt that she ought to write it—indeed, that she had no right under the circumstances to refuse him an answer, considering how entirely unobjectionable his letter was, and that, after all, what he proposed was a great act of generosity indeed, and such as deserved a kind refusal from any one, if it were refused at all.

With these feelings, then, Fanny drew her desk towards her, and commenced writing to Nicholas Lowe; and now, as is the case with many persons when they find they can put off something no longer, she got on much better than she expected, which perchance wholly arose from the fact, that she knew she had not time to be so very critical as she had been.

Her object was vanity, and after a time she produced the following epistle, which, if it did not clearly express all that she wished Lowe to understand, came, at all events, tolerably near to doing so.

"NICHOLAS LOWE,—You have written me a note, which I must wish had remained unwritten, and which I do think, after our interview at the church at Wilsden, might have so remained. But still I cannot refuse you an answer to it, if that answer expresses no more than what I have before stated by word of mouth, and which is, that I cannot, for one moment, considering all that has passed, considering my own position, and considering yours, think of accepting any aid from you. Do not suppose that any feeling partaking of resentment actuates me. You ought to believe me when I say it is not so; but that, still feeling all the gratitude which I can and do feel for the offer, and still believing it to be dictated by the very feelings which you in your note expressed, I feel that I must decline it. Wishing you, for the future, all the happiness that this world can afford,

"I am, with all sincerity, yours truly,

"FANNY ARROWDALE."

This was as kind a refusal as, under the circumstances, Fanny could write, and she felt that there was a great weight off her mind when she had written it. It was an immense relief to feel that she had made such an answer to Nicholas Lowe as would bear future reflections, and to know that, let her encounter what she might now, she could most assuredly do so without any embarrassment, as regarded an affair which might have been most embarrassing. She was glad when the letter was posted and so at once past recall, and then she turned her mind away from the subject, and began collecting together such little things as she considered herself justified in saving from the wreck of her fortune. Some article which Horace had actually given her she thought she had a right to, and nobody interfered with her in taking them, for as all that had come in already, in the shape of a seizure, was the landlord, there was abundance of goods in any one room to satisfy his claim.

And thus, then, Fanny occupied herself until the return of her aunt, who came back, about the middle of the day, with the news that she had found a furnished cottage to let, a short distance off the Notting-hill Road, which was very cheap, and which, she thought, would suit them.

"You know, my dear," she said, "of course it's very different from this place, very different indeed, but still there's a nice little garden, and I think that with a girl we may manage very well."

"Oh, yes," said Fanny, "let the place be ever so humble, aunt, it will do, so long as we can call it our own and be at peace : I have not yet, it is true, seen much of what is called the world, but I have seen enough of it to be tired of all its follies and its sadness—all I pant for now, is quiet."

"Well, my dear, that's very much my opinion as well, for there really are such wretches in the world, that we had a great deal better be out of it, if one can ; I am sick enough of everybody and everything. Oh, if I could but catch them !"

"Catch who ?"

"Never mind—never mind."

It was quite clear that it would take Mrs. Paddlebat an amazing long time to forget her adventure at Nicholas Lowe's, and that if she did happen ever to come across poor little old Gilbert, he would have to trust to what speed he could make to get out of the way of her vengeance, which otherwise, most unquestionably, would fall with some severity upon him.

There can be no doubt but that the good lady fully believed that old Gilbert had placed himself precisely on Nicholas Lowe's step for her to tumble over him, and we certainly do yet anticipate some accidental meeting between them, which, if it be not actually productive of mischief, will be of amusement.

She would fain have got Fanny to go and look at the cottage; but this the latter refused to do, saying that she fully relied upon her, Mrs. Paddlebat's, judgment in the matter, which being rather a something in the shape of a compliment than otherwise, was very acceptable to the lady, who, we know, had no objection to anything of that description. Thus, if Fanny had been inclined to what is called manage her aunt, she could not hit upon a better mode of doing so than by a little well-timed flattery, of which she was so proverbially susceptible.

But alas! who is not? The weak side of human nature, and the blind side likewise, is the love of praise: so that, after all, Mrs. Paddlebat was only like everybody else, although she might be rather deficient in the judgment which enables some to correct the feeling, and to judge between real and deserved commendation and gross flattery. At all events, she took what Fanny said as a compliment, and for the next half hour she continually spoke of what vast experience she had, and what she knew of the world, &c.

To all this Fanny listened quietly and complacently; for nothing in the world could be easier than carrying on a conversation with Mrs. Paddlebat when she got into one of her favourite topics, for all she required of you to say occasionally was, "Oh!—oh, indeed! Yes—really," &c. In fact, if you said any more, she considered you to be a serious interruption to her, and began to consider that you were not worth talking to—in fact, that she was casting the pearls of her great experience, in a manner of speaking, before swine.

"And do you think, aunt," said Fanny, when she saw that Mrs. Paddlebat showed some signs of coming to a finish, "do you think, aunt, we could remove to-day?"

"I see nothing, my dear, to prevent us. All the man wants who lets it is a month's rent in advance and a reference."

"We can manage both those requisites, I think."

"Of course, my dear, we can. So you see, I think, that the best thing we can possibly do is to pack up what few things we want, call a coach, get into it, and go away, leaving the house altogether."

"Be it so."

Fanny felt quite pleased; that is to say, comparatively pleased, at the idea of leaving where they were, for anything in the shape of positive pleasure, alas! she was not likely to enjoy for many a day—for although she knew that no creditors could have any claim upon her, for that the death of Horace had settled all that, yet it was to her mind such a positive horror to be asked for a debt which it was out of her power to liquidate, that she now dreaded every knock that came to the door.

And well she might; for if the servants had not kept off people from intruding upon her by positively denying her, she would, during the absence of her aunt, have been sadly pestered. When Mrs. Paddlebat was at home, the case was different; for she did not mind seeing a dun, and she thought nothing of saying to anybody who came for money, "Good God! what does the man want? Do you wish to eat the dead body of poor Mr. Arrowdale?" and when the creditor would say, "No, that he only wanted his little account," (by some means all demands, however exorbitant, are always called little accounts,) she thought nothing of saying to him, "You can go to the church-yard of Wilsden and ask Mr. Arrowdale for it."

But Fanny could not so manage, and, consequently, no wonder she was so anxious to get away from the house, where she felt she had no longer any right to stay, inasmuch as numerous expenses had been incurred in it, which of course there were ample means of meeting from the dividends of the funded property of Horace, if he had not been so cruelly robbed of all, as he had been, by his rascally cousin.

The man who was in possession remained in the dining-room, where he was quite satisfied with the articles of property he could see around him, as they were more than sufficient to pay three times over the demand which he was sent in for ; therefore Fanny and her aunt, if they had felt so disposed, which they did not, might really have taken away a great many things without hindrance from any one.

This, however, they did not do, for the whole that they took went into two boxes; and about an hour before sunset they got into a coach, and ordered the driver to take them to the cottage which they gave him the address of.

All these arrangements could be made very handily, for the owner of the cottage himself resided quite close to it, and, therefore, they had but to drive to his house first and settle about the terms on which they were to have possession, and then at once step into their new abode, if no unexpected obstacle presented itself to such a course.

As it fortunately happened, the man they had to deal with was of gentlemanly education and manners, so that the whole affair was conducted satisfactorily. The rent in advance, which he required, was paid, and a reference was given him to one of Mr. Paddlebat's old city friends, who could testify to their being what they represented themselves. Indeed, the mild and gentle lady-like appearance of Fanny was quite sufficient to banish the scruples of any one, and the landlord said—

"I am more in the habit of judging for myself than of consulting any one, and I can only say that I am on this occasion abundantly satisfied and much pleased to have got tenants for my cottage so much to my liking as yourselves."

Out of politeness, it will be seen that the gentleman included Mrs. Paddlebat in his compliment, but as he looked at Fanny all the time, and at its conclusion turned to her, it may be fairly presumed that he meant to address it to her alone.

Mrs. Paddlebat answered him, saying, "I'm sure you are very polite, sir, and if you come and see us at any time, a dish of tea will be always at your service, and I dare say we shall be very good neighbours indeed, sir."

"I have no doubt of that whatever."

Armed now with the key of the cottage, they proceeded at once to take possession ; and Mrs. Paddlebat was much pleased to hear Fanny express her approval of the place, and praise the neatness of the little bit of garden-ground behind, which, certainly, although small, was quite a pattern as regarded the laying out.

"And do you think you can be comfortable here?" said Mrs. Paddlebat.

"I think," replied Fanny, "I can be as happy here as it is possible for me to be anywhere, aunt ; but we must not forget that we are not independent people, and that our resources are very limited indeed."

"Oh, there's time enough to think of all that in some months; we have got enough to last some time yet, Fanny, and we shall not run into any great expenses. I'm sure we can manage here upon very little indeed, you know; and I have brought away more than you think, and when you unpack the boxes to-morrow, you will be quite astonished at what I have crammed into them."

"But were we justified, aunt?"

"Were we a fiddlestick?"

"Nay, but you know that many of the things were not paid for, and that we ought to have restored such as we could to the real and proper owners of them. The plate, for instance."

"Fiddle-de-dee! The plate is in very good hands; you know there was not much, for it was intended, if you recollect, to buy it, as it could be found at sales ; so I just collected it all together and popped it into one of the boxes."

Fanny shook her head, for she could hardly consider it right to have done so, but, however, as Mrs. Paddlebat told her, it was too late now to make any fuss about it, so they would just keep what they had got.

"Besides," she said, "it was not seized, and so, of course, every bit of it would have been stolen as a matter of course, by somebody or another ; and I wonder who had more right to it than we, or half so much, if it comes to that?"

The night had now set in, and Mrs. Paddlebat went out on an exploring expedition to discover some shops where she could provide herself with some articles wanted for immediate consumption. She brought in some supper, of which Fanny partook with a better relish than she had done anything for a long time.

They made up their minds to retire to rest early, for what with the removal, and one thing and another, Fanny and her aunt were both much fatigued, and were quite disposed to welcome an early hour for repose.

CHAPTER LXXXV.

THE NIGHT ROBBERY.—THE STRUGGLE FOR LIFE.—THE MURDER OF MRS. PADDLEBAT.

THE night was one of those calm, still beautiful ones which lend such a charm to country scenery, even when it is united with the sombre hues imparted by the night clouds, and when really so little can be seen of the varied beauties of Nature that in the day-time are so rich and so resplendent with all that can charm the senses.

There was not a breath of air to stir the sweet odours from the clematis that twined round the porch of the cottage, and for all the sound of human proximity that could be then heard, they might really have been occupying some lone cottage on some island where no human foot save theirs had trodden since the world's creation.

This state of things ensued for several hours, until, as the hour of midnight passed, the sky grew darker, and one of those soft, fine rains incidental to our climate began to fall.

It was more like a mist than a rain coming down, as it did almost perpendicularly, and in such fine drops, that it fell like a wet cloud upon house, meadow, tree, and flower.

But still it made a low, strange, murmuring noise, which fell upon the ears of Fanny, as she lay in wakefulness on her strange couch in that new cottage-home. She could not at first imagine what it was that made so odd a murmuring sound, and she rose gently and pulled aside the window-curtains for a moment, and then she saw that every object without was drenched with the small, penetrating rain that was falling.

The noise she heard she fancied proceeded from the water collecting upon the leaves of some thick-growing ivy that was outside her window, and which let it drop from leaf to leaf as it collected.

Having satisfied herself, then, as to the cause of the sound, which could not be said to have roused her, but which had struck upon her waking ears, causing her some surprise, she retired to her bed again; and now that the low, gentle noise freed her mind from any feelings of doubt or danger, she could listen to it, and fancy that it had a sedative effect upon her feelings, and disposed her to slumber; so that after a time she dropped into repose.

*   *   *   *   *   *

Who are they who pause now, and ring some of the accumulated rain from their clothing, beneath the garden-fence of the little cottage where sleeps the unhappy Fanny?

They are two men, coarse and vulgar in appearance, and in their attire combining something of the London pickpocket, and the sporting character. They converse in low tones, and their conversation is interlarded with the most horrible oaths. Without that part of it, we will present to the reader what it is they say to each other.

"Are you sure?," said one, "cos if you aint, it's a nice treat to have come all the way out here, on such a night as this. There don't seem to be much rain falling, but I'm wet to the skin."

"Oh, this sort of rain always does, when you aint athinking of it, drench you—

It's horrid. But never mind ; if I don't mistake, our night's work will pay   us ver
well for a wetting."

"You think so, do you? You recollect Bob was wrong once before, and w
nearly got lagged for nothing. You remember that well enough, I suppo se :
wasn't so long ago but you may."

"Oh, I remember it; but we must take our chances. We can't sit down an d d
nothing. We must live, you know, somehow or another, and if so be as we can
live one way, we must another."

"That's true enough, only I hope it's all right, and I can tell you don't feel in
the best of humours to-night. I wouldn't advise anybody to interfere with us
much."

"Who's a going?"

"Why, how do I know? You say there's only two women in the crib; but you can't make sure of that. How do you know but what there's two fellows as well? It's only natural as there should be."

" Oh, you be hanged! You always do try to make the worst of everything, you know; blow you for a fool! I only wonder I came to crack anybody's crib along with such a fellow.

" I'll tell you; it's because you can't get anybody else; that's it."

" Is it?"

" Yes, and for half a pin I'd wring your neck. But what's the use of our quarrelling, I should like to know, when we have got a job in hand? There, I have just wrung out my hat like an old dishclout."

" Ah! I throwed mine away. It came down on my blessed eyes all of a heap like a piece of damp brown paper; and I couldn't stand that, you know, any way."

" Who asked you?. Did Bob, the jarvey, tell you there was two boxes along with the women?"

" Yes, he did tell me so; and they were precious heavy, too, he said; and in one of them he swore he heard the jingle of plate; and what makes me think it was all right is his sticking out so much for his regulars, which he wouldn't have said so much about if he hadn't thought that he would get something worth while by the affair."

" Well, well; if it's all right, it's all right. All I can say is, it don't altogether seem the sort of crib to get anything of that sort in; but there's no saying. Do you think as it's late enough to do the job?"

" I should think so! If they haven't gone to bed now, they won't go at all; and I don't see any light in any of the windows : so come, and let's get it over at once."

" Come on, then; and mind you, I won't be baulked in anything. If they are quiet, well and good—I shan't interfere with them; but if they aint, I'll make 'em : that's all I've got to say about it."

" Stuff! we mustn't have any violence, you know; or else, when we does get to the Bailey, it's sure and certain to come up agin us, and then there's no mercy."

" Mercy be hanged! Who wants their mercy? When they catch me they may have me, but not before; and, in the mean time, I'll crack as many cribs as I can; and woe be to those that try to stop me! Come on, and we'll soon see what the boxes are made of. I wonder if they have opened them yet?"

" It aint at all likely, so we shall have the first pick of what's in them; but if they have, they can't have swallowed the silver plate, you know; and we shall find it laying about somewhere, safe enough."

" Safe, do you say?"

" Well, safe for us, you know; it aint a very difficult thing to get over these palings. I say, you had better tread on the flower beds instead of the gravel paths, and then your footsteps won't be so likely to be heard. You know, if you give 'em any alarm before you get into the house, and women once begin screaming, there's no such thing as getting at 'em in time to stop 'em."

" Lor! have you found that out? You are getting quite a conjuror, you are!"

" None of your gammon; but come on, and, if you do say anything, don't say it quite so loud as what you did just now, or else you may wake 'em up. This way, this way."

The two housebreakers, who had been put upon the scent of the robbery by the hackney coachman who had conveyed Fanny and her aunt to the cottage, crossed the low paling which separated the garden from the open fields, and trod recklessly over those trim and well-kept little flower-beds which had so much excited Fanny's admiration when first she arrived at the place. They made their way, then, without treading upon any of the gravel paths, until they reached the house, round which they trod cautiously, to find at which window it would be easiest to effect an entrance.

For some time the villains were foiled—for, as people usually are when they go into a new house, Mrs. Paddlebat had been amazingly careful about the fastenings.

At length, however, they made their way, which they found they could do with ease, into a little green-house, which was built against one of the walls of the house, and which they hoped would contain a door leading actually into the cottage, as is very frequently the case in such arrangements.

This, then, to their great gratification, they found to be the case, and as this door was of an ornamental character, and actually within the cottage, Mrs. Paddlebat, to whom Fanny had left all the task of fastening up, had neglected to do more than merely close it—therefore, at a touch almost, it presented a ready mode of ingress into the house.

The thieves now proceeded with the very utmost caution, for they knew that, in so small a place, the least noise must have the effect of betraying their presence, and they trod so carefully that their footsteps emitted not the slightest sound.

They hoped that the two chests—in one of which they expected to find plate—had not been removed from the ground floor, and after a very slight search indeed through the precincts of the cottage they were gratified in discovering both the boxes corded up tightly, which convinced them that they had not been opened.

" All's right," whispered one ; " here they are—and if there is anything in either of them worth the taking, it's ours."

" Hush—hush !"

" Well, damn it, a person would need to have cat's ears to hear me."

" Be cautious. Have you a knife to cut the cords?"

" Have I a knife ? What a question to ask a gentleman. Have I a knife ? When did you ever know me without one, I should like to know ? Why, it's one of my tools. Here goes."

In a moment the cords that were round the boxes were cut, but then it was found that they were each locked. That, however, was not much of an obstacle to these practised burglars, for, by the aid of a small but exquisitely-tempered crow-bar, they forced both the locks, and the lids of the boxes at once opened a little way, in consequence of the manner in which Mrs. Paddlebat had crammed them.

" Now then, to work," said one of the fellows; " you hold the glim, and I'll look to the swaggery."

One of them now stood holding the lantern they had lit, while the other took from the chest nearest to them, with great rapidity, every article it contained, and as fortune would have it for them, they had hit upon the one in which Mrs. Pattlebat had placed the silver, the propriety of carrying off which had appeared so doubtful to Fanny.

" Here they are," he said, as he bundled up the spoons and forks, and placed them in his pocket.

" Here's a watch, too."

" Do you think I'm a lass, and can't see the nose upon my face ? Of course there's a watch—I see it—I see it. Hilloa, hilloa ! I say. What's that ?"

" What's what?"

" A noise. Hush ! I hear something. Hush, again—don't you ? Don't say a word. Hush ! it's a coming down the stairs as safe as possible. There will be the devil to pay in a minute."

There came down the stairs a distinct footstep certainly, but it was a very light one, and as they kept their eyes fixed upon the door of the apartment, they saw the head of a very large cat look in.

" A cat," said one. " Well, I'll be hanged if I could make it out." Then he made a slight movement, such as he thought would have the effect of frightening away the animal, and it did, only not in the way he wished, for it darted across the room towards the glass door opening into the conservatory, and not finding it open, the creature shut its eyes, and with one bound went right through one of the squares of glass, shattering it into a thousand pieces, and of course making a most tremendous noise amid the profound stillness of the night.

" It's all up now, by Jove !" cried one of the men, and he made a dart towards the green-house door, but his companion was fully as anxious to escape as he was, so that they impeded each other most desperately, and a short but fierce struggle ensued between them, which ended in the one who had the plate, and who was by far the most powerful man of the two, throwing the other violently on to the floor.

The one who had been thus worsted in the encounter lay for a moment or two half stunned, while his companion ran off and fairly escaped from the cottage with the plunder.

While these affairs were going on in the palour of the cottage, both Mrs. Paddlebat and Fanny of course had been awakened by the loud crash of glass which was consequent upon the means the cat had used to escape..

Fanny sprang from her bed with a cry of terror, and Mrs. Paddlebat did the same.

"Aunt, aunt," cried Fanny, " did you hear that ?"

" Yes, to be sure—it's thieves !"

" Thieves !"

" Why, good God, who else would make that dreadful noise in the night. Oh! the two boxes—oh ! my watch—oh ! the plate—oh ! my dresses. They shan't rob me."

" Beware, aunt, beware; what would you do ? There may be danger."

" But am I not going to be robbed because there's danger. Let go of me, Fanny, for down stairs I will go."

" Let me implore you—"

" Implore a fiddlestick ! Do you think I am going to be robbed quietly while I stay up here. No, indeed, I'll soon settle them. Thieves! thieves! thieves !"

Mrs. Paddlebat, as she raised this cry, rushed down stairs, and Fanny in vain called to her to return, for she, too, felt tolerably confident that the cottage was attacked by thieves, although she had not the courage which her aunt had, to run down and face them. Finding, however, that all her calling to her aunt was fruitless, she stood trembling at the stair-head, and listened.

All was profoundly still for a moment or two—then she heard a scuffle and several oaths uttered in a man's voice ; there was then a loud scream, after which a door was dashed to with great violence ; then silence, as of the very grave, reigned within the precincts of the little cottage.

Yes, all was still, as if no scene of strife had been there enacted; and indeed, as regarded the brief uproar itself which had taken place, it had lasted such a very few seconds, that, after she had stood what appeared to her scarcely time enough to count six, it was all over, and whatever was written in the volume of destiny to happen that night had happened.

Poor Fanny found herself now in a most embarrassing position, for, although she called repeatedly upon her aunt, no answer was returned, and if any mischief had been done to her, how did she (Fanny) know that the perpetrators of it might not be waiting for her to appear, perhaps to take her life ?

" Aunt, aunt," she cried, " speak, I beg of you to speak."

There was no answer ; and, urged by a sort of desperation, Fanny bounded down the staircase, and stood upon a mat that was in the little passage, listening intently. The door leading into one of the ground-floor rooms was open, and through the narrow crevice that it was so open there came the faint glimmer of a light.

It was very strange : a shuddering sensation came across Fanny, and she had not the power to speak, although she more than once tried again to call upon her aunt, as she crept now slowly forward to the door that was so partially open. With her right hand she opened it a little wider, and peered into the apartment. A lantern was upon the floor, lying by the side of Mrs. Paddlebat, upon whose face there was a quantity of blood.

Fanny could see no more. A kind of mist came across her eyes, and with a deep sigh she fell slowly back and fainted in the passage.

CHAPTER LXXXVI.

THE ALARM.—THE FRUITLESS PURSUIT.—THE SYMPATHY WITH FANNY AND
THE REMOVAL.

ALL this had not happened quite so quietly as the thieves would have wished, for although the cottage which had been so recently taken possession of by Fanny Arrowdale and her aunt did stand alone in the fields, the landlord's house was sufficiently near at hand for any alarm to be easily communicated.

And when we come likewise to consider how quiet—how profoundly still everything was, save now and then the gentle pattering of the rain, as it fell from leaf to leaf of the trees, we shall not wonder that even the sudden smashing of the pane of glass in the green-house door should come to somebody's ears.

In fact, it was heard by the landlord of the cottage himself, who happened to be lying awake, ruminating upon what could have made his new tenant so very young a widow; for Fanny in her weeds looked still quite girlish, and she had not given her name, as Mrs. Paddlebat ostensibly took the cottage; although, if she had, the landlord perhaps would not have remembered that that was the name of the gentleman whose sudden death was reported in the daily papers.

In London and its immediate neighbourhood people don't know much or trouble themselves about their neighbours' affairs, and it is no exaggeration to say that a man may cut his throat, have an inquest held on his body, and be buried, without his next door neighbour knowing anything about it.

The sudden smashing of glass, however, at nearly one o'clock in the morning, rather surprised Mr. Davidson, which was the landlord's name, and he could not reconcile himself to sleep again.

"What could it be?" he said. "It came from Vine-cottage, certainly. What can it be?"

While he was asking himself thus whether or not he ought to get up and ascertain what it was all about, he suddenly heard a cry of distress proceeding from the same direction, and this completely settled the question, for he rose instantly, and began to dress himself with all the expedition he could.

"It's quite clear something's amiss," he said. "Hush! is that horses' feet?—perhaps it's the patrol."

He flung open his window, and called loudly,—

"Hilloa! hilloa! are you the patrol?"

"Yes," said a rough voice. "What's the matter?"

"Have you heard anything?"

"What sort of thing?"

"A smashing of glass, and a cry of help from Vine-cottage."

"Not I; for I have been down the road. I stopped a man who was running, but he had nothing suspicious about him. Are you quite sure of what you say, because I'll go there at once, if you are?"

"I am as positive as that I am dressing now, and will go with you in a minute. Just wait for me. There are only two females in the cottage, and God forbid any harm has come to them, although something seems to tell me there has."

"Be quick, then," said the patrol; "for I don't know that I ought to wait for anybody after such news."

The landlord did not keep him waiting above another minute, and then they both proceeded at a rapid pace towards the cottage, at the entrance gate of which the patrol dismounted, and tied his horse.

"I hope it's all a mistake," he said.

"I fear not," replied Mr. Davidson; "for I was lying awake, and heard it most distinctly. My mind, somehow, labours strongly under an impression that something serious has occurred."

"Nothing more serious than a robbery, I suppose?"

"I sincerely hope not.   Let me pull the bell.   It requires a knack and a knowledge of it to make it ring well."

"You seem to understand it?"

"I do.   The cottage belongs to me.   I am Mr. Davidson."

"I beg your pardon, sir," said the patrol; "I have heard of you, but, as I had never happened to see you, I really did not know you at all."

"Don't mention it; you have said nothing offensive to me.   But you perceive that, although we both heard the bell ring, there is no answer, which looks bad. I will try again, and then I am quite willing that an entrance should be forced in some way or another."

"Look," said the patrol, as he held his lantern to the ground, "look how the flowers are all trodden down, and the mould from the beds strewn upon the paths. Somebody not very particular has been here.   We can trace these steps."

They did trace them, and found that they led towards the green-house, the door of which was wide open, thus at once indicating by what route the thieves, for now that there had been thieves there was no longer a matter of doubt, had entered and left the premises.

"This is the way," said the patrol, as he darted forward, "this is the way."

Mr. Davidson closely followed him.   They opened the glass door, one of the shattered panes in which sufficiently explained to Mr. Davidson the noise he had heard and in another moment they were in the room where a fearful tragedy had been enacted.

On the floor, by the side of the burglars' lantern, which was still dimly burning, lay Mrs. Paddlebat, weltering in blood.   One glance was sufficient to assure them that she was dead.

"This is serious," said the patrol.

"Good God!" exclaimed Mr. Davidson, "who would have thought of this? Where is the young widow?"

"They are both murdered, I'll be bound.   It is a dreadful case—a most dreadful case.   We must search the house at once for the other, as you say there was another."

"Oh, yes, yes!" said Mr. Davidson, sinking on to a couch that was in the room, and turning a death-like paleness: "who would have dreamt of this? My God! what an awful catastrophe.   Call for help.   It is too horrible! too horrible!"

"It is bad enough; but compose youself, sir, while I search the cottage. Hilloa, here's the other lying in the passage.   What a pity! and such a sweet young creature too.   No; there's no blood about.   Let me see.   Here, just you come here, Mr. Davidson.   I—I don't think, somehow, the young one is dead."

Mr. Davidson rose, joyful enough at this intelligence, and made his way to the passage, from the floor of which the patrol lifted the light, fragile form of Fanny as easily as he would have lifted a child.

"Carry her up stairs at once, poor thing!" said Mr. Davidson.   "She looks as if she had only fainted.   I hope to God it is so!"

The patrol went up stairs with her, and placed her in the first bed he came to, which happened to be the one she had been occupying, when she showed some signs of returning animation.

"It's all right," he said.   "Lord bless you! she aint hurt.   How are you now, Miss?   What do you bring it in now, Miss, eh?   Are you better?   What a consolation it is, after all, that it's the old 'un that's killed, and not the young 'un."

"Oh! what a dreadful dream," said Fanny.

"There, do you hear her? she thinks it's a dream, you see.   Ah! poor thing, I suppose it's her old mother."

"No; I heard her call her aunt."

"Oh!   Well, it's much the same.   What a duck she is, aint she, sir?"

Fanny now became conscious that she was fully awake, and that two men were in her apartment.   She uttered a loud scream of terror, and cried, in accents of anguish,—

"Oh, spare me! spare me! Life has not many charms for me, but still I would not die a death of violence. Take all, but do not needlessly—oh, do not wantonly kill me!"

"Be at ease upon that score, I pray you," said Mr. Davidson. "We have come here for your protection. Do you not recollect me? I am the landlord of the cottage."

"And I'm a patrol, miss; so your safe enough."

Fanny looked, with a confused expression of countenance, from one to the other of them, as if she could scarcely comprehend the language in which they spoke, and then she said,—

"Something dreadful has happened. I am sure that something dreadful has happened. It could not be so vivid a dream. I saw my aunt lying as if murdered!"

"It's a sad thing to have to say," remarked Mr. Davidson, "but the real fact, which cannot be denied, is, that such is the case. Some thieves have broken into the house, and possibly she has paid the penalty of interrupting them with her life.

Fanny looked for a moment as if she were about to say something expressive of her abundant grief, and then she burst into tears, and sobbed most bitterly.

Even the patrol, who did not seem to be possessed of the finest feelings of humanity, shrank back and looked affected to see that frantic gush of grief.

"Come, miss," he said, for he took Fanny for a miss; "come, cheer up. It can't be helped now; and as for me, I'm so glad they did not interfere with you that I, in a manner of speaking, almost forgot the old woman. However, I must mount my horse again and be off."

"Where to?" said Mr. Davidson.

"To see if I can't overtake the fellow I met on the road; for if he aint the man who did the deed, I am much mistaken. There's no good to be done here just now."

As he spoke, the patrol left the apartment, and Mr. Davidson said to Fanny,—

"I will run back to my house and send over my housekeeper to you at once, who will stay and keep you company; or, if you please, when she comes you can dress yourself and come to my house, for I do not think this is now a proper place for you to stay in, nor is it one which, I am sure, you would choose."

"It is not, indeed," said Fanny; "and with the knowledge that there is such a dreadful spectacle below, I should be most unhappy. For the present, therefore, sir, I will throw myself upon your kindness."

"Very good. You shall receive a most hearty welcome; and we can make you, I dare say, comfortable enough, although I am an old bachelor, and my old housekeeper is not the most active of human beings in all the world. You won't be afraid to be left alone for a few minutes?"

"Oh! no, no!"

Mr. Davidson hastened on his errand, but it took him some time to get the old woman who conducted his domestic affairs in a fit state to go to Fanny; for, first of all, she had to be awakened, and then she had to be convinced that the house was not on fire; and then she took a long time to dress herself—longer than any old woman, surely, ever took before; but at last she did manage to be ready.

During all this time, as our readers may well suppose, poor Fanny was left a prey to the saddest reflections; but she did not stir from her room, for, although she had told Mr. Davidson that she should not be afraid to be left alone, her fears converted every little sound that met her ear into some note of danger.

When she heard, however, the voice of Mr. Davidson, as he came to let his housekeeper into the house, she felt a sense of security again, and that voice was the most welcome to her that she thought she had ever heard.

And, indeed, it was a sad and a fearful thing for her to be alone with the dead—to know that within a few paces of her lay the murdered corpse of one whom she had known so well, and who with all her faults—and, Heaven knows, they were numerous enough—had still some good traits of disposition about her, and was willing to do all she could for Fanny's happiness.

"Alas, alas!" resumed Fanny, "she was the only tie by way of kindred that held me to the world. And she has now gone from me, leaving me utterly desolate. Oh, when will death cease to persecute me ; or why does the fell destroyer with-hold his hand from my own existence ?"

Poor Fanny would gladly at that moment (so absorbed in grief were all her feelings) have laid down her life at once, for the world seemed lost to her, and she felt all that utter desolation of heart which the sad circumstances in which she was placed were likely to induce.

As for the old housekeeper, beyond the mere name of the thing, she certainly was not of much use as a companion, for her own fright, when she was told there was the dead body of a murdered person in the house, was so great, that she did not know whether she was standing on her head or her heels, and she was in such a state of agitation, that, instead of helping Fanny to dress, she sat down upon a chair and stared at her with all her might.

But still it was something to have somebody there ; and Fanny, although she got no assistance from the old woman, was infinitely happier to find that she was in company of the living instead of the dead.

"Oh Lord, deliver us !" said the old woman. "What we are born to, we don't know. The idea, now, of a murder being done here, when we least of all expected it ! Oh, dear me, I almost feel as if somebody was cutting my throat, and I do feel just as if cold water, fresh from some pump, was being poured down my back."

"It is very sad," said Fanny.

"Yes, at my age it is," said the old woman, mistaking Fanny's sympathy for her aunt for sympathy in her symptoms and feelings ; "it is very sad, sure enough, you may well say, and that's a fact ; for what with one thing and an-other I haven't much peace : and Mr. Davidson, although you wouldn't think it to look at him, is a very troublesome man."

"Indeed !" said Fanny, and she spoke rather mechanically, than from any real reflection upon what was being said to her.

"Yes, you would hardly believe it, but he expects his coffee at eight in the morning, and you can imagine what a nuisance that is when I don't want mine till nine ; but, however, as I've been with him now twelve years, I don't like to give him up."

How strangely in this world people deceive themselves ! The old woman had, unconsciously, stated the very reason why Mr. Davidson did not like to give her up, namely, because she had been with him so long, and she fancied that she was doing him a favour by remaining with him.

But this self-delusion is extremely common ; indeed, there are very many per-sons who practise it unconsciously, and are not at all aware of it.

We knew once an old man, who had been in a large wholesale house of business in the city for nearly thirty years, at a small salary ; but he fancied at last that he was the whole and sole prop of the business, and that they could not go on with-out him, so that when, one day, he was called into the private room, and one of the partners said to him, with great kindness—

"Mr. Grover, you have been with us now so long, that we consider you en-titled to repose for the remainder of your existence, and without any reference to whether you have saved any money or not, we intend to give you the same salary you have always had and dispense with your services," he was so astonished and shocked at the firm thinking of doing without him, that he took to his bed, and died in three days.

Fanny made her toilette as quickly as she could, and, casting a look of shud-dering horror at the room in which lay the lifeless remains of her aunt, she left Vine cottage, as it was called, she hoped, never again to set foot across its ill-omened and sad threshold.

"Ah, it's very sad—very sad indeed !" said the old housekeeper ; " was she an elderly person ?"

"Yes, my poor aunt was about sixty."

"Indeed !   Quite in the prime of life too—what a sad thing !"

"Prime of life ?" said Fanny.

"Yes, to be sure," said the old woman rather tartly; "look at me, and I am seventy-one !"

Fanny saw in a moment what it was that made her aunt young, or in her prime, in the estimation of the old housekeeper, and she forbore to say more upon a point which it was in vain to argue with her, even if Fanny had been in the frame of mind to have done so, which Heaven knows she was not.

She was grateful for the shelter which Mr. Davidson's house afforded to her, and although, now and then, a thought of what was to become of her did cross her mind, she was glad to dismiss it, if she could, with a shudder, for how dark and drear did the future now to her appear!

What was to become of her?   If even the thieves at the cottage had not carried away the most valuable portion of the property which Mrs. Paddlebat's foresight had brought from the house in town, for how short a time would it support her! and she felt that, without her aunt to manage such slender resources, she should soon see the end of them.   But she had still to learn that all that was left to her to subsist upon consisted of a few half-worn-out dresses belonging to her aunt, and the sum which the sale of her own wardrobe would produce.

The morning now was breaking—that morning which she hoped to have welcomed from the garden of that little cottage which was now such a ruin, and she fell into a shudder which forced itself upon her, for the small amount of sleep she had had before the alarm at the cottage was not near sufficient to recruit her exhausted energies.

What a great and wonderful change the last few months had wrought upon the position and prospects of Fanny!   When we look back to that happy time when she was an inmate of her uncle's house, and when the good old goldsmith was day by day loading her with caresses, and with every mark of kindness he could show to her, and contrast that blissful state with her present position, alone and dependent upon strangers, we cannot but feel that Fate has dealt harshly with one to whom we would have wished the happiest destiny.

But although the grave cannot be made to give up its dead, and although we cannot hope that Fanny shall ever again know the happiness she has known, we do hope that serenity will be hers, if nothing else; and that in time to come there will be no more rude shocks of misfortune to approach her.

And yet what a sad and poor consolation it is to be able only to say no misfortune of magnitude is to be dreaded because every one of that character has happened!

And yet, such is the only consolation which Fanny can feel at the present time.   There was no living being now in whose fate she felt that abundant interest that could give her such heart pangs as she had endured; for although she had had as many of the purest and best affections of humanity as any one was ever blessed with, death had snatched them all from her now.

First her mother had been taken from her, in the wilds of that country (America) whose wilds are far preferable to the thousand and one bad qualities of those who call themselves its civilised inhabitants.

Then the next person she had taken completely to her heart—her poor old uncle; he had gone the way of all humanity, whether it be loved or not.

And then, oh, severest stroke of fate! the being to whom she had pledged her best affections, and in whose good keeping she had placed the happiness of her life, he too had been torn from her by the ruthless destroyer. Yes, Horace Arrowdale—the noble—the high-spirited—the gifted Horace—he, too, was no more.   And lastly, the sole surviving link that made up the chain of her earthly connexions was snapped asunder by the sudden and violent death of her aunt.   No wonder that to the excited imagination of Fanny there seemed to be something fatal in the mere fact of a connexion with her.

" We can only hope for better days for thee, Fanny, and that they may come quickly too."

CHAPTER LXXXVII.

THE PURSUIT FOR THE MURDERER AND THE WOUNDED PATROL.—THE HUE AND CRY.

WE left the patrol pursuing the supposed murderer on the London road, and as there cannot be any reasonable doubt but that this really was the man who had given her death-wound to Mrs. Paddlebat, we feel some degree of interest in following his proceedings in the chace.

If the man continued upon the high road he considered that he had a very fair chance indeed of capturing him, but that he would do so seemed a very doubtful proposition indeed, and one that involved a great number of considerations.

In the first place, having once met the patrol, he was likely enough to suppose that his danger would be increased by the knowledge which that conservator of the peace would have of his personal appearance.

And then again, of course, putting out of sight every other consideration, it was likely enough that such an individual would find his best safety in by-ways rather than in highways.

But at all events, whether the chances of his capture were great or small, he (the patrol) was determined to make the attempt, come of it what would, and putting his horse nearly to its full speed he went at a good pace down the road.

Knowing well as he did almost everybody and certainly every house for some miles, he frequently drew rein to make an inquiry as regarded any one having seen such a man as he described, and in some instances he got vague and unsatisfactory answers; but when he did get a direct and conclusive answer it was most decidedly in the affirmative.

In two cases in particular he was assured that such a man had passed, and at one public-house where he made the inquiry he was told that a man answering the description had hammered at the door before they were up, and had demanded some refreshment.

"Ah, to be sure!" said the landlord, "he was a biggish lantern-jawed looking fellow. I held quite a talk with him from the window of my bed-room."

"Indeed! and what did he say?"

"Why, he wanted to make out, as he was a traveller, I was bound to get up and serve him with what he wanted, whether it was in my regular hours or not."

"But you did not?"

"I should think not!"

"Well, I only wish you had, and that you had kept him here till I came up, for he has committed a most atrocious and dreadful murder."

"A murder—a murder—a mur—you don't mean that now. Come, you are joking, that's what you are. You are nothing but joking; you know you are. Don't tell me about murder. Why, we haven't had a murder down in these parts Heaven knows when. Come, Mr. Patrol, it's a sell now, is it not?"

"I wish it was, and it would be something for me if I could take him, I can tell you, so I'm off again. I thank you for your news, for it lets me go on now with a better heart than I did before, because it makes me think I am on the right scent after all."

"That you are if you follow your nose—and it's quite long enough," added the landlord to himself, "for you to see it half a mile off I should say."

The patrol did not hear this last most ungracious remark upon the most prominent feature in his face, or he might even, despite his hurry, have been prompted to make some reply to it; but he rode on, much more intent upon effecting the capture of the murderer than anything else, for he felt a sort of *esprit de corps* in the business.

"If I could but catch him now," he said—"if I could but catch a murderer, I should be somebody. It aint every day in the week that a good out-and-out murder like this is committed on a fellow's beat, and when it is it's a great shame if anybody else catches the criminal."

There can be no doubt but that among the police there is some feeling of injury if a malefactor commit a crime in one district and get apprehended in another; and we cannot help thinking that it's a very wrong thing indeed, when a murderer, now-a-days, commits a deed of blood in the district of, we will say, the A division of the great unboiled, that he should think of being taken by B or C, No. something.

Most certainly he belongs to the A division, and by them he ought to be captured.

The patrol was full of similar thoughts to these, when he saw about a quarter of a mile, a-head of him, just in the dim morning light, a man walking along very fast.

The idea that it might be the man he sought was too delightful to be let slip, and, immediately clapping spurs to his horse, he galloped onwards. Scarcely, however, had he got a hundred yards on, when the man glanced round in consequence, no doubt, of hearing the sound of a horse's feet, and then, with great precipitation, he burst through a hedge that was close at hand, and got into some open fields lying between Hammersmith and the western road.

This proceeding on the part of the man at once confirmed his suspicions, although he was not near enough to obtain a sufficiently clear sight of him to be assured he was the same man whom he had stopped on the road before.

He at once turned his horse towards the hedge, but the animal refused the leap, and perhaps it was just as well for his rider's neck that he did so.

After this he had no resource but at once to dismount, and break away—which he did with his sabre—sufficient of the hedge for the horse to get through, and then, mounting him again, he was in full pursuit, for he saw the man skulking along under a hedge.

The patrol's object, however, was to get as near to him as he could, without the man thinking he was observed; so he did not ride close up to him, but kept his eye upon him, and turned the horse's head somewhat to the left, a proceeding which, while it brought him laterally nearly down upon the man, no doubt gave the latter an idea that he was fortunate enough to be not observed.

This *ruse* succeeded; but when the patrol seemed to be upon the very point of trotting past the enclosure close to which the fellow lay crouching, he suddenly turned his horse's head, and cantered right towards him.

This proceeding must have opened the eyes of the murderer, if it were indeed he, in a moment; but, strange to say, it seemed to have no effect upon him, for he did not move from his partial covert.

A few minutes sufficed to bring the patrol quite close to him, and then it was evident why he had not moved, for there was the sharp report of a well-loaded rifle pistol, and in another moment the patrol dropped from his saddle.

The ruffian now sprang forward and rushed up to the wounded man, whose sabre he drew from its sheath, and, with all his force, dealt him several slashing cuts as he lay prostrate.

Deep groans were the only responses of the patrol to the savage and seemingly needless attack; and then the ruffian, casting the sabre on one side, tried to mount the horse, but the animal was frightened and swerved, so that, after several fruitless attempts, he was forced to give up doing so, and again he set off at full speed across the meadow towards Hammersmith; but a retribution awaited him sooner than he expected.

It so happened that a party of gentlemen (five in number) had arranged with each other to go out shooting on that particular morning, and they had met at the house of one of their number, and had just sallied out, and stood on the brow of a hill which commanded a very extensive view of this chace in the meadows between the patrol and the man whom he was so anxious to capture.

They were much too far off to interfere, but they were by no means too far off to see the whole transaction just as we have described it to the reader.

They saw the man hiding, and they saw that, as they at the time thought, the patrol overlooked him. But when the horse was so suddenly wheeled round, they gave the officer full credit for the skill he displayed in manœuvring to catch his prisoner.

But when the shot was fired, and they saw the patrol fall, the affair assumed a much more serious aspect than it had before, but still it was nothing of a nature much to arouse the passions of men until they observed that dastardly attack with the cutlass which was made upon a wounded, if not a dying, man.

The sight of that, however, did rouse them and, being all young men, they resolved upon the punishment, as well as the capture, of the fellow who had committed such an atrocity.

One of their number ran back to the house to get assistance for the wounded patrol, and the remainder of them, with their guns loaded, went by a circuitous route along the meadows, which they were pretty certain would bring them face to face with the criminal.

Gradually they neared him, and he seeing merely a party of gentlemen out shooting, and never suspecting that they would interfere with him, thought it certainly safest to take no notice of them, and, at all events, not to appear anxious to get out of their way, as such a course would at once excite suspicion.

When they neared him closer still, they straggled about as if searching the bushes for small game, so that at last, in one way or another, he was tolerably surrounded, and then, but not till then, a sort of suspicion came over him that all was not right.

The moment this disagreeable suspicion did arise, he made an effort to escape; but, as he did so, one of the young men called out in a loud voice,—

"Here's game!" and at the same moment he discharged his fowling-piece about the fellow's legs.

He raised a shout of pain and turned round, which gave another an opportunity of giving him a taste of the contents of his gun, and that nearly doubled him up with agony.

They kept him at this game completely at bay, until they had each given him a taste of a good charge of small shot, which, although it would not kill him, would give him a most intolerable amount of annoyance.

Then they walked up to him, and one of them said,—

"Now, my friend, if by any nice quibble of the law you should get off for your dastardly attack upon the man you have already disabled, you will, I think, not be able to congratulate yourself upon this day's work."

"I'm a murdered man!" he groaned; "I'm a murdered man!"

"Oh dear no! Such fellows as you take a deal of killing, and I live in hopes that you will come comfortably to the gallows yet, when all the small shot are picked out of you."

"I can't move—oh! I can't move."

"Very good: you can be carried then to Hammersmith, as soon as we can see some field labourers who don't mind the job; and then we shall give you in charge for murder."

"I haven't done anything. Let me go!"

"Oh, no; besides, if you have done nothing, we have, and you know we must answer to you for giving you a shot apiece, which I hope will do you good."

"Oh, gentlemen," he whined, "I'll say nothing about the shots. You have had your joke. I'm a poor fellow, gentlemen, and won't say nothing about them, if you'll only let me go."

"Oh dear no."

"Oh no," cried another, "we couldn't think of doing you such an injustice; and see, Miller, there are some men going to work somewhere. I dare say for a shilling each they will carry the fellow to the watch-house."

"Damn you all!" cried the discomfited ruffian; "if I had a knife, and was not hurt, I'd put it into some of your insides before you were a minute older."

"So, you are now coming out in your true colours."

The labourers who had been observed trudging along the fields were called to, and they readily undertook to convey the prisoner to the town of Hammersmith, which was not now above half or three-quarters of a mile from the spot on which this fracas had taken place.

Resistance on his part was out of the question, but he muttered—

"You won't hear the last of this job. You had no occasion to shoot me, and I'll trounce you all for it yet."

"We have a very fair excuse," said he who was the spokesman of the party, "for firing at you. We saw you fire at the patrol; and not only that, but attack him afterwards, in a manner which showed the brutal ferocity of your disposition : and so, for all we knew to the contrary, you might have other arms concealed."

" Curse you all ! "

" Oh, you will find, I rather think, your curses, like a great many other people's, will go home to roost. Take him along, my men, take him along, we will follow and charge him."

A rude sort of litter was promptly made by the labourers with hedge-stakes, and on it the man was conveyed into the town, where, at that early hour, but few persons were stirring.

They took him direct to the watch-house, and the look of pain, mingled with the most malignant ferocity that his countenance bore, was something dreadful to see.

Several of the police were immediately sent to see after the fate of the wounded patrol, whom the gentlemen had left to the care of one of their number, and the servants of the house, and who they thought, from the savage manner in which he had been attacked with the cutlass, must surely be murdered, even if the pistol-shot had not struck him in some mortal part.

It is most astonishing, however, what injuries the human frame will sustain ; for although he had received the bullet in his shoulder and looked as if he had been almost cut to pieces by the sabre, he yet was sensible and could give directions for his removal.

The owner of the house in the immediate vicinity humanely afforded to him every accommodation, and a surgeon, upon being sent for, said—

" I do not think any of the wounds mortal in themselves, and if no great derangement of the constitution takes place he will get well."

This was a verdict which astonished every one who heard it, as it seemed perfectly incredible that any one could survive so many injuries, and apparently all of them of such a serious nature.

CHAPTER LXXXVIII.

OLD GILBERT TRIES IN VAIN TO FIND A PERFECTLY SECURE INVESTMENT.

Old Gilbert Paddlebat, failing to induce Nicholas Lowe to join him in any nefarious transactions, seemed very much to annoy him.

By some means or another he seemed to have quite calculated upon Nicholas Lowe's willingness to take part in anything, provided it could be shown that money was to be made by it. Perhaps knowing that such was the ordinary course of things as regarded human nature generally, he could hardly make up his mind that it would be any way different as regarded any individual.

It was the sort of acquaintance, and the sort of mutual confidence that had so strangely sprung up between them, was quite of a nature to encourage the old man in such a belief : a belief, however, which it was seen the event was very far from in the smallest degree verifying.

We are no admirers of Nicholas Lowe ; for, although we willingly admit his to be a strangely mixed character of good and of evil, we much fear that the latter has an alarming preponderance over the former.

Certainly there was in his disposition a strange laxity of principle, which seemed very inconsistent with some of his better actions ; but let him, who fancies that he has been sufficiently long a student of human nature, think that he knows something of the complex movements of the human heart, and he will soon find how much he is mistaken, and how completely what really happens will baffle all experience of what has happened.

But to return to old Gilbert, with whom we have at present some concern.

When he found that Lowe would have nothing to do with his schemes for money-making, and when he became convinced that it was not that scheme in particular, but all schemes of such a nature, that he objected to, the old man began to look out for some other mode of investment.

It was truly astonishing that merging, as old Gilbert Paddlebat now was, upon an age which he could not hope much to surpass, he was dreadfully dissatisfied with the amount of interest that his money brought him in ; and thought, although he did not spend one-twentieth part of that amount of income, still it behoved him to seek for some more profitable mode of investment for his cash.

He was not active enough to continue to carry on the same business of money-lending that he had been in so long, and which, with the arts he had brought to bear upon it, he had found to be so abundantly profitable ; so he would be content, he told himself, with a smaller per centage than that brought him ; although the idea of putting up with the proceeds of the public funds was too preposterous to his mind.

While these cogitations and thoughts were going through his mind, a circumstance happened, however, which nearly turned the old man's brain completely.

He had placed merely for temporary security a sum of eighteen thousand pounds in the hands of a banker, who after several interviews had promsed three pounds per cent. upon the amount, if it were undrawn for twelve months certain ; all of which old Gilbert fully promised, and fully intended to perform.

Now, it was the custom of the old man to shuffle out towards the dusk of the evening, and take himself to a neighbouring public-house, into the parlour of which he would sneak, not to order anything—the idea of Gilbert Paddlebat ordering anything in a public-house ;!—but to look at the papers.

How he managed was this—it was a house of good business, and there were two or three waiters continually running in and out of the rooms, so that old Gilbert used to watch until some one was done with a glass of mixed liquor ; and then, when none of the waiters were at hand, he would draw the empty glass towards him, and from one of the water decanters, of which there were two upon each table, he would fill up the glass, and if there was a slice of lemon in it, why, the delusion was all the more perfect.

When a troublesome waiter, then, who perhaps had seen him come in, and marked him for his particular customer, came up to him with a " What would you please to order, sir ?" he would find old Gilbert, to all appearance, provided with a glass of gin and water, and wondered how he had got served so quickly.

Then the stolid look with which the old man would regard him completed the delusion.

Now, one would have thought there would be some little difficulty in getting out without paying something, but there was none in the world, for the waiters had a great jealousy of interference with their separate customers, and could not on any account put up with such a thing from each other ; so if in his progress out old Gilbert were to encounter each of the waiters in turn, each knew that he had not served the old man with anything, and out he marched, therefore, completely unmolested.

By this means was it, therefore, that he got a look at the City articles of all the morning papers, and acquired, without it costing him one penny piece, an accurate notion of what was going on in the commercial world.

This ingenious scheme—for it really was ingenious—lasted for a considerable time, until one evening that old Gilbert went in as usual, a circumstance occurred that rather spoilt it for the future. That circumstance was just as follows :—

He thought himself in amazing luck, because some one who was sipping brandy and water in the same box with him left the place, leaving at the same time about a spoonful of brandy and water at the bottom of the glass, so that when old Gilbert filled it up with water it looked for all the world like a glass of sherry and water.

Full of the idea that he had done the thing nicely on that occasion, he boldly seized a newspaper, and commenced reading the commercial intelligence.

What was his horror, however, to find, under the head of ' City News,' the following to him most terrifying paragraph :—

" 'The failure of Messrs. Mugsley, Dobbs, Phelps, and Underwood, the bankers, has created a great sensation ; and if it be true that parties have recently paid in large sums to that establishment, it falls very hard upon them.''

The paper dropped from old Gilbert's hands, and he uttered a groan that disturbed the whole room, for that was the very firm with which he had deposited the whole of the eighteen thousand pounds for which he was to get three per cent., and which of itself ought to have been a suspicious circumstance.

Several people thought the old man was dying, and the waiters were summoned.

Such, then, was the horrid cadaverous look of old Gilbert, that a medical man was sent for, who came at the top of his speed, but when he arrived he could not tell very well what was the matter.

" I think," he said, "if the old man was to take some stimulant it would be as well."

" He's drinking something, sir," said one of the waiters, as he glanced at the cunningly-manufactured glass of nothing which was before old Gilbert.

" What is it ?"

" Why I—I should say it was sherry and water."

" Indeed ! that could not disagree with him.   Let me see it."

The medical man tasted it again and again, and then he said,—

" If this is the sherry and water you give people, you certainly must get the most good-tempered customers, or the most ignorant, that London can send you. Taste it."

The landlord, who had by this time made his appearance, tasted the compound, and made a wry face as he said,—

" Who served this old gentleman ?"

The waiters one by one repudiated having anything to do with it; and the thing remained a mystery until a young man came forward from one of the boxes and said,—

" I think I can explain about the supposed sherry and water.   I have been a frequenter of this house for some time, and have often noticed this old man come into the room ; there was something about his appearance that irresistibly attracted my curiosity, and I watched him on several occasions.   He never orders anything."

" Not order anything ?"

" Never ; he merely comes to read the papers."

" Indeed ! but how came he by this glass of something or another before him ? "

" He waits until some one goes out, and leaves a glass, with a drain of something or another at the bottom of it, and then he fills it up from one of the water bottles."

This explanation was quite decisive, and the landlord was dreadfully indignant at such a trick being played off in his establishment.

" Hark you," he said to the waiters, "kick him out, if he comes here ever again."

" I'm going," said old Gilbert, "I'm going.   Mugsley, Dobbs, Phelps, and Underwood have stopped, and I'm going.   I'll have Mugsley's heart's-blood, and I'll be the death too of Dobbs.   I—I'm a going—£18,000,   Oh dear !—oh dear ! the interest, at 3 per cent. on £360,000.   Oh, dear !—oh, dear !   I'm going."

" He's out of his mind, I think," said the surgeon.   " It would be cruel to touch him.   When he comes, if he should again, just get him out as quietly as you can, but I caution you against using any violence towards him."

The surgeon really thought what he said ; for no one, to look at old Gilbert Paddlebat, would imagine that he had eighteen thousand pence in the world, or perhaps they would have guessed the eighteen pence without the thousand at all, to be nearer the mark ; and yet, unless there were some men of great substance in that room, which was not very likely, he could have bought up every one of them.

This was, indeed, a terrible blow to old Gilbert, and no doubt it tended very much to unsettle his mind, for when he went home he trotted about the house like a man walking in his sleep, and seemed quite mentally stunned by the, to him, most horrible piece of intelligence he had received.   And it was not in the *Times* that he had read it, so he could not lay, even for that night, the flattering unction to his soul that it was not true.   He took what money he had in his possession, and hid it in old odd corners, as if he thought that it was necessary to do so at once, for fear of further losses, and when, at length, quite exhausted, he lay down to repose, he muttered to himself—

"If—if now I could have persuaded Nicholas Lowe to die five times or so, all would have been well, and I should make up this large amount again, but he won't do it—he won't do it, and I don't know who else I can depend upon."

Alas! that insatiable avarice should take such a hold of its victims as it had done of old Gilbert. What had his gold done for him, but produce for him an amount of misery that deprived him, and had deprived him for a long time past, of the luxury of a night's rest, for he never failed, about the middle of the night, to wake up in a fright! Sometimes, with a loud scream, he would start awake from some frightful dream, and springing to his feet, utter some incoherent words of terror, before he really knew where he was. Then, when he found it was but a vision of his slumbers, he would lapse into a fit of trembling, which would last him some hours, and perhaps until the daylight was dawning he would not again close his eyes in sleep.

This was a horrible state of existence—it was a state of existence which he knew well he had endured for a long time past, and he knew well, likewise, that the cause of it was that he loved gold too much, but yet he clung to his destroyer—yet he clung to that dear possession, which has the peculiarity of being valueless only so long as it is kept, and which to him was utterly and entirely useless, and, so far as the purposes of money were concerned, he might as well have made for himself any number of little pieces of tin to jingle together, which would have answered his purpose, or ought to have answered his purpose, just as well as the little pieces of gold by which he set such amazing store.

But such is the miser's grand mistake. There can be no doubt but that he commences his career with a high appreciation of what money will produce in a country like this ; there can be no doubt but that he in the first instance discovers (and it takes no wonderful amount of discernment to make the discovery) that it is the idol to which all men bow down. He finds that money confers every cardinal virtue under heaven upon any man ; that the silly, the selfish, the brutal, and the lowest of the low, if he have but money, is fawned upon, and flattered, and invested with every virtue by those who have it not, but who hope to get something from the golden calf. No doubt, we say, that this is the first impression of the miser. He thinks that he will make present sacrifices to place himself ultimately in such a glorious position. Perhaps he is one who has felt

> ' The proud man's contumely,'

and is willing and anxious to pay him off in kind, so he begins to amass money, and the wish to do so grows upon him until it becomes a second nature, and until he begins to love the bright and glittering mass, which he knows will purchase the very souls of men.

Thus he loses sight of his first intentions. Old age creeps upon him, and he becomes content to posess a power which he never now dreams of using, any more than Mr. Warner, from his house in the Hampstead-road, thinks of knocking down Camden-town with his powerful projectiles, or giving the dome of St. Paul's a dig with the invisile shell at a long range. Such, we make no doubt, is the miser's true career, until, from an ardent desire to live the master of money and all that it can produce, he dies its most abject and wretched slave.

That this was the case of old Gilbert Paddlebat, is, indeed, enough from the whole tenor of his life, and yet we shall see how strangely the intellect becomes warped by this most unholy passion ; for old Gilbert would have been just as much vexed at the loss of £18 as he was at the loss of £18,000. It was not the amount, but it was the loss of money, that plagued him.

CHAPTER LXXXIX.

RETURNS TO FANNY AT THE HOUSE OF MR. DAVIDSON.

When Fanny awoke from the sleep into which she had fallen at the house of Mr. Davidson, who had so kindly offered her an asylum, she, for some moments, could hardly believe it possible that such startling and dreadful events, as the last night had witnessed, could have really occurred ; but the strange place in which she found herself afforded to her proof positive which could not be gainsayed.

She was in a handsome bed-room, and she had not been many minutes awake when the old housekeeper made her appearance, and said, with a toss of her head and an air of arrogance, " It seems that I am to assist you to rise, and to ask you when you will breakfast, and what you will please to have?"

"Anything," said Fanny, "anything. Pray make my best acknowledgments to Mr. Davidson, and tell him how much indebted to him I am for this great kindness, in affording me a shelter on such an occasion."

"Oh, I dare say; you can do that yourself."

"If you are not disposed," civilly said Fanny, "to do your master's bidding, you had better say so at once, and I can dispense with your services with great ease, as I am well accustomed to attend upon myself."

"Very good, I shall please myself; and all I can say is, if he don't mind I'll leave him at once, and then I wonder what would become of him! Ah, I don't suppose he thinks of that."

Fanny could perceive that the old woman was most sadly put out of her way at the amount of courtesy which Mr. Davidson chose to pay her, but as she did not intend to trespass upon him long, she considered that there would soon be an end of any hard soreness on that point with the housekeeper.

"Heaven forbid," she said to herself, "that I should be the cause of any domstic discomfort anywhere, and I will leave here in the course of the day, although what is to become of me now is more than I can divine, or dare to think."

She dressed herself rapidly: in the happiest and best of times Fanny was never one who devoted much time to the cares of the toilet—and when she had completed her simple attire she went softly down stairs, for she had no one to guide her to any particular room; and she, under the circumstances, naturally felt loth to ring the bell in another person's house.

There was a door nearly close to the bottom of the stairs, which, being partially open, enabled her to see into a handsome apartment, in which were such evident preparations for the morning meal that Fanny entered it once, concluding that it was the breakfast-room.

She found she was quite right, for not only was a good and substantial breakfast laid, but Mr. Davidson was there himself, ready to do the honours of the morning repast.

He rose at her entrance, and handed her a chair, saying, "I hope that you have passed a more quiet night than you expected, and I trust, Mrs. A—A—."

"Arrowdale," said Fanny, observing that he hesitated for want of her name.

"Arrowdale—I beg your pardon, Mrs. Arrowdale; I was going to say that I hope my housekeeper has paid you every attenton."

"Oh, yes, yes," said Fanny.

This was not strictly true, but if it was a little perversion, it would have been very odd and ungracious of Fanny to have commenced the morning with a complaint of any of the establishment, so she could not think of so doing, although the old housekeeper had been far more insolent than otherwise. As for Mr. Davidson, the thought it was all right, and, as he sat down to the table, he said, "I cannot think of attempting to preside here when a lady is present."

"Nay," said Fanny, as her eyes filled with tears, "excuse me, sir; my heart is too surcharged with grief, and my mind is altogether too full of consternations at late events, for me to think of even the most ordinary civilities of life. Pray excuse me; and for the few short hours I shall be your guest, excuse likewise any seeming rudeness."

"Don't say a word about that," said Mr. Davidson, "but just do as you like, and as if the house was your own, you know. Don't mind me, or anybody else here, and don't fancy that I shall think you otherwise than—than—"

Mr. Davidson evidently wanted to perpetrate some compliment, but he upset a cup of coffee instead, which, however, did just as well, so far as Fanny was concerned.

"You see," he added, "what a dreadful blunderer I am!"

At this moment the housekeeper, without the least ceremony, entered the apartment. She looked rather furious, and when she suddenly came up to the breakfast-table and gave it a blow with her fist, both Mr. Davidson and Fanny thought that really she must have gone suddenly out of her senses.

"Mr. D." she said, "attend to me, sir."

"Well, Mrs. Green, what is it?"

"I give you a month's notice, sir. Oh, dear me, you are very comfortable, I dare say; amazingly comfortable, I have no doubt. Mr. D.—Oh, dear!—Yes, of course, sir—of course."

"What are you talking about?"

"What am I talking about, you wretch? You know well enough. But there's no fool like an old fool."

"Well," said Mr. Davidson, "I must say that if I had any doubt before about the truth of that saying you would settle such a doubt by proving that, in your own person, there was no fool like an old fool; and, as you have come here to give me notice to quit, I can only say that I gladly accept such notice, and desire that you immediately leave this apartment."

"You accept it?"

"Most certainly; and what is more, I shall insist upon its being carried out to the very letter. Go you shall; and I can tell you, that had it not been for your age and the many years you have been with me, I should, myself, have given you that notice long ago, for you are utterly useless; but when you come to add insolence to uselessness, I have no hesitation in getting rid of you at once and for ever."

Mrs. Green looked petrified, as well she might, and for a moment or two seemed as if she were half inclined to box her master's ears, for having the intolerable presumption to say so much to her; but if such an idea did cross her mind, she gave it up, and with what she considered a withering laugh, she said,—

"I shall leave you with contempt."

"You will, indeed," said Mr. Davidson, "for your great insolence can be called by no other term, and if you don't go soon I shall call Joe, who, I suppose, is feeding the pigs, to turn you out."

The only reply of Mrs. Green to this was to snatch up a plateful of hot muffins, and throw them at her master's head, about which they fell in a copious shower, to his great astonishment and the alarm of Fanny.

After this devilish act of personal hostility she left the room, and Mr. Davidson with a look of great vexation said,—

"You see, Mrs. Arrowdale, that is the consequence of having a pampered domestic too many years in one's service. But now my eyes are opened. Pray be seated, there is no cause for alarm."

Fanny seated herself again, but she could not possibly help feeling that all this noise and tumult in the house was occasioned by her presence, which somehow gave great umbrage to the housekeeper.

There certainly is a wonderful similarity between old women and cats; they are always either positively troublesome in their affections, or they give you a scratch when you least expect it; and another peculiarity which they show with the feline race is a decided antipathy to any other woman coming upon their premises.

Thus, like some old mouser who has been in a family a long time, and suddenly sees a strange cat comfortably reposing upon the hearthrug, did Mrs. Green put up her back and spread her claws when she saw Fanny was seated at breakfast with Mr. Davidson.

This little tumult being over, the breakfast was finished in peace, and then Fanny said with faltering tones,—

"Sir, I have to thank you for your great hospitality to me, a comparative stranger to you; I shall always entertain the liveliest sense of such kindness, and will no longer intrude upon you."

"It is no intrusion, Mrs. Arrowdale; do not call an intrusion the fact of your doing me the favour of your paying me this visit."

"You are very kind, sir, to call it a favour, but the obligation is great, and all the other way."

"But—but perhaps you will think me rude when I ask you if you have any friends to go to?"

Fanny was silent for a moment, and then she said in a voice of deep emotion,—

"I have not one in the world of which death has not now robbed me; but I ought not to trouble you, sir, with my misfortunes; you are entitled to my warmest thanks."

"Madam," said Mr. Davidson, in a voice which showed that he deeply felt what he said, "Madam, I do hope that you will not allow yourself to be able to say that you have no friend living while I live and am able to be of assistance to you. It is true that I have seen but little of you, but then there are some persons concerning whom if we see them but once, we have more fixed and certain opinions than we have of others whom we know for years. Let us hope that I may be permitted to fill the place of some of those friends of whom death has deprived you."

"You are too—too kind," said Fanny, as the tears, despite all her exertions to restrain them, burst forth.

"No!" exclaimed Mr. Davidson, "hear me, madam, and do not suppose that I speak from any sudden impulse, but from the most deliberate convictions."

Fanny began to have quite a terrible idea of what was coming, and it gave her the greatest uneasiness to think that such was the case; but she dare not say anything, for the idea of anticipating what after all might not be the case, was too hazardous, so she felt herself compelled to let Mr. Davidson go on.

"Do not, I say," he added, "mistake me, and suppose that what I now say to you, I say because I am at the moment gazing upon charms which never before met my eyes. I have lived a life of loneliness and solitude now for many years. I have been married, but she whom I loved was snatched from me by death."

He paused for a moment, as if the memory of the past came crowding upon him too painfully and rapidly, to allow him to speak; and during that pause, Fanny would fain have said something, but it was over, and the opportunity was passed before she could frame the necessary words in which to clothe her sentiments, and Mr. Davidson resumed.

"I throw myself and my fortune, and all I possess at your feet. I offer you a hand and a heart which will be devoted for ever to your happiness. If you think you can accept of such an asylum, I beg of you to do so; but if your feelings prompt you with doubt or hesitation whether to reject what I offer you, I hope still that you will allow me to consider myself, and to show myself your friend.

An offer so nobly and so generously put, as this was, certainly deserved as kind and candid an answer as could be returned to it, and after a pause, to command her feelings, Fanny replied—

"Sir, you have made me so entirely unlooked for, and so kind a proposition, that, banishing all that malignity and reserve which the fashion of the world puts on on such occasions, I tell you frankly that I respect you, but must say no to any proposition which places you in any other situation than that of a dear friend to me."

"It is enough," said Mr. Davidson, with a sigh, "it is enough; and now let me assure you, Mrs. Arrowdale, that you need fear no persecution from me, for never again shall one word upon this subject pass my lips."

"You are as generous, sir, as you can be," said Fanny; "and if I had not suffered so much already, that I am resolved not again to go to my melancholy destiny with that of another, there is no one to whom I could turn with greater confidence than to yourself. Pray, sir, accept of my best and warmest thanks."

"I ought to thank you, and do with all my heart, for tempering a refusal, so that you have deprived it of its greatest pang; you have rejected me, but you have not done so contemptuously."

"That, sir, would be impossible."

"Then, in token of our amity, and of the fact that you do accord to me your friendship, will you allow me to shake hands with you?"

"Most willingly."

Fanny, as she spoke, placed her small hand in that of Mr. Davidson, with all that natural grace which belonged to her; but, before another word could be spoken, bang—crash, went a pane of glass in the window which opened upon a garden, and Mrs. Green's head appeared at the opening.

"I knew it," she said, "I knew it! Oh! you hoary-headed old sinner—I knew it! You are going to marry her. I couldn't hear what you said, but I knew by the look of you, you old reprobate, that you were offering her your hand; and she has just given you hers of course, because she knows you are well off. But you'll live to regret it, you—you old——"

"Mrs. Green, I shall have to get a policeman to you," said Mr. Davidson; "and, as for the square of glass you have broken, I shall of course deduct that from your wages."

Fanny was much annoyed at this false imputation which the maddened jealousy of the old woman had placed upon a most innocent action, and she sat down upon the nearest chair looking much disturbed.

"Oh, you hussey!" screamed Mrs. Green, growing quite hoarse with rage, and breaking another pane of glass with her fist; "oh, you hussey! I only wish I'd known of this before, and I'd soon have put a stop to your goings on; it's all a plan, and the two of you arranged it between you, that one of you was to be murdered, and the other was to get into this house. Oh! it's as clear as——"

What it was as clear as, nobody ever knew, for something upon which Mrs. Green had been standing gave way at this moment, and sent her sprawling among a bed of flowers, with her face into a complete bush of soft nettles, that began to attack her in all directions.

Her shouts brought Joe, the man of all-work, to her assistance, and he lifted her up, exclaiming,—

"Why, missus, what be the matter? Be thee taken with a *plexy?*"

"Take that," said Mrs. Green, and she gave Joe, for his kindness, a swinging box on the ear, that sent him off again at a good pace.

But Mr. Davidson saw something of all this from the window, and he was determined that such a volcano as Mrs. Green should be no longer upon his premises, so he called out loudly,—

"Joe, Joe!"

"Yes, master."

"Go and fetch me a constable directly—I won't have this mad old woman making confusion in my house and gardens—I'm used to a quiet life, and I won't put up with it."

"Yes, sir—all right, sir—right-fol-ol-di-idity, old mother Green's a-going, shan't I have a night of it at the Blue Pig and Snuffer Stand. Rifum-tifum-tifum-tidy-idy-high-gee-woa!"

What further collection of extraordinary sounds Joe would have made, expressive of his delight at the probable absence of Mrs. Green from the premises, were cut short by his jumping over a fence, instead of going round some distance to the gate, for he was enormously eager to obey his master's orders, lest he should retract them before he, Joe, could get a constable.

Mrs. Green probably now saw that her fate was fixed, and that she had already gone too far for a compromise; so she disdained even the attempt to make one, and walked with as much dignity as she could assume, jerking her head so as she went, that the maid of all-work, who was quite as much rejoiced at her going as Joe could be, wondered she did not jerk it off.

But then there was a sort of a kind of an understanding between Joe and this maid of all-work which is no business of ours, so we will say nothing further about it for the present.

Fanny, if she had not been so kind-hearted and too much occupied with her own thoughts to think about such a matter, ought to have felt, that, in being the accidental means of ridding Mr. Davidson of such an annoyance as Mrs. Green, she had done that gentleman, at all events, some service. He, however, thought so if she did not.

"I hope," he said, "that, notwithstanding all that has occurred, you will not think of leaving here."

"Ought I," she said, "to stay after what has occurred?"

He was silent, and after a moment or two, she added,

"I put it to your own judgment, Mr. Davidson, if, situated as you are, and situated as I am, I ought to remain in your house one moment longer than is absolutely necessary to prepare for my departure?"

"You are right—you are right. But whither do you think of going?"

"To London."

"London! Alas, that is no place for one like you."

"It is only in a large city that I can hope to obtain a livelihood, and by my own exertions now I shall be compelled to do so, for the few accomplishments that are mine can only be made marketable in a city. I must endeavour to dispose of my drawings, and, perchance, I may possibly be fortunate enough to get some teaching to do in that as well as in music."

"Alas!" said Mr. Davidson, "you can have no idea how those two arts are overrun by insolent pretenders to science. You will have to contend against such mendacity as you can have no conception of, and more particularly in music; the German influence which the court of this country is so much infested with, has produced such a host of what is called, and not unfrequently miscalled foreign talent, that there is no chance for anything else."

"Still," said Fanny, "I must do the best I can, and in the midst of even the most frightful competition, make an attempt."

The utmost that Mr. Davidson could get her to do was to accept, as a loan from him, the sum of £10, and for that she would give him an acknowledgment, which she was half offended with him for throwing into the fire.

"You are too hasty," she said.

"No," he replied, "I am naturally a little suspicious, and I can assure you that a knowledge of the world has not tended in any degree to make me less so."

"And yet you trust me?"

"Because I know you."

"Because you know me! Mr. Davidson, you cannot know me. What now, if after all you are judging hastily, and not at all in accordance with your usual discernment? What, if after all I am deceiving you, and you should have to regret your generous and trusting confidence?"

"I can hear you say thus much," he replied, unmoved, "but I would not hear such words from any one else; no, Mrs. Arrowdale, if you were capable of being really other than what you seem, you would not need to appear what I know you are."

"You speak in riddles, sir, and I am too foolish to understand you."

"If you were so accomplished an actress that you could play the part of innocence and virtue so well as you have played them here, you would, long ere this, have found out that you possessed such powers, and the stage would not have been without its brightest ornament, nor you without the fortune to which your abilities would have entitled you."

"I am myself defeated," she said, "and will no longer attempt to reason with you, sir, against an opinion in my power which I sincerely hope to be able in time to justify."

Mr. Davidson at length, by great persuasion, induced her to consent to stay for that day, at all events, at his house; in fact, he told her that it would be absolutely necessary that she should be there, for that if she did not remain at his house she would have to go to an inn, for at the inquest, which must be held upon her aunt, her testimony, simple as it was, would be required.

This argument, which she could not deny the validity of, sufficed, and she consented to remain, at all events, until the evening, when she made up her mind to proceed to town.

Mr. Davidson did all in his power to spare her feelings any unnecessary pang, as regarded the investigation into the circumstances attendant upon her aunt's death, but he could not save her from an appearance at the inquest, which we need not trouble the reader further with, except just to say that it terminated in a verdict of wilful murder against the man who was in custody at Hammersmith.

Fanny then dined with Mr. Davidson, who on her behalf took possession of the boxes, which had been brought to Vine Cottage by the unfortunate Mrs. Paddlebat.

As for the plate it was not found upon the person of the thief, who was brought to the coroner's court in order that he might be identified, if possible, and it was believed by the police that he had thrown it away somewhere in the fields as he came along, and that it would be ultimately found, in which event it would be of course restored to her, Fanny.

We must not orget, however, to mention that Joe, duly returned with a constable to take away Mrs. Green from Mr. Davidson's premises, but that as she refueed to go quietly, that functionary was compelled to take her in his arms, which he did despite all her kicking and screaming, and carry her away, after which her boxes and a month's wages, more than were due up to that date, were handed out to her and she was, to the immense joy of the whole household, which joined in one chorus of condemnation of her, fairly got rid of.

In the evening Fanny, accompanied by Mr. Davidson, who would come to town with her, drove into London in his little pony-chaise, in search of some respectable, quiet, and economical lodging, where she could remain until she discovered if the resources she calculated upon would be productive or not.

CHAPTER XC.

THE FATE OF OLD GILBERT, AND THE DISCOVERY OF THE PAPER CRIMINATING LOWE.

A BRIGHTER day was, however, coming for Fanny, and not for long had she to reflect upon the means of obtaining, in the great Babel of London, a subsistence.

The affair at the tavern had completely upset the small portion of intellect which old Gilbert had left, and when he went home he could not be considered to be in his right mind and judgment. It was then that he, in his mad avarice, conceived the idea of burying his money, and commenced an excavation in the cellar of the house for that express purpose.

Our readers will find, upon turning to our first chapter of this veritable history, what was the dreadful issue of this insane plan for the preservation of his gold; the miser dug for himself a tomb, and was buried alive in it!

When the body was found it was a mass of putrefaction, and some sovereigns were found clutched tight in the long, bony fingers. An attentive search in the house discovered a number of jars, the top portions of each of which was covered with size, but below that was gold, and in one of them was a slip of paper distinctly accusing Nicholas Lowe of the murder of Rodwell, and asserting that the body was hidden somewhere in his house.

This scrap of paper was taken to the head police-office, and after much consultation it was determined to send a force of constables, at a time when they would not be expected, to make a thorough search of Lowe's house, and to take him into custody if anything suspicious should be found upon the premises.

It so happened, that at the very time Lowe had opened his heart to tell the only person he had ever admitted to his privacy the secret of his guilt, that visit was made.

The officers of justice thundered at his door while the ghastlyy remains of Rodwell were exposed to observation.

By a strange fatality he had chosen that very evening, of all others, for the purpose of unbosoming himself to one whom he thought he could call his friend, upon the awful subject which had been the bugbear of his thoughts for many a long and weary day.

Little did he suspect how near he was to that awful time towards which he had always looked with a shuddering horror, when it should be said to him, "Nicholas Lowe, you are accused of the murder of Jervis Rodwell, and his ghastly, lifeless remains come up in judgment against you."

Little did he think when, by some strange aberration of mind, he found himself inclined to make the terrific disclosures he did, that such a time was close at hand.

A madness seemed to come over him as he heard the loud demands for admission to the house, and when, at length, the door was burst open, he shouted aloud, and accused himself, in the most frightful terms, of that deed which was but a matter of question, as yet, with others.

Even the person to whom he had made the horrible disclosure had felt inclined to doubt the sanity of the man who could do so, and to think that it might be possible, he only accused himself from the suggestions of a distempered brain.

The officers of justice, although not men of the most refined sensibilities, shrank into a sort of horror, from the scene which presented itself to their observation, in the drawing-room of Lowe's house,—that costly apartment which had now been closed for so long a time, and so completely abandoned to the ghostly tenant who lay beneath its floor.

Without anything in the shape of self-accusation, the finding of that terrific spectacle would have been sufficient to bring conviction to their minds that the memorandum left by old Gilbert Paddlebat was true. Why the old man had left such a damning record of Lowe's guilt behind him it is hard to say; but probably feeling grievously offended that he, Lowe, would not join with him in the projected fraud upon the Life Assurance offices, he fully meant it as a piece of revenge, in case he, Gilbert, should die first.

And if that indeed was his motive, it certainly sufficiently succeeded; for even if Nicholas Lowe had not at that time himself, as it were, exhumed the body, the slightest examination of his house, must have found it in its very inefficient hiding-place, beneath the flooring.

Lowe, before he was removed out of the house, made an ineffectual attempt upon his own life, which was prevented by the officers, who then, upon finding the mood that he was in, took effectual means of preventing a repetition of any such design.

Perhaps it would have been merciful had he been permitted to do the deed, although certainly not in accordance with our notions of right, or at all what popular justice required of one who had taken the life of another in such a manner as he, Nicholas Lowe, had taken the life of Rodwell.

Some of the officers remained in the house with Lowe, while one of them went to the neighbouring workhouse and got a shell, in which was placed the dead body of Rodwell. The officers then got a coach, and, holding Lowe firmly, one on each side of him, they led him down the staircase of his once splendid house to the street-door, which he was now doomed to pass out at for the last time.

Oh, what must have been the thoughts of that wretched man at such a time as this! How fearful must have been the mortal retrospect that presented itself to him!

If his bewildered intellect enabled him to look back at all upon the past, what a world of heartrending, harrowing remembrances must have come over his soul at that time, when he felt that the very worst that could happen to him had come to pass, and he stood before the world in all the hideous aspect of a murderer!

Did he think of her he had deceived in early life, and who had ended her days in the cell of a madhouse? Did the recollection of that one of his deeds help to press him down? Did he think of Fanny Leslie, whom he had loved, and with whom surely he might have been happy, but that he had dipped his hands in human blood, and dared not stand at the altar's foot with her?

We can yet pity Nicholas Lowe. About him there was some good feelings, which, if they had not been overpowered by circumstances, some of which he could have no possible control over, might have blossomed into goodly fruit; but his whole life had been a great mistake—a mistake which could not be redeemed, and he felt that the time had now come when he had to pay the stake he had lost in the great game of existence.

"Come," said one of the officers, "we are ready!"

"I—I come," said Lowe, "I am ready—for death."

And so they led him out from his house,—that house in which he had once taken so great a pride, and to which he thought to have welcomed Fanny Leslie as his wife. Alas! how different a guest had he in it for a long and weary time?

Never could those who chanced to see the countenance of Nicholas Lowe as he was dragged to prison, forget the agonised and horrible expression of it. It was one of those expressions to haunt the rest, and to make the night hideous with frightful dreams. The world of concentrated agony that his face exhibited was truly horrible.

His house became an object of fearful attraction, and it was calculated that when the dead body of Jervis Rodwell was removed, which was done on the following morning, there could not have been less than five thousand persons present. An inquest was held upon the remains, and they were identified, notwithstanding the l ngth of time that had elapsed, principally by the elaborate and showy jewellery that he wore, and which, on that particular morning of all others, he had quite loaded himself with, to dazzle the eyes of Mrs. Paddlebat.

CHAPTER XCI.

THE CONCLUSION.

THUS, then, may we consider that virtually our tale is over, although no doubt our readers would fain know yet something more of the fate of the various personages who, from time to time, have figured in these pages.

There is a laudable amount of literary curiosity which a very few sentences will suffice to gratify, and we forthwith proceed to pen them.

And first let us speak of Fanny, who was now in possession of such ample wealth. She did not forget Arrowdale, but, on the contrary, cherished his image in her heart, and the recollection of his gentleness and unvarying kindness towards her was one of the saddest, as well as one of the most delightful, recurrences of her past life.

Probably few persons had less of a skeleton in their houses than Fanny Arrowdale. She went to live in the country, and took one of those chateau-like looking buildings, which are, alas! fast disappearing from the face of merry England, and thus she was for many a long year the real, and not an ostentatious, Lady Bountiful to the whole neighbourhood.

She was often pressed to marry again ; but to all proposals she gave a most decided negative, and remained single for the remainder of her life, which was lengthened out far beyond the usual limits of humanity.

Mr. Davidson often visited her, and it was through him that she employed every possible means for the purpose of defending Nicholas Lowe, who was tried and committed on the charge of murdering Jervis Rodwell.

His day of execution was fixed, and he laid down to rest on the preceding night in the condemned cell, apparently resigned, even to the dreadful fate that awaited him.

Two men, as is the custom, set up with him, but they only conversed together in low whispers, and did not wish to disturb the repose of the condemned man. Early in the morning the chaplain of Newgate paid him a visit, and desired that he should be awakened, as it really wanted but two hours to the period of his execution.

The men shook him and called upon him by name, and one of them remarked that he slept uncommonly sound. Truly he did so, for it was the long sleep of death that was upon him ! They were striving in vain to arouse a corpse !

The cause of death was a great mystery, and very many reports were in circulation upon the subject ; but it seemed probable that a heart disease, induced by long anxiety and acute mental misery, had been the real cause. Peace be to the erring Nicholas Lowe ! May you yet be happy where there is no skeleton !

And thus, then, have we followed, even to the grave, the fortunes of those individuals with whom we started in the strange eventful game of existence. W^e have, we trust, shown that avarice makes no happiness.   Witness the wretched lif^e and as wretched death of old Gilbert.

We have shown that the gratification of revenge to the utmost produces no satisfaction.   Witness the never-sleeping remorse of Nicholas Lowe, who felt himself for years compelled to reside under the same roof with the ghastly remains of the man whom he hated, and whom he had murdered.

And likewise, we trust, we have shown that single-minded virtue and a constant perseverence in the right, cannot be long under the cloud of misfortune ; and that such is the case, we produce Fanny as our example, showing in her, that when all else had merged into death and wretchedness, she was calm, and only knew that faint and sad melancholy which must oppress a good mind at the loss of those it loved, while at the same time it is cheered with the dear hope that they shall meet again.

THE END.

LONDON: PRINTED AND PUBLISHED BY E. LLOYD, 12, SALISBURY SQUARE, FLEET STREET.